Byrom Bramwell

Anæmia

and some of the diseases of the blood-forming organs and ductless glands

Byrom Bramwell

Anæmia
and some of the diseases of the blood-forming organs and ductless glands

ISBN/EAN: 9783337390648

Printed in Europe, USA, Canada, Australia, Japan

Cover: Foto ©Andreas Hilbeck / pixelio.de

More available books at **www.hansebooks.com**

ANÆMIA

AND

SOME OF THE DISEASES

OF THE

BLOOD-FORMING ORGANS

AND

DUCTLESS GLANDS

BY

BYROM BRAMWELL, M.D., F.R.C.P.ED., F.R.S.ED.

PHYSICIAN TO THE ROYAL INFIRMARY, EDINBURGH ; LECTURER ON THE PRINCIPLES
AND PRACTICE OF MEDICINE AND ON CLINICAL MEDICINE IN THE SCHOOL
OF THE ROYAL COLLEGES, EDINBURGH ; ETC., ETC.

PHILADELPHIA
P. BLAKISTON'S SON & CO.
1012 WALNUT STREET
1899

PREFACE.

— - — —

THIS book, which is essentially based upon my own clinical and pathological experience, represents a great deal of clinical observation and hard work. The abstraction of the cases and the preparation of the tables, for which I am personally responsible, has taken much longer than I had anticipated and has delayed the publication; a considerable portion of the text has been in type for more than a year.

My sincere thanks are due to Professor Robert Muir and to Dr Lovell Gulland for much valuable information and kindly criticism; also to my successive House-Physicians— Drs W. G. Aitchison Robertson, John J. Douglas, D. Chalmers Watson, J. H. Henderson, Edwin Bramwell, Horace C. Colman, John W. Struthers, and George W. Miller—for valuable assistance in the observation and recording of the hospital cases, in making blood-counts, &c.

B. B.

23 DRUMSHEUGH GARDENS,
EDINBURGH, *April* 1899.

CONTENTS.

——⁂——

ANÆMIA

AND

SOME OF THE DISEASES

OF THE

BLOOD-FORMING ORGANS AND

DUCTLESS GLANDS.

Introduction.—The diseases of the blood, blood-forming organs and ductless glands, are of great interest and importance. During the past decade many important facts have been ascertained regarding the functions of the ductless glands; and it is hardly necessary to say that our knowledge of the diseases of these important organs is much more complete than it was a few years ago. I desire specially to emphasise the fact that this advance in our physiological, as well as our pathological and clinical, knowledge is largely due to clinical observation and research. Further, in the case of one of the affections included under this group of diseases— I refer to myxœdema—we are now not only intimately acquainted with the pathology and clinical history of the disease, but, what is much more important, we know how to treat it and how to cure it.

The diseases of the blood, blood-forming organs and ductless glands which I propose more particularly to consider in this work are :—Chlorosis, Pernicious Anæmia, Leucocythæmia, Hodgkin's Disease, Addison's Disease, Myxœdema and Sporadic Cretinism, Exophthalmic Goitre and Acromegaly. Some of these diseases,

A

such as chlorosis and exophthalmic goitre, are common ; others, such as leucocythæmia, Hodgkin's disease, Addison's disease and acromegaly, are rare. The relative frequency of these diseases in 14,777 consecutive cases which have come under my notice is respectively as follows :—

Chlorosis	314
Pernicious Anæmia	45
Leucocythæmia	5
Hodgkin's Disease	12
Addison's Disease	12
Myxœdema and Sporadic Cretinism	40
Exophthalmic Goitre	79
Acromegaly	3

But it must be remembered that these figures do not represent the actual frequency of some of these diseases. The number of cases of pernicious anæmia and myxœdema is, for example, much above the average ; this is due to the fact that a considerable proportion of the cases were seen in consultation practice.

ANÆMIA.

Definition.—Anæmia may be defined as a condition in which, either, (*a*) the blood as a whole; or (*b*) the red blood corpuscles or (*c*) the hæmoglobin, in particular, are diminished in amount.

Some writers make the definition still wider, but that given above is, I think, quite sufficiently comprehensive for all practical purposes.

The term *oligæmia* is sometimes applied to those cases of anæmia in which the blood is deficient as a whole, *i.e.*, in which all of its constituents are diminished *en bloc;* the term *oligocythæmia* to those cases in which the defect is chiefly a reduction of the red blood corpuscles; and the term *oligochromæmia* to those cases in which the defect is chiefly a reduction of the hæmoglobin or colouring matter.

CLASSIFICATION AND ETIOLOGY.

Strictly speaking, anæmia or bloodlessness is, in the great majority of cases, a symptom, comparable to dropsy or jaundice, rather than a disease. It may result from many different morbid conditions.

(1.) In some affections, as in chlorosis and pernicious anæmia, the anæmia or bloodlessness is the most striking clinical and pathological feature of the case. These we at present term the *primary* anæmias, for as yet our information as to their exact cause is somewhat indefinite and obscure.

The terms *essential* and *idiopathic* have also been applied to these forms of anæmia; but since the same terms (*essential* and *idiopathic*) have been by many writers restricted to a special form of primary anæmia (viz., pernicious anæmia), they are apt, if used as synonyms for primary anæmia (all the forms of primary anæmia), to give rise to confusion, and should, therefore, in this sense be discontinued.

Dr Pye-Smith has suggested that the term *cytogenetic* anæmia should be applied to those forms of anæmia in which the bloodlessness is due to functional disturbance or organic disease of the blood-forming organs (the marrow of the bones, the spleen, and the lymphatic glands). But I doubt whether in the present position of our knowledge it is advisable to classify these so-called cytogenetic forms of anæmia under a separate heading. They are in reality primary anæmias, and, if separately grouped under a special term (cytogenetic), should be merely regarded as a sub-group of the primary anæmias.

(2.) In other cases of anæmia, the bloodlessness is obviously secondary—the result of such conditions as :—(a) loss of blood; (b) the presence of a poison introduced into the blood from without; (c) defective nutrition ; or (a) well-defined disease in some of the tissues and organs of the body, other than the blood-forming organs strictly so-called, such for example as cancer of the stomach. These we term the *secondary* or *symptomatic* anæmias.

This classification is clinical and practical rather than strictly pathological and scientific. It is probable that as our etiological and pathological knowledge advances some of the cases of anæmia which we at present consider primary—I refer more particularly to some cases of pernicious anæmia—will be found to be secondary.

Further, it must be remembered that in the present position of our knowledge it is not always possible to differentiate during life (clinically) the different sub-varieties of primary anæmia, nor even (in some cases) to say with absolute certainty whether the anæmia is primary or secondary. There seems, for example, some reason to suppose that in rare cases the clinical condition to which the term pernicious anæmia is applied may be due to a primary disease of the marrow of the bones ; in other words, in some cases this form of primary anæmia, *i.e.*, progressive pernicious anæmia (which, as I will afterwards point out, is usually the result of excessive blood destruction and not of imperfect blood formation), is perhaps the result of imperfect blood formation. Again, there is, I think, some reason to suppose that an anæmia, which is at first merely secondary and symptomatic, may, if sufficiently severe and sufficiently prolonged, ultimately assume all the clinical features of the pernicious form. But I need not enter into details regarding these very difficult and debatable questions. I will refer to them again when I come to consider the pathology of pernicious anæmia in more detail.

From what I have just stated it will be obvious that in the present position of our knowledge it is convenient to divide cases of anæmia into two great groups, viz., primary and secondary; but as soon as we have more accurate information as to the exact causation and pathology of the different forms of primary anæmia this classification will no doubt be discarded.

A scientific classification of anæmia should in my opinion aim at :—

Firstly, dividing all cases of anæmia into two great groups, viz. :—

(1.) Cases of anæmia due to excessive blood destruction, loss of blood, etc. ; and

(2.) Cases of anæmia due to imperfect blood formation.

And *secondly*, determining the exact seat and cause of (*a*) the excessive blood destruction, blood loss, etc., and (*b*) of the imperfect blood formation, respectively.

In some cases in which all the clinical characteristics of anæmia are present and in which the red blood corpuscles are diminished in number and the hæmoglobin deficient, the white corpuscles are enormously increased. To these cases the term *leukæmia* or *leucocythæmia* is applied. Leucocythæmia includes, as we shall presently see, at least two varieties which are perhaps separate diseases, viz., the spleno-medullary and lymphatic forms of leucocythæmia.

Further, there is perhaps reason to suppose that in rare cases leucocythæmia may result from a diseased condition of the bone-marrow, the spleen and lymphatic glands being unaffected, or from a diseased condition of the spleen, the marrow of the bones and the lymphatic glands being unaffected.

The symptomatic and secondary anæmias need not detain us. It is the anæmias included under the first group—the primary anæmias (under which I include the so-called cytogenetic forms)—to which I wish particularly to refer.

The more important causes of anæmia.—But before considering the individual forms of primary anæmia, it may perhaps be well to enumerate the more important causes of anæmia and to classify these causes in certain groups. They are as follows :—

(*a.*) *Hæmorrhage.*—Sudden and profuse hæmorrhage from an external wound or from an internal ulceration such as an ulcer of the stomach, and the prolonged drain of large or small quantities of blood which may result from hæmorrhoids, menorrhagia, etc., only of course require to be mentioned as causes of profound anæmia.

In middle-aged and old people, profound anæmia is not unfrequently due to bleeding piles. I have also seen a profound condition of anæmia, which presented many of the clinical characteristics of the pernicious form, due to a long-continued drain of blood from the uterus.

The profound anæmia which is in some cases associated with the presence in the duodenum of the ankylostoma duodenale is probably in great part due to loss of blood ; these parasites attach themselves to the mucous membrane and suck the blood from the minute vessels. In aggravated cases of this kind, the clinical condition closely simulates, and in some cases is perhaps identical with, that characteristic of pernicious anæmia. Dr William Hunter has suggested that the ankylostoma duodenale leads to the production of this profound form of anæmia, not so much by loss of blood as by the production of a poisonous substance which, being absorbed into the portal circulation, exerts a destructive influence upon the red blood corpuscles. I shall return to this point when I come to describe the pathology of pernicious anæmia in more detail.

(*b.*) *Deficiency of food, improper food, unhealthy surroundings, want of sunlight, etc.*

(*c.*) *Functional derangements or organic disease of the stomach or intestine which interfere with the digestion and absorption of food.*— In some cases of cancer of the stomach, very profound anæmia is developed. In these cases the anæmia is doubtless due to a variety of different causes acting in combination, and not merely to a defect in the digestion and absorption of food.

Under this head are included those derangements and diseases of the gastro-intestinal tract which prevent the absorption of iron from the food into the blood ; this is perhaps an important element in the causation of chlorosis (one of the primary forms of anæmia).

(*d.*) *The presence of certain parasites and poisonous substances (chemical and organic) in the blood (the malarial parasite, lead, arsenic, mercury, etc.).*—Under this head it is convenient to include the anæmia which develops in the course of many febrile and infectious diseases (rheumatic fever, ulcerative endocarditis, typhoid, syphilis, etc.), though in such conditions the anæmia may doubtless be due to a number of different factors.

Dr Robert Muir has suggested to me that *malarial anæmia* should be placed under a separate heading, since the mode in which the malarial parasite destroys the red corpuscles is now so well established.

(*e.*) *Long-continued diarrhœa, prolonged suppuration, a prolonged drain of albuminous material from the blood, as in Bright's disease, leucorrhœa, and other similar conditions.*—And here I may state that one of the most profound cases of anæmia which I have ever seen was due to long-continued diarrhœa in a case of sprue ; possibly this was not merely the result of the diarrhœa, but of the absorption into the blood of some poison (a micro-organism or its toxin).

(*f.*) *Derangement or disease of the blood-forming organs (bone-marrow, spleen and lymphatic glands), which is attended with the defective production and formation of red blood corpuscles.*

(*g.*) *Derangement or disease of the blood-destroying organs (the gastro-intestinal mucosa, the spleen, the liver, and, to a slight extent, the marrow of the bones) associated with an increased destruction of red blood corpuscles.*

In considering the different forms of primary anæmia and their differential diagnosis, I shall have to point out how necessary it is, before coming to the conclusion that the anæmia is primary, to exclude all the possible causes of secondary anæmia which have been enumerated in the foregoing headings. The point is of so much importance that I emphasise it here.

The conditions which are included in the foregoing heads may be arranged in three great groups, viz. :—

Group 1.—This includes those cases (*a*) in which the anæmia is due to conditions which interfere with the elaboration of the materials which are essential to maintain the blood in a condition of health ; and (*b*) in which the anæmia is due to defective blood formation (functional derangement or organic disease of the blood-forming organs properly so called).

Group 2.—This includes those cases in which the anæmia is due (*a*) to direct loss of blood, or to a prolonged drain of the albuminous materials of the blood from the system ; and (*b*) to excessive blood destruction (functional derangement or organic disease of the blood-destroying organs or poisons in the blood).

Group 3.—This includes those cases in which the anæmia is due both to excessive blood destruction and to defective blood formation, acting in combination.

As a matter of fact, in many cases of anæmia the bloodlessness is due to a number of different causes acting in association. The profound anæmia which is present in some cases of rickets, for example, may be partly the result of deficient or imperfect feeding, partly the result of want of sunlight, insanitary surroundings, insufficient clothing, exposure to cold and damp, and partly the result of disease of the blood-forming or blood-destroying organs (the marrow of the bones, liver, spleen, etc.). It is not unreasonable, I think, to suppose that in many cases of rickets the bone-marrow is functionating imperfectly ; further, it must be remembered that in aggravated cases of rickets, more particularly I think in those cases in which congenital syphilis is also present, the liver and spleen are enlarged and diseased. I may take this opportunity of stating that in some cases of this kind (rickets with enlargement of the liver and spleen) the microscopical characters of the blood closely resemble those of pernicious anæmia ; and further, that in children it is sometimes very difficult, from the mere microscopical characters of the blood, to draw a distinction between pernicious anæmia and pseudo-leucocythæmia.

Again, although in many cases of pernicious anæmia the primary change appears to be an increased destruction of the red blood corpuscles, there is at the same time a too rapid and consequently defective blood formation.

The seats of blood formation and destruction in health.— In connection with some of the foregoing statements it may be advisable to point out that in health, the composition of the blood, the number of red blood corpuscles and the total amount of hæmoglobin are maintained at a tolerably uniform standard. The destruction of red corpuscles which is constantly going on is accurately met by the production of new red blood corpuscles.

The average duration of a red blood corpuscle appears to be about two weeks or less.

In health, the red marrow of the bones is the chief, and probably the only, seat of the production of the red corpuscles. And here it may be well to state that the nucleated red corpuscle, which is normally present in the marrow of the bones, is the antecedent of the ordinary non-nucleated red corpuscle which is found in the blood. In some conditions of disease, and especially when the destruction of red blood corpuscles is excessive, the yellow marrow of the long bones may be replaced by red marrow—this is apparently a compensatory increase of the blood-forming tissue. It would appear that in animals (and presumably therefore in man) after very profuse hæmorrhage, red blood corpuscles may be produced in the spleen. Further, it has been suggested that occasionally, after great loss of blood, or excessive blood destruction, however caused, red blood corpuscles may also be produced, but probably only in a very limited degree, in the lymphatic glands. Dr Gulland, however, tells me that this view is probably erroneous.

In health, the chief seats of the destruction of the red blood corpuscles appear to be the gastro-intestinal mucosa and the spleen. A certain amount of destruction of red blood corpuscles also seems to take place in the bone-marrow.

The white corpuscles appear to be chiefly formed in the lymphatic glands partly in the other lymphoid structures (spleen, marrow of the bones, gastro-intestinal lymph follicles, thymus gland, and tonsils).

In health, the hæmoglobin which results from the destruction of red blood corpuscles in the gastro-intestinal mucosa and the spleen is carried to the liver, where it is in part transformed into bile pigment and urinary pigment. It would appear that all of the iron arising from the disintegration of the hæmoglobin is not excreted ; a considerable portion of it is probably retained in the system and re-utilised in blood formation. Stockman concludes as the result of a most careful analysis of the iron in the ordinary dietaries of healthy people with ordinary appetite and digestion that "the iron-metabolism of the body must be very small, and that while the pigment of disintegrated red blood corpuscles is excreted, in part at least, as the colouring matter of bile and urine, their iron is carefully retained in the body for future use." *

We have seen that in some cases of anæmia the bloodlessness is the chief clinical characteristic of the case, that it is convenient to term the anæmia in these cases primary ; that in other cases the anæmia is secondary and symptomatic ; that in some of the cases of primary anæmia the anæmia is due to disease of the cytogenetic or blood-forming organs, *i.e.*, to defective blood formation, and in others to increased blood destruction. In dealing with a case of anæmia at the bedside, it is of the utmost importance to endeavour to determine in which of these groups the anæmia should be placed ; for the treatment of the condition largely depends upon the nature of the primary cause, whether, for example, the anæmia is due to increased destruction or defective formation of the red blood corpuscles, whether it is the result of a deficiency of hæmoglobin, etc. But I repeat that it is not always easy or possible to come to a definite conclusion on some of these points. It is sometimes, for example, extremely difficult to differentiate pernicious anæmia from profound anæmia associated with cancer of the stomach, the presence of parasites in the intestine, etc.

Those who think that pernicious anæmia is a definite and distinct disease say that in these cases the pernicious anæmia is superadded to, or developed upon, the original (secondary) form of anæmia ; others, on the contrary, suppose that the condition which we term pernicious anæmia may be the result of a number of different conditions in all of which the ultimate blood condition, clinically speaking, is very much the same. It seems to me not

* "Journal of Physiology," Vol. xxi., No. 1, 5th February 1897.

improbable that any profound condition of anæmia may, provided that it is sufficiently severe and sufficiently long continued, pass into the pernicious form—I refer more especially to those cases in which the anæmia is the result of loss of blood and increased blood destruction. But I will discuss this question more in detail later.

From what I have already stated, it will readily be understood that a general description of the different varieties of anæmia which are included under these groups (whether primary or secondary) is insufficient; it is essential to consider the more important forms individually and in detail. But before doing so it will certainly be convenient and advisable to give a brief general description of the clinical symptoms which are present, in a more or less marked degree, in all cases in which the red blood corpuscles are greatly deficient in number or in which the hæmoglobin is greatly reduced in amount; and to refer in more detail than I have hitherto done to the etiology and pathology of anæmia, using the term in its widest and most general sense.

THE CLINICAL SYMPTOMS ASSOCIATED WITH ANÆMIA.

The chief clinical symptoms and signs which characterise or are associated with a profound degree of anæmia, however produced, are as follows :—

Pallor of the skin and mucous membranes.—The pallor of the mucous membranes (palpebral conjunctiva, inner surface of the lips, etc.) is much more important as a sign of anæmia than the colour of the skin; for in some cases in which anæmia is very marked, the skin is not pale and white. In many cases of chlorosis, for example, the skin has a greenish tint; in pernicious anæmia it is usually of a lemon-yellow tint, occasionally distinctly, and in rare cases markedly, jaundiced; in Addison's disease, in which there may be some, though there is not generally any marked degree of, anæmia, the skin is brown, in rare cases almost black, while the ocular con-junctiva is very pale and glistening; in tertiary syphilis, in which a certain amount of anæmia is usually present, the skin often has a dingy muddy hue; in cancer, more particularly cancer of the stomach in which the anæmia is often very marked, the skin may have a yellow cachectic appearance. On the other hand it must be remembered that, in many cases in which the skin is pale, the lips and conjunctivæ are well coloured and there is no anæmia.

I repeat that the colour of the mucous membranes is more important than the colour of the skin as a diagnostic sign of anæmia. With very rare exceptions, the mucous membranes are, in well-marked cases of anæmia, markedly pale and bloodless-looking. But in exceptional cases this is not so; in rare cases of splenic leucocythæmia, for example, the lips are blue and the face red and turgid. To this condition the term leukæmic plethora has been given. Further information is required as to the number of red blood corpuscles which are present in cases of this kind, i.e., as to the degree of the anæmia. I may also state that in the rare condition which is termed diffuse melanosis, with which a certain degree of anæmia is sometimes associated, the mucous membranes, instead of being pale, may be of a leaden hue.

The degree of pallor is very variable. The colour of the mucous membranes seems to depend quite as much (perhaps more) upon the total amount of hæmoglobin which the blood contains as upon the number of red blood corpuscles. In some cases of chlorosis, for example, in which the red blood corpuscles are only slightly diminished in number, but in which the hæmoglobin is very deficient, the mucous surfaces of the lips may be almost absolutely bloodless-looking.

Languor, debility, incapability of sustained exertion either of body or mind.—These are prominent symptoms in cases of profound anæmia.

Shortness of breath on exertion and palpitation.—These are very characteristic symptoms, and are prominent both in those cases of anæmia in which the red blood corpuscles are greatly reduced in number and in those cases in which the red corpuscles are only slightly reduced, but in which the hæmoglobin is markedly deficient. In well-marked cases of chlorosis, for example, shortness of breath on exertion and palpitation are always complained of. The shortness of breath on exertion is partly due to the deficiency in hæmoglobin, partly to the altered condition of the heart. In all cases of profound anæmia, if long continued, the heart muscle is apt to become fatty, and is in a condition of irritable weakness. Under such circumstances, palpitation and increased frequency of the heart and pulse are easily excited by comparatively trifling causes, such as slight efforts, mental excitement, etc.

Œdema of the feet.—In profound conditions of anæmia, a certain degree of œdema of the feet is very common. It is no doubt in many cases partly the result of the watery condition of the blood, but is chiefly due to the enfeebled condition of the heart. Œdema of the feet is particularly apt to arise in the later stages of anæmia and in those cases in which the vasomotor nerve tone is enfeebled.

Giddiness, fainting, headache, etc.—In well-marked cases of anæmia, giddiness is usually experienced when the patient stoops the head or suddenly rises from the recumbent to the erect position; and fainting may occur as the result of comparatively slight causes, such as a copious watery evacuation of the bowels. These symptoms are of course due to the defective supply of arterial blood to the brain. Headache, noises in the ear (tinnitus), a painful feeling of throbbing in the head, are also in many cases complained of.

Irritability of temper, peevishness, and diminished emotional control are common. *Neuralgia*, which has been described as a prayer on the part of the nerves for a better supply of blood, is of frequent occurrence. In the advanced stages of profound anæmia, especially in the pernicious form, an extremely painful form of *restlessness*, which is no doubt due to the want of oxygen and the anæmic condition of the nerve centres, is often developed; and *delirium, a semi-comatose condition, epileptiform convulsions and coma* may occur.

Loss of appetite, dyspeptic symptoms, and constipation.—These are common symptoms. In some cases, the dyspepsia and anæmia are due to a common cause, as, for example, cancer of the stomach; in others, the dyspeptic symptoms are the result of the anæmia—the functional and structural alterations which the anæmic condition produces in the tissues of the stomach.

Constipation is a prominent symptom in many cases of anæmia, especially in chlorosis; indeed the late Sir Andrew Clark supposed that chlorosis is due to constipation and the resulting absorption into the blood of excrementitious products produced in the intestine.

In other cases of anæmia there is *diarrhœa*. It is rarely the result of the anæmia. In some cases it appears to be the cause of the anæmia; in others, it is an associated symptom—due to the functional or structural alterations, such as ulceration in the gastro-intestinal tract, with which the anæmia is associated.

In chlorosis, simple perforating ulcer of the stomach is of frequent occurrence; and in such cases, it is often a difficult matter to determine how far the anæmia is due to the chlorosis or how far to the hæmatemesis to which the ulcer of the stomach may give rise.

Hæmorrhages.—In profound conditions of anæmia, bleeding from the mucous surfaces and extravasations of blood into the internal organs are apt to occur. *Epistaxis, bleeding from the throat and bleeding from the gums* are especially common. *Bleeding from the uterus* is met with in some cases. *Hæmatemesis* is of frequent occurrence in those cases of chlorosis in which the stomach is ulcerated, but is comparatively rare in other forms of anæmia. *Bleeding from the bowel* occasionally occurs. *Petechial extravasations in the skin and subcutaneous tissue* are occasionally observed, and minute extravasations of blood into the internal tissues (*pleura, pericardium, etc.*), are frequently found after death. In pernicious anæmia, *retinal hæmorrhages* are very common, and of great diagnostic importance ; they are apt to occur in all conditions in which the red blood corpuscles are very markedly diminished in number ; they are, too, frequently met with in leucocythæmia. In chlorosis, on the contrary, in which the defect is chiefly a diminution of the hæmoglobin, petechial and other hæmorrhages (with the exception of hæmatemesis, which is not the direct result of the anæmia but due to associated ulceration of the stomach) are uncommon.

The general state of nutrition.—In many cases of profound anæmia, the body fat is well preserved, though the muscles are usually soft and flabby. As I have already pointed out, a continued deficiency of hæmoglobin leads to the production of a fatty condition of the internal organs, especially of the heart, and is favourable rather than otherwise to the deposit of subcutaneous fat. Marked emaciation, when associated with profound anæmia, is strongly suggestive of the presence of some associated disease, such as cancer of the stomach ; in other words, is suggestive that the anæmia is secondary and not primary. Nevertheless, it must be remembered that in some cases of pernicious anæmia there is considerable loss of weight and in rare cases decided emaciation ; this, in my experience, is especially apt to occur in those cases of pernicious anæmia in which there is long-continued diarrhœa.

Fever.—In profound conditions of anæmia, intercurrent febrile attacks occasionally occur. They are especially frequent in pernicious anæmia. The pyrexia is in some cases continuous, in others intermittent or remittent. In some cases, the fever seems to be the direct result of the anæmic condition, or perhaps of a poison in the blood which is the cause of the anæmia. To this form of fever, the terms *anæmic fever* or *the essential fever of anæmia* have been applied. In other cases, the fever is the result of associated lesions or complications ; in others, to the unstable condition of the nerve centres. In chlorosis, true anæmic fever is probably very rare. When pyrexia occurs in chlorosis, the elevation of temperature is usually due to over-exertion, excitement, etc., to the development of some associated lesion such as venous thrombosis, etc., or to some independent condition.

The condition of the heart and vessels.—In all profound conditions of anæmia, if long continued, the heart muscle is apt to become fatty, irritable and easily excited, and the heart cavities are apt to become dilated. Palpitation, shortness of breath on exertion and sudden variations in the frequency of the pulse are, as we have seen, prominent symptoms in anæmia, and are partly due to this fatty and dilated condition of the heart and partly to the incompetence of the mitral and tricuspid valvular orifices which is apt to be superadded.

The altered condition of the heart is in some cases less evident on physical examination than one would expect, for the lungs are in many cases—and this is in my experience especially frequent in cases of pernicious anæmia—voluminous and hyper-resonant, the condition being due to a diffuse emphysema. The apex beat may be displaced more or less outwards and to the left. The cardiac impulse is in many cases more diffused than normal; during any temporary excitement it may be forcible, at other times it is usually feeble. The cardiac dulness both to the right and to the left is usually increased. Systolic murmurs may be audible in all the areas. A pulmonary systolic murmur is by far the most frequent; but I shall refer to this point in more detail when I come to describe the condition of the heart in chlorosis. A venous hum is usually present in the neck. In many cases of profound anæmia, the jugular veins are more prominent than normal. Pulsation in the jugular veins, often slight and flickering, but in some cases very definite and marked (and doubtless due to tricuspid incompetence), may also be developed.

Profound anæmia if long continued—but this statement applies more especially to those cases in which the red blood corpuscles are markedly diminished in number (progressive pernicious anæmia, for example), rather than to those cases in which the hæmoglobin is merely diminished in amount (chlorosis)—is apt to produce structural (fatty) changes in the walls of the minute blood vessels. This is in all probability the cause of the hæmorrhages, more particularly of the petechial hæmorrhages (retinal hæmorrhages, for example), which are under such circumstances of frequent occurrence.

The condition of the urine.—In pernicious anæmia more especially, this is of pathological interest and of some diagnostic value. In most cases of anæmia, notably in chlorosis, the urine is paler than normal; in other cases—and this statement more particularly applies to cases of pernicious anæmia, especially during the intercurrent attacks of blood destruction which are apt to be attended with fever and the development of slight jaundice—it may be more highly coloured than natural, the dark colour being partly due to an excess of pathological urobilin.

The condition of the blood in anæmia.—This is of great importance. The characters of the blood, as regards the number of red and white corpuscles, the total amount of hæmoglobin, the richness of the individual corpuscles in hæmoglobin, and the microscopic appearance which the formed elements of the blood present, vary considerably in different forms of anæmia and in the same form of anæmia in accordance with the severity of the case. Further, there can be little doubt that the specific gravity of the blood and the nature and richness of the soluble constituents of the plasma are subject to great variations ; but our knowledge of these alterations is as yet somewhat indefinite.

And here it may perhaps be well to say a few words with regard to—

The clinical examination of the blood.—In the clinical examination of the blood in anæmia, the chief points which should be observed are :—

1. The naked-eye characters of a drop of blood obtained by puncturing the ear, finger, etc.

2. The presence or absence of rouleaux formation.

3. The number of red corpuscles.

4. The total amount of hæmoglobin.

5. The hæmoglobin richness of the individual red corpuscles.

6. The size, shape, and microscopic characters of the red blood globules.

7. The number, size, shape, and microscopic characters of the white corpuscles, and the way in which they react to staining reagents.

8. The number and microscopic characters of the blood platelets (including Max Schultze's granular masses, which seem to be masses of blood platelets).

9. The presence of other formed elements, such as microorganisms, pigment granules, crystals, etc.

10. The rapidity with which the fibrin filaments are formed and the density of the fibrin network in a drop of blood examined under the microscope.

11. The specific gravity of the blood.

12. The " reaction " of the blood.

In this preliminary sketch of the condition of the blood in anæmia, I shall not attempt to describe in detail the minute alterations which are characteristic of the different forms of anæmia, but it may perhaps be well to direct attention to some of the more important points.

The number of red blood corpuscles.—The average number of red blood corpuscles is, in the healthy adult male, 5,000,000, and in the healthy adult female, 4,500,000 per cubic millimetre.

In all forms of anæmia and in all cases in which anæmia is actually present, some cases of slight chlorosis excepted, the red blood corpuscles are diminished in number. The degree of diminution varies with the form of anæmia and the severity of the case. In chlorosis, the diminution is in the great majority of cases comparatively slight. In pernicious anæmia, on the other hand, the degree of diminution is extremely great.

The total amount of hæmoglobin.—In normal blood, the total amount of hæmoglobin as estimated by the hæmoglobinometer should be 100 per cent.; but as a matter of fact I rarely find that it is possible by means of Gowers' instrument to obtain a higher percentage than 85 to 90 per cent. In all forms of profound anæmia the *total* amount of hæmoglobin is diminished, but the degree of diminution varies considerably in different cases.

The relative richness of the individual corpuscles in hæmoglobin.—This is a most important point, for, as I have already stated, in some cases of anæmia the red blood corpuscles are proportionately much more diminished than the hæmoglobin, while in other cases the hæmoglobin is proportionately much more diminished than the red corpuscles.

In chlorosis, the anæmia is chiefly due to diminution of the hæmoglobin. Even in cases of severe chlorosis the diminution of the red corpuscles may be comparatively slight. In a case of well-marked chlorosis, for example, which was recently under observation, the red blood corpuscles, instead of numbering 4,500,000, were 3,000,000; while the hæmoglobin, instead of being 85 to 90 per cent. (as estimated by Gowers' instrument) only amounted to 25 per cent.

In this case of chlorosis the condition of the blood would therefore be represented by the following formula :—

$$\frac{\text{H. (Percentage of Hæmoglobin)}}{\text{R.C. (Percentage of Red Corpuscles)}} = \frac{25}{60}.$$

But since Gowers' instrument reads low—say 85 to 90 per cent. instead of 100 per cent.—the amount of hæmoglobin actually present would be 28 per cent.

Further, since the average number of red blood corpuscles in the female is 4,500,000 (not 5,000,000), the 3,000,000 red corpuscles = 66 and not 60 per cent. Hence the fraction should be $\frac{28}{66}$. The relative richness of the individual red corpuscles was consequently in this case less than half; in other words, the colour-index was .42.

In pernicious anæmia, on the other hand, the individual red

blood corpuscles may contain an excess of hæmoglobin. In a case which was recently under my observation, the red corpuscles were reduced from 5,000,000 to 1,125,000 = about 25 per cent. (the patient was a male), and the hæmoglobin (as registered by Gowers' instrument) equalled 31 per cent. In this case of pernicious anæmia the condition of the blood would therefore (without correction) be represented by the fraction $\frac{H.}{R.C.} = \frac{31}{25}$; but allowing for the low reading of Gowers' instrument, the individual corpuscular richness of hæmoglobin was in reality greater than this fraction represents. It ought to be 34.4 instead of 31 per cent.—$\frac{H.}{R.C.} = \frac{34}{25}$; in other words, the colour index was 1.3.

The size and shape of the red blood corpuscles.—In health, the red blood corpuscles are non-nucleated, bi-concave, circular discs of a pale yellow colour. They go into rouleaux with great readiness.

In some cases of anæmia, more especially in those cases in which the red corpuscles are greatly diminished in number, and in which there is marked poikilocytosis, as in most cases of pernicious anæmia for example, the rouleaux formation is often completely absent.

In some cases of anæmia in which the red blood discs are greatly diminished in number, as for example in pernicious anæmia, the red corpuscles usually present very marked alterations in size and shape —some are larger, some smaller than normal, while many of them are misshaped (poikilocytosis).

In other cases of anæmia, more especially in those cases in which the red blood corpuscles are only slightly diminished in number, as in most cases of chlorosis, though the corpuscles are paler than normal they may present little or no alteration in size and shape.

The average diameter of the normal red blood corpuscle varies from 7 to 8 micromillimetres (7μ. to 8μ.).

Unusually large red corpusles (*megalocytes*) measuring from 9μ. to 12μ. or even larger are seen in various forms of profound anæmia, but especially in pernicious anæmia; hence they are of some though not perhaps *per se* of any great diagnostic importance. Their exact significance has not been definitely determined. By some authorities they are supposed to be imperfectly formed red corpuscles, by others degenerated red corpuscles.

Unusually small red corpuscles (*microcytes*) measuring in diameter from 2μ. to 5μ. or even less also occur in a variety of circumstances; they occur after extensive hæmorrhages and are present in advanced conditions of blood degeneration, notably in pernicious anæmia; they are suggestive of very rapid and imperfect blood formation, which may either be the result of increased blood destruction with (consequently) too rapid formation, or of a primary defect or lesion in the blood-forming organs—especially the marrow of the bones.

Small red corpuscles, *distinguished from the last* by their deeper colour, and known under the term of *Eichhorst's corpuscles*, are highly suggestive though perhaps not pathognomonic of pernicious anæmia. So far as my observation enables me to judge, they only occur in a small proportion of cases of pernicious anæmia.

Irregularity in the shape of the red blood corpuscles (*poikilo-cytosis*) occurs in many conditions, but more especially in cases in which the blood corpuscles are excessively reduced in number, in which the blood is very watery and in which the formation of the red blood corpuscles is being carried on too rapidly or in an im- perfect manner. By some authorities these irregularly formed corpuscles are regarded as degenerated red corpuscles, but I am strongly disposed to think that they are imperfectly formed red corpuscles.

Dr Robert Muir tells me that in those cases of anæmia in which the red corpuscles present marked alterations in size he has found that the nucleated red corpuscles in the bone-marrow also show greater variations in size than in the normal condition—a condition corresponding with that which obtains in the fœtus.

Marked alterations in size and shape of the red blood corpuscles are, as we shall afterwards see, suggestive of pernicious anæmia.

Nucleated red blood corpuscles occasionally occur, more especially in spleno-medullary leucocythæmia and in some cases of pernicious anæmia; but they cannot be satisfactorily seen without staining reagents. These nucleated corpuscles vary in size. They are espe- cially frequent in spleno-medullary leucocythæmia and in children affected with profound anæmia. They represent the passage of the red corpuscles into the blood stream before they have lost their nuclei, and are probably indicative of an excessive and imper- fect blood formation—an effort on the part of Nature to compensate for the increased corpuscular destruction; this view is confirmed by the fact that nucleated red corpuscles may readily be made to appear in the blood of animals by bleeding them, as Dr Robert Muir and others have shown.

The number, size, and microscopic characters of the different forms of white blood corpuscles.—In many cases of anæmia there is little or no change in the white corpuscles. A slight or moderate increase in the number of white blood corpuscles is met with in a great variety of different conditions, such as suppuration, inflammatory lesions, and in some forms of fever. In leucocythæmia, the number of white blood cells may be greatly increased; instead of being 8,000 per cubic millimetre, which is about the normal average in health, they may number 400,000 or more per cubic millimetre; instead of being in the proportion of 1 to 400 or 500 red blood corpuscles as they usually are in health, they may number 1 to 50 or less. In leukæmia or leucocythæmia it is by no means uncommon to find one white corpuscle to every 4 or 5 red cells, and it is said that in rare cases the white blood cells may be as numerous as the red. In estimating the number of white corpuscles which are present, the actual number per cubic millimetre should be taken; the older method of estimating the proportion of white to red corpuscles is fallacious (for the red corpuscles are often diminished in number) and should be discontinued.

Recent methods of observation—the examination of dried and stained specimens—have shown that several different forms of white blood corpuscles are normally present in the blood. The more important forms are :—

1. *Small uninucleated corpuscles* (*lymphocytes*) measuring about 7μ. to 9μ. in diameter. The nucleus is relatively very large, the protoplasm, which does not contain granules, merely consisting of a narrow rim round the nucleus. In normal blood they usually equal about 25 per cent. of the total white corpuscles.

2. *Large uninuclear leucocytes.*—These are considerably larger than the red blood corpuscles, measuring up to 12μ.; their nuclei are larger than the nuclei of the small uninucleated leucocytes; the protoplasm is, relatively to the nucleus, abundant and non-granulated.

3. *Transitional forms* between 2 and 3.

The large nucleated and transitional forms of the uninucleated corpuscles usually constitute from 3 to 6 per cent. of the total leucocytes in normal blood.

4. *Large polymorphonuclear* (*multinucleated* or *multipartite-nuclear*) *corpuscles*—*Ehrlich's neutrophiles*—Most of them measuring from 9μ. to 10μ. in diameter, some being larger (13μ. to 14μ.). The protoplasm is finely granular. These are the most numerous form; in normal blood they usually equal about 65 to 70 per cent. of the whole white corpuscles.

5. Large leucocytes, with one or more nuclei, containing coarse granules which stain deeply with eosin, hence they are termed *eosinophile cells*. In normal blood they usually equal about $\frac{1}{2}$ to 4 per cent. of the total leucocytes. Ehrlich, to whom we are so greatly indebted for our knowledge of the different characters of the leucocytes and the way in which they react to different staining

agents, originally thought that an increase of these eosinophile cells was indicative of myelogenic leucocythæmia; but this view seems now to have been quite abandoned by all authorities.

In cases of anæmia in which the leucocytes are greatly increased (*i.e.*, cases of leukæmia or leucocythæmia) the character of the leucocytes and the relative proportion of the different forms vary greatly.

These differences are manifested not only by the size of the leucocytes and the character of their contained nuclei, but also by the way in which the white blood corpuscles react to various stains. I shall return to this point when I come to describe leucocythæmia. All I need say now is, that in some cases of leucocythæmia, the splenic or spleno-medullary form of leucocythæmia as it is now generally termed, several different forms of white corpuscles are usually present; but the chief alteration consists in the presence in the blood of *large uninucleated corpuscles*, which measure from 12μ. to 20μ., and which do not contain eosinophile granules; some of these cells seem to be identical with marrow cells, hence they have been termed *myelocytes;* in some cases the *eosinophile cells*, which are present in normal blood in small proportion ($\frac{1}{2}$ to 4 per cent. of the total leucocytes), may be greatly increased, but this alteration is inconstant. Whereas in other cases of leucocythæmia (in which the spleen is often also greatly enlarged and in which the lymphatic glands are usually but not always enlarged) the increase of the white corpuscles is for the most part (some authorities say almost entirely) due to an enormous increase of the uninucleated white corpuscles of small size (the *lymphocytes*) which are normally present in the blood. Hence these cases have been termed cases of lymphatic leucocythæmia.

Blood-plates or blood-platelets.—These are the smallest formed elements of normal blood. They are circular or oval in form with a well-defined margin, and they consist of a highly refractile plasmic material. Their usual size is from 1 to 3 micromillimetres in diameter; they vary in number from 125,000 to 250,000 per cubic millimetre (some writers say 300,000 or even more). They seem to be most numerous in cachectic conditions, after long-continued bleeding, etc. In pernicious anæmia they are usually (and sometimes markedly) diminished. Hayem regards them as immature red blood corpuscles; according to other authorities they are the result of blood destruction. They seem to be the active agents in the process of coagulation and the formation of coagula (especially white thrombi). Dr Robert Muir tells me that he has " found that there is no relationship between the number of the blood-plates and the rate of blood formation. After a large hæmorrhage followed by rapid regeneration and no cachexia their number was little increased. Whereas after several hæmorrhages with the development of some general cachexia and impairment of blood regeneration their number was sometimes very great." He thinks that probably the impoverished condition of the serum is the chief condition associated with their increase.

Max Schultze's granular masses are irregular bodies composed of colourless granular protoplasm ; they seem to consist of collections of blood-platelets or perhaps of broken-down leucocytes.

From these statements, it will be seen that the exact characters of the blood vary considerably in different forms of anæmia. Speaking generally, three great groups of anæmia may be described, namely :—

1. *Cases in which the red blood corpuscles and the hæmoglobin are diminished in the same proportion.*—In these cases, the chief change is a watery condition of the blood, a hydræmia. The term oligæmia, which literally means deficiency of the blood as a whole, has been applied to this form of anæmia. It is characteristic of many of the secondary forms of anæmia (anæmia due to hæmorrhage, wasting discharges, etc.).

2. *Cases of anæmia in which the hæmoglobin is proportionally much more diminished than the red blood corpuscles.*—This condition is highly characteristic of chlorosis, though it also occurs in other conditions. Dr Stephen Mackenzie has also shown that it occurs in some cases of cancer, and my own observations confirm his views on this point.

3. *Cases of anæmia in which the red blood corpuscles are more diminished than the hæmoglobin.*—This condition occurs in pernicious anæmia, rarely if ever, so far as we know, in other conditions.

Let us now consider some of the more important forms of primary anæmia individually and in detail.

CHLOROSIS.

Definition or Short Description.—This disease, to which the synonyms *chloræmia*, *chloranæmia*, *green sickness*, etc., have been applied, is by far the most common form of primary anæmia. It varies very greatly in severity in different cases. It is characterised by all the typical symptoms of profound anæmia—weakness, pallor, shortness of breath, palpitation, giddiness, etc. The essential blood change is a marked deficiency of hæmoglobin ; and since in the great majority of cases the red blood cells are comparatively little diminished in number, the richness of the individual red blood corpuscles in hæmoglobin (as well as the total amount of hæmoglobin in the blood) is markedly below the normal. In the vast majority of cases the disease is rapidly cured by the administration of iron.

ETIOLOGY.

Age and Sex.—Chlorosis is essentially a disease of the female, and in the vast majority of cases is developed at or about the time of puberty ; but cases of apparently causeless anæmia, in which the blood presents all the characters of chlorosis and which are curable by iron, are sometimes met with in older women. Cases which appear to be closely allied to (and in some cases apparently identical with) chlorosis are also occasionally met with in children, and also perhaps in men, though some authorities doubt whether true chlorosis ever occurs in adult males.

In 314 typical cases of chlorosis of which I have notes, the ages were as follows :—

TABLE I.—SHOWING THE AGE IN 314 CASES OF CHLOROSIS.

Years.	No. of Cases.	Years.	No. of Cases.
12	1	24	8
13	1	25	10
14	6	26	9
15	6	27	9
16	19	28	2
17	31	29	5
18	41	30	2
19	47	31	2
20	39	32	1
21	33	33	1
22	18		——
23	23	Total	314

The result of this analysis is graphically represented in Fig. 1; the curve is a very remarkable one. The apex corresponds to the 19th year, the rise and fall on each side of this point being singularly symmetrical.

Of my 314 cases, 251 occurred between the ages of 16 and 23 inclusive; but it must be remembered that this does not represent the age at which the disease commenced, but the age at which the patients came under my observation. In many of the cases the patients had suffered from the disease for several months or years before I saw them. Hence the average age at which the disease commenced in these cases was certainly somewhat lower than is shown in the table. But there is little doubt that in the great majority of cases of chlorosis the disease develops between the ages of 15 and 23; comparatively few cases are met with before the age of 15 or after the age of 24; and in most of the cases which are met with after the age of 24, the disease commenced at an earlier period of life.

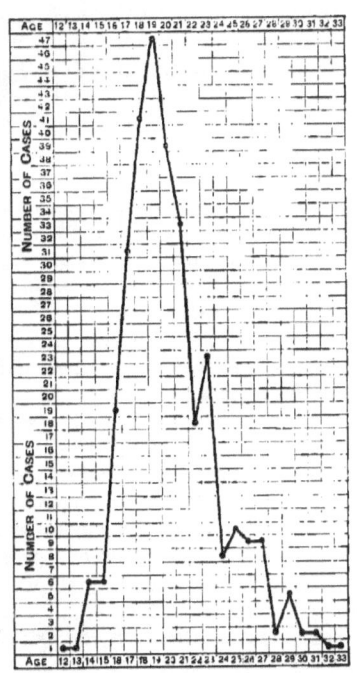

Fig. 1.—Graphic Representation of the Age Frequency of 314 Cases of Chlorosis.

Occupation, locality, etc.— The disease occurs amongst all classes of society, but in my experience it is most common in young servant girls. Sedentary habits, want of exercise, want of fresh air and sunlight, late hours, excessive fatigue, over-pressure at school, mental anxiety, prolonged grief, home-sickness, etc., undoubtedly seem in some cases to predispose to its production; but in other cases these factors seem to be wanting. The disease appears to be more common in towns than in the country. Country girls who come into service in town are, it is said, particularly apt to be affected.

Influence of heredity.—In some families there appears to be a hereditary tendency to the disease; and many authorities are agreed that there is a certain relationship between tuberculosis and chlorosis; in other words, it would appear that in families predisposed to tuberculosis the girls have a stronger tendency to chlorosis than the girls of other families in which there is no tubercular tendency. An analysis of my own cases gives some support to this view.

In the 80 cases included in Table 2, the details of the family history are stated in 72 cases. In these 72 cases, there was a definite history of some tubercular affection in the near relatives (parents, brothers and sisters, uncles and aunts) in 22 cases or 30 per cent.

But it is probable that these figures do not exactly represent the tubercular tendencies of patients affected with chlorosis, and that for the following reasons :—

On the one hand, in many of the cases in which no definite tubercular history could be elicited, it was stated that some near relative was delicate, but the exact cause of the delicacy could not be ascertained ; no doubt in a certain proportion of these cases the ill health was due to tubercle. Again, in a considerable proportion of the cases in which no tubercular history in the near relatives was elicited, the exact cause of death of some of the near relatives (parents, brothers, sisters, etc.) was unknown to the (chlorotic) patients ; in a certain number of these cases death was no doubt due to tubercle.

On the other hand, the 80 cases included in the Table were all hospital patients, in whom the mortality from tubercular diseases is somewhat greater than in the average population, and certainly greater than in the more fortunately situated ranks of society.

Theories as to the cause of chlorosis.—The exact causation of chlorosis has given rise to a great deal of difference of opinion.

It used to be thought that the disease was due to disappointment in love ; and there can be no doubt that mental anxiety and grief may act as contributory or exciting causes, but only perhaps in persons predisposed to chlorosis or already suffering from it.

Derangement or disease of the uterus and ovaries has been suggested as a cause. Amenorrhœa is usually present in severe cases of chlorosis, but it appears to be the result, not the cause, of the disease. Proof of this is found in the fact that in a not inconsiderable proportion of well-marked cases the menstruation is perfectly regular. It is true that in many of the cases of chlorosis in which the menstruation is regular in time, the discharge is deficient in quantity and too pale in colour ; but in some cases, the menstruation is perfectly natural in every respect. In rare cases, there is menorrhagia.

But although amenorrhœa is not the cause of chlorosis, there can, I think, be little doubt that the active strain which is thrown upon the tissues and organs of the female at the time of puberty and during the first few years of menstrual life is an important factor in the production of the disease. According to Niemeyer, chlorosis is invariably developed in girls who begin to menstruate before the mammæ and genital organs are developed. My own view is that the unusual strain, so to speak, which is thrown upon the blood-forming organs by the rapid development of the tissues and organs which occurs at the time of puberty, and especially by the development and establishment of the function of menstruation, is a most important factor in the production of the condition. This view seems to me to be supported by the fact that as the patient gets older (in other words, as the organism becomes accustomed to the strain on the blood-forming organs which menstruation entails) the disease and the tendency to relapse which is such a striking feature of the disease gradually disappear.

Virchow thought that chlorosis was due to defective development of the aorta and arterial system; but narrowing of the aorta and thinness of the arterial coats are not always present; in some cases they are perhaps the result and not the cause of the chlorosis; or perhaps the narrowing of the aorta and thinness of the arteries and the chlorosis are the result of a common cause—a congenital or developmental condition, *i.e.*, some imperfection in the development of the blood-forming organs and blood vascular system. Further, as Stockman has pointed out, Virchow's theory seems contradicted by the fact that cases of chlorosis are *rapidly* cured by appropriate treatment.

Trousseau and others have suggested that the primary cause is a nervous derangement which produces alterations in the blood; this may be so, but there can I think be little doubt that many of the nervous symptoms which are so frequently associated with the disease are a result rather than the cause of the bloodlessness; this is not, of course, an argument against the (primary) nervous origin of the disease. Cases such as that mentioned by Clifford Allbutt, in which a profound degree of chlorosis was developed (or rather redeveloped, for the patient had just recovered from the disease) after a nervous shock, lend some support to the view that the bloodlessness is the result of a trophic nerve change acting either directly on the blood-forming organs, or indirectly on the blood by the production perhaps of some toxic product of metabolism; but as yet there are not, so far as I know, any definite facts in favour of such a mode of causation. Further, the condition of the blood in cases of chlorosis seems strongly opposed to the view that the anæmia is the result either of the defective production of red corpuscles, or of a destruction of red blood corpuscles due to a toxic agent.

Sir Andrew Clark supposed that chlorosis was the result of auto-intoxication from the intestine (copræmia) due to constipation. Constipation is certainly very common in cases of chlorosis, but it is by no means always present. In quite a number of well-marked cases which have come under my own observation, more especially amongst girls belonging to the upper orders of society, constipation has been entirely absent. In some of these cases, I have satisfied myself that the bowels were not only opened, but sufficiently freely opened, every day. It must, however, be remembered that auto-intoxication from the intestine may probably occur even when there is no constipation. That constipation may in some cases have an influence in the production of the disease is I think highly probable, but it cannot be regarded as the essential and fundamental cause. Further, Rethers * and Mörner† claim that their analyses of the urine in cases of chlorosis show that there is no evidence of excessive sepsis in the alimentary canal. Again, if intestinal sepsis and auto-intoxication were the cause, the disease ought to occur in men and to be frequently developed in women during the middle and later periods of adult life ; but this is not the case.

It has also been theorised that chlorosis is due to deficiency of hydrochloric acid in the gastric juice and the presence of an excess of sulphuretted hydrogen in the intestines, and that these conditions produce the disease by interfering with the assimilation of iron.

Bunge‡ in particular has advocated the view that the presence of an excess of sulphuretted hydrogen and of alkaline sulphides in the intestinal tract produces a continuous non-assimilation of iron by combining with the organic iron of the food and forming an inorganic and therefore insoluble iron compound ; and that the chlorotic condition results from the non-assimilation of iron produced in this way. But in opposition to this view it has been shown by Rethers and Mörner (a) that there is no increase of aromatic sulphates in the urine of chlorotics, and therefore no indication of excessive putrefaction in the intestine ; and by Stockman § (b) that

---

* Dissertation, Berlin, 1891.
† Zeitschr. f. Physiol. Chemie, xviii. 1893.
‡ Lehrbuch der Physiolog. und Patholog. Chemie, 1887.
§ " British Medical Journal," 1893, Vol. i., pp. 881 and 942.

the administration of sulphide of iron (enclosed in keratin capsules, so as to ensure its reaching the intestine) is capable of curing chlorosis ; and (c) that other drugs, such as bismuth, which are as capable of neutralising sulphuretted hydrogen in the intestine as iron is, do not cure the disease.

Ulceration of the stomach and gastric hæmorrhage have been suggested as causes of the disease ; possibly these conditions may in some cases act as predisposing causes, and they may, of course, undoubtedly aggravate the anæmia when they happen to be associated with chlorosis ; but there can I think be little doubt that in most cases they are results rather than causes of the disease. Dilatation of the stomach and tight-lacing (which is apt to produce dilatation of the stomach) have also been blamed ; but here again I regard the dilatation of the stomach rather as a consequence than a cause of the disease.

Stockman is of opinion that the essential causes of chlorosis are two, or possibly three, namely :—

"(1.) Excessive menstrual loss, or (much less frequently) other blood loss. This," he states, " may be relative, that is, too much for a weakly or rapidly-growing organism to bear, or it may be actually large.

"(2.) Insufficient ingestion of iron with food. Anything which diminishes the appetite diminishes the consumption of iron ; therefore dyspepsia, constipation, heated rooms, insufficient exercise, unhealthy atmospheres, mental depression, etc., all predispose to the affection by lessening the amount of food consumption. It is probably owing to change of habits, confinement indoors and want of fresh air—all leading to small consumption of food—that so many girls from the country become anæmic on going into towns to live.

"The dyspepsia and constipation which are so common in chlorotic patients lead," he says, "to the consumption of a totally inadequate amount of food, and therefore of a totally inadequate amount of iron."

From an analysis of the dietaries of fifteen healthy persons, and from four analyses of the daily dietary of two girls suffering from chlorosis, he concludes that the amount of iron in the food of chlorotic patients is very much smaller than normal—about one-third only of that of healthy persons. Further, he has shown that the quantity and kind of food consumed exercise an important influence on the amount of iron available for blood formation.

At the same time, he admits that "patients suffering from chlorosis fed on even a rich and varied diet, containing plenty of iron, do not, as a rule, recover until inorganic iron is administered."

He states that in a very large number of cases of chlorosis there is a combination of the two causes just enumerated; but he adds

"(3.) It is possible that certain persons are born inherently weak in blood-forming power and tend to become anæmic under very slight provocation."

Stockman's observations as to the amount of iron in the food of chlorotics are highly suggestive and important; but it seems to me that further observation and a much more extended series of analyses are required before they can be applied to chlorotics as a whole, i.e., before we can definitely conclude that in all cases of chlorosis the iron in-take is insufficient.

And even if it be allowed that the iron "in-take" is deficient in all well-marked cases of chlorosis, it does not follow that this is one of the chief causes of the disease. It does not follow, because in well-marked cases of chlorosis and in the advanced stages of the disease the iron "in-take" is insufficient, that the iron "in-take" is deficient in the pre-chlorotic period, as it may be termed, and in the earlier stages of the disease. The deficient iron "in-take" in the advanced stages may be the result of the disease, i.e., of the defective appetite and dyspeptic conditions which are due to the chlorosis. It seems premature to conclude that one of the chief causes of chlorosis is a deficient "in-take" of iron, unless it can be shown that at the onset of the disease and during the period immediately preceding the onset of the disease, the iron "in-take" is deficient.

Further, if the cause, or one of the chief causes, of chlorosis is a deficiency of iron in the food, the chlorotic condition ought, in its earlier stages at all events and in slight cases, to be readily cured by (1) removing the dyspeptic condition and by the administration of a liberal (iron-containing) diet—but this is not the case; by (2) the administration of small doses of the organic compounds of iron —but almost all authorities are agreed that the organic compounds of iron are less effective than the inorganic; and by (3) the administration of small quantities of iron in any form—but this is not the case.

Stockman has recently shown that in health the iron "in-take" and the iron "out-put" in the urine and fæces are very small— in the cases which he most carefully investigated the quantity of metallic iron in ordinary dietaries seldom exceeded 10 milligrams per diem, and might be as low as 6 milligrams, in people of ordinary appetite and digestion. These observations seem to show that the amount of iron which must be absorbed from the intestine under ordinary conditions in order to maintain the body in a state of health is extremely small (rarely more than 10 milligrams per diem). Consequently, if chlorosis is due to a deficient "in-take" of iron, the disease ought to be rapidly cured by very minute doses of iron—but this is certainly not the case, in most instances at least.

Further, as regards loss of blood, it must be remembered that chlorosis is sometimes developed in girls who have never menstruated, and that in a large proportion of cases of chlorosis menstruation (though perhaps it may be relatively excessive and too much, as Stockman states,* for a weakly or rapidly-growing organism to bear) is much less profuse than normal—I refer, of course, to the condition of menstruation at the onset of the disease and not to the condition of menstruation when the disease is thoroughly established; for in the majority of cases of chlorosis at this stage, amenorrhœa is present.

Lloyd Jones concludes, as the result of a long series of observations on the blood in normal girls and chlorotic patients, that "chlorosis is an exaggeration of a physiological blood condition, an exaggeration of a change which occurs in the blood of healthy females at puberty, and which shows itself in many females at each menstrual period. Further, he suggests that appearances point to the likelihood of chlorosis being a chronic auto-intoxication brought about by some substances which are possibly the products of uterine, Fallopian, or ovarian metabolism, and which produce their effects on the blood by inducing changes in the gastro-intestinal canal by the medium of the nervous system."†

As I have already stated, the essential clinical feature of chlorosis is a diminution of the hæmoglobin—a deficiency of the iron of the blood. Further, in order to understand the causation of the disease it must be remembered:—(a) that chlorosis is essentially a disease of the female sex; (b) that it is in the vast majority of cases developed at or about the period of active sexual development; and (c) that in the great majority of cases it is speedily and easily cured by the administration of iron—provided only that the iron is given in sufficiently large quantities and that the gastro-intestinal tract and its contents are in a condition to permit of the absorption of the remedy.

There seem to be no sufficient reasons for supposing that the deficiency of hæmoglobin in the blood which is the essential feature of chlorosis is primarily due to defective action of the blood-forming

---

* "British Medical Journal," 14th December 1895.
† "Chlorosis," by Dr E. Lloyd Jones, p. 56.

organs properly so called (the marrow of the bones, etc.). This view seems supported by the following facts :—

That in the earlier stages of the disease and in slight cases of chlorosis the only alteration in the blood is, practically speaking, a deficiency of hæmoglobin ; the red corpuscles may be little if at all reduced in number, and they may present little or no alterations in size and shape ; and

That there appears to be no inability on the part of the red blood corpuscles to take up iron, provided only that they have the chance of doing so. It would appear that in the earlier stages of chlorosis, at all events, the red corpuscles are normally formed by the bone-marrow but are sent off without their normal supply of hæmoglobin. The diminution in the number and the alterations in size and shape of the red corpuscles, which only become marked in the advanced stages of severe cases of chlorosis, may quite well be accounted for (as my son Dr Edwin Bramwell has pointed out to me) by the effects which a long-continued and marked deficiency of oxygen (*i.e.*, of hæmoglobin) produces on the blood-producing organs.

The essential cause of chlorosis, then, would appear to be a deficiency of hæmoglobin in the blood—a deficiency which is produced in some way or another by the strain which is put upon the tissues and blood-forming organs of the female by the rapid development which takes place at or about the time of puberty, and especially perhaps by the unusual strain which the development and establishment of the function of menstruation entail. Further, functional derangements of the gastro-intestinal tract, or rather perhaps the presence in the intestinal tract of some substance or substances, which prevent the absorption of the iron of the food, or which split up the soluble iron compounds and render them unfit for absorption into the blood, may perhaps have some influence in the production of the condition. Constipation, though it cannot in my opinion be regarded as the essential and fundamental cause of the disease, probably acts as a contributory cause, in some cases at all events. Again, if Stockman's analyses as to the small amount of iron in the food of chlorotic patients are of general application, it must be allowed that this (the deficiency of iron in the food), if it is present at the onset of the disease, probably plays some part in the production of the disease, though, so far as I see, there is no reason to suppose that it is the chief or essential cause.

CLINICAL HISTORY.

The onset of the disease is usually insidious. The patient gradually loses colour, complains of debility, and inability for exercise, becomes short of breath, and suffers from palpitation and giddiness—in short, the disease is characterised by the presence of symptoms which are associated with profound anæmia or a marked deficiency of hæmoglobin in the blood, and which result from the irritable and enfeebled condition of the heart, which the deficiency of hæmoglobin and the consequent imperfect oxygenation of the heart muscle occasion.

In order to understand the clinical features of chlorosis and to intelligently and successfully treat cases of chlorosis, *it is essential to remember that the fundamental feature of the disease is a deficiency of hæmoglobin in the blood.* And since the function of the hæmoglobin is to carry oxygen to the tissues, a deficiency in hæmoglobin means a deficient supply of oxygen to the tissues. Now, when the supply of oxygen to the tissues is deficient, they are apt to undergo fatty degeneration; hence in cases of chlorosis the heart muscle and the other tissues and organs of the body are apt to become fatty. In consequence of the deficiency of hæmoglobin the nutrition of the cardiac muscle becomes impaired, a condition of irritable weakness of the heart, and, if the chlorosis is severe and long continued, cardiac dilatation and fatty degeneration are developed. In consequence of nutritive disturbances in the walls of the stomach, dyspepsia, dilatation, and it may be ulceration are in some cases produced; etc.

The exact manner in which chlorosis leads to the production of ulceration of the stomach is still somewhat uncertain. One view is that the anæmia produces lowered vitality in the gastric mucous membrane; another that there is hæmorrhagic extravasation in the mucous membrane; a third that embolic or thrombotic destruction of the nutrient vessels causes necrotic softening; and that the mucous membrane the vitality of which is lowered in any of these ways is acted on and eroded (digested so to speak) by the gastric juice.

General appearance.—Patients who are affected with a high degree of chlorosis are, as a rule, well covered with fat, but their muscles are usually soft and flabby. In some of the cases, more especially in those cases in which dyspepsia or ulceration of the stomach are associated with the anæmia, there is more or less emaciation.

In many cases, the mammæ are full, the external genitals and the pubic hair well developed; but in other cases the reverse is the case, the mammæ and genital organs being imperfectly developed.

The skin and mucous membranes are pale, and the skin often has a greenish-yellow colour ; hence the term "green sickness" which has been given to the disease. The green hue is usually more marked in dark-complexioned than in fair-complexioned girls. In blondes, the complexion often has a beautiful rosy-red tint when the patient first comes under the notice of the physician ; patients suffering from chlorosis flush readily ; their skin is usually thin and delicate ; the temporary tinting of the skin which results from the flushing is very becoming, for many of the girls who are affected with chlorosis are very pretty. After the temporary excitement subsides, the face becomes pale ; and in severe cases both the lips and skin may look almost entirely bloodless. Pallor of the buccal mucous membrane and conjunctiva is, from a diagnostic point of view, of more importance than pallor of the skin. In some cases in which the buccal mucous membrane is pale, the palpebral conjunctiva is injected with fine vessels.

Symptoms and complaints.—Patients affected with chlorosis complain of weakness and debility, inability for prolonged and sustained efforts either of body or mind, shortness of breath on exertion, palpitation, giddiness on stooping the head and on suddenly rising from the recumbent to the erect position. In advanced stages of the disease, the feet and lower part of the legs may be œdematous, but marked dropsy is rare. In some cases the eyelids are somewhat swollen and puffy-looking. The œdema is probably due partly to the watery condition of the blood, and partly to the enfeebled condition of the heart. A slight degree of exophthalmos is sometimes present. The thyroid gland is not unfrequently somewhat enlarged. I do not of course refer to cases of exophthalmic goitre which are complicated with chlorosis—a combination of diseases which is not uncommon.

The physiognomy is usually so characteristic and the symptoms associated with the anæmia so constant that in well-marked cases of chlorosis it is usually possible to predict most of the symptoms from which the patient is suffering before a single question has been asked.

The condition of the blood.—This is of the greatest importance. A drop of blood obtained by pricking the ear or finger is thin, pale and watery-looking. In many cases, the puncture bleeds more freely than one would expect considering the markedly bloodless appearance of the patient.

In slight cases, the red blood corpuscles are little if at all diminished in number. In more severe cases, they usually number from 3,500,000 to 2,500,000 per cubic millimetre. In exceptional cases the reduction is much more considerable. Hayem has reported a case of chlorosis in which the blood corpuscles numbered only 1,300,000; in four of my cases, the red corpuscles numbered 1,800,000, 1,675,000, 1,600,000 and 1,425,000 per cubic millimetre respectively; but such a marked decrease is quite exceptional.

In 77 cases of chlorosis, observed by Cabot (" Clinical Examination of the Blood," p. 134), the red corpuscles averaged 4,050,000 per cubic millimetre. In the 80 cases which I have included in Table 2, the red corpuscles averaged 3,437,300 per cubic millimetre. With few exceptions these cases were all in-patients, and as only the more severe cases were admitted to hospital, and as many of the cases included in the table were also suffering from dyspepsia, or slight ulceration of the stomach, they may be regarded as aggravated and severe cases of the disease.*

The essential blood change is a diminution in the hæmoglobin. The total amount of hæmoglobin may be reduced to 20 per cent. or even lower. In the 80 cases included in Table 2, the average amount of hæmoglobin as estimated by Gowers' instrument equalled 34 per cent.; but since Gowers' instrument reads low, the average amount of hæmoglobin (calculated on the basis that Gowers' instrument reads 90 instead of 100 per cent.) equalled 37.7 per cent. In four of my cases, the percentage of hæmoglobin as estimated by Gowers' instrument equalled 16, 10, 15 and 19 per cent. respectively.

Now, since the reduction of the red corpuscles is in the great majority of cases proportionately much less than this, the individual richness in hæmoglobin of the red corpuscles is considerably below the normal. In many cases the individual richness of the red blood corpuscles in hæmoglobin is less than half the normal—for example, $\frac{H}{R.C.} = \frac{30}{66}$.

In the 80 cases included in Table 2, the hæmoglobin averaged 34 per cent. as estimated by Gowers' instrument; and the individual corpuscular richness in hæmoglobin equalled 44 per cent.; or, after correction (taking the normal amount of hæmoglobin as estimated by Gowers' instrument at 90 instead of 100 per cent.), 37.7 per cent. and 49.4 per cent. respectively.

In the 77 cases tabulated by Cabot, the hæmoglobin averaged

---

* In none of the cases included in the table were the symptoms of ulceration of the stomach prominent; in all cases of combined chlorosis and ulceration of the stomach, in which the ulceration of the stomach was *the* prominent condition, the case has been classified under the head of ulcer of the stomach.

TABLE 2.—CHLOROSIS.

No.	Case-book. Vol.	Case-book. Page	Age.	Red Corpuscles.	Per'ge Hæmo. (Flowers).	Colour Index (corrected).	Menstruation.	Bowels.	Remarks.
1	1	27	23	2,920,000	55	.92	Amenorrhœa.	Constipated.	Dyspepsia.
2	1	102	22	4,030,000	50	.61		Constipated.	Dyspepsia. ? Ulcer of stomach. Headache.
3	1	130	17	3,610,000	54	.77	Normal.	Regular.	Rheumatism.
4	3	18	17	2,860,000	32	.55	Amenorrhœa.		Dyspepsia. ? Ulcer of stomach. Headache.
5	4	114	26	3,560,000	43	.60	Normal.		Dyspepsia.
6	4	108	22	3,820,000	40	.54	Normal.	Constipated.	
7	6	100	18	3,820,000	43	.58		Constipated.	Erythema of legs.
8	8	71	23	4,160,000	35	.41		Constipated.	Slight dyspepsia.
9	8	54	18	3,460,000	32	.45	Normal.	Constipated.	Thin.
10	8	117	20	3,800,000	32	.41	Amenorrhœa.	Regular.	Headache. Vomiting.
11	9	120	17	4,030,000	50	.61		Constipated.	Epigastric pain. Sickness. Headache.
12	10	5	15	1,600,000	16	.48	Amenorrhœa.	2 or 3 motions daily.	Headache.
13	10	16	21	1,675,000	10	.29	Amenorrhœa.	Constipated.	
14	10	24	27	3,337,000	36	.54	R. Scanty and pale.	Regular.	Thirst. Neuralgia. Headache. Nervous vomiting.
15	10	39	25	4,000,000	48	.60	Normal.	Regular.	Epigastric pain.
16	10	47	21	3,220,000	50	.77	Amenorrhœa.	Constipated.	Thirst. Ulceration of stomach.
17	10	56	18	2,212,000	15	.32		Constipated.	Headache. Backache.
18	10	102	31	4,000,000	60	.75	Normal.	Constipated.	Backache.
19	11	58	18	3,860,000	19	.24		Constipated.	Infra-mammary pain. Morning sickness.
20	11	92	26	3,750,000	30	.39	Amenorrhœa.		Severe headache.
21	11	96	19	3,725,000	35	.46		Regular.	
22	12	87	16	1,425,000	28	.96			Gastric pain. Vomiting. Enlarged thyroid.
23	12	109	18	3,750,000	30	.39	R. Scanty & pale.	Constipated.	
24	12	150	23	2,500,000	40	.81	R. Dysmenorrhœa Leucorrhœa.		Very bad teeth.
25	12	158	14	3,000,000	26	.42		Regular.	Vomiting. Swollen glands in neck.
26	13	97	18	3,300,000	30	.45	R. Scanty & pale.	Regular.	
27	15	132	18	3,450,000	40	.58	Normal.	Regular.	
28	16	108	19	2,240,000	25	.55		Regular.	Mild articular rheumatism.
29	20	131	19	4,900,000	58	.59			Enl'ged glands in neck.
30	21	91	19	4,700,000	50	.52	Amenorrhœa.	Constipated.	Great thirst.
31	22	10	21	2,800,000	24	.41	Irregular.	Constipated.	Thirst. Headache.
32	22	31	21	3,000,000	40	.66	Normal.	Constipated.	Dyspepsia.
33	22	51	16	3,850,000	40	.51	Amenorrhœa.	Constipated.	Sickness. Infra-mammary pain.
34	22	99	17	2,000,000	38	.95	Amenorrhœa.	Constipated.	
35	22	157	18	2,800,000	20	.35	Amenorrhœa.	Constipated.	Dyspepsia. Headache.
36	23	34	17	3,100,000	35	.55	Amenorrhœa.	Constipated.	
37	24	37	20	3,400,000	30	.41	Amenorrhœa and Leucorrhœa.	Constipated.	Vomiting. Frontal headache.
38	24	43	21	2,900,000	20	.34	Normal.	Constipated.	
39	24	47	25	3,300,000	26	.38		Constipated.	
40	24	98	16	3,500,000	30	.42	Never menstruated.	Constipated.	
41	24	116	19	2,890,000	40	.68	Amenorrhœa.	Regular.	
42	26	16	21	2,200,000	22	.50	Irregular.	Constipated.	Headache. Vomiting.
43	32	10	23	3,200,000	38	.50	Normal.	Constipated.	

No.	Case-book. Vol.	Case-book. Page	Age.	Red Corpuscles.	Perc'ge Haemo. (Gowers).	Colour Index (corrected).	Menstruation.	Bowels.	Remarks.
44	35	113	26	3,520,000	35	.49	Amenorrhœa.	Constipated.	
45	35	131	16	4,100,000	26	.30	Amenorrhœa.	Constipated.	Headache. Vomiting.
46	36	72	21	4,800,000	65	.64	Irregular.	Constipated.	
47	36	78	29	4,800,000	40	.41	Amenorrhœa.		
48	36	119	18	4,100,000	35	.41	Amenorrhœa.	Constipated.	
49	37	59	22	3,200,000	25	.38	Amenorrhœa.		
50	38	8	13½	4,360,000	40	.45	Never menstruated.	Constipated.	
51	39	32	21	4,320,000	20	.24	Amenorrhœa.	Regular.	
52	39	69	17	4,000,000	40	.50	Amenorrhœa.	Constipated.	
53	40	117	17	4,640,000	30	.33	Irregular.	Constipated.	Dyspepsia. Headache.
54	41	123	18	3,000,000	30	.50	Irregular.	Constipated.	Pain in chest. Congenital syphilis.
55	42	124	26	4,230,000	38	.44	R. Scanty & pale.	Constipated.	Cramps in legs at night.
56	45	133	19	2,880,000	29	.50	Normal.	Constipated.	
57	47	104	18	2,840,000	24	.41	R. Scanty and pale.	Constipated.	
58	48	52	20	4,860,000	28	.20	Amenorrhœa.	Constipated.	Occasional vomiting.
59	49	25	24	3,500,000	45	.64	Irregular.	Constipated.	Vomiting. Headache.
60	49	68	26	4,700,000	52	.54			
61	50	81	20	2,300,000	30	.64	Slight menorrhagia.	Regular.	Slight mitral stenosis. Sickness.
62	50	64	17	3,500,000	30	.42			Dyspepsia.
63	50	114	25	2,430,000	26	.51	Amenorrhœa.	Constipated.	Thirst.
64	51	20	18	3,800,000	35	.45	R. Scanty & pale.	Constipated.	Dyspepsia.
65	53	95	24	5,200,000	48	.46	Irregular.	Constipated.	Epigastric pain.
66	53	131	23	3,500,000	40	.58	Irregular.	Constipated.	
67	54	125	22	2,800,000	35	.61	Amenorrhœa.	Constipated.	
68	55	68	21	1,800,000	20	.55	Irregular. Leucorrhœa.		Dyspepsia.
69	55	74	21	3,300,000	35	.52	Amenorrhœa.	Constipated.	Headache. Backache.
70	55	127	24	4,480,000	35	.38	Amenorrhœa.	Constipated.	Pains in arms and legs.
71	56	56	17	3,200,000	30	.46	Amenorrhœa.	Constipated.	Dyspepsia. Headache.
72	57	106	29	3,600,000	35	.47			
73	10	77	19	3,500,000	40	.57			
74	13	117	17	3,400,000	30	.44			
75	13	193	19	3,590,000	35	.48	Amenorrhœa.		
76	13	159	20	3,500,000	25	.35	Amenorrhœa.		
77	40	63	19	3,200,000	26	.39			
78	40	151	12	3,100,000	25	.39			
79	49	217	17	3,160,000	24	.37		Constipated.	
80	53	167	19	2,100,000	20	.45	R. Scanty & pale.	Constipated.	
Average =			20	3,437,300	34	.49			

Note.—The colour index or the hæmoglobin richness of each individual red blood corpuscle is arrived at by dividing the percentage of hæmoglobin by the percentage of red corpuscles. Thus the average number of red corpuscles in the 80 cases of chlorosis included in the table was 3,437,300 per cubic millimetre ; and taking the average number of red corpuscles per cubic millimetre in the female at 4,500,000, the average percentage of red corpuscles in the 80 cases included in the table was 76 per cent. The actual average percentage of hæmoglobin in the 80 cases included in the table (as estimated by Gowers' instrument) was 34. But Gowers' instrument reads low (85 to 90 instead of 100 per cent.). Therefore, taking the reading of Gowers' instrument at 90 instead of 100 per cent., the average percentage of hæmoglobin in the 80 cases of chlorosis included in the table should be 37 per cent. The colour index would therefore be :—

$$\frac{\text{Average percentage of hæmoglobin}}{\text{Average percentage of red corpuscles}} \text{ or } \frac{37.7}{76.3} = .49.$$

Strictly speaking, the normal percentage of hæmoglobin in the female should be represented as less than 90 °/₀ (as estimated by Gowers' instrument), and consequently the colour index should be higher than .49 ; for the amount of hæmoglobin in the blood of the female is probably, on the average, 8 °/₀ or 10 °/₀ less than in the blood of the male—which is usually taken as the standard.

41 per cent.; and the individual corpuscular richness in hæmoglobin (the colour index, as he terms it) equalled 50 per cent.

In chlorosis, the blood corpuscles are markedly paler than normal; many of the red corpuscles are somewhat smaller than normal, but in most of the cases which I have carefully observed, the alterations in size and shape have not been marked; in the advanced stages of aggravated cases unusually large red corpuscles (megalocytes) are occasionally present, but very small red corpuscles (the smallest sized microcytes) are in my experience very rare. In those cases of profound chlorosis in which the red blood corpuscles are greatly reduced in number (but this, it must be remembered, is quite exceptional), and in which this marked reduction is of long duration, in other words, in those rare cases of chlorosis in which an excessive production of red blood corpuscles is demanded for a length of time, one would naturally expect that the red blood cells would be imperfectly formed and consequently altered in size and shape. As a matter of fact, the extreme alterations in size and shape of the red blood corpuscles, which are so characteristic of pernicious anæmia, have rarely been present even in the most severe cases of chlorosis which have come under my own notice. I have, however, noticed a considerable degree of poikilocytosis in some cases.

With regard to the alterations in size and shape of the red corpuscles, Cabot states (p. 136): "Deformities in size and shape are very common in all advanced cases, but often absent in mild or moderate ones. They present no special peculiarities except that macrocytes are relatively rare and microcytes relatively common. In the severest cases, however, the macrocytes begin to get more numerous and we approach the picture of pernicious anæmia."

In chlorosis, the large white blood corpuscles are usually less numerous than in health; the small white corpuscles (lymphocytes) may be more numerous than normal.

The blood-plates are usually increased in number, and Max Schultze's granular masses are often numerous and prominent.

The blood usually coagulates rapidly and the fibrin network is well marked.

Nucleated red blood corpuscles and myelocytes are, it is said, occasionally present in the blood; Dr Muir informs me that in his experience this only occurs in very extreme cases.

In some cases I have seen appearances which seemed to be suggestive of the presence of micro-organisms; but in all of the cases of chlorosis in which I have inoculated sterilised gelatine with the blood—and I have from time to time made quite a number of observations of this kind—the results have been negative.

Lloyd Jones states that the specific gravity of the blood in chlorosis is always considerably diminished (from 1050-1060, the normal, to 1030-1045). He further concludes that since his observations show that the specific gravity of the serum obtained from chlorotic blood, as a rule, differs little if at all from the serum of the healthy (while it may be increased or more rarely diminished), the marked diminution of the specific gravity of the whole blood in chlorosis must be largely either due to an absolute diminution of the number of red corpuscles, or an absolute increase in the amount of plasma.*

The following notes descriptive of the condition of the blood in three well-marked cases of chlorosis may be taken as fairly typical and illustrative :—

Case 1 (No. 35 in Table 2).—Female, aged 18 : profound and typical chlorosis.

The condition of the blood on 19th December, 1894, was as follows :—Red corpuscles, 2,800,000 ; hæmoglobin = 20 per cent. ; colour index, .35 ; slight excess of white corpuscles, both small and large ; blood-plates numerous and Max Schultze's granular masses in excess ; a strong tendency to fine fibrin-felt formation.

The red corpuscles for the most part go into rouleaux ; they are pale, the majority of them of normal size or perhaps slightly smaller than normal ; a few larger and a few distinctly smaller than normal, but no very large corpuscles and no small microcytes. A few of the red corpuscles appeared to be nucleated in consequence of the concentration of the hæmoglobin in one part of the corpuscle. A few of the red corpuscles are mis-shaped, tailed and biscuit-shaped (a moderate degree of poikilocytosis). Some small, pale, apparently actively-moving, minute masses of protoplasm (? organisms) ; some of them are rod-shaped, one distinctly swollen at each end.

Case 2 (No. 39 in Table 2).—Female, aged 25: typical chlorosis.

The condition of the blood was as follows :—Red corpuscles, 3,300,000 ; hæmoglobin = 26 per cent. ; colour index, .38. The red corpuscles go into rouleaux ; they are pale ; no poikilocytosis ; a few microcytes ; no megalocytes ; no apparently or actually nucleated red corpuscles. There is no excess of white corpuscles ; those which are present are mostly of large size and coarsely granular. The blood-plates and Max Schultze's granular masses are in some excess.

Case 3 (No. 40 in Table 2).—Female, aged 16: typical chlorosis.

---

* "Chlorosis," by Dr E. Lloyd Jones, p. 23.

The condition of the blood was as follows : Red corpuscles, 3,500,000 ; hæmoglobin = 30 per cent. ; colour index, .42. The rouleaux formation is somewhat imperfect ; the red corpuscles are pale ; a moderate degree of poikilocytosis ; a few microcytes ; no megalocytes. Leucocytes less numerous than normal. Blood-plates and Max Schultze's granular masses about normal in number.

Cabot sums up the characters of the blood in chlorosis as follows :—

" 1. Blood as a whole: Very pale in marked cases, very fluid, but coagulates rapidly. Fibrin not increased. Specific gravity usually low, running parallel with the hæmoglobin.

2. Red cells : Average 4,000,000 when patient is first seen, very rarely go below 1,000,000. The majority of them are *small-sized, pale*, often deformed. Nucleated corpuscles are rare (normoblasts as a rule).

3. White cells, not increased.

Lymphocytosis ; occasionally eosinophilia.

4. Blood-plates increased." *

The condition of the heart and pulse in cases of chlorosis is very important. As I have already stated, palpitation is a frequent symptom ; it is due to the irritable weakness of the heart muscle. Slight excitements whether of body or mind produce an unusual effect upon the irritable heart. The pulse is readily excited. In the earlier stages of the disease, the pulse tension is usually good, in fact it may be higher than normal ; but when the chlorosis is long-continued or severe, the pulse tension has, in my experience, been invariably low. Sphygmographic tracings often show the undue irritability of the heart in a striking way.

When the patient is perfectly tranquil and at rest the cardiac impulse is usually feeble and diffuse ; under excitement, the apex beat becomes much more forcible and well defined ; the apex beat is usually displaced somewhat downwards and outwards to the left; epigastric pulsation is often present. The area of cardiac dulness is usually increased both to the right and to the left. The ventricles, particularly the left ventricle, are usually more or less dilated. On auscultation, a systolic murmur is usually present in the pulmonary and often in the mitral and tricuspid areas. Less frequently a systolic murmur is also audible in the aortic area. The mitral and tricuspid murmurs are doubtless due to regurgitation, apparently the result of muscular and relative incompetence.

---

* "Clinical Examination of the Blood," p. 139.

The exact mode of production of the pulmonary murmur is more difficult to explain. In my opinion the balance of evidence seems to show that it is due partly to the altered condition of the blood, partly to the altered relationship of the pulmonary orifice to the pulmonary artery, and partly to the altered mode of contraction of the heart. In cases of chlorosis the pulmonary artery is usually somewhat dilated and the action of the heart is, at all events under excitement, quick and the contraction of the cardiac muscle more rapid and sudden than in health. The sudden propulsion of a wave of hydræmic blood into the pulmonary artery which is, in comparison to the orifice, relatively dilated, seems to me the most reasonable explanation of the mode of production of the pulmonary murmur.

I am quite unable to accept Dr George Balfour's theory that the murmur is a systolic mitral murmur propagated to the pulmonary area through the appendix of the left auricle, which he states comes to the surface and overlaps the pulmonary artery in the 2nd left interspace. I need not discuss the question in detail, for I have considered it at great length in my work on the heart. I need only repeat that Dr Balfour's theory seems contradicted by the following facts :—(1) That in some of the cases of chlorosis in which the systolic murmur in the pulmonary area is well marked, there is no mitral murmur, *i.e.*, no murmur can be heard in the mitral area ; (2) That in cases of profound anæmia which prove fatal (cases of pernicious anæmia, for example, in which the same pulmonary murmur is present), the appendix of the left auricle, as Dr William Russell was the first to point out and as my pathological experience abundantly confirms, rarely if ever overlaps the pulmonary artery ; owing to the dilatation of the right heart and the twisting of the organ on itself which results therefrom, the left auricular appendix is usually entirely concealed by the pulmonary artery and does not come to the surface of the chest at all ; (3) The aortic systolic murmur is clearly not the result of mitral regurgitation, but in some cases at all events appears to be produced at the aortic orifice (in other cases it is perhaps the pulmonary systolic murmur heard in the aortic area). Now, if a systolic murmur can in cases of chlorosis be produced at the aortic orifice, there is every reason to suppose that it may also be produced at the pulmonary orifice ; (4) That the point of maximum intensity of the pulmonary systolic murmur in cases of anæmia and chlorosis is not situated as Balfour states at a point an inch and a half or more outside the sternum, but at the inner end of the 2nd left interspace, just outside the sternum, *i.e.*, over the position of the pulmonary artery.

Many other theories have been advanced to account for the pulmonary murmur of anæmia ; for example, Potain is of opinion that the murmur is exocardial and produced in the borders of the lung which surround the heart ; * William Russell supposes that it is due to the stretching and compression of the pulmonary artery during its systolic filling by the distended left auricle ; † Sansom thinks that the cause of the murmur is a fibrillary tremor initiated at the overstrained portion of the right ventricle, the conus just below the valves, and perhaps communicated to the valves themselves so that they vibrate in the blood current ; ‡ and Kingston Fowler believes that it is due to the altered condition of the blood and the relatively dilated condition of the pulmonary artery to the blood in anæmia. Dr Fowler's explanation seems to me important; his statement on the point is as follows:§—

" The theory which to my mind most satisfactorily explains the mode of production of this murmur, and also that heard in the veins of the neck, is the one first advocated by Chauveau, ‖ and may be stated thus :—' In anæmia there is a general reduction in the volume of the blood ; the blood-vessels generally with two exceptions adapt their diameter to the reduced volume. The exceptions are (1) the aorta and pulmonary artery, which, owing to the absence of the contractile and the preponderance of the elastic element in their walls, cannot reduce their diameter proportionately to that of the current passing through them ; (2) the roots of the innominate veins are fixed and kept permanently dilated by the cervical fascia, which not only ensheaths them but is connected with the sternum, clavicle, and first rib. · Hence, whilst the jugular and subclavian veins above accommodate themselves to the reduced diameter of their respective currents, the commencing portion of the innominate vein is incapable of a reduction of calibre and becomes relatively dilated.' The blood-stream, therefore, at these points passes through a narrow orifice into a portion of the vessel having a wider calibre, which, as we have seen, is one of the conditions necessary for the production of a murmur. There is an interesting confirmation of the truth of this theory in the fact

---

* An important abstract and criticism of Potain's views are given by Dr Gordon Sanders in the "Edinburgh Medical Journal," 1897, Vol. i., p. 522.

† "Investigation into Some Morbid Cardiac Conditions," by Dr William Russell, p. 53.

‡ "The Diagnosis of Diseases of the Heart and Aorta," by Dr A. E. Sansom, p. 285.

§ "On the Origin of Anæmic Murmurs," by Dr J. K. Fowler, p. 28.

‖ "Gaz. méd. de Paris," 1855.

that a similar bruit to that audible in the innominate veins may occasionally be heard over the cerebral sinuses at the torcular Herophili where the same conditions as to non-contractility are present, and also in the fact which I have observed, that in anæmic subjects who suffer from deafness not dependent on disease of the auditory nerve and in whom the conduction of the skull vibrations is normal, a similar sound becomes audible on the affected side. This is, no doubt, the bruit produced in the lateral sinus conveyed to the ear through the medium of the temporal bone."

Some authorities state that a diastolic aortic murmur is occasionally also present; but the correctness of this opinion is doubtful. Dr Sansom has suggested that what appears to be the diastolic portion of a double aortic murmur is probably the venous murmur in the neck heard at the aortic orifice during the diastole of the heart.

In the great majority of cases a venous hum (*bruit de diable*) can be heard, and in some cases very distinctly felt by the finger, at the root of the neck. Occasionally, more especially in children affected with chlorosis, a loud blowing murmur is audible over the torcular Herophili.

In many cases of profound chlorosis the veins of the neck are dilated. A flickering pulsation can not unfrequently be observed in the dilated external jugular vein on careful observation. In those cases in which a considerable degree of tricuspid regurgitation is present, true venous pulsation in the external jugulars may be well marked.

Venous thromboses occasionally occur. In my experience, they are much more frequent than some writers have stated. The veins of the calf are usually affected. The clot not unfrequently extends up to the femoral vein. The onset is usually rapid. The patient complains of pain in the calf, which becomes considerably swollen, hard and exceedingly tender ; the foot and ankle swell ; there is often at the same time a marked elevation of temperature. In rare cases, the condition is bilateral, one vein being first affected and the corresponding vein on the opposite side after an interval of time becoming involved. In very rare cases, the venous sinuses within the cranium may become thrombosed, or a portion of clot which has been detached from the femoral veins may be swept through the circulation and may produce fatal plugging of the pulmonary artery. No cases of this kind have come under my own observation.

The condition of the alimentary system.—Dyspeptic derangements are very common ; there is usually loss of appetite ; not unfrequently the appetite is capricious. In some cases there is flatulent dyspepsia with pain some time after eating; in these cases the dyspepsia is probably the result of the nutritive altera- tions in the stomach and intestine which the anæmic condition pro- duces, and of the impairment of the digestive power which results therefrom. In a considerable proportion of cases the stomach seems to be dilated. In other cases, ulceration of the stomach is present. Chlorosis and simple perforating ulcer of the stomach are often met with in combination. I do not of course mean to say that most chlorotics are the subjects of ulceration of the stomach, but I do say that in a large proportion of cases of simple (perforating) ulcer of the stomach the patients are chlorotic. The anæmic condition undoubtedly predisposes to the production of ulceration, perhaps by producing a debilitated condition of the gastric mucous mem- brane, structural changes in the gastric mucous membrane (fatty, hæmorrhagic, etc.), or by leading to the formation of embolic or thrombotic plugging of the nutrient vessels.

In many cases of chlorosis, the tongue is pale, flabby, indented by the teeth and slightly furred; in others, it is pale and clean.

Constipation is usually present, but, as I have already pointed out, it is not an essential or invariable symptom; in many of the cases which have come under my own notice the bowels have been quite regular. In the 80 cases contained in Table 2, in 49 the bowels were constipated; in 13 there was no constipation (in one of these cases there was diarrhœa); and in 18 cases the condition of the bowels is not specially mentioned in the notes.

In many cases, the teeth are carious.

The condition of the uterine and ovarian functions.—There is usually some utero-ovarian derangement, generally amenorrhœa. This, as I have already stated, is a result and not a cause of the disease. As I have already pointed out, in a not inconsiderable proportion of cases of chlorosis the menstruation is perfectly regular in time, though in most cases of this kind it is too pale and scanty; in some cases the menstruation is perfectly natural in every respect; in other cases (but they are rare) there is menorrhagia. In the 80 cases analysed in Table 2, in 29 cases there was amenorrhœa; in 9 cases the menstruation was irregular; in 7 cases the menstrua- tion was regular in time but scanty and pale; in 2 cases the patients had never menstruated; in 1 case there was slight menor- rhagia; in 1 case there was dysmenorrhœa; in 11 cases the men- struation was perfectly normal; and in 20 cases the condition of menstruation is not specially mentioned in the notes.

In some cases of chlorosis there is leucorrhœa, doubtless the result of the enfeebled tone, both general and local; in 3 of the 80 cases analysed in Table 2, there was leucorrhœa. Dysmenorrhœa is occasionally present, but it is very doubtful whether it is the result of the disease ; I am strongly disposed to think that its occasional occurrence is purely accidental.

The condition of the nervous system.—Nervous symptoms, such as giddiness, which is of course due to defective blood supply to the brain, tinnitus, headache, a feeling of weight on the top of the head and of tightness round the head, and neuralgia are often complained of. The late Dr Anstie used to say that neuralgia was a prayer on the part of the nerves for a better supply of blood. Pain in the region of the heart and under the left breast (infra-mammary myalgia or neuralgia) is a common symptom. In many cases the temper is irritable and uncertain. Hysterical symptoms are of frequent occurrence. Sleeplessness is comparatively common. Fainting may occur after slight effort, such for example as suddenly rising from the recumbent to the erect position, after a watery evacuation of the bowels, etc. A nervous cough is not uncommon.

The condition of the fundus oculi and optic discs.—In a small proportion of cases of chlorosis, optic neuritis (papillitis) occurs. It is especially apt to be developed in those cases in which there is hypermetropia ; and since patients affected with chlorosis frequently suffer from headache, the combination of headache with double optic neuritis may lead the physician to suppose that he has to deal with the presence of a cerebral tumour.

The condition of the urine.—There is rarely any characteristic change. In my experience the urine is generally normal in colour or paler than normal, and of low specific gravity, but free from any abnormal constituents.

The temperature.—Intercurrent attacks of fever occasionally occur. A slight degree of pyrexia may be the result of some agitation or excitement ; a decided degree of pyrexia is usually due to the development of venous thrombosis or some other accidental complication. Anæmic fever properly so-called, such as is frequently seen in cases of pernicious anæmia, is exceedingly rare, indeed it is doubtful if it actually occurs.

Hæmorrhages. — Epistaxis occasionally occurs, but other hæmorrhages are exceedingly rare, except in those cases in which hæmatemesis results from associated ulceration of the stomach ; in cases of this kind, the hæmorrhage is, as I have already pointed out, an indirect, not a direct, result of the disease, or an accidental and associated condition. When the hæmatemesis is profuse it may of course materially aggravate the anæmic condition. In rare cases, as has just been mentioned, there is menorrhagia.

DIAGNOSIS AND DIFFERENTIAL DIAGNOSIS.

The diagnosis of chlorosis rarely presents any difficulty. In well-marked cases the anæmia is self-obvious and the symptoms highly characteristic; while the history of the case and the absence of any obvious cause for the bloodlessness, such as severe hæmorrhage, show that the anæmia is a primary anæmia.

The chief difficulty occurs in those cases in which ulceration of the stomach is associated with the chlorosis and in which there has been profuse hæmatemesis. As has been already stated, the two conditions are often met with in combination.

The Differential Diagnosis of Chlorosis and of Dyspepsia and Ulceration of the Stomach.—In cases in which dyspeptic symptoms are associated with chlorosis, the stomach symptoms may, as I have already stated, be the result either of anæmic changes with loss of functional activity in the walls of the stomach, or of ulceration. In those cases in which hæmatemesis occurs and in which the patient comes under observation for the first time after the occurrence of the bleeding, it is important to determine whether the patient was bloodless before the hæmatemesis, or whether the anæmia is the result of the bleeding. There is usually no difficulty in deciding this point by a careful investigation of the previous history of the case.

The Differential Diagnosis of Chlorosis and Phthisis.—In some cases of phthisis, there is a considerable degree of anæmia at the onset of the disease; but these cases are not likely to be mistaken for chlorosis by a careful and competent observer. The diagnosis must of course be chiefly based upon the presence of physical signs indicative of lung disease, and the examination of the sputum; but the associated symptoms (more especially loss of weight, pyrexia and a tendency to night sweats) are also of importance.

The Differential Diagnosis of Chlorosis and of Bright's disease.—Bright's disease may also be mistaken for chlorosis by a careless observer. The condition of the urine at once shows the true nature of the case.

The Differential Diagnosis of Chlorosis and of Lead poisoning.—In some cases of lead poisoning a profound degree of anæmia is present, and if, as is often the case, the patient should happen to be a young woman, the case may easily be mistaken for chlorosis. In both conditions, constipation and amenorrhœa are usually present. The presence of a blue line on the gums, the fact that the patient has been exposed to lead poisoning, the occupation of the patient and the presence of other symptoms suggestive of plumbism (such as dry colic, rheumatism, wrist-drop, etc.) are usually sufficiently distinctive of the true nature of the condition. It must, however, be remembered that the two conditions may occur in combination, *i.e.*, lead poisoning may be developed in a patient already affected with chlorosis.

The Differential Diagnosis of Chlorosis and of Organic Mitral disease.—The differential diagnosis of a primary cardiac lesion and of the chlorotic heart is not always easy. In the earlier stages of chlorosis in which a pulmonary systolic murmur is alone present, there is usually no difficulty. It is in the advanced stages when the heart cavities become dilated, when murmurs are developed at the mitral and tricuspid orifices that the chief difficulty of diagnosis occurs. In cases of this kind, the patient suffers from palpitation and shortness of breath, and œdema of the feet may be present. The condition may consequently be easily mistaken by an inexperienced observer for a case of primary heart disease. But the profound anæmia and the condition of the blood (the marked deficiency of hæmoglobin) at once suggest the true nature of the case. It is only in those cases in which there is a history of previous rheumatism, or where there is reason to suppose that the heart was affected before the bloodless condition developed, that the diagnosis presents any real difficulty.

In doubtful cases, the effects of treatment are most important in deciding the true nature of the condition. Chlorosis is, as I have already stated, easily cured by appropriate treatment, and with the disappearance of the anæmia, the heart symptoms and physical signs subside and gradually disappear. With the supply of iron to the blood, the nutritive alterations and fatty changes in the heart muscle disappear, the dilatation subsides and the heart becomes normal. It must be remembered that while in some cases fatty degeneration of the heart muscle is a very grave disease, in others, as in aggravated and long-continued cases of chlorosis, it is eminently curable. It cannot be too forcibly insisted on that the prognosis in cases of fatty heart depends entirely upon the cause of the condition—whether that cause is removable by treatment or not.

The Differential Diagnosis of Chlorosis and Ulcerative Endocarditis.—This rarely presents any difficulty, although the two conditions are, as regards some of their symptoms, very similar. In both diseases, a profound condition of anæmia, a greenish-yellow or lemon-yellow tint of the skin, cardiac murmurs, a dilated and unduly irritable condition of the heart, with arterial murmurs, a jerking visible condition of the pulse and a distended and pulsating condition of the veins in the neck may be present. In ulcerative endocarditis there is usually more or less fever, and some cases of chlorosis are, as I have already stated, attended with slight and temporary pyrexia.

The chief points of distinction are :—The age and sex of the patient ; the condition of the blood ; the exact condition of the heart ; the character of the febrile disturbance ; the condition of the spleen ; and the presence or absence of symptoms indicative of embolic infarction.

Chlorosis is, as we have seen, essentially a disease of young women. Ulcerative endocarditis may, of course, occur at the same age, but it is comparatively speaking uncommon in young women. The sex of the patient and the age of the patient are consequently of some importance.

In chlorosis, the anæmia, and especially a deficiency of hæmoglobin, are the fundamental features of the case, while the altered condition of the heart is secondary. But in ulcerative endocarditis, the anæmia is secondary to and the result of the cardiac lesion. The history of the case and the way in which the anæmia has developed are consequently of importance for the purposes of diagnosis. Further in some cases of ulcerative endocarditis, staphylococci or other micro-organisms can be detected in the blood by staining or cultivation.

In most cases of ulcerative endocarditis the cardiac lesion and the cardiac symptoms are far greater than can reasonably be accounted for by the degree of anæmia which is present ; whereas in chlorosis the reverse is the case—the cardiac symptoms and the degree of cardiac dilatation are more or less proportionate to the degree of the anæmia and the length of time it has existed.

In chlorosis, fever is rare except as the result of some well-marked complication such as thrombosis of the veins of the leg ; while, in ulcerative endocarditis, fever is almost always present and is usually a striking feature of the case.

In ulcerative endocarditis, the spleen is usually enlarged and symptoms indicative of embolic infarctions and of peripheral inflammations, the result of minute emboli, are often developed. These conditions are absent in chlorosis, though venous thromboses, especially in the calf, sometimes occur.

Further, in cases of ulcerative endocarditis, it is obvious that the patient is seriously ill ; the general condition is suggestive and indicative of gravity and danger. This is rarely the case in chlorosis, although in any profound condition of anæmia, the patient may look extremely ill and manifest great exhaustion after effort. I recently had in hospital a case in point—a profound case of chlorosis—in which the patient walked some distance to the hospital. On admission, she looked extremely ill and her condition was suggestive of great danger, but a few days' rest in bed and appropriate treatment were immediately followed by marked improvement and a striking change in the appearance of the case.

Lastly, and this is a most important point, the effects of treatment are of the greatest diagnostic value.

The Differential Diagnosis of Chlorosis and Pernicious Anæmia.—When the observer has satisfied himself that the anæmia is primary, that there is no obvious disease in any of the organs to account for it, and that the bloodlessness is the chief clinical characteristic of the case, the question arises whether the case is one of chlorosis or of pernicious anæmia. In the great majority of cases there is no difficulty in deciding this point.

The chief points to which attention should be directed in order to decide the question are:—(1.) *The age and sex of the patient.*— Pernicious anæmia rarely occurs in young women, while chlorosis is almost exclusively a disease of young women. In my 314 cases of typical chlorosis, no case occurred after the age of 33 (though I have seen three or four cases, apparently of primary anæmia of the chlorotic type, in middle-aged or old women), and only 11 cases after the age of 28 ; while in my series of 45 cases of pernicious anæmia only 3 cases occurred below the age of 28.

(2.) *The condition of the blood.*—In pernicious anæmia, the red blood corpuscles are enormously reduced in number ; though the total amount of hæmoglobin is often markedly diminished, the richness in hæmoglobin of the individual red blood corpuscles is usually equal to or above, the normal ; the red blood corpuscles do not form rouleaux, and they present marked variations in size and shape. Whereas, in chlorosis the red blood corpuscles may be almost up to the normal average number, or in the more severe cases only moderately decreased in number ; though in exceptional cases they are greatly reduced, the lowest figure I have met with being 1,425,000 per cubic millimetre (average in my cases, 3,437,300 per cubic millimetre). The total hæmoglobin is not only decreased but the richness in hæmoglobin of the individual red blood corpuscles is markedly below the normal—average 49.4 per cent. in my own cases. Apart from the pallor of the red blood corpuscles and the fact that many of the red corpuscles are somewhat smaller than normal, the microscopical characters of the blood do not as a rule present any marked or characteristic alterations, though a moderate degree of poikilocytosis is common. The extreme variations in size and shape which are so characteristic of pernicious anæmia are comparatively rarely present in chlorosis.

The concentration of the hæmoglobin in localised parts of the red corpuscles (apparent nucleation) which is such a constant feature in pernicious anæmia is rarely seen, at all events in a marked degree, in chlorosis.

Nucleated red corpuscles which frequently occur in pernicious anæmia, though they may only be present in small number, are very rarely met with in chlorosis (only in very severe cases of long duration).

In pernicious anæmia the blood coagulates less rapidly than in health, the blood-plates are usually diminished in number, sometimes markedly so, and the fibrin network is deficient ; whereas in chlorosis the blood-plates and Max Schultze's granular masses are usually more numerous than in health, and the fibrin network is usually abundant.

(3.) *The therapeutic effect of iron.*—In pernicious anæmia, iron usually produces no improvement, in fact in many cases it seems to do harm rather than good ; while in the vast majority of cases of chlorosis the patients rapidly improve under the administration of iron (together with rest in bed, etc.), provided always that the iron is given in sufficiently large doses and that the gastro-intestinal tract is in a healthy condition.

(4.) *The presence of pyrexia.* — In chlorosis, fever is rarely developed except as the result of some intercurrent complication such as thrombosis of the veins of the leg ; whereas in pernicious anæmia intercurrent and apparently causeless attacks of pyrexia (true anæmic fever) are of frequent occurrence and of considerable diagnostic value.

(5.) *The condition of the urine.*—This, though an uncertain guide, is, in some cases, of considerable diagnostic importance. In chlorosis, the urine is usually normal in colour or paler than normal. In pernicious anæmia, the urine may be of normal colour or pale, but is apt from time to time (during the temporary exacerbations) to be darker than normal.

PROGNOSIS.

In cases of chlorosis the prognosis is eminently favourable, unless the disease should happen to be attended with some grave complication, such as ulceration of the stomach, thrombosis of the cerebral sinuses, etc. There are few diseases which are more amenable to treatment than chlorosis. Nevertheless, a marked degree of chlorosis should never be made light of; for so long as the profound anæmia continues, complications of a serious kind are apt to be developed. I have already referred to the frequency with which ulceration of the stomach is developed in cases of chlorosis; consequently the possibility of the occurrence of this serious complication should always be kept in view. Further, in a certain proportion of cases of chlorosis, thrombosis of the veins is developed. When the tibial or femoral vein is affected, the condition is almost always recovered from; but in rare cases the cerebral veins may become thrombosed, or a portion of clot from the thrombosed femoral vein may be detached and may be swept through the circulation with the production of fatal plugging of the pulmonary artery. Again, the development of an acute disease in the course of chlorosis, such, for example, as endocarditis or acute croupous pneumonia, is always a serious matter. An example in point occurred a few years ago in my hospital practice. A young woman who, for several months, had suffered from profound chlorosis, was admitted suffering from an attack of acute croupous pneumonia. Although the lung lesion was only moderate in extent, the patient died notwithstanding the most careful treatment. The fatal issue was, I believe, mainly due to the anæmic condition of the blood and the chlorotic condition of the heart. In acute croupous pneumonia, the prognosis, as every one knows, largely turns upon the condition of the heart. The enfeebled and dilated (and in some cases fatty) heart of chlorosis is unable to bear the strain of a severe attack of continued fever or of a severe attack of acute croupous pneumonia.

Further, it would appear that chlorosis predisposes to the occurrence of endocarditis. Acute nephritis and pernicious anæmia are also, it is said, occasionally developed in the course of the disease.

For the reasons just stated, it will be apparent that it is eminently advisable to cure cases of chlorosis as speedily as possible, and, so long as the chlorotic condition continues, to guard the patient as carefully as possible from exposure to the causes of acute febrile disease and from conditions likely to produce intercurrent complications.

But although in the great majority of cases the prognosis is eminently favourable and the disease rapidly cured by appropriate treatment, this, it must be remembered, is not invariably the case. In a small proportion of uncomplicated cases the disease is most obstinate.

Further, it must be remembered that in most cases of chlorosis there is a strong tendency to relapse and recurrence. Hence the importance, after the disease has been temporarily cured, of persistent care and watchfulness and of continued treatment—the continued administration of iron in small doses. After the age of 25, provided that no complications are present, the disease usually cures itself.

TREATMENT.

In the treatment of chlorosis, the essential point is to supply iron to the blood. I will presently refer to the method which in my experience is most effectual for this purpose. But before doing so, let me say a word or two with regard to the general management and hygienic treatment.

In all cases in which the bloodlessness is marked, I attach the greatest importance to keeping the patient persistently at rest in bed. One reason why the disease is so much more easily cured in hospital than in private practice is, I think, because the hospital patients are kept in bed. The absolute rest in the recumbent position removes all strain from the heart (a most important point) and aids the recuperative powers. In chlorosis, anything which excites the body or mind and which is apt to suddenly accelerate the heart's action should be avoided.

While the patient is lying in bed, her surroundings should be as bright and pleasant as possible. It is very desirable that she should have plenty of fresh air and an abundance of sunlight when it can be obtained. There can, I think, be no question that sunlight hastens the cure.

The temperature of the bedroom should be kept about 55°, rather on the cool than on the hot side.

The food should be nutritious and easily digestible. When there are no dyspeptic symptoms, an ordinary mixed diet, consisting of milk, milk foods, fish, white meat, butcher meat, a moderate amount of vegetables, and fruit, may be allowed. Some chlorotic patients seem to have a special liking for oranges and lemons; they sometimes have a craving for acids. As I have already pointed out, it has been suggested that the disease is the result of a deficiency of hydrochloric acid in the gastric juice. While I see no reason to accept this view (or indeed to believe that in most cases of chlorosis there is any deficiency of hydrochloric acid), I nevertheless think it advisable to allow the patient to satisfy this natural craving when it is present.

The function of the bowels should be carefully regulated. This is a most important point, for although I do not agree with the late Sir Andrew Clark in thinking that the chlorotic condition is the direct result of the constipation with which it is so often associated, careful regulation of the bowels seems to aid recovery. The object of the physician should be to see that the bowels are not only evacuated daily, but that the evacuation is sufficiently copious. Cascara, or aloin with nux vomica, ipecacuanha and belladonna may be given each night, or some purgative mineral water first thing in the morning in sufficient quantity to produce a copious and soft but not liquid motion. The tendency which iron has to produce constipation should be remembered; and in prescribing a laxative it is well to remember that the constipation in chlorosis probably depends, in part at least, upon loss of muscular tone, and to select a drug which stimulates the muscular coat of the intestine.

When dyspeptic symptoms are prominent, it is of great importance to restore the stomach and gastro-intestinal tract to a normal healthy condition. This is an important point in the treatment. In some of the dyspeptic cases, iron is badly borne, or at all events it cannot be given as freely as in other cases of chlorosis in which there is no dyspepsia. It must, however, be remembered that the dyspepsia which is so frequently associated with chlorosis may be due to different causes. In most cases the anæmia is the cause of the stomach disorder. In such cases, the dyspeptic symptoms disappear with the removal of the chlorosis. As a matter of experience, I find that in those cases of chlorosis in which the tongue is flabby, furred and indented by the teeth, in which the breath is foul and the patient troubled with flatulence, a preliminary course of alkalies is often most helpful. In my experience, there is nothing more efficacious than a combination of bicarbonate of potash, bicarbonate of soda, aromatic spirits of ammonia, tincture of rhubarb and infusion of calumba.* With this alkaline mixture given before meals, a tonic containing hydrochloric acid, nux vomica and gentian may be given after meals.

As soon as the tongue begins to clean, iron should be freely given; but in most cases I find that the iron may be given from

---

* This alkaline mixture which I give largely and with great advantage in cases of chronic gastritis and flatulent dyspepsia is as follows:—

    ℞   Potassi Bicarb.,
            Sodii Bicarb.,
            Sp. Amm. Arom. āā ℨiii.
            Tr. Rhæi ℨiss.
            Inf. Calumbæ ad ℥vi.

Sig.—A tablespoonful in water three times daily twenty minutes before meals.

the first together with these other remedies. In some cases I give a bitter tonic before meals and the iron after meals. This is, I think, the most effective plan of treatment in those cases in which the dyspeptic symptoms seem to be entirely the result of the chlorotic condition. Dr Lauder Brunton has pointed out that in cases of dyspeptic chlorosis the astringent preparations of iron are often better borne than the ordinary forms ; but, speaking for myself, I find that Robertson's Blaud's pill capsules are usually well borne even in the dyspeptic cases. I have found this preparation of iron far more efficacious than any other which I have hitherto employed.

In those cases in which the stomach is ulcerated, the diet must of course be carefully regulated. It should consist of milk, beef extracts, milk foods and, when the symptoms are severe, peptonised milk alone. Raw beef juice or finely pounded raw meat is, in some of these cases, well borne. In those cases in which the stomach is very irritable, I have found the greatest advantage from rectal feeding. In many cases a blister applied over the region of the stomach is beneficial. The bowels should, of course, be carefully regulated in the manner that I have already described, and iron and arsenic should be given internally.

In cases of chlorosis, the essential part of the treatment is, as I have already mentioned, the administration of iron ; and one great secret of success is to give a sufficient quantity of iron. It matters perhaps comparatively little what the particular preparation is, provided only that enough of it is given, but some preparations are better borne and are more effective than others. Personally, I have been most successful with Robertson's Blaud's pill capsules.* Robertson's capsules are made of different strengths, corresponding to one, two and three Blaud's pills. Unless there is any reason to the contrary, I begin with the No. 3 capsule, which contains the same amount of carbonate of iron as three Blaud's pills, and give one capsule three times daily, after meals ; but I do not stop there ; I gradually increase the dose. During the first week I give one

---

* Messrs Robertson inform me that they attribute the medicinal value of the preparation to the use of the dried salts and the medium used for forming the mass. The disintegration being gradual, the nascent ferrous carbonate is slowly formed in the stomach and is as quickly absorbed by the system, and hence the good results. That the ferrous carbonate is formed after the administration is, they say, also proved by the slight aperient effect which the capsules have, owing to the formation of an alkaline sulphate. They claim that this aperient action does away with the necessity of patients having to take an aperient ; but with this opinion my experience does not altogether agree.

(No. 3) capsule, three times daily; during the second week, two
(No. 3) capsules; during the third week, three (No. 3) capsules;
and during the fourth and succeeding weeks, four (No. 3) capsules
three times daily—equivalent to thirty-six Blaud's pills per diem. In
some cases I have given much larger doses even than this. In one
case which was recently under treatment in hospital, I gave, as an experiment, ten No. 3 capsules three times daily—equivalent to ninety
Blaud's pills per diem. Such enormous doses are in the great
majority of cases altogether unnecessary; four (No. 3) capsules,
three times daily (corresponding to twelve ordinary Blaud's pills,
three times daily), are abundantly sufficient.

In addition to the iron, I often prescribe arsenic; but I do not
attach any great importance to the influence of the arsenic in
chlorosis, except in the rare cases in which the red blood corpuscles
are markedly reduced in number; in such cases arsenic is, I think,
of great value In the great majority of cases of chlorosis, iron is a
far more efficacious remedy than arsenic. In those cases in which
I think it advisable to prescribe arsenic, I usually give two minims
of Fowler's solution three times a day for the first week; three
minims the second; four minims the third; and five minims three
times daily during the fourth and succeeding weeks.

If the plan of treatment which I have now described is faith-
fully and diligently carried out, there is in my experience very rarely
any difficulty in speedily curing even the most severe and obstinate
cases of chlorosis, provided of course that no grave or serious complications are present. I have, I think, obtained greater credit and
reputation from the treatment of severe and obstinate cases of
chlorosis, both in private and hospital practice, than from the treatment of any other disease. I rarely fail to cure even the most
severe cases in the course of from four to six weeks' time. The
points on which I lay most stress are :—(1) rest in bed ; (2) careful
regulation of the diet and bowels; and (3) the administration of
large doses of iron.

Speaking theoretically, the iron should be continued in full
doses until the hæmoglobin, as estimated by the hæmoglobinometer,
reaches the normal amount (85 to 90 per cent. as estimated by
Gowers' instrument). This I consider a most important point. It
should always be aimed at; for no case of chlorosis is really cured
until the hæmoglobin has reached the normal amount, but it is often
difficult to attain to in actual practice. One has often to be content
with a percentage of from 65 to 75 per cent. (as estimated by
Gowers' instrument) After the case is cured (or apparently cured)
the iron should still be persistently administered for several months

in smaller doses—one No. 3 capsule, equal to three Blaud's pills, three times a day.

There are, of course, many other preparations of iron which are very effective. Griffith's mixture, the saccharine carbonate, the sulphate, the bi-palatinoids of Oppenheimer, the oxalate, the lactate, are all admirable preparations; but with none of them have I obtained such satisfactory results as with Robertson's Blaud's pill capsules.

In children, in whom a profound anæmia exactly corresponding to the chlorosis of young women is occasionally met with, the saccharine carbonate is perhaps the most effective remedy; it is easily taken and should be freely given. A very convenient way is to give it mixed with brown Demerara sugar.

In some of the dyspeptic cases, I have found a combination of the tincture of the perchloride of iron with sulphate of magnesia a very efficacious form.

In the anæmia of young males, which in my experience is often attended with emaciation and dyspeptic symptoms, and which appears, in some cases at all events, to be of the chlorotic type, this combination of perchloride of iron and sulphate of magnesia is, I think, particularly efficacious. In passing, I may also say that this is a most useful remedy in cases in which sores which are difficult to heal break out about the nose, and in cases of recurring boils. In some of these conditions, the symptoms are perhaps due to absorption into the blood of poisonous products developed in the intestine. In cases of this kind, constipation is often a prominent symptom. The combination of perchloride of iron and sulphate of magnesia acts both as a laxative, an intestinal disinfectant and as a blood tonic.

In the treatment of chlorosis, sulphur is also a useful remedy; its beneficial effect is probably due to its action as a laxative.

Other remedies which have been recommended for the treatment of chlorosis are oxygen inhalations and the administration of bone-marrow. I have no personal experience to offer with regard to either of them. I am so successful with the rest-iron plan of treatment, which I have described above, that I have never found it necessary to give any other plan of treatment a prolonged trial.

In the course of three or four weeks, the patient may be allowed to get out of bed and to pass part of the day on a sofa or to take carriage exercise. In cases of chlorosis walking exercise is, I think, better avoided, so long, at all events, as the heart symptoms—the shortness of breath on exertion, the palpitation, etc.—continue.

As the colour returns and the hæmoglobin increases, the patient may gradually be allowed to return to her ordinary mode of life.

During the earlier part of the treatment while the patient is confined to bed, massage is often a valuable adjunct to the treatment. It promotes the muscular nutrition and gives the patient, as it were, a sufficient amount of exercise without throwing any undue strain upon the heart.

It is essential to remember that chlorosis is a condition which is very apt to relapse. As I have already stated, the iron should be persistently continued for some time—several months at least—after the case is apparently cured ; and after all treatment has been suspended, the patient should be closely watched for a year or two at least. If any indications of a relapse (such as pallor, breathlessness, palpitation, etc.) again develop, another course of iron should be immediately prescribed ; but, provided that the onset of the relapse is recognised at an early stage, it is rarely necessary to confine the patient to bed. Careful regulation of the bowels, avoidance of cardiac strain and the administration of iron are, in such circumstances, usually all that are required to effect a cure.

I have described the treatment of chlorosis in considerable detail ; it is an important subject, for the disease is very common and it is a most satisfactory disease to treat. Niemeyer used to say that he gained great credit in practice by the successful administration of Blaud's pills ; and, as I have already stated, my personal experience is identical with his on this point.

To sum up, the essential points in the treatment of chlorosis are in my opinion persistent rest in bed in a well-ventilated and sunny room, careful regulation of the diet and bowels, and above all the administration of large doses of iron, Robertson's Blaud's pill capsules being in my experience more effective than any other preparation.

PERNICIOUS ANÆMIA.

Definition or Short Description. — This very interesting disease, to which the synonyms *Idiopathic* anæmia, *Essential* anæmia, *Progressive pernicious* anæmia, etc., have been applied, is characterised by profound anæmia, which usually develops insidiously and without apparent cause. It tends to pursue a progressive course and with rare exceptions ultimately terminates in death.

The essential feature of pernicious anæmia is the great diminution in the number of the red blood corpuscles. The total amount of hæmoglobin in the blood is also markedly decreased, but the diminution of the hæmoglobin is usually less than that of the corpuscles ; in fact, the richness of the individual corpuscles in hæmoglobin is in most typical cases considerably above the normal.

The essential and primary lesion in pernicious anæmia seems to be a destruction of the red blood corpuscles. Dr William Hunter, whose observations have added so much to our knowledge of the pathology of the disease, thinks that the blood destruction is due to a poison absorbed from the gastro-intestinal tract ; and that this poison leads to the rapid destruction of the red blood corpuscles in the portal circulation (more especially in the spleen and liver) and at the same time exerts a disturbing influence upon the liver cells. Some years ago, I ventured to suggest to Dr Hunter that, if this view were correct, the disease might be appropriately termed *gastro-intestinal-hepatic* anæmia.

Historical Note.—The celebrated Dr Addison of Guy's Hospital, the discoverer of Addison's disease, was the first to give a complete description of the disease ; he termed it *idiopathic anæmia*. Addison's description was published in the year 1855.

Though well known to Dr Wilks and the physicians of Guy's Hospital, it was for a time lost sight of until it was redescribed by Professor Biermer of Zurich in the year 1872. In 1876 and 1877 I published two clinical lectures on the subject in the Medical Times and Gazette, and a series of cases in the " Edinburgh Medical Journal " ; in the latter communication I figured the blood changes and directed attention to the value of arsenic in the treatment of the disease. In Vol. xxvi. Guy's Hospital Reports (1882), Dr Pye-Smith published an important contribution to the subject, in which he gives a very complete résumé of the literature of the disease up to that date and an abstract of 102 cases collected from various sources. Of recent years, numerous cases have been recorded and our knowledge of the nature and causation of the disease has been very materially increased.

Before considering the pathology of pernicious anæmia in detail, it will perhaps be advisable to describe the clinical history of the disease and the morbid alterations which are present in the bodies of patients who have died of the disease.

CLINICAL HISTORY.

Addison's description of Pernicious Anæmia. — Addison's description of pernicious anæmia, or idiopathic anæmia as he termed it, was as follows :—

" For a long period I had from time to time met with a very remarkable form of general anæmia occurring without any discoverable cause whatever, cases in which there had been no previous loss of blood, no exhausting diarrhœa, no chlorosis, no purpura, no renal, splenic, miasmatic, glandular, strumous, or malignant disease.

" Accordingly, in speaking of this form in clinical lectures, I, perhaps with little propriety, applied to it the term 'idiopathic' to distinguish it from cases in which there existed more or less evidence of some of the usual causes or concomitants of the anæmic state.

" The disease presented in every instance the same general character, pursued a similar course and, with scarcely a single exception, was followed after a variable period by the same result.

" It occurs in both sexes ; generally, but not exclusively, beyond the middle period of life ; and, so far as I at present know, chiefly in persons of a somewhat large and bulky frame, and with a strongly-marked tendency to the formation of fat.

" It makes its approach in so slow and insidious a manner that the patient can hardly fix a date to his earliest feeling of that languor which is shortly to become so extreme. The countenance gets pale, the whites of the eyes become pearly, the general frame flabby rather than wasted : the pulse perhaps large, but remarkably soft and compressible, and occasionally with a slight jerk, especially under the slightest excitement ; there is an increasing indisposition to exertion, with an uncomfortable feeling of faintness or breathlessness on attempting it ; the heart is readily made to palpitate ; the whole surface of the body presents a blanched, smooth, and waxy appearance; the lips, gums, and tongue seem bloodless; the flabbiness of the solids increases; the appetite fails; extreme languor and faintness supervene, breathlessness and palpitations being produced by the most trifling exertion or emotion; some slight œdema is probably perceived about the ankles. The debility becomes extreme; the patient can no longer rise from his bed; the mind occasionally wanders; he falls into a prostrate and half-torpid state, and at length expires. Nevertheless, to the very last, and after a sickness of perhaps several months' duration, the bulkiness of the general frame and the obesity often present a most striking contrast to the failure and exhaustion observable in every other respect.

"With perhaps a single exception, the disease, in my own experience, resisted all remedial efforts, and sooner or later terminated fatally.

"On examining the bodies of such patients after death I have failed to discover any organic lesion that could properly or reasonably be assigned as an adequate cause of such serious consequences; nevertheless, from the disease having uniformly occurred in fat people, I was naturally led to entertain a suspicion that some form of fatty degeneration might have a share at least in its production; and I may observe that, in the case last examined, the heart had undergone such a change, and that a portion of the semilunar ganglion and solar plexus, on being subjected to microscopic examination, was pronounced by Mr Quekett to have passed into a corresponding condition.

"Whether any or all of these morbid changes are essentially concerned—as I believe they are—in giving rise to this very remarkable disease, future observation will probably decide.

"The cases having occurred prior to the publication of Dr Bennett's interesting essay on 'Leucocythæmia,' it was not determined by microscopic examination whether there did or did not exist an excess of white corpuscles in the blood of such patients."

The passage is taken from Addison's classical treatise "On the Constitutional and Local Effects of Disease of the Suprarenal Capsules." It was while investigating and trying to detect the cause of idiopathic anæmia, that he came to discover the disease of the suprarenal capsules which bears his name.

From this account, it will be seen that the onset of pernicious anæmia, or idiopathic anæmia as Addison termed it, is, as a rule, gradual and the course progressive, though cases are occasionally observed in which the onset is more or less rapid (in one of my most marked cases the condition had developed certainly in three and probably in less than two months' time); that in most cases the condition arises without any apparent cause; that it is chiefly characterised by debility and prostration, increasing pallor, a profoundly bloodless condition of the mucous membranes and other tissues and organs, shortness of breath and palpitation, and, I may add, in many cases by slight œdema of the feet and eyelids, retinal hæmorrhages, recurring attacks of fever, temporary darkening of the urine, and it may be of jaundice, etc. Though, in the advanced stages of the disease, some swelling of the feet and eyelids is of common occurrence, a marked degree of general dropsy and effusion into the internal cavities are rare.

Let us take a typical case in a fully developed stage and consider some of the symptoms in more detail.

Colour of the skin and mucous membranes. — In well-marked cases of pernicious anæmia, the observer is at once struck by the remarkable pallor of the mucous membranes and of the skin. The skin rarely presents the white pallor which is seen after hæmorrhage or in cases of Bright's disease; it usually has a lemon-yellow or canary-yellow tint. In some cases, this yellow tint is so marked that the patient looks as if he were jaundiced. As a matter of fact, jaundice is in many cases present; it is usually slight in degree, though in rare instances, as in a case which I recently reported,* the jaundice is very marked. In many cases, the yellow tint of the skin is not due to jaundice. In some cases it is probably due to the presence of a pigment derived from the destruction of red blood corpuscles. This, as we shall presently see, is a point of some importance from an etiological point of view. In some cases the yellowness of the conjunctiva is due, as I pointed out several years ago, to the presence of little deposits of fat beneath the conjunctiva. In those cases in which true jaundice occurs, the whole of the conjunctiva, as well as the skin, is of course stained yellow.

In some cases, pigmented patches are present in the skin; and, in rare cases, this pigmentation is so marked or so diffused as to suggest the presence of Addison's disease. I have met with five cases in which the skin was so deeply pigmented as to give rise to the suspicion that Addison's disease and pernicious anæmia were combined. In two of these cases there was an autopsy and in both cases the suprarenal capsules were normal. In two cases in which there was no post mortem the pigmentation of the skin was, I think, due to the arsenic which the patient had been taking in large doses for some time before death.

In one case which came under my notice some years ago a high degree of leucoderma was present. In two of my cases the hair turned rapidly grey during the development of the anæmia; in

---

* "Lancet," Vol. I., 1897, p. 197.

both of these cases the colour was partly regained as the anæmia disappeared under the administration of arsenic.

Excessive weakness, languor and debility.—These are constant and, on the whole, perhaps, the most prominent symptoms of the disease ; they are often the first symptoms which are complained of ; towards the termination of the case the debility is always profound. Great prostration and weakness were complained of in every one of my 45 cases (see Table 3).

The general state of nutrition.—In most cases of pernicious anæmia emaciation is not a prominent symptom, though exceptions to this general statement are occasionally met with. The subcutaneous fat is in many cases well preserved ; the muscles are usually soft and flabby and more or less (in some cases considerably) wasted, but the marked emaciation which is so characteristic of malignant disease is rarely present. This is a point of considerable diagnostic importance, for in some cases it is by no means an easy matter to distinguish pernicious anæmia and cancer of the stomach. It must, however, be remembered that cases are sometimes met with in which there is considerable emaciation, and that in most cases there is some loss of weight.

In my series of 45 cases, there was loss of weight in 34 cases ; in 15 of these 34 cases, the loss of weight was slight, in the remaining 19 the loss was more or less considerable.

The *skin* has usually a soft velvety feel—another point of distinction between pernicious anæmia and most cases of cancer of the stomach, for in malignant disease the skin is apt to become wrinkled and atrophied, and often dry and harsh.

In some cases, but in my experience they are rare (I have only met one well-marked instance), the bones, more especially the sternum and ribs, are tender to pressure and, it may be, affected with localised swellings.

The condition of the blood.—This is most important. Owing to the profoundly bloodless condition, it is often difficult or impossible by simply puncturing the finger (puncturing without bandaging), to obtain a sufficient amount of blood for the purposes of accurate examination. A prick may produce little or no bleeding. This fact, the relatively dry condition of the tissues, and the small amount of blood which is present in the heart and blood vessels after death seem to show that the total amount of blood in the body is reduced in quantity.

When a drop of blood is obtained by simple puncture of the finger, or, preferably, by puncturing the lobe of the ear, it is usually found to be thin and watery-looking ; it usually looks like very thin

TABLE 3, SHOWING THE MORE IMPORTANT SYMPTOMS IN 45 CASES OF PERNICIOUS ANÆMIA.

No.	Age	M.	F.	Number of Red Corpuscles (Lowest Count)	Hæmoglobin	Megalocytes	Microcytes	Poikilocytosis	White Corpuscles	Prostration and Weakness	Loss of Weight	Retinal	Other.†	Dropsy	Vomiting	Diarrhœa	Jaundice	Anæmic Fever.‡	Colour.‡	Albumen.§
1	43	1	..	Much dimd.	..	Numerous	Numerous	Marked	Excess of lymphocytes	1	1	?*	0	0	0	0	0	0	N.	T.
2	20	1	..	Much dimd.	..	Numerous	Numerous	Marked	....	1	0	1	Epis.	1	1	1	1	1	N.	0
3	34	1	..	Much dimd.	..	Numerous	Numerous	Marked	Diminished	1	1	1	0	1	1	0	0	0	N.	0
4	28	1	..	Much dimd.	..	Numerous	Numerous	Marked	Diminished	1	1	1	0	1	0	1	0	0	P.	T.
5	29	..	1	....	1	....	....	....	....	1	0	1	0	0	1	0	..	..	P.	0
6	38	1	..	Much dimd.	..	Numerous	Numerous	Marked	Diminished	1	1	1	0	1	1	1	0	1	P.	c
7	31	1	..	Much dimd.	..	Numerous	Numerous	Marked	No excess	1	0	1	0	1	1	0	..	..	N.	0
8	47	1	..	Much dimd.	..	Numerous	Numerous	Marked	No excess	1	1	1	0	1	0	1	0	0	N.	0
9	17	1	..	Much dimd.	..	Numerous	Numerous	Marked	Slight excess	1	1	0	0	1	1	0	1	0	N.	0
10	51	..	1	Much dimd.	..	Numerous	Numerous	Moderate	....	1	0	1	0	0	1	0	0	..	P.	0
11	54	1	..	Mod. dimd.	..	Few	Some	Moderate	No excess	1	0	..	0	0	1	0	0	..	N.	0
12	50	1	..	1,470,000	46%	Numerous	Numerous	Marked	....	1	1	..	Piles.	0	0	1	1	..	D.	T.
13	38	1	..	Much dimd.	..	Few	Some	Moderate	No excess	1	1	1	Epis.	0	1	1	1	1	D.	1
14	41	..	1	....	..	....	....	....	....	1	0	1	0	1	0	0	0	1	N.	0
15	42	..	1	Much dimd	..	Numerous	Numerous	Marked	....	1	1	0	0	1	0	0	0	..	N.	0
16	53	1	..	Much dimd.	..	Some	Numerous	Marked	Excess of lymphocytes	1	1	0	0	1	0	0	0	..	N.	0
17	54	1	..	....	..	....	....	....	....	1	1	1	0	1	1	0	..	..	N.	0
18	62	..	1	....	..	....	....	....	....	1	0	0	0	0	1	1	1	..	N.	T.
19	63	1	..	1,125,000	35%	Numerous	Numerous	Marked	No excess	1	1	1	0	1	0	0	1	1	D.	0
20	53	1	..	Much dimd.	..	Some	Numerous	Marked	No excess	1	1	?	0	1	0	0	0	0	D.	T.
21	51	1	..	900,000	..	....	....	Marked	....	1	1	1	0	1	1	1	..	1	N.	0
22	66	1	..	....	..	....	....	....	....	1	1	1	0	1	1	1	1	..	N.	0
23	57	1	..	Much dimd.	..	Some	Numerous	Moderate	No excess	1	1	1	0	0	1	1	1	1	D.	0
24	49	1	..	650,000	20%	Some	Numerous	Moderate	4,000	1	1	0	Epis.	0	1	1	1	1	D.	0
25	54	..	1	995,000	28%	Few	Numerous	Moderate	....	1	1	0	0	1	1	0	1	..	D.	0
26	53	1	..	810,000	20%	Numerous	Numerous	Marked	Excess of lymphocytes	1	1	1	0	1	0	1	1	..	D.	1
27	52	..	1	1,180,000	33%	Numerous	Numerous	Moderate	Excess of lymphocytes	1	1	0	Epis.	0	0	0	1	0	D.	0
28	36	1	..	Much dimd.	..	Few	Numerous	Moderate	Excess of lymphocytes	1	0	0	0	0	1	1	1	..	D.	0
29	49	..	1	Much dimd.	..	Numerous	Numerous	Marked	....	1	1	1	0	1	1	1	..	..	N.	0
30	40	..	1	....	..	....	....	Marked	....	1	1	0	0	0	1	0	0	..	N.	0
31	16	..	1	450,000	5%	Some	Some	Moderate	....	1	1	1	Hæm.	1	1	0	0	1	D.	0
32	42	1	..	Much dimd.	..	Few	Numerous	Marked	No excess	1	1	1	Hæm.	0	1	0	0	..	N.	0
33	54	1	..	1,000,000	..	....	....	Marked	....	1	0	0	0	0	0	1	..	..	N.	0
34	46	1	..	800,000	18%	Numerous	Numerous	Marked	Diminished	1	1	0	0	0	0	1	0	..	N.	0
35	72	1	..	....	..	....	....	....	....	1	1	0	0	1	0	0	..	..	N.	0
36	50	..	1	....	..	....	....	....	....	1	0	..	0	1	0	1	..	..	D.	0
37	71	1	..	Much dimd.	..	Numerous	Numerous	Marked	....	1	1	1	0	1	1	1	1	..	N.	0
38	58	1	..	....	..	....	....	....	....	1	1	1	0	0	1	0	1	..	D.	0
39	67	1	..	Much dimd.	..	Numerous	Numerous	Marked	Excess of lymphocytes	1	1	1	0	1	1	1	1	..	N.	0
40	37	1	..	816,000	28%	Some	Numerous	Moderate	4,370	1	1	1	0	0	1	1	1	1	D.	0
41	51	1	..	Much dimd.	..	Numerous	Numerous	Marked	....	1	1	1	0	1	1	0	1	1	D.	0
42	31	..	1	780,000	29%	Numerous	Numerous	Marked	Excess of lymphocytes	1	0	1	0	1	1	0	1	1	D.	0
43	65	..	1	1,300,000	32%	Numerous	Numerous	Marked	Excess of lymphocytes	1	1	1	Epis.	1	0	1	1	1	N.	T.
44	44	..	1	459,000	14%	Some	Some	Moderate	Excess of lymphocytes	1	1	1	0	..	1	0	1	1	D.	0
45	58	1	..	541,670	20%	Numerous	Numerous	Marked	Excess of lymphocytes	1	1	0	Piles.	..	1	0	1	1	N.	0

* In this case retina not well seen owing to opacity of the media. † Epis. = Epistaxis. Hæm. = Hæmatemesis.
‡ N. = Normal. P. = Pale. D. = Dark. § T. = Trace.

claret, and in some cases immediately separates into a clear watery part and a more deeply stained part. In some cases there is a tendency of the puncture to continue bleeding.

In order to obtain a drop of blood of sufficient size for the purposes of accurate examination, it is usually necessary, after making the patient hang the hand down over the side of the bed so as to allow the blood to gravitate into the tips of the fingers, to bandage one of the fingers tightly from the meta-carpo-phalangeal joint down to the termination with a strip of tape. By this procedure all the blood which is contained in the finger is pressed into the tip. Owing to the concentration of the corpuscles, the drop of blood which is now obtained by a deep puncture is more deeply coloured, and the number of red blood corpuscles may, when counted in the ordinary way, appear to be much more numerous, than is actually the case. Hence it is advisable if possible to avoid ligaturing the finger and to estimate both the hæmoglobin and the red blood corpuscles in a drop of blood which has been obtained by simple puncture. As I have just stated above, a drop of blood can usually be obtained without any difficulty by puncturing the lobe of the ear. It is important that the instrument with which the puncture is made should be perfectly clean and very sharp.

The most striking alteration in the blood is the diminution in the number of red blood corpuscles. In well-marked cases of pernicious anæmia the red blood corpuscles, instead of numbering 5,000,000 (male) or 4,500,000 (female) per cubic millimetre, are usually found to be reduced to less than 1,500,000. It is quite common to find only 1,000,000 or less. In several of the recorded cases only 500,000 red corpuscles were present, and in one case described by Quincke the number of red blood corpuscles only reached 143,000; but, as Dr Stephen Mackenzie has pointed out, Quincke's figures always read low. In the great majority of cases in which the red blood corpuscles have been reduced to 500,000 per cubic millimetre, the patient has died from the disease. In Quincke's case recovery took place.

In 15 of my 45 cases blood counts are recorded; the average corpuscular richness of the first counts in these 15 cases was 1,250,384, and of the lowest counts 829,600, the lowest figure being 370,000 per c.mm. (see Table 4). In 52 cases tabulated by Cabot, the red corpuscles averaged 1,200,000 per c.mm.

In the advanced stages of the disease, the total amount of hæmoglobin is always greatly reduced, but the reduction of the hæmoglobin is, in most cases, relatively less than that of the red blood corpuscles. Consequently the individual richness of the red blood corpuscles in hæmoglobin is usually equal to or above the normal. In a case, for example, which I had under my observation when this lecture was written, the red blood corpuscles numbered 1,125,000 per c.mm., while the hæmoglobin (estimated by Gowers' instrument) equalled 31 per cent. This gives the following formula :—$\frac{H}{R.C.} = \frac{31}{25}$, instead of $\frac{H}{R.C.} = \frac{100}{100}$, which represents the relative proportion of hæmoglobin to red corpuscles as estimated in health. But since Gowers' instrument reads low (85 per cent. to 90 per cent. instead of 100 per cent.), the formula should really be $\frac{H}{R.C.} = \frac{36}{25}$ (instead of $\frac{31}{25}$) = a colour index 1.4. In 13 of the cases included in Table 3, the percentage of hæmoglobin was estimated ; the results are set forth in Table 4 ; the average percentage of hæmoglobin in these cases when the patient came under observation (first counts) was 30 per cent., and the average colour index 1.3.

TABLE 4.—CONDITION OF BLOOD IN 15 CASES OF
PERNICIOUS ANÆMIA.

No, in Table 3.	Age.	Sex.	First Count.			Lowest Count.		
			Number of Red Corpuscles.	Hæmo-globin.	Colour Index corr'ct'd.	Number of Red Corpuscles.	Hæmo-globin.	Colour Index corr'ct'd.
				Per cent.			Per cent.	
12	50	M	1,470,000	46	1.7	1,470,000	46	1.7
19	63	M	1,250,000	35	1.5	1,250,000	35	1.5
21	51	M			...	900,000	...	...
24	49	M	1,450,000	46	1.7	650,000	20	1.7
25	54	F	995,000	28	1.4	995,000	28	1.4
26	53	M	810,000	20	1.3	810,000	20	1.3
27	52	F	1,400,000	25	.8	1,118,000	33	1.5
31	16	F	900,000	15	.8	450,000	5	.5
33	54	M			...	1,000,000	...	...
34	46	M	2,500,000	30	.6	800,000	18	1.3
40	37	M	1,200,000	44	2.	370,000	16	2.4
42	31	F	780,000	20	1.4	780,000	20	1.4
43	65	F	1,328,000	32	1.2	1,050,000	28	1.3
44	44	F	1,160,000	34	1.4	459,000	14	1.5
45	58	M	642,000	16	1.4	542,090	30	2.2
Average	-		1,250,384	30	1.3	829,000	23	1.5

These characters of the blood (the marked diminution of the red corpuscles and the fact that while the total hæmoglobin is greatly reduced the individual corpuscular richness in hæmoglobin is usually equal to, and often greater than, the normal) are of the greatest diagnostic importance ; they are the direct opposite of the condition of the blood in chlorosis ; and they differ notably from the characters of the blood in cases of secondary anæmia (anæmia due to loss of blood, cancer of the stomach, etc.) in which the blood corpuscles and the hæmoglobin are (usually) proportionately diminished. I will return to this point when I come to speak of the diagnosis.

In estimating the individual richness of the corpuscles in hæmoglobin it must be remembered that in pernicious anæmia a large number of very minute red corpuscles (microcytes) are almost always present. Now in counting the red corpuscles the presence of these very minute corpuscles is usually ignored ; the smaller microcytes, at all events, are usually omitted from the count. It is obvious that there is a source of fallacy here. If all the minute corpuscles are included in the count, the individual richness of the red blood corpuscles in hæmoglobin (the colour index) will in many cases be found to be much less than it is usually stated to be. On the other hand, it is obvious that the very small microcytes can only carry a very minute quantity of hæmoglobin (though the amount of hæmoglobin which they contain may be larger, in proportion to their relative sizes, than that contained by the megalocytes—this is strikingly seen in the case of Eichhorst's corpuscles) ; and since the blood in pernicious anæmia usually contains large numbers of megalocytes which ought to carry a larger quantity of hæmoglobin than the normally sized red corpuscles (but which do not perhaps always do so), this fallacy, due to counting the normally sized or large red corpuscles only, is perhaps more apparent than real. But allowing for both sources of fallacy (the presence of microcytes and megalocytes), there can, I think, be little doubt that in typical cases of pernicious anæmia the individual richness of the corpuscles in hæmoglobin is usually above the normal.

In my 15 cases in which the blood was counted, the hæmoglobin was also estimated in 13 ; the average percentage of hæmoglobin in the first counts was (uncorrected) 30 per cent., and (corrected for the low reading of Gowers' instrument) 33 per cent., and the average colour index (after correction) was 1.3, the highest colour index being 2. and the lowest .6 (see Table 4).

In 39 cases of pernicious anæmia observed by Cabot, in which the red cells were counted and the hæmoglobin estimated, the red corpuscles averaged 1,200,000 or 24 per cent., while the hæmoglobin averaged 26 per cent., the individual corpuscular richness in hæmoglobin (the colour index) being consequently (uncorrected) 1.08 and corrected 1.2 per cent.*

The microscopical alterations which the red blood corpuscles present are, when taken in connection with the other characters of the blood (more especially the number of red corpuscles and the colour index), also of great diagnostic significance. There is no disease in which the red blood corpuscles are so markedly altered in size and shape as in some cases of pernicious anæmia. In typical cases, the red blood corpuscles do not go into rouleaux; some of them are larger than normal, measuring, it may be, 12μ. or even more (*megalocytes*); others are smaller than normal, measuring 3μ. or even less (*microcytes*). Many of them are tailed, horse-shoe-shaped, pear-shaped, battledore-shaped, biscuit-shaped, etc. (*poikilo-cytes*).

Apparently active amœboid movements can not unfrequently be observed in the irregular-shaped red corpuscles; when they occur in the very minute red corpuscles, seen sideways on, they may closely resemble the active movements of bacteria. For the same reason, the larger-sized red corpuscles, when seen sideways, may resemble gigantic bacteria. Dr Muir tells me that he has never seen anything to suggest that the red corpuscles in pernicious anæmia have independent movement; and Dr Gulland informs me that in his opinion the movements of the irregular projections of the poikilocytes, which are not unlike amœboid movements to the eye, are due to physical causes and not to actual vital movement. While this is doubtless correct, the movements have in some of my cases been so marked that I was at one time disposed to think that they were perhaps vital.

In many cases, nucleated red blood corpuscles are present, though often only in small numbers.

In the original series of cases of pernicious anæmia which came under my observation in the year 1875, I minutely described the microscopical characters of the blood and published an illustrative plate. My description was as follows:—

A drop of blood drawn from the finger in the usual way was found to be thin and watery. It speedily separated into two parts, one coloured, the other colourless, looking as if a drop of colourless oil had been added to a red liquid. On microscopical examination it presented the following characters:—The red globules were diminished in numbers, and did not form rouleaux. They were markedly altered in shape, some of them being large, and no longer biconcave; others irregular, and with one or more tailed-like pro-

---

* "Clinical Examination of the Blood," p. 122.

E

jections ; others appeared nucleated ; the nucleus was of a pinkish-red colour. There were also numerous small red globules ; indeed, they (the red globules) seemed to be of all sizes, from minute masses of protoplasm to the abnormally large oval corpuscles which I have described. (A coloured plate illustrative of these appearances was published with the original paper.) The white corpuscles were not increased. In addition there were many small colourless granules ; some of these formed irregular masses, somewhat larger than white blood corpuscles. In one specimen an emerald-green rod-shaped body about $\frac{1}{7000}$th of an inch in length was observed ; it seemed to move with a slight vibratile movement. Nothing of the sort was again observed ; its occurrence was therefore probably accidental.

In the drawing which illustrated this description I represented many of the blood corpuscles as nucleated. I now know that the nucleated appearance was, for the most part, apparent only. The appearances which I supposed were indicative of a nucleus were shortly afterwards shown by Drs Mackern and Davy to be due to a concentration of the hæmoglobin in a particular part of the corpuscle. This apparent nucleation of the red corpuscles due to concentration of the hæmoglobin is, in my experience, invariably present in pernicious anæmia. Although it may occur in a slight degree in other conditions, I am disposed to think that it is an important characteristic of the disease.

But although the appearances suggestive of nucleation of the red corpuscles are in unstained preparations usually due to concentration of the hæmoglobin in a particular part of the corpuscle, it is certain that in the great majority of cases of pernicious anæmia, nucleated red blood corpuscles are actually present ; they can only be satisfactorily seen in stained preparations.

Some of the red blood corpuscles—and this statement more particularly applies to the unusually large corpuscles (megalocytes)—contain little or no colouring matter (*shadow-corpuscles*) ; others are uncoloured in their centres (apparent vacuolation); others appear to be really vacuolated.

Deeply stained microcytes, which were first described by Eichhorst and are consequently termed "*Eichhorst's corpuscles*," are sometimes present, though in my experience much less frequently than some observers seem to indicate—indeed, I have seen them in only two or three cases. When present, they are of considerable diagnostic importance.

Several different observers have claimed to have seen organisms in the blood of pernicious anæmia ; in more than one case of the disease, flagellated organisms have been described. In several cases which have come under my own notice, I have seen appearances which seemed to me suggestive of organisms ; and in one case, observed some years ago, I made a series of cultivations from the blood, and a very definite growth was obtained in gelatine. Dr Arthur Hare examined the cultivations for me and stated that they consisted of a short thick bacillus with rounded sides which was growing very rapidly. He further stated :—"I cannot recognise it " (the bacillus) " as any with which I am acquainted, but from its character and rapidity of growth I am inclined to think it saprophytic." The presence of this organism was probably accidental ; for in three recent cases in which the disease was extremely well marked, Dr Robert Muir failed to detect any organisms in the blood either in stained films or in gelatine tubes after incubation. As I have already stated, the apparently actively moving minute microcytes, if seen sideways on, are very apt to be mistaken for micro-organisms.

In uncomplicated cases of pernicious anæmia, the white blood corpuscles are almost always diminished, sometimes markedly so ; though after hæmorrhage, or with any inflammatory complication there may be a considerable leucocytosis.

The percentage of lymphocytes is usually much increased, while the polymorphonuclear oxyphiles (or neutrophiles) are diminished. Eosinophiles are sometimes increased, and myelocytes are occasionally present in small numbers. As the disease approaches its termination, the number of leucocytes is usually still further diminished.

The blood-plates are usually diminished in number, sometimes markedly so. The fibrin network usually forms less quickly and is less dense than under normal circumstances, consequently the blood usually coagulates less quickly than normal.

The hæmoglobin stability is markedly impaired. I have already pointed out that the hæmoglobin tends to become concentrated in a particular part of the corpuscle and to give an appearance of apparent nucleation. Dr Copeman has also shown that the hæmoglobin tends to separate readily out of the corpuscles when the blood is removed from the body. This instability of the hæmoglobin appears to be of importance in connection with the pathology of the disease.

The specific gravity of the blood is diminished.

Cabot sums up the characters of the blood in pernicious anæmia as follows :—

" 1. *Red cells about* 1,000,000 *per cubic millimetre.*

2. *White cells much diminished.*

3. Hæmoglobin variable, *sometimes*" (I would say in the great majority of cases) "*increased* relatively (= high-colour index).

4. Deformities in size and shape of red cells in many" (I would say in almost all well-marked) " cases.

5. *Increase in average diameter of red cells.*" (I do not feel satisfied as to this, if the microcytes are included, as they ought to be, in the calculation.)

" 6. Polychromatophilic red cells.

7. *Megaloblasts more numerous than normoblasts.*" (I have not always observed this.)

" 8. Lymphocytosis.

9. Small percentage of myelocytes.

The items italicised are the most important and characteristic." *

To these characters I would add :—

10. Marked defect in rouleaux formation.

11. Marked tendency for the hæmoglobin to be concentrated in localised parts of the red corpuscles, giving an appearance of apparent nucleation.

12. The presence in many cases of truly nucleated red corpuscles.

13. Diminished stability of the hæmoglobin.

14. Great frequency, in well-marked cases, of microcytes, often of very minute size—from mere points up to the average-sized red corpuscles.

15. The occasional presence of deeply-stained microcytes (Eichhorst's corpuscles).

16. Blood-plates usually diminished in number and in some cases markedly so ; and the fibrin network less quickly formed and less dense than normal.

Such, then, are the most important microscopic changes in the blood. Though highly significant and characteristic, it is perhaps premature to conclude that these changes are absolutely pathognomonic of a single definite disease — a single clinical entity. What I mean to say is, that it has not yet been definitely shown that the same changes may not occur in other conditions in which the red blood corpuscles are for a long time profoundly reduced in number (as from a long-continued drain of blood) and in which the red-blood-forming organs (the marrow of the bones) are for long periods of time called upon to rapidly produce an excessive number of red blood cells—in other words, in cases in which, as the result

---

* " Clinical Examination of the Blood," p. 128.

of a long-continued and excessive strain on the blood-forming organs, the production is too rapid and consequently defective, *i.e.*, in cases in which many immature and imperfectly-formed red blood corpuscles are thrown into the circulation.

The condition of the heart and pulse.—Palpitation and shortness of breath on exertion are constant symptoms. Præcordial pain is occasionally complained of, but a more frequent symptom is a feeling of sinking or "goneness" in the region of the stomach (epigastric region). Giddiness, fainting and tinnitus aurium are very common. As I have already remarked, in well-marked cases of pernicious anæmia the cardiac cavities are usually dilated and the heart muscle is in the great majority of instances found after death to be in an advanced state of fatty degeneration; in fact, if I may judge from my own pathological experience, there is no disease in which fatty degeneration of the heart is so marked as in pernicious anæmia. As in chlorosis, the heart muscle, which is affected in this way is not only weak but abnormally irritable. Quite exceptionally, in severe and long continued cases of the disease, the heart muscle is not fatty; a striking illustration came under my notice quite recently (Case 45).

The cardiac impulse is usually diffused, the præcordial dulness (unless, as is not unfrequently the case, the lungs should be emphysematous) usually increased.

The pulse is usually quicker than normal; sometimes large, but more frequently small; soft, of low tension and often dicrotic in character; in the advanced stages of the disease the pulse may be jerking in character; the jerking collapsing character is in some cases so marked as to suggest the presence of aortic regurgitation. Trivial excitements are apt to increase the frequency of the pulse and to produce palpitation.

A venous hum can almost always be heard in the neck. In the advanced stages of the disease, the external jugular veins are often knotted and distended, or the seat of true venous pulsation indicative of tricuspid regurgitation.

A systolic murmur is generally present in the pulmonary area; in many cases a systolic murmur may also be heard in the mitral, tricuspid and, less frequently, in the aortic areas. The cardiac impulse while at rest and unexcited is diffused, feeble, flickering and the transverse dulness in particular increased. In many cases, the lungs are emphysematous and the increased area of cardiac dulness is consequently less marked than one would expect from the appearance of the heart after death. The condition of the heart is, in short, similar to that which is met with in aggravated and long-continued cases of chlorosis ; but in the advanced stages of pernicious anæmia the cardiac alterations are much more marked and the heart symptoms usually more prominent than in the most severe cases of chlorosis.

Retinal and other hæmorrhages.—In the majority of well-marked cases of the disease, hæmorrhages are present in the retina. In my 45 cases, retinal hæmorrhages were present in 28 ; there were no retinal hæmorrhages in 12 ; and in the remaining 5 cases the presence or absence of retinal hæmorrhages is not mentioned in the notes, or the fundus was not examined or could not be examined owing to opacities of the media. The presence of retinal hæmorrhages is consequently of considerable diagnostic importance.

The hæmorrhages are usually of small size, scattered here and there over the retina. In some cases larger hæmorrhages are seen, usually in the course of the larger vessels. Striated flame-like hæmorrhages extending out from the margin of the disc are not, however, uncommon. In some cases, the central part of the hæmorrhage is paler than the circumference ; it may be of a pale yellow colour or almost white. In exceptional cases, there is some swelling and inflammation of the optic discs (papillitis). Further, I may here state that in well-marked cases of the disease the pallor of the fundus oculi is very striking.

Other hæmorrhages.—According to most authorities, hæmorrhages (other than retinal hæmorrhages) are common in the advanced stages of pernicious anæmia, but in the cases which have come under my own notice they were rare. Epistaxis, hæmatemesis, and bleeding from the throat and gums are the most frequent. Bleeding from the bowel, uterus and vagina occasionally occurs. In the advanced stages of the disease, petechial hæmorrhages are sometimes found in the skin, more particularly on the lower extremities. In one of my cases in which there were no hæmorrhages, the skin bruised very readily, slight injuries producing extensive subcutaneous extravasations.

In my series of 45 cases, epistaxis occurred in 5 cases, hæmatemesis in 2 cases, and in 2 there was bleeding from piles.

As I shall point out when I come to describe the post-mortem appearances, hæmorrhages beneath the pericardium, the pleura, the peritoneum and into the delicate tissue of the brain are very generally present in the bodies of patients who have died from the disease. I am strongly of opinion that these petechial hæmorrhages are the result, not the cause, of the disease ; there can I think be little doubt that they are due to the structural (fatty) changes which are apt to be produced in the walls of the minute blood vessels in all cases of profound and long-continued anæmia in which the red blood corpuscles are greatly reduced in number.

I may take this opportunity of saying that in cases of anæmia the occurrence of hæmorrhages seems to depend chiefly upon the number of red blood corpuscles which are present and the duration of the anæmia. Whenever the red blood corpuscles are for any length of time greatly reduced in number, retinal and other hæmorrhages are apt to occur.

Febrile attacks.—During the course of pernicious anæmia temporary attacks of pyrexia are of frequent occurrence and of considerable diagnostic value.

In some cases, the fever is continuous ; in others—and this is more common—intermittent or remittent. The fever has been termed "*anæmic fever*" or "*the essential fever of anæmia.*" In many cases, the febrile attacks seem to be associated with a rapid destruction of red blood corpuscles, which is apt to occur from time to time in what may be termed a paroxysmal manner. During these paroxysms there is usually an exacerbation of the symptoms, the urine often becomes deeply pigmented, the patient may become jaundiced, and, as has just been stated, fever may be developed. In many cases in which little or no febrile disturbance is noticed during the course of the disease, the temperature runs up, sometimes to a high point, just before death. In a few cases recurring attacks of chilliness or actual rigors occur.

In my series of 45 cases, irregular attacks of fever were noted in 17 cases ; in 7 cases it is definitely stated in my notes that there was no fever ; in the remaining 21 cases the presence or absence of fever was not ascertained or was not noted ; many of these cases were seen only once in consultation.

The exact cause of the febrile attacks which so frequently occur during the course of pernicious anæmia has not, so far as I am aware, been definitely determined. As I have just stated the febrile paroxysms seem to occur in association with paroxysmal exacerbations of blood destruction. The fever, like the blood destruction, is perhaps the result of the presence of a poison (a toxin or ptomaine) in the blood, it may be the same poison which produces the blood destruction, or possibly of some fever-producing substance developed during the process of blood destruction.

The condition of the urine.—In the majority of the cases of pernicious anæmia which have come under my own notice the urine has presented no abnormal appearance ; as a rule, it has been normal in colour or paler than normal.   During the paroxysmal exacerbations and in the advanced stages of the disease it may, as I have already mentioned, be more deeply coloured than normal.   In some cases, at all events, this excessive pigmentation appears to be due to the presence of pathological urobilin.   Dr William Hunter and Dr Mott think that the deep pigmentation of the urine is an important clinical indication of the excessive blood destruction which is taking place.   When the blood destruction is excessive, part of the pigment is excreted by the kidneys ; and after death microscopical deposits of pigment, which give the iron reaction with hydrochloric acid and ferrocyanide of potassium, have been found in the renal tubules. Dr Hunter states that in some cases in which the urine is deeply coloured, not only is pathological urobilin present in the urine in large quantities, but the presence of blood pigment may be recognised in the urine in the form of microscopical granules and on analysis the iron excreted in the urine is increased in amount.   In some cases the urine contains an excess of indican.

In my series of 45 cases, the urine was normal in colour in 23 ; dark in 16; and pale in 5 ; in one case the colour of the urine is not noted.   There can, however, be little doubt that if the condition of the urine had been carefully observed throughout the course of the 28 cases in which it is noted as normal or pale, deep pigmentation would have been observed in many, perhaps in all of them, at some period or other of their course.

In some cases, the urine deposits large quantities of uric acid ; a very striking case of this kind came under my observation some years ago ; the same condition was present in the deeply jaundiced case to which I have already referred.

In some cases the urine contains albumen ; it is usually small in amount and unattended with tube casts ; in most cases it is merely temporary ; in some cases it disappears with the improvement which in many cases results from arsenical treatment.   In my series of 45 cases albumen was present in 9 cases ; in 7 of these only in small quantity (a trace) ; in 36 cases there was no albumen ; and in the remaining 10 cases the presence or absence of albumen is not mentioned in the notes.

In some cases the combined sulphates are in marked excess.

The condition of the respiratory system.—Shortness of breath on exertion is always present even in the earlier stages of the disease.   In the later stages, attacks of shortness of breath may occur independently of effort (anæmic dyspnœa).   Cough (unless a nervous cough) is not usually observed except as the result of some complication (pneumonia, bronchitis, œdema of the lungs, hydrothorax).

All of these conditions are rare, though in my experience pneumonia is sometimes, and œdema of the lungs frequently a cause of death.

The condition of the digestive system.—Symptoms indicative of functional derangement of the stomach and intestines are almost invariably present.

Anorexia is usually a prominent symptom (in one of my cases the appetite was excessive) ; flatulent dyspepsia is common ; nausea and vomiting are of frequent occurrence ; in some cases the vomiting occurs in paroxysms.

In my series of 45 cases, vomiting was present (though in many of these cases only as an occasional and slight symptom) in 31 ; there was no vomiting in 14 cases.

In at least half of the cases there is diarrhœa ; in other cases the bowels are normal ; in a small proportion of cases constipated. In my 45 cases, diarrhœa occurred in 24 cases ; in many of these the diarrhœa was very troublesome. I may further say that in some of the cases which have come under my notice, the development of the disease has been preceded by intractable diarrhœa ; and in more than one of these cases I have found the intestines ulcerated after death. I am disposed to think that prolonged diarrhœa is in some cases an important factor in the production of the disease ; though, in cases of this kind, the diarrhœa and the pernicious anæmia may of course be due to a common cause—the presence of some organism or other irritant in the intestine.

These conclusions as to the frequency of vomiting and diarrhœa are quite in accord with the observations of Dr Hale White ; he states, " We may therefore conclude that dyspeptic symptoms, particularly vomiting and diarrhœa, are very common in genuine pernicious anæmia, being present in almost half the cases, that they are often very severe, and that constipation is one of the least common of the dyspeptic symptoms." *

The tongue is usually very pale ; in many cases, it is remarkably smooth, apparently destitute of its surface epithelium, but rarely raw-looking ; I attach considerable diagnostic significance to this condition of the tongue ; it has been a notable feature in many of my cases. In other cases, the tongue is flabby and indented by the teeth ; in some cases it is furred ; in the later stages of the disease it is frequently dry. In two or three of my cases an ulcerated or inflamed condition of the gums has been present ; in one case this condition of the gums and buccal mucous membrane, which was

---

* Guy's Hospital Reports, Vol. 47, 1890.

perhaps an indication of a similar condition in the whole gastro-intestinal tract, preceded the development of the pernicious anæmia.

During the later stages of the disease—and sometimes in the earlier stages—the patient often suffers from distressing thirst.

On physical examination, the stomach is in some cases found to be dilated; the free hydrochloric acid in the gastric juice is, it is said, in most cases much diminished in amount, or it may be entirely absent.

In some cases the fæces contain parasitic organisms or their ova; hence in all cases of pernicious anæmia a careful microscopic examination of the fæces should be made. In all of my recent cases the stools have been carefully examined for parasites; but in no case have parasites been found.

The condition of the nervous system.—Giddiness on rising from the recumbent to the erect position and on stooping, fainting on slight exertion or after a free evacuation of the bowels, tinnitus aurium, buzzing and throbbing sensations in the head and headache are very common symptoms. The temper is in many cases unduly irritable. The patient is unable to carry out any sustained mental effort; he easily becomes exhausted and tired. The memory is in some cases impaired. In many cases the patient complains of dimness of vision, of black specks floating before the eyes; these symptoms are especially marked in those cases in which the retinal hæmorrhages are numerous, and in the cases in which the optic discs are swollen and inflamed. In some cases there is slight deafness.

Symptoms indicative of derangement of the functions of the spinal cord are met with in a certain proportion of cases and are readily explained by the very marked and definite lesions in the cord (usually sclerotic changes in the posterior and lateral columns) which in some cases have been found after death. These symptoms chiefly consist of numbness or tingling in the toes, feet, legs, fingers and hands; muscular weakness, especially in the lower extremities; and inco-ordination. In some cases there are shooting pains, resembling the lightning pains of locomotor ataxia; in other cases there is rigidity and spasticity; in rarer cases, marked and localised muscular atrophy. In some cases the knee-jerks are exaggerated, in others abolished. The functions of the bladder and rectum are rarely deranged, except in the later stages of those cases in which the spinal lesions are extensive and advanced.

Lichtheim was the first to direct attention to these cord changes. Minnich, Nonne, James Taylor, Risien Russell and several other physicians have published important observations on the subject.

The cord lesions are admirably illustrated and a complete résumé of the literature up to date is given in Taylor's communication [*] and in Risien Russell's paper.[+]

In the advanced stages of the disease, sleeplessness and an extremely distressing and painful condition of uneasiness and restlessness are often present. Finally, the patient may pass into a drowsy semi-comatose condition ; in other cases, delirium, epileptiform convulsions or profound coma occur. It is needless to say that these symptoms are usually the precursors of death.

The frequency of occurrence of some of the more important symptoms in my 45 cases of pernicious anæmia is shown in Table 3.

ETIOLOGY.

Age.—Pernicious anæmia usually occurs in adults, most frequently if I may judge from my own experience between the ages of 35 and 55.

In the 45 cases which I have personally observed, 27 occurred between the ages of 35 and 54 inclusive ; 8 cases occurred below the age of 35, and 10 cases above the age of 54. The number of cases occurring in each of the five years between 15 and 74 in my series of cases is shown in the following table :—

TABLE 5.—SHOWING THE AGE DISTRIBUTION IN 45 CASES OF PERNICIOUS ANÆMIA.

Years.	Cases.	Years.	Cases.
15 to 19	2	50 to 54	13
20 „ 24	1	55 „ 59	3
25 „ 29	2	60 „ 64	2
30 „ 34	3	65 „ 69	3
35 „ 39	4	70 „ 74	2
40 „ 44	6		—
45 „ 49	4	Total	45

I do not wish to attach too much importance to these figures, for the total number of cases is too small to allow of a definite conclusion, and my results are not in accord with the statistics of some other observers. Thus, in 103 cases collected by Pye-Smith [‡] from various sources the average age was thirty-four years and four months ; and in 36 American cases collected by Musser [§] 19 occurred below the age of 40.

---

* Medico-Chirurgical Transactions, Vol. 78, 1895.
+ "Lancet," 1898, 2nd July, p. 4.
‡ Guy's Hospital Reports, Vol. xxvi.
§ On Idiopathic Anæmia, by Dr J. H. Musser, Proceedings of the Philadelphia County Medical Society, 1885.

Sex.—The statements of different observers differ as to the frequency with which the two sexes are liable to be affected ; in some of the lists of cases which have been published, females were more frequently affected than males. In my 45 cases, 29 of the patients were males and 16 females.

Distribution.—The disease seems to occur in all countries and in persons of all occupations. From the observations of Biermer and Immermann it would seem to be specially common in Switzerland ; but as Dr Gulland has pointed out to me this great frequency in Switzerland may perhaps be due to the fact that cases of anæmia due to the ankylostoma duodenale (which appear to be unusually frequent in Switzerland) are included.

Rank in life.—About half of the cases which have come under my own notice have occurred in fairly well-to-do or well-to-do people, but it is probable I think that the disease is more common amongst the lower orders of society and amongst those whose diet, social habits and sanitary surroundings are unsatisfactory.

Influence of heredity.—So far as I know, a hereditary tendency to pernicious anæmia can very rarely be traced ; indeed the only instance with which I am acquainted in which the disease appeared to be inherited occurred in the practice of Dr Allison of Kettering. The patient, a man aged 53, was under Dr Allison's care with all the typical symptoms of pernicious anæmia and died from the disease. Dr Allison writes me :—" I venture to think that in this case there is a distinct hereditary taint. His mother died here aged 60, certified cardiac weakness and chronic diarrhœa ; before she died she consulted Dr Francis, one of the physicians to the Northampton Infirmary, who said that she had a peculiar disease of the blood which would probably be fatal. One aunt died at Mansfield in 1879, aged 55, the certificate gave the cause of death anæmia. Another aunt died at Croydon, aged 46, of morbus cordis. An uncle died at Kettering in 1885, aged 51, certificate congestion of the liver ; his widow tells me that he suffered a good deal from vomiting and feverish attacks during the last year of his life and that he looked exactly like his nephew is at present (typical and advanced pernicious anæmia). An uncle died this year (February) at Wakefield, aged 74 ; the cause of death was certified by Dr Eddison of Leeds as pernicious anæmia. The patient has a brother, aged 51, at Willesden very ill just now, like himself in symptoms, I am told."

Other exciting or predisposing causes.—In many of the reported cases the patients have, up to the onset of the disease, enjoyed good health. In a considerable proportion of cases, the disease is preceded by dyspeptic troubles or diarrhœa. In some cases the onset has been preceded by mental anxiety, strain, etc. In a small proportion of cases the patients have suffered from a prolonged drain of blood. A profound form of anæmia, somewhat similar to that characteristic of pernicious anæmia, appears sometimes to be developed as the result of long-continued malarial poisoning. In two of my cases the disease seemed to have its starting point in an attack of yellow fever. A profound condition of anæmia, resembling pernicious anæmia, may also be developed after prolonged lactation, pregnancy and parturition. In some of these cases the anæmia is without doubt of the pernicious form, but in others it would appear to be of the simple (chlorotic or secondary) type; probably, therefore, the importance of pregnancy and lactation as causes of pernicious anæmia has been exaggerated. In some cases, intestinal parasites (the ankylostoma duodenale and the bothriocephalus latus) have been found in the intestine. A profound form of anæmia, which in many of its clinical features closely resembles pernicious anæmia, was very prevalent amongst the miners in the St Gothard tunnel, and was proved to be due to the ankylostoma duodenale; in these cases the anæmia seems, in part at least, to be the direct result of the abstraction of blood from the intestinal mucous membrane. In some cases, the condition appears to be developed in patients affected with cancer of the stomach, but this is rare; in the great majority of cases of this description there seems to be little doubt that the anæmia (judging from the characters of the blood) is of the "secondary" type.

Mode of Onset.—The onset is usually slow and gradual, but in exceptional cases (and the jaundiced case to which I have already referred was a case in point) the disease is rapidly developed and the patient becomes profoundly anæmic and manifests all the symptoms characteristic of an advanced stage of the disease in the course of two or at most three months.

MORBID ANATOMY.

Before considering the exact manner in which the anæmia is produced, it may perhaps be well to direct attention to the morbid anatomy of the disease.

The bodies of patients who have died of pernicious anæmia are remarkably *bloodless ;* the brain is probably more anæmic than in any other condition, death from hæmorrhage not excepted. In more than one case I have diagnosed pernicious anæmia in the post-mortem room from the bloodless condition of the brain alone (without of course knowing anything of the clinical history or seeing the whole of the post mortem—going into the pathological theatre and seeing the exposed brain, I have, from the remarkably bloodless condition, said to the pathologist, "That is surely a case of pernicious anæmia"). The heart and large vessels usually contain extremely little blood.

The *subcutaneous fat* is usually well preserved and in most cases of a lemon or canary yellow colour. In some cases the tissues are distinctly bile-stained. The subcutaneous tissues of the feet and legs and eyelids, more especially the upper eyelids (and it may be of the body generally, though this is not usually the case), may be slightly œdematous. The *internal cavities* (pericardium, pleura, much less frequently the peritoneum) may contain a certain amount of dropsical effusion, though this is not as a rule extensive.

The *somatic muscles* are usually somewhat wasted; in some cases they are of a deep red colour, like the muscles of a horse; in others—and this in my experience is more common—they are paler than normal.

Small petechial extravasations are in the great majority of cases present in the retina and in many cases in the pericardium, pleura, beneath the endocardium, and peritoneum, sometimes in the skin, less frequently on the surface, or in the substance, of the brain, etc. In rare cases more extensive hæmorrhages have been noted on the surface of the brain, etc.

The *heart muscle* is usually in a condition of advanced fatty degeneration; there is, in fact, no disease in which such splendid examples of fatty degeneration of the heart are found as pernicious anæmia. The cardiac cavities are usually more or less dilated.

In some cases, the *lungs* are pale, dry and emphysematous; in others, œdematous.

In a considerable proportion of cases, morbid changes are present in the *stomach or intestine*. The mucous membrane of the stomach is sometimes atrophied; in others affected with fibroid changes. In three of my cases it presented a mammillated appearance towards the pylorus, and the same condition has been noted by other observers. In some cases, as Samuel Fenwick and others have pointed out, the gastric tubules are affected with fatty degeneration or completely atrophied. Ulceration of the intestine is sometimes present; I have seen it in several instances. The mucous coat of the small intestine is also in many cases atrophied; but this is often masked by an œdematous condition which is probably developed in many instances shortly before death. Worms or other parasites are occasionally found in the intestine. Changes have been described in the pancreas and in the abdominal sympathetic, but they are probably accidental or secondary to the anæmic condition.

The *spleen* is in some cases somewhat enlarged; in others shrunken. Dr Hunter has suggested that the difference depends upon the condition as regards blood destruction which was going on just before death.

The *liver* is usually enlarged and markedly fatty. On microscopical examination it presents, in most typical cases, a highly important and characteristic alteration, viz., the presence of yellowish brown pigment granules situated within the liver cells. The pigmentation is usually most marked in, or confined to, the outer two-thirds of the portal area. This pigment contains iron in a comparatively simple combination, so that when treated with hydrochloric acid and ferrocyanide of potassium the Prussian blue colour is obtained. Sulphide of ammonium blackens the granules. In some cases, the amount of iron in the liver has been ascertained to be ten times the normal. According to Dr William Hunter, this change (excess of iron and its peculiar characters and distribution in the cells of the liver) is characteristic and pathognomonic of pernicious anæmia. In two of the cases which I described many years ago, I recognised the abnormal pigmentation and its peculiar distribution, but I did not attach any importance to it. In all of my recent cases in which a post-mortem examination was obtained, a considerable excess of iron was present in the liver and in some instances also in the spleen and kidney.

Whether this excess of iron in the liver is, as Dr Hunter supposes, a constant feature of pernicious anæmia remains to be proved by further information. In one case which presented all the typical clinical characters of pernicious anæmia, Dr W. B. Ransom found no excess of iron in the liver after death. As I will presently point out, the question has not as yet been definitely decided whether the clinical condition pernicious anæmia is always due to excessive blood destruction in the portal area or not; if it is not always due to excessive blood destruction in the portal area, it must of course be admitted that an excess of iron in the liver is not an essential feature of the disease.

The *kidneys* are usually enlarged, the cortex pale, the epithelium of the tubules fatty; deposits of pigmented granules containing iron are in some cases present within the tubules, and, when well marked, present a highly striking and characteristic appearance.

The *marrow of the bones* is usually (? always) more or less distinctly altered; the yellow marrow of the long bones (the femur, for example) is replaced by red marrow and the marrow tissue is evidently in a state of active change and proliferation. Instead of presenting the yellow fatty appearance of the bone-marrow of the adult, the marrow is of a deep red or violaceous colour like the marrow of the fœtus. On microscopical examination, the fat may have for the most part, or entirely, disappeared and the marrow may contain an enormous increase of nucleated red corpuscles; while the marrow cells may be much less numerous than normal. In some cases, enormous nucleated red blood corpuscles ("giganto-blasts"), which are not found in the normal marrow, are present in large numbers. There may also be some absorption of the bone trabeculæ. In all of my cases in which the condition of the bone marrow was noted, these characteristic alterations were present.

Dr Muir sums up his observations on the condition of the bone-marrow in a series of five cases of pernicious anæmia as follows :—

" 1. The changes most frequently observed in the marrow in pernicious anæmia may be said to be : (*a*) increased number of nucleated red corpuscles in the marrow ; (*b*) transformation of the fatty marrow in the shafts of the long bones into red marrow ; (*c*) absorption of the bone trabeculæ between the red marrow.

" 2. A further change, which may be found in the long-standing cases, is the occurrence, in large numbers, of large nucleated red corpuscles (giganto-blasts), reaching 20μ. or even more in diameter, often with fragmented and apparently degenerated nuclei. Along with these is generally a distinct pre-ponderance of coloured over colourless elements in the marrow. The condition of the marrow in this advanced stage appears to be peculiar to pernicious anæmia.

" 3. The newly formed marrow in its cellular constituents and structural arrangement closely resembles normal marrow. The eosinophile cells are specially few at first, but become more numerous afterwards. The giant cells, whose development can be traced from marrow cells, are generally compara-tively small and few in number.

" 4. In the transformation of the fatty into the red marrow there are two main factors, viz., a widening of certain capillaries to form 'venous capillaries,' and an accumulation of marrow cells (leucocytes) around them. Afterwards the demarcation of the vessels becomes deficient, and the usual marrow structure is reached.

" 5. No special cells are concerned in the process of the absorption of bone which occurs ; gradual softening and simple atrophy appear to take place, associated with the hyperplasia of the marrow.

" 6. Pigment, much of which gives the iron reaction, may be present in the newly formed marrow in considerable amount, occurring both in the free state and also within cells. I have found it specially abundant where the anæmia has been severe and progressing at the time of death.

" 7. The earlier changes can only be interpreted as an extension of blood-forming tissue of compensatory nature, due to blood destruction ; the changes (*a*) and (*b*) being similar to those produced by hæmorrhage, and also found in other diseases.

"8. The further changes found in advanced cases (2) are also secondary, and are due to a long continuance of the same conditions, the nucleated red corpuscles showing a return to an embryonic type." *

Whether these *changes* in the bone-marrow are constant or not in cases of pernicious anæmia is, however, another point ; in some of the cases which have been examined they have been only slightly marked or (?) altogether absent. Further, these same changes have been observed in other conditions than pernicious anæmia (other forms of profound anæmia, cancer, etc.) ; consequently they cannot be regarded, so far as our present knowledge enables us to judge, as pathognomonic of the disease.

Pathological changes are sometimes present in the *spinal cord*. In most cases in which the cord lesion is advanced and marked, a condition of postero-lateral sclerosis, very similar in appearance and distribution (as Dr Risien Russell has pointed out) to the lesions in cases of ataxic-paraplegia, is present. In some cases, the posterior columns are sclerosed very much in the same way as they are in locomotor ataxia. In others, again, the crossed or direct pyramidal tracts are sclerosed. In some cases, the cord changes consist of scattered patches of myelitis, perhaps produced around minute petechial hæmorrhages. It remains, however, to be shown whether in all of the cases such as Dr Taylor has described (in which the pathological changes in the spinal cord were very marked and striking) the anæmia was the cause of the cord changes ; and, if so, whether the anæmia was "pernicious." Dr Taylor thinks that these extensive cord lesions are probably the result of some toxic substance. This view seems to me very probable, though some of the sclerotic changes in the spinal cord are perhaps developed around, and as the result of, minute petechial hæmorrhages.

The *brain*, as has been already stated, is remarkably bloodless ; and I have little doubt that careful microscopical examination will show pathological changes in the brain tissues, more especially in the nerve cells. In one case, which came under my notice some years ago, numerous small petechial hæmorrhages were present both on the surface and in the substance of the brain.

In Vol. 47, Guy's Hospital Reports (1890) Dr Hale White gives a valuable abstract of the post-mortem findings in all the cases of pernicious anæmia (31 in number) which have died in Guy's Hospital from 1855 to 1889, both years inclusive.

---

* "The Journal of Pathology and Bacteriology," February 1894.

F

PATHOLOGICAL PHYSIOLOGY.

There is still considerable difference of opinion as to the exact manner in which the anæmia is produced—in other words, as to the exact nature and causation of the condition which is termed pernicious anæmia. In the present state of our knowledge it is perhaps impossible to come to a positive conclusion and to give an explanation which will embrace all cases. In considering the nature and causation of the disease, the following questions have to be taken into account :—

1. Is the condition which we term pernicious anæmia a separate and distinct disease, *a definite clinical entity*, or may the *clinical* condition which we term pernicious anæmia be the result of several different pathological conditions and morbid states?

2. Is the anæmic condition the result of blood destruction or defective blood formation.

3. What is the fundamental and underlying cause of the condition ?

All of these questions are more or less intimately bound up together, and it is difficult to answer one without considering and trying to answer the others. In the present state of our knowledge it is perhaps impossible to give a decided and dogmatic answer to any one of them.

Dr William Hunter is of opinion that there is a separate and distinct disease, pernicious anæmia ; that it is due to blood destruction ; that the blood destruction takes place chiefly in the portal circulation ; and that the blood destruction is the result of the absorption of some poisonous substance, probably a chemical substance or cadaveric ptomaine, produced in the intestine by some definite and specific micro-organism.

He thinks that the blood destruction chiefly occurs in the spleen and liver ; and that the iron which is liberated from the red corpuscles which are destroyed in the spleen is carried to the liver and is there stored up in the liver cells in the outer two-thirds of the portal area.

Dr Hunter therefore supposes that the poison which is absorbed from the intestine causes destruction of the red blood globules in the spleen and has an effect on the liver cells which leads them to store up the iron in the form of pigment granules—in other words, to functionate in an abnormal manner.

Dr Hunter summarises his conclusions in the following propositions :—

" 1. Pernicious anæmia is to be regarded as a special disease both clinically and pathologically. It constitutes a distinct variety of *idiopathic* anæmia.

" 2. Its essential pathological feature is an excessive destruction of blood.

" 3. The most constant anatomical change to be found is the presence of a large excess of iron in the liver.

" 4. This condition of the liver serves at once to distinguish pernicious anæmia post mortem from all varieties of *symptomatic* anæmia, as also from the anæmia resulting from loss of blood.

" 5. The blood destruction characteristic of this form of anæmia differs both in its nature and its seats from that found in malaria, in paroxysmal hæmoglobinuria, and other forms of hæmoglobinuria.

" 6. The view can no longer be held that the occurrence of *hæmoglobinuria* simply depends on the quantity of hæmoglobin set free.

" 7. On the contrary, the *seat* of the destruction and *the form assumed by the hæmoglobin* on being set free are important conditions regulating the presence or absence of hæmoglobinuria in any case in which an excessive disintegration of corpuscles has occurred.

" 8. In paroxysmal hæmoglobinuria the disintegration of corpuscles occurs in the general circulation, and is due to a rapid dissolution of the red corpuscles.

" 9. In pernicious anæmia the seat of disintegration is chiefly the portal circulation, more especially that portion of it contained within the spleen and the liver, and the destruction is effected by the action of certain poisonous agents, probably of a cadaveric nature, absorbed from the intestinal tract." *

Dr Hunter regards the changes in the bone-marrow as secondary to the blood destruction ; and with this opinion I entirely agree, at all events so far as the great majority of cases are concerned ; at the same time it is I think quite possible that future observations may show that a condition of blood identical with that of pernicious anæmia (in other words the clinical condition which we term pernicious anæmia) may perhaps in rare instances be due to a *primary* lesion of the bone-marrow.

Before I became acquainted with Hunter's observations, I was in the habit (with, I suppose, most other clinicians and pathologists) of regarding the great diminution in the number of the red blood corpuscles, which is the essential characteristic of pernicious anæmia, as the result of defective blood formation. The presence of large numbers of immature red blood corpuscles and the occasional occurrence in the blood of nucleated red blood corpuscles seemed to me to be strongly in favour of this view—defective formation rather than of increased destruction. At the time when Dr Hunter first told me of his experiments and observations, I had the advantage of his assistance in the Out-Patient Department of the Edinburgh Royal Infirmary. I put the following questions to

---

* An Investigation into the Pathology of Pernicious Anæmia, Lancet, Sept. 22, 29 and Oct. 6, 1888.

him, "How do you account for the large number of immature red blood corpuscles in the blood?" and "Are not these immature red corpuscles indicative of defective blood formation rather than excessive blood destruction?" He met this by saying that if you have excessive destruction of red blood corpuscles at one end of the circulation (*i.e.*, in the portal circulation), this will necessarily give rise to excessive production at the other (*i.e.*, in the bone-marrow); in other words, he allowed that there was defective blood formation, but he explained the defective formation of the red blood globules as the result of the excessive strain thrown on the blood-forming tissues—the bone-marrow—in consequence of the excessive blood destruction which he argued was the essential cause of the anæmia. This argument, which supposes that a large number of immature and imperfect red blood cells are thrown into the circulation in order to meet, as it were, and compensate the excessive blood destruction which is going on at the other end of the circulation, seems to me a satisfactory explanation; but the question is whether it represents the whole truth.

It is quite possible, I think, that in many cases of pernicious anæmia the diminution of the red blood corpuscles is the result both of excessive blood destruction and defective blood formation. Even if we admit with Dr Hunter that in the great majority of cases of pernicious anæmia the primary cause of the anæmia is excessive blood destruction, it must also I think be allowed that, in the later stages of the disease at all events, there is imperfect and defective, or perhaps it is more correct to say too rapid and therefore imperfect, blood formation in the bone-marrow. Now, it is not difficult to conceive, if this condition (too rapid and therefore imperfect formation of red blood corpuscles, due to an excessive and pathological strain, so to speak, on the blood-forming tissue— the bone-marrow) continues and lasts, as we know it must do, for long periods of time, that an actual diseased condition of the bone-marrow may ultimately become produced. We may suppose that there is, in the first instance, as the result of the excessive strain which is thrown upon the bone-marrow, a condition of irritable weakness; and that this, which is at first a functional condition, as in many other cases of irritable weakness, may ultimately pass on to organic disease. It seems to me probable that although the fundamental change in typical cases of pernicious anæmia (those— and they seem to comprise the vast majority of cases—in which there is an excess of iron in the liver) is the result of excessive blood destruction in the portal circulation, the defective blood formation in the bone-marrow is an important consideration which cannot be ignored. To cases of this kind in which there is an excess of iron in the liver, the term "*gastro-intestinal-hepatic type of hæmolytic anæmia*" may I think be appropriately applied. I think it probable that even in these cases—the Hunterian type of the disease, as I am in the habit of terming it—a double cause for the bloodlessness is present, viz., increased blood destruction in the portal circulation and too rapid and therefore defective blood formation in the bone-marrow.

Further, as I have already suggested, it is perhaps the case—though this requires to be definitely proved—that in some cases a primary lesion of the marrow of the bone may lead to the production of a form of anæmia which is very closely allied to, if not identical with, the pernicious variety of the disease. If this is so, we may term these cases the *myeloid type of pernicious anæmia of hæmogenetic origin*. And in this connection it is interesting to note that so long ago as the year 1875 Professor Pepper of Philadelphia, who was one of the first to direct attention to the changes in the bone-marrow, proposed the term "myelogenous anæmia" or the "medullary form of pseudo-leukæmia" for the disease.

If it should be proved, as I have suggested above, that excessive blood destruction, however produced, may ultimately, *provided only that it is continuous and sufficiently long continued*, lead to an abnormal and diseased condition of the red-blood-forming tissue (the bone-marrow), it must be allowed that the group of *clinical* symptoms to which we give the term pernicious anæmia may be due to a variety of processes, *i.e.*, may be the ultimate result of many conditions.

I am not then prepared to deny (for I think before this is granted further information is required) that a drain of blood, which lasts continuously for a sufficiently long period of time, may not ultimately perhaps produce a form of anæmia which is clinically identical, so far as the condition of the blood is concerned and so far as our present methods of clinical examination enable us to judge, with pernicious anæmia.

That the most marked poikilocytosis may occur as the result of a long-continued drain of blood is shown by the following case which came under my observation some years ago. The patient had suffered for years from a bloody vaginal discharge, the result of a diseased condition of the ovary and uterus. She was profoundly anæmic, the red blood corpuscles were greatly reduced in number and of all shapes and sizes, in many of them the hæmoglobin was concentrated in a localised area of the corpuscle; in short the microscopic condition of the red blood globules exactly corresponded to that which is characteristic of pernicious anæmia. (I have no note of the condition of the white corpuscles, of the percentage of hæmoglobin, or of the "colour index.") In this case the excessive and long-continued loss of red blood corpuscles from the uterus was apparently the cause of an excessive and imperfect formation of red blood corpuscles in the bone-marrow, while the resulting anæmia was an anæmia which, clinically speaking, seemed to me at the time to correspond to the usual type of the disease. Whether the blood characters, if they had been examined by modern and improved methods of research, would have been identical with those of pernicious anæmia, I am not of course prepared to say.

But notwithstanding this suggestion (that a drain of blood if sufficiently severe and long continued may perhaps produce a clinical condition corresponding to that characteristic of pernicious anæmia), I am quite unable to agree with the theory which Professor Stockman has advanced that pernicious anæmia is due to the small capillary hæmorrhages which are so often found after death in fatal cases of the disease. I look upon these capillary hæmorrhages as a consequence—the result and not the cause of the anæmia. In proof of this it is, I think, only necessary to state :— That in many cases of pernicious anæmia very few petechial hæmorrhages are found after death ; that there is no correspondence between the number of petechial hæmorrhages found after death and the degree of the anæmia ; in some of my most marked cases of pernicious anæmia there were practically no petechial hæmorrhages present ; that the petechial hæmorrhages which we can see during life (the retinal hæmorrhages and the petechial hæmorrhages which are occasionally though rarely seen in the skin and subcutaneous tissues in the advanced stages of the disease) are not developed in the early stages of the disease, but only when the anæmia becomes marked ; and that in other diseases in which numerous petechial and other hæmorrhages are developed, and recurringly developed for long periods of time, as in some cases of Henoch's purpura for example—and I will afterwards record a case in point—the symptoms and blood conditions characteristic of pernicious anæmia are not developed.

Now, if a form of anæmia undistinguishable during life, except by its mode of causation, from progressive pernicious anæmia, can ultimately result from a long-continued loss of blood, there is no reason to suppose that in such a case the liver would contain an excess of iron pigment.

Hunter, if I understand him aright, would exclude from the

category of pernicious anæmia all cases of anæmia in which there is no excess of iron in the liver. But it seems to me that further information is required before this proposition can be absolutely accepted, though I admit that it applies to the vast majority of cases. At the Newcastle Meeting of the British Medical Association, Dr W. B. Ransom brought before the Medical Section a case in which all the characteristic symptoms of pernicious anæmia were present during life and in which no excess of iron in the liver was found after death.

And even if Hunter's view (that pernicious anæmia is a separate and distinct clinical entity) is correct, the clinical physician would still be left in doubt and perplexity as regards the diagnosis of some cases during life ; for, if I understand him correctly, Hunter regards the condition of the liver, in respect to the presence or absence of an excess of iron, as the fundamental characteristic of the disease. He considers that those cases of anæmia in which the liver contains a great excess of iron during life are cases of pernicious anæmia ; but that those cases in which there is no excess of iron in the liver are not. But even if this point be granted, the condition of the liver is a post-mortem change which cannot be determined during life, unless the new photography can demonstrate its presence ; but this, as Dr Gulland has pointed out to me, is very unlikely since the iron in the liver is in organic combination. In short, as I have already stated, in the present position of our knowledge, it is perhaps premature to conclude that a profound anæmia which proves fatal and in which there is no excess of iron in the liver is never pernicious.

I doubt, too, whether we can absolutely rely upon the condition of the urine as a clinical test of pernicious anæmia. So far as my experience enables me to judge, a highly pigmented condition of the urine is often absent ; and even in those cases in which it is present, it is usually merely temporary and evanescent.

Further, if future observation should show that a condition undistinguishable during life from pernicious anæmia may be the result of long-continued hæmorrhage, it may further, perhaps, be allowed that the same group of clinical symptoms (which we regard as characteristic of pernicious anæmia) may sometimes be due to long-continued diarrhœa and perhaps to other conditions which lead to long-continued and excessive blood destruction on the one hand, and which consequently throw a long-continued and abnormal strain upon the blood-forming tissue (the marrow of the bones) on the other. Again, it seems certain that a condition closely resembling, though it may perhaps be doubted whether it is identical with pernicious anæmia may be the result of intestinal parasites. Further, it has been stated that in some cases which commence as chlorosis, a condition of pernicious anæmia is ultimately established. The exact nature of these transitional cases is doubtful. The blood seems seldom to have been examined with sufficient accuracy to make sure of either the original or ultimate diagnosis ; but Case 31 of my series seems a case in point.

The same statement perhaps also applies to some cases of gastric cancer.

I am, then, disposed to think in the present state of our knowledge :—

(1.) That pernicious anæmia should be regarded as a *clinical condition ;* in other words, that the term pernicious anæmia should be applied to any profound and (apparently) causeless anæmia which is characterised by the peculiar alterations in the blood which I have described above, and in which the anæmia tends to pursue a progressive or pernicious course.

(2.) That until further information is obtained, the question whether the clinical condition termed pernicious anæmia may result from a variety of causes, or whether it is a single clinical entity the causation of which is always one and the same, should be left an open one.

(3.) That in many of the most typical cases of pernicious anæmia the two conditions (excessive blood destruction and defective blood formation, or perhaps it would be better to say too rapid and, therefore, defective blood formation) are probably combined.

(4.) That in those cases in which the condition is due to excessive blood destruction, the blood destruction may perhaps be due to a variety of different causes and conditions ; though there seems good reason to suppose that in the vast majority of typical cases the condition is due, as Dr Hunter has shown, to increased blood destruction in the portal circulation, and that this increased destruction is probably the result of the absorption of some poisonous substance from the gastro-intestinal tract.

(5.) Whether a true pernicious anæmia can result from a long-continued drain of blood from the intestine (as in cases of ankylostoma duodenale), from the uterus, etc., from long-continued diarrhœa, or as the result of the malarial, syphilitic, and cancerous cachexia must in the meantime I think remain an open question.

(6.) That the condition is in some cases perhaps due to primary changes in the bone-marrow (though this has not as yet been definitely established) ; and, if so, is the result of defective blood formation.

Before we can come to a definite conclusion regarding the exact nature and causation of pernicious anæmia, it is essential to determine (1) whether the excess of iron in the liver which Hunter and others have described is invariably present in all fatal cases in which the clinical group of symptoms characteristic of pernicious anæmia was present during life; and (2) whether such an excess of iron in the liver is necessarily indicative of excessive blood destruction in the portal circulation alone. It is only after these questions have been decided by a sufficiently wide series of observations that it will be possible to determine whether the condition which we term pernicious anæmia is a definite disease, a single clinical entity, which is always the result of blood destruction in the portal circulation, or whether it may not be the ultimate clinical result of a number of different pathological conditions.

The solution of the question whether pernicious anæmia is a distinct clinical entity or not and more especially the determination of the further questions—if pernicious anæmia is always due to excessive blood destruction in the portal area, what is the exact nature of the ptomaine or toxin which produces that destruction, and how is that toxin or ptomaine produced—are of great importance for the purposes of diagnosis, prognosis and treatment.

In concluding this discussion on the pathology of pernicious anæmia, I may add that during the past six months I have had the opportunity of observing, both during life and after death, a considerable number of typical cases of the disease, and that in all of them an excess, and with one exception a very large excess, of iron has been present in the liver. A careful consideration of these and of the other cases which have come under my notice during the past two years has led me to believe that Dr Hunter's conclusions as to the nature and causation of the disease are correct, in the vast majority of cases at all events. Whether all cases of pernicious anæmia are due to one and the same cause remains, I think, to be proved by future observation.

DIAGNOSIS.

In well-marked cases of pernicious anæmia, the diagnosis does not, as a rule, present any difficulty. The clinical features which are most important for the purposes of diagnosis are :—

1. The (usually) insidious development and progressive course, unless of course the disease is arrested and (? temporarily) cured by treatment.

2. The profound asthenia and anæmia, the lemon tint of the skin with, in some cases, the presence of distinct jaundice.

3. The absence of any organic disease or obvious cause of the anæmia (such as loss of blood) to account for the anæmic condition—in other words, the primary or idiopathic character of the anæmia.

The absence of local or visceral disease capable of accounting for the anæmia is a most important diagnostic point.

4. The characters of the blood, more especially :—(a) the great diminution in the number of the red blood corpuscles ; (b) the comparatively small diminution of the hæmoglobin and the consequent fact that the individual red blood corpuscles contain at least the normal amount, and usually more than the normal amount, of hæmoglobin ; (c) the marked alterations in size and shape which the red blood corpuscles present ; (d) the presence of apparently nucleated and in most cases of truly nucleated red corpuscles ; (e) the occasional occurrence of the small dark red microcytes described by Eichhorst ; and (f) the occurrence of lymphocytosis in many cases, and probably in all severe cases.

5. The retinal hæmorrhages.

6. The inutility of iron and the beneficial effect of arsenic. I attach somewhat less importance to this point than I did some years ago, for in more than one case of pernicious anæmia which I have seen of recent years remarkable benefit has speedily resulted from the combined use of iron in the form of Robertson's capsules, and large doses of liquor arsenicalis. I think it probable that in these cases the improvement was due to the arsenic, but I cannot of course say that the iron may not also have been beneficial ; in the cases to which I refer it certainly was not prejudicial. Further, a few cases have been recorded — and Case 7 in my series seems a case in point — in which marked improvement occurred under the administration of iron alone. But speaking generally, the therapeutic effect of iron on the one hand and of arsenic on the other is undoubtedly helpful for the purposes of diagnosis. It is certain, I think, that in most cases of pernicious anæmia iron is useless and in many cases distinctly harmful ; whereas in many cases of the disease (provided they are seen sufficiently early and the patient is able to take sufficiently large doses of the remedy) arsenic is beneficial.

7. The occurrence of febrile attacks, apparently due to the anæmic condition, i.e., to the presence of a toxin in the blood which is perhaps also the cause of the blood destruction or of some product of blood destruction, and not due to any other (obvious) cause.

8. The presence of dark-coloured urine. As I have already stated, excessive pigmentation of the urine is often absent; and when present is usually only temporary and evanescent. Nevertheless, I agree with Dr Hunter in thinking that the occurrence of highly pigmented urine, which in many cases is associated with fever and a paroxysmal exacerbation of the anæmia and other symptoms characteristic of the disease, is, when present, of considerable diagnostic significance. With reference to this point Dr Hunter says :—

"In addition to this, their pathological significance, these changes are, I am inclined to think, of no little importance from a diagnostic point of view. The high colour of the urine observed, unaccompanied as it was by any diminution in quantity or any rise in specific gravity, and the presence of granules of blood-pigment in the urine, pointed so unmistakably to the nature of the pathological process at work in the blood, that they establish conclusively the diagnosis of the case as one of pernicious anæmia.

"One must, however, in this connexion guard one's-self against a misconception that may not improbably arise. The urine in pernicious anæmia need not *always* show these well-marked and, when present, characteristic changes. It may be said, however, with some degree of assurance, that they will be found more or less marked in all cases at some period or other of their history.

"In all cases, as in the foregoing one, there will be times corresponding to the periods when the patient is gaining ground, when the colour of the urine will be that of health, and nothing abnormal will be microscopically recognisable.

"The aggravations of weakness will always, however, be evidenced by a higher colour of the urine, it may be also by the appearance of blood-pigment granules in the urine ; both changes marking the nature of the process within the blood which is the occasion of these attacks, namely excessive hæmolysis."*

9. The age and sex of the patient. These points are in some cases of considerable diagnostic value, more particularly in determining whether a profound anæmia is the result of chlorosis or pernicious anæmia.

The differential diagnosis of chlorosis and pernicious anæmia.—I have already considered this point in connection with chlorosis (see page 47). The distinction must, as I have previously stated, be chiefly based upon :—(*a*) The condition of the blood ; (*b*) the presence of retinal hæmorrhages ; (*c*) the therapeutic effect of iron on the one hand and of arsenic on the other ; and (*d*) the age and sex of the patient.

The difficulty of distinguishing pernicious anæmia and chlorosis is chiefly likely to arise :—(1) in those cases—but they are comparatively rare—in which pernicious anæmia is developed in a young

* Observations on the urine in pernicious anæmia, Practitioner, November, and December 1889.

woman (*i.e.*, at the chlorotic period); and (2) in those cases of chlorosis—but they are most exceptional—in which the chlorotic condition is developed in middle-aged or old women (*i.e.*, after the chlorotic period), or in men, or in children (*i.e.*, before the chlorotic period). In my 314 cases of typical chlorosis, no case occurred after the age of 33 (though I have seen three or four cases apparently of idiopathic anæmia of the chlorotic type in middle-aged or old women), and only 11 cases after the age of 28; while in my series of 45 cases of pernicious anæmia only 3 cases occurred below the age of 28. The facts that pernicious anæmia comparatively rarely occurs in young women, whereas chlorosis is essentially a disease of young women, are, therefore, in some cases of distinct diagnostic value.

There is reason, I think, to believe that in some of the cases which have been reported as cases of pernicious anæmia in which recovery took place under iron, the condition was chlorosis and not pernicious anæmia. A profound and causeless anæmia in a young woman is in the *vast* majority of cases chlorotic. In such cases a definite diagnosis of pernicious anæmia should be given with hesitation and should only be ventured upon when (*a*) the characters of the blood are very definite and very distinctive of pernicious anæmia (rather than of chlorosis); and (*b*) when iron given in large doses fails to produce benefit. *Vice versâ*, in cases of profound anæmia in which rapid improvement results from the administration of iron the diagnosis of pernicious anæmia should always be regarded with suspicion, and this is more especially the case when the patient is a young woman.

The differential diagnosis of pernicious anæmia and primary heart disease.—This can rarely give rise to any difficulty. The same points which are important in distinguishing chlorosis and primary heart disease are of importance here, together with the condition of the blood and the fact that the cardiac symptoms were developed after the anæmia.

The differential diagnosis of pernicious anæmia and cancer of the stomach.—In some cases of cancer of the stomach in which there is no discoverable tumour, and especially in those cases in which the body of the stomach is involved, the orifices being free, the symptoms may closely resemble those of pernicious anæmia.

In both conditions there is progressive asthenia, anæmia and more or less emaciation, without, perhaps, any definite and discoverable organic cause.

In the great majority of cases the differential diagnosis can be satisfactorily arrived at by a judicial survey of the whole symptoms and physical signs of the case. The condition of the blood, the severity of the stomach symptoms, the presence or absence of tenderness on pressure over the region of the stomach, the absence of free hydrochloric acid in the stomach contents, and especially of hæmatemesis, of a tumour or localised hardness in the epigastric region or of difficulty in swallowing due to obstruction of the lower end of the œsophagus, are the most important points to which attention should be directed in doubtful cases. The exact characters of the blood and the presence or absence of a tumour in the region of the stomach are the most important points.

Cabot lays stress upon the fact that in pernicious anæmia there is no leucocytosis, whereas in cases of profound anæmia due to malignant disease there is leucocytosis. His statement is as follows:—"As will be seen in the chapter on malignant disease, leucocytosis is by no means invariable in the anæmia of cancerous growth, but *in those cases* which cause such an anæmia as to resemble the counts of pernicious anæmia, leucocytosis is invariable."*

The occurrence of hæmatemesis is strongly in favour of cancer, for in my experience bleeding from the stomach is rare (though it does occasionally occur) in cases of pernicious anæmia.

But I know from my own experience that the differential diagnosis of pernicious anæmia and of cancer of the stomach or liver is in some cases extremely difficult, more especially when the patient is seen in consultation practice and when the means of ascertaining the exact characters of the blood are not forthcoming.

The differential diagnosis of pernicious anæmia and of Bright's disease.—There is rarely if ever any difficulty in distinguishing these conditions. The diagnosis of course turns upon the condition of the urine (presence of albumen, casts, etc.) on the one hand, and the condition of the blood (the presence of the alterations characteristic of pernicious anæmia) on the other. The latter (the condition of the blood) is the more important, for in some cases of pernicious anæmia the urine contains albumen. In 9 of my series of 45 cases, albumen was present; the amount was usually small—in most cases a trace—but in 2 cases it was considerable.

The differential diagnosis of pernicious anæmia and of leucocythæmia and pseudo-leukæmia.—This presents no difficulty, except in children. The two conditions are at once distinguished by (a) the microscopical characters of the blood; and

---

* "Clinical Examination of the Blood," p. 130.

(*b*) the marked enlargement of the spleen, or of the lymphatic glands, or of both (spleen and lymphatic glands).

The differential diagnosis of pernicious anæmia and of splenic anæmia without leucocythæmia.—In some cases in which the spleen is enlarged, there is profound anæmia but no increase of the white blood corpuscles. This form of anæmia is extremely rare; no case has come under my own observation. The essential points of distinction from pernicious anæmia are the enlargement of the spleen, which can, of course, be distinguished during life, and the characters of the blood ; in cases of splenic anæmia without leucocythæmia (*a*) the hæmoglobin appears to be diminished more than the corpuscles, in other words the anæmia is of the chlorotic rather than of the pernicious type; and (*b*) the red corpuscles do not (usually) present the extreme variations in size and shape and the other features which are characteristic of pernicious anæmia.

The differential diagnosis of pernicious anæmia and of medullary anæmia.—In considering the etiology and pathology of pernicious anæmia, I have stated that in (? all) cases of pernicious anæmia of long standing, pathological changes are ultimately produced in the medulla of the bones ; and that it has been supposed (though this has not as yet been definitely proved) that a form of anæmia, presenting all the clinical characteristics of pernicious anæmia, may in rare instances result from a primary lesion of the bone-marrow. I know of no means by which such a condition could be distinguished from the usual (Hunterian) type of pernicious anæmia during life, except by the presence of swelling and tenderness over the bones and sternum, and it is doubtful whether such swelling and tenderness are always and necessarily present. Whether in such cases, if they occur, the liver contains an excess of iron or not is, as I have already pointed out, a matter which requires to be determined by future observation. It is one of the facts which require to be settled before we can come to a definite conclusion as to whether the condition which we term pernicious anæmia is a definite and distinct disease, or whether it is a clinical condition which may result from a variety of morbid lesions, or rather of different causes.

PROGNOSIS.

The prognosis of pernicious anæmia is always very grave. Many cases steadily progress in spite of treatment, and the vast majority of cases ultimately terminate in death. Until the year 1873, when I first employed arsenic in the treatment of the disease, no known method of treatment seemed to be attended with even temporary benefit, at all events in any considerable proportion of cases, though in isolated instances the patients had got well under iron and phosphorus, and in some cases which had been diagnosed as pernicious anæmia by competent authorities, a (? temporary) cure had spontaneously resulted, *i.e.*, without any treatment. Up to the time that I directed attention to the value of arsenic in the treatment of the disease, the opinion expressed by Addison practically represented the experience of all clinical observers ; and as regards the *ultimate* result, that opinion probably correctly represents the experience of almost all physicians at the present time, *provided only that the cases, which are temporarily relieved and apparently cured, are followed up and watched for a sufficiently long period of time.* But under arsenical treatment, the *immediate* prognosis is certainly more hopeful. No one who has had large experience of the disease, and has given arsenic a fair trial, in a considerable number of cases, can fail, I think, to have come to the conclusion that some cases improve in the most remarkable way under the administration of large doses of the drug. Many independent observers have published cases in which the results of the arsenical treatment were markedly beneficial.*

In some cases, the improvement which follows the administration of arsenic is so marked and rapid that, in them, the remedy seems almost to be a (temporary) specific ; in other cases, arsenic produces little or no benefit. I have used the term *temporary* specific advisedly, for as Dr Hale-White has pointed out, in the vast majority of the cases which are temporarily relieved and it may be for the time apparently cured by arsenic (and I may add by every other plan of treatment which has as yet been employed), a relapse subsequently occurs and the disease ultimately proves fatal. This at all events represents my own experience. A tendency to relapse is one of the most striking features of the disease. In this respect pernicious anæmia closely resembles chlorosis ; but while in chlorosis the natural tendency in all, or almost all, uncomplicated cases is

---

* The following amongst others in this country have reported cases successfully treated by arsenic :—Byrom Bramwell, "Ed. Med. Journ.," 1877, and "Lancet," 1897 ; Lockie, "British Medical Journal," 1878 ; Stephen Mackenzie, "Lancet," 1879 ; Finny, "British Medical Journal," 1880 ; Broadbent, "British Medical Journal," 1880 ; Mitchinson, "Lancet," 1881 ; Withers Moore, "British Medical Journal," 1881 ; Pye-Smith, "Guy's Hosp. Rep. xxvi. (New Series)," 1882 ; Padley, "Lancet," 1883 ; Willcocks, "Practitioner," 1883 ; Wilks, "Lancet," 1885 ; Hale-White, "Guy's Hosp. Rep.," 1890 ; Handford, "British Medical Journal," 1891 ; Risien Russell, "British Medical Journal," 1894 ; &c.

towards recovery and spontaneous cure, in pernicious anæmia the very reverse is the case—the natural tendency in all cases seems to be towards relapse and death.

It remains for future observation to show whether relapses can be prevented by the continued administration of arsenic or of bone-marrow (for, as I will presently point out, bone-marrow appears to be beneficial in some cases of the disease), and by minute attention to the general health, to the hygienic surroundings, and to the condition of the gastro-intestinal tract. I am not without hope that this may be the case.

Immediate prognosis.—In cases of pernicious anæmia the immediate prognosis largely, of course, depends upon *the severity of the individual case*—and this, when the patient first comes under notice (*i.e.*, before the effects of treatment can be taken into account), must be chiefly judged of by *the degree of the anæmia* and *the exact characters of the blood changes* which are present, and by *the severity of the general (constitutional) symptoms.*

The disease is almost always rapidly fatal in cases in which the number of blood corpuscles sinks below 600,000 per c.mm.; though in one remarkable case reported by Quincke in which the red corpuscles are said to have numbered only 143,000 per c.mm., the patient recovered under the transfusion of 185 c.c. of defibrinated blood. It is worthy of note, and confirmatory of Dr Stephen Mackenzie's statement that Quincke's figures read low, that in this case, on recovery, the red corpuscles are said to have numbered only 1,234,000 per c.mm.

Cabot thinks that the microscopic characters of the blood are of importance for the purposes of prognosis. He states that although "the prognosis is always bad, the following scheme indicates the presence of a severe or of a mild type of the disease :—

" 1. *Severe (rapidly fatal).*
(*a.*) Extreme progressive anæmia.
(*b.*) High-colour index.
(*c.*) Increase in size of red cells.
(*d.*) Degenerative changes.
(*e.*) Numerous megaloblasts.
(*f.*) Few or no normoblasts.
(*g.*) Lymphocytosis.

2. *Less Severe (slower course).*
(*a.*) Remissions.
(*b.*) Normal or low-colour index.
(*c.*) Normal-sized cells.
(*d.*) No degenerative change.
(*e.*) Few megaloblasts.
(*f.*) Numerous normoblasts.
(*g.*) Normal percentage of adult cells."*

* "Clinical Examination of the Blood," p. 131

While these conclusions no doubt hold true in most cases, it must be remembered that exceptions to them occur. Thus, in a remarkable case in which pernicious anæmia and Addison's disease appeared to be combined, although the red corpuscles only numbered 450,000 per c.mm. (with one exception the lowest number which I have personally observed in any case) there was little alteration in the size of the red corpuscles and comparatively little poikilocytosis. In that case, too, the hæmoglobin was very greatly reduced, indeed more reduced than the red corpuscles (the colour index was only .55). It should, however, be noted that the diagnosis in this case was attended with difficulty; the condition seems to have been originally chlorosis and ulceration of the stomach, and even in its later stages the colour index and characters of the blood were more suggestive of chlorosis than of pernicious anæmia (see Abstract, Case 31).

The length of time that the disease has existed and *the stage at which it comes under treatment* are also very important points so far as the immediate prognosis is concerned; for, in the later stages of aggravated cases arsenic is, as a rule, useless, though this is not invariably the case.

I am disposed to think that, in those cases in which the disease is of short duration and in those cases in which it is rapidly developed, arsenic is more likely to be beneficial, and the prognosis consequently somewhat more favourable, than in the chronic and old-standing cases; but I speak with reserve on this point.

Many of the cases of pernicious anæmia which have come under my notice of recent years were seen once only in consultation, some of them only a short time before the fatal termination took place—in some of them, the disease was in such an advanced stage that recovery could not be expected under any plan of treatment.

Repeated relapses are unfavourable indications; in all of my cases in which more than one relapse occurred, the patients ultimately died. My experience goes to show that arsenic has a less beneficial influence upon the relapses than upon the original attack.

The age of the patient.—Whether the prognosis is more favourable in young subjects than in middle-aged adults and old people, I am unable to say.

The patient's ability to take arsenic in sufficient (full) doses is a most important (personally I am disposed to think *the* most important) point. This is very clearly brought out in the analysis of the results of treatment in my 45 cases. I will refer to this point in more detail presently.

Provided that the case is not too far advanced, that it is not of too long duration, *and that large doses of arsenic are well borne*, there is in many cases a reasonable hope of marked temporary improvement or complete temporary recovery.

The immediate prognosis is always very grave in those cases *in which hæmorrhages* (other than retinal hæmorrhages) occur; epistaxis, in some cases, should also perhaps be excepted; but in my own cases epistaxis was usually a late symptom.

The frequent recurrence of febrile attacks with jaundice and dark-coloured urine is also I think unfavourable, since these conditions are indicative of exacerbations of the blood destruction which is the fundamental feature of the disease. But too much importance must not be attached to this point. In the case in my series (Case 26) in which jaundice was most marked, the beneficial effect of arsenic was perhaps greater than in any other   Again, in Case 40, in which the urine was persistently very dark in colour and the symptoms most profound, though the patient ultimately relapsed and died, he improved for a time in a very marked degree under large doses of the remedy.

The presence of obstinate and intractable diarrhœa is also in most cases unfavourable. *Profound nervous symptoms*, such as extreme restlessness, delirium, semi-coma, convulsions, or coma, are of the gravest significance; such symptoms are usually the immediate precursors of death.

To sum up, in trying to form an *immediate prognosis* in cases of pernicious anæmia attention should be chiefly directed to the following points :—The degree of the anæmia ; the exact character of the blood (colour index and microscopic characters) ; the severity of the general constitutional symptoms (debility, dropsy, etc.) ; the length of time which the disease has continued ; the patient's ability to take arsenic in large doses for long periods of time ; and the presence or absence of grave symptoms and of complications, such as severe and obstinate diarrhœa, hæmorrhages, nervous symptoms, etc.

Ultimate prognosis.—As regards the ultimate prognosis, my experience shows only too clearly that in the vast majority of cases, even in those in which a complete cure seems for the time to have resulted from arsenical treatment, a relapse sooner or later occurs, and death ultimately takes place. But I repeat that I am not without hope that if arsenic is steadily given for long periods of time after (temporary) recovery, the tendency to relapse which is such a striking feature of the disease may perhaps be prevented.

In one of my cases the patient remained well for 12 years and then relapsed and died from the disease (13¾ years after the first attack). In no other of my cases, in which the result is known, has the patient lived more than 3 years after he first came under observation ; in one case death was due to an intercurrent attack of pneumonia—not directly at all events to pernicious anæmia ; in three cases only, in which the ultimate result of the treatment is known, do the patients still survive ; two of them are in good health.

TREATMENT.

So far as my own experience is concerned—and I think I may correctly say that the experience of most other observers is entirely corroborative of it—the only remedy with which we are at present acquainted which is likely to produce benefit, in any considerable proportion of cases of pernicious anæmia, is arsenic.

I was led to try the administration of arsenic in pernicious anæmia by the following chain of reasoning :—I knew from pathological observation that in cases of pernicious anæmia the most striking naked-eye appearance was the extreme fatty degeneration of the heart. I further knew that arsenic was a remedy of undoubted value in the treatment of many cases of fatty heart. I consequently said to myself, Why not try the effect of arsenic in pernicious anæmia ? I happened about this time to have several cases of pernicious anæmia under my care in the Newcastle Infirmary. In three of the cases in which I first tried the remedy, rapid and immediate improvement took place ; and the result of my whole experience, which now extends over twenty-three years, goes to show that the arsenical treatment is in many cases attended, for a time at least, with marked benefit.

Unfortunately, as I have just pointed out, the beneficial effects of arsenic are in the vast majority of cases only temporary. But instead of merely making general statements I will now describe in detail the results of the treatment in the 45 cases which have come under my own notice. These results are particularly valuable since the number of cases is large, and especially since they have, with few (seven) exceptions, been followed to their ultimate termination.

The results of the treatment in *all* of the 45 cases of pernicious anæmia which have come under my own observation are detailed in Table 6 and in the following analysis. I append to this paper an Abstract of the chief clinical and pathological details of all of these cases.*

---

* Since this Analysis and Table 6 were set in type, I have met with three additional cases of the disease. The chief facts in their clinical history are detailed below. (See Abstract, Cases 46, 47, and 48.)

TABLE 6.—SHOWING THE RESULTS OF ARSENICAL TREATMENT IN 45 CASES OF PERNICIOUS ANÆMIA.

No.	Age	Sex	Treatment Adopted.	Arsenic well or ill borne.*	Maximum Dose in Drops of Fowler's Solution Daily.	Immediate Result.	Subsequent Progress.	Ultimate Result.	Duration of life after first seen.
1	43	M	Iron, quinine, cod-liver oil, lime juice — without improvement. Then arsenic	W	18	Complete (?temporary) recovery	Not known	Not known	
2	20	M	Arsenic	W	12	Complete (?temporary) recovery	Not known	Not known	
3	34	M	Iron, quinine, lime juice, stimulants	..	..	No improvement		Death	14 days
4	28	M	Quinine, astringents, and stimul'nts	..	..	No improvement		Death	16 days
5	29	F	Iron, astringents, stimulants	..	..	No improvement		Death	12 days
6	38	M	Iron, quinine, and phosphorised cod-liver oil for 3 weeks, without improvement. Then arsenic	W	48	Complete recovery	Relapse 12 years after	Death	13¾ years
7	31	F	Arsenic tried, but disagreed. The carbonate of iron	B	6	Complete (?temporary) recovery	Not known	Not known	
8	47	M	None—would not remain in hospital	..	..	No change	Not known	Not known	
9	17	M	Arsenic, iron, q'nine, & stomachics	W	27	No improvement		Death	53 days
10	51	F	Arsenic (but it disagreed), Beta-naphthol, thymol	B	6	No improvement		Death	21 days
11	54	M	Arsenic	W	..	Temp'rary impr'vm't	Relapse	Death	1 year
12	50	M	Arsenic	B	?	Not known	Not known	Not known	
13	38	M	Arsenic	W	30	Complete (?temporary) recovery	Relapse 1 year after	Death †	15 month
14	41	F	Arsenic	W	42	Rapid disappear'nce of anæmia	Relapse (abscess of kidney)	Death ‡	4 months
15	42	F	Arsenic and iron	W	30	Complete (?temporary) recovery	Relapse 1 year after	Death	18 months
16	53	M	Arsenic and iron	W	18	Marked and rapid improvement	Relapse when arsenic discontinued	Death §	2 years
17	54	M	Arsenic and iron	W	15	Marked temporary improvement	Relapse 9 mths. after	Death	18 months
18	62	F	Arsenic	?	?	Marked impr'veinn't	Not known	Not known	
19	63	M	Arsenic and bone-marrow advised, but would not take	o	o			Death	2 days
20	53	M	Arsenic and iron	W	20	Decided temporary improvement	Relapse 4 months after, and arsenic not subsequently given	Death	5 months
21	51	M	Arsenic	W	12	Marked impr'v'm'nt	Relapse 11 mths. after	Death	16 months
22	66	M	Arsenic (could only take small doses) and bone-marrow	B	9 (for a few days)	No improvement		Death	3 weeks
23	57	M	Arsenic (could only take small doses), iron (it disagreed) and salicylate of bismuth	B	6	No improvement		Death	2 months
24	49	M	Arsenic, and after relapse arsenic and bone-marrow	W	36	Temporary recovery	Relapse 9 mths. after ; again recovered under arsenic. Second relapse 5 months later	Death	17 months
25	54	M	Arsenic	W	42	Slight temporary improvement	..	Death	5 months
26	53	M	Arsenic	W	60	Complete (? temporary) recovery	Slight relapse 10 months after	Well	1 year
27	52	F	Arsenic	W	57	Very slight improvement	Not known	Not known	
28	36	M	Arsenic	W	60	Complete (?temporary) recovery	Remains well	Well	1 year
29	49	F	Arsenic and salicylate of bismuth	B	9 (for a few days only)	No improvement		Death	4 months
30	40	F	Arsenic advised—could not take	B	9 (for a few days only)	No improvement		Death	11 days
31	16	F	Arsenic and iron	B	12 (for a short time)	No improvement		Death	2 months
32	41	M	Arsenic and iron	W	24	Complete temporary recovery	Relapse 10 mths. after ; again improved with arsenic. Second relapse 5 mths. later; again improved. Third relapse 6 mths. later.	Death	2½ years
33	54	M	Arsenic. After relapse, arsenic and bone-marrow	W	40	Complete temporary recovery	Relapse a year after; again improved under arsenic. Second relapse	Death	2 years
34	46	M	Arsenic, iron and bone-marrow	W	45	Slight temporary improvement		Death	3 months
35	72	F	Arsenic	?	?	Slight tem. improve.		Death	3 months
36	50	F	Arsenic and iron advised—patient refused to take	o	o	No improvement		Death	1 month
37	71	M	Arsenic	?	?	Marked temporary improvement	Relapse 5 mths. later	Death	8 months
38	55	F	Arsenic and iron	?	?	Temporary improvement	Relapse	Death	1 year
39	67	M	Arsenic and salicylate of bismuth	B	9 (for a few days only)	No improvement		Death	1 month
40	37	M	Arsenic and salicylate of bismuth	W	63	Marked temporary improvement	Relapse	Death	4 months
41	51	M	Arsenic, strychnine, &c.	W	15	No improvement		Death	8 days
42	31	F	Arsenic, oxygen inhalations, strychnine and digitalis	W	30	No improvement		Death	5 days
43	65	F	Arsenic, bone-marrow, transfusion	R'fus'd to take	5	Slight improvement (transfusion)		In statu quo	6 months
44	44	F	Arsenic, bone-marrow, oxygen inhalations, strychnine, &c.	W	45	Slight temporary improvement		Death	6 weeks
45	58	M	Arsenic, oxygen inhalations, &c.	W	42	No improvement		Death	18 days

* W = well borne : B = badly borne. † Immediate cause, cerebral hæmorrhage. ‡ Abscess of kidney found post mortem.
§ Pneumonia.

ANALYSIS OF THE RESULTS OF TREATMENT IN 45 CASES OF
PERNICIOUS ANÆMIA.

Cases in which arsenic was not given.—In seven of the forty-five cases, no
arsenic was given (Cases 3, 4, 5, 8, 19, 36 and 43).   In four of these cases (3, 4, 5
and 8) arsenic was not prescribed ; these patients came under my notice before I
appreciated the value of arsenic in the treatment of the disease.   In the remaining three cases (19, 36 and 43), arsenic was prescribed, but the patients refused
to take it.

In five of the seven cases in which no arsenic was given, the patients died
within a month, and usually much sooner, namely, in 14, 16, 12, 2 and 30 days
respectively.   In one of the remaining cases, the patient refused to stay in
hospital and submit himself to treatment ; the ultimate result in that case is
not known.   In the other case (43), there was some improvement under
transfusion.

Cases in which arsenic was administered.—In thirty-eight of the forty-five
cases, arsenic was given.

In *ten* of these cases (1, 2, 6, 13, 15, 24, 26, 28, 32 and 33), complete (temporary) recovery resulted ; in *eight* (14, 16, 17, 18, 20, 21, 37 and 40), there was
marked temporary improvement ; in *seven* (11, 25, 27, 34, 35, 38 and 44), there
was *slight temporary improvement ;* in *twelve* cases (7, 9, 10, 22, 23, 29, 30, 31,
39, 41, 42 and 45), there was *no improvement ;* (in one of these cases—7—in
which arsenic disagreed and was discontinued the patient recovered under
carbonate of iron ; in another—43—there was some improvement under transfusion) ; and in *one* case (12) the *result is not known*.

Thus in twenty-five out of thirty-eight cases in which arsenic was administered
there was more or less improvement ; in seven the improvement was slight, in
eight marked, and in ten there was complete (temporary) recovery.

**Ultimate result in the cases in which complete temporary recovery took
place.**—In *seven* of the ten cases in which complete (temporary) recovery resulted,
a relapse subsequently occurred (Cases 6, 13, 15, 25, 26, 32 and 33) ; in *one* (28),
there has been *no relapse* and the patient *remains well* (one year after the treatment was commenced) ; in the remaining *two* cases (1 and 2), *the result is
unknown*.

In *six* of the seven cases in which a relapse occurred, the patients have *died*
(6, 13, 15, 24, 32 and 33) ; in *one* case (26), the patient has *again completely
recovered*, for the time, under arsenic.

In the seven cases which completely recovered for a time and then relapsed
and died, in one case (6) the patient remained well for 12 years and died at the
end of 13¾ years ; in all the other cases (13, 15, 24, 26, 32 and 33), a relapse
occurred within a year (the exact date of occurrence of the relapse is given in
Table 5).

In seven of the eight cases in which there was marked improvement but not
complete (temporary) recovery under the treatment, death ultimately occurred ;
and in the remaining case (18), the ultimate result is not known.

In the seven cases in which there was slight improvement, six died (Cases
11, 25, 34, 35, 38 and 44) ; and in one case (27), the result is not known.

An analysis of the immediate results of the treatment in those cases in which
arsenic was well and badly borne shows very clearly that the prospect of

immediate improvement under this treatment largely depends upon the patient's ability to take full doses of the drug.   The analysis is as follows :—

Results of the treatment in those cases in which arsenic was well borne.— In the total number of thirty-eight cases in which arsenic was given, the remedy was well borne in twenty-four cases.

The results of the treatment in these twenty-four cases was as follows :—In ten, there was complete (temporary) recovery (Cases 1, 2, 6, 13, 15, 24, 26, 28, 32 and 33) ; in six, there was marked temporary improvement (Cases 14, 16, 17, 20, 21 and 40) ; in four, there was slight temporary improvement (Cases 25, 27, 32 and 44); and in four, there was no improvement (Cases 9, 41, 42 and 45).

The maximum dose of arsenic which each of these patients was able to take *per diem* was as follows :—

Cases which completely recovered.—Case 1 = 18 drops ; Case 2 = 12 drops; Case 6 = 48 drops ; Case 13 = 30 drops ; Case 15 = 30 drops ; Case 24 = 36 drops ; Case 26 = 60 drops ; Case 28 = 60 drops ; Case 32 = 24 drops ; Case 33 = 40 drops.

Cases in which there was marked improvement.—Case 14 = 42 drops ; Case 16 = 18 drops ; Case 17 = 10 drops ; Case 20 = 20 drops ; Case 21 = 12 drops ; Case 40 = 63 drops.

Cases in which there was slight improvement.—Case 25 = 42 drops ; Case 27 = 57 drops ; Case 34 = 45 drops ; Case 44 = 45 drops.

Cases in which there was no improvement.—Case 9 = 27 drops ; Case 41 = 15 drops ; Case 42 = 30 drops (this patient died five days after commencing the treatment) ; and Case 45 = 42 drops.

Results of the treatment in those cases in which arsenic was badly borne.— In the total thirty-eight cases in which arsenic was given, it was badly borne in nine cases.

The results of the treatment in these nine cases was as follows :—Complete recovery in one case (7) under carbonate of iron after arsenic had failed ; no improvement in seven cases, namely, 10, 22, 23, 29, 30, 31 and 39 ; and the result not known in one case (12).

Results of the treatment in those cases in which the dose of arsenic is not known.— In the remaining five of the total number of thirty-four cases in which arsenic was given, I am unable to state whether the remedy was well or ill borne, or to give the maximum dose which the patient took.

The result in these five cases was as follows :—Marked temporary improvement in two cases (18 and 37); slight temporary improvement in three cases (11, 35 and 38).

SUMMARY.

The immediate and ultimate result of the treatment in the 45 cases included in Table 6 is therefore as follows :—

Ultimate Result in 45 Cases of Pernicious Anæmia under Various Plans of Treatment.

In good health at present time · ·	2 cases.	
Still under treatment · · ·	1	,,
Dead · · · ·	35	,,
Result not known · · · ·	7	,,
Total · ·	45	,,

Immediate Result in 45 Cases of Pernicious Anæmia under Various Plans of Treatment. '

Complete (temporary) recovery - - -	10 cases.
Marked (temporary) improvement - - -	8 ,,
Slight (temporary) improvement - - -	8 ,,
No improvement - - - - -	17 ,,
Immediate result not known - - -	2 ,,
Total - -	45 ,,

Immediate Result in 7 Cases not Treated with Arsenic.

No improvement - - - - -	5 cases.
Slight temporary improvement - - -	1 ,,
Result not known - - - - -	1 ,,
Total - -	7 ,,

Immediate Result in 38 Cases Treated with Arsenic.

Complete (? temporary) recovery - - -		10 cases.
No relapse - - - -	1	
Relapse and recovery - - -	1	
Relapse and death - - -	8	
Marked (temporary) improvement - - -		8 .,
Slight (temporary) improvement - - -		7 ,,
No improvement - - - - -		12 ,,
Result not known - - - - -		1 ,,
Total - -		38 ,,

Immediate Result in the 24 Cases in which Arsenic was Well Borne.

Complete recovery - - - - -		10 cases.
With no relapse - - - -	1	
With relapse and recovery - -	1	
With relapse and death - -	6	
Result unknown - - -	2	
Marked (temporary) improvement - - -		6 ,,
Slight (temporary) improvement - - -		4 ,,
No improvement - - - - -		4 ,,
Total - -		24 ,,

Immediate Result in the 9 Cases in which Arsenic was Badly Borne.

Complete (? temporary) recovery (under iron) -	1 case.
No improvement - - - - -	7 ,,
Result not known - - - - -	1 ,,
Total - -	9 ,,

Immediate Result in the 5 Cases in which the Dose of Arsenic is Not Known.

Marked temporary improvement - - -	2 cases.
Slight temporary improvement - - -	3 ,,
Total - -	5 ,,

General treatment.—Before referring to the dose of arsenic and the mode of administration, let me say a few words with regard to the general treatment of the disease ; for in this form of anæmia, as in chlorosis, attention to the hygienic surroundings and the feeding of the patient are of great importance.

It is essential, I think, that the patient should be kept at absolute rest in bed, or at all events in the recumbent position, until recovery is well advanced. I attach the greatest importance to this point. It is, I think, one of the reasons why advanced cases of the disease are more successfully treated in hospital than in private practice.

The patient should have plenty of fresh air and, if possible, an abundance of sunlight.

The diet should be light and nutritious. Owing to the impaired digestive power of the stomach, the patient is usually unable to digest solid food. Milk and milk foods, meat extracts (of which Wyeth's is perhaps the best), raw beef juice, finely grated and pounded raw meat, and whipped-up eggs should form the basis of the dietary. On the view that pernicious anæmia is the result of blood destruction in the portal circulation and that the individual red corpuscles contain more than the normal amount of hæmoglobin, a milk diet should theoretically be preferable to a red meat diet ; but I have not been able to satisfy myself that the administration of meat extracts, beef juice, or pounded raw meat is harmful. On the contrary, I am disposed to think that a meat diet is in some cases beneficial.

The condition of the bowels must be carefully regulated. If there is constipation—but this is rare—gentle laxatives should be given ; aloin, cascara and sulphur are probably the best. If there is diarrhœa, it should be arrested as soon as possible ; salicylate of bismuth is one of the best remedies for this purpose. When there is reason to suppose that excessive decomposition is going on in the intestine, intestinal antiseptics (Beta-naphthol, thymol, menthol or salol) may be tried ; thymol, one grain three times a day, is perhaps the most effective.

It is unnecessary to say that in those cases in which the patient is losing blood from the uterus, piles, etc., the hæmorrhage should be arrested as speedily as possible.

In rickety children who are suffering from profound anæmia (which it is sometimes difficult to distinguish from pernicious anæmia), the appropriate treatment for rickets is of course essential, and arsenic and iron may at the same time be given. These cases can hardly, however, be included under the term pernicious anæmia, though the blood condition is very similar, so far at all events as the shape and size of the red blood corpuscles is concerned.

Dose and Mode of Administration of Arsenic.—In administering arsenic, I usually begin with a small dose—two drops of Fowler's solution three times a day, given in plenty of water, soon after food. I gradually increase the dose by one drop every third day (and in severe and advanced cases every second or even every day unless the remedy disagrees), so that on the fourth day the patient is taking three drops, on the seventh day four drops, on the tenth day five drops, and so on. Many patients affected with pernicious anæmia can ultimately take ten, fifteen, or even twenty drops of Fowler's solution three times daily. In two of my cases, the patients took as much as sixty drops per diem. The object of the treatment is to gradually increase the dose until the maximum quantity that the patient can take without any discomfort is reached. When the patient begins to complain of itching of the eyeballs, pain in the stomach or diarrhœa, the dose should be immediately and considerably reduced ; subsequently it may again be increased and the remedy continued in the largest dose which can be comfortably and satisfactorily borne.

The long-continued administration of arsenic in some cases produces pigmentation of the skin, and in others peripheral neuritis. I have observed both effects in a few cases.

Many patients who are suffering from pernicious anæmia seem to have a remarkable tolerance for the drug ; and my experience very definitely shows that it is precisely in those cases of pernicious anæmia (in which large doses of arsenic are well borne) that the remedy is most likely to produce benefit. The same thing is seen in many other diseases in which a remedy is markedly beneficial ; for example, iodide of potassium in syphilis, opium in peritonitis, iron in chlorosis, chloral hydrate in some cases of nervous spasm, etc.

In those cases in which the arsenic agrees and is attended with benefit, it should be steadily continued in full doses until the number of red blood corpuscles reaches the normal, and until the symptoms of the disease disappear.

When the patient is apparently cured, the dose should be reduced, *but the remedy should still be given in small doses*—three or four drops of Fowler's solution three times a day—for a long period of time. I am of opinion that these small doses should be continued for several months at least, and probably, if relapses are to be prevented, for several years. I attach great importance to this point, and I am hopeful that if this plan of treatment is systematically carried out, relapses will in future be found to be less common than they have been in the past.—

Probable Mode of Action of Arsenic.—The exact manner in which arsenic produces its beneficial effects in pernicious anæmia is not yet determined. Dr Hunter suggests that it probably acts by producing a healthier condition of the gastro-intestinal tract, that is to say by preventing the formation and absorption of the toxic product which he thinks is the essential cause of the disease. Dr Copeman has shown that under the administration of arsenic in pernicious anæmia, the hæmoglobin is much more stable; it does not tend to separate from the corpuscles after withdrawal from the body in the way which it does before the arsenic was administered. It is probable, I think, that the remedy acts both in the manner that Dr Hunter has suggested and as a blood tonic, that it exerts a beneficial effect upon the bone-marrow, enabling the marrow to form healthier red blood corpuscles —blood corpuscles which are more resistant, and in which the hæmoglobin is more stable and intimately combined. But be this as it may the beneficial effect of the remedy in many cases of the disease is undoubted.

Bone-marrow.—Professor T. R. Fraser * has recommended the administration of bone-marrow and has published a case in which remarkable improvement occurred under the combined administration of bone-marrow and arsenic. He concluded that in that case the improvement was due to the bone-marrow rather than the arsenic and other remedies which the patient was taking. It remains to be seen whether further observation will confirm this opinion or not; and it is only right to state that (I am informed) in that case, as in so many other cases of pernicious anæmia, the disease relapsed and the patient died some little time after his discharge from hospital.

Drs Barrs and Danforth have also published cases, and I have heard of some other cases which have not been published, in which bone-marrow was beneficial when arsenic had failed.†

So far as present experience enables us to judge, bone-marrow appears to be a much less efficacious remedy than arsenic. Further information is required before it is possible to pronounce a positive opinion as to the value of bone-marrow in this disease. Bone-marrow has not appeared to produce any benefit in the

---

* "British Medical Journal," 1894, Vol. i., p. 1172.

† "British Medical Journal," 16th February 1895; "Chicago Clinical Revue," October 1895.

cases in which I have prescribed it; but it is only fair to say that I always commence the treatment with arsenic, and that it is only in those cases in which arsenic fails to produce a (temporary) cure—in other words, marked improvement—that I prescribe bone-marrow. In most of the cases in which I have prescribed bone-marrow, it has in the course of a short time disagreed with the stomach.

Bone-marrow is perhaps best administered, as Dr Lauder Brunton has pointed out to me, in the raw state mixed with mashed potato.

Iron.—In most cases of true pernicious anæmia, iron usually fails to produce any beneficial effect; indeed, in some cases it seems to be prejudicial. But, as I have already stated, I speak with less confidence on this point than I did some years ago, for in some of my recent cases most marked improvement has occurred under the simultaneous administration of Robertson's capsules together with large and gradually increasing doses of arsenic. Cases have however been reported in which an apparent (? temporary) cure has resulted from the administration of iron alone[*]; and Stockman argues that if a case of pernicious anæmia is curable at all (excluding those which are necessarily fatal) then iron is bound to be of value, as it is whenever a deficiency of hæmoglobin has to be made good[†]; but I fail to follow his reasoning. If iron is prescribed, the effects of the remedy should be very carefully watched, for I am satisfied (both from the observation of my first and recent cases) that in some cases it is prejudicial; in a recent case the patient himself volunteered the statement that it did harm and increased the diarrhœa which in his case was a prominent symptom.

Intestinal antiseptics.—Believing that the disease is due to the absorption of a poison from the intestines, Dr Hunter has recommended the administration of intestinal antiseptics (Beta-naphthol, etc.); Dr George Gibson has published a case in which this plan of treatment seemed to produce a remarkably beneficial effect. In the only two cases in which I have tried this plan of treatment, no improvement resulted.

Anthelmintics.—If there is reason to suspect the presence of

---

[*] Amongst others, the following cases which recovered under iron have been reported :—Quincke (Deut. Archiv., Vol. xx., p. 3); Byrom Bramwell (Edin. Med. Jour., Nov. 1877); Wilks (Lancet, Vol. i., 1885, p. 653); Finlay (Lancet, Vol. i., 1885, p. 358).

[†] On the Nature and Treatment of Pernicious Anæmia, "British Medical Journal," May 4th, 11th, and 18th, 1895.

intestinal worms or parasites (and in all cases of pernicious anæmia the fæces should be examined for ova, parasites, etc.), such remedies as thymol or santonin should be given.

Yellow santonin, a remedy which has recently been said to be a specific in sprue, in which disease the most profound anæmia is sometimes developed (but it is, so far as my experience enables me to judge, of the chlorotic and not of the pernicious type), deserves, I think, a thorough trial in cases of this kind, and, perhaps, in all cases of the disease in which the diarrhœa continues and the patient does not improve under arsenic and salicylate of bismuth.

Oxygen inhalations have also been recommended. I have tried the remedy in a few cases in which the arsenic and bone-marrow failed to produce improvement, but without any beneficial result.

Transfusion of blood or saline solution has been tried by various observers. In the great majority of cases the effect was negative or prejudicial. From the results of his experimental observations on the lower animals, Dr Hunter is strongly disposed to think that transfusion will be likely to do more harm than good. The only possible effect which, in his opinion, it is likely to produce is temporary benefit. But notwithstanding these theoretical objections, which seem to be based on satisfactory reasoning, good results have undoubtedly been obtained in a few cases.* In one of my cases (a private patient) in which blood was directly transfused, a very temporary rally took place, but the patient died the day after the operation; in another case in which the patient was unable to take either arsenic or bone-marrow, decided temporary improvement has resulted from transfusion. This case is still under observation. (See Abstract, Case 43.)

If further observation should show that pernicious anæmia is a *clinical* condition and not a separate disease (*i.e.*, if pernicious anæmia may result from several different causes and not merely from one cause), it is reasonable to suppose that some cases will improve under one remedy and some under another (in other words, that in some cases arsenic, in others bone-marrow, will be beneficial); and if this should be the case it is not unreasonable to hope that further observation and experience may enable us to differentiate the cases in which arsenic, bone-marrow and other remedies, which may ultimately be employed in the treatment of the disease, are most beneficial.

---

* Quincke, "Deutsches Archiv.," Vol. xx., p. 1; Brakenridge, "British Medical Journal," 1892; Affleck, "British Medical Journal," 1892.

Let me repeat that in the advanced stages of grave cases of pernicious anæmia it is unreasonable to expect improvement under any of our present plans of treatment, though exceptions to this statement occasionally occur.

Cases of pernicious anæmia which have been temporarily cured by arsenic or other remedies should, as I have already stated, be closely and continuously watched. The blood should be examined from time to time. If any indications of a relapse develop, the dose of arsenic should be immediately increased. The tendency to relapse is so great that the arsenic should be continued in small doses for many months or even years after an apparent cure has been effected. As I have already stated, I attach the greatest importance to this point.

ABSTRACT OF 48 CASES OF PERNICIOUS ANÆMIA (ADDISON'S IDIOPATHIC ANÆMIA) OBSERVED BY THE AUTHOR DURING LIFE.

CASE I.—Male, aged 43, cabman, was admitted to the Newcastle Infirmary on 18th March 1875, suffering from profound anæmia and spinal symptoms.

Duration.—3 years.

Apparent cause.—None.

Symptoms.—Profound anæmia ; loss of weight ; shortness of breath and palpitation on exertion ; red corpuscles much diminished in number ; many megalocytes and microcytes ; marked poikilocytosis ; some excess of white corpuscles ; heart sounds weak ; soft systolic mitral murmur ; area of cardiac dulness small ; radial pulse 56, very soft, weak, slightly visible and jerking ; retinæ not seen because of opacity of vitreous ; urine normal in colour ; trace of albumen ; numbness, weakness and inco-ordination in arms and legs ; superficial reflexes markedly exaggerated.

Treatment.—Iron, quinine, cod-liver oil and lime juice were at first prescribed ; there was some, but only slight, improvement ; arsenic was then substituted (maximum dose, 18 drops daily).

Immediate result.—Marked and rapid improvement under arsenical treatment ; the patient was discharged, apparently quite well, and saying he was fit for work, on 22nd July 1875, after being in hospital 126 days.

Subsequent progress and Ultimate result.—Not known.

Case recorded in the " Edin. Med. Journal," Nov. 1877.

CASE II.—Male, aged 20, sailor, admitted to the Newcastle Infirmary on 21st March 1875, suffering from all the characteristic symptoms of profound pernicious anæmia.

Duration.—3 months.

Apparent cause.—An attack of yellow fever four-and-a-half months previously.

Symptoms.—Profound anæmia ; great weakness and prostration ; no loss of weight; shortness of breath and palpitation on exertion; red corpuscles markedly diminished in number; many megalocytes and microcytes; marked poikilocytosis; apparent nucleation of red corpuscles (colour plate of blood published in "Edin. Med. Journal," Nov. 1877); heart of normal size; soft systolic mitral murmur, heard also in other areas; pulse 112, very weak, compressible and visible; retinal hæmorrhages; epistaxis; slight dropsy of face; tongue smooth, clean and pale; occasional vomiting; severe diarrhœa; slight jaundice; intermittent attacks of fever; urine dark; no albumen; thirst; restlessness.

Treatment.—For two days he was treated with iron, but as it made him worse (before admission to hospital he had taken large quantities of iron and quinine without benefit) arsenic was then substituted (maximum dose = 12 drops daily).

Immediate result.—Under the arsenic rapid and remarkable improvement took place. At the end of 88 days the patient was discharged from hospital apparently quite well.

Subsequent progress and Ultimate result.—Not known.

Case recorded in the "Edinburgh Medical Journal," November 1877.

CASE III.—Male, aged 34, grocer's assistant, admitted to the Newcastle Infirmary on 10th June 1875, suffering from all the typical symptoms of pernicious anæmia.

Duration.—2 years.

Apparent cause.—None.

Symptoms.—Profound anæmia; great weakness and prostration; some loss of weight; shortness of breath and palpitation on exertion; red corpuscles greatly diminished in number; many megalocytes and microcytes; marked poikilocytosis; apparent nucleation of red corpuscles; white corpuscles diminished in number; area of cardiac dulness somewhat increased; well-marked mitral systolic murmur; loud venous hum in the neck; dilatation of external jugular veins; pulse 100, very weak, irregular; retinal hæmorrhages; some swelling of feet; tongue smooth, pale, moist; occasional vomiting; occasional fever; great restlessness; urine normal in colour.

Treatment.—Iron and quinine, lime juice and stimulants.

Result.—No improvement; death a fortnight after admission.

Post-mortem appearances typical.

Case recorded in the "Edinburgh Medical Journal," November 1877.

CASE IV.—Male, aged 28, foreign sailor, was admitted to the Newcastle Infirmary on 16th August 1875, suffering from profound pernicious anæmia.

Duration.—7 months.

Apparent cause.—Attack of yellow fever seven months previously.

Symptoms.—Profound anæmia; profound prostration; loss of weight and emaciation; shortness of breath and palpitation on exertion; great diminution of red corpuscles; many megalocytes and microcytes; marked poikilocytosis; apparent nucleation of the red corpuscles; white corpuscles diminished in number; soft systolic murmur at the base of the heart; loud venous hum in the neck; pulse 84, small and weak; retinal hæmorrhages; slight œdema of eyelids;

diarrhœa; tongue smooth, pale, moist; constant thirst; urine pale, trace of albumen.

Treatment.—Quinine, astringents and stimulants were administered.

Result.—No improvement; death 16 days after admission.

Post-mortem appearances characteristic.

Case recorded in the "Edinburgh Medical Journal," November 1877.

CASE V.—Female, aged 29, married woman, seen in consultation 14th September 1875, suffering from profound pernicious anæmia.

Duration.—8 months.

Apparent cause.—None; the anæmia developed after the last confinement (labour easy, no excessive loss of blood).

Symptoms.—Profound anæmia and prostration; no loss of weight; shortness of breath and palpitation on exertion; blood not examined; heart slightly increased in size; loud blowing murmurs at the base of the heart and in the vessels of the neck; retinal hæmorrhages; vomiting; diarrhœa; urine very pale, no albumen.

Treatment.—Iron, astringents and stimulants.

Result.—No improvement; the patient died 12 days after the consultation.

Post-mortem examination not allowed.

CASE VI.—Male, aged 38, a chemical worker, was admitted to Newcastle Infirmary on 26th November 1873, suffering from profound pernicious anæmia.

Duration.—$7\frac{1}{2}$ months.

Supposed cause.—Exposure to cold, wet and working in "gas."

Symptoms.—Profound anæmia and prostration; slight loss of weight; shortness of breath and palpitation on exertion; great debility; red corpuscles markedly diminished in number; many megalocytes and microcytes; marked poikilocytosis; apparent nucleation of red corpuscles; white corpuscles diminished in number; heart of normal size; loud blowing systolic murmurs at all the cardiac orifices, the mitral being most marked; pulse 76, regular, of fair strength; loud venous hum in the neck; external jugular veins distended and prominent; retinal hæmorrhages; some dropsy of feet and face; tongue clean, pale and moist; occasional vomiting; frequent diarrhœa; occasional fever; urine very pale; numbness of hands and feet; exaggeration of superficial reflexes.

Treatment.—For the first three weeks after admission, iron, quinine and phosphorised cod-liver oil were administered without benefit; arsenic was then given in gradually increasing doses (maximum dose, 48 drops daily).

Immediate result.—Remarkable and rapid improvement under the arsenical treatment; the patient was discharged apparently quite well on 20th January 1876, 55 days after admission.

Subsequent progress.—He remained well for 12 years; then relapsed; was again admitted to Newcastle Infirmary under the care of Professor Philipson; arsenic again administered with temporary improvement.

Ultimate result.—Again relapsed and finally died from the disease thirteen years and nine months after the first attack.

Case recorded in the "Edinburgh Medical Journal," November 1877, and Atlas of Clinical Medicine," Vol. iii., p. 142.

CASE VII.—Female, aged 31, married woman, seen in consultation on 27th March 1877, suffering from profound anæmia, apparently pernicious in character.

Duration.—5 months.

Apparent cause.—None ; the anæmia developed during the last pregnancy ; the confinement was easy, there was no excessive loss of blood.

Symptoms.—Profound anæmia and prostration ; no loss of weight ; shortness of breath and palpitation on exertion ; red corpuscles markedly diminished in number ; many megalocytes and microcytes ; marked poikilocytosis ; apparent nucleation of red corpuscles ; no excess of white corpuscles ; some swelling of feet ; retinal hæmorrhages ; vomiting ; diarrhœa.

Treatment.—Arsenic was tried, but disagreed even in small doses (maximum dose of arsenic = 6 drops daily). The patient ultimately recovered under large doses of carbonate of iron (a fact which perhaps throws some doubt upon the diagnosis).

Subsequent progress and Ultimate result.—Not known.

Case recorded.—" Edin. Med. Journal," Nov. 1877.

CASE VIII.—Male, aged 47, pitman, was admitted to Newcastle Infirmary on 6th September 1877, suffering from all the characteristic symptoms of pernicious anæmia.

Duration.—1 year.

Apparent cause.—None.

Symptoms.—Profound anæmia ; great debility ; slight loss of weight ; shortness of breath and palpitation on exertion ; red corpuscles markedly diminished in number ; many megalocytes and microcytes ; marked poikilocytosis ; apparent nucleation of the red corpuscles ; no excess of white corpuscles ; heart's action feeble ; pulse very weak ; retinal hæmorrhages ; some swelling of feet ; frequent diarrhœa ; slight jaundice ; thirst.

Treatment.—The patient remained in hospital only 4 days ; then insisted on going home ; no treatment adopted.

Subsequent progress and Ultimate result.—Not known.

Case recorded in the " Edinburgh Medical Journal," November 1877.

CASE IX.—Male, aged 17, errand boy, admitted to the Newcastle Infirmary on 21st February 1878, suffering from profound anæmia and vomiting.

Duration.—1 year.

Apparent cause.—Not known ; the anæmia developed (or perhaps was first noticed) after an attack of vomiting. When 10 years of age had an attack of inflammation of the bowels.

Symptoms.—Profound anæmia and prostration ; some loss of weight ; shortness of breath and palpitation on exertion ; red corpuscles markedly diminished in number, many megalocytes and microcytes, marked poikilocytosis ; apparent nucleation of the red corpuscles ; slight excess of whites ; loud venous hum in the neck ; heart of normal size ; soft mitral systolic murmur ; pulse very quick (120-130), and of low tension ; no retinal hæmorrhages ; slight swelling of feet ; frequent vomiting ; thirst ; dulness, apparently due to hydrothorax, over the base of each lung.

Diagnosis difficult; but as there did not appear to be any evidence of local disease (in stomach, etc.), and as the microscopical characters of the blood appeared to be characteristic, I concluded, though with hesitation, that the case was one of pernicious anæmia. I feel considerable doubt as to the correctness of this view.

Treatment.—Arsenic in gradually increasing doses (maximum dose, 27 drops daily), iron, quinine, stomachics.

Immediate result.—No improvement. After being in hospital for 53 days, the patient was seized with pain in the abdomen, vomiting and collapse, and died somewhat suddenly.

Post-mortem examination not allowed.

CASE X.—Female, aged 51, married woman, seen in consultation on 31st March 1889, suffering from profound pernicious anæmia.

Duration.—Said to be 2 or 3 months; short of breath for 2 or 3 years, but not markedly anæmic till 2 months ago.

Apparent cause.—Formerly very subject to diarrhœa and bleeding piles. No diarrhœa or loss of blood for more than a year; hæmatemesis a year ago.

Symptoms.—Profound anæmia and prostration; no loss of weight; shortness of breath and palpitation on exertion; red corpuscles markedly diminished in number; many megalocytes and microcytes; moderate poikilocytosis; apparent nucleation of red corpuscles; ? organisms; heart somewhat dilated; systolic murmurs at base and apex; veins in the neck distended; pulse markedly jerking in character; retinal hæmorrhages; occasional vomiting; no diarrhœa lately; some swelling of feet; marked leucoderma.

Treatment.—Arsenic was tried but only in small doses as it disagreed (maximum dose=6 minims daily); then Beta-naphthol and thymol.

Immediate result.—None of these remedies produced any benefit. Patient died 3 weeks after consultation.

Post-mortem appearances typical of pernicious anæmia; some petechial hæmorrhages in pericardium, stomach, and on outer surface of intestine; heart markedly fatty and dilated; liver fatty and containing a large excess of iron; spleen slightly enlarged and dark in colour; suprarenal capsules normal; some (slight) old ulceration of the ilio-cæcal valve.

CASE XI.—Male, aged 54, Indian Civil Servant, was seen in consultation on 14th September 1886, suffering from profound anæmia.

Duration.—1 year.

Apparent cause.—None; ? gout.

Symptoms.—Profound anæmia; great prostration; no loss of weight; shortness of breath and palpitation on exertion; red corpuscles moderately diminished in number; few megalocytes, some microcytes; moderate poikilocytosis; no excess of whites; heart slightly dilated; mitral systolic murmur; occasional angina-like pains; no sign of aneurism; occasional vomiting; tongue clean, smooth and moist; urine rather pale, no albumen.

Treatment.—Arsenic in gradually increasing doses (maximum dose = ?).

Immediate result.—Improved considerably for a time under arsenic; then developed acute gout (from which he had previously suffered); again improved.

Subsequent progress and Ultimate result.—Died (from the disease) in the South of England about two years after the consultation.

CASE XII.—Male, aged 50, medical man, seen in consultation on 24th October 1890, suffering from typical pernicious anæmia.

Duration.—9 months.

Apparent cause.—Several attacks of gastric influenza, with diarrhœa.

Symptoms.—Profound anæmia and prostration ; slight loss of weight ; shortness of breath and palpitation on exertion ; red corpuscles markedly diminished in number (1,470,000 per c.mm.) ; hæmoglobin=46 per cent. ; many megalocytes and microcytes ; marked poikilocytosis ; apparent nucleation of red corpuscles ; no excess of white corpuscles ; marked venous hum in the neck ; heart of normal size ; systolic pulmonary murmur ; no retinal hæmorrhages (pupils very small) ; occasional diarrhœa ; urine normal in colour ; occasional temporary trace of albumen.

Treatment.—Small doses of arsenic ($\frac{1}{100}$th to $\frac{1}{60}$th of a grain) had been tried but disagreed, producing gastro-intestinal irritation. Advised to try gradually increasing doses of Fowler's solution (maximum dose = ?).

Immediate result, Subsequent progress and Ultimate result.—Not known.

CASE XIII.—Male, aged 38, banker, seen in consultation 9th September 1890, suffering from profound pernicious anæmia.

Duration.—2 years.

Apparent cause.—Gastro-intestinal catarrh and diarrhœa, thought to be due to defective sanitary surroundings (manure heap 10 feet from office window).

Symptoms.—Profound anæmia and prostration ; slight loss of weight ; shortness of breath and palpitation on exertion ; red corpuscles markedly diminished in number ; a few megalocytes, some microcytes ; moderate poikilocytosis ; no increase of white corpuscles ; marked venous hum in the neck ; no retinal hæmorrhages ; slight loss of blood from piles ; some diarrhœa ; slight jaundice ; urine very dark ; an occasional trace of albumen.

Treatment.—Arsenic was given in gradually increasing doses (maximum dose=60 drops daily).

Immediate result.—Marked and rapid improvement. On 23rd February 1891, his doctor wrote me : " Mr B. is now quite well ; after his visit to you he steadily improved and is now stout and strong."

Subsequent progress.—In March 1891 got cold, followed by relapse of the anæmia ; the arsenic then discontinued by the advice of his doctor (from March 1891 until June 1891). Seen again 16th June 1891 ; profoundly anæmic and skin so deeply pigmented that doctor suggested Addison's disease. (The pigmentation was probably due to arsenic ; the patient had taken double the dose ordered ; the remedy produced numbness in fingers and toes.) Arsenic resumed ; again improved.

Ultimate result.—In November 1891 again relapsed. During December 1891 confined to bed with profound anæmia and gastro-intestinal catarrh. At beginning of January 1892 died suddenly, doctor thought from cerebral hæmorrhage.

Post-mortem examination.—None.

CASE XIV.—Female, aged 41, married woman, seen in consultation 24th March 1891, suffering from profound anæmia apparently pernicious in character.

Duration.—18 months.

Apparent cause.—From July to December 1890 was extremely ill with pneumonia and recurring pyrexia from which she recovered ; this was followed by profound anæmia, paralysis and inco-ordination of legs.

Symptoms.—Profound anæmia and prostration; some loss of weight; shortness of breath and palpitation on exertion; blood not examined ; venous hum in the neck; systolic pulmonary and mitral murmurs ; retinal hæmorrhages ; repeated attacks of epistaxis ; jaundice; occasional fever ; urine dark—the specimen which I examined contained no albumen.

Treatment.—Arsenic was given in gradually increasing doses (maximum dose reached, 42 drops daily).

Immediate result.—The anæmia almost entirely disappeared in the course of a few weeks ; the skin became much bronzed.

Subsequent progress.—On 8th May a considerable quantity of pus was suddenly discharged in the urine (apparently due to pyelitis). After this the patient suffered from recurring pyrexia, the temperature going up to 105° ; the anæmia returned ; epistaxis recurred, and dropsy developed; the arsenic had to be discontinued ; quinine, digitalis and stimulants substituted.

Ultimate result. —The patient died in July 1891.

Post-mortem examination.—The patient's doctor informs me that both kidneys contained numerous abscesses ; the other parts of the body were not examined.

NOTE.—I had no doubt when I saw this patient that the case was one of pernicious anæmia ; it is unfortunate, since it was complicated with abscesses in the kidney, that a complete post-mortem examination was not made.

CASE XV.—Female, aged 42, widow and washerwoman, seen on 2nd October 1892, suffering from profound anæmia.

Duration.—2 years ; worse 6 months.

Apparent cause.—Loss of blood (pulling of tooth 2 years ago); attack of influenza and profound grief (loss of husband and father) 3 months ago ; overwork and insanitary surroundings.

Symptoms.—Profound anæmia and debility ; no loss of weight ; shortness of breath and palpitation on exertion ; red corpuscles markedly diminished in number ; many megalocytes and microcytes; marked poikilocytosis ; apparent nucleation of red corpuscles ; heart dilated ; systolic pulmonary and mitral murmurs ; venous hum in the neck ; retinal hæmorrhages ; swelling of feet.

Treatment.—Large doses of iron (Robertson's capsules) and increasing doses of arsenic (maximum dose reached, 30 drops daily).

Immediate result.—Rapid and remarkable improvement. In two-and-a-half months (15th December 1892) the doctor wrote me saying "our patient is now in perfect health, the recovery has been remarkable and rapid, and has made much talk."

Subsequent progress.—The patient remained well for nearly a year and was able to work as a washerwoman. Then (in March 1893) had two attacks of hepatic colic, followed by a return of the anæmia. Iron and arsenic again administered, but without effect. Seen on 3rd May 1894 ; profoundly anæmic ; temperature 104°; profoundly exhausted and restless. Bone-marrow and arsenic by rectum prescribed. Unable to take medicine.

Ultimate result.—Died two days after my visit.

Post-mortem examination.—None.

CASE XVI.—Male, aged 53, hotelkeeper, seen on 15th December 1892, suffering from profound pernicious anæmia.

Duration.—10 months.

Apparent cause.—Chill while curling.

Symptoms.—Profound anæmia and debility; considerable loss of weight (1½ stone); some shortness of breath on exertion; red corpuscles markedly diminished in number; some megalocytes; many microcytes; marked poikilocytosis; apparent nucleation of red corpuscles; some excess of lymphocytes; heart of normal size; action feeble; slight systolic murmur in aortic and mitral areas; no retinal hæmorrhages; some swelling of feet; urine normal in colour; tongue pale, smooth and moist.

Treatment.—Arsenic in gradually increasing doses, and Blaud's pill capsules, prescribed (maximum dose of arsenic reached, 18 drops daily).

Immediate result.—Rapid and marked improvement.

Subsequent progress.—His medical attendant wrote me on 4th April 1896:—" He improved very much after you saw him, and was able to go about and do his business until December 1894—two years afterwards."

Ultimate result.—In the end of December 1894 he got a chill; died from *congestion of the lungs* (pneumonia) in the beginning of January 1895. He took the arsenic nearly constantly; indeed, whenever he stopped it he fell back."

Post-mortem examination.—None.

CASE XVII.—Male, aged 54, shopkeeper, seen in consultation in July 1894, suffering from profound anæmia.

Duration.—Several months.

Apparent cause.—None.

Symptoms.—Profound anæmia and debility; some loss of weight; shortness of breath and palpitation on exertion; blood not examined; retinal hæmorrhages; some swelling of feet; occasional vomiting and diarrhœa; urine of normal colour.

Treatment.—Iron (Robertson's capsules) and arsenic in gradually increasing doses (maximum dose reached, 10 drops daily) prescribed.

Immediate result.—Marked temporary improvement.

Subsequent progress and Ultimate result.—Relapse 9 months, and death 18 months afterwards.

Post-mortem examination.—None.

CASE XVIII.—Female, aged 62, married woman, seen in consultation on 17th August 1894, suffering from profound anæmia.

Duration.—1 year.

Apparent cause.—None.

Symptoms.—Profound anæmia and debility; some loss of weight; shortness of breath and palpitation on exertion; blood not examined; a systolic murmur in all the cardiac areas; heart somewhat dilated; venous hum in the neck; no retinal hæmorrhages; some swelling of feet; occasional vomiting and diarrhœa; tongue pale, smooth and moist; slight jaundice; urine of normal colour, and contains some albumen (temporary).

Treatment.—Arsenic in gradually increasing doses prescribed (maximum dose = ?).

Immediate result.—Patient improved considerably.

Subsequent progress and Ultimate result.—Not known.

CASE XIX.—Male, aged 63, banker, seen in consultation on 16th December 1894, suffering from profound pernicious anæmia.

Duration.—6 months.

Apparent cause.—None.

Symptoms.—Profound anæmia and debility; some loss of weight; shortness of breath and palpitation on exertion; red corpuscles number 1,125,000 per c.mm.; hæmoglobin = 35 per cent.; many megalocytes and microcytes; marked poikilocytosis; apparent nucleation of red corpuscles; no excess of white corpuscles; heart somewhat dilated; soft blowing murmurs in all the cardiac areas; jugular veins markedly distended and pulsating; venous hum in the neck; retinal hæmorrhages; slight swelling of feet; occasional vomiting and diarrhœa; slight jaundice; irregular fever; urine dark in colour. No albumen.

Treatment.—Had been treated with iron and tonics without any benefit. Arsenic and bone-marrow advised; but the day after consultation patient became very excited, and talked in a confused incoherent way; he denounced all sorts of drugs and poisons, spoke rather boastingly of what he could do for himself, that he knew " to a grain " what amount of food he should take, etc. At times he got quite ravelled and used wrong words to express himself. In the evening he was more composed and rather disinclined to speak. Next morning doctor hurriedly summoned (at 8 A.M.) as he was greatly distressed by palpitation. When doctor arrived was unconscious.

Result.—Patient died shortly afterwards—2 days after the consultation.

Post-mortem examination.—None.

CASE XX.—Male, aged 53, carter, seen as an out-patient at the Edinburgh Royal Infirmary on 21st February 1893, suffering from profound pernicious anæmia.

Duration.—Several months.

Apparent cause.—None.

Symptoms.—Profound anæmia and debility; some loss of weight; marked shortness of breath and palpitation on exertion; red corpuscles markedly diminished in number; some megalocytes; many microcytes; marked poikilocytosis; apparent nucleation of red corpuscles; no excess of white corpuscles; heart's action feeble; no murmur; retinæ not well seen; some swelling of feet; urine dark in colour; trace of albumen.

Treatment.—Iron, and arsenic in gradually increasing doses prescribed (maximum dose reached, 20 drops daily).

Immediate result.—Between February and June he improved very much, the œdema of the legs disappeared and he was able to get about.

Subsequent progress.—In June 1893 the anæmia returned and the patient consulted another medical man, who diagnosed kidney disease. The arsenic was discontinued.

Ultimate result.—After this the patient got rapidly worse and died 30th July 1893. The medical man who sent him to me wrote me on 2nd April 1898, saying : " His widow tells me to-day that all the time he was under your treatment he did well, and when he gave it up he got rapidly worse. Indeed, there was a scene between her and Dr A., during which she forgot herself and told Dr A. that her husband had been killed."

Post-mortem examination.—None.

CASE XXI.—Male, aged 51, publisher, seen in consultation on 6th February 1895, suffering from profound pernicious anæmia.

Duration.—Several months.

Apparent cause.—None.

Symptoms.—Profound anæmia and debility; some loss of weight; shortness of breath and palpitation on exertion; red corpuscles markedly diminished in number (lowest count 900,000); hæmoglobin not estimated; marked poikilocytosis; loud venous hum in neck; heart somewhat dilated; systolic murmurs at base and apex; during relapse, distension and pulsation of jugular veins; retinal hæmorrhages; slight jaundice; occasional vomiting; no diarrhœa; tongue pale, smooth and moist; urine normal in colour.

Treatment.—Arsenic was prescribed (maximum dose reached, 12 minims daily).

Immediate result.—Marked improvement took place and the patient was able for a time to resume his business.

Subsequent progress.—In January 1896, the anæmia relapsed; another consultant was called in and diagnosed the condition as dyspepsia; patient was treated accordingly, the arsenic being discontinued. No improvement took place. Seen again 2nd June 1896, in the last stage of pernicious anæmia. Arsenic and bone-marrow prescribed. Could not take the arsenic. On 8th June 1896, very much worse. Transfused with blood on 9th June 1896.

Ultimate result.—Died 10th June 1896.

Post-mortem examination.—None.

CASE XXII.—Male, aged 66, stockbroker, seen in consultation on 28th September 1895, suffering from profound pernicious anæmia.

Duration.—Several months.

Apparent cause.—Dyspepsia and diarrhœa (doubtful if diarrhœa the cause or consequence).

Symptoms.—Profound anæmia and debility; slight loss of weight; shortness of breath and palpitation on exertion; blood not examined; retinal hæmorrhages; swelling of feet; occasional vomiting and diarrhœa; occasional fever; urine normal in colour.

Treatment.—Arsenic in gradually increasing doses prescribed; was only able to take the arsenic in small doses (3 drops, subsequently reduced to 1 drop —maximum dose reached, 9 drops daily, but only for a few doses). Bone-marrow was also tried, but did no good.

Subsequent progress and Ultimate result.—There was no improvement; the patient died 3 weeks after the consultation.

Post-mortem examination.—None.

CASE XXIII.—Male, aged 57, engineer, seen in consultation on 8th April 1896, suffering from profound anæmia and diarrhœa.

Duration.—18 months.

Apparent cause.—None. Dyspeptic for 12 or 15 years. For 18 months excessive appetite and recurring attacks of diarrhœa, with heat and excoriation of anus (increased by butcher meat and stimulants).

Symptoms.—Profound anæmia and debility; slight loss of weight; shortness of breath and palpitation on exertion ; red corpuscles markedly diminished in number; some megalocytes ; many microcytes; moderate poikilocytosis; apparent nucleation of red corpuscles ; no excess of white corpuscles ; retinal hæmorrhages ; frequent diarrhœa ; tongue pale, smooth and moist; no febrile attacks ; urine of normal colour.

Treatment.—A milk diet, salicylate of bismuth for diarrhœa, iron and arsenic. The iron disagreed ; it brought on diarrhœa. Was only able to take very small doses of arsenic, 2 minims three times a day (maximum dose reached, 6 minims daily).

Immediate result.—No improvement.

Subsequent progress.—Seen again 10th June 1896. Very much worse in every way ; profoundly anæmic ; temperature 100° ; tongue dry; delirious.

Ultimate result.—Died on 12th June 1896.

Post-mortem examination.—None.

CASE XXIV.—Male, aged 49, formerly a shunter now a cart-weigher, seen as an out-patient at the Edinburgh Royal Infirmary on 3rd December 1896, suffering from profound pernicious anæmia.

Duration.—1 year.

Apparent cause.—In October 1893, run over by an engine ; right arm and leg amputated ; never so well since, but able to work till lately.

Symptoms.—Profound anæmia and debility ; no loss of weight ; shortness of breath and palpitation on exertion ; red corpuscles markedly diminished in number; few megalocytes ; many microcytes ; marked poikilocytosis ; apparent nucleation of red corpuscles ; no excess of white corpuscles ; venous hum in neck ; heart somewhat dilated ; systolic murmur in pulmonary area ; no retinal hæmorrhages ; occasional vomiting; slight jaundice ; urine dark in colour.

Treatment.—Gradually increasing doses of arsenic (maximum dose reached, 36 drops daily).

Immediate result.—Made rapid and continuous improvement.

Subsequent progress.—Able to return to work on 15th February ; worked (as a cart-weigher) till 13th August ; was then laid up with slight return of the anæmia ; off work six weeks ; again cured by arsenic. Worked till 9th of January 1898, when had again to leave off because of the anæmia ; has not worked since ; lost his wife at the beginning of February 1898 and has been much worse since. Is taking 30 drops of arsenic daily ; for a time tried bone-marrow, but could not take it as it made him sick.

Profoundly anæmic and debilitated ; no retinal hæmorrhages ; urine dark in colour ; no albumen ; depositing large quantities of uric acid ; red corpuscles markedly diminished in number ; moderate poikilocytosis ; some megalocytes ; many microcytes ; apparent nucleation of the red corpuscles ; white corpuscles not increased ; skin very dark (arsenic).

The dose of arsenic was increased to 36 drops daily, but the patient did not improve.

Admitted to the Edinburgh Royal Infirmary on 3rd May 1898 in a state of extreme anæmia and exhaustion ; some œdema of feet and face ; no albumen. On the 17th and 20th May there was some epistaxis.

Ultimate result.—Died on 20th May.

Post-mortem examination.—Not allowed.

The following table shows the condition of the blood during the final illness :—

Date.	Red Corpuscles.	Hæmoglobin.	Colour Index (Corrected).	White Corpuscles.
4th April 1898	1,450,000	46 per cent.	1.7	3,220
11th ,, ,,	1,000,000	28 ,,	1.5	4,000
18th ,, ,,	1,075,000	38 ,,	2.	
25th ,. ,,	1,050,000	40 ,,	2.	3,500
6th May ,,	916,700	28 ,,	1.6	2,500
12th ,, ,,	867,000	30 ,,	1.9	1,870
18th ,, ,,	650,000	20 ,,	1.6	4,375

CASE XXV.—Female, aged 54, married woman, admitted to Edinburgh Royal Infirmary on 30th September 1896, suffering from profound pernicious anæmia.

Duration.—10 months.

Apparent cause.—None. For 20 years has had large ulcers on both legs. Before admission, treated with iron, arsenic (9 drops daily) and bone-marrow, without improvement.

Symptoms.—Profound anæmia and debility ; considerable loss of weight ; shortness of breath and palpitation on exertion ; red corpuscles 995,000 ; hæmoglobin = 28 per cent. ; colour index 1.4 ; few megalocytes ; many microcytes ; moderate poikilocytosis ; apparent nucleation of red corpuscles ; heart's action very feeble ; heart somewhat dilated ; systolic murmurs in pulmonary and other areas : pulse 80, of fair volume, weak ; no retinal hæmorrhages ; occasional vomiting and diarrhœa ; tongue clean, smooth and moist ; occasional slight fever ; urine dark ; tenderness of sternum and tibiæ.

Treatment.—Arsenic in increasing doses prescribed (maximum dose reached, 42 drops daily).

Immediate result.—Marked improvement so far as appearance and symptoms were concerned, but no improvement in blood condition. On 2nd November, red corpuscles 1,100,000 ; hæmoglobin = 33 per cent. Patient was discharged on 2nd November 1896.

Subsequent progress and Ultimate result.—After leaving hospital the patient gradually got worse and died on 2nd February 1897. In writing to tell me of her death, the doctor stated "she was much improved by her treatment in hospital."

Post-mortem examination.—None.

CASE XXVI.—Male, aged 53, gamekeeper, admitted to the Edinburgh Royal Infirmary on 3rd May 1897, suffering from profound pernicious anæmia and marked jaundice.

Duration.—Probably 2 (at most 3) months.

Apparent cause.—None.

Symptoms.—Profound anæmia and debility; slight loss of weight; marked jaundice; shortness of breath and palpitation on exertion; red corpuscles numbered 810,000; hæmoglobin = 20 per cent. ; many megalocytes and microcytes ; marked poikilocytosis; apparent nucleation, but no true nucleation of red corpuscles; a few Eichhorst's corpuscles; white corpuscles not increased; blood-plates about normal; no organisms in blood; heart's action feeble; no murmurs; pulse 96, small, weak; some swelling of feet; retinal hæmorrhages; occasional vomiting; constipation ; stools bright orange colour ; no parasites in stools ; tongue thickly furred; occasional fever ; urine very dark and containing (temporarily) albumen and casts, and on several occasions deposited large quantities of uric acid crystals.

Treatment.—Was treated with gradually increasing doses of arsenic (maximum dose reached, 60 drops daily).

Immediate result.—Remarkable and rapid improvement took place. On patient's admission (3rd May 1897) the red corpuscles numbered 810,000; hæmoglobin = 20 per cent. At the date of the patient's discharge (14th June 1897) the red corpuscles numbered 3,420,000 and the hæmoglobin = 64 per cent. On 20th July 1897, the red corpuscles numbered 4,010,000 ; hæmoglobin = 88 per cent.

Subsequent progress.—The patient made steady progress after leaving the Infirmary. He continued to take the arsenic regularly until the end of October 1897, when by the advice of his local medical man he almost entirely gave it up.

In March 1898, he caught a slight chill; this was followed by a slight relapse of the anæmia. Advised to at once begin the arsenic again and take it regularly.

On 4th May 1898, was examined at the Edinburgh Royal Infirmary. Says that he has almost completely recovered from the recent relapse ; weight 12 stone ; does not look anæmic ; conjunctiva slightly bile-stained ; urine dark and contains a distinct quantity of albumen and excess of indican ; red corpuscles number 2,360,000 ; hæmoglobin = 60 per cent.; a few megalocytes and microcytes ; slight poikilocytosis; white corpuscles diminished in number (3,440 per c.mm.) ; is taking 36 drops of Fowler's solution daily.

The condition of the blood at different dates is shown in the following table :—

Date.	Number of Red Corpuscles.	Hæmoglobin.	Colour Index (Corrected).	Whites.
5th May 1897	810,000	20 per cent.	1.3	...
10th „ „	970,000	28 „	1.6	13,000*
18th „ „	1,710,000	40 „	1.2	12,000*
23rd „ „	2,650,000	42 „	.8	...
8th June „	2,700,000	64 „	1.3	...
14th „ „	3,420,000	64 „	1.	12,000*
20th July „	4,010,000	88 „	1.2	14,000*
4th May 1898	2,360,000	60 „	1.4	3,440
13th „ „	2,958,340	70 „	1.3	3,439

Case recorded in the "Lancet" of 24th July 1897, p. 197.

* These counts were probably erroneous.

CASE XXVII.—Female, aged 52, single, children's nurse, was admitted to the Edinburgh Royal Infirmary on 17th May 1897, suffering from profound anæmia, weakness and pigmentation of the skin.

Duration.—2 years.

Apparent cause.—None. The disease commenced with weakness and loss of flesh and anæmia; these symptoms were followed by pigmentation of the skin, epistaxis and jaundice. Six months ago Dr Garnet of Massachusetts Hospital diagnosed the case as Addison's disease.

Symptoms.—Profound anæmia and debility; considerable loss of weight; shortness of breath on exertion; considerable diffused pigmentation of the skin, no pigmentation of nipples, no pigmentation of buccal mucous membrane; red corpuscles numbered 1,400,000, and the hæmoglobin = 25 per cent.; many megalocytes and microcytes; moderate poikilocytosis; apparent, but no true, nucleation of red corpuscles; some excess of lymphocytes; heart's action feeble; no murmurs; venous hum in neck; pulse 90, small, weak; no retinal hæmorrhages; severe epistaxis and jaundice some months before admission; urine dark in colour.

Diagnosis.—The case seemed to me to be pernicious anæmia, perhaps complicated with Addison's disease.

Treatment.—Arsenic was given in gradually increasing doses (maximum dose reached, 57 minims per diem).

Immediate result.—The patient improved considerably both in appearance and as regards her symptoms, but the blood condition remained much *in statu quo*. She was discharged on 26th June 1897. Shortly before this date the red corpuscles numbered 1,310,000 and the hæmoglobin equalled 44 per cent. She had gained 5½ lbs. in weight.

The following table shows the condition of the blood at different dates :—

Date.	Red Corpuscles.	Hæmoglobin, per cent.	Colour Index (Corrected).	Whites.
18th May 1897	1,400,000	25	.8	
	1,118,000	33	1.5	
...	1,131,000	44	1.9	...

Subsequent progress and Ultimate result.—Not known.

CASE XXVIII.—Male, aged 36, reporter, seen on 30th June 1897, suffering from profound and causeless anæmia, apparently pernicious.

Duration.—Several months.

Apparent cause.—None.

Symptoms.—Profound anæmia and debility; shortness of breath on exertion; red corpuscles markedly diminished in number; few megalocytes; many microcytes; a few Eichhorst's corpuscles; moderate poikilocytosis; lymphocytes in excess; venous hum in neck; systolic murmurs in all the areas, loudest in pulmonary and tricuspid; slight jaundice; no retinal hæmorrhages; occasional vomiting and diarrhœa; urine dark; no albumen.

Treatment.—Arsenic in gradually increasing doses (maximum dose reached,

60 drops of Fowler's solution daily) ; and salicylate of bismuth for the diarrhœa, which was a prominent symptom.

Immediate result.—Rapid and continuous improvement.

Subsequent progress.—On 12th April 1898, his medical man wrote me : "Patient is perfectly well. I pushed up the arsenic until he took one drachm of the liquor daily."

Ultimate result.—Cure (? *pro tem.*).

CASE XXIX.—Female, aged 49, single, no occupation, seen in consultation on 20th July 1897, suffering from advanced pernicious anæmia.

Duration.—1 year.

Apparent cause.—None. Had for a time improved under iron and arsenic ; then relapsed ; only able to take the arsenic in very small doses (two or three minims) as it caused irritation of the stomach.

Symptoms.—Profound anæmia and debility ; considerable loss of weight ; shortness of breath and palpitation on exertion ; red corpuscles markedly diminished in number ; many megalocytes and microcytes ; marked poikilocytosis ; blowing murmurs in all the cardiac areas ; venous hum in neck, also over occiput ; retinal hæmorrhages ; occasional vomiting and diarrhœa ; some swelling of feet ; urine normal in colour ; no albumen.

Treatment.—Advised to make another attempt to take the arsenic in larger doses ; salicylate of bismuth also prescribed for the diarrhœa, which was very troublesome. The patient's medical man informs me that " she could never take more than 3 drops of arsenic (maximum dose reached, 9 minims daily), and that only for a few days at a time."

Result.—There was no improvement ; the patient died on 21st November 1897.

Post-mortem examination.—The doctor informs me that " the post-mortem appearances were highly characteristic of pernicious anæmia ; portions of the organs were sent to one of the laboratories in Edinburgh, but have been mislaid."

CASE XXX.—Female, aged 40, single, no occupation, seen in consultation on 25th September 1897, suffering from advanced pernicious anæmia.

Duration.—9 months.

Apparent cause.—None. Ten years previously the patient had been profoundly anæmic but had recovered. The patient had been treated with arsenic, but had not been able to take it except in small doses (maximum dose reached, 9 drops daily, and this only for a short time).

Symptoms.—Profound anæmia and debility ; some loss of weight ; shortness of breath and palpitation on exertion ; the blood was not examined ; heart dilated ; systolic murmurs in pulmonary, mitral and tricuspid areas ; pulsation in veins of neck ; loud venous hum ; retinal hæmorrhages ; diarrhœa ; urine normal in colour ; no albumen.

Treatment.—Advised to make a fresh attempt to take the arsenic in gradually increasing doses. Was unable to do so, as it produced vomiting.

Result.—There was no improvement ; the patient gradually became weaker, without any fresh developments, and died eleven days after the consultation.

Post-mortem examination.—None.

CASE XXXI.—Female, aged 16, child's nurse, was admitted to Edinburgh
Royal Infirmary on 19th September 1890, suffering from profound
anæmia, apparently pernicious.

Duration.—3 years.

Apparent cause.—Vomiting of blood, the result apparently of ulceration of
the stomach 3 years previously; quite well before this; never well since; has
vomited frequently and become paler and weaker. On 3 or 4 occasions (since
the first attack) has vomited blood or "coffee-grounds"; has several times improved and several times relapsed; got better before under Blaud's pills; the
condition seems therefore to have been chlorosis and ulceration of the stomach;
worse since an attack of influenza in January 1890. No pain in stomach.
Some constipation.

Symptoms.—Profoundly anæmic and debilitated; some loss of weight;
shortness of breath and palpitation on exertion; menstruation regular every
three weeks and too profuse till last period which she missed; red corpuscles =
900,000; hæmoglobin = 15 per cent.; on microscopical examination the blood
changes were much less marked than I had expected, considering the extreme
diminution of the red corpuscles; there were some megalocytes, some microcytes and a moderate degree of poikilocytosis; loud venous hum in neck;
systolic murmur in pulmonary and mitral areas; retinal hæmorrhages; some
swelling of feet; urine dark in colour; no albumen; skin in places deeply
pigmented as if from Addison's disease; areolæ of nipples dark brown; several
dark bands round waist where clothes tied; no pigmentation of mucous
membranes.

Diagnosis.—Difficult; the case seemed without doubt to be originally
chlorosis and ulceration of the stomach; when admitted to hospital the great
diminution of the red corpuscles, the retinal hæmorrhages and the progressive
course of the anæmia notwithstanding the administration of large doses of iron
were suggestive of pernicious anæmia; the pigmentation of the skin was
suggestive of Addison's disease. After carefully watching the case, I came to
the conclusion that the case was probably a combination of pernicious anæmia
and Addison's disease following chlorosis and ulceration of the stomach.

Treatment.—Iron and arsenic in increasing doses were administered
(maximum dose of arsenic reached, 12 drops).

Result.—No improvement; progressive diminution of the red corpuscles
and of the hæmoglobin without any obvious cause. The arsenic was badly
borne. On 8th October, the patient complained of pain in the stomach and
vomited; pulse 130; M.T. 99°.6, E.T. 102°; arsenic and iron discontinued;
peptonised milk and rectal feeding. 10th October :—Vomiting less; pulse 140;
respirations 60; M.T. 99°.6, E.T. 101°; patient very prostrate; commencing
pneumonia at the base of right lung. On 12th October, pneumonia of the right
lung more advanced; the temperature, which in the morning was 100°.2, at
12 A.M. began to rise rapidly; at 10 P.M. it reached 105°.4; the patient died
at 11 P.M.

The following table shows the condition of the blood at different dates :—

Date.	Number of Red Corpuscles.	Hæmoglobin.	Colour Index (Corrected).	
21st Sept. 1890	900,000	15 per cent.	.8	
28th ,, ,,	600,000	10 ,,	.85	
3rd Oct. ,,	650,000	10 ,,	.78	
6th ,, ,,	450,000	8 ,,	.88	
9th ,, ,,	550,000	8 ,,	.73	
11th ,, ,,	450,000	5 ,,	.55	

Post-mortem examination.—Not allowed.

CASE XXXII.—Male, aged 41, a farmer, seen in consultation on 2nd April 1894, suffering from profound pernicious anæmia.

Duration.—Six months.

Apparent cause.—None. Has for some time been taking iron and arsenic in small doses.

Symptoms.—Profound anæmia and debility ; slight loss of weight ; shortness of breath ; palpitation ; red corpuscles markedly diminished in number ; few megalocytes ; many microcytes ; moderate poikilocytosis ; apparent nucleation of red corpuscles ; white corpuscles not in excess ; venous hum in neck ; retinal hæmorrhages ; tongue pale, smooth and moist ; urine normal in colour ; no albumen.

Treatment.—Iron (Robertson's capsules) and arsenic in increasing doses (maximum dose reached, 24 drops daily).

Immediate result.—On 24th June 1895, his doctor wrote me :—Vomited blood (coffee-grounds) a few days after consultation. Took three Robertson's capsules three times daily and arsenic until he reached 24 drops daily. He rapidly improved, in the course of a short time got perfectly well, and was able to do his ordinary (farm) work. The patient's own statement was : "After the consultation I went away with a bound ; within a week after commencing the arsenic was better."

Subsequent progress.—*In February 1895* (11 months afterwards) had a relapse during the intense cold ; again soon got well under the same treatment.

In July 1895 (6 months afterwards) had a second relapse ; stomach symptoms developed and the arsenic had to be stopped. As he was not improving he came to Edinburgh to see me.

He was then (on *23rd October 1895*) profoundly anæmic, but not much thinner ; appetite fair ; no diarrhœa ; no retinal hæmorrhages ; red corpuscles greatly reduced ; many megalocytes and microcytes ; very marked poikilocytosis ; white corpuscles not increased. Was advised to remain at absolute rest in bed and to continue the iron and arsenic, increasing the dose of arsenic if he can manage it.

The subsequent progress of the case is fully detailed in the following statement which the patient's doctor has kindly sent me :—" When you saw Mr H.
in October 1895, you advised rest with Blaud's pills and arsenic. He came
home and went to bed, and, with the exception of getting up to have his bed
made, remained in bed until the middle of January 1896. During that time, he
was taking five and six minims of liquor arsenicalis with two and sometimes
three No. 3 Blaud's capsules three daily. His appetite was good—better
than when he was going about, he was able to take considerable quantities of
nourishment, nothing seemed to disagree with him ; he was cheerful and in
good spirits ; his colour improved a good deal. About the middle of January
1896, he began to get out of bed for a short time daily, gradually extending
the time as he gained in strength. As the season advanced, he began to get
out of doors, and in the month of March did a little light work. As he felt
none the worse of this, he gradually increased the amount, until by the middle
of April 1896 he was doing something nearly all day. From January 1896 to
April 1896 I did not see him much, but I suppose he was going on with the
arsenic and iron, though I believe not with the same regularity as before.

About the middle of *April 1896*, I was sent for and found him in a semi-
collapsed condition, pallid, breathless and the other anæmic symptoms returned.
On enquiry I found that on the previous day he had done a full day's garden
work at what is known in this district as 'putting in' the garden. Rest,
arsenic and iron capsules were again resorted to. For a time he seemed as if
he would improve, but he did not respond to the treatment in the same way as
before. Towards the end of May 1896, his appetite began to fail and he had
occasional attacks of vomiting (food and mucus). I diminished the dose of
arsenic and the stomach improved a little—I had got him up to six minims
three times daily but could not get beyond that, as on every attempt to do
so the stomach rebelled. About the end of July 1896, he had an attack of
hæmatemesis. After this date, he had three attacks of vomiting of the same
nature. No growth or hardness could be felt in the region of the stomach,
and as he was pretty much emaciated I think this could have been made out
had it existed."

Ultimate result.—Patient died from the disease on 11th August 1896.

Post-mortem examination.—None.

CASE XXXIII.—Male, aged 54, clergyman, seen in consultation on 23rd
     January 1895, suffering from marked pernicious anæmia.

Duration.—Four months.

Apparent cause.—None.

Symptoms.—Profound anæmia and debility ; marked shortness of breath
on exertion ; palpitation ; frequent fainting and giddiness ; heart's action very
feeble and irregular ; heart somewhat dilated ; systolic murmurs in pulmonary
and mitral areas ; venous hum in neck ; blood not examined ; no retinal
hæmorrhages ; frequent and troublesome diarrhœa ; tongue pale, smooth and
moist ; urine of normal colour ; no albumen.

Treatment.—Arsenic in gradually increasing doses (maximum dose reached,
40 drops).

Immediate result.—Marked improvement ; in the course of a few months the
patient appeared to be quite well.

Subsequent progress.—A year afterwards, a relapse ; the red corpuscles fell
to 1,000,000 ; arsenical treatment with bone-marrow and iron again followed by

marked improvement (maximum dose of arsenic reached, 40 drops daily); the red corpuscles went up to 4,600,000.

After some months, another relapse, the red corpuscles falling to 1,200,000; the patient became very depressed mentally and complained of numbness in the fingers and toes. Seen again in consultation on 23rd October 1896; the red corpuscles now numbered 3,000,000; there was considerable poikilocytosis. Advised to continue the arsenic, if possible in larger doses.

Ultimate result.—After several ups and downs the anæmia again became profound and the patient ultimately died from the disease on 11th February 1897.

Post-mortem examination.—None.

CASE XXXIV.—Male, aged 46, an American Judge, seen in consultation on 5th August 1895, suffering from pernicious anæmia.

Duration.—2 years.

Apparent cause.—Overwork and change from an active outdoor to a sedentary indoor life.

Symptoms.—Profound anæmia and debility; considerable loss of weight (1½ st.); anæsthesia, stiffness and heaviness in the legs and some difficulty in walking; knee-jerks absent; red corpuscles markedly diminished in number; alteration in shape slight; slight poikilocytosis; heart's action very feeble; no retinal hæmorrhages; urine normal in colour; no albumen.

Treatment.—Iron and arsenic in gradually increasing doses was advised.

Immediate result.—Some improvement.

Subsequent progress.—Dr Ewart of Eastbourne has kindly sent me the following notes of the subsequent progress of the case :—After consulting you he went to Leamington where, without advice, he took the waters, but says he was well, only feeling weak. He then ate largely of fruit; this produced diarrhœa. When I saw him a month afterwards, he was extremely anæmic and very weak, unable to sit up for more than half-an-hour at a time. On the 23rd of September he had an attack of faintness so severe as to suggest some internal hæmorrhage. The red corpuscles on this day numbered 2,500,000 and the hæmoglobin = 30 per cent.; colour index .66; the leucocytes were unusually scanty; the red corpuscles were very variable in size, some large and pale, some very small, some oval, pear-shaped or tailed.

The iron and arsenic were continued and 3 ozs. of bone-marrow and 3 ozs. of raw meat in each 24 hours, added on 24th September. He took the bone-marrow well at first, but had no appetite for any other food. Drank largely of milk.

On 5th October, he looked better, but could not take the bone-marrow, though it was tried in various ways. Troublesome diarrhœa developed and the arsenic (he had been taking five drops of the liquor) had to be discontinued. Food confined to Benger and arrowroot; and astringents (at first bismuth and opium, then bismuth and coto) were prescribed.

On 12th October, the diarrhœa was better; arsenic (2½ drops) again prescribed; has lost ground; increased on 15th October to 5 drops.

18th October.—Doing very well. More appetite; eats toast and bread which he could not do before. Tongue looks more natural, not so red. Bowels act daily; no diarrhœa. Arsenic increased to 7 drops. No retinal hæmorrhages found. Red corpuscles number 1,675,000; hæmoglobin = 28 per cent.; no excess of leucocytes; there are many megalocytes, microcytes and poikilo-cytosis. Patient to-day began Benger, extract of bone-marrow (ʒi twice a day) with one drachm of Dr Pfeiffer's hæmoglobin.

22nd October.—Arsenic increased to 10 drops.

4th November.—Patient is making no progress; sometimes wanders in his conversation; arsenic increased to 12 drops daily; and on 7th November to 15 drops.

8th November.—Red corpuscles numbered 800,000; hæmoglobin = about 15 to 20 per cent.; colour index 1.1; a great number of extraordinarily large and very pale red corpuscles present in the blood.

21st November.—Since last report the patient's condition varied to a most remarkable extent from time to time. At the morning visit he was often found insensible, stertorous, and to all appearance at the point of death. In the evening he would say he was "first rate," but though he often appeared clear and asked rational questions, he could never sustain a conversation.

Ultimate result.—On 22nd November he was taken to Southampton and shipped for America. He died before reaching New York.

Post-mortem examination.—None.

CASE XXXV.—Male, aged 72, seen in consultation on 28th August 1896, suffering from profound anæmia and spinal symptoms.

Duration.—Several months.

Apparent cause.—None.

Symptoms.—Marked anæmia and debility; some loss of weight; numbness and loss of power in the legs; absence of knee-jerks; considerable muscular atrophy both in legs and thighs; at first, no affection of the bladder or rectum; blood not examined; occasional diarrhœa.

Treatment.—Arsenic in gradually increasing doses (maximum dose reached, 9 drops daily); strychnine, massage and the faradic current.

Immediate result.—Slight temporary improvement as regards the anæmia; no improvement in the spinal symptoms.

Subsequent progress and Ultimate result.—Increase of the paralysis; paralysis of the bladder and rectum; death, three months after consultation.

Post-mortem examination.—None.

CASE XXXVI.—Female, aged 50, married woman, seen in consultation on 18th September 1895, suffering from profound pernicious anæmia.

Duration.—9 months.

Apparent cause.—None.

Symptoms.—Profound anæmia and debility; no loss of weight (patient was a very stout woman); shortness of breath and palpitation; heart sounds very feeble; venous hum in neck; blood not examined; slight jaundice; urine dark coloured; occasional vomiting; tongue pale, smooth and moist.

Treatment.—Arsenic and iron in gradually increasing doses prescribed, but patient refused to take the medicine.

Result.—Her medical attendant wrote me that "the patient's strength gradu-ally but steadily declined. She was very self-willed and refused to take any medicine on the plea that everything made her sick. She died exactly a month after you saw her."

Post-mortem examination.—None.

CASE XXXVII.—Male, aged 71, seen in consultation on 16th March 1893, suffering from profound pernicious anæmia.

Duration.—Several months.

Apparent cause.—None.

Symptoms.—Profound anæmia and debility; shortness of breath on exertion; palpitation; swelling of feet; slight jaundice; red corpuscles greatly diminished in number ; many megalocytes and microcytes ; marked poikilocytosis ; apparent nucleation of red corpuscles; venous hum in neck; heart's action feeble ; somewhat dilated ; systolic, pulmonary and mitral murmurs ; retinal hæmorrhages ; occasional vomiting and diarrhœa.

Iron had been given for some time without benefit.

Treatment.—Arsenic in increasing doses was prescribed (maximum dose reached, 2 or 3 drops) ; larger doses produced vomiting.

Immediate result.—The patient improved remarkably for a time ; the dropsy of legs disappeared ; able to get about.

Subsequent progress and Ultimate result.—Relapsed in September and finally died on 17th November 1893.

Post-mortem examination.—None.

CASE XXXVIII.—Female, aged 58, single, shopkeeper, seen in consultation June 1892, suffering from profound pernicious anæmia.

Duration.—Several months.

Apparent cause.—None.

Symptoms.—Profound anæmia and debility; some loss of weight; shortness of breath on exertion; palpitation ; no opportunity of examining the blood ; venous hum in neck; heart's action feeble; systolic, mitral and pulmonary murmurs ; retinal hæmorrhages ; occasional vomiting ; slight jaundice ; urine dark, no albumen.

Treatment.—Arsenic in gradually increasing doses ; and iron (maximum dose of arsenic reached ?).

Immediate result.—Decided improvement.

Ultimate result.—Relapse ; death a year after consultation.

Post-mortem examination.—None.

CASE XXXIX.—Male, aged 67, ironmonger, seen in consultation on 9th January 1898, suffering from profound pernicious anæmia.

Duration.—Several months.

Apparent cause.—Dyspepsia and diarrhœa (doubtful if diarrhœa the cause or consequence).

Symptoms.—Profound anæmia and debility; considerable loss of weight ; shortness of breath and palpitation on exertion; loud venous hum in neck ; systolic murmur at base of heart, loudest in aortic area ; red corpuscles markedly diminished in number ; many megalocytes and microcytes ; marked poikilocytosis ; lymphocytes in excess ; retinal hæmorrhages ; some swelling of feet ; frequent vomiting and diarrhœa ; tongue very smooth and moist ; slight jaundice ; urine of normal colour ; no albumen.

Treatment.—Arsenic in gradually increasing doses prescribed, but patient could only take very small doses because of gastric irritation (maximum dose reached, 9 drops daily and that only for a few days) ; bone-marrow and iron subsequently tried ; oxygen inhalations advised, but patient refused to have it.

Result.—No improvement ; patient died on 12th February 1898.

Post-mortem examination.—None.

I

CASE XL.—Male, aged 37, pitman, admitted to Edinburgh Royal Infirmary on 16th April 1898, suffering from profound pernicious anæmia.

Duration.—2 years ; worse for 3 or 4 months.

Apparent cause.—None.

Symptoms.—Profound anæmia and debility ; considerable loss of weight (1½ stone) ; shortness of breath and palpitation on exertion ; great giddiness, headache and buzzing in the ears ; slight swelling of the face ; occasional vomiting ; frequent diarrhœa ; occasional chilly feelings (rigors) ; red corpuscles numbered 1,200,000 ; hæmoglobin = 44 per cent. ; white corpuscles numbered 3,400 ; on microscopical examination, a few megalocytes, many microcytes, moderate poikilocytosis, apparent nucleation of red corpuscles, some truly nucleated red corpuscles ; excess of lymphocytes ; blood plates less numerous than normal ; retinal hæmorrhages ; slight jaundice ; urine dark, containing a marked excess of indican and an enormous excess of combined sulphates ; large uric acid deposits ; no albumen ; considerable pigmentation of the skin (patient sent to hospital as a case of Addison's disease).

Treatment.—Arsenic in gradually increasing doses and salicylate of bismuth for diarrhœa ; bone-marrow, oxygen inhalations, etc. Maximum dose of arsenic reached, 63 drops daily.

Immediate result.—Marked temporary improvement, after the arsenical treatment was pushed.

Subsequent progress of the case.—On 24th May, the patient looked and felt very much better.

On 28th May, he began to complain of itchiness of the eyeballs and pain in the stomach ; the dose of arsenic was therefore reduced.

Towards the end of June, pains, numbness and anæsthesia in the feet, legs, arms, and hands, obviously due to peripheral neuritis, developed, and the knee-jerks became abolished. The arsenic was consequently stopped ; strychnine was prescribed, together with phenacetin and morphia for the relief of the pains.

4th July.—Bone-marrow tabloids prescribed.

7th July.—The anæmia has become more marked since the arsenic was stopped ; the eyes are still sore, and the pains in the feet severe, especially at night.

22nd July.—More anæmic ; skin desquamating ; pains less, but anæsthesia in feet and hands more marked.

30th July.—Temperature went up to 104° ; pulse rapid (100) and dicrotic ; anæmia more marked ; urine very dark ; very prostrate ; fresh retinal hæmorrhages ; arsenic recommenced (10 minims daily).

3rd August.—Very anæmic, feeble and emaciated ; looks very much as he did at the time of his admission to hospital ; tongue dry ; very thirsty. Fresh bone-marrow mixed with mashed potato prescribed.

10th August.—Patient died at 10 P.M.

The following table shows the condition of the blood at different dates :—

Date.	Red Corpuscles.	Hæmoglobin.	Colour Index (Corrected).	White Corpuscles.
18th April	1,200,000	44 per cent.	2.	3,438
27th „	816,000	28 „	1.9	4,370
29th „	975,000	30 „	1.7	3,125
10th May	1,234,000	38 „	1.7	5,312
18th „	1,600,000	44 „	1.5	3,125
23rd „	1,670,000	62 „	2.	2,190
2nd June	1,366,700	60 „	2.6	5,156
14th „	1,683,334	62 „	2.	1,600
20th „	1,416,667	60 „	2.3	2,223
28th „	1,350,000	50 „	2.	4,531
4th July	1,475,000	48 „	1.4	2,600
12th „	1,333,334	30 „	1.2	3,500
22nd „	940,000	32 „	1.9	4,700
29th „	642,000	24 „	2.1	2,100
5th August	370,000	16 „	2.4	1,900

Post-mortem examination.—Made by Dr Fleming on 12th August, at 1 P.M. The appearances were typical of uncomplicated pernicious anæmia.

Body somewhat emaciated and very anæmic. Both *pleuræ* uniformly adherent ; the *lungs* weighed 1 lb. 4 ozs. and 1 lb. 9 ozs. respectively, and were markedly œdematous ; a few old tubercles in the upper lobe of the right lung. The *heart* and great vessels contained very little blood ; the heart weighed 15 ozs., and was very fatty. The *liver* weighed 3 lbs. 5 ozs., was very fatty, and contained a large excess of iron. The *spleen* weighed 8 ozs., and gave no iron reaction. The *kidneys* weighed 4 ozs. and 5 ozs. respectively; they were markedly fatty and did not give the iron reaction. The *suprarenal capsules* were normal. The mucous coat of the *stomach* was atrophied ; the mucous and submucous coats of the upper end of the *small intestine* were œdematous and bile-stained ; some of the coils of the intestine were bound together by old adhesions ; there was no ulceration of the intestines. The *brain* was markedly anæmic. The *spinal cord* was anæmic, but otherwise normal to the naked eye. The peripheral nerves were normal to the naked eye. The *marrow of the bones* was of a deep purple colour. A few very minute *petechial hæmorrhages* were present on the peritoneal surface of the stomach ; there were several retinal hæmorrhages, but no petechial hæmorrhages elsewhere.

The *microscopical examination* of the organs and tissues has not yet been completed.

CASE XLI.—Male, aged 51, clergyman, seen in consultation on 25th April 1892, suffering from profound pernicious anæmia.

Duration.—1 year.

Apparent cause.—None.

Symptoms.—Profound anæmia and debility; some loss of weight; shortness of breath on exertion, palpitation, slight swelling of feet; red corpuscles markedly diminished in number; many megalocytes and microcytes; marked poikilo-cytosis; systolic pulmonary and mitral murmurs; venous hum in the neck ; retinal hæmorrhages; bowels constipated (diarrhœa 9 months ago); frequent vomiting ; urine normal in colour, no albumen.

Treatment.—Advised to increase the dose of arsenic which he has been taking (maximum dose reached, 5 drops three times daily); rest in bed ; strychnine.

Result.—Died eight days after consultation.

Post-mortem examination.—None.

CASE XLII.—Married woman, aged 31, admitted to Edinburgh Royal In-firmary on 9th June 1898, suffering from profound pernicious anæmia.

Duration.—3½ months.

Apparent cause.—Pregnancy. Always enjoyed good health until the present illness commenced. Has been married nine years and has had five children. The anæmia developed when she was 6½ months pregnant, without apparent cause, and has gradually increased. Was delivered at the full term, on 24th May 1898 ; labour easy; no loss of blood. For a week after confinement,. improved slightly ; then, got rapidly worse.

Symptoms.—Very profound anæmia and debility: no jaundice; great short-ness of breath ; frequent palpitation ; no swelling of the feet (they were swollen before her confinement); face slightly swollen ; some dulness and fine crepita-tions over the base of each lung ; systolic, mitral, and pulmonary murmurs ; venous hum in the neck ; temperature 104.8°; pulse 146 ; respirations 44; occa-sional vomiting ; no diarrhœa ; urine pale and free from albumen ; a scanty and rather fœtid vaginal discharge ; tongue pale and dry; very thirsty; innumerable very small hæmorrhages scattered over both retinæ, and a few flame-like hæmor-rhages at the margins of the discs ; red corpuscles, 780,000 per c.m. (blood obtained from bandaged finger, simple puncture of the finger and ear yielding no blood); hæmoglobin = 20 per cent.; colour index = 1.4 ; white corpuscles numbered 6,250 per c.m.; many megalocytes and microcytes, marked poikilo-cytosis.

Treatment.—Arsenic, oxygen inhalations, strychnine, and digitalis.

Result.—For two days some improvement ; then œdema of the lungs sud-denly developed, and the patient died on 14th June—five days after admission.

Post-mortem examination.—Made by Dr Fleming on 15th June, at 1 P.M. The appearances were typical of uncomplicated pernicious anæmia ; there was. no puerperal septic condition.

Body well nourished and very bloodless. The right *pleural cavity* contained

15 ozs., the left 17 ozs., and the pericardial sac 4½ ozs. of clear serous fluid. The *heart* weighed 14 ozs.; it was covered with a thick layer of fat; the muscle was in an advanced condition of fatty degeneration. The *lungs* weighed 1 lb. 15 ozs. and 1 lb. 9 ozs. respectively; both were markedly œdematous; at the apex of the right, the pleura was adherent, the lung puckered and the seat of some old (healed) tubercles. The *liver* weighed 5 lbs. 4 ozs. and was very fatty and gave a very marked iron reaction. The *spleen* weighed 1 lb.; its capsule was thickened, its tissue soft and congested; it gave a marked iron reaction. The *kidneys* weighed 7 ozs. and 7½ ozs. respectively and were somewhat fatty and affected with cloudy swelling. The mucous membrane of the *stomach* presented a mammillated appearance towards the pyloric end; it was elsewhere atrophied (apparently the result of post-mortem change); the mucous and submucous coats of the upper end of the *small intestine* were œdematous and bile-stained. The *uterus* was enlarged; its cavity, which measured 3 inches in length, contained a small quantity of partly adherent broken-down blood clot which was not septic. The *brain* weighed 2 lbs. 14 ozs. and was pale and somewhat œdematous. The *retina* contained numerous small hæmorrhages; there were no petechial hæmorrhages in other parts of the body. The *spinal cord* was anæmic, but otherwise normal to the naked eye. The bone-marrow was of a deep purple colour, highly characteristic of the disease.

Microscopical examination not yet completed.

CASE XLIII.—Female, widow, aged 65, seen in consultation on 23rd May 1898, suffering from profound pernicious anæmia.

Duration.—Several months.

Apparent cause.—Patient herself blames mental worry; a year ago she began to be troubled with sore gums (inflammation of the gums, buccal mucous membrane and side of the tongue).

Symptoms.—Profoundly anæmic and debilitated; considerable loss of weight; very short of breath; frequent palpitation; throbbing in the head; some swelling of the feet; slight swelling of the face; occasional headache; very occasional vomiting; no diarrhœa; no jaundice; skin of a yellow lemon tint; urine pale, contains a small quantity of albumen; retinal hæmorrhages; for the past two days has had some (slight) epistaxis. The condition of the blood (which was examined by Dr Robert Muir) was as follows:—Red corpuscles number 1,328,000; many megalocytes and microcytes; marked poikilocytosis; hæmoglobin = 32 per cent.; colour index = 1.2; leucocytes much diminished—2,000; blood plates much diminished—about 20,000; a few truly nucleated red corpuscles of moderate size with homogeneous nucleus staining very deeply; the relative proportion of lymphocytes was slightly increased; there were no myelocytes.

Treatment.—Rest in bed and arsenic in gradually increasing doses prescribed.

Result.—Patient could not take, or would not take, the arsenic and other remedies (bone-marrow, strychnine, digitalis, etc.) which were from time to time prescribed.

10th June 1898.—Patient much worse; temperature last night 102°; looks extremely ill; face more swollen; arsenic to be given unknown to the patient, and if it does not agree, transfusion advised. (Only one dose, 5 drops, of arsenic given, as it was followed by vomiting.)

12th June.—Patient transfused (four ounces of blood with four ounces of phosphate of soda solution); bore the operation very well; same afternoon became unconscious; rallied under stimulants and then steadily improved for three weeks.

5th July 1898.—Blood counted by Dr Muir.   Red corpuscles = 1,050,000; haemoglobin = 28 per cent.

9th July 1898.—Looks very much worse; has run down very rapidly during the past two or three days; temperature 102.4°; face more swollen; slightly jaundiced; urine dark.

As transfusion undoubtedly produced temporary benefit, advised that should be transfused again and the operation regularly repeated at short intervals, and not delayed until its beneficial effects have passed off.

12th July.—Again transfused, but the operation unsuccessful (the boy who was giving the blood fainted and the transfusion had to be stopped).

27th July.—Transfusion again performed, most successfully; for some days was followed by shortness of breath; after this the patient improved considerably.

12th August.—Looks very much better and more vigorous; lips and tongue have more colour; conjunctivæ still very bloodless and slightly yellow; face less swollen; is eating very well; says she feels greatly better; is very bright and talkative.

Advised to be again transfused and the operation to be regularly repeated at short intervals. My recommendation was not carried out.

Her medical attendant informs me that she remained pretty well until the end of September, when the mouth again became irritable. During the second week in October another relapse took place. She was again transfused on 16th October; the operation was followed, as on previous occasions, by a rigor and rise of temperature (103° F.).

1st November.—Patient again seen to-day; looks very much worse; profoundly anæmic; much thinner; several petechial hæmorrhages on the surface of the tongue, buccal mucous membrane and lower extremities; feet more swollen; hands slightly swollen; urine dark and containing a small quantity of albumen; the temperature, which for some days after the last transfusion was considerably elevated, is again normal; for the past two days a good deal of wandering; since last visit had an attack of diarrhœa.

The question of renewed transfusion again considered. It was decided, as the patient would certainly die, probably in the course of a few days, if nothing was done, to recommend that transfusion should be again tried; and that, if improvement should again result, the operation should be repeated at short intervals and at the time when the improvement is most marked. This was the course which I had previously advised. It seems useless to transfuse and after improvement has taken place to wait until the patient has again relapsed before repeating the operation. *If any permanent benefit is to be obtained in severe cases of pernicious anæmia from transfusion the operation ought, in my opinion, to be repeated at short intervals and to be performed when the patient is at the height of the improvement curve;* it is only, I think, in this way that permanent benefit can possibly be expected, for the beneficial effect of a single transfusion seems to pass off in the course of a few weeks. In this particular case, there was little improvement for the first week after the operation; the patient then slowly improved (after every operation except the last), for three or four weeks, and then again got rapidly worse. In this particular case, the operation ought, I think, to be repeated every three weeks.

CASE XLIV.—Married woman, aged 44, admitted to the Edinburgh Royal Infirmary on 16th June 1898.

Duration.—12 months ; worse for the past 5 months.

Apparent cause.—None.

Symptoms.—Profound anæmia and debility ; considerable loss of weight (used to be very fat) ; shortness of breath ; palpitation ; slight swelling of feet and face ; slight yellowness of conjunctivæ ; areolæ of the nipples very dark (this is quite recent) ; no pigmented patches on buccal mucous membrane ; systolic, mitral, and pulmonary murmurs ; venous hum in the neck ; some giddiness ; beating in the head ; some headache ; no retinal hæmorrhages (but they developed before death) ; temperature on admission normal (subsequently became elevated) ; very occasional vomiting ; no diarrhœa ; tongue clean and moist, not abnormally smooth ; red corpuscles number 1,160,000, rouleaux formation imperfect ; a few megalocytes and microcytes and comparatively slight poikilocytosis (the alterations in the size and shape of the red corpuscles much less marked than in most cases of profound pernicious anæmia) ; hæmoglobin = 34 per cent. ; colour index = 1.4 ; white corpuscles number 3,438 (50 per cent. being multinucleated and 50 per cent. being uninucleated) ; some apparent nucleation of the red corpuscles ; no true nucleation seen ; urine amber-coloured (subsequently became dark) ; no albumen ; heavy phosphatic cloud.

Treatment.—Arsenic in gradually increasing doses (maximum dose reached = 45 drops per day), bone-marrow, oxygen inhalations ; strychnine, strophanthus.

Result.—For a short time there was slight (but very slight) improvement ; as the result of the large doses of arsenic peripheral neuritis (pains in the hands, feet, arms and legs, tingling, numbness and loss of the knee-jerks) developed. The arsenic was consequently stopped. After this, notwithstanding the administration of bone-marrow, oxygen inhalations, strychnine, strophanthus, &c., the patient rapidly got worse ; œdema of the lungs developed ; and she died on 30th July. The temperature rose repeatedly above the normal during her stay in hospital and the urine became very dark in colour.

The condition of the blood is shown in the following table :—

Date.	Red Corpuscles.	Hæmoglobin.	Colour Index (Corrected)	White Corpuscles.
17th June	1,160,000	34 per cent.	1.4	3,438
24th ,,	900,000	30 ,,	1.6	3,000
1st July	1,541,500	32 ,,	1.	3,755
8th ,,	1,158,333	36 ,,	1.6	2,000
17th ,,	841,700	20 ,,	1.2	1,600
22nd ,,	660,000	20 ,,	1.5	1,100
29th ,,	459,000	14 ,,	1.5	1,900

Post-mortem examination.—Made by Dr Fleming on 31st July. The appearances were in every respect typical of pernicious anæmia.

The body was fairly well nourished and very bloodless; there was slight œdema of the feet and legs. The pericardial sac contained 1 oz. of clear serum; the pleural cavities were obliterated by old adhesions. There were several small petechial hæmorrhages on the surface of the *heart, stomach,* and *dura mater.* The *heart* weighed 13 ozs.; it was covered with a considerable layer of yellow fat; its cavities were empty; its muscle in an advanced stage of fatty degeneration. The right *lung* weighed 1 lb. 8 ozs. and the left 1 lb. 1 oz., and were markedly œdematous. The *liver* weighed 3 lbs. 5 ozs., was markedly fatty, and gave a very marked iron reaction. The *spleen* weighed 11 ozs. and was of a deep purple colour; it gave no iron reaction. The *kidneys* weighed 6 ozs. and 7 ozs. respectively, and gave a slight iron reaction; the tissue was soft, somewhat fatty, and presented slight interstitial change. The *stomach* was healthy; its mucous membrane was somewhat thin (? post-mortem change). The mucous and submucous coats of the *upper* end of the *small intestine* were œdematous and bile-stained, but otherwise normal. The *suprarenal capsules* were normal. The *brain* weighed 2 lbs. 12½ ozs. and was markedly anæmic. The *spinal cord* was markedly anæmic, but otherwise normal to the naked eye. The peripheral nerves were normal to the naked eye. The *retinæ* contained several recent hæmorrhages.

The *microscopical examination* has not been completed.

CASE XLV.—Male, aged 58, mast-maker, admitted to the Edinburgh Royal Infirmary on 16th June 1898, suffering from profound pernicious anæmia.

Duration.—18 months.

Apparent cause.—Patient attributes his illness to mental worry and overwork; has suffered from bleeding piles for 12 years, bleeding at times very profuse, but little or none for the past year. At the beginning of the present illness, he suffered from gastric catarrh; throughout this illness, the bowels have been constipated.

Symptoms.—Profound anæmia and debility; skin lemon yellow coloured; considerable loss of weight; very short of breath on exertion; frequent palpitation; appetite poor; very thirsty; occasional vomiting; no diarrhœa; bowels constipated; tongue slightly furred and rather dry; some œdema of feet, face and body generally; some yellow tinging of conjunctiva; venous hum in the neck; heart sounds very feeble; pulse markedly jerking in character; no pulmonary systolic murmur; urine markedly pale and free from albumen; no retinal hæmorrhages; a few minute petechiæ on the wrists and legs; blood highly characteristic; red corpuscles number 642,000; hæmoglobin = 16 per cent.; colour index = 1.4; white corpuscles number 2,500 (uninucleated 50 per cent., multinucleated 50 per cent.); blood plates much diminished in number); many megalocytes of large size; many microcytes; very marked poikilocytosis; much apparent nucleation; some truly nucleated red corpuscles; no micro-organisms (stained films and incubated gelatine tubes).

Treatment.—Arsenic in gradually increasing doses (maximum dose reached, 42 drops per diem); laxatives.

Result.—Felt better after a free evacuation of bowels, but no real improvement.

On 3rd July, œdema of the lungs suddenly developed and the patient died on 4th July.

The condition of the blood at different dates is shown in the following table :—

Date.	Red Corpuscles.	Hæmoglobin.	Colour Index (Corrected).	White Corpuscles.
17th June	642,000	16 per cent.	1.4	2,500
24th ,,	650,000	20 ,,	1.6	3,125
1st July	542,000	20 ,,	2.2	4,000

Post-mortem examination.—Made by Dr Fleming on 5th July.

Body very anæmic, somewhat emaciated ; slight œdema of the legs ; a few minute petechial hæmorrhages on the hands and trunk. The left *pleural cavity* contained 40 ozs., the right 45 ozs., and the pericardium 11 ozs. of clear serum. The *heart* weighed 11 ozs. ; the endocardium and chordæ tendineæ were slightly thickened ; the muscular substance presented no evidence to the naked eye of fatty degeneration, but was in a marked condition of brown atrophy. The *lungs* weighed 1 lb. 7 ozs. and 1 lb. 6 ozs. respectively; the upper lobes were markedly emphysematous, the lower lobes markedly œdematous. The *liver* weighed 3 lbs.; it presented little or no evidence of fatty degeneration to the naked eye and gave a slight (blue) reaction to the iron test. The *spleen* weighed 9 ozs. ; it gave a slight iron reaction. The *kidneys* weighed 6 ozs. and 5 ozs. respectively, both showed decided interstitial change, but gave no iron reaction. The *suprarenal capsules* were normal. A few minute petechial hæmorrhages on the outer surface of the *stomach ;* the mucous membrane was for the most part atrophied ; near the pylorus there were about six mammillated projections. A few minute hæmorrhages on the outer surface of the *small intestine* (jejunum); mucous and submucous coats œdematous and bile-stained, no ulceration. *Bone-marrow* of a dark purple colour, highly characteristic of pernicious anæmia. The *brain* weighed 3 lbs. 4 ozs., and was very anæmic and œdematous. There were no hæmorrhages in the *retina.*

The *microscopical examination* of the tissues and organs not yet completed.

Note.—In this case, in which the clinical symptoms and the condition of the blood were most typical, and the disease of long (18 months) duration, there was no fatty degeneration of the heart and the liver only contained a slight excess of iron, as determined by the ferrocyanide test.

CASE XLVI.—Male, aged 48, estate manager, seen in consultation on 25th March 1897, suffering from profound anæmia and angina pectoris.

Duration.—Several months.

Apparent cause.—None. A year ago the patient suffered from gouty glycosuria ; he was strictly dieted and lost more than 2 stone in weight ; he weighed at that time 18½ stone. For several months past he has been losing colour. During the past three months the anæmia has markedly increased, he has become very breathless on exertion and has had several attacks of severe substernal pain (angina pectoris).

Symptoms.—Profound anæmia and debility ; no jaundice ; great shortness of breath on exertion ; occasional severe angina-like pain on exertion ; frequent palpitation ; no dropsy ; heart slightly dilated ; a soft systolic murmur in the aortic and mitral areas ; venous hum in the neck ; urine free from albumen and sugar and not abnormally dark in colour ; red corpuscles markedly diminished in number ; some microcytes and megalocytes ; moderate poikilocytosis ; no retinal hæmorrhages.

Treatment.—Arsenic, strychnine, iron (Blaud's pill capsules) and subsequently bone-marrow tabloids.

Subsequent progress and Result.—For the first month after the treatment was commenced, the patient improved considerably. The stomach then became irritable and the arsenic had consequently to be diminished and then altogether stopped (the maximum dose reached was 9 drops per diem). After this date, the patient rapidly got worse and died some two months after he first came under my observation.

CASE XLVII.—Male, aged 60, clergyman, was seen in consultation on the 17th August 1898, suffering from profound pernicious anæmia.

Duration.—18 months.

Apparent cause.—None.

Symptoms.—Profound debility and anæmia ; marked loss of flesh ; tongue clean and smooth ; marked shortness of breath and palpitation on exertion ; heart's action very feeble ; venous hum in the neck ; (no opportunity of examining the blood); no retinal hæmorrhages ; no diarrhœa ; no vomiting ; urine pale ; occasional attacks of fever.

Treatment.—Has been treated with arsenic, iron and bone-marrow. For a time improved, but has recently again relapsed. Advised to continue the arsenic and bone-marrow in gradually-increasing doses ; and if there is no improvement, the question of transfusion to be considered.

Result.—No improvement ; death ten days after first seen.

CASE XLVIII.—Male, aged 35, veterinary surgeon, seen in consultation on 27th September 1898, suffering from profound pernicious anæmia.

Duration.—Several months ; worse for six weeks.

Apparent cause.—None ; prior to the commencement of the present illness was an extremely robust, active, and hard-working man ; has occasionally over-indulged in alcohol.

Symptoms.—Profoundly anæmic and debilitated, has fainted on getting out of bed ; has lost a good deal of weight, but is still well covered with fat ; marked shortness of breath and palpitation on exertion ; conjunctivæ slightly yellow ; urine extremely pale (a specimen made in my presence) and has been so throughout the illness ; no albumen ; soft systolic murmur in the mitral, pulmonary and aortic areas ; venous hum in the neck ; bowels regular ; diarrhœa a month ago, said to be due to purgative medicine ; no vomiting ; tongue clean and somewhat dry ; very thirsty ; gums bleeding ; a few petechial hæmorrhages under the tongue and on the neck and upper part of the trunk ; double optic neuritis ; numerous retinal hæmorrhages, some flame-shaped, round the discs, others petechial over the retinæ ; a few yellowish-white spots, the remains of former hæmorrhages in the retinæ ; no œdema ; blood examined by medical attendant— red corpuscles = 1,000,000 per cubic millimetre ; hæmoglobin not estimated ; moderate degree of poikilocytosis ; temperature for some weeks persistently above normal, highest point reached 103° F.; no evidence of disease (except the profound anæmia and its results) in any of the organs ; knee-jerks normal.

Treatment.—Has been taking arsenic and bone-marrow. Advised to continue these remedies in increased doses.

Result.—Rapidly got worse and died a few days after the consultation.

LEUCOCYTHÆMIA.

Definition or Short Description.—The terms *leukæmia* (white blood) and *leucocythæmia* (white-celled blood) are applied to a condition of the blood in which the white blood corpuscles are greatly increased in number, both (*a*) absolutely and (*b*) relatively to the red cells; while the red blood corpuscles and the hæmoglobin are at the same time diminished in amount—often considerably so. In other words, in cases of leucocythæmia there is also more or less, and sometimes great, anæmia.

The increase of the white cells is not merely temporary as it is usually in leucocytosis. Further, in leucocythæmia the increase of the white corpuscles is for the most part due to the presence in the blood of myelocytes (spleno-medullary form), or of lymphocytes (lymphatic form); whereas in leucocytosis the increase of the white corpuscles is for the most part, or entirely, due to an increase of the polymorpho-nuclear form of white corpuscles.

Leucocythæmia is usually a chronic condition, which is slowly developed, and which usually progresses more or less steadily to a fatal issue. In rare cases, the disease runs a rapid, or comparatively rapid, course (*acute leucocythæmia*).

In most cases of leucocythæmia (but especially in the spleno-medullary form) the spleen is greatly enlarged; in other cases (more especially in the lymphatic variety) the lymphatic glands are enlarged. In the great majority of cases, the marrow of the bones is diseased; and it is now generally held that in the spleno-medullary form the marrow of the bones is in all probability the primary seat of the lesion.

Historical Note.—Leucocythæmia is a very interesting condition. It was first described in the year 1845 by the late Professor Hughes Bennett as a *primary* suppuration of the blood; but it is only fair to Bennett to state that, in discussing the nature of the blood change in this, his first, communication on the subject, he qualified this opinion by the following statement:—" Unless therefore it could be shown that inflammation and fever were like processes, we must conclude that the alteration of the blood in this case *was independent of inflammation properly so called"* (no italics in the original).

Very shortly (a few weeks) afterwards,* Virchow published a case, which had been independently observed by him prior to the publication of Bennett's first communication on the subject, and pointed out that the white corpuscles found in the blood were white blood corpuscles and not pus cells ; he consequently termed the condition " weisses Blut " or leukæmia.

A keen controversy was waged for some time between these two celebrated men and their supporters, both as to the question of priority of discovery and as to the correctness of their respective interpretations of the blood condition. Bennett used to give a most entertaining lecture on the subject. Every one who attended his lectures on Physiology or Clinical Medicine will remember what a treat it was. Hughes Bennett was a man of acute intellect and of great dramatic power. He was, however, an advocate rather than a judge; and I need hardly say that in describing his controversy with Virchow and Virchow's supporters he left us students completely under the belief that his (Bennett's) opponents had not a leg to stand upon. I now take a somewhat different view of the position. It must, I think, be allowed that while Bennett was the first to observe and publish an accurate and detailed description of the pathological appearances and blood changes in leucocythæmia,† Virchow was the first to give an intelligent explanation of the peculiar alteration in the blood which is the essential characteristic of the disease. Further, it is important to note that very shortly after his first publication on the subject the great German pathologist recognised the fact that, in some cases of leucocythæmia, the increase of the white corpuscles is due to an increase of the large white cells of the blood, while, in others, it is due to an increase of the small white cells ; and that in some cases the spleen is enlarged, while in other cases the lymphatic glands are enlarged. Basing the distinction upon these points of difference, Virchow consequently divided cases of leukæmia, as he termed the condition, into two varieties—the splenic and the lymphatic forms of leukæmia respectively.

---

* Bennett's first case was observed on 19th March 1845, and published on 1st October 1845. Virchow's first case was observed on 1st August 1845, and published in the second week of November 1845.

† One or two individual cases had been reported, before Bennett and Virchow described the condition, without their peculiar nature and character being recognised.

In the years 1851 and 1852, Hughes Bennett published a series of papers and a systematic work on the subject, in which he advanced the view that the lymphatic and other ductless glands secrete the blood, and proposed that the name leucocythæmia or white-celled blood (from λευκος = white, κυτος = cell, and αιμα = blood), which has since been generally adopted as a more appropriate term than leukæmia or white blood (from λευκος = white, and αιμα = blood), should be applied to the disease.

Varieties.—In most cases of leucocythæmia the spleen is markedly enlarged; and until comparatively recently it was supposed that the spleen was the primary and fundamental seat of the lesion; hence the term *splenic* leucocythæmia was for a long time applied to the disease. But recent observations have shown that in some of the cases in which the spleen is markedly enlarged and the blood is loaded with white corpuscles the marrow of the bones is not only diseased but is in all probability the primary seat of the lesion. To these cases the term *spleno-medullary* or *lieno-medullary* leucocythæmia is now generally applied.

In other cases of leucocythæmia in which the spleen is also generally, but not necessarily, enlarged, though the enlargement is not usually so great as in the spleno-medullary form, the lymphatic glands are enlarged; to this variety the term *lymphatic* leucocythæmia is usually applied.

But this use of the terms *splenic* and *lymphatic* leucocythæmia (founded upon the presence or absence of enlargement of the spleen and lymphatic glands) is not strictly accurate for the following reasons:—

(*a*) In both the spleno-medullary and the lymphatic forms of leucocythæmia the spleen may be greatly enlarged; (*b*) in some cases of spleno-medullary leucocythæmia, more especially in the later stages of the disease, the lymphatic glands are enlarged; and (*c*) in some (apparently quite exceptional) cases of lymphatic leucocythæmia, the spleen is enlarged while the lymphatic glands are not enlarged.

Hence, as Dr Robert Muir has recently pointed out, the lymphatic form of leucocythæmia is not synonymous with a leucocythæmia in which the lymphatic glands are enlarged. In other words, the distinction between the spleno-medullary and lymphatic varieties of leucocythæmia cannot be based merely upon the presence, in the one case, of an enlarged spleen, and, in the other, of enlarged lymphatic glands, but should be based upon the exact microscopical characters of the white corpuscles to which the leucocythæmic condition is due.

In spleno-medullary leucocythæmia, a great variety of different white corpuscles are usually present in the blood ; but, in most (typical) cases, the increase of the white corpuscles is in great part due to the presence of large nucleated white corpuscles, which do not stain with eosin and which appear to be identical with certain cells of the marrow of the bones (hence the term *myelocytes* which has been given to them) ; in some cases of spleno-medullary leucocythæmia, the eosinophile cells, which are normally present in the blood in small proportion ($\frac{1}{2}$ to 4 per cent.), are also greatly increased in number ; but this is by no means always the case, or perhaps it would be more correct to say that while the total number of eosinophile cells in the blood is (usually) increased, the percentage of eosinophile cells to the total number of white corpuscles is usually less than the normal.

In the lymphatic form of leucocythæmia, the increase of the white corpuscles of the blood is almost entirely due to an increase of the uninucleated white corpuscles, and, in most cases, of the small uninucleated corpuscles (lymphocytes), which are normally present in the blood in considerable proportion (25 to 30 per cent.).

A few rare cases of leucocythæmia have also been described in which neither the spleen nor the lymphatic glands were affected, but in which the lesion seemed to be situated in the medulla of the bones ; to these cases the term *medullary* leucocythæmia has been applied. There is, however, considerable doubt as to the exact nature, indeed as to the actual occurrence of cases of this kind, though for *a priori* reasons I am disposed to think that cases of pure medullary leucocythæmia probably occur.

It has also been suggested that a *pure splenic* leucocythæmia may occur ; but this is still more doubtful.

In some cases of leucocythæmia, the marrow of the bones, the spleen and the lymphatic glands are all involved ; in other cases, all the lymphoid tissues throughout the body are affected (enlarged), and lymphoid deposits may even be developed in organs and tissues in which they are not normally present or apparent.

We may say, then :—(1) That leucocythæmia is (usually) a chronic and slowly progressive condition which is characterised clinically by :—(*a*) An enormous increase of the white blood cor-puscles ; (*b*) more or less, and in some cases marked, diminution of the red blood corpuscles and hæmoglobin ; and (*c*) in some cases, by enlargement of the spleen ; in others by enlargement of the lymphatic glands ; and in others by a combination of these conditions (enlargement of the spleen and lymphatic glands). (2) That so far as our present knowledge enables us to judge, the spleno-medullary and lymphatic forms of leucocythæmia appear to be distinct conditions or varieties. (3) That other varieties of leucocythæmia (a purely medullary form, for example), may perhaps occur.

Further, it should be added that the spleno-medullary is far more common than the lymphatic variety of the disease.

The exact relationship of the lymphatic form of leucocythæmia to Hodgkin's disease has not yet been satisfactorily determined. To the naked eye, the glandular lesions in the lymphatic form of leucocythæmia and in Hodgkin's disease are very similar, and some observers state that they are identical in character; but so far as my observation enables me to judge, the enormous glandular enlargements which are met with in some cases of Hodgkin's disease are never developed in cases of lymphatic leucocythæmia. Further, Dr Robert Muir tells me that his observations show that the lymphatic glands, when affected in leucocythæmia, are simply crowded with leucocytes, similar in character to those which are present in excess in the blood, and the enlarged lymphatic glands do not present the proliferative changes in the stroma, leading to indurations, which are common in Hodgkin's disease.

When I come to describe Hodgkin's disease I will point out that the peculiar form of glandular enlargement (a hard painless enlargement of many different groups of lymphatic glands), which is its chief clinical characteristic, may undoubtedly be due to more than one pathological process, for example to Hodgkin's disease and to tubercle, and that in some cases it is difficult or impossible to differentiate these conditions during life.

Some writers advocate the view that lymphatic leucocythæmia is a combination of Hodgkin's disease and leucocythæmia. But to my mind this view is not altogether satisfactory. It merely expresses the fact that, in some cases of disease in which the lymphatic glands are enlarged and in which that enlargement presents the same clinical characters as the glandular enlargement characteristic of Hodgkin's disease, the spleen is also enlarged and the blood contains a large excess of white corpuscles. It does not afford any satisfactory explanation of the fact that in many (most) typical cases of Hodgkin's disease the white corpuscles are not increased, or at all events not markedly increased; and it takes no account of the exact character of the white blood corpuscles which are present. In some cases of Hodgkin's disease in which the white corpuscles are in excess—and this seems chiefly to occur in the later stages of the disease—the condition appears to be a leucocytosis and not a lymphatic leucocythæmia. Further, as has been already stated, I very much doubt whether the glandular enlargement is identical in the two conditions.

ETIOLOGY.

In this country, leucocythæmia is a very rare disease. In 14,777 consecutive cases of medical disease which I have analysed, there were only five cases of leucocythæmia.*

Age and Sex.—Leucocythæmia is much more common (probably at least three times more common) in men than in women. In the great majority of cases, the disease is developed during active adult life, between the ages of 25 and 50, though cases also occur in childhood ; the disease is very rare in old age. The spleno-medullary form is more common in adults, the lymphatic form appears to be more common in children.

Locality, race, etc.—The disease occurs in all parts of the world and affects all races, though, according to Eichhorst, it is particularly apt to affect Jews ; it appears to be more frequent in the lower than the upper ranks of society.

Influence of malaria, traumatic injury, etc.—In a considerable proportion (according to Gowers 20 per cent.) of cases, the disease occurs in persons who have previously suffered from malaria ; but, so far as I know, it has not been shown that the disease is more prevalent in tropical and malarial districts than in temperate climates. The disease would, however, appear to be much more common in certain parts of America than it is in this country. Thus, Stengel states that he has seen 15 cases during the past four years in Philadelphia, and at least 12 during the past year in the hospital service and private practice of himself and colleagues.+ Whether the greater frequency of malaria accounts for the frequency with which leucocythæmia seems to occur in America or not I cannot say. Further, the nature of the connection which seems to prevail between certain cases of leucocythæmia and malaria is entirely unknown.

In some cases, traumatic injuries (blows over the spleen, etc.) appear to have been the exciting cause of the condition. In other cases, the onset of the disease has been preceded by mental anxiety or overwork. In one of my cases the disease seemed to develop after an attack of influenza. It is probable that these conditions merely act as contributory or predisposing causes ; it can hardly be supposed that they are the actual causes of the disease.

---

* I have, of course, seen and had under my care several other cases.

+ "Twentieth Century Practice of Medicine," Vol. vii., p. 401.

Since in women the disease appears as a rule to occur at a somewhat later age than in men, it has been supposed that, in some instances at least, its development in women is related to the occurrence of the menopause. Pregnancy, lactation and uterine or ovarian derangements appear in some cases to have an influence as predisposing or exciting causes of the disease; though this relationship may perhaps, as Muir has suggested, be merely accidental.

In rare cases, the disease appears to be hereditary or to affect more than one member of the same family.

The ultimate cause; possibly an irritant in the blood; ? microorganisms.—The true (the fundamental) cause of leucocythæmia is as yet unknown. It has been suggested (and some of the clinical and pathological characters of the disease seem to favour this view) that the disease is due to some form of intoxication—to the introduction into the body of an irritant which has a special and specific influence upon the organs in which the white blood corpuscles are formed (the marrow of the bones, the lymphatic glands and the spleen); and in some cases micro-organisms have actually been detected in the blood. But in other cases in which micro-organisms have been carefully searched for, none have been found. Further information is, therefore, required before any definite statement can be made on this point. It is possible that future observation may show that in some cases leucocythæmia is due to micro-organisms, while in others it is not. The same line of argument which has been advanced with regard to the rôle which micro-organisms may possibly play in the production of pernicious anæmia may perhaps be applied to leucocythæmia.

With regard to the exact nature and ultimate causation of the disease, Muir states:—" In the absence of knowledge regarding the agent producing the excessive proliferation of leucocytes, we cannot definitely assign the place of leucocythæmia in the category of disease. On the whole, it presents most points of analogy to the growth of tumours, the analogy being especially striking in the lymphatic variety; but, on the other hand, it is not absurd to suppose that it may yet prove to be due to a microparasite." *

The primary seat of the lesion.—Two views have been held as to the primary seat of the disease, viz., (1) That the increase of leucocytes takes place in the blood itself, and that the lesions in the bone-marrow, spleen, lymphatic glands, etc., are secondary: (2) That the increase of the leucocytes is due to an abnormal or patho-

---

* Article on Leucocythæmia in Clifford Allbutt's " System of Medicine," Vol. v., p. 652.

logical over-production of white cells in the organs (bone-marrow, spleen, lymphatic glands) in which the white corpuscles of the blood are normally formed.

The latter view is the one which is now generally held and is in all probability correct; though in some cases evidence has been found that in leucocythæmia the leucocytes may go on increasing in the blood itself or in the tissues and organs in which they are extravasated or deposited from the blood, just as they seem to do in normal blood to a certain extent. The presence of leucocytes containing nuclei in an active state of division seems to show that this may occur.

Some authorities have supposed that the increase of the leuco-cytes in leucocythæmia is due to defective destruction, an abnormal accumulation of leucocytes in the blood, so to speak ; but the evidence seems strongly to support the contrary opinion, viz., that the increase is the result of over-production in the blood-forming organs. Probably, as has been already suggested, this over-production may be due to more than one cause, and, in different cases and in different forms of leucocythæmia, may have its chief seat in different parts of the blood-forming organs and tissues (marrow of the bones, spleen, lymphatic glands, etc.).

I have already stated that cases of leucocythæmia (in both of which the spleen may be enlarged) may be divided into two main varieties, which have been termed (a) the *spleno-medullary* and (b) the *lymphatic* types or forms of leucocythæmia respectively. The different characters of the blood (the white corpuscles) would seem to show that these two varieties of leucocythæmia are separate and distinct diseases. It has been suggested that the two forms are occasionally met with in combination, but so far as I know this has not as yet been actually demonstrated. If the two forms do occur in combination, it must of course be admitted that the distinction between the spleno-medullary and lymphatic forms of leucocythæmia is not always so definite and distinct as the statement which has just been made would imply.

In the great majority of cases of leucocythæmia in which the spleen is enlarged, the marrow of the bones is found diseased after death ; and in this, the spleno-medullary form as it is now usually termed, the lesion of the marrow of the bones is regarded by most modern authorities as the primary and fundamental lesion. This opinion is based upon the microscopical characters of the white corpuscles which are present in this form of leucocythæmia, and particularly upon the presence in the blood of large uninucleated corpuscles which do not stain with eosin and which appear to be identical with certain cells which are normally present in the bone-marrow (myelocytes). This opinion seems to be corroborated by the fact that in this variety of leucocythæmia nucleated red blood corpuscles are present in the blood, often in considerable numbers. Further, cases of leucocythæmia have, as I have already stated, been described in which the spleen and lymphatic glands were normal, and in which the only lesion appeared to be a lesion of the marrow of the bone. Again, it is probable, I think, that the diminution of the red blood corpuscles, which constitutes one of the clinical characteristics of spleno-medullary anæmia, is due to the changes in the bone-marrow—in other words, is the result of defec-tive production, rather than excessive destruction, of red blood corpuscles. So far as I know, there is nothing to show that in the spleno-medullary form of leucocythæmia there is an excessive destruction of red blood corpuscles.

And here I may state that the great majority of physiologists now admit that the red blood corpuscles are formed from nucleated red cells, and that they are, under normal circumstances, produced in the marrow of the bones. The view which was at one time held, that the red blood corpuscles are produced from the white blood cells and that the diminution in red blood corpuscles in splenic leukæmia is the result of defective formation of red blood cells from white corpuscles, is rapidly losing ground and may in fact be said to be abandoned by almost all authorities.

MORBID ANATOMY.

On examining the bodies of patients who have died from leucocythæmia, the remarkable condition of the blood and the great enlargement of the spleen are the two most constant and striking naked-eye features.

The conditions of the blood and blood vessels.—The con-dition of the blood is very remarkable. In many typical cases, the blood vessels are over-distended with brick-red-coloured or choco-late-brown-coloured blood, or contain pale purulent-looking clots. The clots which are present in the heart usually have a peculiar yellowish-green colour. In some cases the cardiac cavities seem to be filled with pus. The purulent appearance is due to the fact that the white blood corpuscles are apt to separate from the red corpuscles and collect together, forming a greenish-yellow, creamy-looking fluid which closely resembles pus.

The *veins* and smaller blood vessels in the different organs may be over-distended with white corpuscles.

In one case which I examined some years ago, and recorded in the "British Medical Journal," 1886, Vol. ii., p. 1098, the veins on the surface of the brain were enormously distended with brick-red and chocolate-coloured blood; the brain looked as if it were covered with large red worms. The appearance was a very remarkable one.

Hæmorrhagic extravasations.—A tendency to hæmorrhage, both into the internal organs and from the mucous surfaces of the body, is one of the most striking features of the disease when it is severe and advanced. In the case to which I have just referred, numerous hæmorrhages, most of them microscopic but some of large size, were scattered throughout the brain substance. The small vessels in the interior of the brain were all engorged and over-distended with white blood corpuscles. Many of them were dilated, presenting here and there a varicose or aneurismal appearance.

Exactly the same condition may be seen in other organs. The vessels of the liver and kidney, for example, may be engorged with white blood corpuscles, and the lymphatic sheaths and tissues round the distended vessels may also contain large numbers of white blood cells. In the case to which I have just referred, the vessels of the spinal cord as well as the vessels of the brain and all the organs of the body were enormously distended with white blood cells.

Localised collections of white corpuscles and lymphoid deposits, which in many cases appear to be the result of the multiplication *in situ* of white blood cells which have escaped from the blood vessels, may be seen in the different tissues and organs. These infiltrations of leucocytes in the different tissues and organs, giving rise to localised lymphatic deposits and enlargements, appear to be much more common and prominent in the lymphatic than in the spleno-medullary variety of the disease.

The distended condition of the veins and the difficulty with which the white blood corpuscles circulate through the distended vessels is one cause of the thromboses, which are apt to occur in the course of the disease.

The *microscopical characters of the blood* will be more appropriately considered in connection with the clinical history.

Spleen.—The spleen is in some cases so much enlarged that it occupies a large part of the abdominal cavity; it not unfrequently weighs six or seven pounds, and one case has been recorded in which it reached the enormous weight of eighteen pounds. The capsule is very often thickened; in some cases, dense adhesions bind the enlarged spleen to the surrounding organs and to the adjacent wall of the abdomen. The organ is usually, and especially in long-standing cases, firmer and harder than normal. The enlargement appears to the naked eye to be a simple hypertrophy, with an increased production of fibrous tissue. In the more rapidly developed cases, the spleen is usually less enlarged and softer in consistence than in the more common (chronic) cases.

On section, the spleen usually has a uniform, brownish-yellow, brownish-grey, or reddish-brown colour. In most cases, the Malpighian corpuscles cannot be differentiated by the naked eye from the splenic pulp. In other cases, the Malpighian bodies stand out as pale points in the midst of the darker splenic tissue. In some cases, hæmorrhagic extravasations, in others, infarctions, usually wedge-shaped and in various stages of decoloration, are present.

In some cases of (lymphatic) leucocythæmia, nodules of a whitish colour are scattered here and there throughout the spleen. In these cases, the enlargement of the spleen is not usually great.

On microscopical examination, the splenic tissue is seen to be infiltrated and the splenic sinuses crowded with white corpuscles ; in some, more especially long-standing, cases, the fibrous tissue is greatly increased in amount. The white cells are for the most part ordinary leucocytes, but myelocytes and nucleated red blood corpuscles are present in the spleno-medullary variety of the disease. Dr Robert Muir informs me that his observations seem to show that the character of the leucocytes in the splenic pulp correspond more or less closely to those in the blood—in the spleno-medullary form they consist chiefly of myelocytes, the eosinophile cells being often also in excess ; in the lymphatic form, they consist chiefly of lymphocytes. Pigment granules or crystals of hæmatin, the results of previous hæmorrhages, may be seen in different parts of the section. Small colourless octahedral crystals, which were first described by the late Professor Charcot, are sometimes found in the blood and splenic tissue after death.

Lymphatic glands and other lymphoid tissues.—In the great majority of cases of lymphatic leucocythæmia, the *lymphatic glands* are more or less, and in some cases considerably, enlarged. In the spleno-medullary form, the lymphatic glands may also be enlarged, but this is not usually the case. The enlarged glands may be firm or soft. On section, they have generally a yellowish-pink or reddish colour.

On microscopical examination, the gland tissue is found to be crowded with white corpuscles, usually of small (lymphocytes), but in some cases (spleno-medullary form) of larger size.

The *tonsils, thymus gland,* the *Peyer's patches* and *solitary glands* in the intestine are in some cases affected ; and *lymphoid deposits* are sometimes also present in the *stomach, lungs,* the *serous membranes, retina* and even in the *skin.* The lymphoid deposits in the intestine are in some cases ulcerated. These lesions are much more common in the lymphatic variety of the disease.

Bone-marrow.—Changes in the marrow of the bones are constantly present in the spleno-medullary variety, but are usually less marked and characteristic in the lymphatic form. Neumann was the first to direct attention to the changes in the marrow of the bones which are now regarded by most authorities as the primary lesion in the spleno-medullary form of the disease.

On naked-eye examination, the marrow is seen to be of a yellowish-grey or reddish colour, to which Neumann applied the terms *pyoid* and *lymphoid* respectively ; the latter is much the more frequent.

On microscopical examination, it is found that the fat cells, which are normally present in the marrow in great abundance, have for the most part disappeared. In the spleno-medullary form, the marrow tissue contains an excessive number of large uninucleated marrow cells, eosinophile cells and nucleated red blood corpuscles, and lymphoid corpuscles. In the lymphatic variety, the marrow tissue is infiltrated with uninucleated white corpuscles similar to those which are present in excess in the blood. The trabeculæ and even the shaft of the bone may be atrophied.

Heart.—The muscular tissue is usually flabby, pale and more or less fatty, the cardiac cavities being in some cases considerably dilated. Petechial hæmorrhages may be present in the pericardial or endocardial surfaces.

On microscopical examination, the minute blood vessels in the cardiac wall may be greatly distended with leucocytes, and minute collections (extravasations) of white blood corpuscles may be present here and there in the sub-pericardial tissue or between the muscular fibres.

Liver.—The liver is usually considerably enlarged, its surface smooth and its consistency usually firm. On section, it generally presents a more or less uniform dull-red colour ; in some cases, the surface of the section is markedly mottled, the peripheral parts of the lobules being pale owing to the leucocytic infiltration along the portal tracts. Small whitish-yellow deposits, which to the naked eye resemble tubercles, but which consist of lymphoid tissue, may be scattered here and there in the midst of the liver tissue.

On microscopic examination, the minute blood vessels are usually found to be markedly distended with leucocytes, and large numbers of leucocytes may be infiltrated and scattered in the midst of the hepatic tissue. In some cases, nucleated red blood corpuscles and evidences of active nuclear division (*mitosis*) in the white corpuscles have been seen in the liver—changes which have been thought to indicate a return to the fœtal blood-forming function of the organ. In many cases, the leucocytes are collected in small masses which are evidently the starting points of the lymphoid nodules previously described.

Kidneys.—The kidneys are usually more or less enlarged ; the surface is generally smooth, the capsule unadherent, and the section paler than normal. In some cases, lymphoid nodules can be seen with the naked eye on the surface of the organ.

On microscopical examination, the minute vessels may be greatly distended with white corpuscles, and enormous numbers of leucocytes may be infiltrated and extravasated through the renal tissues. The renal epithelium is usually more or less fatty or in a condition of cloudy swelling.

In the description which has just been given of the morbid appearances met with in the bodies of patients who have died from leucocythæmia, I have not thought it necessary to give a separate description of the morbid appearances in the two varieties of leucocythæmia—the spleno-medullary and the lymphatic forms ; though, as has already been stated, these two varieties seem, so far as our present knowledge enables us to judge, to be distinct diseases. As I have previously stated, some authorities suppose that the two varieties may occur in combination ; while this is theoretically possible, further observation seems to be required before this view can be definitely accepted.

CLINICAL HISTORY.

Mode of onset and Course.—The onset of leucocythæmia is usually slow and insidious, and the course chronic. In rare cases (which are almost invariably cases of the lymphatic variety) the onset is acute and the course rapid. In many of the chronic cases, paroxysmal exacerbations of the symptoms occur from time to time.

Symptoms and complaints.—In the great majority of cases, the patient slowly and gradually begins to lose strength and colour, and complains of a feeling of fulness, weight and heaviness in the abdomen, due to the presence of the enlarged spleen. Intercurrent attacks of pain in the region of the spleen are of frequent occurrence. In some cases, the pain is probably due to acute congestion and stretching of the capsule; in others, to perisplenitis or localised peritonitis. As the disease advances, the patient becomes breathless on exertion, suffers from palpitation and the other symptoms characteristic of anæmia. In some cases, intercurrent attacks of fever every now and again occur. Priapism has been noted in a considerable proportion of cases ; in some cases, it is an early symptom. It is probably the result of over-distension or of thrombosis of the corpora cavernosa with leucocythæmic blood.

Tenderness of the bones (sternum, tibiæ, etc.) is occasionally complained of, and, when it does occur, is highly suggestive of implication of the bone-marrow.

General appearance.—On examination, the abdomen is found to be distended, often enormously so. In the majority of cases, the distension is chiefly due to the enlarged spleen, partly to the enlarged liver ; but in a few cases it is in some degree the result of associated ascites.

In the vast majority of cases, the complexion (skin and mucous membranes) is pale, but this is not invariably so ; for cases are occasionally met with in which the skin of the face and the mucous membranes of the lips are well, indeed too deeply, coloured. I happen to possess an admirable water-colour drawing by Mr John Williamson of a case in point.

The patient was a woman, aged 33 ; the spleen was enormously enlarged ; the face (cheeks, nose, chin) and lips were deeply injected and mottled ; the red corpuscles numbered 3,120,000 and the white corpuscles 310,000 per cubic millimetre ; the case was one of spleno-medullary leucocythæmia.

To this exceptional condition the term "*leucocythæmic plethora*" has been applied. It apparently is the result of an over-distended condition of the peripheral vessels of the face and lips. It is not unreasonable to suppose that the vessels of the face and mucous membrane of the lips may in some cases be chronically over-distended with chocolate-coloured blood just as the vessels on the surface of the brain may be. But this condition (leucocythæmic plethora) is quite exceptional. In the great majority of cases of leucocythæmia the face is pale and the buccal and conjunctival mucous membranes more or less anæmic. In some cases in which the face is pale the lips are well coloured. I happen to have a case of this kind in the hospital at the present time.

General state of nutrition.—One important point in which leucocythæmia differs from chlorosis and pernicious anæmia is the fact that, when the disease is thoroughly established, the patients are usually more or less emaciated, often markedly so. In many cases, the enlarged abdomen forms a striking contrast to the emaciated condition of the upper and lower extremities and of the face. In this respect the clinical picture resembles to some extent that of cirrhosis of the liver.

Dropsy.—Œdema of the feet and ankles is common in the advanced stages, especially in those cases in which the anæmia is marked. The face is sometimes puffy. Localised swellings in the face, neck, etc., may be the result of the pressure of enlarged glands upon the vessels.

The condition of the spleen.—On examining the abdomen, the enlarged, hard and weighty spleen is easily recognised. The normal shape of the organ is usually well preserved ; the anterior border is usually sharply defined, and in it one or more notches can usually be felt—points of distinction between the enlarged spleen and the enlarged left kidney. Further, the splenic tumour moves with respiration, is not overlapped by the colon (though this cannot always be demonstrated), and does not usually distend the left loin so fully (*i.e.*, does not extend so far back towards the spinal column in the lumbar region) as a tumour of the left kidney does.

In some cases, there is tenderness on pressure over the enlarged spleen. In others, a friction fremitus may be felt with the hand, or a friction sound may be heard when the stethoscope is placed over the splenic tumour. Pulsations can, it is said, be occasionally felt in the enlarged spleen ; in one of my cases a loud blowing murmur was audible with the stethoscope ; but these conditions (pulsation and murmur) are quite exceptional.

The enlarged spleen may vary considerably in size from time to time ; these variations are chiefly seen in the earlier stages of the disease (*i.e.*, before the development of fibrous overgrowth).

The condition of the liver.—As I have already said, the liver is usually considerably enlarged. Free fluid is sometimes present in the peritoneal cavity ; but a marked degree of ascites appears to be quite exceptional ; in none of my cases was ascites present. The abdominal dropsy is usually supposed to be due to the pressure of the enlarged spleen or of enlarged lymphatic glands upon the portal vessels.

The condition of the blood.—A drop of blood obtained by puncturing the finger may be well coloured, or paler or more opaque (turbid) than normal ; in some cases it may look like a mixture of blood and pus.

On microscopic examination, the white blood corpuscles are found to be enormously increased in number, while the red blood corpuscles and the hæmoglobin are usually diminished, sometimes in a marked degree.

In health, the number of white blood corpuscles varies considerably, the average number being usually about 8,000 per cubic millimetre. In cases of leucocythæmia, the white cells may number 200,000, 300,000, 400,000, or even more, per cubic millimetre.

The proportion of white to red corpuscles (which should not, however, be taken as the standard) is greatly altered. The white corpuscles are enormously increased, while the red corpuscles are diminished in number though not (usually) in a very marked degree. In leucocythæmia it is not uncommon to have one white to every five or six red corpuscles, and cases have been recorded in which the white corpuscles have actually, it is said, been as numerous as the red.

In thirty cases of leucocythæmia observed by Cabot, the average number of white corpuscles was 438,000 per cubic millimetre.

In leucocythæmia, as in health, the number of white blood corpuscles may vary considerably from time to time. A remarkable case has been recorded by Stricker in which, at one period of the case, the white blood corpuscles were more numerous than the red, but, at a subsequent period, there was only one white blood corpuscle to every 150 red cells. Dr Muir makes the following statement, which is of great diagnostic importance, that even in those (rare) cases of (spleno-medullary) leucocythæmia in which the excess of white corpuscles disappears, temporarily or before death, the abnormal form of cells (large uninucleated non-amœboid leucocytes, nucleated red corpuscles, etc.) which are characteristic of the disease remain in the blood.[*] I can confirm Dr Muir's observations on this point, for in a case which is at present under my care the white corpuscles have fallen, as the result of treatment, from 210,000 per cubic millimetre to 1,600 per cubic millimetre, and yet amongst the very scanty number of white corpuscles which are present a considerable proportion of myelocytes are still to be found.

The character of the white blood corpuscles differs in different cases of leucocythæmia in which the spleen is enlarged. As has been already stated, Virchow originally recognised these differences and described two varieties of the disease, the splenic and lymphatic varieties respectively ; and for many years past I have been in the habit of teaching that in cases of splenic anæmia (or splenomedullary anæmia as it is now termed) the white corpuscles are

---

* Clifford Allbutt's "System of Medicine," Vol. v., p. 640.

large and coarsely granulated; whereas in cases of lymphatic leucocythæmia the white corpuscles are of small size and not coarsely
granulated. Modern methods of staining, for the introduction of
which we are chiefly indebted to Ehrlich, have shown that these
differences are well founded and of the greatest diagnostic
importance.

**The microscopical characters of the blood in the spleno-
medullary form of leucocythæmia.**—In the spleno-medullary form
of leucocythæmia, several different forms of white corpuscles are
present. Some of these forms exist normally in the blood, others
do not. The most characteristic is a large uninucleated cell, which
does not generally contain eosinophile granules and which, unlike
the normal white blood corpuscles, does not exhibit active amœboid
movements on the warm stage. In freshly drawn blood, these cells
are usually about twice the size of the normal red blood corpuscles
(about 16 μ. in diameter), though in dried films they may, in consequence of flattening out during the process of preparation, appear
to be considerably larger. Their exact nature has given rise to a
good deal of debate. It has been supposed that they are degenerated white corpuscles, but most observers are now agreed that they
are identical with certain cells which are normally present in the
marrow of the bones. They have therefore been termed *myelocytes*.
Though occasionally present in small number in other conditions
(chiefly in severe forms of anæmia, whether primary or secondary,
and in wasting diseases), myelocytes are, so far as is known, never
present in the blood, in large numbers, except in leucocythæmia;
and since in the spleno-medullary form of the disease they usually
constitute a large proportion of the white corpuscles—30 per cent.
or even more—they are of the highest diagnostic significance.
They are sometimes met with in small numbers in the lymphatic
form of leucocythæmia.

In 18 cases of spleno-medullary leucocythæmia observed by
Cabot, the average percentage of myelocytes to the total number
of white corpuscles in the blood was 37.7 per cent., rising in one case
as high as 60 per cent. and never lower than 20 per cent. He
states :—

"Taking the average total number of leucocytes as 438,000 per cubic millimetre, the absolute number of myelocytes would be over 162,000 per cubic
millimetre. So far as I am aware the highest count of myelocytes in any other
disease is that mentioned on page 128 in a case of pernicious anæmia, namely,
1,150 per cubic millimetre. The contrast is sufficiently striking. I wish to
insist upon this point, namely, that the blood of splenic-myelogenous leukæmia
is absolutely peculiar and characteristic, and could not be confused with that of
any other disease. Certain writers of late years have concluded that because

myelocytes do occur in a great variety of diseases as well as in leukæmia, therefore there is nothing peculiar about the blood of the latter affection. It would
be as logical to say that because albumin and casts occur occasionally in the
urine of persons practically well, therefore there is nothing characteristic about
the urine of acute nephritis.

"Between the largest number of myelocytes ever recorded in any disease
other than leukæmia, and the smallest number ever found in the latter disease,
there is as great a difference as there is between the minute traces of sugar to
be found in normal urine and the marked glycosuria of diabetes mellitus." *

Cases of spleno-medullary leucocythæmia are, however, occasionally met with in which the myelocytes, either as the result of
treatment or of some other cause, become very few in number.   I
have at the present time a case of this description under observation ; and it is interesting to note that in it the coarsely grained
eosinophile cells are very few, and nucleated red-blood corpuscles
are very scanty.   The details of this somewhat exceptional case are
recorded below (see page 171).

In some cases of spleno-medullary leucocythæmia, the *eosinophile cells* (which are normally present in the blood in small proportion—only ½ to 4 per cent. of the total leucocytes) are also greatly
increased (to 20 per cent. or more of the total leucocytes); but this
is by no means always the case ; and of late years much less
significance has been attached to the presence of these (eosinophile)
corpuscles, as a characteristic feature of leucocythæmia, than Ehrlich
originally claimed for them.   In the spleno-medullary form of
leucocythæmia, the actual number of the eosinophile cells in the
blood is probably always greater than in health, but they are not
always relatively increased in proportion to the other forms of
white corpuscles ; and they may be greatly increased in other conditions (certain skin diseases, for example).

Some of the eosinophile cells are of large size ; Dr Robert Muir
states that they are never present in normal blood, and hence they
are of considerable diagnostic importance.

The total number of *polymorpho-nuclear leucocytes* is also increased, but their relative proportion to the total number of leucocytes is considerably decreased.   In the 18 cases analysed by Cabot,
the average proportion of 'polymorpho-nuclear cells to the total
number of white corpuscles was 49.2 per cent. instead of 65 to 70
per cent. as in health.

The total number of *lymphocytes* in the blood is also increased
in some cases, but their relative proportion to the total number of
white corpuscles is markedly diminished.   Dr Muir states that the

---

* "Clinical Examination of the Blood," page 144.

lymphocytes are not increased.* In the 18 cases observed by Cabot, the average was 7.6 per cent. instead of 20 to 30 per cent. (the normal average).

In the spleno-medullary form, *nucleated red blood corpuscles* are usually present in the blood and generally in considerable numbers —in far larger numbers than in any other condition. They are sometimes of large size (megaloblasts); in some cases their nuclei are seen to be in an active state of division.

Further, in some cases there is distinct evidence that some of the white corpuscles, more especially the large uninucleated myelocytes, are undergoing active division (*karyokinesis*). The white corpuscles containing nuclei in an active state of division (*mitotic figures*) are rarely seen in normal blood, and the number of white corpuscles in leucocythæmia which show this change is always, relatively to the total number of white corpuscles which are present, very small.

The microscopical characters of the blood in the lymphatic form of leucocythæmia.—In the lymphatic form of leucocythæmia (in which the spleen may also be enormously enlarged, though the enlargement is usually much less than in cases of lymphatic leucocythæmia, and in which, as Dr Muir has shown, the lymphatic glands are not necessarily, though they are in the great majority of cases, enlarged) the increase of the leucocytes is for the most part due to an enormous increase of the *uninucleated white corpuscles*, either small or large, but, in most cases, of the small lymphocytes, which normally exist in the blood in moderate proportion (20 to 25 per cent. of the total leucocytes). It has indeed been stated that the increase of the white corpuscles in this form of leucocythæmia is entirely due to an increase of the uninucleated white corpuscles; but this view appears to be a mistake. Dreschfeld and other writers have shown that in this form of leucocythæmia other varieties of leucocytes (*eosinophile cells* and even *myelocytes*) may also be present; but the uninucleated white corpuscles generally form 90 to 95 per cent. of the total white corpuscles present.

In the lymphatic form of leucocythæmia, nucleated red corpuscles are rarely present, and if they occur are only present in very small numbers.

In both varieties of leucocythæmia, the *red blood corpuscles* are usually diminished in number, sometimes markedly so. In well-marked cases of the disease they usually number from 2,500.000 to 3,500,000 per cubic millimetre; but in some cases—and this state-

---

* Clifford Allbutt's "System of Medicine," Vol. v., p. 639.

ment more particularly applies to the lymphatic variety—the reduction is even more marked (1,500,000 or even less). In the cases observed by Cabot, the average number of red corpuscles per cubic millimetre was 3,000,000, the hæmoglobin being diminished in the same proportion—in other words, the individual richness of the corpuscles in hæmoglobin (or the colour index) was about normal. In some cases, the colour-index is, at certain periods of the case at all events, above the normal (see Case, page 171).

In some cases of leucocythæmia, the red corpuscles are mis-shapen (*poikilocytosis*); but in the cases which have come under my own notice, the alterations in size and shape have not been striking.

As has been already stated, nucleated red blood cells, many of which are of large size (megaloblasts), may be present, more especially in the spleno-medullary form of the disease.

The *hæmoglobin* is usually proportionately diminished with the red blood corpuscles, sometimes more so. In some cases, the hæmoglobin separates more readily from the corpuscles after death than in normal conditions ; and Charcot's crystals, which are often found on post-mortem examination in the blood of leucocythæmia, have, it is said, been seen in microscopic preparations of blood freshly-drawn during life from the spleen or finger-tip.

The blood-plates are in some cases markedly increased in number.

The leading characters of the blood in the two varieties of leucocythæmia are summarised by Cabot as follows :—

"(*a*.) *Splenic-myelogenous Form.*

" 1. Red cells about 3,000,000 ; nucleated forms very numerous.

" 2. White cells about 450,000, of which

" 3. Myelocytes form about 30 per cent.

"(*b*.) *Lymphatic Form.*

" 1. Red cells about 3,000,000 or lower ; nucleated forms rare.

" 2. White cells about 100,000 or lower, of which

" 3. Lymphocytes form over 90 per cent. (the large or the small forms may predominate).

" 4. Myelocytes and eosinophiles very scanty.

"(*c*.) *Mixed forms* occasionally occur, partaking of the characteristics of each of the above."

The condition of the skin.—In some cases of leucocythæmia, pigmented patches are developed in the skin. In one of my cases, characteristic patches of leucoderma were scattered here and there over the surface of the body. In another case, which is at present under observation, a diffuse erythematous eruption attended with high fever and followed by desquamation of the skin was developed during the treatment (see *infra*). Petechial hæmorrhages in the skin occasionally occur in the later stages of the disease. In rare cases, lymphoid nodules are, it is said, developed in the skin and subcutaneous tissue and can be seen and felt during life. In some cases of the disease, excessive sweating is present.

In a considerable proportion of cases, and as has already been remarked this statement chiefly applies to the lymphatic variety of the disease, the superficial lymphatic glands are enlarged.

The condition of the heart.—The heart's action is extremely feeble ; this is one of the most characteristic features of the disease. The weakness of the heart of course largely accounts for the shortness of breath on exertion, the palpitation and the tendency to giddiness and faintness which are in many cases very striking and prominent symptoms. A venous hum is usually present in the neck and a systolic murmur in the pulmonary area. Mitral, tricuspid and systolic murmurs may occur, just as in other forms of advanced anæmia. The aortic second sound is in some cases accentuated ; and in this respect cases of leucocythæmia may differ from pernicious anæmia. The accentuation of the aortic second sound is probably due to the fact that the leucocythæmic blood has greater difficulty than normal blood in circulating through the vessels ; the white blood corpuscles cling to the sides of the vessels, and when they are unduly numerous tend to choke the vessels and to produce obstructions (thromboses). As I have already pointed out, this is probably one of the reasons why hæmorrhages are so common in this disease. In the advanced stages of leucocythæmia, when the heart's action is much enfeebled, the accentuation of the second aortic sound may, of course, disappear. The pulse is usually increased in frequency, often considerably so ; and is generally soft and weak.

Hæmorrhages.—Hæmorrhage may occur from the external surfaces ; epistaxis and bleeding from the gums are particularly common ; bleeding from the stomach and bowel are by no means rare ; occasionally there is hæmaturia. Hæmorrhages into the retina occur in a certain proportion of cases. On ophthalmoscopic examination, the fundus is usually found to be paler than normal ; the retinal veins are in some cases enormously distended ; localised deposits of white blood corpuscles resembling little lymphoid growths may be found in the retina after death and are occasionally seen with the ophthalmoscope during life ; in some cases the optic discs are swollen and inflamed (papillitis). To these retinal changes the term *leucocythæmic* or *leukæmic retinitis* has been applied.

The condition of the digestive organs.—Symptoms indicative of derangement of the digestive functions are very common. As a rule, the appetite is markedly impaired. Vomiting is of frequent occurrence; in some cases it seems to be due to the irritation which the splenic tumour produces on the stomach. Constipation is common, and obstruction of the bowels may even result from the pressure of the splenic tumour on the intestine. Diarrhœa is apt to occur, and in many cases it is the immediate cause of death. Intercurrent inflammations of the peritoneum, usually localised to the region of the spleen, are common.

The condition of the urine.—The urine does not as a rule present any characteristic naked-eye alterations. The uric acid is increased in amount. Albuminuria and hæmaturia sometimes occur, especially in the later stages of the disease.

The condition of the nervous system. — Head symptoms of various kinds (hæmorrhage, vertigo, fainting fits, somnolence, epileptiform convulsions, coma, etc.) are apt to occur during the terminal stages of the disease. Ollivier and Ranvier have described these symptoms in great detail. They sum up the chief points in the clinical history as follows :—

" In some cases, prodromal symptoms are observed ; some patients, in fact, complain of headache for a longer or shorter time before the more serious symptoms develop. Later, swimming sensations in the head, vertigo, buzzing in the ears, sometimes even fainting fits, occur. In the more advanced stages, hebetude, soon succeeded by somnolence, is observed. Lastly, the patient may pass into a condition of coma, which may be more or less prolonged, but which always terminates in death.

To these three successive periods there correspond three degrees of alteration in the brain. The first degree (headache, vertigo, and the other phenomena which have been mentioned above) is explained by the accumulation of white globules, which produce slowing of the circulation, and consequently anæmia of the brain.

A more advanced accumulation of white blood corpuscles increases the blood pressure ; the capillaries dilate, the cerebral pulp is compressed, in consequence of which hebetude and somnolence are developed.

In the third degree, hæmorrhages form and destroy more or less extensive portions of the brain. This is the terminal period, during which coma comes on, and death ultimately supervenes." [*]

To sum up, *cerebral anæmia, cerebral compression,* and *cerebral hæmorrhage with destruction of the brain tissue* are, according to

---

[*] " Archives de Physiologie," 1870, p. 114.

these authorities, the three conditions which determine the cerebral symptoms which are seen in patients suffering from leucocythæmia.

Convulsions sometimes precede death. In some cases maniacal excitement occurs.

The following are the leading pathological details of a case which came under my observation while I was pathologist to the Edinburgh Royal Infirmary. In it the head symptoms were prominent and the vascular lesions in the brain tissues more marked than in any other case with which I am acquainted :—

Case of Leucocythæmia with very extensive vascular lesions in the brain.— The patient, a shoemaker, aged 40, died on 18th May, and was examined post mortem on 19th May 1884. He had suffered for some time from the usual symptoms of leucocythæmia, but, shortly before death, had complained of headache, and had become maniacal.

It is unnecessary to detail the exact condition of every organ. Suffice it to say, that the case was, in every way, a typical one.

The *blood* throughout the body was thick, and of a brick-red colour, exactly resembling thick anchovy sauce. *On microscopic examination*, the white corpuscles appeared to be quite as numerous as—indeed, in some slides, more numerous than—the red blood discs ; many of them were of large size, and coarsely granular.

The *spleen* weighed 4 lbs. 8 ozs. ; the *liver*, 10 lbs. 8 ozs. ; the *kidneys*, 14 and 13½ ozs. respectively; the *pericardium* was in a condition of early inflammation, and there were *numerous punctiform ecchymoses* in the inflamed membrane, under the endocardium, in the pleura, and in the other parts of the body ; the *bone-marrow* was of the same brick-red colour and thick consistence as the blood.

The *brain* weighed 3 lbs. 1 oz., and presented a very remarkable appearance. The vessels, on the surface, were enormously distended with the thick, brick-red-coloured blood, and looked like masses of huge worms ramifying over the surface of the hemispheres. In vertical sections made through the whole brain, innumerable extravasations of blood were found in the brain-substance. Some of them were chocolate-coloured and of large size, the largest being fully the size of a hen's egg ; others were just visible to the naked eye. *On microscopic examination*, the whole brain-tissue (more especially the white matter) was riddled with capillary hæmorrhages. The blood vessels and capillaries throughout the brain were enormously dilated and distended with white corpuscles, multitudes of which had escaped into the lymphatic sheaths surrounding the larger vessels. The vessels of the brain, even the large trunks, were almost entirely destitute of red blood corpuscles. Collections of red discs were present in the large (naked-eye) extravasations, but the large hæmorrhages were for the most part, and the small (microscopic) hæmorrhages were (apparently) entirely, composed of white corpuscles.

The vessels of the *spinal cord* were dilated in the same way as the vessels of the brain, and were stuffed with white blood corpuscles.

Several hæmorrhages were seen with the naked eye in the *retina ;* the optic papillæ were much swollen, and, on microscopic examination, large numbers of white blood corpuscles were found scattered between the fibres of the optic discs, and between the bundles of the optic nerves behind the lamina cribrosa.

L

A careful search was made in the different tissues for micro-organisms. No organisms were found in the brain. The superior cervical ganglion of the sympathetic was infiltrated throughout with fine, highly refractile, granular particles of uniform size, which exactly resembled unstained micrococci, but which did not take on any of the ordinary dyes (gentian-violet, methyl-violet). Before examination, the sympathetic ganglia had been kept for a considerable time in a solution of gum, sugar, and carbolic acid; whether this solution prevents the staining of micro-organisms I do not know, but I have on several previous occasions suspected that such was the case. That the fine granular particles, which looked like micrococci, were not due to the gum and sugar solution I feel quite certain; for, in the course of a research on the normal and pathological condition of the sympathetic ganglia of the neck and abdomen, which extended over three years, I examined a very large number of ganglia which had been kept in the same solution, and in no case, except in this one, was this peculiar granular micrococcus-like appearance seen. Whether any importance is to be attached to the condition I am unable to decide.

The condition of the respiratory system.—Pressure symptoms of various kinds may also of course be developed in those cases in which the bronchial or mediastinal glands are enlarged. I need not refer to these symptoms in detail; they will be more appropriately considered in connection with Hodgkin's disease.

Intercurrent attacks of bronchitis, œdema of the lungs and a low form of pneumonia are in many cases the immediate cause of death.

Acute leucocythæmia.—Ebstein's observations * show that in cases of acute leucocythæmia the onset is sometimes sudden, the course rapid and attended with considerable fever; hæmorrhages from the gums and nose sometimes occur; purpuric spots may be developed in the skin, and hæmorrhages may be poured out into the viscera or from the mucous surfaces; the lymphatic glands, spleen, and liver enlarge; in some cases there is tenderness over the bones; the patient becomes profoundly anæmic and asthenic; the blood contains a large excess of leucocytes (the white corpuscles in some of the cases were said to be as numerous as the red); finally, the patient may sink into a typhoid state; or delirium, coma, or convulsions may be developed.

In the sixteen cases (all verified by post mortem) which Ebstein tabulated and analysed, the average age was 29 years, the youngest patient being 5 years and the oldest 59 years; while the average duration of the disease was 5.8 weeks, the shortest duration being 2½ and the longest 9 weeks.

In acute leucocythæmia, unhealthy and rapidly formed ulcerations in the mouth are of frequent occurrence, and are highly characteristic; ulceration in other parts of the gastro-intestinal tract may also occur.

---

* "Deutsches Arch. f. Klin. Med.," Leipzig, 1889, B. xliv., p. 343.

The clinical features and course of this acute form of leucocythæmia are highly suggestive of an infective process, and in some cases micro-organisms (staphylococci and streptococci) have been found in the blood during life, and in the organs after death. In a case recorded by Dr J. S. Fowler a bacillus was present in all the blood films which were examined.*

Diagnosis and Differential Diagnosis.

In well-marked cases the diagnosis of leucocythæmia can usually be at once made by a microscopical examination of the blood. Until recently, physicians were in the habit of regarding all cases of leucocythæmia in which the spleen was enlarged as cases of splenic leucocythæmia, and of considering those cases of leucocythæmia in which the lymphatic glands were enlarged either as cases of lymphatic leucocythæmia or as a combination of leucocythæmia and of Hodgkin's disease.

But recent observations as to the exact character of the blood in cases of leucocythæmia show that the diagnostic problem is by no means so simple as these statements would imply.

Further, it must be remembered that in some cases of leucocythæmia the white corpuscles are not very greatly increased in number; and in some cases in which they are, at one period of the case, greatly increased in number, at another period the increase is far less marked.

If the patient should be seen at a period at which the total number of leucocytes is not increased or is only slightly increased (but this is, of course, quite exceptional) the diagnosis can only be made by the examination of stained films—*i.e.*, by the detection in the blood of myelocytes.

It is hardly necessary to state that leucocytosis may occur in a large number of different conditions (inflammatory and cachectic conditions, after profuse hæmorrhage, etc.) ; and that a slight degree of leucocythæmia (which it may be impossible to differentiate from excessive leucocytosis by the *mere number* of the white corpuscles) may, as I have already stated, be the result of disease of the lymphatic glands, and probably of disease of the marrow of the bones, the spleen being unaffected.

But leucocytosis is usually a temporary condition, and in leucocytosis the increase of the white corpuscles is always due to an increase of the polymorpho-nuclear white corpuscles—the reverse of the condition which occurs in leucocythæmia ; for although the

---

* "Edinburgh Hospital Reports," Vol. v., 1898, p. 13.

total number of polymorpho-nuclear corpuscles is increased in leucocythæmia, the relative proportion of polymorpho-nuclear corpuscles to the total number of white corpuscles is usually greatly diminished (49.2 per cent. instead of 65 or 70 per cent.—the normal proportion).

Again, enlargement of the spleen is often met with without leucocythæmia. In rare cases (cases of so-called splenic anæmia), as I have previously pointed out in considering the diagnosis of pernicious anæmia, the spleen is enlarged with a pronounced condition of anæmia, but without any increase of the white blood cells. The spleen is often enlarged as the result of chronic malarial poisoning ; but in malarial enlargement, whether acute or chronic, there is usually a diminution rather than an increase of the white blood corpuscles. Considerable enlargement of the spleen without leucocythæmia may also, of course, be the result of portal congestion, of waxy disease, and (rarely) of hydatid cysts and other forms of new growth.

Further, in very rare and exceptional cases, the spleen is greatly enlarged, the blood contains an enormous excess of white blood corpuscles, and rapid recovery takes place under treatment. It is doubtful whether cases of this kind should be placed in the same category as cases of ordinary spleno-medullary leucocythæmia ; they are perhaps due to a different cause and represent a distinct disease. When I was in practice in North Shields, a remarkable case of acute leucocythæmia came under my notice. The notes of the clinical history are briefly as follows :—

Case of Acute Leucocythæmia : Rapid Recovery under Quinine.*—A labourer, aged 35, who lived in a damp insanitary house on the banks of the Tyne, came under my care in the year 1870. He had been ill for two or three weeks before I saw him. The disease had developed rapidly ; it was, in short, acute. There was some, though not marked, febrile disturbance. I have no note as to whether the onset was attended with rigors. The patient was remarkably pale and cachectic-looking ; his colour resembled that of pernicious anæmia more than anything else. The spleen was greatly enlarged ; it extended down almost to the pelvis, filling at least one half of the abdomen ; the lymphatic glands were not enlarged ; there were no hæmorrhages. The blood contained an enormous excess of white blood cells. Under the microscope, the white blood corpuscles seemed quite as numerous as the red. At that time, clinical physicians were not in the habit of counting the blood, and I cannot say what the exact proportion of white to red blood cells was ; further, we were not then able to differentiate the different forms of white corpuscles in the way that we can do now ; I can say nothing therefore on this point, but the appearance of the blood was in every

---

* This case is not included in the five cases I have observed in my series of 14,777 consecutive cases of medical diseases.

way characteristic and typical of leucocythæmia. I was well acquainted with the disease, splenic leucocythæmia or leucocythæmia as it was then simply termed, from Bennett's teaching and from cases which I had seen in the Edinburgh Royal Infirmary. I of course came to the conclusion that the patient was suffering from leucocythæmia and that he would die ; but taking into account his insanitary surroundings, I determined to try the effect of large doses of quinine and of the tincture of the perchloride of iron. Under this treatment, the symptoms rapidly subsided and the enlargement of the spleen and the excess of white corpuscles disappeared in the course of a few weeks' time.

I was at the time disposed to think that in this case the condition was more closely allied to malaria than to leucocythæmia; but I now know that in ordinary malarial poisoning a marked excess of white blood corpuscles such as was present in this case is not developed. In acute malarial poisoning, there is rapid destruction of the red blood cells, and diminution of the leucocytes.*

I mention the case in proof of the fact that the presence of an enlarged spleen and of an enormous increase in the white blood corpuscles is not necessarily indicative of the chronic and usually fatal disease to which the term splenic leucocythæmia used to be applied.

A considerable number of cases of acute lymphatic leucocythæmia have of recent years been described—Stengel states that the total number is now more than 40†—but they appear always to have been fatal. The case which I have just recorded is, so far as I know, unique, inasmuch as it ended in complete recovery, and that, so far as I could judge from the mere microscopical characters of the unstained blood, the white corpuscles were of large size and coarsely granulated, in other words the case was one of acute spleno-medullary (and not of lymphatic) leucocythæmia.

Whether cases of acute leucocythæmia are due to the same cause (acting in a more intense and virulent degree) as the ordinary chronic form of leucocythæmia has not as yet been determined.

The differential diagnosis of spleno-medullary leucocythæmia

---

* With regard to the condition of the white cells in malaria Cabot makes the following statement :--The number of leucocytes is usually subnormal, but shows a slight increase at the beginning of the paroxysm. Following this increase there is a rapid decrease continuing throughout the paroxysm. The small number of leucocytes is to be seen at the end of the paroxysm when the temperature is subnormal. From this time it shows a gradual increase until the beginning of the next attack (Billings).

In a general way the white cells follow the same course as do the red.

The differential count shows a lymphocytosis whenever the white cells are subnormal, the larger forms of young cells being especially numerous, while the adult cells and eosinophiles are scanty.

† "Twentieth Century Practice of Medicine," Vol. vii., p. 436.

and of lymphatic leucocythæmia.—In both, the blood may contain an enormous excess of white blood corpuscles ; and in both, the spleen and lymphatic glands may be enlarged. The more important points of distinction are as follows :—

(1.) The enlargement of the spleen is usually much greater in spleno-medullary leucocythæmia than in lymphatic leucocythæmia.

(2.) In spleno-medullary leucocythæmia many of the white corpuscles are large and coarsely granulated ; the increase of the white blood corpuscles is chiefly due to an increase of the large nucleated cells which do not stain with eosin, which do not exhibit active amœboid movements on the warm stage, and which appear to be identical with cells which are normally present in the medulla of the bones (*myelocytes*); the eosinophile cells may be, but are not necessarily, greatly increased in number. In the spleno-medullary form of leucocythæmia, nucleated red blood corpuscles, often of large size (megaloblasts), are usually present in considerable numbers.

In typical cases of lymphatic leucocythæmia, the increase of the leucocytes is almost entirely due to an increase of the uninucleated white corpuscles, large or small, but especially of the small lymphocytes which are normally present in the blood in moderate proportion ; while myelocytes are either absent or present only in small proportion, and nucleated red blood corpuscles are not present, or are only present in very small numbers.

In short, in typical and uncomplicated cases of spleno-medullary and lymphatic leucocythæmia respectively, the microscopical characters of the blood are totally different, and enable us to distinguish the two conditions with absolute certainty. The essential feature of the blood in most (typical) cases of spleno-medullary leucocythæmia is the great excess of myelocytes (which constitute on the average 30 per cent. at least of the total white corpuscles which are present) ; while the essential feature of the blood of the lymphatic variety is the great excess of the uninucleated white corpuscles (which constitute on the average at least 90 per cent. of the total white corpuscles which are present).

(3.) In many (most) cases of spleno-medullary leucocythæmia the lymphatic glands are not enlarged ; whereas in the great majority of cases of lymphatic leucocythæmia the lymphatic glands are enlarged. But, as I have already pointed out, the distinction between the two varieties of leucocythæmia should not be based upon the condition of the lymphatic glands, for in some cases of spleno-medullary leucocythæmia the lymphatic glands are in some degree, though even then usually only slightly, enlarged, and in some exceptional cases which the microscopical examination of the blood shows are cases of lymphatic leucocythæmia the lymphatic glands are (as Dr Robert Muir has shown) not enlarged, while the spleen is greatly enlarged.

The differential diagnosis of leucocythæmia and Hodgkin's disease.—There is no difficulty in distinguishing typical and uncomplicated cases of leucocythæmia (whether of the splenomedullary or lymphatic variety) on the one hand, from typical and uncomplicated cases of Hodgkin's disease on the other. The distinction is at once made by a microscopic examination of the blood ; for in typical and uncomplicated cases of Hodgkin's disease the white blood corpuscles are only slightly or not at all increased in number.

Further, even in those cases of Hodgkin's disease in which the white corpuscles are increased, there is usually no real difficulty in diagnosis. The distinguishing point is the different character of the white corpuscles which are present, viz. :—(1) In the splenomedullary form of leucocythæmia the large number of myelocytes ; (2) in the lymphatic form of leucocythæmia the large number of lymphocytes ; and (3) in Hodgkin's disease with leucocytosis, the large number of polymorpho-nuclear leucocytes.

From this statement it will be gathered that the differential diagnosis of the lymphatic form of leucocythæmia and of Hodgkin's disease can, in most cases, be made by a microscopical examination of the blood. As has been already remarked, the etiological and pathological relationships of these two conditions has not yet been determined, though I am personally disposed to think that they are separate and distinct conditions and not merely (as some authorities suppose) different stages of one and the same disease. Further, I doubt the correctness of the view which supposes that in those cases of Hodgkin's disease in which the white blood corpuscles are in excess, the condition is usually due to a combination of Hodgkin's disease and leucocythæmia, as many authorities seem to suppose.

The differential diagnosis of the spleno-medullary form of leucocythæmia and of the myeloid form of leucocythæmia.—I have already mentioned that some cases of leucocythæmia have been recorded in which the spleen was not enlarged, and in which it was supposed that the lesion was situated in the marrow of the bones. Cases of this kind are exceedingly rare. They are differentiated from cases of the spleno-medullary form of leucocythæmia by the fact that the spleen is not enlarged. But whether spleno-medullary leucocythæmia and pure medullary leucocythæmia (if it occurs) are separate and distinct diseases, or merely, as is perhaps more probable, varieties of the same disease, has not as yet been definitely determined. Indeed, Stengel doubts whether such a condition as pure myeloid leucocythæmia occurs.

The differential diagnosis of spleno-medullary leucocythæmia and of splenic anæmia.—Cases of splenic anæmia (profound anæmia with marked enlargement of the spleen, in which there is no increase of the white blood corpuscles) are, as I have already stated, rare ; no case has come under my own notice. The differential diagnosis can usually be at once made by a microscopical examination of the blood; but it must be remembered that in rare cases of leucocythæmia the excess of white corpuscles disappears either temporarily as the result of treatment or before death. Now if the case should happen to be seen for the first time, when the blood is free from an excess of white corpuscles, the true nature of the case might, and probably would, be overlooked.

The differential diagnosis of leucocythæmia and of pernicious anæmia.—This presents no difficulty. The enlargement of the spleen and the enormous increase in the white blood corpuscles are quite distinctive. Some authorities have assumed that there is some relationship between spleno-medullary leucocythæmia and pernicious anæmia ; for cases have, it is said, been met with in which the blood, which in the earlier stages presented the characters of leucocythæmia, assumed in the later stages the characters, or some of the characters, of pernicious anæmia, the excess of white blood corpuscles entirely disappearing and the blood changes characteristic of pernicious anæmia being ultimately developed. That some such alterations in the blood may occur is perhaps not to be wondered at, considering that in both diseases (splenomedullary anæmia and pernicious anæmia) the medulla of the bones is diseased ; but that leucocythæmia may be transformed into true pernicious anæmia is another matter and requires, I think, further demonstration before it can be accepted as a fact.

PROGNOSIS.

This is most unfavourable. In the vast majority of cases of spleno-medullary leucocythæmia, the disease progresses steadily downwards and ultimately terminates in death, though intercurrent periods of improvement not unfrequently occur. A fatal issue is, however, not invariable. I have already referred to a case of acute splenic leucocythæmia in which complete recovery took place ; and in the ordinary chronic variety of the disease recovery is said occasionally, though very rarely, to have occurred under the influence of arsenic, oxygen inhalations, and other measures of treatment to which I will presently refer. But speaking generally, in the present position of our therapeutic knowledge, the treatment of leucocythæmia is most unsatisfactory.

The average duration of the disease in typical and well-marked cases is usually said to be from one to three years. The lymphatic variety seems in most cases to run a more rapid course than the spleno-medullary form, the usual average being from four weeks to four months.

The marked tendency to hæmorrhages and to inflammatory lesions is a very important point in connection with the prognosis. In those cases in which external or internal bleeding (epistaxis in some cases excepted *) occurs, and in which vomiting and diarrhœa are prominent symptoms, the prognosis is most unfavourable. A rapid diminution of the red corpuscles in spite of treatment is also unfavourable.

The occurrence of head symptoms, which are usually only developed shortly before death, is of the gravest significance. Intercurrent attacks of bronchitis, œdema of the lungs and pneumonia are usually fatal.

TREATMENT.

The same general measures which have been previously recommended in cases of chlorosis and pernicious anæmia should be adopted. The patient should be kept at rest in bed in a well-ventilated, sunny room. Anything which is likely to cause cardiac strain or mental excitement should be avoided. If there is any suspicion of malaria the patient should be removed to a more salubrious district.

The diet must be carefully regulated ; anything which is likely to produce vomiting and diarrhœa should be prohibited.

Laxative and purgative medicines should be prescribed with caution, for in leucocythæmia as in Addison's disease intractable diarrhœa may be produced by a comparatively mild purgative and may prove fatal.

Amongst drug remedies, quinine and arsenic are by far the most important, more especially arsenic. There is no doubt that

---

* The mere occurrence of epistaxis is not necessarily of serious significance ; slight bleedings from the nose may occur in the course of chronic cases without any marked deterioration of the general condition ; continued bleeding from the nose and large bleedings are unfavourable.

in some cases of leucocythæmia temporary improvement has resulted from the continued administration of gradually increasing doses of arsenic. In those cases in which vomiting is prominent, the arsenic may be given subcutaneously. So far as I know, it has not yet been definitely determined whether arsenic is more beneficial in the spleno-medullary or the lymphatic forms of the disease, though I am disposed to think that it is probably more beneficial in the lymphatic variety. Feeding with bone-marrow also, I think, deserves a trial; it may possibly produce benefit, for there is reason, as I have previously stated, to believe that in spleno-medullary leucocythæmia the bone-marrow is always diseased and is in fact the primary seat of the lesion.

Feeding with splenic extract or splenic tissue has also been recommended. I have not had the opportunity of observing the effects in any case; so far as I know it is useless; and this is, in fact, only what one would on *à priori* grounds have anticipated.

Inhalations of oxygen have in some cases been attended with marked benefit, and in any future cases which come under my notice I shall certainly give this plan of treatment a thorough trial. In other cases this plan of treatment has proved useless.

In those cases in which the anæmia is marked, iron may be tried. Iodine has also been recommended. Possibly in some cases the iodide of iron may be beneficial; I have tried it and I think in one case with some temporary benefit.

Local measures have also been recommended with the object of producing contraction of the enlarged spleen—painting with iodine, the application of mercurial ointment, of cold, and of the faradic current over the enlarged spleen. In some cases these measures are perhaps attended with a certain measure of temporary success. The faradic current is perhaps the most effective; under its use, the enlarged spleen in some cases undoubtedly contracts, but the effect so far as I know is merely temporary; I doubt whether it produces any definite or distinct influence upon the course of the disease. Several years ago, I tried the effect of galvano-puncture in one case of spleno-medullary leucocythæmia which was under my care in the Newcastle Infirmary. The result was unsatisfactory; for although properly insulated needles, such as are used in the treatment of aneurism, were employed, a local peritonitis resulted. The patient died shortly afterwards; but it is only right to say that the operation was practised as a last resource, after all other means had been employed, and when the patient had apparently only a few days to live.

Excision of the spleen has also been practised, but the results of the operation are not in the least encouraging. In the great majority of cases, the operation has only been attempted in the last stages of the disease in which there is a strong tendency to death from bleeding. In the earlier stages, the operation is perhaps attended with less danger, but the results in the cases which have been operated upon (according to Stengel one success in twenty operations) prove, in my opinion, that the operation is unjustifiable. Further, it is extremely doubtful, even if the enlarged spleen could be safely removed, whether the effect would be satisfactory and curative.

In the present position of our knowledge, the systematic administration of arsenic in gradually increasing doses, of quinine, and of oxygen inhalations seem to be the measures which are most likely to be attended with benefit. But there is, I think, every *à priori* reason to believe that in the future, when our knowledge of the exact pathology and etiology of the disease is more advanced, some more efficient and satisfactory means of treatment will be discovered.

Quite recently Dr William Ewart has advised the administration of carbonic acid gas in the form of inhalations.* The details of a case in which I have employed the remedy are given below. I am disposed to think that the rapid disappearance of the leucocytes from the blood, which took place in that case during the treatment, was probably due to the arsenic or to the oxygen, or to both of these remedies, rather than to the mercurial inunctions or the carbonic acid inhalations. The notes are as follows :—

A Case of Spleno-Medullary Leucocythæmia, in which, under treatment, the white corpuscles rapidly fell from 210,000 per cubic millimetre to 1,600 per cubic millimetre.

A. H., aged 44, schoolmaster, married, was admitted to the Edinburgh Royal Infirmary on 23rd September 1898, suffering from spleno-medullary leucocythæmia.

Previous history.—The patient enjoyed excellent health until a year ago. For some years he has resided in a healthy seaside place ; he has never suffered from malaria. Seven years ago, he had an attack of influenza ; for some years he has been somewhat liable to take cold and has had several sharp attacks of coryza.

Last Christmas, he had an attack of influenza and has never felt quite well since ; he has been less vigorous and has got somewhat paler and thinner.

In March last, he suffered for some days from a stabbing pain in the left side (region of the spleen) ; it was thought to be rheumatic. *Some six weeks ago,* he

---

* "British Medical Journal," 23rd July 1898, p. 235.

had an attack of diarrhœa. *Three weeks ago*, he had an attack of localised peritonitis ; it commenced with a shiver and was characterised by severe pain and tenderness on pressure in the left side of the abdomen, and fever, the highest temperature reached being 102° F. A large tumour was then found to be present in the left side of the abdomen. During this illness, he was confined to bed for a fortnight ; as soon as he was able to travel (9th September), he was sent to me, and I prescribed arsenic.

On 23rd September 1898, the patient was admitted to the Infirmary.

Family history.—Unimportant.

Present condition.—Is a tall, somewhat spare, man, not very muscular, though fairly well nourished. His complexion, which is naturally florid, is somewhat yellow and sallow, but there is no marked anæmia to the naked eye, the lips being well coloured. The temperature is 99° F.; pulse 80.

Spleen.—The abdomen is considerably distended, the greater part of the left half and a portion of the right half of the cavity being occupied by a solid tumour which presents all the characteristic features of an enlarged spleen.

Below, the tumour extends to within an inch of the middle of Poupart's ligament ; to the right, it extends at its lower end fully two inches to the right of the umbilicus ; above, in the mid-axillary line, to the 6th rib ; to the left, not quite back to the spinal column.

The anterior border of the tumour is sharp and well defined, and in the anterior border a very distinct notch can be felt. The tumour moves with respiration and seems to overlap the colon. The tumour is very firm and resisting ; its surface appears to be smooth. Over the lower end of the tumour the patient still complains of some tenderness on pressure (the remains of the attack of peritonitis described above). On 9th September, rough friction could be heard over the middle part of the enlarged spleen.

Blood.—On microscopical examination, the blood was found to contain a very large excess of leucocytes, most of them of large size. The exact character of the blood, on 19th September, was as follows :—

A drop of blood obtained by puncturing the ear looked quite normal to the naked eye. The red corpuscles numbered 2,600,000 per cubic millimetre ; and the hæmoglobin equalled 54 per cent. The red corpuscles formed rouleaux in the normal manner ; and, with very few exceptions, were of normal size and shape, a few being tailed (slight poikilocytosis), and a few larger and smaller than normal. In the numerous stained films which were examined I was only able to detect two nucleated red corpuscles ; one was of normal size, the other, which contained two nuclei, was twice the size of a normal red corpuscle.

The white corpuscles numbered 210,000 per cubic millimetre. They consisted almost entirely of ordinary polymorpho-nuclear leucocytes and of myelocytes ; the uninucleated white corpuscles (lymphocytes) were (relatively) much reduced in number ; very few eosinophile cells were present. In a few, but very few, of the white corpuscles karyokynetic figures were observed.

On 28th September, the relative proportion of the different forms of white blood corpuscles was, I calculated after very careful counting of three microscopic films, as follows :—

Polymorpho-nuclear - -	67 per cent. (normal=65 to 70 per cent.).
Myelocytes - - -	29 per cent. (normal=0).
Uninucleated (lymphocytes)	$3\frac{1}{2}$ to 4 per cent. (normal=25 per cent.).
Eosinophile cells - -	$\frac{1}{2}$ or less per cent. (normal=$\frac{1}{2}$ to 4 per cent.).

Dr Gulland was kind enough to make an independent count ; his results, which are practically speaking identical with my own, are given in the following table :—

TABLE SHOWING THE PERCENTAGE OF THE DIFFERENT FORMS OF WHITE CORPUSCLES AT DIFFERENT DATES.

Form of White Corpuscles.	1,000 Corpuscles counted.		500 Corpuscles counted (not enough to count more).		
	28th Sept.	9th Oct.	15th Oct.	21st Oct.	4th Nov.
	Per cent.	Per cent.	Per cent.	Per cent.	Per cent.
Polymorpho-nuclear neutrophiles - - - -	69	70	91	75	62
Myelocytes - - - -	26½	25	3	5	7
Lymphocytes - - -	3½	4	5	20	31
Eosinophiles - - -	1	1	1+	...	...
Total - -	100	100	100	100	100
	B*	G†	G	B	G

Nucleated red corpuscles.—In the count of 28th September, there was *one* nucleated red corpuscle—a normoblast ; this was the only nucleated red corpuscle seen in the whole series of films.

The lymphatic glands are not enlarged.

Heart.—The apex is somewhat higher than normal, being situated in the 4th interspace, just below the left nipple. A soft systolic murmur, not heard in the back, is present in the mitral area. A well-marked *venous hum* is present in the neck. The *pulse* numbers 80 per minute, and is soft in character. The *feet* are slightly swollen. *Lungs* normal. *Liver* apparently normal ; in the line of the nipple the liver dulness extends from the 4th rib above to the costal margin below. *Kidneys.*—The urine is normal in quantity, acid, specific gravity 1,015 ; it deposits a copious sediment of urates and on heating throws down a precipitate which is only partly cleared by the addition of an acid (both albumen and phosphates). No casts were detected in the sediment and in the course of a few days after the patient's admission to hospital the albumen almost entirely disappeared. The albumen which was present on admission was serum albumen ; there was no peptone and no blood or sugar. *Nervous system* normal. The *optic discs* are pale ; there are no hæmorrhages in the retinæ.

Treatment.—From the 9th to the 23rd of September, the patient was treated with arsenic.

After his admission to the hospital, the arsenic was continued in gradually increasing doses, the maximum dose reached being 49 drops per diem.

On *24th September,* mercurial ointment was rubbed over the spleen ; the inunctions were continued daily until 27th October ; no ptyalism or other indications of constitutional disturbance resulted.

* B = Dr Bramwell's films.   † G = Dr Gulland's films.

On *27th September*, inhalations of carbonic acid gas and oxygen were commenced ; the inhalations were given three times daily, at first, for five minutes at a time, the duration of the inhalations being gradually increased to half an hour, three times daily. The gas from a cylinder of compressed carbonic acid gas and from a cylinder of compressed oxygen was conducted through a large bottle of water, and the mixture inhaled by the patient. No perceptible effect (alteration in colour, or dyspnœa, etc.) was observed as the result of the inhalations ; and the patient stated that he felt no difficulty in breathing or other uncomfortable effects (sensations). On *17th October*, the carbonic acid was stopped.

Subsequent Progress of the Case.—*26th September.*—Less pain over the enlarged spleen.

27th September.—Red corpuscles = 2,184,000 per c.mm.; white corpuscles = 130,000 per c.mm.; hæmoglobin = 50 per cent.

29th September.—No pain or tenderness over the enlarged spleen.

5th October.—Complains of slight pain over the enlarged spleen ; for the past two days there has been some diarrhœa ; the enlargement of the spleen is distinctly less.

9th October.—The abdomen at the level of the umbilicus measures 34 inches.

20th October.—Circumference of abdomen = 30 inches ; spleen considerably less enlarged. Red corpuscles = 2,300,000 ; white corpuscles, 6,200 per cubic millimetre ; hæmoglobin = 60 per cent.

25th October.—The temperature rose to 101° F.

27th October.—Is still feverish (temperature = 102.2° F.) ; a papular erythema covers the abdomen, trunk and upper part of the thighs ; tongue slightly furred ; no sore throat. The red corpuscles have fallen to 1,500,000 and the white corpuscles to 1,600 per c.mm.; the hæmoglobin = 35 per cent. The mercury to be discontinued.

1st November.—The eruption is fading ; the temperature is to-day 99°, and the patient feels better ; the enlargement of the spleen is considerably less. On microscopical examination, the freshly-drawn (unstained) blood appears to be quite normal ; the red corpuscles are normally shaped, and the white corpuscles are not in excess. In stained films the few white corpuscles which are present are seen, with few exceptions, to be lymphocytes and polymorpho-nuclear neutrophiles ; a few myelocytes and a few small eosinophile corpuscles are present.

4th November.—The temperature rose last night to 103° ; the rash is brighter and more extensive to-day, and is more marked on the back of the trunk, the limbs and face.

5th November.—Morning temperature normal, evening temperature 103.6° ; pulse 114 ; respirations 20.

7th November.—On the left arm and lower part of the back the eruption is purpuric in character. The upper eyelids are much swollen ; spleen smaller ; friction heard over it.

10th November.—Eruption fading, and skin beginning to desquamate ; face and eyelids still swollen. Dr Welsh examined films of blood, taken from the purpuric patch over the lower part of the back, for micro-organisms, but found none.

12th November.—Temperature normal ; very free desquamation on the face, limbs and trunk ; one or two small unhealthy-looking ulcers on the sides of the tongue ; no sore throat ; diarrhœa. Urine not dark ; heavy deposit of mucus, urates ; small quantity of albumen.

23rd November. — Looking and feeling much better ; desquamation still present ; eczema of right ear ; spleen considerably smaller.

The condition of the blood at different dates was as follows :—

TABLE SHOWING THE CONDITION OF THE BLOOD AT DIFFERENT DATES.

Date.	Red Corpuscles.	Hæmoglobin.	Colour Index (corrected).	White Corpuscles.	Proportion of Whites to Reds.
		Per cent.			
19th September.	2,600,000	54	1.1	210,000	1 to 12
25th „	2,000,000	56	1.5	200,000	1 „ 10
28th „	2,184,000	50	1.2	130,000	1 „ 16
1st October.				156,000	
3rd „	2,000,000	50	1.3	109,000	1 „ 18
9th „		...		81,450	...
11th „	2,640,000	56	1.1	62,500	1 „ 42
15th „	2,070,000	54	1.4	36,000	1 „ 57
18th „	3,000,000	56	1.	7,000	1 „ 428
20th „	2,300,000	60	1.4	6,200	1 „ 370
23rd „	3,000,000	60	1.1	4,500	1 „ 666
27th „	1,500,000	35	1.3	1,600	1 „ 937
3rd November.	2,100,000			2,400	1 „ 875
11th „	1,250,000	45	2.	4,500	1 „ 277
17th „	3,125,000	50	.8	2,600	1 „ 1201

Remarks.—This case of spleno-medullary leucocythæmia presents several points of great interest. The more important are :—(1) The small number of eosinophile cells ; (2) the relatively small number of lymphocytes ; (3) the remarkable diminution in the number of leucocytes which occurred during, and apparently as the result of, the treatment ; (4) the fact that when the leucocytes had fallen to 1,600 per c.mm., some myelocytes were still present in the blood ; (5) the very scanty number of nucleated red corpuscles which were present, even when the leucocythæmia was at its height ; (6) the fever and skin eruption which occurred during the course of the disease, the cause of which is not apparent ; (7) the great diminution of the red corpuscles which occurred as the result of this febrile attack ; (8) the absence of any leucocytosis during the febrile attack ; (9) the fact that the individual red corpuscles contained more than the normal amount of hæmoglobin (high colour-index) ; in this respect the condition of the blood resembled that of pernicious anæmia.

HODGKIN'S DISEASE.

Definition or Short Description.—The essential features of Hodgkin's disease, to which the synonyms *Lymphatic Anæmia, Lymphadenosis, Pseudoleukæmia, Malignant Lymphoma, Lymphadenoma, Adénie, Lymph-adénie*, etc., have been applied, are :—(1) A widespread non-caseating and non-suppurating enlargement of the lymphatic glands (a generalised hypertrophy of the lymphatic glands, Trousseau termed it); and (2) certain constitutional symptoms, amongst which weakness and emaciation are the most important.

In the advanced stages of the disease, nodules or deposits, as they have been termed, of adenoid or lymphoid tissue may be developed in the spleen and other parts of the body, in which adenoid or lymphoid tissue normally abounds (tonsils, solitary glands of the intestine, Peyer's patches, thymus gland, etc.), and, in some cases, in organs and tissues in which adenoid tissue is only very sparingly present, or is not present, normally (liver, kidney, suprarenal capsules, skin, etc.).

Enlargement of the spleen is a clinical feature of the disease, which is of considerable diagnostic importance. A certain amount of anæmia is present in most cases of the disease, at some period or other of their course ; but, in other cases (though this, perhaps, only occurs at certain stages of the case), the red blood corpuscles are more numerous than normal.

In some cases, in which the glandular enlargements and constitutional symptoms characteristic of Hodgkin's disease are present, the blood contains a large excess of white corpuscles. Some authorities regard cases of this kind as cases of Hodgkin's disease to which lymphatic leucocythæmia has been superadded ; but, as I have already pointed out, the correctness of this opinion is, in many cases at all events, extremely doubtful.

Hodgkin's disease is usually a chronic, progressive, and incurable condition, though acute cases, and cases which end in recovery, occasionally occur.

Future observation will probably show that several different conditions have hitherto been grouped together under the common term Hodgkin's disease; in other words, it is highly probable that more than one morbid process may produce the group of *clinical* symptoms (the form of enlargement of the lymphatic glands and the constitutional symptoms) which are supposed to be characteristic of Hodgkin's disease. By this statement I do not mean to imply that Hodgkin's disease is not a definite and distinct clinical entity; but merely to emphasise the great difficulty of recognising the condition during life, and of distinguishing the clinical entity, which we term Hodgkin's disease, from the other conditions which more or less closely resemble it.

Historical Note.—Cases of this interesting disease had been described before the year 1832 ; indeed, Hodgkin himself refers to two cases figured by Carswell, and termed by him " Cancer cerebriformis of the lymphatic glands " ; but it was not until Hodgkin published his important paper, " On some Morbid Appearances of the Absorbent Glands and Spleen," that the distinctive features of the disease were definitely recognised, that the relationship of the enlargement of the lymphatic glands with disease of the spleen was appreciated, and that the peculiar form of the glandular enlargement which characterises the disease was differentiated from the scrofulous and cancerous enlargements of the lymphatic glands with which it had been previously confounded.*

Hodgkin described the glandular enlargement in the following terms :—

" It may be observed that notwithstanding some differences in structure, to be noticed hereafter, all these cases agree in the remarkable enlargement of the absorbent glands accompanying the larger arteries—namely, the glandulæ concatenatæ in the neck, the axillary and inguinal glands, and those accompanying the aorta in the thorax and abdomen. That, as far as could be ascertained from observation, or from what could be collected from the history of the cases, this enlargement of the glands appeared to be a primitive affection of those bodies rather than the result of an irritation propagated to them from some ulcerated surface or other inflamed texture, through the medium of their inferent vessels, and that although, in some instances, the glands so enlarged may contain a little concrete inorganisable matter, such as is known to result from what is called scrofulous inflammation, it is obvious that this circumstance is not an essential character, but rather an accidental concomitant to the idiopathic interstitial enlargement of the absorbent glandular structure throughout the body. That unless the word inflammation be allowed to have a more

---

* As I have already pointed out, the distinction between the glandular enlargements due to Hodgkin's disease and to scrofula is by no means so certain, during life, as this statement implies.

indefinite and loose meaning than is generally assigned to it, this affection of the glands can scarcely be attributed to that cause, since they are unattended with pain, heat, and other ordinary symptoms of inflammation, and are not necessarily accompanied by any alteration in the cellular and other surrounding structures, and do not show any disposition to go on to the production of pus or any other acknowledged product of inflammation, except where, as in the cases above alluded to, inflammation may have supervened as an accidental affection of the hypertrophied structure. Nor can the enlargement in question, with any better reason, be attributed to the formation of any of those adventitious structures, the production of which I have already had occasion to describe, and have referred to the type of compound adventitious serous cysts. Notwithstanding the different characters which this enlargement may present, it appears, nearly in all cases, to consist of pretty uniform texture throughout, and this rather to be the consequence of a general increase of every part of the gland than of a hard structure developed within it, and pushing the original structure aside, as when ordinary tuberculous material is deposited in these bodies. At the same time, it must be admitted that the new material by which the enlargement is effected presents various degrees of organisability, which in some instances is extremely slight, and appears incompetent to maintain the vitality of the affected gland. In such cases the new structure will generally become opaque, soften, or break down, and, acting as a foreign irritating body, excite irritation and lead to the formation of abscess." *

Since the year 1832, numerous important papers and monographs have been written on the subject, some of the most valuable being contributed by physicians in this country. In the year 1855, Sir Samuel Wilks independently described the disease in a paper entitled, "Cases of a Peculiar Enlargement of the Lymphatic Glands frequently associated with Disease of the Spleen." † In a subsequent communication, he proposed to give the name "Hodgkin's Disease" to the disease. ‡ Lymphatic anæmia is another term which the same authority (Wilks) has applied to the disease. Bonfils and Trousseau, whose descriptions of the disease are of great value and importance, applied the term *Adénie* to it. One of the best accounts of the disease in any language is that of Gowers, in Russell Reynolds' *System of Medicine* (vol. v., p. 306).

Hodgkin's disease, or true lymphadenoma (provided that the tubercular cases which are apt to be confounded with it are rigidly excluded), is probably a very rare disease. In my series of 14,777 consecutive cases of medical disease, 12 cases were diagnosed as Hodgkin's disease; but I have no doubt that in some of these cases the glandular enlargement was in reality tubercular.

---

* "Medico-Chirurgical Transactions," vol. xvii., p. 85.
† Guy's Hospital Reports, vol. ii. (1855), p. 131.
‡ Guy's Hospital Reports, vol. xi. (1855), p. 56.

Morbid Anatomy.

As has been previously stated, the essential lesion in Hodgkin's disease is a peculiar enlargement of the lymphatic glands, together with, in many cases, the development of deposits of lymphoid or adenoid tissue in the spleen and other organs and tissues of the body. Whether the presence of lymphoid deposits in the spleen or other organs and tissues is a necessary and essential feature of the disease is perhaps a debatable point ; in other words, it is questionable whether only those cases should be considered to be cases of Hodgkin's disease in which, in addition to the enlargement of the lymphatic glands, lymphoid deposits are present in the spleen and other organs and tissues.

The Condition of the Lymphatic Glands.—The *extent and distribution* of the glandular enlargement varies in different cases. In some cases, all the glands in the body (external and internal) are involved, and lymphatic glands may become apparent in situations (such as the popliteal space and at the bend of the elbow) in which they cannot be detected (during life) in conditions of health. In other cases, the glandular involvement is less extensive ; but, as has already been pointed out, the glandular enlargement is not merely *local* (confined, for example, to the cervical glands), as a scrofulous enlargement usually is.

The *size* to which the individual glands and glandular masses may attain is very variable.

In many cases, the individual glands remain separate and distinct ; in other cases, the enlarged glands are firmly adherent, and matted or welded together in the form of large masses or tumours. In cases of this kind, various secondary alterations and lesions due to pressure, inflammation, or infiltration may be developed in the tissues and organs with which the masses of enlarged glands are in contact. When, for example, the bronchial and mediastinal glands are enlarged, the root of the lung, the lung tissue itself, the great veins in the thorax, the recurrent laryngeal nerve, etc., may be implicated ; or pleurisy and empyema may be developed.

The *consistency* of the enlarged glands varies in different cases. In most cases, the enlarged glands are firm, though they have not the stony hardness of the enlargement due to cancer ; in other cases, the consistency is softer. Consequently, two varieties—a hard and a soft form—are described.

To the naked eye, the character of the glandular enlargement is very similar to that which occurs in the lymphatic form of leucocythæmia.

On section, in both the hard and the soft varieties, the enlarged glands present a more or less homogeneous appearance ; there is usually no appearance of softening, breaking down, caseation, or suppuration. In well-marked and typical cases of the disease, the distinction between the cortical and medullary portions of the gland can no longer be recognised.

But it is important to note that, although in typical cases of Hodgkin's disease the glandular enlargements present the pathological characters which have just been described, in some cases in which the glandular enlargements during life present all the characteristic *clinical* features of Hodgkin's disease, the enlarged glands are found after death to be caseous and tubercular. I have seen several cases of this kind, and I have been so impressed with the difficulty that there is in some cases, more especially in children and in young subjects, of differentiating during life the glandular enlargements due to Hodgkin's disease from that due to tubercle, that I now have great hesitation in committing myself to a definite diagnosis of Hodgkin's disease and in excluding tubercle, unless the spleen is distinctly enlarged, or unless there is evidence of the presence of lymphoid deposits in the other organs and tissues. It is certain, I think, that the frequency with which enlarged glands, which during life present all the appearances characteristic of Hodgkin's disease, are found after death to be tubercular has been much under-estimated.

On *microscopical examination,* it is seen that, in typical cases, the affected glands are for the most part composed of small round cells, resembling leucocytes or ordinary lymph cells, and of fibrous tissue, arranged in the form of a network or in trabeculæ. A few large multi-nucleated corpuscles are in some cases also present, and the presence of myelocytes and nucleated red blood corpuscles have in exceptional cases been described.

The relative proportion of the cells to the fibroid tissue varies in different cases. In the soft variety, the whole section may, at first sight, appear to be composed of cells, the delicate fibrous network, in the meshes of which the cells are situated, being only seen after special methods of preparation (pencilling or teasing). In the hard variety, the fibrous tissue is relatively much more abundant ; the fibrous septa of the gland are thickened, and, in some cases, dense bands of fibrous tissue may be seen crossing the section in various directions, and forming the trabecular structure described above.

In some cases, spindle cells with oval nuclei are present in addition to the ordinary fibroid elements.

Spleen.—In the great majority of cases of Hodgkin's disease, the spleen is enlarged, though the enlargement is not as a rule very great.

In most cases, the enlargement of the spleen is due to localised deposits of lymphoid tissue, which look like whitish nodules or masses of suet or bacon-fat, deposited here and there in the splenic substance. The nodules in the spleen are for the most part due to pathological alterations in the Malpighian bodies (lymphoid tissue), similar in nature to those which are present in the lymphatic glands.

In some cases, the enlargement of the spleen is uniform, and no lymphoid deposits are visible to the naked eye.

Liver.—The liver is in some cases enlarged, and studded with lymphoid deposits.

Lymphoid deposits in other organs and tissues.—Lymphoid deposits and nodules are frequently developed in the gastro-alimentary tract, especially in the *stomach* and the *small intestine* (the Peyer's patches and solitary glands are very apt to be affected) ; and are sometimes seen at the back of the *tongue*, in the *tonsils*, and even in the walls of the *œsophagus*.

The *thymus gland* is in some cases enlarged and infiltrated with lymphoid cells. Lymphoid deposits and nodules may also be present in the *marrow of the bones, kidneys, suprarenal capsules, thyroid gland, heart, pleura, ovary, skin, etc.*

The deposits of lymphoid tissue in the spleen, liver, and other organs, present the same histological characters as those which are present in the enlarged glands themselves ; in other words, they consist of lymphoid cells embedded in a fibrous reticulum.

In some cases, the vessels of the enlarged glands, of the spleen, liver, kidney, etc., present evidences of waxy (amyloid) degeneration ; but the waxy change is not usually extensive.

Bone-marrow.—The changes in the bone-marrow, when they occur, appear to be very similar to those which occur in the lymphatic form of leucocythæmia ; but, so far as I know, it has not yet been shown that the character of the leucocytes which infiltrate the bone-marrow in the two affections is identical. As has been already stated, I am disposed to think that Hodgkin's disease and the lymphatic form of leucocythæmia are distinct conditions, and that this statement applies to most of the cases of Hodgkin's disease, at all events, in which the blood contains an excess of white corpuscles.

ETIOLOGY AND PATHOLOGY.

Age.—Hodgkin's disease may occur at any age, but is most common during childhood, youth, and early adult life. Of 100 cases tabulated by Gowers, 50 occurred before the age of 30, and 64 before the age of 40. In my series of 12 cases, 7 (or 56 per cent.) occurred before the age of 30, and 8 (or 66 per cent.) occurred before the age of 40.

Sex.—Males are much more frequently affected than females. In the 100 cases analysed by Gower, 75 were males, and 25 were females. In my series of 12 cases, 10 (or 83 per cent.) were males, and 2 (or 16 per cent.) were females. From these figures it would therefore appear that the disease is at least three times as common in the male as in the female.

Influence of depressing circumstances, etc. — Depressing influences of all kinds, such as previous ill-health, insufficient food, deficient clothing, insanitary surroundings, intemperance, mental anxiety, etc., seem to favour the production of the disease, but they are clearly only predisposing causes. In some cases, the disease is developed in the midst of perfect health, in persons who have never previously had any severe illness, and in those whose sanitary surroundings and circumstances are altogether satisfactory. Malaria and rickets have in some cases been thought to be causes of the disease. Syphilis does not appear to be a cause of the disease. In some cases, the subjects of Hodgkin's disease have previously suffered from scrofulous enlargement of the lymphatic glands, or have inherited a strong tendency to scrofula; but whether there is any real relationship between scrofula and Hodgkin's disease (true lymphadenoma) is doubtful. In a few (apparently exceptional) cases, active tubercular lesions have been found in the lungs or other organs after death; but whether all of these cases were in reality Hodgkin's disease (true lymphadenoma) is I think very doubtful; for, as I have already stated, cases are not unfrequently met with, especially in young subjects, in which the clinical symptoms and the condition of the enlarged glands during life were typically those of Hodgkin's disease rather than of scrofula, but in which post-mortem examination showed that the glandular enlargement was without doubt tubercular.

Probable exciting cause.—The exact condition or conditions which produce Hodgkin's disease are as yet entirely unknown. On theoretical grounds it is not unreasonable, I think, to suppose that the disease is due to the presence in the blood of some substance or substances which excite the overgrowth or development of lymphoid tissue—possibly some chemical substance (irritant) produced within the body, or some chemical or germ poison or its toxin introduced from without.

Or perhaps the essential cause of the disease consists in some peculiarity of constitution, inherited or acquired, which, in the subjects of Hodgkin's disease, favours the production of an overgrowth of lymphoid tissue, or allows some irritant, which in ordinary healthy individuals would be inoperative, to excite the production of a lymphatic overgrowth.

In some cases, more especially in some of the cases in which generalised lymphatic enlargement is preceded by a strictly local glandular enlargement, local irritation seems to be the exciting cause of the primary (local) glandular swelling. In one of my own cases, chronic irritation and inflammation in the nose, and in another of the throat, seemed undoubtedly to be the starting-point of the condition. In both of these cases the cervical glands were first enlarged. The influence of local peripheral irritation in exciting the primary glandular enlargement has been especially insisted upon by Trousseau. In speaking of the etiology of the disease, he says :*—

"We are thus constrained to conclude that there is a new *special* diathesis, the essential nature of which is unknown, which we call the *lymphatic diathesis.* This diathesis may be described as a tendency in certain persons to present, under the influence of a determining cause, glandular engorgements, at first local, and becoming general in from eighteen months to two years. This glandular engorgement, as I have seen, may consist in a hypergenesis of the normal cellular elements of the lymphatic glands, a hypergenesis which in some cases may invade the glandular corpuscles of the spleen and intestine. The patient, consequently, has anæmia and cachexia, unaccompanied by leucocytosis.

"Adenia, I have said, is a diathesis which has a determining cause. What is this cause, and what is its most common seat? When we attentively peruse the reports of cases of adenia, whether described by others or observed by ourselves, we are struck by the fact that, in the first instance, only one or two glands have been enlarged: some weeks, or it may be two or three months, after the appearance of these swellings, a veritable explosion of glandular tumours occurs in different parts of the body, while, at the same time, the original tumours rapidly increase in size. In the majority of cases the submaxillary are the glands which first become affected : sometimes, however, the first seat of the affection is in the axillary or inguinal glands.

"Whenever there is an acute or chronic engorgement of glands, we must search in the regions which they depurate for some organic lesion to explain the glandular irritation. This rule, which is absolute, will be found to lead to many important results. It is natural, therefore, in a case of general adenia, to inquire what local lesion has occasioned the original engorgement. There are many cases, however, in which no light is thrown upon this question : we must be

---

* "Clinical Medicine," Sydenham Society's Edition, vol. v., p. 206.

satisfied to note that the engorgement commenced in the axillary, inguinal, or maxillary glands—which is provoking.   Viewed along with these incomplete cases, there are others—the cases of Leudet, Potian, and Perrin, and the case of my Stockholm patient—which possess great interest in relation to this question. I have thrice observed that there existed acute or chronic irritation at the great angle of the eye, or in the external auditory passage : and observe, Gentlemen, that the glands first attacked were situated on the same side as the ocular, nasal, or aural lesion, and that the submaxillary and cervical glands of the opposite side, as well as the other glands of the body, were only secondarily attacked. It is, therefore, well worthy of remark that, in the five cases to which I have referred, there were four with inflammatory lachrymal tumour, chronic coryza, and otorrhœa.   One cannot help being struck with this alteration of the skin and mucous membranes, and with the primary glandular alteration.   I ought, however, to remind you that, in one of Leudet's cases, and also in the case for which we are indebted to Perrin, the patients stated that the glandular engorgement began in the axillary region.   Subsequently, however, MM. Leudet and Perrin discovered submaxillary engorgement, so that we may suppose the possibility of that engorgement having existed at the commencement of the adenia, but to so small an extent as not to attract the notice of the patients.

"Be that as it may, it is a fact that, in twelve cases of adenia, there were four in which.there existed lachrymal tumours, a chronic coryza, and an otorrhœa.

"It is not a matter involved in the least doubt—it is a positive fact—that there is a relation between the primary adenopathia and the superficial lesions of skin and mucous membrane.

"As to general consecutive adenia, I cannot understand admitting certain persons to have a predisposition to such a special nature, that one or two lymphatic glands being engorged for a certain short period, in general of variable duration, but nearly always of recent date, should be the starting-point of the generalisation of the malady to the other glands."

In some cases of Hodgkin's disease, micro-organisms have been detected in the blood ; in others, in which a careful search has been made, no micro-organisms have been found.   The probability that the glandular enlargement is due to some form of irritation is very great, and the occurrence of acute cases, such as those described by Dreschfeld, and the frequent development of fever in the course of the disease lend support to this supposition.   Further information and observation on this point are, however, required.   In the present position of our knowledge I do not think one is warranted in going further than this, that the theory which supposes that some of the conditions which are at present grouped together under the common term Hodgkin's disease are due to micro-organisms or their toxins is probable, but as yet not proven.

The exact nature of Hodgkin's disease, or rather of the conditions which may produce the group of clinical symptoms characteristic of Hodgkin's disease, will be further considered in connection with the clinical history, the clinical types, and the diagnosis of the disease.

CLINICAL HISTORY.

Onset and Course.—The onset is usually slow and gradual, and the course usually chronic and progressive, though in some cases periods of distinct improvement occur. In rare cases, the onset is rapid and the course acute. A number of cases of this kind have been recorded by Dreschfeld and other observers.

Clinical Features.—The symptoms which characterise Hodgkin's disease (and the symptoms and physical signs which result from the glandular enlargements which are the essential feature of the disease) are partly local and partly constitutional. The more important may be classed as follows :—

1. Enlargement of the lymphatic glands—visible, tangible, or demonstrable by means of physical examination (*e.g.*, percussion, etc.).

2. Weakness, emaciation, cachexia, and symptoms associated therewith.

3. Anæmia—diminution of the red blood corpuscles, with, in some cases, an excess of white blood corpuscles—and the symptoms which result therefrom.

4. Loss of appetite, dyspepsia, and other symptoms indicative of derangement of the gastro-intestinal functions.

5. Pyrexia.

6. Enlargement of the spleen.

7. Enlargement of the tonsils, of the liver, and it may be of other internal organs, such as the thymus gland or suprarenal capsules.

8. Symptoms and physical signs due to the pressure of the enlarged lymphatic glands upon adjacent structures and parts.

9. Symptoms and physical signs due to inflammatory complications in the neighbourhood of the enlarged glands, and to associated lesions.

It must be clearly and definitely understood that all of the symptoms and clinical alterations, which have just been enumerated, are by no means always present. The clinical picture which different cases of Hodgkin's disease present is, in fact, a very variable one. This is only what one might expect from the fact that the symptoms and physical signs, which are due to the pressure which the enlarged glands exert upon, and the inflammation which the enlarged and diseased glands excite in, the tissues and organs with which they are in immediate contact, necessarily vary in different cases ; and to the circumstance that more than one different pathological condition may probably produce very similar clinical results, viz., glandular enlargements and constitutional symptoms suggestive of Hodgkin's disease.

The only clinical symptoms which can be regarded as constant, though they are not pathognomonic, for they occur in some cases in which the glandular affection is tubercular, are—*firstly*, enlargement (not a mere local but a more or less widespread enlargement) of the lymphatic glands ; and, *secondly*, weakness, emaciation, and (usually) more or less anæmia.

But even with regard to these symptoms, it must be remembered that, in some cases, which appear to be undoubted cases of Hodgkin's disease, the internal lymphatic glands are chiefly, or almost exclusively, affected, and that in such cases a visible and tangible enlargement of the lymphatic glands may not be present; and that, in other cases, even when the enlargement of the lymphatic glands is widespread and well marked, there is little or no anæmia —little or no diminution in the number of the red blood corpuscles as measured by the hæmocytometer, in fact in some cases the number of red blood corpuscles is increased.   Some diminution of the red blood corpuscles is, however, usually present, when the disease is fully developed, and it is probable that a certain degree of anæmia is met with in all typical cases of Hodgkin's disease, at *some period or other of their course.*

In typical cases of Hodgkin's disease, the spleen is usually enlarged ; and pyrexia is generally present.   An excess of white corpuscles in the blood is observed in a certain proportion of cases.

The symptoms and physical signs due to pressure and to local inflammations in the neighbourhood of the enlarged glands are inconstant, and may in fact be termed accidental symptoms.

It may be, and indeed it has been, questioned whether those cases in which the internal lymphatic glands (such as the mediastinal, bronchial, and retro-peritoneal glands) are alone involved, are actually cases of Hodgkin's disease.

As I have more than once pointed out, it is probable that more than one form of lymphatic enlargement is included under the common term Hodgkin's disease ; though in the present position of our knowledge we are unable to differentiate these different varieties of glandular enlargement in the living patient, and perhaps not even in the dead-house.   Perhaps the most satisfactory statement which can at present be made with regard to the glandular enlargement is this :—that only those glandular enlargements should be considered as characteristic of Hodgkin's disease in which several different groups of lymphatic glands are affected, and in which the glandular enlargement is painless, non-suppurating, and non-caseating.   But even this definition is not altogether satisfactory ; for (1) in some cases which, so far as our present means of observation enable us to judge, are cases of Hodgkin's disease, the enlarged lymphatic glands do soften and ulcerate; and (2) in some cases in which the glandular enlargement is widespread, painless, and non-suppurating, the condition is tubercular.

From these statements, and from what I have previously stated in connection with the pathology and etiology of the disease, it will be obvious that our knowledge of the true nature of Hodgkin's disease is in a very unsettled and unsatisfactory condition.

As I have already pointed out in the article on leucocythæmia, I am strongly inclined to think that Hodgkin's disease and lymphatic leucocythæmia are separate and distinct conditions.

Let us now consider the chief symptoms of Hodgkin's disease individually and in detail.

Enlargement of the Lymphatic Glands.—As I have already pointed out, this is the fundamental and characteristic feature of the disease. The clinical features of the glandular enlargement (which are supposed to be special and peculiar) are as follows :—

In the *first* place, the glandular enlargement is not a mere local condition, but is more or less widespread. In the earlier stages of the disease, the enlargement may for a time be limited, or may appear to be limited, to one group of glands; but in well-marked and typical cases, such as those represented in my Atlas of Clinical Medicine, Plates VIII. and IX., and especially in the advanced stages of the disease, all, or almost all, the lymphatic glands throughout the body may be implicated.

The *order* in which the different groups of lymphatic glands are involved is, according to Gowers, as follows :—(1) The cervical; (2) the axillary; (3) the inguinal; (4) the retro-peritoneal; (5) the bronchial; (6) the mediastinal; and (7) the mesenteric.

In some cases, enlarged glands may be felt in the popliteal space or about the elbow; and in rare cases, adenoid deposits may develop in the skin or subcutaneous tissues. In a remarkable case which came under my notice when I was in practice in North Shields, all the glands (external and internal) throughout the body seemed to be enlarged; the skin was thickly studded with innumerable nodules of lymphoid tissue, the largest of which were the size of a pea; the spleen and liver were much enlarged; and both ovaries were transformed into large round tumours, fully the size of cricket balls.

In the *second* place, the glandular enlargement is painless, non-suppurating, and non-caseating in character. In this respect it differs from a simple inflammation or a typical scrofulous enlargement of the glands.

This statement does not, of course, imply that the enlarged glands in Hodgkin's disease are never painful, and that they never suppurate and never caseate. In exceptional cases, some of the enlarged glands may be painful and tender to the touch; in fact, in advanced stages of the disease inflammation of the capsule of the enlarged glands and of the cellular tissue which surrounds the enlarged glands is not uncommon. In other cases, which undoubtedly seem to have been cases of Hodgkin's disease, one or more of the enlarged glands may caseate or suppurate. But these conditions (pain, tenderness on pressure, caseation, and suppuration) are exceptional. They are accidental features. They are in no way characteristic of the disease; in fact, in the great majority of cases, they are absent altogether.

It may perhaps be questioned whether some of the cases in which suppuration and caseation were observed were true examples of the disease. Suppuration and caseation appear to be so exceptional, that in any case of supposed Hodgkin's disease in which several or many of the enlarged glands soften, suppurate, or caseate, the diagnosis should be regarded with suspicion. It must, however, be admitted that suppuration and caseation do occasionally occur. I see no reason why a gland which is enlarged by Hodgkin's disease may not, under certain conditions (irritation, defective blood-supply, etc.), suppurate or caseate or become tubercular, just as I see no reason why a gland or group of glands which is chronically enlarged as the result of scrofula may not become implicated in the general enlargement of Hodgkin's disease. But suppuration and caseation in Hodgkin's disease are exceptional, and should therefore be regarded as accidental, associated, or secondary results.

But, notwithstanding this statement, it must be allowed that cases are every now and again met with in which the clinical symptoms, the nature of the glandular enlargement and the course of the disease, are all characteristic of Hodgkin's disease, and in which the widespread enlargement of the lymphatic glands (painless and non-suppurating) is found on post-mortem examination to be undoubtedly tubercular. The following is a case in point :—

Case of Tubercular Disease of the Cervical, Axillary, Inguinal and Abdominal Glands, with Enlargement of the Liver and Spleen, resembling Hodgkin's Disease.

A. B., aged 16, a scullery-maid, was admitted to Ward 27, Edinburgh Royal Infirmary, on 15th October 1893, suffering from general weakness and glandular enlargements in various parts of the body.

Previous History.—Some of the cervical glands have been enlarged as long as the patient can remember; they never gave her any trouble; they never softened nor suppurated ; the glandular enlargements have never been painful. For several years her teeth have been very bad. Her general health was very good till two years ago ; about this time she was very hard worked as a scullery-maid, and she noticed that lumps (enlarged glands) were developing in both armpits and in both sides of the neck. For the past year she has been getting thinner and weaker, and has occasionally suffered from diarrhœa.

Family History.—None of her near relatives have, so far as she knows, suffered from any tubercular affection ; her parents, brothers, and sisters are strong and well.

Condition on Admission.—The patient is thin and anæmic ; the feet and face are slightly swollen.

Numerous enlarged lymphatic glands are present on both sides of the neck from the chin to the clavicle and behind the angles of the jaw, in both axillæ and in both groins. The enlarged glands are hard and painless, none of them present the slightest indication of softening or suppuration. The enlarged glands vary in size from a hazel-nut to a pigeon's egg ; with few exceptions they are isolated and freely movable, being unadherent either to one another, to the skin, or the surrounding tissues. On the right side of the neck some of the enlarged glands are adherent and matted together. The skin over the enlarged glands is quite natural in appearance.

The abdomen is moderately distended ; the spleen and liver both appear to be enlarged ; a mass of enlarged glands can be felt in the centre of the abdominal cavity ; there is some fluid in the peritoneal cavity.

The temperature is above the normal—about 99° in the morning ; 101°, 102° in the evening. The skin is dry and harsh.

The patient is distinctly anæmic ; the red corpuscles number 3,320,000, and the hæmoglobin = 58 per cent.; the polymorpho-nuclear leucocytes are in slight excess.

There is some impairment of the percussion note in the right infra-scapular region, but no increase of vocal resonance and no moist sounds. There is no cough or expectoration.

The appetite is poor ; the patient complains of thirst ; the bowels are usually moved twice daily ; there have been several attacks of diarrhœa.

The urine contains a considerable quantity of albumen (equal parts of serum albumen, and globulin), no blood, some casts.

The patient has never menstruated.

Diagnosis.—Hodgkin's disease and nephritis, probably amyloid degeneration of the kidneys and intestines.

Treatment.—Arsenic, Easton's syrup, quinine, digitalis, together with nourishing foods, were administered.

Progress of the Case.—There was no improvement. On *23rd* and *31st October* there was troublesome diarrhœa. On *6th November* severe vomiting and collapse. On *9th November* the patient died.

Post-mortem examination made by Dr Leith on 10th November.

External appearances.—Rigidity and lividity present. The lymphatic glands on both sides of the neck, in both axillæ and in both groins, are enlarged, forming firm nodules. The glandular masses in the axillæ are especially large. The individual glands are not greatly enlarged. On section the enlarged glands are found to be caseous, almost without exception ; subsequent microscopical examination showed that they were all tubercular. The *left lung* weighs 14 ozs. ; a depressed scar at apex passes into the lung tissue in the form of fibrous pigmented bands ; no tubercles can be seen around this cicatrix, but it is extremely suspicious of a tubercular origin.   Over the whole section of the lung substance a few small firm nodules, apparently of recent miliary tubercle, are scattered ; these are especially frequent in the deep pleural lymphatics.   The *right lung* weighs 14 oz. ; it shows a similar scar at apex ; in the lung tissue surrounding it there are several caseous areas, evidently tubercular ; and over the general section of the lung there are scattered tubercular nodules of recent origin.

The *heart* is small, but quite healthy.

The *omentum* is everywhere adherent to the pelvis and lateral abdominal walls.   A very large mass of enlarged and caseous glands is present in the abdomen.   The surface of the intestine is covered here and there with flaky-looking organised lymph ; the coils are not glued together.   The pelvic contents are quite shut off from the abdomen by old adhesions.   All the pelvic contents are much matted together.   The left ovary is fairly free and healthy. The right ovary is surrounded by enlarged and indurated glands.

In typical cases, and in the earlier stages of the disease, at all events, the enlarged glands preserve their individuality of contour ; they are not matted or fused together and adherent as scrofulous glands usually are.   The individual glands can be felt as oval or rounded and movable nodules, the surface of which is smooth and even.   The skin covering the enlarged glands is neither adherent nor discoloured.

The degree of density varies in different cases, and, as has been already stated in connection with the morbid anatomy, two varieties —a hard and a soft—have been described.   The consistency of the enlarged glands seems chiefly to depend upon the amount of fibrous tissue which is present.   In some cases, the enlarged glands feel so soft and elastic that they almost appear to fluctuate ; in others, they feel firm and solid throughout, but even in these (fibroid) cases they have not the dense, cartilaginous, or stony hardness which cancerous glands have.   In the earlier stages of those cases in which the glandular enlargements are rapidly developed, the soft form of enlargement is apt to occur.

The size of the individual glands varies greatly in different cases ; the individual glands may attain to the size of a hen's egg, or even larger ; while the glandular masses, as a whole, may be as large as a child's head (see Atlas of Clinical Medicine, Plates IX. and X.).

In the advanced stages of the disease, the corresponding glandular groups on the opposite sides of the body (two sides of the neck, two axillæ, two groins, etc.) are usually both involved ; but the enlargement generally begins on one side and subsequently involves the other ; it rarely happens that the glandular enlargement is so equal and symmetrical as in the case represented in my Atlas, Plate VIII.

In some cases, the glandular masses in the neck, axilla, thorax, abdomen, and groin are all joined together by bands of enlarged glands.

In consequence of the glandular enlargement, marked deformity may be produced (see Atlas of Clinical Medicine, Plate IX.); and the adjacent parts may be displaced or subjected to injurious pressure; the enlarged glands in the neck and sub-maxillary regions may join, and encircle the greater part of the neck.

The symptoms and signs which may be produced by the pressure of the enlarged glands are multifarious; the more important are detailed below.

In those cases in which the enlarged gland itself or its capsule becomes inflamed, or in which the capsule becomes perforated, pain and tenderness on pressure may be complained of, and the structures in the vicinity of the affected gland may become involved in the inflammatory process. It has been already stated that under such circumstances suppuration may occur.

Weakness, Emaciation, and Cachexia.—Asthenia is one of the most marked features of the disease. Emaciation is often extreme, more especially in advanced stages of the case. In acute cases (*i.e.*, cases in which the glandular enlargement is rapidly developed) and in the later stages of many of the more chronic cases, a marked condition of cachexia is often developed.

The weakness and cachexia are, as a rule, developed gradually, and are, in my experience, usually proportionate to the extent and degree of the glandular enlargement.

So long as the glandular enlargement is localised, so long, more especially, as one or two groups of the external glands are alone affected, there may be little or no emaciation—in short, little or no constitutional disturbance.

In those cases, on the other hand, in which the glandular enlargement is widespread, in which the internal glands are involved, in which the spleen and the glandular structures in the intestine are affected, in which the disease is quickly and actively progressing, in which the febrile disturbance is considerable, and in which inflammatory complications such as empyema are present, the emaciation may be very great indeed. In at least three cases of Hodgkin's disease, I have seen the glutei muscles almost completely atrophied, and the pelvic bones laid bare, as it were, by the emaciation. Such a condition is of very serious significance; for in my experience, marked wasting of the glutei muscles is rarely, if ever, produced unless the emaciation of which it is part and parcel is extreme. A high degree of atrophy of the glutei muscles and of the thick cushion of fat which normally overlies the buttocks is indicative of a very profound disturbance of nutrition.

Anæmia and the condition of the blood.—In well-marked cases of Hodgkin's disease, the skin and mucous membranes are usually pale, and the red blood corpuscles are diminished in numbers.   Some writers, indeed, state that anæmia is always present when the glandular enlargement is widespread and well marked ; but with this statement I am unable to agree.   I have myself met with two well-marked cases of the disease in which the red blood corpuscles were respectively 5,390,000 and 4,550,000 per cubic millimetre.   In the case represented in my Atlas of Clinical Medicine (Plate VIII.), Dr Handford found that the red blood corpuscles numbered 4,807,000, and seven weeks later 4,895,000, per cubic millimetre.   In a case reported by Osler, in which the cervical and axillary glands were enormously enlarged, the red blood corpuscles numbered 4,250,000 per cubic millimetre, and did not undergo any diminution in numbers during the three weeks that the patient was under observation in hospital.   In the case which is represented in my Atlas (Plate IX.), the red corpuscles, which in December 1886 numbered 2,930,000, had increased in February 1887 to 4,180,000 per cubic millimetre.

It is impossible to suppose that in all of these cases, in which the observations were made by four independent observers, the results were erroneous.   It must, I think, be allowed (if it be granted that in these cases the glandular enlargement was due to Hodgkin's disease and not to tubercle) that, in certain stages of the disease, the red corpuscles are not diminished, or are only very slightly diminished, in numbers.   But this is exceptional.   In most cases of Hodgkin's disease anæmia is present ; and it is probably correct to say that in all well-marked cases of the disease the red blood corpuscles are diminished in numbers (*i.e.*, there is more or less anæmia) at some period or other of their course.

The degree of anæmia varies in different cases.   Gowers states that anæmia is one of the most conspicuous features of the disease ; he found the red corpuscles reduced to sixty per cent. of the normal, in some patients affected with the disease in whom the face was well coloured.

The red corpuscles are usually normal as regards their size and shape, but in some cases a number of small (imperfectly developed) red corpuscles are present ; in other cases, more especially, I think, in those cases in which the anæmia is well marked, the red corpuscles do not form rouleaux in the normal manner.   Poikilocytosis is in my experience rarely present, at all events in any marked degree ; but the statements of different observers differ on this point.

The condition of the white blood corpuscles is variable. In most of the cases which have come under my own notice, the white corpuscles have been slightly increased in numbers, and for the most part of small size ; but an excess of white corpuscles appears to be exceptional, for Gowers states : " In the majority of cases there is no excess of white corpuscles in the blood. In a minority of cases, there is an excess, slight or considerable. Out of sixty-four cases in which the blood was examined by the microscope, there was no excess of white corpuscles in thirty-nine. In the remaining twenty-five cases, there was an excess, which in nineteen was moderate, in three was slight. In three others, there was no excess of leucocytes during the early period of the case, but a slight excess was present during its later stages." * Trousseau, in his well-known lecture on the subject, also says : " Gentlemen, I cannot tell you what special action in the composition of the blood is caused by general hypertrophy of the glands ; I do not know whether it notably diminishes the leucocytes, but I am certain that it does not increase them." †

In exceptional cases, the white blood corpuscles are in considerable excess ; this is especially apt to occur in the later stages of the disease. Many writers speak of cases of this kind as a combination of Hodgkin's disease, and of lymphatic leucocythæmia ; but the correctness of this view is, I think, very questionable ; in many cases of this kind, the increase of the white corpuscles appears to be the result of a terminal leucocytosis, and in no way indicative of lymphatic leucocythæmia.

Dr Robert Muir informs me that in the only typical case of lymphadenoma (with characteristic lesions in the spleen, etc.) which he has examined post mortem, "the leucocytes were between 20,000 and 30,000 per c.mm., and the proportion of polymorphonuclear leucocytes are very much increased—a true leucocytosis." He adds : " In two cases, in which the blood was examined during life, I found a slight excess of lymphocytes—they were both young subjects—and I have noticed that in early life the proportion of lymphocytes tends to be raised more readily than in adults. I should say that in lymphadenoma the increase of leucocytes is never very great ; sometimes there is an excess of lymphocytes, sometimes an ordinary leucocytosis."

---

* Russell Reynolds' *System of Medicine*, vol. v., p. 334.
† Sydenham Society Translation, vol. v., p. 201.

Cabot sums up the characters of the blood in Hodgkin's disease as follows:—

"Normal blood in early stages.

"Later often marked anæmia.

"Sometimes leucocytosis." *

In those cases of Hodgkin's disease in which the anæmia is marked, shortness of breath, palpitation, and the other well-known symptoms associated with a deficiency of the red blood corpuscles (oxygen-carriers), may, of course, be present; but Hodgkin's disease, or lymphatic anæmia, as Sir Samuel Wilks has termed it, differs from other forms of anæmia (chlorosis and progressive pernicious anæmia, for example) in the fact that the patients affected by it are usually emaciated as well as anæmic.

The Condition of the Heart and Pulse.—The action of the heart is usually quick and feeble, and in many cases the organ is found to be more or less atrophied after death.

The pulse is usually quick, small, and weak; in some cases it is markedly dicrotic, more particularly in the advanced stages of the disease, and in those cases in which the pyrexia is considerable.

Œdema of the feet is of frequent occurrence in the later stages of the disease; in some cases, it is merely the result of anæmia, debility, or cachexia; in others, it is due to the pressure of the enlarged glands upon the iliac or femoral veins, or the inferior vena cava.

Hæmorrhages.—Epistaxis occurs in some cases; purpuric eruptions, and unhealthy inflammations of the skin or other parts (erysipelas, boils, stomatitis, etc.), may develop in those cases in which the anæmia and cachexia are great.

Loss of Appetite, Dyspepsia, and other Symptoms indicative of Derangement of the Gastro-Intestinal Functions.—In well-marked cases of Hodgkin's disease, the appetite is usually much impaired or entirely lost; and dyspepsia, vomiting, and diarrhœa are of frequent occurrence. In some cases, these symptoms are merely the result of the anæmia, debility, and cachexia; in others, they are associated with deposits of lymphoid tissue, or the presence of ulcerations, in the stomach or intestine.

Difficulty in swallowing is in some cases due to the pressure of enlarged glands upon the œsophagus.

Pyrexia.—In several of the cases of Hodgkin's disease which have come under my own observation (it would perhaps be more

---

* "Clinical Examination of the Blood," p. 157.

correct to say which were diagnosed as cases of Hodgkin's disease), there has been little or no febrile disturbance ; but elevation of temperature is of frequent occurrence during the course of the disease.

The degree of fever is not usually great (101°, 102°, or 103° F.), but temperatures of 104° and 105° F. are occasionally met with.

Gowers describes three types of fever in Hodgkin's disease. " In one the temperature is continuously raised, presenting very slight diurnal variations of a degree or a degree and a half. The highest temperature is sometimes in the morning, sometimes in the evening. Occasionally the temperature may descend to the normal and rise again. The degree of elevation is usually from 100° to 103°. A second type is characterised by periods of pyrexia, in which for several days a high temperature is maintained, the daily variation being slight. Alternating with these pyrexial periods are intervals of several days in which the temperature is normal, or nearly so. The height attained by the fever may be considerable, sometimes reaching 105°, as in the case from which a chart is given. A third type is characterised by morning remissions, the temperature being always higher in the evening than in the morning. The daily variations are from one to three degrees, the morning temperature being at or below 100°, sometimes normal, and the evening temperature being from 101° to 103°." *

Fever is most apt to occur in acute cases, in young subjects, and in those cases in which inflammatory complications, such as broncho-pneumonia, empyema, etc., are developed. In some of the cases in which fever is prominent, the glandular enlargement is undoubtedly tubercular.

Enlargement of the Spleen.—This occurs in the majority of cases of the disease. The degree of enlargement is not, as a rule, great, but sometimes (as in the case represented in my Atlas of Clinical Medicine, Plate VIII.) it is very considerable. The surface of the enlarged spleen is usually smooth ; in rare instances it may be nodulated. Perisplenitis, with thickening of the capsule, and perhaps the formation of adhesions to the surrounding parts, is not uncommon in the later stages of the disease. In those cases in which perisplenitis is present, pain and tenderness on pressure over the enlarged organs may be complained of.

The enlargement of the spleen may be due either to the presence of disseminated lymphoid nodules or an increase (hypertrophy) of the splenic tissue. In many cases both of these conditions are

---

* Russell Reynolds' *System of Medicine*, vol. v., p. 336.

present. The presence of nodules of lymphoid tissue in the spleen is seldom *per se* (*i.e.*, in the absence of hypertrophy) the cause of marked enlargement of the organ. In short, in the great majority of cases of Hodgkin's disease the enlargement of the spleen, though in many cases it is sufficient to enable one to detect it by palpation, is not great.

Enlargement of the Tonsils, Liver, and other organs.— Enlargement of the *tonsils* occasionally occurs ; when considerable, and especially if associated with great swelling of the cervical glands, and the presence of lymphoid deposits in the pharnyx and adjacent parts, it may be attended with alterations in voice, deafness, difficulty in swallowing, and shortness of breath. The enlarged tonsils may ulcerate, and in rare cases—one has come under my notice—may be the seat of diphtheritic deposits.

Enlargement of the *liver*, sufficiently great to be detected during life, is present in a certain number of cases ; in a few cases the enlargement is great.

The *testicle* is occasionally the seat of lymphoid deposits. In a remarkable case which, through the kindness of Mr Alexis Thomson, I was able to record and figure in my Atlas (see Plate X), the *mammæ* were enormously enlarged. The *thymus gland, suprarenal capsules, kidneys,* and *ovaries* are in some cases affected, but it is seldom that the enlargement of these organs (the thymus, perhaps, most frequently excepted) is sufficient to enable one to detect it during life. In the North Shields case to which I have already referred, the enlarged ovaries could, however, be very distinctly felt in the abdomen ; they were as large as cricket balls.

In some cases in which the marrow of the bones is more markedly affected than it is in the great majority of cases of Hodgkin's disease, some of the bones (sternum, tibiæ, etc.) may be painful and, perhaps, in places distinctly swollen.

Symptoms and signs due to the pressure of the enlarged lymphatic glands upon adjacent structures and parts.—The "pressure-symptoms and signs" which may be present in Hodgkin's disease are very numerous ; in some cases, as for instance in those cases in which the internal glands are chiefly affected, they may be the most striking clinical features of the case.

The enlarged *cervical glands* may displace or compress the trachea, the œsophagus, or the nerves, veins, and arteries in the neck. Difficulty in breathing, alterations in voice, cough, difficulty in swallowing, inequality in the size of the pupils, vomiting, irregularity of the action of the heart, swelling of the head and face, and various cerebral symptoms due to impeded venous circulation or defective arterial supply to the brain (such as mental obfuscation, giddiness, convulsions, coma) may result.

The enlarged *glands within the cavity of the thorax* (the bronchial and mediastinal glands, and the enlarged thymus) may displace or compress the root of the lung, the bronchi, the trachea, the œsophagus, the recurrent laryngeal nerve, the superior vena cava, the aorta and its branches, the pulmonary artery, and even the heart itself. Difficulty in breathing, cough, alterations in voice, stridor, difficulty in swallowing, œdema of the head and neck, paralysis of the left vocal cord, inequality in the size of the pupils, murmurs due to displacement of the heart or compression of the great vessels, displacement of the apex-beat, extensive dulness on percussion—in short, all the symptoms and signs which may be present in cases of solid intra-thoracic tumour—may result.

The enlarged *glands in the cavities of the abdomen and pelvis* may compress the lumbar, sacral, or solar plexuses, the stomach, portal vein, inferior vena cava, etc., and may produce a great variety of symptoms, such as œdema of the feet, ascites, jaundice, vomiting, shooting pains in the lower extremities, paralysis of the lower limbs, etc.

The enlarged *glands in the axillæ and groins* may interfere with the free movement of the upper or lower limbs, and may press upon the nerves, veins, and arteries in their neighbourhood ; pains in the limbs, paralysis, and œdema may result.

The pressure of lymphoid deposits *on the spinal cord* may produce paraplegia. Osler has recorded a case in point.

Symptoms due to inflammatory complications in the neighbourhood of the enlarged glands and associated lesions.—As I have already stated, inflammation of the capsule of the enlarged glands (periadenitis) not unfrequently occurs ; pain and tenderness on pressure, with matting together (fusion, as it were) of the individual glandular masses may in consequence be developed.

In some cases, the adjacent structures become implicated in the inflammatory process ; adhesion of the glandular masses to the skin, and, in rare cases, ulceration of the skin overlying the enlarged glands, may result. The question arises whether in these cases the glandular enlargement is tubercular or due to Hodgkin's disease.

In exceptional cases, the enlarged glands themselves suppurate or caseate. The suppuration is, so far as I know, always local, *i.e.*, confined to a limited number of the enlarged glands. I am not acquainted with any case of Hodgkin's disease in which all the enlarged glands, or many of them, in different parts of the body, have softened and suppurated; though widespread caseation without suppuration is, in some cases, which during life appeared to be cases of Hodgkin's disease, found after death. I have already detailed a case in point. In any case of supposed Hodgkin's disease in which widespread suppuration or caseation were present and obvious during life, I should be disposed to doubt the correctness of the diagnosis, and to suppose that the primary glandular enlargement (on the top of which, so to speak, the suppuration or caseation was developed) was due to some pathological condition other than Hodgkin's disease, *e.g.*, to tubercle.

It is not unlikely that in some cases of Hodgkin's disease in which one or more of the enlarged glands suppurate or caseate, they were, previous to the development of the Hodgkin's disease, the seat of an inflammatory or scrofulous lesion. Again, as I have already pointed out, I see no *à priori* reason why tubercle should not be engrafted upon Hodgkin's disease.

Thrombosis of the veins which are embedded in, and compressed by, the enlarged glands is developed in some cases. Complete venous obstruction produced in this manner is usually attended with great œdema in the area from which the obstructed vein draws its blood supply. Effusion into the pleural, pericardial, or peritoneal cavities is sometimes produced in this manner. In some cases, pleurisy, empyema, pericarditis, and peritonitis, which is usually localised, are developed. As has been already stated, stomatitis, diphtheria, and erysipelas occasionally occur.

The condition of the respiratory apparatus.—In addition to the disturbances of the respiratory apparatus which have been already mentioned, lung complications, such as bronchitis, bronchopneumonia, and less frequently croupous pneumonia, which is usually localised, are of frequent occurrence. A low form of chronic inflammation of the pulmonary tissue, probably due to compression of the vascular and nervous structures in the root of the lung, is occasionally developed in those cases in which the bronchial and mediastinal glands are implicated.

The condition of the urine.—The kidneys are sometimes the seat of inflammatory or degenerative changes; the characteristic symptoms and signs of Bright's disease (general dropsy, albuminuria, tube casts in the urine) may, of course, be developed in such cases.

Nervous Symptoms.—Drowsiness, mental apathy, coma, or convulsions occasionally occur in the later stages of the disease. These symptoms are not usually indicative of any actual lesion (such as lymphoid deposits) in the brain tissue, but are rather the result of the anæmic and cachectic condition, alterations in the venous or arterial blood supply of the nervous tissues, and the defective nutrition which results therefrom.

CLINICAL TYPES, DURATION AND COURSE.

From the description which has just been given, it will be apparent that different cases of Hodgkin's disease present differences in respect to their symptoms. When we study the manner in which the chief symptoms—the glandular enlargements and the local symptoms which result therefrom, on the one hand, and the constitutional symptoms (debility, emaciation, anæmia, cachexia, fever, etc.), on the other—are grouped together; the order in which the symptoms are developed; and the rapidity with which the disease progresses, it is possible to arrange different cases of Hodgkin's disease into certain *clinical* groups. It must, however, be distinctly understood that the division is a rough one, and, so far as our present knowledge enables us to judge, artificial, and that the different groups or types run insensibly one into the other. Nevertheless, some such classification as that which is adopted below is of use to the practical physician, chiefly for the purposes of prognosis.

In most cases, the disease develops gradually and runs a slow and chronic course, the duration (dating the commencement from the period at which the glandular affection is first observed) being, in the majority of cases, at least eighteen months, and in some cases considerably longer.

In a minority of cases, the progress of the disease is much more rapid, the fatal termination being reached within a few weeks or months from the period at which the symptoms were first noticed.

These two groups (*i.e.*, cases of Hodgkin's disease which run a chronic or protracted course, and cases of Hodgkin's disease which run a rapid or acute course) are not sharply defined; they are connected by cases having an intermediate duration. But it is often possible, when the patient first comes under observation, to predict with tolerable accuracy whether the case is likely to run a rapid or a protracted course. Hence this division into *acute* and *chronic*, though not, so far as our present knowledge enables us to judge, founded upon any distinct etiological or pathological differences, is of practical use for the purposes of prognosis.

In most cases of Hodgkin's disease, the constitutional symptoms are developed later than, and are apparently the result of, the glandular enlargements. This statement chiefly applies to the more common (chronic) form of the disease.

Some authorities divide the disease into three stages, viz. :—first, a stage of localised glandular enlargement ; second, a stage of generalised glandular enlargement ; and third, a stage of anæmia, cachexia, and profound constitutional disturbance. Trousseau terms these three periods, the latent period, the period of progress and generalisation, and the cachectic period.

In many cases, these three stages can undoubtedly be observed. But as I shall presently point out, in speaking of the diagnosis, so long as the glandular enlargement is merely local, and there are no constitutional symptoms, although the presence of the disease may be suspected, it cannot be positively diagnosed. It is only when the glandular enlargement has become generalised that Hodgkin's disease can with any degree of certainty be recognised, and even then it is often difficult, as I have more than once pointed out, to exclude tubercle.

Again, in some cases the stage of local enlargement is wanting, or at all events appears to be wanting ; and the several groups of glands in different parts of the body appear to be simultaneously, or to all intents and purposes simultaneously, affected. It is probable that in many of these cases the generalised enlargement was preceded by a local enlargement of some of the external glands which had escaped notice, or by an enlargement of some of the internal glands which could not be detected.

In another group of cases, the constitutional symptoms are developed, or appear to be developed, simultaneously with the glandular enlargement.

In still another group, the constitutional symptoms are developed, or appear to be developed, before (prior to) the glandular enlargements.

It is probable that in many of the cases which are included in the last two groups, enlargement of the internal glands does actually precede the development of the constitutional symptoms. Cases in which this occurs are not in reality exceptional ; clinically they appear to be exceptional, but pathologically and as a matter of fact they conform to the general rule, viz., that the constitutional symptoms follow the glandular enlargement.

In another group, the internal glands (the bronchial and mediastinal glands, and the thymus, for instance) are alone affected. It is probable that in some of these cases the glandular enlargement is not in reality due to Hodgkin's disease ; but it is nevertheless true that our present methods of pathological research do not enable us to differentiate them.

It may be stated, as a general rule, that those cases run a rapid course in which cachexia and constitutional symptoms are developed early, in which several groups of glands are simultaneously, or apparently simultaneously, affected,* and in which the glandular enlargement is rapidly developed. The cases analysed by Gowers seem to show that after the age of 50, and still more after the age of 60, the course of the disease is usually rapid; but further observation is probably required before this conclusion can be finally accepted.

Mode of Death.—Gradual failure of the vital powers, the result of the progressive asthenia and cachexia, is the most frequent mode of death; in some cases, the fatal termination is due to asphyxia, the result of the pressure of the enlarged glands upon the trachea, larynx, or bronchi; in many cases, the immediate cause of death is the development of some intercurrent illness or complication, such as pneumonia, pleurisy, pericarditis, diphtheria, etc. Epistaxis and diarrhœa, in some cases, precede and hasten the fatal issue.

DIAGNOSIS.

In typical and advanced cases of the disease, the diagnosis does not as a rule present any great difficulty. The peculiar characters of the glandular enlargement, more especially the absence of caseation and suppuration, and the fact that the enlarged glands have not the cartilaginous and stony hardness of cancer; the fact that the glandular enlargement is not merely local, but that different groups of glands throughout the body (groups of glands which are not, as it were, in direct anatomical continuity) are affected; the absence of any primary, local, malignant lesion, such as cancer of the mamma, stomach, or other internal organ; the presence of enlargement of the spleen, without, in many cases, any marked increase in the number of the white blood corpuscles; the presence of lymphoid deposits in the tonsils or (but this is rare) in the skin; the presence of enlargement of the liver, thymus gland, etc. (suggestive of lymphoid deposits in these organs); and the presence of the characteristic constitutional symptoms (asthenia, anæmia, emaciation, cachexia, etc.), usually enable us to distinguish the disease from the other conditions with which it is likely to be confounded.

But even these characteristics are not absolutely conclusive; for it cannot be too frequently repeated that in some cases in which

---

* Wunderlich's opinion was different on this point. He thought that in those cases in which several groups of glands were simultaneously affected, the disease was apt to develop slowly.

the clinical symptoms and the character of the glandular enlargement are typical of Hodgkin's disease, the enlarged glands are
found on post-mortem examination to be the seat of a widespread
tubercular lesion. I have already expressed the opinion that these
cases are probably much more common than is usually supposed.

In the earlier stages of the disease, the diagnosis is very difficult
and often impossible; in some cases, for example, in which the
cervical and axillary glands are enlarged, hard, painless and non-
suppurating, and in which there are no constitutional symptoms, it
is extremely difficult to come to a conclusion as to the exact nature
of· the glandular enlargement, more especially in which the
glandular enlargement is of long duration. Several cases of this
kind have come under my own notice.

Hodgkin's disease has to be differentiated from the other affections in which the enlargement of the lymphatic glands occurs,
and especially from local lymphatic overgrowth (simple or local
lymphoma), from scrofulous enlargement, and from cancer and
sarcoma (true malignant disease) of the lymphatic glands. In
some cases, the differential diagnosis is difficult, if not impossible.
The chief points of distinction are as follows :—

**The differential diagnosis of Hodgkin's disease and of
local lymphatic overgrowth (simple, or local, non-malignant
lymphoma).**— In fully-developed cases of Hodgkin's disease—
cases in which the lymphatic enlargements are generalised and
the characteristic constitutional symptoms (asthenia, anæmia,
emaciation, fever, and cachexia) are developed—there is, of course,
no difficulty; but in some cases of the disease, the generalised
glandular enlargement is, as we have seen, preceded by a stage
in which the glandular swelling is local. Now in such cases,
so long as the glandular enlargement is localised, it is impossible to distinguish the condition from simple, local, non-
malignant lymphoma by any means with which we are at present
acquainted. The local glandular enlargement may present exactly
the same characters in both conditions—it may be painless, non-
suppurative, non-caseating, the individual glandular nodules being
isolated, and not adherent either to one another or to the surrounding parts.

So long as the glandular enlargement presents these characters,
and is localised and limited to one group of glands, we may hope
that it is merely a simple, local, non-malignant lymphoma, but we
cannot positively assert that it may not be the precursor of a
generalised glandular enlargement, in other words, of Hodgkin's
disease.

In connection with the differential diagnosis in such cases, Osler makes the following statement: "A single bunch in the neck, particularly if sub-maxillary, persisting for over a year or eighteen months without involvement, however slight, of the glands on the same or the opposite side, or in the axilla, is almost certainly non-malignant lymphoma." *

The whole question turns upon the definition and meaning which ought to be attached to the term Hodgkin's disease. In those cases in which a local glandular enlargement has existed for a considerable period of time (many months or years) as a mere local enlargement, and has ultimately been followed by Hodgkin's disease (i.e., by generalisation of the glandular swellings and constitutional symptoms), it would, perhaps, be more correct to say that the Hodgkin's disease followed a simple, local, non-malignant lymphoma, than to affirm that the primary, local, glandular enlargement was one and the same throughout the whole course of the case (i.e., was from the first identical with that characteristic of Hodgkin's disease).

In those cases in which a local glandular enlargement is followed, soon after its development, by enlargement of other groups of glands (by generalisation of the glandular enlargement) and by constitutional symptoms, there is, of course, no difficulty in supposing that the primary (and apparently localised) glandular enlargement was in reality part and parcel of (the first stage of) the Hodgkin's disease.

The differential diagnosis of Hodgkin's disease and of scrofulous enlargement of the lymphatic glands must be chiefly based upon:—the character of the glandular swellings; the presence or absence of tubercular lesions, such as phthisis, in other parts of the body; the condition of the spleen; the presence or absence of lymphoid deposits in other tissues and organs; the nature of the constitutional symptoms; and the family history and hereditary tendencies of the patient.

The glandular enlargement of Hodgkin's disease is usually a firm, more or less hard, painless enlargement, which slowly and gradually, but (in most cases) progressively, increases in size, and which (in typical cases) has no tendency to soften, suppurate, or caseate; the individual glands can, in the earlier stages of the disease, at all events, be felt as smooth, round, or oval, movable lumps, which are neither adherent to one another nor to the adjacent parts.

---

* Pepper's *System of Medicine*, vol. iii., p. 929.

But these characters are not invariably present, for in some cases the glandular enlargements are soft and almost fluctuating.

The glandular enlargement due to scrofula is usually painful and tender to the touch, and tends—and this is one of its essential characteristics—to soften, caseate, and suppurate, and after reaching a certain size to diminish in size rather than to increase, but exceptions to this statement are by no means uncommon. In typical cases, the individual (scrofulous) glands cannot be distinctly defined, even at a comparatively early stage of their development; they tend to become adherent to one another, and to the surrounding parts, and to form a soft, ill-defined mass. But here again it must be remembered that in some cases in which the glandular enlargement during life presents all the characters of Hodgkin's disease (rather than of scrofula), post-mortem examination shows that the condition is tubercular.

The skin overlying the enlarged glands in Hodgkin's disease is usually natural in appearance, whereas in scrofulous cases it is usually injected, reddened or purple in colour, and often altered in texture.

In scrofulous cases, cicatrices, indicative of former suppuration, are often present.

The fact that the glandular enlargement is of very large size, more especially when there is no appearance of softening or suppuration, is in favour of Hodgkin's disease rather than of scrofula; but exceptions to this statement are not very uncommon.

Marked emaciation, anæmia, and cachexia, when there is no suppuration and no internal tubercular lesion, such as phthisis, to account for their presence, are suggestive of Hodgkin's disease.

Enlargement of the spleen, in the absence of chronic phthisis and waxy (amyloid) degeneration, is strongly in favour of the glandular enlargement being due to Hodgkin's disease.

A marked hereditary tendency to scrofula; the existence of scrofulous lesions, such as phthisis, in other parts of the body; the presence of the tubercle bacillus in the sputum or in the discharge from any inflamed or suppurating gland or sinus; the fact that the glandular enlargement is localised (*i.e.*, limited to one group of glands or to groups of glands which are in direct anatomical continuity); and non-enlargement of the spleen are, in addition to the other points which have been enumerated above (see the special characters of enlarged scrofulous glands), in favour of scrofula.

The differential diagnosis of Hodgkin's disease, and of scrofulous enlargement of the lymphatic glands is especially difficult in the following circumstances :—

1. *In the early stages of those cases of Hodgkin's disease in which the sub-maxillary and cervical glands are the only glands which are affected.*

In such cases the diagnosis must be based upon the characters of the glandular swellings which have been described above, though it must be admitted that these characters are not conclusive.

In those cases in which it is impossible to give a positive opinion when the patient first comes under observation, the physician must either be content to watch the future progress of the case, and to wait for the development of distinctive symptoms (generalisation of the glandular swellings and the appearance of constitutional symptoms), or (as I have in some recent cases done) have some of the enlarged glands removed by the surgeon, and the true nature of the glandular affection definitely determined.

Another method of diagnosis which has recently suggested itself to me, but which I have not as yet put into actual practice, is the tuberculin test—the injection of Koch's tuberculin into the body of the patient with the object of determining whether a reaction results or not.

2. *In those exceptional cases of Hodgkin's disease in which some of the enlarged glands soften, suppurate, or caseate.*

Under such circumstances, a differential diagnosis can only be made by a careful and judicial consideration of the whole facts of the case. I should strongly doubt the case being merely one of Hodgkin's disease if several of the glandular swellings were to suppurate or caseate. There seems reason to suppose that scrofula and Hodgkin's disease may (actively) co-exist in the same patient; this fact must not be forgotten in the diagnosis of doubtful cases.

3. *In those exceptional cases of tubercular disease in which the glandular affection is widespread* (the inguinal as well as the cervical and axillary glands, for example, being affected), *in which the individual glands remain isolated, and in which they are firm, hard, painless, in which there is no softening and suppuration and no adhesion to the overlying skin.*

Tubercular cases of this description are rare; but when they do occur they cannot, so far as I know, be distinguished during life from cases of Hodgkin's disease, unless it be by observing whether they react or not to the hypodermic injection of tuberculin; for the clinical characters of the glandular enlargement are identical in both cases.

In cases of this kind, the age of the patient, his hereditary tendencies as regards tubercle, the presence or absence of marked enlargement of the spleen and of lymphoid deposits in the tonsils, skin, etc., and the presence or absence of fever may, however, as I have previously pointed out, throw some light upon the nature of the case.

The differential diagnosis of Hodgkin's disease and of cancerous enlargement of the lymphatic glands.—Here there is seldom any great difficulty.

The lymphatic enlargement due to cancer is usually harder (more cartilaginous, stony, and knobby) than that due to Hodgkin's disease. The glandular enlargement due to cancer is seldom, if ever, so generalised and widespread as that in typical cases of Hodgkin's disease. In cancer, the lymphatic enlargement is secondary rather than primary; the symptoms and signs of a primary cancerous lesion on the surface of the body (skin, mamma, etc.) or in some of the internal organs, such as the stomach, are therefore usually present; and the enlarged glands are usually in direct anatomical (lymphatic) relationship to the primary growth.

Enlargement of the spleen is in favour of Hodgkin's disease and against cancer.

In doubtful cases the age of the patient may be of importance : cancer is much more likely to occur in old people.

The differential diagnosis of Hodgkin's disease and of true malignant sarcoma of the lymphatic glands.—Here the distinction is often, I believe, impossible; it is probable, I think, that some of the cases of lymphatic enlargement which are described as Hodgkin's disease are in reality malignant sarcomata.

The facts that the lymphatic enlargement is limited to one or more groups of lymphatic glands which are in direct anatomical continuity; that the lymphatic swellings directly invade the surrounding tissues; that such organs as the mamma and testicle are affected ; and especially that the lymphatic enlargements are secondary to a primary tumour in these, or in some of the internal organs ; and that the spleen is not enlarged—are in favour of true malignant sarcoma of the lymphatic glands rather than of Hodgkin's disease.

Vice versa, widespread enlargement of several groups of lymphatic glands in different parts of the body ; the absence of a primary tumour ; enlargement of the spleen ; the early development of cachexia ; implication of the tonsils and other organs in which lymphoid tissue normally abounds, are in favour of Hodgkin's disease.

The differential diagnosis of Hodgkin's disease and of true malignant sarcoma is especially difficult, in fact, impossible during life in many of the cases in which the glandular enlargement is internal—*i.e.*, in which the bronchial and mediastinal glands are affected. In the present position of therapeutics this point of differential diagnosis is of no importance to the practical physician; in such cases it is a matter of indifference, so far as prognosis and treatment are concerned, whether the glandular enlargement is due to a true malignant sarcoma or to Hodgkin's disease; for we are unable by any therapeutic means, with which we are at present acquainted, to cure either the one affection or the other.

In his work on the clinical examination of the blood, Cabot makes the following statements with regard to the nature of Hodgkin's disease and its diagnosis. The subject is one of so much difficulty, and, in the present position of our knowledge, of so much uncertainty, that I quote his remarks in full :—

"The diagnosis of this disease is impossible without the blood count. Its pathology is identical with that of leukæmia, and even post-mortem the two diseases are indistinguishable so far as the lesions outside of the blood are concerned. Yet the blood is in no way peculiar, but presents in most cases all the characteristics of the normal tissue. Its value is as negative evidence, telling us in a given case that leukæmia is absent even though all the other signs and symptoms may be those of leukæmia.

(1.) Transitions from Hodgkin's disease to leukæmia have taken place under the eyes of competent observers, but they are very rare. Only three such cases are on record so far as I know, that of Fleischer and Penzoldt,[*] that of Mosler,[†] and one reported by Senator,[‡] where two sisters came under observation, both suffering from Hodgkin's disease. One died of it ; in the other the blood changed to that of leukæmia before death.

Doubtless many of the other cases supposed to exemplify a similar transition were really cases in which a leucocytosis arose owing to some inflammatory complication, as not uncommonly occurs.

From the existence of these very rare cases of a transition to leukæmia it has been supposed, especially by French observers, that Hodgkin's disease is simply an early stage of true leukæmia, and that this would always become apparent were it not that the patients die of some intercurrent disease before the signs of leukæmia have time to show themselves in the blood. One difficulty with this view is, that there occur chronic cases which last from eight to ten years without any change in the blood. Another difficulty is, that the transition is in fact rare despite the relative frequency with which the disease is met with.

(2.) Undoubtedly many cases diagnosed as Hodgkin's disease are in fact cases of glandular hypertrophy due to syphilis or tuberculosis, and this fact has led many to the belief that *all* cases called Hodgkin's disease are in reality only syphilitic or tubercular adenitis. In a considerable number of cases, however, tuberculosis has been disproven by careful inoculation experiments with the glandular tissue, and there is no reasonable doubt that *some* cases at any rate

---

[*] Deut. Arch. f. klin. Med., vol. 17.

[†] Ziemssen's "Handbuch d. Path. und Therap.," vol. 8.

[‡] Berl. klin. Woch., 1882, p. 533.

are not due to tuberculosis or syphilis. Probably the diagnosis can never be made with absolute certainty during life.

(3.) The frequent occurrence of fever and other symptoms characteristic of an infectious disease has led some writers to class it as such. In a certain percentage of cases the disease (like leukæmia) has run an acute course, lasting not more than six weeks from the first symptom to death. In some chronic cases the same sort of evidence of an infectious nature has been brought forward. Ulcerations occur in the mouth and intestine through which morbid products might gain admission. Various bacteria (pyogenic and others) have been found in the blood and tissues from time to time, but numerous negative examinations for micro-organisms are also on record, and the evidence is insufficient to establish the infectious nature of the disease. None the less, there is a growing tendency, among the leading writers and observers in Germany and elsewhere, to believe that the disease will ultimately be shown to be infectious.

(4.) Meantime most surgeons continue to regard it as a form of sarcoma, and to treat it like malignant disease." *

The differential diagnosis of Hodgkin's disease and of leucocythæmia has already been considered (see p. 167).

(see p. 167)

PROGNOSIS.

In undoubted cases of Hodgkin's disease the prognosis is most unfavourable ; so far as is at present known, the disease almost invariably terminates sooner or later in death. So long as the glandular enlargement is local, the prognosis is, of course, much more favourable ; but, as I have previously pointed out, it is often impossible at this stage of the disease to distinguish the condition from simple, local, non-malignant lymphoma.

In trying to form a correct estimate of the probable duration of the disease in any particular case, after the glandular enlargement has become generalised, the following points have to be taken into · account :—(1) The length of time the disease has already existed ; (2) the rapidity with which it appears to be progressing ; (3) the position of the glandular groups which are chiefly affected ; (4) the presence or absence of complications ; (5) the state of the patient's health prior to the onset of the disease ; (6) the age of the patient ; and (7) the effects of treatment.

The simultaneous enlargement of many different glandular groups; the rapid enlargement of the affected glands; the early development of constitutional symptoms; the fact that the asthenia, anæmia, emaciation, fever, and cachexia are pronounced ; the fact that the enlarged glands are pressing upon and interfering with the function of important structures, such as the respiratory passages, the œsophagus, etc.; the fact that the bronchial and mediastinal

---

* "Clinical Examination of the Blood," p. 154.

glands are involved; the presence of grave symptoms, such as great dyspnœa, general dropsy, ascites, etc., and of serious complications such as pleurisy, pericarditis, pneumonia, diphtheria, etc.; the facts that the patient is old, and that prior to the onset of the disease he was in bad health; and the fact that there is no improvement under treatment, are highly unfavourable indications, and suggest that the duration of the case will be short.

TREATMENT.

In the present state of our therapeutic knowledge the treatment of Hodgkin's disease is a most unsatisfactory subject. So far as I know, arsenic is the only remedy which is of any use, once the glandular enlargements have become generalised. I am satisfied that in two cases of the disease which were under my own observation, temporary arrest in the development of the glandular swelling, and marked, though temporary, improvement in the constitutional symptoms, occurred under the use of this drug. But in both cases the improvement was merely temporary. In both cases after three or four months, the disease appeared to take on new activity; both cases terminated fatally. The drug may be given either by the mouth, or it may be injected into the enlarged glands. I have no personal experience of the subcutaneous method. In all cases I have given the drug by the mouth, in the form of Fowler's solution, well diluted. I begin with a small dose (two or three drops), and gradually increase the dose until the maximum quantity which can be satisfactorily borne is reached. The object is to saturate the system with arsenic without producing toxic symptoms. Should toxic symptoms arise, the remedy should be discontinued for a time, and then, after an interval, again administered in small doses. It might be expected that the injection of the drug into the enlarged glands would produce irritation and inflammation, but this is certainly not always the case; indeed, a case which I have figured and detailed in my Atlas of Clinical Medicine (Plate VIII), shows that very large doses may, in some cases, be injected into the enlarged glands without producing any untoward effects. In that case Dr Handford injected as much as thirty drops of Fowler's solution into the enlarged glands, daily; the injections did not cause any local irritation or inflammation; though after a time they did produce disturbance of the stomach.

In treating cases of Hodgkin's disease, the general health must, of course, be kept in the highest possible state of efficiency. The patient

O

should be carefully and well fed, well clothed, well housed, and diligently protected from cold and all causes of depression. During the summer months he should spend as much of his time as possible in the open air, and especially at the seaside—for in some cases sea air has seemed to be beneficial (it is highly probable that some of these cases were tubercular).

Cod-liver oil, quinine, and Easton's syrup are, in addition to arsenic, perhaps the most useful remedies which we possess. I have no personal experience of phosphorus, but its administration appears to have been followed by temporary improvement in some cases. Possibly the interstitial injection of chloride of zinc, which has recently been introduced by M. Lannelongue for the treatment of tuberculosis, may be beneficial. Iodide of potassium and the syrup of iron have not, in my hands, yielded any good result; and this appears to be the experience of almost all observers.

Local counter-irritation (by iodine, blisters, the iodide of mercury ointment, etc.) seems to be of little or no use. Cold douches applied to the enlarged glands, friction and massage have been recommended by some authorities, but at the best they can be merely palliatives. Galvano-puncture has been employed, but without benefit; the application of the constant electric current to the enlarged glands, with the object of producing absorption of the lymphoid tissue and promoting a healthier state of nutrition in the diseased glands, is of very doubtful value.

Excision of the enlarged glands is useless once the glandular enlargement has become generalised.

In those cases in which the glandular enlargement is local, excision is advisable, provided that the glandular mass can be safely and satisfactorily removed by operation.

The difficulty of distinguishing the glandular enlargement due to simple non-malignant lymphoma and that due to Hodgkin's disease, in its early localised stage, has already been insisted upon. Excision of a simple adenoma, provided that the tumour can be safely and satisfactorily removed, though it may not be absolutely necessary, can do no harm; should, however, the glandular enlargement be due to Hodgkin's disease, excision is eminently advisable while the lymphatic swelling is still localised; the operation may, perhaps, give the patient a chance of recovery. But owing to the difficulty of distinguishing simple lymphoma and the glandular enlargement of Hodgkin's disease, conclusions based upon the successful removal of lymphatic enlargements, supposed to be due to Hodgkin's disease, are apt to be fallacious.

In one case, in which a glandular enlargement in the neck and thorax presented all the clinical characters of Hodgkin's disease, the glandular enlargement has subsided and the patient gained strength and weight under the administration of thyroid extract, arsenic and cardiac tonics internally, and the application of iodide of potassium ointment externally.

ADDISON'S DISEASE.

Definition or Short Description.—Addison's disease, to which the synonyms *Morbus Addisonii*, *Melasma supra-renale*, *Bronzed-skin disease*, *Maladie bronzée*, *Asthenie surrénale*, etc., have been given, is a distinct clinical entity, characterised during life by certain well-marked symptoms (of which asthenia, remarkable feebleness of the heart's action and of the pulse, vomiting, pains in the abdomen and back, and pigmentation of the skin and mucous membranes, are the chief), and associated after death with a lesion of the suprarenal capsules (usually a fibro-caseous destruction of both capsules).

The onset of the disease is usually slow and insidious, and the course is usually chronic, though in exceptional cases the onset is more acute and the course rapid. The disease is almost invariably fatal, though recovery does appear to have occurred in very rare instances.

That the disease is a distinct clinical entity is conclusively proved by the fact that over and over again, in instances too numerous to mention, the existence of the capsular lesion has been predicted (because of the presence of the symptoms enumerated above) during life, and the presence of the capsular lesion has been demonstrated after death, without any other local change or visceral lesion capable of explaining the clinical symptoms, or sufficient to account for the fatal issue.

There is still much difference of opinion as to the pathological physiology of the disease, *i.e.*, as to the exact manner in which the symptoms are produced, the relationship of the symptoms to the lesion of the capsules and to the lesions in the sympathetic nervous system which are present in many cases of the disease.

Historical Note.—The celebrated physician, Dr Addison, directed attention to the relationship of anæmia and diseases of the suprarenal capsules in the year 1849, though he did not publish his well-known treatise, entitled *On the Constitutional and Local Effects of Disease of the Suprarenal Capsules*, until 1855. His description of the symptoms was singularly complete, and (with some few additions) practically represents our clinical knowledge at the present time (see *infra*).

Cases of Addison's disease had undoubtedly been observed and recorded before the year 1849, though the connection between the symptoms and the lesion of the capsules does not seem to have been suspected. Thus Dr Frederick P. Henry, in the historical summary which he gives of the disease, states :—" The first case of Addison's disease on record is to be found in Lobstein's treatise, *De nervi sympathici humani fabrica et morbis*, Paris, 1823, from the English translation of which, by the late Professor Joseph Pancoast, I take the following extract : ' I have myself observed the nerves forming the suprarenal plexus much thickened in disease, where the suprarenals, which were more than twice as large as usual, had degenerated into tuberculous substance. The patient was an unmarried woman, twenty-five years of age, who died in convulsive spasms analogous to the epileptic. . . . Nothing unusual was discovered in the body of this woman, but the aforesaid change in the suprarenal glands and the enlargement of the nerves.' Notwithstanding," says Dr Henry, "the fact that there is no record of the darkening of the complexion, the above was undoubtedly a typical case of Addison's disease, in which, moreover, death by convulsions is not uncommon. The observation regarding the thickening of the nerves in this, the first recorded instance of the disease, is of remarkable interest. The second case was recorded in the *Halle Hospital Reports*, by Dr Schotte, in October 1823, and is published in vol. vii. of the *Deutsches Archiv.f. klin. Med.*, by Risel, in the course of his article *Zur Pathologie des Morbus Addisonii*. The third case came under the observation of Dr Richard Bright, at Guy's Hospital, in 1829. It is contained in Bright's classical *Reports of Medical Cases*, and also figures as Case v. in Addison's original memoir. The lesions of the capsules were characteristic ; there was no other affection of any consequence, and for the first time in the history of the disease, it was noted that the complexion was very dark. A few other cases were reported before the year 1855, when Addison published his work *On the Constitutional and Local Effects of Disease of the Suprarenal Capsules*, but it was reserved for his sagacity to detect the relation between the well-marked constitutional symptoms of the affection, the peculiar pigmentation of the skin, and the structural changes in the suprarenal capsules."[*]

From these statements it will be apparent that Addison was the first to give a detailed description of the clinical symptoms of the disease, and to show that the lesion in the suprarenal capsules and the well-marked and characteristic clinical symptoms are associated as cause and effect.

---

[*] Buck's *Reference Handbook of the Medical Sciences*, vol. i., p. 74.

Further, it must be noted that Addison's discovery of the relationship of the symptoms of the disease to the lesion of the capsules was not merely a happy hit—it was no mere fluke—but was the outcome of a well-planned and deliberate search, the object of which was to discover the cause of that form of anæmia which he termed *idiopathic—the pernicious anæmia* of the present time.

ETIOLOGY.

In the great majority of cases of Addison's disease the lesion of the capsules is tubercular.   Hence it may be assumed that conditions which favour the production of tubercle in other parts of the body predispose to the production of Addison's disease.

Age.—The disease is most frequently met with between the ages of twenty and forty ; it is exceedingly rare before ten, and after fifty years of age.   Cases are, however, occasionally met with in children and in old people.   In a case which I have at present under observation the patient is aged eight and a half years (see Case VI.).   Dr T. W. M'Dowall, of the Northumberland County Asylum, sent me a few years ago the suprarenal capsules from a case which terminated fatally at the age of seventy ; in that case, in which the lesion was quite typical, it seems certain that the disease must have developed after the age of sixty-one.

Sex.—Males are much more frequently affected than females. Of 183 unequivocal cases collected by Greenhow, 119 (or 65 per cent.) were males, and 64 (or 35 per cent.) females ; of 127 cases analysed by Jaccoud, 79 (or 62 per cent.) were males, and 48 (or 38 per cent.) females.   In my 12 cases, 7 were males and 5 females.

Occupation : Social Position.—The great majority of cases of the disease occur in hospital patients, amongst the working classes and lower orders of society, and especially in those whose occupation exposes them to injury and strain.

Blows and injuries to the back seem undoubtedly to be the exciting cause of the disease in a certain proportion of cases ; and this is just what one might expect seeing that the lesion is tubercular.   There can be no doubt that local injury (probably by affording a suitable nidus for the development of the tubercle bacillus or its spores, which are already in the body) may favour the production of tubercular lesions in some organs—such, for example, as tubercular tumours in the cerebellum.   In my 12 cases, a definite history of injury to the back could only be obtained in one case.

So much difference of opinion still exists regarding the pathological physiology of Addison's disease, that it will perhaps be advisable, before describing the morbid anatomy and pathology, to consider the clinical history of the disease.

CLINICAL HISTORY.

Although a large number of cases of morbus Addisonii have been recorded during the past forty-three years, and many important papers and monographs have been written on the subject, the original description of the disease which Addison published in the year 1855 remains singularly complete, and (with some additions) practically represents our clinical knowledge at the present time. The following is his description of the disease (I omit the paragraphs relating to idiopathic anæmia which have already been quoted on page 57):—

Addison's description of the disease.—" It was whilst seeking in vain to throw some additional light upon this form of anæmia that I stumbled upon the curious facts which it is my more immediate object to make known to the profession ; and however unimportant or unsatisfactory they may at first sight appear, I cannot but indulge the hope that, by attracting the attention and enlisting the co-operation of the profession at large, they may lead to the subject being properly examined and sifted, and the inquiry so extended as to suggest, at least, some interesting physiological speculation, if not still more important practical indications.

" The leading and characteristic features of the morbid state to which I would direct attention are—anæmia, general languor and debility, remarkable feebleness of the heart's action, irritability of the stomach, and a peculiar change of colour in the skin, occurring in connection with a diseased condition of the ' supra-renal capsules.'

" As has been observed in other forms of anæmic disease, this singular disorder usually commences in such a manner that the individual has considerable difficulty in assigning the number of weeks, or even months that have elapsed since he first experienced indications of failing health and strength ; the rapidity, however, with which the morbid change takes place varies in different instances.

" In some cases that rapidity is very great, a few weeks proving sufficient to break up the powers of the constitution, or even to destroy life, the result, I believe, being determined by the extent, and by the more or less speedy development, of the organic lesion.

" The patient, in most of the cases I have seen, has been observed gradually to fall off in general health ; he becomes languid and weak, indisposed to either bodily or mental exertion ; the appetite is impaired or entirely lost ; the whites of the eyes become pearly ; the pulse small and feeble, or perhaps somewhat large, but excessively soft and compressible ; the body wastes, without however presenting the dry and shrivelled skin and extreme emaciation usually attendant on protracted malignant disease ; slight pain or uneasiness is from time to time referred to the region of the stomach, and there is occasionally actual vomiting, which in one instance was both urgent and distressing ; and it is by no means uncommon for the patient to manifest indications of disturbed cerebral circulation.

" Notwithstanding these unequivocal signs of feeble circulation, anæmia, and general prostration, neither the most diligent inquiry nor the most careful physical examination tend to throw the slightest gleam of light upon the precise nature of the patient's malady ; nor do we succeed in fixing upon any special lesion as the cause of this gradual and extraordinary constitutional change.

" We may, indeed, suspect some malignant or strumous disease —we may be led to inquire into the condition of the so-called blood-making organs—but we discover no proof of organic change anywhere—no enlargement of spleen, thyroid, thymus, or lymphatic glands—no evidence of renal disease, of purpura, of previous exhausting diarrhœa, or ague, or any long-continued exposure to miasmatic influences ; but with a greater or less manifestation of the symptoms already enumerated, we discover a most remarkable and, so far as I know, characteristic discoloration taking place in the skin—sufficiently marked, indeed, as generally to have attracted the attention of the patient himself or of the patient's friends.

" This discoloration pervades the whole surface of the body, but is commonly most strongly manifested on the face, neck, superior extremities, penis, and scrotum, and in the flexures of the axillæ and around the navel.

" It may be said to present a dingy or smoky appearance, or various tints or shades of deep amber or chestnut-brown ; and in one instance the skin was so universally and so deeply darkened, that but for the features the patient might have been mistaken for a mulatto.

" This singular discoloration usually increases with the advance of the disease ; the anæmia, languor, failure of appetite, and feebleness of the heart, become aggravated ; a darkish streak usually appears on the commissure of the lips ; the body wastes, but without the emaciation and dry, harsh condition of the surface, so commonly observed in ordinary malignant diseases ; the pulse becomes smaller and weaker ; and, without any special complaint of pain or uneasiness, the patient at length gradually sinks and expires."

Detailed description of the symptoms of Addison's disease.
—The symptoms of Addison's disease, or, to speak more accurately, the chief symptoms and signs of typical and uncomplicated cases of Addison's disease, may be described as partly positive and partly

negative; and may for the purposes of description be arranged in the following groups, which are by no means artificial :—

1. Asthenia, feebleness of the action of the heart, and the symptoms and signs which result therefrom.

2. Nausea, vomiting, and other symptoms indicative of gastro-intestinal irritation.

3. Pain, and in some cases tenderness on pressure, in the epigastric, hypochondriac, and lumbar regions; in other words, symptoms due to irritation of sensory nerve fibres in the neighbourhood of the suprarenal bodies.

4. Pigmentation of the skin and mucous membranes.

5. Anæmia.

6. Symptoms due to derangement of the cerebro-spinal (more especially the cerebral) nerve apparatus, such as headache, anæsthesia, muscular twitchings, delirium, convulsions, etc.

7. The absence of any elevation of temperature ; in fact, in most cases the presence of a subnormal temperature.

8. The absence of any marked emaciation.

9. The absence of symptoms and signs indicative of local organic disease (other than the disease of the suprarenal capsules) to account for the asthenia and other symptoms which characterise the condition.

It must of course be distinctly understood that all of these symptoms are not necessarily present even in typical and uncomplicated cases of the disease. Thus, the anæmia is in some cases only slight, in others absent ; in some cases there is marked wasting (loss of weight and muscle) ; in others, pain in the back is absent, etc.

Let us now consider some of the more important symptoms individually and in detail.

Asthenia and Feebleness of the Action of the Heart.— Asthenia is the most constant, and consequently, in some respects, the most important symptom of Addison's disease. Although it varies considerably in degree in different cases, and indeed often very notably from time to time in the same case, it is the one symptom which is never altogether absent in well-marked cases of the disease ; usually, too, it is the first symptom of which the patient makes complaint. Now, since in most cases the weakness is developed very gradually, since it usually arises insidiously, without being preceded by any illness or other obvious exciting cause, and since in most cases, in the earlier stages of the disease at all events, it is unattended with any marked loss of flesh, it seems reasonable to conclude that it (the asthenia), and the lesion of the capsules on which it directly or indirectly depends, have in all probability, in many cases at least, been gradually and slowly developing for months, possibly in some cases for years, unknown to the patient. This statement is quite in accord with what we know of the morbid anatomy of the disease. Many cases of Addison's disease have been reported, in which, although the symptoms were only of a few months' duration, the capsules were found after death to be completely destroyed and *in an advanced stage of caseo-calcareous degeneration.* In such cases, as Sir Samuel Wilks pointed out in some of his earlier writings on the subject, the capsules had, in all probability, been destroyed for years before the date at which the disease is said (from the clinical history) to have commenced. The date at which the patient *first complains* of symptoms, and the date at which a disease commences and at which the symptoms actually begin to develop are, as I have pointed out in speaking of the development of myxœdema, not always synonymous. Now there are probably no cases to which this statement applies with greater force than to most cases of Addison's disease. The onset is so insidious, and the loss of strength, which, be it observed, is in many cases the only symptom at the commencement of the disease, is, in the earlier stages of the case, so slight, that the patient slowly and insensibly, as it were, passes from a state of health into a condition of disease. It is probable, I think, that in many cases it is only after the disease has been in existence for some considerable time that the languor and debility become sufficiently accentuated to attract the attention of the patient, or, at all events, to make him suspect that he is really ill, and to lead him to take medical advice.

The asthenia seems to be the direct result of the lesion of the suprarenal capsules.

As the case goes on the asthenia becomes more and more marked, and the patient complains of feeling "weak," "tired," "languid," "unfit for any exertion, either of body or mind," "good for nothing," "quite done up," "completely exhausted," "utterly prostrated," etc.

Loss of vasomotor nerve tone and feebleness of the heart's action are important features—I am disposed to think perhaps the most important features—of the disease.

The nerve tone, reserve force, recuperative and resisting powers, soon become seriously impaired; and comparatively trivial causes, such as slight bodily exertion, mental excitement, an ordinary dose of purgative medicine, an attack of vomiting, or a trivial intercurrent illness, which in a healthy man would cause little or no disturbance, may produce the most profound prostration and exhaustion. This lack of resisting power and want of proper recuperative energy are, from a therapeutic point of view, most important features of the disease. In more than one of the recorded cases death resulted from an ordinary dose of purgative medicine. It cannot be too forcibly pointed out, that in the treatment and management of cases of Addison's disease it is of paramount importance to protect the patient from everything which (in him) will be likely to cause exhaustion and depression. There can, I think, be little doubt that the duration of many cases of Addison's disease depends upon the nature of the patients' surroundings and the care with which the patients are protected from everything likely to be in the least injurious and to produce depression.

Paroxysmal exacerbations of the debility and languor are of frequent occurrence. These exacerbations are apparently in some cases the result of attacks of nausea and vomiting, or of gastro-intestinal irritation, to which I will presently refer in more detail.

The asthenia is reflected externally in the appearance of the patient; his facial expression and whole bearing are, when the disease is at all advanced, suggestive of languor and debility.

The condition of the heart and pulse afford corroborative evidence of this depression.

The pulse is always weak, and in the great majority of cases small, though in some, as Addison himself pointed out, it is full and soft. In some cases, more especially in the later stages, the pulse may be jerking in character. The same condition of pulse is seen in the later stages of some cases of pernicious anæmia.

During the paroxysmal attacks of exhaustion and depression, the pulse may be so small as to be almost or even entirely imperceptible. The feebleness and smallness of the pulse are sometimes so marked that the condition of the pulse has been compared to that of the collapse stage of Asiatic cholera. It must, however, be noticed that in many cases of Addison's disease in which the pulse is imperceptible, the patient, while at rest and in the recumbent position, is not, strictly speaking, in other respects collapsed. But so far as the condition of the heart and pulse are concerned, many patients in the advanced stage of Addison's disease may be said to be in a constant (chronic) condition of collapse.

The weakness of the action of the heart is very apparent on physical examination. The impulse of the apex beat is always feeble, often altogether imperceptible ; the heart sounds are in many cases faint and distant. In some cases, the area of cardiac dulness appears to be diminished ; after death the heart is often found to be smaller than normal. This atrophy of the heart, which has been recorded in several cases, and which was present in a very notable degree in a case which came under my observation a few years ago, has hardly, I think, received the attention which it deserves. I am disposed to regard it as a very important pathological feature of the disease.

This opinion is corroborated by the experimental observations of Schäfer and Oliver ; they have shown that the medullary portion of the suprarenal capsules contains (secretes) a substance which has a remarkably stimulating effect upon the muscular system, and especially upon the heart and arteries. Consequently, when the secretion of the suprarenal capsules is suppressed, we would expect muscular weakness and atrophy, and especially cardiac muscular weakness, to be developed.

The smallness and weakness of the pulse are perhaps not entirely due to weak action of the heart. In many cases of Addison's disease there is disease or irritation of the abdominal sympathetic (the suprarenal and solar plexuses of nerves) ; and we know that irritation of the abdominal sympathetic produces, amongst other results, dilatation of the blood-vessels in the abdomen, and that this overloading of the abdominal vessels is sometimes so great that the vessels in other parts of the body are depleted of their blood, and consequently under-filled. Possibly the smallness of the pulse in Addison's disease is produced, in part at least, in this way.

The remarkable feebleness of the heart's action, and the inadequate supply of blood to the brain and peripheral organs, afford a satisfactory explanation of many of the symptoms which are met with in Addison's disease. The *palpitation of the heart and shortness of breath*, which are so apt to occur on exertion, the *tendency to fainting*, the *giddiness* which results from stooping the head or suddenly rising from the recumbent to the erect position, the *temporary disturbances of vision*, and many of the *cerebral symptoms*, which are apt to occur in the later stages of the disease, are doubtless due to these conditions.

The facility with which cerebral anæmia and fainting are produced by effort, as, for example, by suddenly rising from the recumbent to the sitting or erect position, should always be kept in view. Several cases have been reported in which slight efforts have been followed by fatal syncope.

Nausea, Vomiting, and other symptoms indicative of Gastro-intestinal Irritation.—In almost all cases of Addison's disease the *appetite* is markedly impaired, and in some entirely lost. Kussmaul, however, has recorded a case in which there was an insatiable appetite, but this is altogether exceptional. Some patients seem to have a special distaste or actual repugnance for butcher's meat. A "sinking feeling" in the pit of the stomach is often complained of. *Thirst* is in some cases complained of.

Irritability of the stomach, sickness, nausea, retching, and vomiting are highly characteristic symptoms, and are present in most cases of the disease at some period or other of their course. The nausea and vomiting are usually developed after the asthenia, but in some cases they are the first symptoms to attract the attention of the patient.

In many cases, the sickness and vomiting occur in paroxysms, often without any apparent exciting cause; the vomiting may or may not be associated with pain or tenderness on pressure in the epigastric or hypochondriac regions. In more than one case, these attacks have appeared to me to resemble most closely the gastric crises of locomotor ataxia. The attacks of sickness and vomiting are often accompanied or followed by intense prostration and depression. The vomited matters in some cases contain large quantities of mucus, and occasionally (though quite exceptionally) blood. It may be pointed out in this connection that after death the stomach has often been found to contain an abnormal amount of mucus, and that its mucous membrane in many cases shows distinct evidence of irritation—it may be deeply congested, ecchymosed, or even superficially ulcerated.

The *tongue* is generally clean and moist; it is often pigmented in the manner which is described below.

The *bowels* are usually constipated, but in many cases diarrhœa is very readily produced, and paroxysmal attacks of diarrhœa occasionally occur without any apparent cause. This tendency to diarrhœa should always be borne in mind; strong purgatives should never be given in Addison's disease; and even mild aperients should only be prescribed with the greatest care, for violent diarrhœa, followed by intense prostration, and even death itself, have been known to follow an ordinary dose of purgative medicine.

The *spleen* has in many cases been enlarged after death, and the increase can, in some cases, be detected during life.

The condition of the *liver* calls for no special remark.

Pains in the abdomen and back.—In many cases, although the fact does not seem to have come under Addison's own observation, pain and sometimes tenderness on pressure are experienced in the epigastric, hypogastric, or lumbar regions, and over the lower dorsal or lumbar portions of the spinal column.

These pains are doubtless due to irritation of the suprarenal nerves and solar plexus. In some cases, the attacks of pain are paroxysmal, and not unfrequently associated with nausea and vomiting. As I have already stated, these paroxysmal attacks of pain, when accompanied by nausea and vomiting, may resemble very closely the gastric crises of locomotor ataxia.

In some cases, pain is complained of when pressure is made from behind over the position of the suprarenal capsule.

Dr Greenhow states that the abdominal pain and tenderness are not infrequently associated with an almost spasmodic rigidity of the abdominal muscles, as if they were instinctively contracted in order to protect the more deeply-seated parts from pressure.

Pigmentation of the skin and mucous membranes.—Discoloration of the skin and mucous membranes (more especially of the mucous membrane of the mouth) is perhaps the most remarkable, and, from the point of view of a positive diagnosis, certainly the most important symptom, or rather sign, of Addison's disease.

It must however be remembered that the pigmentation is by no means always well marked, and, in fact, in some rare cases, especially cases which run an unusually rapid course, it is absent altogether.

In the great majority of cases, the pigmentation is developed either subsequently to, or simultaneously with, the asthenia and other constitutional symptoms ; as a general rule, the pigmentation of the skin is not noticed until the asthenia has been in existence for some considerable time ; but numerous cases have been reported in which the discoloration of the skin was the first symptom to attract attention. Thus, in a case reported by Dr Rankin,[*] discoloration of the face and hands was the symptom which first attracted the attention of the patient, " and she was often annoyed, when making calls, by friends offering her water to wash her hands." Dr Greenhow gives a number of instances in which the discoloration of the skin was developed several months,[†] and in one case, it is said even as much as eight years, before the asthenia and other characteristic constitutional symptoms were noticed. But it may perhaps be doubted whether the discoloration of the forehead, face, and neck, which developed in this remarkable case eight years before the constitutional symptoms became marked, was actually due to the capsular lesion.

In many of the cases in which the pigmentation is the first

* " Medical Times," 24th May 1856, p. 518.
† " Croonian Lectures on Addison's Disease," p. 20.

symptom to attract notice, it will, I suspect, be found on careful inquiry that a certain degree of asthenia is at the same time present ; the very gradual and insidious manner in which the constitutional symptoms are usually developed, and the fact that some asthenia is often present for months before the languor and weakness become sufficiently marked *to be complained of*, have obviously a very important bearing on this point. Probably the statement which Dr Pye-Smith makes in the second edition of Hilton Fagge's great work,* is as precise a statement as it is possible to make with regard to the period at which the pigmentation is developed. He says : " The skin is always darker when the symptoms of Addison's disease have lasted more than a year."

The discoloration is in many cases so marked, that, even in the earlier stages of the case, it may at once be noticed by persons with whom the patient is brought in contact. Thus, in a case reported by Dr Henry Davy, " the patient, a male, aged 25, obtained employment as a baker, but after he had continued his employment for a few months, he was dismissed by his master on account of his ' dirty appearance,' for the discoloration had by this time so increased that his hands, arms, and face were quite ' dark coloured.' "†
In another case, reported by Dr Langdon Down,‡ it is stated that "the patient's master noticed that his face was very dark when he engaged him, but the man replied that he had been helping his brother painting a greenhouse, and had got sunburnt. The indoor life, however, did not diminish the discoloration ; on the contrary, it rapidly increased, and his fellow-servants gave him the name of ' The Missionary.' "

As regards its *extent, depth*, and *colour*, the pigmentation varies very considerably in different cases.

In some rare and quite exceptional cases, the pigmentation, as has been previously stated, is entirely absent.

In a small proportion of cases of the disease, the discoloration is so limited in distribution that it may easily escape notice unless very carefully looked for. More than one case of this kind has come under my notice (see Cases II., III., and XI.).

The lesson which Case III. taught me, viz., that in cases of profound and apparently causeless asthenia, the whole surface of the skin, and especially the buccal mucous membrane, should be carefully examined in a good light, since the asthenia may be due to Addi-

---

* " Practice of Medicine," 2nd edition, Vol. ii., p. 736.
† " Transactions of the Pathological Society of London," 1882, p. 360.
‡ *Ibid*, 1869, p. 389.

son's disease, has since proved valuable. I would particularly
emphasise the fact that in this case, and also in Case II., rapid
and extreme emaciation and loss of weight were very prominent
features.   In Case III. the patient had lost 3 st. in six months ;
and in Case II., 4 st. in nine weeks.

In the majority of cases in which the asthenia and other symptoms
have lasted for any length of time, the discoloration of the skin
is marked and extensively distributed over the body. It may be
diffused, though by no means equally so, over the whole surface of
the body.   In some cases, the whole skin is so deeply pigmented
that the patient, originally of fair complexion, comes to resemble
one of the darker races.   In a case reported by Merkel, the patient,
who used during his illness frequently to come to the hospital, was
known to the inmates of the institution by the nickname of "Turko."*
In the case which is represented in Plate VI. of my Atlas, the skin,
which was originally white and fair, became as black as that of a
negro.   The clinical features of that case (Case I.), which is a highly
typical and characteristic one, are fully detailed below.

The pigmented patches are rarely, if ever, abruptly defined, as
the dark portions of the skin in leucoderma are; in Addison's
disease, the pigmented portions, and the more deeply pigmented
patches in those cases in which the whole skin is discoloured,
merge insensibly into the surrounding skin.

The discoloration is usually most marked—(1) in those situations which are exposed to the atmosphere, such as the face and
back of the hands ; (2) in those parts of the skin (such as the
areolæ of the nipples, the genital organs in the male, the perineum,
the sides of the axilla, the groins, and the skin around the umbilicus)
in which there is normally most pigment ; and (3) in those parts
of the skin which are exposed to friction or irritation of any kind.

In well-marked cases of Addison's disease, the areolæ of the
nipples are usually very deeply stained ; in the case which is represented in my Atlas, Plates VI. and VII., the nipples and their areolæ
were as dark as in a pregnant woman. But this is not invariable, even
in those cases in which the pigmentation is extensive. Two well-
marked cases have come under my own notice in which the pigmentation was very marked over almost the whole body, but in which
the nipples and their areolæ were not specially dark-coloured ; and
many similar instances are to be found amongst the recorded cases.
Nevertheless, as Dr Greenhow has pointed out, deep pigmentation
of the areolæ of the nipples is very generally present, and is of con-

---

* "Ziemssen's Cyclopædia," Vol. viii., p. 648.

siderable diagnostic importance in distinguishing the discoloration of Addison's disease from some other forms of skin pigmentation. The same writer lays great stress upon the presence of "small, well-defined black specks, like black freckles or moles, on already discoloured portions of skin," as indicating that the discoloration is due to Addison's disease. In Plate X. of Addison's memoir, in which the appearance of the skin in a case of cancer of the stomach with secondary deposits in the renal vein, and apoplectic destruction of the left suprarenal capsule are represented, these small deeply pigmented spots are well seen. Sir Samuel Wilks and many other authorities have denied that this was a case of Addison's disease. It must, however, be admitted, that if the Plate accurately represents the appearance of the patient, the discoloration of the skin was very remarkable, and unlike anything which is usually seen in cancer.

The penis and scrotum are usually deeply pigmented; in a case recorded by Dr Welford, the discoloration of the genital organs was so extreme (after death) that the friends asked if the parts were not mortified.

Parts of the skin which have been subjected to friction or irritation are apt to become very deeply pigmented. Portions of skin to which blisters have been applied are usually very deeply pigmented, but this is only an exaggeration of what takes place in many perfectly healthy persons. Deeply stained bands have in some cases been met with above the knee, due to the pressure of garters, and around the waist in women, due to the pressure of petticoat-strings and clothes; and in one case (the patient was a baker's boy) the shoulders were marked with dark stripes, corresponding in position to the parts which had been pressed upon by the bands by which a heavy basket was slung on the patient's back.

The skin over the vertebral spines is apt, as the result of the pressure and irritation to which it is subjected (more especially when the patient is thin, and confined to bed for any length of time), to become deeply stained; and in rare cases, of which III. and XI. are examples, this is the only part of the skin which is pigmented. This point should be remembered, for it may be of great diagnostic significance.

Superficial cicatrices and portions of the skin which have been the seat of superficial eruptions are usually deeply stained; whereas, according to Dr Greenhow, the cicatrices of deeper injuries usually remain pale and white. In the case which is represented in my Atlas, Plate VI., the lupoid-like patches, which were situated on the lower part of the abdomen, were almost black; and in Case IV., in which very marked improvement resulted from feeding with suprarenal extract, the pitmarks left by a previous attack of small-pox were much more deeply pigmented than the surrounding portions of the skin of the face.

The exact tint or shade of the discoloration varies in different cases; brown, or some mixture of brown, is usually the predominant tint ; the discoloration which is produced by staining the skin with walnut juice exactly represents the colour in many cases of Addison's disease. The following are some of the terms in which the discoloration has been described : "dingy," "dusky," "smoky," " various shades or tints of deep amber or chestnut brown," "dirty brown," "yellowish brown," "greenish yellow," "dark brown," "deep bronze," " almost black," " mulatto-coloured," etc.

In some cases, it is stated that the hair and iris shared in the discoloration, and became darker as the disease advanced.

The nails are very rarely pigmented. I only know of two cases in which the nails were discoloured. In the first, a very remarkable case, reported by Dr Finny,[*] which seems undoubtedly, so far as one can judge from the symptoms, to have been a case of Addison's disease, " the nails of both hands and of a few of the toes were stained ; in many, the pigment was along the free border, and also over the body, a space one-eighth of an inch in which no staining existed separating them. Again, in some the pigment was laid down in longitudinal streaks of a black colour, the lunulæ of several being discoloured equally with the body of the nail. The pigmentation of the nails and fingers are such that the more observant would be at once struck by it." In the second case, which is reported by Drs Alezais and Arnaud,[†] and which was in every way typical, the pigmentation was very marked over the whole body, the discoloration being especially deep on the face, scrotum, penis, *and the lunulæ of the nails ;* pigmented patches were also present on the buccal mucous membrane.

In one case, the teeth were, it is said, discoloured. [‡]

In some cases, the discoloration of the skin seems to vary in intensity and depth from time to time. In one of my cases (Case I.) the discoloration of the face and hands was said to become distinctly darker during the menstrual periods.

Even in those cases in which the discoloration is very marked,

---

[*] " Dublin Medical Journal," 1882, p. 293.

[†] " Revue de Médecine," 10th April 1891, p. 296.

[‡] Case 34 in Jaccoud's list of cases, reported by Gromier, " Gaz. Médec." Lyon, 1857.

the skin usually retains its normal softness, elasticity, and pliability ; it does not become rough and wrinkled, shrivelled, or dry. Exceptions to this, as to almost every other general statement connected with the disease, do, however, occasionally occur. In a case reported by Dr Bristowe, "the surface of the skin was neither dry nor moist, but was covered with a very fine scurf." * In the case depicted in Plate VI. of my Atlas, the scalp was thickly coated with furfuraceous scales ; and, at the time when the drawing was made, although the skin of the body generally was beautifully silky, soft, and pliable, there were one or two slightly rough patches on the face.

Eczematous and other skin eruptions have occasionally been noted ; patches of leucoderma are by no means very unfrequent : in one of my cases (Case I.) several lupoid-like patches were present on the lower part of the abdomen and one in the left groin.

Pigmentation of the Mucous Membranes.—Deposits of pigment on the lips, gums, buccal mucous membrane, tongue, and palate are of frequent occurrence, and are of the greatest diagnostic value.

On the *lips, gums,* and *tongue,* the pigmented patches are usually of a bluish-black colour ; in tint they closely resemble ink-stains or stains produced by blackberry juice. On the *buccal mucous membrane* the pigmented patches are usually (always in my experience) of a dirty brown tint, but in some cases they are bluish-black, or almost black.

On the *lips,* the deposits of pigment, which are usually situated along the line of contact of the upper with the lower lip, or near the junction of the mucous membrane and of the outer skin, generally take the form of bluish black streaks running longitudinally. In some cases the lips have been so deeply stained as at first sight to suggest sordes.

On the *gums,* the pigmentation usually occupies very much the same position as it does in lead-poisoning ; and, in fact, the discoloration of the gums, due to Addison's disease, has actually been mistaken for that due to plumbism. In some cases, the pigmentation infiltrated the gum tissue below the free margin (Case VI.).

On the *buccal mucous membrane,* the pigmented deposits are most frequently met with about the angle of the mouth, and on the inner side of the cheek opposite the line of junction of the closed teeth. As Dr Greenhow has pointed out, the localisation of the pigmented deposits on the buccal mucous membrane appears in

---

* "Addison's Disease," by Dr Greenhow, p. 132.

some cases to be determined by the irritation of rough, sharp, or projecting teeth.

On the *tongue* the pigmented patches are usually situated near the free margin of the organ ; but in the case represented in my Atlas, Plates VI. and VII., in which the pigmentation of the tongue was unusually well marked, the deposits were chiefly situated on the dorsum, and especially about the root. In that case, too, several small, round, ball-like collections of pigment were present under the tongue, on each side of, and apparently adhering to, the lingual arteries. Such a condition has, so far as I know, not been previously observed in the disease. It is also present in another case which I have at present under observation (see Case VI.).

Deposits of pigment may also occur in other parts of the body, such as the *nymphæ*, the *labia majora* and *minora*,* the *vagina*,† and the *upper part of the œsophagus*. In a few cases (but whether the staining in these situations was actually the result of the lesion of the capsules has been doubted) deposits of pigment have been found after death in the *peritoneum* and *pleura*.‡

Anæmia.—Addison, in the passages which I have quoted, and in other parts of his memoir, lays great stress on anæmia as a symptom of the disease. In this he differs from Sir Samuel Wilks, who states positively that anæmia is not present. Sir Samuel Wilks says :—" An opinion has prevailed amongst many who have had no experience of the complaint, that the constitutional symptoms of Addison's disease are characterised by anæmia and wasting. This is not the case, as neither of these conditions is present." §

Now, at the first glance, a patient affected with typical Addison's disease certainly does look profoundly anæmic ; the remarkably pale, pearly conjunctiva—" *the anæmiated eye*," as Addison himself termed it—contrasting so forcibly as it does with the dark hue of the face, is highly suggestive of marked anæmia ; but in most cases of the disease—and this is a very striking feature of the

---

* See cases by Drs Hadden and Seymour Taylor, "Path. Soc. Trans.," 1885. pp. 435 and 449.

† Dr Dixon Mann's case, "Lancet", 21st March 1891, p. 653.

‡ See Dr Hadden's case, "Path. Soc. Trans.", 1885, p. 436. Also case 21 in Sir Samuel Wilks' series ; in this case specks of pigment of a dark colour were present in the omentum and peritoneum, and on the surface of the ovaries and mucous membrane of the stomach, near the pylorus.—"Guy's Hospital Reports, vol. viii. (1862).

§ Russell Reynold's "System of Medicine," vol. v., p. 357.

case which is represented in my Atlas, Plate VI.—the lips, gums, and tongue are well, indeed it may be deeply, coloured.

But although a high degree of bloodlessness is rarely met with, I cannot help thinking that a moderate degree of anæmia, as estimated by the number of red blood corpuscles, is not unfrequently present. In a typical case reported by Greenhow, the patient is stated to have been "remarkably anæmic, the lining membrane of the eyelids, the lips, tongue, and gums being pale and bloodless." * In at least three of the cases which have come under my own observation, the buccal mucous membrane covering the inside of the cheeks, the conjunctiva covering the lower lid as well as that covering the eyeball itself, and the nails, were paler than normal. In one case (Case I.), for example, the red corpuscles numbered 3,250,000 as compared with 4,500,000, which may be taken as the average standard of health in the female; while the hæmoglobin as estimated by Gowers' instrument equalled 80 per cent. The condition of the blood in this case—some diminution of the red blood corpuscles, but no diminution of the hæmoglobin—has been present in some other cases which I have examined. In another case which came under my notice a few years ago (the patient was a male), the red blood corpuscles numbered 3,500,000 per cubic millimetre.

Now, as I have previously pointed out (see p. 16), 80 per cent. of hæmoglobin, as estimated by Gowers' instrument, is, in my experience, little if at all short of the average standard of health. But whether this be allowed or not, it is certain that the corpuscular richness in hæmoglobin (the percentage of hæmoglobin in each individual red blood corpuscle), was, in this case, at least equal to the normal. Such a condition of the blood is very different from that in chlorosis. It is hardly necessary to add that the comparatively slight diminution in the number of the red blood corpuscles at once distinguishes the anæmia of Addison's disease (granting that some anæmia is often present) from the idiopathic anæmia of Addison—progressive pernicious anæmia, as it is now termed; though in some cases of Addison's disease, as in pernicious anæmia, the colour index may be above the normal.

On microscopical examination the red corpuscles are usually normal in size and shape. In some cases, a slight excess of white corpuscles is present; but, so far as my experience enables me to judge, this is inconstant. Buhl and Laschkewitsch (quoted by Merkel †) lay stress upon the absence of the tendency of the

---

* "Addison's Disease," p. 101.　† Ziemssen's "Cyclopædia," vol. viii., p. 655.

blood corpuscles to form rouleaux. I have not observed this in any of the cases I have examined ; and Dr Greenhow's opinion on this point coincides with mine, for he states that in the cases which he examined microscopically the blood appeared to be normal.

In one or two cases free pigment granules have been described in the blood, but confirmation of the fact is required before any importance can be attached to their presence. In none of the cases which I have examined were pigmented particles present.

Nervous Symptoms.—During the course of Addison's disease various nervous symptoms are apt to occur. In addition to the pains in the abdomen and back, and the paroxysmal attacks of (? nervous) vomiting, diarrhœa, and cardiac debility, which have already been described, headache, vertigo, temporary dimness of vision, flashes of light before the eyes, noises in the ears, temporary deafness, are of frequent occurrence.

Numbness, anæsthesia, and hyperæsthesia are occasionally, though rarely, met with. Merkel states that he has observed severe pains in the joints, which resembled in character the arthritic neuroses of hysterical patients ; these pains were unaccompanied by swelling, and were not increased by direct pressure over the joints.

An excessive tendency to sleep occurs in some cases ; in others, more especially during the paroxysmal exacerbations, and particularly during the periods of depression in the later stages of the disease, that form of restlessness and sleeplessness, which is so frequently associated with profound exhaustion and anæmia, may be a prominent symptom.

Rigors, subsultus tendinum, choreic-like twitchings, and general or localised epileptiform convulsions (which sometimes occur in the earlier stages of the disease), are not unfrequent before death ; in fact, in several of the reported cases, the patient has died in an epileptic fit.

The intellectual faculties usually remain unaffected, at all events until the later stages of the case. Before death, the patient often passes into a listless, torpid, or "typhoid" state ; stupor, delirium, or coma frequently occur during the last few hours or days of life. When these symptoms are developed, the end is usually near at hand ; but this is not always so. In a remarkable case, which was under the care of Dr Burdon Sanderson, "the patient remained for several days in a state of noisy, talkative delirium, frequently endeavouring to get out of bed, making grimaces, singing, vociferating rapidly and incoherently, or shrieking out as if in terror." She, however, recovered from this condition (which was perhaps hysterical), and died nearly a year afterwards from the disease, death being preceded by an epileptic fit.* The question naturally occurs whether the delirium in this case was not hysterical.

Some of the nervous symptoms, such as pains in the back and abdomen and paroxysmal attacks of nervous vomiting, are due to implication of the suprarenal nerves or branches of the solar plexus. Others, such as numbness or anæsthesia in the legs, are perhaps the result of lesions of the spinal cord—for such lesions have been described in some cases of the disease.

The Temperature in Addison's disease is usually normal or subnormal. Absence of febrile disturbance is one of the characteristic (negative) signs of the disease.

Patients affected with Addison's disease usually bear both heat and cold, but especially cold, badly ; as I have previously pointed out, their vasomotor nerve tone and resisting power are seriously enfeebled. They require to be carefully protected from cold, and from all the vicissitudes of the weather.

The state of Nutrition.—The absence of any marked degree of emaciation is an important feature of most uncomplicated cases of Addison's disease. In the earlier stages, there may be absolutely no loss of flesh, and this even when the asthenia is very pronounced. As the case goes on, the patient does, as a rule, lose weight, the muscles, as one might naturally expect, becoming soft, flabby, and more or less atrophied. But in uncomplicated cases the body usually remains well covered with fat even up to the time of death. In many of the recorded cases, in which emaciation was said to have been present during life, a considerable layer of fat was, on post-mortem examination, found in the front wall of the abdomen, and over the body generally.

The very striking atrophy which is in some cases met with in the heart has already been alluded to.

The absence of emaciation, so far as the fat is concerned, is not, however, as some writers have stated, an invariable characteristic of Addison's disease. Some exceptional cases have been recorded, and Cases II. and III. are excellent illustrations, in which considerable emaciation was present, even in uncomplicated cases. Distaste for food, and unusually severe and long-continued vomiting, were, perhaps, the causes of the emaciation in some cases of this kind ; but this is certainly not always so. When the lesion of the capsules is complicated by extensive phthisis, active caries of the spine, or, as it sometimes is, with suppuration (psoas abscess, etc.), and with

---

* "Transactions of the Pathological Society of London," Vol. xx., p. 378.

hectic fever, marked emaciation may of course be present ; but even when complicated with lesions of this kind, there is seldom, if ever, in Addison's disease, the extreme emaciation and the dry withered appearance which are characteristic of the cachexia of advanced malignant disease.

In some cases emaciation, more especially wasting of the muscles, seems to be part and parcel of the disease. In Addison's original description, wasting is mentioned as a feature of the disease.

Dr Greenhow used to lay great stress upon the absence of emaciation ; indeed, in one case about which I consulted him some twenty years ago, he went so far as to say that the fact that the patient was emaciated negatived the view of Addison's disease.

Now, while I admit that in most cases of Addison's disease, there is no emaciation—at all events so far as the body fat is concerned—I know, from cases which have come under my own observation, that most marked and rapid emaciation, without any associated visceral disease to account for it, is in some cases developed. I believe that in the great majority of cases of Addison's disease the muscles, including the heart muscle, become atrophied ; indeed, as I have stated, I am disposed to think that the atrophy of the heart muscle is one of the most important clinical and pathological facts connected with the disease. In one of my cases (Case II.) the patient lost no less than 4 stones in weight in a period of nine weeks. I am disposed to think that this great loss of weight was chiefly due to the disease of the suprarenal capsules ; it can hardly, I think, be satisfactorily accounted for by the very recent deposit of tubercle, with practically speaking little or no peritonitis, which was found in the peritoneum after death. In another case (Case III.), the patient lost 3 st. in weight during a period of six months ; and it was the recollection of the facts of Case III. which led me, after I had excluded some of the conditions which are more common causes of asthenia and emaciation, to look for the symptoms of Addison's disease in Case II. I repeat, that in some (exceptional) cases of Addison's disease there is marked and rapid loss of weight and flesh.

The urine in Addison's disease does not as a rule present any striking or characteristic change. The daily amount is sometimes less, sometimes greater, than the normal ; the specific gravity is usually low. The amount of urea *per diem* is usually considerably below the normal, but this is partly at least accounted for by the small amount of food, and the kind of food, which the patient takes ; there seems good reason, however, for supposing that in Addison's disease the tissue metabolism is below the normal standard.

In a few of the recorded cases, an excess of indican has, it is said, been present in the urine, but this seems exceptional. In a case which came under my notice a few years ago, but in which I had no opportunity of making a detailed analysis of the urine, the addition of nitric acid produced an exceedingly dark discoloration of the urine. In the case which is reproduced in Plate VI. in my Atlas of Clinical Medicine, in which the pigmentation of the skin was extremely marked, the urinary pigments were by no means increased—in fact, rather the reverse. Dr William Hunter kindly made an analysis for me of the urinary pigments in this case.

In a small number of the reported cases of Addison's disease, albumen, pus, or other abnormal constituents have been present in the urine ; but their occurrence was clearly accidental, and due to some complicating condition.

Non-development or atrophy of the genital organs and of the mammæ.—In a case, that of a man aged twenty-nine, which I examined post mortem a few years ago, the genital organs were completely undeveloped, the testicles being no larger than small filberts. The same fact has been recorded in a few other cases. In the case of a girl, aged eighteen, reported by Dr Dixon Mann, " the uterus was infantile, and the external genitals like those of a young child ; the ovaries were small, and showed one or two cicatrices, but not of recent origin." *

The mammæ are not unfrequently much atrophied in the later stages of the disease, but this is certainly not always so, even in very long standing cases (see Case I.).

The *menstruation* is usually irregular or entirely suppressed. In one of my own cases (Case XI.) there was dysmenorrhœa and menorrhagia.

Fœtid odour of the body.—In a few of the recorded cases a fœtid odour, said sometimes to resemble the odour given off from the bodies of the darker races of mankind, has been observed. In some cases, especially towards the termination and shortly before death, a cadaveric smell has been exhaled from the body ; in others the breath had a heavy, ethereal, or acetone-like odour.

The frequency of occurrence of the more important symptoms, in my twelve cases of Addison's disease, is shown in Table 7.

---

* " Lancet," 21st March 1891, p. 653.

TABLE 7.—SHOWING THE MORE IMPORTANT SYMPTOMS IN TWELVE CASES OF ADDISON'S DISEASE OBSERVED BY THE AUTHOR DURING LIFE.

No.	Age	Sex	Asthenia	Feebleness of heart's action.	Emaciation.	Vomiting.	Diarrhœa.	Pain in Back.	Pearliness of Conjunctivæ.	Anæmia.	Pigmentation.				Result.	Total Duration.	Post mortem.
											Skin.	Freckles.	Areolæ of Nipples.	Buccal Mucous Membrane			
1	26	F.	M.	M.	o	1	o	o	1	1	M.	o	1	M.	Death	13 to 14 years	None
2	50	M.	M.	M.	M.(4 st.)	o	o	1	1	1	1	o	o	1	Death	3 years	Typical fibro - caseous change
3	36	M.	M	M.	M.(3 st.)	o	o	1	1	V.s	o	o	1	Death	6 months	Simple fibrous atrophy
4	37	M.	M.	M.	o	o	1	1	o	M.	1	1	M.	Death	3 years	Fatty transformation of capsules
5	41	M.	M.	M.	S.	o	1	1	1	1	M.	o	1	o	?	1 year ‡	
6	8½	F.	M.	1	o	1	o	o	o	o	M.	1	1	1	I.s.q.	7 months	
7	18	F.	M.	M.	1	o	o	o	1	1	M.	o	o	M.	?	2 years ‡	
8	46	M.	M.	M.	o	1	o	1	1	1	M.	o	o	1	?	4 months ‡	
9	19	F.	M.	M.	1	o	o	1	1	1	M.	1	1	o	Death	2½ years	None
10	49	M.	M.	M.	o	o	o	1	1	1	M.	o	1	o	?	1½ years ‡	
11	23	F.	M.	M.	1	1	o	1	1	1	V s.	o	?	1	Recovery	3½ years ‡	
12	45	M.	M.	1	1	o	1	?	1	1	M.	?	?	o	Death	7 months	Left capsule enlarged and caseous ; right normal †

M = Marked.   1 = Present.   o = Absent.   V.s. = Very slight.   I.s.q. = In statu quo.

* Complicated with enlargement of glands ; itchiness of skin (dermatitis herpetiformis).   † Intrathoracic tumour ; cyst in right frontal lobe.   ‡ Before coming under my observation.

COMPLICATIONS AND ASSOCIATED LESIONS.

In many cases of Addison's disease, the case remains uncomplicated to the end, and no associated lesions, except those which may easily be explained by the disease itself (such, for example, as the secondary lesions in the gastro-intestinal tract), are found in the body after death.

Tubercular lesions in the lungs are by far the most common complications. In many cases, these pulmonary lesions are old, clinically insignificant, and incapable of being recognised during life ; but in a certain proportion of cases the clinical signs indicative of more extensive, and it may be actively progressive and widespread, tubercular lesions are present.

Active caries of the spine and lumbar abscesses have been met with in a considerable number of cases; and curvature of the spine, the result of old and cured spinal caries, occasionally also occurs.

Occasionally extensive *tubercular deposits* are developed *in the peritoneum* and *other parts of the body.*

CLINICAL TYPES.

Different cases of Addison's disease present considerable differences in respect to their mode of development, duration, clinical history, and course ; they may, I think, be divided into the following clinical types or varieties :—

(1.) **Typical and uncomplicated cases of the disease.**—This group includes the great majority of cases. The onset is insidious, and not usually preceded by any apparent cause or illness. The characteristic symptoms which have been described above in detail (asthenia, extreme feebleness of the heart and pulse, vomiting, pigmentation, and usually some anæmia, and pain in the abdomen and back) are well marked. There is no obvious local or visceral disease to account for the symptoms and ill health. The average duration (in the case of hospital patients) is probably about two years after the asthenia and other symptoms have become sufficiently striking to attract the attention of the patient. In most cases, temporary exacerbations of the symptoms occur ; in others, there are temporary periods of improvement ; but the course of the case is on the whole progressively downwards, and the termination, with very rare exceptions, is in death.

(2.) **Atypical and exceptional cases.**—This group includes at least two varieties of sub-groups, viz. :—

(a.) *Cases in which the development of the disease is (or appears to be) rapid, and the duration short.* Looking at the clinical features of these cases, they may not incorrectly be termed acute. Dr Greenhow cites a number of cases of this kind.* One well-marked case has come under my own notice (Case III.).

(b.) *Cases in which there is no pigmentation, or in which the pigmentation is so slight as to easily escape observation.* Cases in which the pigmentation is entirely absent are exceedingly rare, but they do undoubtedly occur.

Cases in which the pigmentation is so slight as to escape attention, unless it is carefully looked for, are more common. Between these two extremes—cases in which the pigmentation is so slight as to make the case exceptional, and cases in which the pigmentation is excessively developed—there are all degrees of variety ; it is only the cases in which the pigmentation is entirely absent or very sparingly developed which can be termed exceptional.

(3.) **Cases in which the symptoms of Addison's disease are**

---

* "On Addison's Disease," p. 18.

superadded to the symptoms of some other disease, such as phthisis.—Clinical observation would seem to show that cases of this kind are by no means very rare, but the correctness of this conclusion is not, so far as my experience enables me to judge, borne out by examination after death, for in several cases of phthisis, in which the discoloration was so marked as to suggest the presence of Addison's disease, the suprarenal capsules were at the post mortem found to be healthy to the naked eye. The diagnosis (so far as the recognition of a lesion of the capsules is concerned) is, in cases of this kind, attended with great difficulty.

Pathological Classification.—I need hardly say that this classification is entirely clinical. If a pathological basis of classification were adopted, cases of Addison's disease might be divided into the following groups :—

(A.) *Typical cases*, in which both capsules are affected, and usually completely destroyed, by the fibro-caseous (tubercular) lesion.

(B.) *Atypical and exceptional cases.* Under this head there are several sub-groups, viz. :—

(*a.*) Cases in which one capsule only is affected with the characteristic fibro-caseous (tubercular) lesion, the other being sound.

(*b.*) Cases in which both capsules have been completely destroyed, apparently by cirrhotic or simple atrophy.

(*c.*) Cases in which both capsules have apparently been replaced by fat.

(*d.*) Cases in which both capsules are congenitally absent.

(*e.*) Cases in which the symptoms (or some of the symptoms) of the disease are associated with cancerous destruction of the capsules.

And (*f.*) cases in which the symptoms (or some of the symptoms) of the disease are associated with disease of the abdominal sympathetic (as in Gowers' and Paget's cases), the capsules themselves being sound.

Duration.—The average duration of cases of Addison's disease in hospital cases is probably about two years, if we date the duration from the time of appearance of the first symptoms, *i.e.*, from the time at which the patient first distinctly complained of asthenia, or at which the pigmentation was first noticed.

A duration of five or six years, more especially amongst well-to-do patients, is probably not very uncommon. In the case which I have illustrated in Plate VI. of my Atlas of Clinical Medicine (see Case I.), the patient lived for at least nine years after the characteristic symptoms of the disease were developed.

In some cases, the course is much more rapid—six months to a year; and a few cases have been recorded in which the duration was said to be only a few weeks. It is probable that in many of the rapid cases, the lesion in the suprarenal capsules was of much longer duration than the clinical duration of the case would seem to indicate; for, as Sir Samuel Wilks has pointed out, there is every reason to suppose, from the pathological characters of the capsular lesion found after death—the extensive caseation and calcification which are found after death—that in many cases the capsules have been entirely destroyed for months, probably in some cases for years, before the symptoms of the disease become sufficiently prominent to attract attention. In the cases which run a rapid course, the pigmentation is usually less marked than in the ordinary typical (chronic) cases, and in very exceptional instances may indeed be altogether absent.

Termination.—The vast majority of cases of Addison's disease terminate sooner or later in death; indeed, many writers deny that the disease is ever recovered from. A few cases have, however, been reported in which recovery does appear to have taken place. In the discussion on Addison's disease at the International Medical Congress of London, Sir William Gull mentioned a case in which a patient, aged 57, who had presented all the symptoms of the disease, had completely recovered.* Dr Finny† has reported a very remarkable case, in which all the characteristic symptoms of the disease appear to have been present, in which there was no evidence of any local or visceral disease, and in which complete recovery took place. In a case of my own, in which there is, I think, reason to suppose that the patient was affected with the disease, recovery has also occurred (see Case XI.).

On theoretical grounds, and granting that the lesion is usually tubercular, there is every reason for supposing that recovery may occasionally occur.

Mode of Death.—In most cases, death is gradual, the result of asthenia and gradually increasing exhaustion and debility; in many cases, the patient sinks, for some days or hours before death, into a semi-comatose or typhoid state. In some cases, death is preceded by a period of extreme restlessness; in others, by delirium, coma, a convulsion, or a series of epileptic fits. As we might expect, sudden death sometimes occurs as the result of cardiac

---

* "Transactions of the International Medical Congress of London," Vol. ii., p. 75.
† "Dublin Medical Journal," 1882, p. 293.

syncope. A very striking case of this kind (which shows the importance of guarding the subjects of Addison's disease from any sudden excitement or effort) is reported by Dr Kendal Franks. A girl aged 14, affected with Addison's disease, and in whom the asthenia was intense, suddenly awoke hearing the noise occasioned by a row in the street in front of the hospital; she jumped up in bed with a shriek of terror, and immediately fell backwards, dead.[*]

DIAGNOSIS.

In some cases of Addison's disease the diagnosis is easy, in others most difficult, or impossible.

Pigmentation of the skin, and especially pigmentation of the mucous membranes, is, for the purpose of diagnosis, by far the most important symptom, or rather sign, of the disease.

It is perhaps hardly necessary to say that pigmentation of the skin *per se* (*i.e.*, without asthenia and other constitutional symptoms) is not sufficient to justify a diagnosis of Addison's disease. The pigmentation of the skin in Addison's disease is in no way peculiar; it is not pathognomonic; but it may, with confidence, be stated that such extreme pigmentation as is present in the case represented in Plate VI. of my Atlas (Case I. Illustrative Cases) is very rarely indeed developed except as the result of Addison's disease. One case has, indeed, come under my own notice, in which very marked discoloration of the skin, identical in character with that of Addison's disease, developed apparently as the result of chronic scurvy, and independently of any disease of the suprarenal capsules or the adjacent nerves; but such cases are so infinitely rare that for the purposes of practical diagnosis they may be safely ignored. Sir Samuel Wilks puts the value of extreme pigmentation very forcibly, when he says: "I do not know of any other disease which changes a white man into the appearance of a black one."[†]

Pigmentation of the mucous membranes may, however, for the purposes of practical diagnosis be said to be pathognomonic; for although a few cases have indeed been reported—all, so far as I know, cases of phthisis or tubercular disease—in which pigmentation of the buccal mucous membranes, identical with that of Addison's disease, was present during life, and in which the capsules were found, to the naked eye at least, to be healthy after

[*] "Dublin Medical Journal," 1882, p. 279.
[†] "Guy's Hospital Reports," vol. viii., 1862, p. 14.

death, such cases are so exceedingly rare that for practical purposes they may be left out of account. Possibly in some of these
cases microscopical examination might have demonstrated a tubercular lesion of the capsules ; but to this point I shall again refer in
speaking of the pathology of the disease.

In order to warrant a *positive* diagnosis of Addison's disease
three factors are necessary, viz. :—

(1.) The presence of the characteristic constitutional symptoms
(asthenia, vomiting, and in most cases the absence of marked
emaciation, and the presence of some anæmia, and of pain in the
abdomen and back).

(2.) Pigmentation of the skin (with the characters described
above), and, still more, pigmentation of the mucous membranes.

(3.) The absence of any local visceral disease (other than the
lesion of the suprarenal capsules) capable of accounting for the
symptoms (asthenia, pigmentation, etc.).

When these three factors are all present, a positive diagnosis
may be confidently made. In other words, the recognition of
typical cases of Addison's disease is no more difficult than the
recognition of many other well-marked clinical entities.

It is the atypical and complicated cases in which the diagnosis
is difficult or impossible.

**The diagnosis of the atypical cases in which there is little
or no pigmentation.**—In cases of this kind the diagnosis is most
difficult ; in fact, in the absence of pigmentation, although the
presence of Addison's disease may be suspected, a positive diagnosis
is rarely possible.

We may strongly suspect the presence of Addison's disease
when marked and progressive asthenia, unassociated with emaciation and without fever, develops without any apparent cause. The
suspicion is strengthened if the patient is young (in other words,
in cases in which obscure internal disease of a malignant kind is
not likely to occur), if there is no profound anæmia, and if symptoms of gastro-intestinal irritation (which seem to be of nervous
origin, and which do not appear to be due to local stomach
disease, such as simple ulceration) and lumbar pains are also
present. Further, it must be remembered that marked loss of
weight does not exclude Addison's disease.

In cases of this description, the value and correctness of the
diagnosis depend upon the fact that all other causes of the constitutional symptoms (asthenia, vomiting, etc.), except Addison's
disease, can be excluded. Now, every experienced physician knows
that diagnosis by exclusion is always difficult and hazardous.

Hence the statement, which has been more than once insisted upon, that for the purposes of a positive diagnosis the pigmentation is the most valuable symptom of Addison's disease.

As a positive sign of Addison's disease, the discoloration of the skin, and especially the pigmentation of the mucous membranes, may be ranked with the rashes of the eruptive fevers. Many different conditions may produce fever ; but in the absence of the physical signs of a local inflammation, and in the absence of a skin eruption and the symptoms or signs of a characteristic local lesion, the diagnosis may be very difficult or impossible. From the character of the temperature curve, it may be possible, even in the absence of a rash or local lesion, *always provided that one can rely upon one's powers of excluding a local inflammatory lesion*, to suspect, with more or less probability, and in some cases even to positively diagnose, a particular form of febrile disease ; but in most cases of this kind the diagnosis must necessarily remain more or less uncertain. So too with regard to Addison's disease. In the absence of pigmentation, one may suspect that the asthenia and other constitutional symptoms which are present are due to disease of the suprarenal capsules ; but unless one can be very sure of one's powers of exclusion, it may be impossible to definitely diagnose that condition. The presence, however, of the characteristic discoloration of the skin and mucous membranes gives a different complexion to the case, and enables us to make a positive diagnosis. Hence, in all cases of suspected Addison's disease, the presence of discoloration of the skin, and more particularly of those parts of the skin which are exposed to the atmosphere, which are subjected to pressure or irritation, and in which pigment deposits are normally most abundant, and especially the presence of pigmented patches on the lips, gums, tongue, and the under surface of the tongue and buccal mucous membrane, should be most carefully looked for. I attach the highest diagnostic value to the presence of pigmented deposits on the mucous membranes.

The diagnosis of those atypical cases in which there are no constitutional symptoms.—In not a few cases of Addison's disease, the discoloration of the skin is, as we have seen, the first symptom to attract attention, and in some rare cases it seems to be well marked in the earlier stages, and before the asthenia and other constitutional symptoms are sufficiently developed to be noticed.

In cases of this kind, a positive diagnosis may be very difficult, or even impossible. One may suspect that the pigmentation is due to Addison's disease ; but in the absence of asthenia, and other constitutional symptoms, it is rarely, if ever, possible to make a positive diagnosis.

In order to carry the diagnosis farther than a mere supposition, all other possible causes of skin pigmentation must be excluded. Even in those cases in which all these conditions can be excluded, and in which there is no obvious cause for the discoloration of the skin, it is impossible to do more than suspect Addison's disease. When constitutional symptoms are entirely absent, it is rarely, if ever, justifiable to conclude that disease of the suprarenal capsules is the cause of the pigmentation. In cases of this kind, we may strongly suspect Addison's disease, but we must be content to wait for the development of constitutional symptoms before committing ourselves to a positive diagnosis of that condition.

The diagnosis of complicated cases.—The diagnosis of Addison's disease in complicated cases (*i.e.*, in cases in which the pigmentation and other symptoms of the disease are superadded to those of some other affection, such as chronic phthisis or spinal caries) is usually a matter of great difficulty and uncertainty.

The difficulty is especially great in cases of chronic phthisis, and is due, *firstly*, to the fact that asthenia and constitutional symptoms (which more or less closely resemble those of Addison's disease) are frequently met with as the result of the primary disease (phthisis or spinal caries), and, *secondly*, that in some cases of chronic phthisis, marked discoloration of the skin, and in rare and exceptional cases, of the tongue and buccal mucous membrane, identical in character with the discoloration of Addison's disease, is developed. It may, however, be stated that in chronic phthisis the discoloration is usually limited to the face (forehead and skin about the nose more especially), and that it rarely becomes diffused over the whole body, as in Addison's disease. Further, it may not unreasonably be suggested that in some of the cases of phthisis in which the skin is discoloured, the suprarenal capsules are probably affected (tubercular), and that the skin pigmentation is in reality a symptom of Addison's disease. I am fully aware that in many cases of phthisis with skin discoloration the suprarenal capsules have been described as perfectly healthy after death; but it may, I think, be doubted whether they were absolutely normal in all of these cases. Drs Alezais and Arnaud have shown that in a considerable proportion of cases of phthisis taken at random, and in which there were no symptoms indicative of Addison's disease during life, the suprarenal capsules were actually tubercular on microscopical examination. Now if this is so, we may expect *a fortiori* that in those cases of phthisis in which symptoms of Addison's disease are actually present, the suprarenal capsules will be tubercular in a much larger proportion of cases. Further, it must be remembered that, according to these observers, a comparatively slight tubercular deposit in the fibro-vascular zone, which surrounds the suprarenal capsules, and especially that part of the fibro-vascular zone which is situated on the posterior surface of the capsules, may, by implicating the pericapsular nervous ganglia of the sympathetic, lead to the production of skin pigmentation and perhaps of the other symptoms of Addison's disease. Future observers will not have to be content with a mere naked-eye examination of the capsules; in future, before concluding that the skin pigmentation in cases of chronic phthisis is due to the phthisis and not to Addison's disease, it must be shown by microscopic examination that the suprarenal capsules and the pericapsular ganglia are sound. Until the exact (microscopical) condition of the suprarenal capsules and of the pericapsular ganglia has been determined in a sufficient number of cases of phthisis, with skin pigmentation, it is altogether premature to conclude that the skin pigmentation associated with phthisis is due to the phthisis and not to Addison's disease.

Fortunately, in cases of this kind the diagnosis is a matter of scientific interest rather than of practical importance; for so far as prognosis is concerned, the result is very much the same in both conditions. Chronic phthisis with pigmentation of the skin is, like Addison's disease, a condition which usually, sooner or later, terminates in death.

In cases of this kind the physician has to ask himself whether the local lesion in the lung satisfactorily and sufficiently accounts for the constitutional symptoms. In cases of chronic phthisis it is only when the constitutional symptoms seem greater than can reasonably be accounted for by the pulmonary lesion that the pigmentation of the skin can with any degree of certainty be attributed *during life* to a lesion of the suprarenal capsules.

The differential diagnosis of Addison's disease, and of other conditions in which there is pigmentation of the skin.—Before leaving the important question of diagnosis, it may perhaps be well to mention some of the conditions in which discoloration of the skin, resembling more or less closely the discoloration of Addison's disease, may occur, and to indicate very briefly the chief points of differential diagnosis. It may, however, be emphatically stated that a careful observer, who is practically acquainted with Addison's disease, will rarely feel any great difficulty in distinguishing these conditions from Addison's disease.

The following are some of the conditions which (owing to the skin discoloration with which they may be associated) have been mistaken for Addison's disease :—

(1.) *Chronic phthisis with skin pigmentation.*—The differential diagnosis has already been considered.

(2.) *Vagabond's discoloration.*—In this condition, which is usually observed in old and extremely dirty vagrants infested with lice, the discoloration is not uniform ; it is best marked on the exposed parts of the body (hands and face) ; the skin is rough, harsh, and inelastic, and often marked with scratches ; the buccal mucous membrane and tongue are never pigmented ; the patients are generally old (whereas Addison's disease is very rarely indeed met with in old people). The constitutional symptoms suggestive of Addison's disease are absent ; or, if asthenia or other constitutional symptoms suggestive of Addison's disease are present, they are readily accounted for by the presence of some obvious disease or local lesion. The history of the case, the occupation of the patient, and the fact that in many cases the discoloration to a large extent disappears under soap and water, friction, alkaline baths, good feeding, rest and tonics, afford corroborative evidence of the true nature of the condition.

(3.) *Nitrate of silver discoloration.*—The discoloration is only or chiefly marked on those parts which are exposed to light ; the tint is quite different from that of Addison's disease (more leaden and grey, and not so brown) ; the patient has either recently or at some former period been treated with nitrate of silver ; and the constitutional symptoms of Addison's disease are absent.

(4.) *Arsenic discoloration.*—This is also readily distinguished from Addison's disease by :—the history of the case (the fact that the patient has been taking arsenic in full doses) and the presence of other symptoms indicative of chronic arsenical poisoning, such as dryness of the throat, itching of the conjunctivæ, a moist condition of the palms and soles, pains in the abdomen, chronic diarrhœa, vomiting, etc.

In (5) *chronic scurvy,* (6) *pregnancy,* (7) *malarial poisoning,* (8) *syphilis,* (9) *malignant disease,* (10) *exophthalmic goitre,* and (11) *osteoid arthritis,* the skin may become pigmented and discoloured. The history of the case, the associated symptoms, the presence or absence of definite local lesions, the progress of the disease and the effect of treatment, would enable an experienced observer to distinguish these conditions without any difficulty.

(12.) *Diffuse melanosis with pigmentation of the skin.*—In these rare cases the tint of the discoloration is different—it (always?) resembles the discoloration produced by nitrate of silver rather than that of Addison's disease; the conjunctivæ may be discoloured as well as the skin; free pigment granules can often be detected in the blood; the urine becomes black on exposure to the air, and (usually) deposits pigment granules; the sputum may contain pigment granules; the patient is emaciated and usually cachectic-looking; the starting-point of the disease may be apparent in a pigmented mole which has taken on malignant action, or in a tumour of the eye-ball; symptoms and signs indicative of secondary deposits in the internal organs (liver, brain, etc.) are usually (always?) present, and the superficial lymphatic glands may be enlarged, and are in some (rare) cases obviously melanotic.

(13.) *Leucoderma.*—The sharply-defined character of the pigmented areas (the circular form of the white patches and their clean-cut edges) at once distinguish simple uncomplicated leucoderma from Addison's disease. It must, however, be remembered that leucoderma is sometimes associated with Addison's disease. In the sixth case described by Addison, leucoderma was (probably) present, and in another case, which is beautifully represented in his memoir by a coloured drawing, but in which there was no post mortem, he states:—"I entertain no doubt whatever that the capsules were diseased." A case of the same kind (supposed Addison's disease with leucoderma, not, however, verified, by post-mortem examination) came under my own notice several years ago (Case V.). Amongst the recorded cases of Addison's disease the presence of leucoderma is several times mentioned.

(14.) *Pigmentation of the skin, associated with chronic peritonitis, malignant disease in the abdomen, pelvis, etc.*—In cases of this kind the differential diagnosis is often most difficult, and sometimes, I believe, impossible. Nor is this to be wondered at when it is remembered that pigmentation of the skin exactly similar to that of Addison's disease has in some cases resulted from malignant disease involving the abdominal sympathetic, and that in malignant diseases of the abdomen all the other constitutional symptoms of Addison's disease may be present.

The mode of onset of the disease, the rapidity of its course, the age of the patient, especially the presence of marked emaciation, and the fact that there is evidence (in the form of symptoms and signs) of localised organic disease in the abdomen or pelvis, are the points of most importance in distinguishing such cases from cases of Addison's disease.

(15.) *Localised pigmentation due to exposure to the sun, and especially to the sun and sea-air, and discolorations of the skin due to pityriasis versicolor, and other forms of skin disease* have in some cases been mistaken for the discoloration due to Addison's disease. The diagnosis in such cases is so obvious that the points of distinction need not be enumerated in detail.

(16.) *Chronic pigmentation of the skin resembling that of Addison's disease, but without any constitutional symptoms, and not due to any obvious cause.*—Two cases of this kind are described in the "Transactions of the Clinical Society of London," for the year 1881, the first by Dr Crocker, and the second by Dr Carrington. (See pages 152 and 157.) In Dr Crocker's case, the discoloration had lasted for eight years. I simply mention these cases because of their rarity and obscurity, and in the hope that some future observer may be able to explain their true nature, and to decide whether they are in any way related to Addison's disease. Fortunately for diagnosis, cases of this kind are exceedingly rare. It is obvious that if, in either of these cases, the patient had been temporarily debilitated from any cause, or had been suffering from gastro-intestinal irritation or from pain in the abdomen or back, the distinction from Addison's disease might (for the time at least) have been impossible.

(17.) *Pernicious anæmia.*—In some cases of pernicious anæmia, in which no arsenic has been administered, the skin becomes pigmented and the clinical picture closely resembles that of Addison's disease. Several cases of this kind have come under my own notice (see Cases XXVII., XXXI., XL., and XLIV.); in two of these cases (XL. and XLIV.) the suprarenal capsules were found, on post-mortem examination, to be normal; in the other two cases, there was no autopsy. The similarity of the constitutional symptoms (profound and causeless asthenia, little or no loss of fat, debility of the heart's action, attacks of causeless vomiting and diarrhœa), the absence of any local visceral disease to account for the symptoms, the fact that in both diseases the colour-index may be above the normal, and the fact that the pigmentation of the skin may be identically the same in the two diseases, are points of close resemblance. But the condition of the blood is distinctive. In pernicious anæmia, the bloodlessness is profound; whereas, in Addison's disease, there is either no anæmia or the degree of anæmia is slight. In most cases of Addison's disease, the lips are well, indeed in some cases too highly, coloured. By an accurate estimation of the red corpuscles, and by observing the microscopical characters of the red corpuscles, it is, so far as my observation enables me to judge, always possible to determine with certainty whether the case is one of uncomplicated pernicious anæmia, on the one hand, or of uncomplicated Addison's disease on the other. But whether it is possible to definitely exclude Addison's disease in those cases of pernicious anæmia in which the skin is deeply pigmented, and in which the pigmentation is not the result of arsenic, is another question. It is possible that the two conditions may occur in combination, but, so far as I know, no case has hitherto been recorded in which it has been proved by post-mortem observation that this actually was the case. In two of my cases of pernicious anæmia in which Addison's disease was suspected during life, the suprarenals were healthy after death. I have not seen any case of pernicious anæmia in which the pigmentation of the mucous membranes characteristic of Addison's disease was present. If any case of pernicious anæmia should come under my notice in which the mucous membranes were pigmented as in Addison's disease, I should feel justified in diagnosing a combination of the two conditions.

(18.) *Diabetic bronzing.*—In some cases of hypertrophic cirrhosis of the liver associated with the presence of sugar in the urine, the skin becomes so markedly pigmented that the term *diabète bronzé* has been given to the condition by Hanot and Chauffard.* The condition is at once distinguished from Addison's disease by the clinical features (enlargement of the liver, pigmentation of the skin, and the presence of sugar in the urine—diabetes).

MORBID ANATOMY.

Typical lesion.—In the great majority of cases of Addison's disease, both suprarenal capsules are more or less completely destroyed by a fibro-caseous degeneration, as it has been termed. Most authorities are now agreed that this lesion is tubercular in character, although in several cases which have been carefully examined no tubercle bacilli have been found; and in one instance in which Delepine injected the caseous material into a guinea-pig, no tubercles were developed.

In the great majority of cases, the capsules are enlarged; but in some they are of normal size, and, in a few cases, they are smaller than normal.

In typical cases the capsules are enlarged, firm, nodulated, irregular in shape, and adherent to the surrounding structures.

The appearances which the diseased capsules present on section vary with the stage of the disease and the nature of the secondary (degenerative) changes which have taken place. In most cases, the

---

* " Revue de Médecine," 1882, p. 386.

distinction between the cortical and medullary parts of the organ is no longer recognisable. In fresh specimens, the cut surface usually has a mottled or marbled appearance, due to "the admixture of two materials of different colour and consistence.

"One of these materials is a translucent tissue of firm consistence and of a grey or greenish-grey colour, at least when freshly cut, but which rapidly assumes a reddish hue on exposure to air.

"The other material is of an opaque yellow or cream colour, and generally assumes the form of irregular, roundish masses of a more or less friable consistence embedded in the translucent tissue from which they can in many cases be easily enucleated." * The yellow opaque masses are caseous foci. In some cases, gritty calcareous nodules are present in the midst of the caseous material. In long-standing cases, the whole capsule may be converted into a cheesy, putty-like, or calcareous mass. In other cases, the caseous portions, instead of becoming dry, cheesy, or calcareous, soften and liquefy; numerous small cavities containing a thick creamy fluid may then be formed in the interior of the diseased organ, or the whole capsule may be converted into a cyst containing a thick yellow fluid which looks like pus. The fibrous, caseous, or calcareous changes appear to be simply the ultimate result of a tubercular lesion.

The relative proportions of the translucent, exudation-like, and of the fibrous, caseous, or calcareous materials, vary greatly in different cases, and depend, in great part at least, upon the length of time which the lesion has existed.

In the early stages of the disease, the translucent exudation-like material predominates, and the capsules may then be very much enlarged. In the later stages, when the fibrous, caseous, and calcareous changes are far advanced, the capsules may be smaller than normal.

In the great majority of cases of Addison's disease, both capsules are affected and usually completely destroyed by the fibro-caseous (tubercular) lesion; but in some cases the lesion of the capsules is more advanced on one side than on the other. In a few of the recorded cases the lesion of the capsules has been limited to localised areas; and in rare cases one capsule only has been involved.

Simple fibrous atrophy and fatty transformation of the suprarenal capsules.—In most of the cases in which the capsules are smaller than normal and replaced by fibrous tissue, the fibroid change seems to be merely a late (secondary) result of the typical

---

* "Addison's Disease," by Dr Greenhow, p. 24.

fibro-caseous (tubercular) lesion which I have just described. But cases are occasionally though rarely met with in which the atrophy does not seem to be satisfactorily accounted for in this way. A considerable number of cases of Addison's disease have been recorded—and Case III. is an illustration—in which the capsules were represented by a mere shell of fibrous tissue (simple atrophy); or in which the capsular (secreting) tissue seemed to be replaced by fibrous tissue (cirrhotic atrophy).

In some cases of this kind, there were no indications of any preceding inflammatory lesion, and so far as I can see, no reason whatever to suppose that the atrophy or fatty change was the result of the fibro-caseous (tubercular) lesion described above.

In other and still rarer cases, the suprarenal capsules appear to have been completely absent, or replaced by fat. I have recorded a remarkable case in point (see Case IV.).

Dr Sydney Coupland has thrown out the suggestion that in these cases the atrophy of the capsules is a secondary (and presumably, if I understand him aright, trophic) result of a primary lesion of the abdominal sympathetic; but, so far as I know, there are no facts in favour of this hypothesis. There can, I think, be little doubt that in typical cases of Addison's disease, the lesion of the capsules is primary, and the lesions in the sympathetic secondary thereto; and, so far as I see, there is no reason to suppose that this pathological sequence is reversed in the rare cases to which I am at present more particularly referring.

The condition of the suprarenal nerves and the abdominal sympathetic.—As I have already stated, in typical cases of Addison's disease the enlarged and indurated capsules are usually more or less firmly adherent (clearly as the result of inflammatory changes) to the surrounding parts (kidneys, vena cava, aorta, pancreas, stomach, etc.).

The nerves which pass in such abundance between the capsules and the semilunar ganglia, and the semilunar ganglia themselves, are in a considerable proportion of cases implicated in these inflammatory changes. On naked-eye examination, they may be seen to be enlarged, thickened, indurated, and sometimes injected and redder than normal. On microscopic examination, appearances clearly indicative of inflammatory induration (increase of connective tissue, infiltration with leucocytes, enlargement and engorgement of the blood-vessels) may be present in the fibrous covering of the nerves; and, in some cases, the proper nervous elements (nerve tubes and ganglion cells) are also inflamed, degenerated, or atrophied.

These inflammatory changes in the nerve tubes and semilunar ganglia are probably secondary—the result of irritation and inflammation excited by the (primary) fibro-caseous (tubercular) lesion of the capsules.

Further, it is important to note—for this point has a very distinct bearing upon the pathological physiology of the disease—that in a considerable number of cases in which the suprarenal capsules have been completely destroyed by the typical fibro-caseous (tubercular) lesion, no pathological alterations have been found, even on careful microscopical examination, in the semilunar ganglia and the large nerve trunks forming the solar plexus ; and that in other cases in which the suprarenal capsules are completely atrophied, absent, or replaced by fat, the suprarenal nerves and the solar plexuses have appeared to be quite normal. Nevertheless, it may, I think, be confidently stated that in most cases of Addison's disease in which the lesion is typical the nerve tubes which are directly connected with the diseased capsules are involved and inflamed.

The condition of the suprarenal nerves in Addison's disease has been very minutely studied by two French observers, Drs Alezais and Arnaud. They have shown that true sympathetic nervous ganglia, which they have termed *pericapsular nervous ganglia*, are situated on the surface of, and sometimes actually in the substance of, the fibrous capsule which envelops the suprarenal bodies.

They claim to have demonstrated, *firstly*, that in several cases of Addison's disease, in which the pigmentation and other characteristic symptoms were present, these pericapsular nervous ganglia were invaded by the tubercular process which originated in the capsule ; and, *secondly*, that in some cases in which the characteristic fibro-caseous (tubercular) lesion of the capsules was present, but in which there was no pigmentation, the pericapsular nervous ganglia were not implicated.

They, therefore, conclude that the essential cause of the pigmentation and other characteristic symptoms of Addison's disease is implication of these *pericapsular nervous ganglia* by a tubercular process which extends from the suprarenal capsules.

In the article on Addison's disease in my Atlas of Clinical Medicine I have quoted these observations in full (vol. i., pp. 64, 65, and 66).

Cancerous destruction of the capsules.—Most authorities deny that the symptoms of Addison's disease are produced by cancerous destruction of the suprarenal capsules. Sir Samuel Wilks, for example, says:—"There is very strong evidence in favour of the opinion that the change in the capsules is peculiar, uniform in character, and primary in its nature. We mean by this that it does not consist of various forms of disease, and is not a mere accidental part of a malady affecting the body generally, but that it is as much a primary and essential disease as cirrhosis of the liver or a granular degeneration of the kidney. It is unfortunately true that Addison, not content with placing on record his few genuine examples of the complaint, hazarded a conjecture that cancer or any other destructive agency might develop the symptoms, but he gave no instances in corroboration of it, and no single writer has published a single case where cancer, tubercle, or, indeed any form of benignant or malignant growth has been productive of the genuine symptoms, nor, indeed, has any case been recorded where degenerative changes other than those previously described have given rise to the complaint. In all cases, where the symptoms have been well marked, the change in the capsules has been of one kind, and essentially primary." And again, "We might mention that in several articles to be found both in French and German works on the subject of Addison's disease, the authors have collected some hundreds of cases where the suprarenal organs were diseased, also cases where the skin was discoloured, and where asthenic symptoms prevailed. On carefully perusing these, the position we have taken up is clearly proved, viz., that the symptoms which Addison described can be associated with only one form of disease of the capsules, although this is not the conclusion of the authors themselves, who have also mistaken cases of leucoderma and other cutaneous affections for it." *

With this opinion I cannot altogether agree. That malignant disease (cancer and sarcoma) of the suprarenal capsules very rarely indeed results in the production of all of the symptoms characteristic of Addison's disease I fully admit; but I do not feel in a position to say dogmatically that it cannot produce them.

And in this connection I would especially emphasise the fact that in the majority of cases of cancerous destruction of the capsules, the symptoms of Addison's disease have been said to be absent *because pigmentation of the skin and mucous membranes was not present.* But it must be remembered that in typical (tubercular) destruction of the capsules, pigmentation may be very slight, or indeed altogether absent; and that this is particularly apt to occur in those cases (as in cancer) in which the lesion runs a rapid course,

---

* Russell Reynolds' "System of Medicine," Vol. v., pp. 361, 362.

in other words in which the destruction of the suprarenal capsules is more quickly produced than in the average run of (typical) cases.

The argument, then, that because pigmentation is absent the symptoms of Addison's disease are absent, is a fallacious one. One might as well say that in the typical (tubercular) cases in which pigmentation is absent the disease is not Addison's disease.

Further, every one now admits that simple (non-tubercular) atrophy of the capsules may produce all the characteristic symptoms of Addison's disease; and, as Case IV. shows, fatty transformation of the capsules may produce all the characteristic symptoms of Addison's disease.

I see no *a priori* reason, therefore, why malignant disease (cancer, sarcoma) of the capsules may not produce the characteristic symptoms of Addison's disease; and, as a matter of fact, a case reported by Dr Gage of Boston seems to me to support this view. Dr Greenhow, it is true, while fully admitting that the symptoms were characteristic of Addison's disease, says: " In this case there appears to have been no microscopical examination of the diseased organs, and although the description is less clear than in the two previous cases, it presents on the whole a greater resemblance to the lesion in Addison's disease than to cancer." But with his opinion as to the nature of the lesion I cannot agree. The lesion of the capsules was, in my opinion, more like cancer than the fibro-caseous (tubercular) lesion characteristic of Addison's disease. Further, the patient's breast had been removed two years previously for cancer; and on post-mortem examination a secondary deposit, such as might quite well occur in cancer, but which, so far as I know, has never been observed in connection with the ordinary (fibro-caseous) lesion of Addison's disease, was found in the liver. In addition, the medical men who made the post mortem, and who saw the morbid condition in its recent state, report, without any apparent doubt, that it was a case of cancer. The following is the report of the pathological appearances :—

" *Autopsy.*—Not much emaciation ; flesh soft and flabby. Discoloration somewhat faded, but well marked. One inch of fat overlies sternum and abdomen ; much fat inside abdomen. On removal of stomach and intestines two large, almost spherical, tumours are observed, occupying the place of the suprarenal capsules, joined together across the vertebræ by a thickened, corrugated mass of enlarged and diseased lymphatic glands. Tumour on the right side somewhat larger than that on the left, being two and a half inches in diameter, and adhering by a strong and broad attachment to the under surface of the liver. From this point of attachment several broad lines of reddish-white soft deposit radiate into the substance of the liver for one and a half inches, resembling soft cancer, as sometimes seen infiltrated in that organ.

"The tumours, externally, *present a soft uniform glistening surface.* (No italics in the original.)

"On section, *a dense, firm, fibrous texture, making a smooth surface, at first white, but soon covered by a bright orange-yellow exudation, which, after exposure to the air, became a dingy, greenish-brown. The diseased lymphatic gland was of a very similar texture, but gave, on section, none of the yellow fluid.* (No italics in the original.) Nothing else abnormal in thorax or abdomen. Head not examined." (Gage, "Boston Medical and Surgical Journ.," vol. lxxi., p. 69 ; quoted by Greenhow, p. 190.)

In a recent paper, Drs Rolleston and Marks make the following statement with regard to the presence of symptoms of Addison's disease in cases of primary malignant disease of the suprarenal capsules :—" The consensus of experience and opinion is decidedly against the view that secondary malignant growths in these bodies induce symptoms of Addison's disease, and probably this may be explained by supposing that the primary malignant disease kills the patient before there is time for the characteristic symptoms of Addison's disease to appear. Much the same appears to be the case with regard to primary growths in the suprarenal bodies. It does not appear that the complete clinical picture of Addison's disease has been presented by any one case of primary malignant disease of suprarenal bodies, even when both organs have been invaded ; but some of the symptoms of Addison's disease may occur in primary adrenal new growths. Pigmentation has been observed very rarely. Vomiting, probably due to irritation of the abdominal sympathetic, was a marked symptom in some cases. Asthenia was very notable in some cases, but is perhaps generally not more marked than in patients dying of malignant disease elsewhere. Pain in the back, often seen in Addison's disease, may also occur in malignant disease, and suggest an aneurism or deep-seated new growth." They sum up their conclusions in the following remarks :—" The clinical picture of Addison's disease is not presented, but in some rare instances it is partially, though imperfectly, suggested in cases of primary malignant disease of the suprarenal capsules." *

On theoretical grounds, and granting, as I think, that the symptoms of Addison's disease are partly due to destruction of the capsules, and partly to secondary disturbances, probably irritative in character, which are produced in the nerves which surround and are in connection with the suprarenal bodies, I see no reason why any lesion of the capsules, provided only that it is sufficiently destructive, sufficiently chronic and (perhaps) sufficiently irritative

---

* " American Journal of the Medical Sciences," October 1898, p. 396.

in character, may not produce the symptoms of Addison's disease.*

The absence of the characteristic symptoms in cases of malignant destruction of the capsules may probably be due to a variety of circumstances, viz. :—

(*a.*) That the cancerous destruction is incomplete :

(*b.*) That accessory suprarenal bodies, which were not involved in the cancerous lesion, were present :

(*c.*) That the cancerous destruction usually runs too rapid a course to allow of the production of the symptoms of Addison's disease : or,

(*d.*) That the cancerous lesion is not sufficiently irritating to the nerves. For some years past I have suggested in my lectures that the tubercle bacillus perhaps secretes some chemical substance which exerts a special and peculiarly irritative effect upon the nerves.

Drs Alezais and Arnaud, who think that the symptoms of Addison's disease are due to involvement of the pericapsular sympathetic ganglia, explain the absence of symptoms of Addison's disease, in cases of cancerous destruction of the capsules, by the fact that new growths which originate in the suprarenal capsules usually grow from within outwards, and that they are limited by the fibrous covering of the gland, which, in many cases, becomes thickened and, as it were, bars further progress of the new growth, and prevents the invasion and implication of the pericapsular nervous ganglia and other adjacent structures.

Suprarenal capsules healthy; disease of abdominal sympathetic.—In some rare and quite exceptional cases, in which bronzing of the skin and the other symptoms of Addison's disease were present during life, the suprarenal capsules were found, on post-mortem examination, to be healthy, but the abdominal sympathetic (solar plexus and semilunar ganglia) was involved in a mass of new growth. Thus, in a case of Hodgkin's disease, reported by Sir William Gowers, "the glandular enlargement was general, but in the thoracic and abdominal cavities it was very great. The suprarenal body on each side was healthy, but the nerves from each passed into the mass of gland growth by which the solar

---

* This part of the article was written before I had read the important article of Drs Alezais and Arnaud ; but I see no reason to modify it, though it must be noted that if the views of these observers are correct, the disease is due not to irritation but to destruction of the nervous structures in the immediate neighbourhood of the capsules—*destruction of the pericapsular nervous ganglia of the sympathetic.*

plexus was involved. The bronzing of the skin was striking, and had the distribution characteristic of Addison's disease."[*] In another case of Hodgkin's disease recorded by Professor Paget, in which very marked pigmentation resembling in all respects that met with in Addison's disease was present during life, the supra-renal capsules appeared normal in every respect, but the splanchnic nerves, semilunar ganglia, and solar plexus, were enveloped in a mass of enlarged retro-peritoneal glands lying in front of the spine. The semilunar ganglia could not be found.[†]

Unilateral disease of the suprarenal capsules.—In the great majority of cases of Addison's disease, both capsules are affected and usually completely destroyed by the fibro-caseous (tubercular) lesion. In many cases, however, the lesion of the capsules is much more advanced on one side than on the other ; in a few cases the lesion of the capsules is localised and limited to the surface of the capsules and the adjacent pericapsular tissues ; and in rare cases one capsule only is involved.

Some writers deny that the lesion of the capsules is ever limited to one capsule ; but in this they are, I think, mistaken. I have myself recorded a case (Case XII.), which was, I believe, a case of Addison's disease, in which one capsule only (so far as the naked-eye examination enabled me to judge) was affected. Dr Greenhow, in his work on Addison's disease, details more than one case of the same kind (see p. 67). In one of the cases recently reported by Drs Alezais and Arnaud,[‡] the right capsule only was affected. This case, which was complicated with phthisis, is of special value and importance, for the pigmentation affected the buccal mucous membrane as well as the skin, and the suprarenal capsules were carefully examined with the microscope.

If the view of the pathology of the disease which I think the most probable is correct, viz., that some of the symptoms of Addison's disease are due to destruction of the capsules, while others are due to implication of the nervous structures with which they are connected, it is reasonable to suppose that the characteristic symptoms may be developed in some cases in which one capsule only is diseased. The fact that in many cases of Addison's disease the lesion is much more advanced in one capsule than in the other is in favour of this view ; for it is probable that if, in some cases of this kind (*i.e.*, cases in which the capsular lesion is much more

---

[*] Russell Reynolds' "System of Medicine," Vol. v., p. 316.

[†] "Lancet," 1879, Vol. i., p. 258.

[‡] "Revue de Médecine," 10th April 1891. Obs. III., p. 298.

advanced on one side than the other), the patient had died, and the capsules had been examined at an early stage of the disease, it would have been found that one capsule only was affected.

Pathological alterations in other organs.—In addition to the lesions of the capsules and of the abdominal sympathetic which have just been described, other pathological changes are not infrequently met with in Addison's disease.

The *abdominal glands* are, in many cases, enlarged, and in some caseous; *old or recent tubercular lesions in the lungs* are comparatively common; *deposits of recent miliary tubercle in the peritoneum or other parts* occasionally occur; *spinal caries*, both old and recent (healed and active), is present in a certain proportion of cases; and *inflammatory deposits or abscesses in the neighbourhood of the capsules* have been recorded in some instances.

The *spleen* is sometimes enlarged.

The *stomach* often contains an excess of mucus; its mucous membrane, in many cases, presents a mammillated appearance, and in some is ecchymosed or even superficially ulcerated.

The *solitary glands* and *Peyer's patches* are usually enlarged, and the glandular structures in the large intestines are sometimes affected in the same manner. Hyperæmia, ecchymosis, or even superficial ulceration of the intestinal mucous membrane, is sometimes present.

These changes in the stomach and intestine are of such frequent occurrence that they can hardly be regarded merely as accidental or associated lesions; they are perhaps secondary (trophic) results of the (? irritative) alterations in the abdominal sympathetic, which have been previously described.

The *muscles* are in some cases profoundly atrophied.

The *heart* is, in many cases of Addison's disease, markedly atrophied. I have been very much impressed by the smallness of the heart in more than one case which I have examined. The exact cause of the atrophy of the heart is not clear. Possibly it may be a secondary (trophic) result of the lesion of the abdominal sympathetic nerves; possibly the suprarenal capsules may be concerned in elaborating some substance which is of special importance for the nutrition of the heart; or possibly the vagi nerves, or the cardiac ganglia, may be degenerated or diseased. I make these suggestions with the view of stimulating investigation; for I am disposed to think that the atrophy of the heart is a feature in the pathology of Addison's disease which has not, so far, received anything like the degree of attention which it deserves. The observations of Schäfer and Oliver, which were made after this paragraph was written, are strongly in favour of the view that the atrophy of the heart is the direct result of suppression of the function of the suprarenal glands ; in other words, that the suprarenal glands secrete some substance which exerts an active influence on the nutrition of the heart (and muscular system).

Changes in the spinal cord (hyperæmia, perivascular exudations, collections of leucocytes around the central canal, and degenerative changes in the nerve cells and fibres, have been described in a few instances. The significance of such alterations and their relation, if any, to the disease have not as yet been definitely determined.

The nature of the capsular lesion.—The exact pathological nature of the fibro-caseous change, which is the typical and characteristic lesion of Addison's disease, has given rise to much discussion. It has usually been termed scrofulous or tubercular, but some authorities, doubting its tubercular character, have described it simply as inflammatory.

In my opinion, the evidence in favour of the tubercular nature of the lesion is conclusive. The chief facts in support of this view are :—

Firstly, That in many of the cases in which the morbid change is not too far advanced, the lesion of the capsules presents all the characters of a tubercular lesion. Merkel, for example, states :— "My own observations have shown me, in cases where the entire structure has not been broken down into a mass of detritus, that it consists in a proliferation of small cells, lying in a fine reticulum, which includes giant-cells in great numbers. I have never," he says, "seen any appearance which so forcibly reminded me of Schueppel's drawings as a tuberculosis of the suprarenal capsules." [*] Alezais and Arnaud,[†] who are also emphatic as to the tubercular character of the lesion, make the very important statement—and in this they differ from almost all previous observers—that tubercle of the suprarenal capsules, whether primary or secondary to tubercle in other organs, is usually met with in the form of a *diffuse tubercular infiltration*, rather than as true grey, semi-transparent granulations (miliary tubercles).

Secondly, That, in a considerable number of cases, tubercle bacilli have actually been demonstrated in the diseased capsules. It is perfectly true that in others—a larger number of cases—no tubercle bacilli could be detected ; but in the examination of old (caseous and calcareous) tubercular lesions, negative results are of

[*] Ziemssen's "Cyclopædia of Medicine," Vol. viii., p. 651.
[†] "Revue de Médecine," 10th April 1891, p. 289.

comparatively little value. In such conditions one positive observation (so far as the detection of the tubercle bacillus is concerned)
is of much greater weight than several negative ones. It must, too,
be remembered that the opportunity of examining the capsules in
the early stages of the lesion, in typical cases of Addison's disease,
very rarely occurs. It is probable, I think, that future observations will show that the tubercle bacillus is usually present in the
early stages of the disease. With the object of deciding this point,
and of definitely determining whether the lesion is usually tubercular or not, the presence of the tubercle bacillus should be diligently
and carefully looked for in every case of Addison's disease in
which the capsular lesion is in an early stage of development. I
may further add, that the search for the tubercle bacillus should not
be limited to the capsules themselves, but that the lymphatic
glands in the neighbourhood of the capsules should also be carefully examined.

Thirdly, Phthisis, spinal caries, and other tubercular lesions,
such as recent deposits of acute miliary tubercle in the peritoneum, are by far the most common associated lesions which are
met with in cases of Addison's disease.*

It may perhaps be objected that if the capsular lesion were
tubercular, other evidences of tubercle (in the form of secondary
deposits) ought to be more frequently present. This argument is,
to my mind, inconclusive. It is probable, I think, that the proportion of cases of Addison's disease, in which associated tubercular
lesions are present, is as great as in the case of other localised
tubercular lesions in the adult. Even in cases of phthisis, if we
exclude those secondary lesions which are obviously due to direct
infection by tubercular sputum (tubercular deposits in the larynx
and intestine), and the glandular and other lesions which result
therefrom, secondary deposits in the various organs of the body, and
generalised (acute) tuberculosis, are by no means common. Possibly, too, the anatomical structure of the suprarenal capsules, and
the arrangement of their lymphatics, may make the diffusion of
tubercular processes, which originate in the capsules, more difficult
than in the case of some other organs.

PATHOLOGICAL PHYSIOLOGY.

The manner in which the lesion of the suprarenal capsules
produces the symptoms of Addison's disease has given rise to a

---

* The lesion of the stomach and intestine, and the atrophy of the heart,
should, in my opinion, be regarded as direct results of the disease, rather
than mere associated lesions or complications.

vast deal of discussion, and is still unsettled. The question is one of great difficulty and complexity; in the present state of our knowledge, it is difficult to explain all the facts by any single hypothesis. The theory which, in my judgment, is by far the most satisfactory, is that which supposes (1) that the lesion of the capsules is primary; (2) that as a result of that lesion the nervous structures in the neighbourhood of, or connected with, the capsules are in many cases implicated; and (3) that the symptoms of the disease are due partly to suppression of the function of the suprarenal glands, and partly to the associated lesions or functional (irritative) changes in the nervous structures which result therefrom.

Two theories have been advanced, viz. :—

The Theory of the Arrest of Suprarenal Function.—That the symptoms of Addison's disease are due to destruction of the capsules—that is, to abolition of the functions of the suprarenal bodies or suprarenal glands, as they may be termed.

The Nervous Theory.—That the symptoms of Addison's disease are not directly due to destruction of the suprarenal bodies, but that they result from the derangements in the abdominal sympathetic and, perhaps, other nervous structures, which the lesion of the suprarenal capsules produces.

In the present state of our knowledge, it is extremely difficult to reconcile all the facts in accordance with either one or other of these theories.

In favour of the first view, are the facts (a) that in the vast majority of cases of Addison's disease both capsules are completely destroyed; (b) that in some cases, apparently of simple atrophy or fatty change, in which both suprarenal capsules are completely destroyed, and in which, so far as post-mortem examination showed, there was no lesion of the abdominal sympathetic, typical symptoms of Addison's disease are nevertheless developed; and (c) that in some cases of Addison's disease the administration of suprarenal extract is undoubtedly attended with benefit.

Against this view are : (a) The fact that cancerous destruction of both capsules does not (except, perhaps, in very rare instances) produce the symptoms of Addison's disease * ; (b) that in many cases of Addison's disease there is strong pathological evidence to show that the suprarenal capsules have been completely destroyed for months or even years before the death of the patient, and before

---

* The question is whether in cases of cancerous destruction of the capsules, in which the symptoms of Addison's disease were present during life, the suprarenal glands were completely destroyed.

the symptoms of the disease were developed in a marked degree ; and (*c*) that in many of the cases of this kind (cases in which the capsules are completely destroyed) remarkable temporary improvement may occur.

In favour of the nervous theory of the disease are the facts : (*a*) that in the great majority of cases of Addison's disease the lesion is one and the same—a fibro-caseous (tubercular) destruction of both capsules ; (*b*) that cancerous destruction of both capsules rarely (in the opinion of some authorities never) produces the symptoms of Addison's disease * ; (*c*) that in rare cases one capsule only, or (according to two French observers, Drs Alezais and Arnaud) a part—the peripheral part—of one capsule only is involved ; (*d*) that in almost all cases of Addison's disease the nerves surrounding the capsules, and (in many) the semilunar ganglia and large nerve cords of the solar plexus are embedded in a highly irritative (tubercular and inflammatory) tissue ; (*e*) that in a considerable number of cases naked-eye and microscopical changes can be demonstrated in the semilunar ganglia and solar plexuses, and that (according to Alezais and Arnaud) microscopical alternations are always present in the pericapsular ganglia ; (*f*) that (according to Alezais and Arnaud) in some cases in which the tuberculosis of the capsule is limited to the centre of the organ (that is, does not invade the cortical portion), and in which the pericapsular ganglia and the abdominal sympathetic are healthy, the symptoms of Addison's disease are not developed ; (*g*) that in a few rare cases in which the symptoms of Addison's disease have been present during life, the suprarenal capsules have been perfectly healthy, but the semilunar plexus and solar ganglia have been diseased (enveloped in a mass of new growth) ; (*h*) that in most of the cases of Addison's disease in which suprarenal extract has been administered no improvement in the symptoms has occurred.

Against this view (the nervous theory of the disease) are :—

(*a*) That in many cases of Addison's disease no changes have been found in the semilunar ganglia or great cords of the solar plexus. It must, however, be remembered, that the nerve fibres which are in

---

* Possibly, as Dr Robertson has suggested (the Goulstonian Lectures on the Suprarenal Bodies, "British Medical Journal," 30th March 1895, p. 680), in such cases death has occurred before symptoms characteristic of Addison's disease have had time to develop ; or "that some compensation for the destruction of the suprarenal glands is present in accessory suprarenal bodies, and that, as in the case of the thyroid gland, symptoms due to the destruction of the main glands are thus avoided" (loc. cit., 5th April, p. 746).

the immediate neighbourhood of the capsules, are probably always involved in cases in which the typical fibro-caseous lesion of the capsules is present ; and that, as Dr Dixon Mann has pointed out, it is quite possible that an irritation, which is not sufficiently marked to produce visible (naked-eye or microscopic) changes, may nevertheless produce very marked functional disturbances in the nervous system ; and so may perhaps produce the symptoms of Addison's disease. Further, Drs Alezais and Arnaud, as I have already more than once pointed out, claim that the pericapsular ganglia are affected in all cases of Addison's disease,* though they allow that in many cases no alterations can be detected in the semilunar ganglia or large nerve cords of the solar plexus.

(*b*) That simple atrophy and (as my case seems to show) fatty destruction of the capsules (independently of any obvious nervous irritation) is occasionally the cause of the disease ; and

(*c*) That in some cases of Addison's disease—Case IV. is one of the most striking which has as yet been published—the administration of suprarenal extract is attended with marked benefit.

The theory that the symptoms of Addison's disease are due to arrested or defective secretion of the suprarenal glands is undoubtedly a seductive one, and the knowledge which we have obtained during the past few years regarding the important influence which the thyroid and other ductless glands have in regulating the metabolism and nutrition of the tissues renders it much more probable than it was a few years ago. It cannot, I think, be lightly put aside. As I have stated elsewhere, it is not improbable that both theories (the glandular and the nervous) are correct. It is not improbable, I think, that, while some of the symptoms of Addison's disease are the direct result of abolition of the glandular function of the suprarenal capsules, others may be due to the secondary lesions in the abdominal sympathetic, which the primary lesion in the suprarenal capsules, when of the typical fibro-caseous form, seems almost always to be associated with. Cases such as Cases III. and IV., afford strong support to the glandular theory of the disease, and I am disposed to argue more strongly in favour of this theory than I did when I published the article on Addison's disease in 1892.†

Nevertheless, for the reasons already given, it must, I think, be

---

* It is probable that this statement only holds good for the typical (tuberculous) cases. There is no reason to suppose, in cases of simple fibrous atrophy, apparent absence, or fatty transformation (the condition which seems to have been present in Case IV.), that the pericapsular ganglia are affected.

† "Atlas of Clinical Medicine," Vol. i., p. 69.

allowed that in most cases of Addison's disease the lesions in the abdominal sympathetic play, at all events, some part, and probably an important part, in the production of some of the symptoms. The facts (a) that in some rare cases in which the characteristic pigmentation and some of the other constitutional symptoms of the disease were present during life, the suprarenal capsules were found to be healthy after death, while the abdominal sympathetic was involved in a mass of new growth; and (b) that in the great majority of the cases which have been recorded in which both suprarenal capsules were completely destroyed by malignant deposits there were no symptoms of Addison's disease, are extremely difficult to reconcile with the purely and exclusively glandular origin of the disease.

The theory that the symptoms of Addison's disease and the lesion of the suprarenal capsules are both due to a primary lesion of the abdominal sympathetic.—This view, which, so far as I know, was first suggested by Professor Semmola of Naples, to account for all cases of Addison's disease, and which has also been advanced by Dr Sydney Coupland to explain those rare cases in which the symptoms of Addison's disease appear to result from a simple atrophy of the capsules, has, so far as I know, no positive facts to support it.

It is impossible, I think, to conceive that the ordinary fibro-caseous (tubercular) lesion of the capsules is in all cases of Addison's disease a secondary (trophic) result of a lesion of the ganglionic nerve centres, as Professor Semmola suggests; and Dr Coupland's limitation of the theory, though more plausible, could only, I think, be provisionally accepted, as a mere temporary working hypothesis (for, so far as I know, there are no positive facts to support it), if it were allowed—and this I am not prepared to admit—that the other theories advanced above have completely failed to afford a reasonable explanation of the facts. I am firmly of opinion that in the vast majority of cases of Addison's disease, in the ordinary typical cases at all events, the capsular lesion is primary, and that the alterations in the nervous structures are secondary.

The exact mode of production of the pigmentation of the skin has not as yet been determined. One view is that it is due to an increased supply of blood pigment, and another that it is a trophic change the result of perverted innervation. The former view is, I think, the more probable, for it is extremely difficult to account for the pigmentation of the mucous membranes on the latter supposition.

Dr M'Munn believes that "the adrenals remove from the circulation useless and worn-out pigments and their accompanying proteids;" and that "when the adrenals are diseased, these effete pigments and effete proteids circulate in the blood ; the former, or their incomplete metabolites, producing pigmentation of skin and mucous membrane and appearing often in the urine as uro-hæmatoporphyrin, the latter producing toxic effects, and leading to further deterioration of the blood, with its consequences." *

PROGNOSIS.

The prognosis in Addison's disease is most unfavourable. Almost all cases terminate sooner or later in death ; this is the experience of all observers. Very few cases have been reported in which recovery has taken place. At the International Medical Congress of London, Sir William Gull related the case of a man, aged 51, who had presented all the characteristic symptoms of the disease, in which complete recovery had taken place.† Dr Finny has also recorded a case in which the symptoms were typical, the pigmentation affecting not only the skin but the buccal mucous membrane, in which there was a complete absence of any other discoverable disease or local lesion to account for the condition, in which the symptoms, including the discoloration of the skin, disappeared under treatment, and the patient eventually got well.‡ In one of my own cases (Case XI.), in which, however, I admit that the diagnosis was not perhaps absolutely clear, though the balance of evidence seems to me strongly in favour of Addison's disease, complete recovery also took place.

Seeing that tubercular lesions in other parts of the body are so frequently arrested and recovered from, it is not improbable that if we could recognise and actively treat the lesion in its early and presumably curative stage, recovery might more frequently occur. Unfortunately, there is reason to suppose that in most cases of the disease the lesion is already far advanced, and that, in some, the suprarenal capsules are completely destroyed before the symptoms become sufficiently pronounced to lead the patient to consult a doctor.

Complete destruction of the capsules is, as we have already seen, not necessarily fatal; and there are, I think, good grounds for

---

* " British Medical Journal," 4th February 1888, p. 233.
† "Transactions of the International Medical Congress of London," Vol. ii., p. 75.
‡ " Dublin Medical Journal," 1882, p. 293.

supposing that the prognosis, as regards the duration of life, is more favourable than is generally believed. In hospital patients, the average duration of life after the symptoms of Addison's disease have developed sufficiently to be recognised and to necessitate the patients taking medical advice, is probably, at the most, two years.

In those cases in which the patient is more favourably circumstanced, in which he is able to carefully protect himself from all causes of depression, and in which the exacerbations of the disease are carefully and intelligently treated, the prognosis, as regards the mere duration of life, is probably more favourable.

TREATMENT.

If Addison's disease is, in the great majority of cases, due to tuberculosis of the capsules, it is obvious that the first indication for treatment is to cure the tubercular condition of the capsules, or to remove the diseased glands by means of operation. Successful excision of the suprarenal capsules, or rather of one suprarenal capsule, has, so far as I know, only once been performed in the human subject; and although it would be rash in the extreme in these days of brilliant surgical achievement to affirm that the operation cannot be safely and satisfactorily performed, yet it may, I think (in the present state of our knowledge), with confidence be stated that, in such a disease as Addison's disease, in which even trivial causes are apt to be followed by the most profound and even fatal prostration and collapse, the risks of the operation are so great as to render the operation one of extreme danger, in the great majority of cases at all events.

Further, there is, as we have seen, good reason to suppose that in many cases the lesion is already so far advanced that the capsules are to all intents and purposes destroyed at the time when the patient first comes under observation. In such cases, all treatment, so far as the capsules themselves are concerned, is, of course, utterly useless.

Fortunately, in the adult at all events, the suprarenal capsules do not seem to be essential for life. There is good reason to believe that in many cases of Addison's disease, life is prolonged for months, perhaps even for years, after the capsules have been completely destroyed and entirely converted into caseo-calcareous masses, provided always (1) that there is no progressive lesion in the surrounding nerves; (2) that all sources of active irritation in the neighbourhood of the solar plexuses have been removed; (3) that the patient is carefully protected from all depressing and injurious external conditions; and (4) that there are no other lesions in the body. I see no reason why life should not be prolonged under such circumstances for (to speak cautiously) a very considerable period of time.

General Treatment.—In the early stages of the case, and granting that the view which has been advocated above is correct, viz., that in the vast majority of cases of Addison's disease the capsular lesion is tubercular, the same measures should be adopted as are useful in the treatment of tubercular lesions elsewhere. Koch's plan of treatment—whatever value it may ultimately be proved to have in phthisis and the tubercular lesions of some other organs—is, I consider, absolutely unjustifiable here. The violent constitutional reaction which it is apt to produce would in all probability kill a patient affected with well-marked or advanced Addison's disease.

At every stage of the disease, the most careful precautions should be taken to prevent gastro-intestinal irritation, to allay such irritation when it does arise, and to protect the patient from everything which is calculated (in him) to produce exhaustion and depression. In hospital cases, it is especially important to take care that the patient is not "over-examined." In one of Dr Greenhow's patients, the mere fatigue of being submitted to careful examination in bed, on several occasions brought on paroxysms of retching, sickness, hiccough, and intense temporary depression.

It is essential, both with the object of endeavouring to cure the tubercular lesion of the capsules, in its early and curable stages, and with the object of prolonging life after the capsules have been destroyed, to maintain the general health in the highest possible state of efficiency. The patient should, if possible, be well housed, well clothed, and carefully fed. Protection from cold and all causes of bodily fatigue and mental excitement is essential. It may be confidently affirmed that a laborious occupation is, in Addison's disease, incompatible with the prolongation of life. The diet should consist chiefly of milk, butter, eggs, farinaceous foods, fish, and white meats ; in some cases, the patient has an actual distaste for red (butcher) meat, and this indication on the part of nature should be borne in mind. Well-cooked potatoes and tender, well-cooked vegetables may be allowed in small quantities unless they appear to disagree.

Small quantities of alcoholic stimulant seem, in many cases, more especially when the prostration and exhaustion are extreme, to be beneficial.

Drastic purgatives should never be prescribed ; when there is constipation, the bowels should, if possible, be regulated by diet; or, if this is ineffectual, an enema or a small dose of a mild laxative should be cautiously employed.

Cod-liver oil should be given in those cases in which it is well borne; in those cases in which it is satisfactorily assimilated, and in which it does not produce nausea and sickness, it is, without doubt, eminently useful; unfortunately in many cases it is not well borne. Dr Greenhow states that cod-liver oil did not agree well with any of the patients who were under his care for Addison's disease. Glycerine, in doses of two drachms, given two or three times a day, in conjunction with either the citrate or the tincture of the perchloride of iron, seemed to him to be more effectual than any other medicine for keeping up the general health and strength.

The syrup of the iodide of iron, arsenic, and strychnine are some of the most useful drug remedies. But here again—and the caution applies especially to arsenic—caution in administration is necessary. Until the physician is assured that the drug is well borne, small doses only, carefully and gradually increased, should be prescribed.

Mild counter-irritation over the position of the suprarenal capsules is probably beneficial. Painting with tincture of iodine is the method which I am in the habit of employing.

During the paroxysmal exacerbations of the disease, and in advanced stages when the asthenia is marked, the patient should be confined to bed; further, he should be warned against rising suddenly from the recumbent position and making any sudden effort.

Vomiting and diarrhœa, when they occur, must be carefully treated. For the relief of vomiting, a mustard blister to the pit of the epigastrium, small doses of morphia, either hypodermically or by the stomach, bismuth, hydrocyanic acid, creasote or carbolic acid, with small quantities of champagne or brandy, ice and appropriate food (milk, or milk and lime-water, in small quantities, frequently repeated), are perhaps the most useful measures.

Complications and associated lesions, such as phthisis and caries of the spine, must, of course, be treated in accordance with their exact nature; but in dealing with these conditions, the physician must always remember that the patient is suffering from Addison's disease.

Specific Treatment.—There seems good reason to believe that some of the symptoms of Addison's disease at all events (some authorities advocate the view that *all* of the symptoms of the disease) are due to defective suprarenal secretion, *i.e.*, to destruction of the suprarenal glands and abolition of the suprarenal function. Now if this view of the pathology of the disease is correct, the specific treatment of the disease—the administration of suprarenal extract—ought to produce benefit and ought to remove the symptoms of the disease, just as the administration of thyroid extract produces such marked benefit and removes the symptoms of the disease in cases of myxœdema. And as a matter of fact this is sometimes the case. In Case IV. of my series most marked benefit undoubtedly resulted from the administration of the remedy; and other cases have been reported in which a beneficial result has been produced. But such cases appear to be exceptional. It must, I think, be allowed, so far as our present information enables us to judge, that it is only in a small proportion of cases of Addison's disease that the administration of suprarenal extract produces any marked benefit. This is perhaps due to the facts (1) that in Addison's disease the lesion is tubercular, and (2) that some of the symptoms of the disease are due, not to suppression of the function of the suprarenal gland, but to the associated secondary lesions which are produced in the abdominal sympathetic. In those cases of Addison's disease (such as Cases III. and IV.) in which the function of the suprarenal glands is simply suppressed, and in which there is no tubercular lesion and no involvement of (lesions in) the abdominal sympathetic (i.e., in which there is simple fibrous atrophy of the capsules, in which the capsules are replaced by fat, or are congenitally absent), the administration of suprarenal extract would a priori be expected to produce more marked benefit than in those cases of Addison's disease in which the lesion of the capsules is tubercular and in which the abdominal sympathetic is extensively involved. I may, perhaps, make my meaning more clear by saying, that if the thyroid body were completely destroyed by a tubercular lesion, symptoms of myxœdema would result; but that in cases of complete tubercular destruction of the thyroid gland (if such a condition occurs), the results of thyroid treatment would in all probability be less satisfactory than in the ordinary everyday cases of myxœdema, in which the tissue of the thyroid gland is simply destroyed by a process of cirrhotic atrophy.

Now in typical cases of Addison's disease there is not only a tubercular lesion and abolition of the function of the suprarenal capsules, but there is associated disease of the abdominal sympathetic. Hence perhaps the explanation of the fact that while thyroid extract speedily cures myxœdema, suprarenal extract does not as a rule produce marked benefit in cases of Addison's disease.

These therapeutic considerations lend, I think, additional support to the theory which I have for long advocated, that some of the symptoms of typical (tubercular) cases of Addison's disease are probably due to the tubercular character of the lesion and to the associated disease in the abdominal sympathetic, which the tubercular lesion in the capsules seems almost invariably to produce, while others are the result of abolition of the function of the suprarenal glands.

The suprarenal extract may be administered either in the form of a liquid extract or of compressed tabloids; or the raw gland, finely minced and given in rice paper, or mixed with some article of food, may be given. The suprarenal extract seems to pass undestroyed through the stomach; consequently the hypodermic method has no advantage, and has distinct disadvantages (risk of sepsis, greater difficulty of administration, etc.), over the method of administration by the stomach. In Case IV. the raw gland produced irritation of the stomach and vomiting; the liquid extract (ten drops three times daily) agreed perfectly. In a case which I have at present under observation, the patient at first took ten drops of Brady & Martin's liquid extract three times daily; recently, this dose has been increased to twenty drops three times daily, and I intend to still further increase the dose, if the remedy continues to be well borne. In this case (Case VI.) sufficient time has not as yet elapsed to enable me to say whether the remedy is likely to be beneficial or not; but the patient's mother states most emphatically that, since the treatment was commenced, six weeks ago, the debility and prostration which were, in addition to the pigmentation, the only symptoms, have been decidedly less marked. As yet, no perceptible change in the pigmentation has taken place.

Illustrative Cases of Addison's Disease observed by the Author during life.

CASE I.— *Typical Addison's Disease of At Least Ten Years' Duration; Excessive Languor and Debility; Feebleness of the Heart's Action; No Emaciation; Extreme Pigmentation of the Skin and Buccal Mucous Membrane; Pearliness of the Conjunctivæ; Some Anæmia; Paroxysmal Exacerbations of the Languor and Debility; Attacks of Vomiting; Occasional Hiccough; Great Susceptibility to Cold; Deeply Pigmented Lupoid Patches on the Abdomen. Death. No Post-mortem Examination.*
Female, aged 26, seen in consultation in May 1886.

Complaints.—Extreme weakness and prostration, paroxysmal attacks of vomiting, pigmentation of the skin.

Duration.—At least four, and probably eight, years.

Previous History.—Until eight or nine years ago the patient enjoyed good health, and was active and well nourished. At that time, she became languid and debilitated without obvious cause. The debility developed very gradually and insidiously. For the past four years, it has been much more marked. Some months after the debility developed, her friends noticed that the skin was becoming darker ; the pigmentation was first noticed on the face and back of the hands, especially over the knuckles. As a young girl she had a white skin and fine clear complexion, though her hair and eyes are naturally dark.

During the second year of her illness, the asthenia and pigmentation gradually increased ; the weakness and feeling of languor and depression were at times extreme ; the pigmentation gradually extended over the whole body, and became much darker in colour ; attacks of vomiting, which usually lasted several days at a time, and which used to render her completely prostrate, now frequently occurred ; the appetite failed ; she became short of breath, suffered from palpitation on exertion, and was giddy on stooping or rising suddenly from the recumbent to the erect position ; the menstruation, which had previously been regular and natural, now became scanty and irregular, and at times disappeared for months together.

During the first four or five years of her illness, she remained plump and fat ; during the past three or four years, she has got decidedly thinner, but she is still well nourished.

She has not had any pains in the abdomen or back, and she has not suffered from diarrhœa.

For several years past she has kept indoors, and for the most part has remained in her own room, during the winter months.

During the past autumn and winter (1889), she was in the house for eight months—never once out of doors during the whole of that time ; she always feels worse during the winter, but picks up again during the summer ; she does not get up until 11 A.M., and takes the greatest care of herself in every way. Since her illness commenced she has been very susceptible to cold, and very easily upset by the slightest excitement or exertion.

Family History.—The patient is one of five children ; one died at the age of 4½ years of "water in the head" ; the other three (boys), aged 22, 19 and 13 respectively, have all been "terribly troubled with their stomachs" ; as a child, the youngest suffered very much from "enlarged glands in the neck."

Her father died at the age of 37, of heart disease, complicated with pleurisy and disease of the liver. Her mother is a strong, healthy, active woman, aged 51.

So far as is known, none of either her father's or her mother's relatives have died from consumption.

There is no "black blood" in the family.

Present Condition.—The patient is a bright, intelligent young woman. She looks more like a mulatto than a European. The skin of the face and body generally is of a dark brown colour ; the contrast between the dark brown face and the white pearly conjunctiva is most striking.

Her chief, in fact her only, complaint is a feeling of excessive languor and debility ; she says that she is easily fatigued and exhausted, and that she is unequal for any sustained effort either of body or mind. The feeling of tiredness and debility are much greater at times than at others ; during the periods of increased exhaustion (paroxysmal exacerbations of the disease) she feels "terribly languid" and depressed in mind, as well as fatigued in body. She is naturally of a cheerful disposition, and rapidly picks up and regains her spirits after the temporary exacerbations of the languor and depression pass away. During the past winter (1889) she has felt less languid than she did for some years previously.

Though distinctly thinner than she was a few years ago, she is well nourished ; the limbs are rounded, the breasts plump and well developed, and the body well covered with fat.

The pulse is remarkably small and weak ; it is usually somewhat quick, ranging from 84 to 108.

The heart's impulse is imperceptible, and the heart-sounds are feeble, the first sound in particular being short and faint ; there is, however, no evidence of cardiac or vascular disease. Palpitation is readily induced either by excitement or exertion ; the slightest effort makes the patient feel short of breath ; she occasionally feels faint ; she is giddy when she stoops, looks up to the ceiling, or suddenly rises from the recumbent to the erect position. She takes great care to avoid any exertion or excitement ; she never walks quickly ; she lives on the ground-floor, and never attempts to go upstairs.

The appetite, though still small, is better than it used to be a year or two ago ; she rarely eats butcher-meat, and lives chiefly on milk, water, bread, and butter ; her digestion is good, and the bowels regular ; as has been previously stated, she has not, during the whole course of her illness, suffered from diarrhœa. For the past year she has been almost entirely free from the periodical attacks of vomiting, which were of frequent occurrence during the earlier periods of her illness, and which used to exhaust her terribly. She occasionally suffers from hiccough. Her teeth are very bad, but they do not ache and do not cause her any trouble. Her tongue is clean and moist, but deeply pigmented, as will be presently described.

The pigmentation affects the skin of the whole body ; in certain situations the colour is much darker than in others. The areolæ of the nipples, the nipples themselves, and the sides of the abdomen about the waist (lumbar regions), are very dark ; a dark brown line extends from the pubes towards the umbilicus, but the skin around the umbilicus is not more deeply pigmented than that of the rest of the abdomen ; the skin of the face, back of the hands, and front folds of the axillæ, is very dark brown (walnut-juice coloured) ; the lower extremities are less deeply stained than the abdomen and back ; the palms of the hands and the soles of the feet are the parts which are least pigmented ; but even in these situations the skin is uniformly stained of a pale golden-brown colour.

The pigmentation varies in depth from time to time, and is increased during the menstrual period.

The skin, generally speaking, is beautifully smooth, soft, elastic, and pliable. The odour of the skin is in no way remarkable.

The scalp is dry, rough, and thickly covered with furfuraceous scales (pityriasis).

Three lupoid-like patches, which measure from $\frac{1}{2}$ to 1 inch in length, and from $\frac{1}{4}$ to $\frac{1}{2}$ an inch in breadth, are situated over the lower part of the abdomen ; there is also a similar patch in the left groin. All of these lupoid patches are very deeply pigmented—almost black ; the patient says they have been present for about a year ; they do not itch, and do not give her any inconvenience whatever.

The lips, gums, tongue, and buccal mucous membrane are all pigmented.

On the lips, the pigment deposits are situated along the commissure (the line of contact of the lips when the mouth is closed) ; they are bluish-black in colour, and remind one of ink-stains, or stains produced by blackberry juice.

On the gums, the pigmentary deposits are of the same colour as on the lips ; they are situated on the outer surface of the gums, chiefly at, and immediately below, the insertion of the incisor teeth ; the gums are of a deep red colour.

On the buccal mucous membrane, the pigmentary deposits are not numerous ; they are of a dirty brown (not a bluish-black) colour ; and are situated opposite the line of junction of the closed teeth, *i.e.*, along a line drawn horizontally backwards from the angle of the mouth.

On the tongue, the pigmentary deposits are unusually well marked ; they are of a bluish-black (blackberry juice) colour, rather more blue and not quite so black as the deposits on the lips and gums ; they are chiefly situated on the dorsum of the tongue near the root, a situation which, according to Dr Greenhow, is exceptional. Under the tongue, and distributed on each side along the course of lingual arteries, there are several small deposits of pigment of a rich golden-brown colour ; they appear to be adhering to the outer coats of the vessels, and are only seen along the line of the lingual arteries.

The fundus oculi seemed to me to be more deeply pigmented than normal, but Mr George Berry, who very kindly saw the patient with me, did not think that this was the case.

Though the conjunctivæ are so white and pearly, the patient is not profoundly anæmic. The lips, gums, and tongue are all well, in fact deeply, coloured ; while the buccal mucous membrane covering the cheeks, the conjunctiva covering the lower lids, as well as the portions of the membrane which cover the sclerotic, and the nails, are distinctly paler than normal. A drop of blood obtained by pricking the finger was very deeply coloured—a dark claret colour. The red corpuscles numbered (average of several counts) 3,250,000 and the hæmoglobin = 80 per cent.; consequently, the colour index, after correction (allowing for the low reading of Gower's instrument) is above the normal, and equals 1.2 ; the white corpuscles are not in excess. The red corpuscles form rouleaux, and are quite normal in size and shape. No free pigment granules were detected in the blood.

The urine is copious (80 oz. in 24 hours), very pale, slightly acid, specific gravity 1012, no albumen, urea = 400 grains in 24 hours.

For the past few years, the patient has menstruated more or less irregularly during the winter, and has ceased to menstruate altogether during the summer. On 13th September 1890, she began to menstruate for the first time for several months.

The patient sleeps remarkably well ; she generally goes to sleep at 10 and is wakened at 8 o'clock ; her aunt says she thinks she could easily sleep for twelve hours every night ; she is not, however, sleepy during the day.

She is very sensitive to cold ; during the winter she can never, she says, get her hands and feet warm. The temperature is usually a little below the normal ; on 12th September 1890, it was 97° Fahr.

There is no pain or tenderness, even on firm pressure, over the vertebral spines or in the region of the suprarenal capsules.

The muscularity is poor ; the knee-jerks are present, but very considerably diminished in degree.

The pupils are equal, and moderately dilated. There is nothing to be noted regarding the sensory side of the nerve apparatus.

The liver and spleen are not enlarged, they appear to be normal in every respect. The lungs are perfectly normal.

Physical examination fails to detect any evidence of local or visceral disease (other than the Addison's disease) to account for the symptoms.

Result.—The patient died on 19th June 1891. She had been over-fatigued a few days previously while visiting a "dairy school"; this was followed by vomiting, intense depression, collapse, and death. Up to the time of this slight over-exertion, she had continued exceedingly well; the discoloration of the skin had, her mother says, faded considerably.

Post-mortem examination could not be obtained.

Case recorded.—"Atlas of Clinical Medicine," vol. I., p. 73, and represented in Plates VI. and VII.

CASE II.—*Typical Addison's Disease; Profound Asthenia; Pigmentation of the Skin and Buccal Mucous Membrane (the areolæ of the nipples not dark); Very Great and Rapid Emaciation; No Vomiting, Abdominal Pain or Diarrhœa; History of a Severe Blow on the Small of the Back. Death: Both Capsules extensively Affected with the Typical Fibro-caseous Change; Extensive Deposit of Recent Tubercle in the Peritoneum; Old Tuberculous Lesion at the Apex of the Left Lung.*

Male, aged 50, a miner, was seen as an out-patient at the Edinburgh Royal Infirmary on 30th June 1895, and was subsequently admitted as an in-patient.

Complaints.—Weakness and loss of flesh.

Previous History.—Enjoyed good health till three years ago. At that time he received a severe blow in the back with an iron rod—was laid up in bed for a week. Has gradually "failed" since this injury, but worked till three months ago, when he had an attack of influenza; has been much worse since.

Family History.—Unimportant; no hereditary tendency to tubercle.

Present Condition.—Extreme asthenia and prostration; expression indicative of great lassitude (in going from the out-patient room to the wards he collapsed and was found lying on the ground, quite conscious, but unable to get up); marked emaciation—he stated that he had lost 4 st. during the past nine weeks. Heart's impulse imperceptible; heart sounds scarcely to be heard; pulse small, very soft and weak. Appetite poor, tongue slightly furred on the dorsum, red at the edges and tip; no vomiting, no diarrhœa, no abdominal pain or tenderness. No rise in temperature. His medical attendant subsequently informed me that there had been no abdominal pain, diarrhœa, and no pyrexia throughout the course of the illness (*i.e.*, since the attack of influenza). Skin generally dark, especially so on the face, neck, back of the hands, wrists, and back (his wife stated that the colour of the skin was distinctly darker than it was before this illness commenced); areolæ of the nipples not darker; a distinct pigmented patch on the inner side of the left cheek. Urine normal. No evidence of local disease in any of the viscera.

Result.—For a few days after his admission to hospital, he remained in an extremely prostrate and semi-delirious condition, the head symptoms being suggestive of some form of intoxication. He refused to take the suprarenal extract and other medicines which were prescribed. He died four days after admission.

Post-mortem examination.—Both suprarenal capsules markedly enlarged and showing the fibro-caseous lesion typical of Addison's disease. Peritoneum studded with recent grey miliary tubercles. One or two old fibrous (tubercular) deposits at the apex of the left lung. The right lung and the other organs healthy.

Case recorded.—"British Medical Journal," January 1897, p. 1.

CASE III.—*Case of Addison's Disease Characterised by Profound Asthenia and Feebleness of the Heart's Action, Localised Pigmentary Deposits over One or Two Vertebral Spines and on the Buccal Mucous Membrane; Great Emaciation: Diagnosis Verified on Post-mortem Examination; Simple Fibrous Atrophy of Both Suprarenal Capsules.*

Male, aged 36, a seaman, was seen as an out-patient at the Edinburgh Royal Infirmary on 25th March 1887, and was subsequently admitted as an in-patient.

Complaints.—Progressive weakness and debility.

Duration.—Six months.

Previous history.—Prior to the present illness was a robust and healthy man. The asthenia developed gradually and without any obvious cause.

Present condition.—Extreme prostration; considerable anæmia; marked emaciation—the patient stated that he had lost 3 st. in weight since his illness commenced, and he was by no means a big-made man. Heart sounds remarkably feeble, impulse imperceptible, pulse extremely small and weak. The red corpuscles numbered 3,500,000 per c.mm.; they formed rouleaux and were normal in size and shape; white corpuscles not increased. Tongue clean, appetite poor, digestion fairly good, no vomiting, no diarrhœa. No pains in the back.

Two or three brown discolorations over the skin of the dorsal spines; no other discoloration of the skin; areolæ of the nipples not pigmented; *one* small and quite characteristic pigmented patch on the buccal mucous membrane, on the inner side of the left cheek, just opposite the angle of the mouth.

No evidence of local disease in any of the viscera.

Result.—Death a few days after first seen.

Post-mortem Examination.—The suprarenal capsules were reduced to small masses of fibrous tissue. Heart markedly atrophied.

No disease in any of the viscera.

Case recorded, "Atlas of Clinical Medicine," Vol. I., p. 54.

CASE IV.—*Typical Addison's Disease, Characterised by Profound and Causeless Asthenia, Deep Pigmentation of the Skin and Buccal Mucous Membrane, Pain in the Back, occasional Vomiting and slight Emaciation: Marked Improvement in all the Symptoms, including the Skin Pigmentation, under the Administration of Suprarenal Extract. Death from Influenza. On Post-mortem Examination, Absence of the Capsules, their place being taken by Masses of Fat: in the position of the Left Suprarenal a peculiar Histological Change in the Fatty Tissue, probably indicative of the Remains of the Degenerated Suprarenal Capsule.*

The patient, a grocer, aged 37, married, was sent to me by Dr Mossop of Bradford, on 8th October 1893, suffering from all the characteristic symptoms of Addison's disease.

Previous history of the present illness.—The present illness commenced two years ago; it followed a comparatively slight attack of influenza. After influenza, he noticed that his skin was gradually getting darker. The discoloration is not worse than it was twelve months ago.

Previous history prior to present illness.—Has never been a very strong man. When 22 years of age he had to give up his original employment, that of a compositor, because of "weakness." Has not, however, suffered from any special form of disease. He never had a fall or received any injury or strain of the back ; has never been engaged in hard or laborious work.

Family history.—Unimportant ; none of his relatives have suffered from consumption or scrofula. The patient is married and has four children, all of whom are fairly healthy.

Present Condition.—Is naturally of a pale complexion ; is much pitted with small-pox, the result of a severe attack thirty years ago. He complains of extreme languor and debility. Is not appreciably thinner. Since the illness commenced he has felt some pain in the small of the back ; it has been worse during the past three months.

The skin is of a dark, yellowish-brown colour. The numerous small-pox pits on the face are much more deeply pigmented than the other parts of the skin ; in places they are almost black. This appearance was so peculiar that I photographed the patient. There are numerous small deep-brown moles on various parts of the skin. The pigmentation is most marked on the face, neck, hands and genital organs, and it is over these parts that the small black moles and freckles are most abundant. There are also numerous pigmented patches on the lower lip, and on several parts of the buccal mucous membrane.

The patient complains of palpitation, faintness, and giddiness on stooping. He is short of breath on exertion. On several occasions during the past three months he has vomited. His expression and bearing are suggestive of extreme debility. The heart sounds are so feeble that they can hardly be heard, and the cardiac impulse cannot be felt. The blood is quite normal ; a drop drawn for microscopical examination is of a dark purple colour. The red blood corpuscles number 5,600,000 per c.mm., and the hæmoglobin = 85 per cent. There is no excess of white corpuscles. No pigment granules were detected in the specimen of blood which was examined. The urine is normal.

Treatment.—I advised that the patient should be protected from cold, over-fatigue and everything, such as over-exertion, likely to produce exhaustion ; that the diet and condition of the bowels should be carefully regulated ; and that arsenic, the syrup of the phosphates and suprarenal extract should be administered internally.

Subsequent progress of the Case.—I heard no more of the patient until 20th November 1894, when Dr Mossop sent me the kidneys, suprarenal capsules and portions of the liver and spleen.

Dr Mossop subsequently sent me the following notes of the progress of the case from the time that I saw the patient until his death :

"Early in the month of July 1893, I accidentally met W. H. G.—who had been a patient of mine in Bradford for several years previous to 1891—at a seaside resort. I was so struck with his appearance that it occurred to me that he was the subject of Addison's disease. I requested him to call upon me on his return home, which he did on 19th July. He then gave me the following history :—

He had never been an ailing man, though not robust, until two years previously, when he had an attack of epidemic influenza ; since then he had never fairly recovered his wonted strength and energy, and in fact had gradually become weaker and less fit to follow his occupation—that of a grocer. When I met him in July 1893, he was totally unable to do anything, and had spent a month at the seaside in the hope of recruiting his strength, but he stated that

S

he was worse than when he left home. His chief complaints were extreme weakness, loss of appetite, and sickness on the least exertion. He was so feeble that he was only just able to dress and undress himself, and had to crawl up to his bedroom on his hands and knees.

His condition was as follows :—Has a mournful, emaciated look, as if he was in the last stage of phthisis, stooping gait and listless movement, with breathlessness on walking. Face and neck as far as the shoulders deeply bronzed. His face is marked from small-pox from which he suffered in his youth, the pits being deeper in tint than the rest of the skin. The whole cutaneous surface is discoloured, the backs of the hands contrasting strongly with the whiteness of the palms. The mucous membrane of the lips, mouth, and tongue looks mottled and blotched. The conjunctivæ show unmistakably the usual pearly whiteness. There are also a number of small darker petechial spots about the size of a millet seed scattered over the face more particularly, doubtless pigmentary. The finger nails are not affected. The penis and scrotum are also especially discoloured. He first noticed his skin darker a year previously. He does not remember having a fall or a blow. He complains of vertigo, yawning, and sickness, the latter chiefly in the morning ; on stooping or exertion he experiences faint feelings. His pulse in the recumbent position was 114, when standing 120; temperature 98°; respirations 24. His bowels are somewhat constipated ; urine normal. Had a slight discharge of blood from the anus due to pile. Tongue clean and moist, appetite indifferent, attacks of indigestion. Heart sounds normal but action weak. Lungs healthy. I advised rest and nourishing diet, with the compound syrup of hypophosphates.

Three weeks later, on 5th August, I again saw him and found him a little better. Temperature 99°, pulse 92, respirations 20. I suggested that he should see Dr Bramwell, with a view to the treatment by suprarenal capsule juice. He accordingly went to Edinburgh on 7th October 1893, and my opinion was confirmed and a line of treatment adopted which I may say proved entirely successful.

Results of the treatment.—The patient was kept in bed for three weeks, and twice a week I injected with every care and precaution 15 minims of the sterilised suprarenal capsule juice prepared for me by Messrs Brady & Martin, the glands of one rabbit in ʒj. of the extract. It was injected alternately over the kidney region, and in a fortnight a manifest improvement took place in the colour of the skin. Towards the end of October, I tried the capsules of a sheep minced and put into beef-tea. This brought on a severe gastric disturbance. I then ordered him to take 10-drop doses of the sterilised juice every other day by the mouth ; this answered admirably. I ordered him also " Levico " water (arsenio-ferrated), for a time the mild and then the strong, which suited him well. His appetite improved, and a marked change in his general health took place. He was able to indulge in a fair amount of physical exertion, and to attend to his business as before. His colour was decidedly better, which fact was observed by other medical men who saw him from time to time casually. Ten days before his death he took an unusually long walk in the country (about eight miles) and was much fatigued by it.* At that time his wife and children

---

* The fact that after a year's treatment with suprarenal extract the patient could walk a distance of eight miles, whereas before the treatment was commenced "he was so feeble that he was only just able to dress and undress himself, and had to crawl up to his bedroom on his hands and knees," speaks volumes in favour of the remarkable improvement which the treatment produced in this case.

were ill with influenza, his nights were disturbed, and on the Friday night before his death, which occurred on the Sunday morning at 5 o'clock, he slept in the sitting-room on a couch before the fire. He thought that he had caught a chill, and for the rest of the following day appeared in a semi-comatose condition. A medical man who lived near at hand was suddenly sent for; he requested my attendance. At 11 P.M. I found him in a collapsed condition, with pallor of skin, dilated pupils, and temperature 104°, pulse 140, barely conscious, evidently sinking. Restoratives were tried, but he died at 5 A.M. (six hours afterwards)."

Post-mortem examination by Dr Mossop.—"The post-mortem was made on 20th November 1894. In addition to myself, Dr Walter Nenby and Dr Frith, House-Surgeon to the Children's Hospital, Bradford, were present. I was not allowed to make a complete examination. The abdomen and thorax alone were examined.

The skin of the body had a bronzed hue. Half an inch of fat was present in the anterior abdominal wall. The patient was well nourished, the muscles being firm and of normal colour. The pericardium and heart were normal. The apex of the left lung was adherent by old pleuritic adhesions to the front of the chest wall, but the lungs were otherwise normal.

The omentum was adherent on the right side to the adjacent structures. There were also some old adhesions about the liver and spleen. The gall bladder was distended with bile. There were no enlarged glands in the abdomen. The spleen was somewhat enlarged, but to the naked eye the liver and spleen appeared to be normal.

After removing the liver, spleen, and stomach, each kidney with the whole of the fatty tissue in its neighbourhood and (as was supposed) the suprarenal capsules were removed *en masse*. These parts were immediately forwarded, together with portions of the liver and spleen, to Dr Bramwell for further observation." Dr Mossop subsequently wrote saying, "Absolutely nothing was left in the body which could possibly represent a suprarenal capsule."

The Naked-eye Condition of the Kidneys and Fatty Masses representing the Suprarenal Capsules. — The tissues received from Dr Mossop consisted of: (1) The two kidneys and large masses of fat attached to the upper end of each kidney, in which it was supposed the suprarenal capsules were embedded; and (2) portions of the liver and spleen.

The masses of fat which were supposed to contain the suprarenal capsules were first detached from the kidneys and carefully examined. They were of considerable size, measuring 3½ inches by 3 inches and 4 inches by 3¼ inches respectively. An incision from above downwards was first made into the mass of fat corresponding to the right suprarenal capsule, but no suprarenal capsule was found. This mass of fat was then cut up into small pieces, but the most careful examination failed to detect any appearance whatever suggestive of a suprarenal gland. The mass of fat corresponding to the left suprarenal capsule was then carefully cut into a series of transverse sections. In the centre of the fat, a faint, brown, wavy discoloration, which seemed to correspond exactly, in respect to shape and size, to the outline of a normal suprarenal capsule, was seen. The portions of fat in which this supposed suprarenal was embedded were immediately placed in Müller's fluid and handed to Dr Muir, who kindly undertook to make the microscopic examination. The kidney, liver and spleen, which were carefully examined both with the naked eye and the microscope, were found to be perfectly normal.

Dr Muir's Report on the Microscopical Examination of the Mass of Fat

in which the Left Suprarenal Capsule was Supposed to be Embedded. — " I have examined three separate pieces of the tissues, and all show similar appearances. The tissue is composed of lobules of fatty tissue with vessels running in the central part. Some of these vessels are of considerable size. The cells at the periphery do not differ from ordinary fat cells, but those arranged around the vessels show a peculiar appearance. They are filled with small globules of oil, between which is a slightly granular material, which colours of a brown tint with the rubin-orange stain. These globules are smaller, and there is more granular material in the more centrally-placed cells, whilst towards the periphery they become larger, apparently by coalescence and disappearance of the granular material. The appearance is as if cells were becoming filled with droplets of oil, which afterwards run together so as to produce an ordinary fat cell—a condition suggesting the appearances seen in advanced fatty infiltration of the liver. There are no cells which one can identify as being of epithelial type, and there is no arrangement of the cells in columns, etc. All the tissue examined corresponds to this description. Amongst the cells undergoing this change are a few leucocytes here and there, but there is no trace of inflammatory change.' There is nothing, therefore, in the sections which would enable one to identify the tissue as part of a suprarenal. If it is so, the change is an extreme fatty infiltration, with ultimate transformation into ordinary adipose tissue. I am not familiar with these appearances as occurring in ordinary adipose tissue. I may state further that when Dr Bramwell brought to me the piece of tissue for examination, the brownish sinuous outline in the fat certainly resembled that of a suprarenal ; and I was greatly surprised to find, on microscopic examination, no trace of suprarenal structure. In view of the absence of anything else which could represent the suprarenal, I agree with Dr Bramwell that the suprarenals were entirely absent or had been replaced by fat, and the facts stated are in favour of the latter view."

Conclusion.—It must, I think, be allowed, either, that the capsules were entirely absent, or that they were replaced by fat. The only other explanation is that the suprarenal capsules were not removed from the body and were not sent to me, and that the portions of fat which Dr Muir and I examined were merely portions of the fat in which the kidney is embedded. This explanation is, in my opinion, quite untenable. It is of course quite possible in making a hurried post-mortem examination to miss the suprarenal capsules. I have, for example, often seen the right suprarenal capsule removed with the liver by an inexperienced pathologist, and supposed for the moment to be absent ; but in this case the conditions were altogether different. That the fat which was attached to the kidneys did actually represent the remains of the suprarenal capsules cannot, I think, be doubted for the following reasons :—

1. The patient had suffered during life from symptoms which were typical and characteristic of Addison's disease, and had been treated for thirteen months with suprarenal extract on account of the Addison's disease. The case was, in fact, regarded as a typical case of Addison's disease in which notable improvement had occurred as the result of this treatment.

2. Three qualified medical practitioners made the post-mortem examination, with the express object of removing the suprarenal capsules. I am not acquainted with two of these gentlemen, but the third I have known for twenty-five years, and those who know him as well as I do will not doubt his competence and reliability.

3. This gentleman assures me that everything was removed which could

possibly represent a suprarenal capsule, and was sent, along with the kidneys, immediately to myself. He states definitely that nothing was left in the body which could possibly represent a suprarenal capsule.

4. In the specimens which I received I found a large mass of fat attached to the upper end of each kidney. These masses of fat exactly occupied the position of the suprarenal capsules. Until I cut into these masses of fat and examined them I never for one moment doubted that the suprarenal capsules would be found in their interior.

5. In the mass of fat which occupied the position of the right suprarenal I did not find anything suggestive of a suprarenal capsule; but in the mass of fat which occupied the position of the left suprarenal, a dark, apparently pigmented, sinuous outline, which exactly corresponded in size and shape with the outline (size and shape) of a normal suprarenal body, could be seen with the naked eye.

6. Although the microscopical examination subsequently made by Dr Muir failed to show anything which could be definitely identified as the remains of the suprarenal capsule, it showed appearances which are peculiar, and with which neither Dr Muir nor myself are familiar as occurring in ordinary adipose tissue. Whether small localised hæmorrhages could produce such appearances or not I do not know.

Now, for the reasons which I have just stated, there can, I think, be little or no doubt that the suprarenal bodies were absent, and that they were replaced by fatty tissue. Absence of the suprarenal capsules has been noted before.*

From a practical point of view, the marked improvement which was produced by the administration of suprarenal extract is the most important point in the case. It raises a question of great interest and practical importance— namely, Why does the administration of suprarenal extract prove beneficial in some cases of Addison's disease, whereas in others—and so far as our present information enables us to judge they constitute the large majority of cases—it seems to do little or no good? As Dr Muir suggested to me, this case perhaps affords an answer to this question. In cases such as this, in which the function of the suprarenal capsules is simply, as it were, suppressed, and in which there is no tubercular lesion and no involvement of (lesion in) the abdominal sympathetic, the administration of suprarenal extract would *a priori* be expected to produce more marked benefit than in those cases of Addison's disease in which the lesion of the capsules is tubercular, and in which the abdominal sympathetic is extensively involved. I may make my meaning perhaps more clear by saying that if the thyroid body were completely destroyed by a tubercular lesion, symptoms of myxœdema would result; but in cases of complete tubercular destruction of the thyroid gland (if such a condition occurs), the results of thyroid treatment would in all probability be less satisfactory than in the ordinary everyday cases in which the tissue of the thyroid gland is simply destroyed by a process of cirrhotic atrophy.

Now in typical cases of Addison's disease there is not only a tubercular lesion and abolition of the function of the suprarenal capsules, but there is associated disease of the abdominal sympathetic. Hence perhaps the explanation of the fact that while thyroid extract speedily cures myxœdema, suprarenal extract does not as a rule produce marked benefit in cases of Addison's disease.

It remains to be seen whether, as this case seems to suggest, the administra-

---

* By Dr Rispal ("Le Progres Medical," 29th August 1896, and quoted by Dr Hunter, Glasgow, "Medical Journal," January 1897).

tion of suprarenal extract is chiefly beneficial in those cases of Addison's disease in which the lesion is a simple atrophy or fatty degeneration. If this should turn out to be the case, we may in future be able to form, by means of this therapeutic test, a more accurate idea as to the exact nature of the lesion of the suprarenal capsules in cases of Addison's disease than is possible by any of our present means of diagnosis.

These therapeutic considerations lend, I think, additional support to the theory which I have for long advocated, that some of the symptoms of typical tuberculous cases of Addison's disease are probably due to the tubercular character of the lesion, and to the associated disease in the abdominal sympathetic, which the tubercular lesion in the capsules seems almost invariably to produce, while others are the result of abolition of the function of the suprarenal glands.

Case recorded.—" British Medical Journal," 9th January 1897, page 68.

CASE V. — *Typical Addison's Disease with Leucoderma : Profound Debility and Languor ; Little Loss of Flesh ; Pearliness of the Conjunctivæ ; Some Anæmia ; Extreme Feebleness of the Heart's Action : Occasional Sick Feeling ; Occasional Diarrhœa ; Tenderness over the Suprarenal Capsules ; Marked and Characteristic Pigmentation of the Skin ; No Pigmentation of the Buccal Mucous Membrane ; Patches of Leucoderma on Face and Hands ; No Obvious Visceral Disease. No Post-mortem.*

Male, aged 41, admitted to the Newcastle-on-Tyne Infirmary on 1st March 1876.

Complaints.—Extreme weakness and pigmentation of the skin.

Duration.—Six months.

Previous history.—The debility developed gradually and without apparent cause. Patient was previously healthy ; has not had syphilis and has not received any back injury.

Family history.—A sister died of phthisis.

Present condition.—Profound debility and exhaustion ; expression indicative of great lassitude ; rather thin, but little loss of flesh ; conjunctivæ pearly ; somewhat anæmic, the blood shows a slight poikilocytosis, and no increase of the white corpuscles ; heart's impulse and sounds extremely feeble ; pulse small, soft and weak ; frequently feels sick, but does not vomit ; occasional attacks of causeless diarrhœa ; pigmentation of the skin very marked, especially on the face, neck, hands, genitals and axillæ ; areolæ of nipples very dark ; patches of leucoderma on the face and hands ; no pigmentation of the buccal mucous membrane, tenderness on pressure over the position of the capsules ; no visceral disease detectable in any of the organs.

Result.—No improvement under treatment ; the pigmentation of the skin gradually increased. The patient remained under observation for six months and was then lost sight of. The ultimate result is not known.

CASE VI.—*Typical Addison's Disease : Marked Debility and Languor ; No Emaciation ; Occasional Vomiting ; No Diarrhœa ; No Back Pain ; No Anæmia ; Very Marked Pigmentation of the Skin ; Numerous Small Black Moles or Freckles ; Pigmentation of the Lower Gum ; Several Small Ball-like Collections of Pigment in the Course of the Lingual Arteries.*

Female, aged 8½, seen on 8th October 1898.

Complaints.—Weakness and lassitude and pigmentation of the skin ; absolutely nothing else.

Duration.—Six months.

Previous history.—In May 1897, the patient developed ringworm. A great many remedies were tried, and as a result of the treatment her temper and health were perhaps a little upset ; but, except that she did not play and romp about so much as usual, nothing special was noticed wrong with her until March 1898. It was then noticed that the skin of her face was distinctly browner than formerly. It was thought that the discoloration might perhaps be due to an ointment of creolin, iodine, carbolic acid and sulphur which had been applied to the head a few days previously ; the discoloration seemed to spread from the hair over the face. But this theory was soon given up, for the discoloration soon extended all over the body. During the past five months, the feeling of lassitude and tiredness have increased ; and there have been occasional attacks of causeless vomiting. Has never had a fall or received any injury to her back. Before this illness commenced, the patient was a particularly strong, active and lively child.

Family history.—The father, mother, brothers and sisters are healthy ; there are nine other living children, all healthy ; three are dead (two of scarlet fever and one prematurely born) ; a maternal aunt died of consumption, and a cousin suffers from scrofulous glands.

Present condition.—Is a well developed and well nourished (fat and muscular) child ; she has not got any thinner since the disease commenced. Height= 4 ft. ¾ in. ; weight=3 st. 10 lbs. She complains of nothing except debility and muscular weakness. She is very listless and depressed—a great contrast to her former activity and liveliness. Her mother says that if it were not for this listlessness and the discoloration one could not notice anything amiss with her. Appetite good, digestion good, occasional vomiting, no diarrhœa. No pain in the back. Conjunctivæ not pearly, rather leaden-coloured. Not anæmic ; blood of a dark purple hue and perfectly natural on microscopic examination both of fresh blood and stained films ; no pigmented particles in the blood. Ringworm now almost healed ; scalp not pigmented. The whole skin is deeply pigmented of a brown colour, so that the patient resembles one of the darker races of mankind ; the face, back of the hands, elbows, anterior and posterior folds of the axillæ, the areolæ of the nipples and the abdomen are especially dark ; many minute black points, like pigmented moles or freckles, are present on the face, and some on the trunk, forearms and legs. The gum of the lower jaw is distinctly pigmented (of a golden-brown shade), and several small accumulations of pigment are present under the tongue along the course of, and apparently adhering to, the lingual arteries. No pigmented patches on the tongue or other parts of the buccal mucous membrane. The pigmentation of the skin has varied in depth from time to time since it became general ; her mother thinks it is now less deep on the face than when it was first noticed.

Urine normal in colour and in every respect.

Treatment.—Avoidance of all fatigue, causes of exhaustion and exposure to cold ; careful regulation of the diet and bowels ; and the administration of suprarenal extract.

Result.—Patient has only been under observation for six weeks ; as yet there is no apparent alteration in the pigmentation, but the patient's mother is quite satisfied that the debility and languor are decidedly less.

CASE VII.—*Typical Addison's Disease: Profound Asthenia and Feebleness of the Heart's Action; Considerable Emaciation; Marked Pigmentation of the Skin and Buccal Mucous Membrane; Areolæ of the Nipples not dark.*

Female, aged 18, seen as an out-patient at the Edinburgh Royal Infirmary on 25th March 1887.

Complaints.—Extreme prostration and weakness ; some headache.

Duration.—Two years.

Previous history.—Prior to the onset of the present illness was in good health ; the weakness and emaciation developed gradually without any obvious cause.

Present condition.—Extreme prostration and weakness ; considerable anæmia, conjunctivæ very white and pearly ; considerable loss of flesh. Heart's impulse very weak, heart sounds very feeble, pulse small and weak. Conjunctivæ pearly; patient looks anæmic ; the red corpuscles (not counted) normal in size and shape ; slight excess of white corpuscles. Tongue slightly furred, appetite poor, no vomiting, no diarrhœa. Has had a good deal of headache ; it has not been severe until lately. No pain in the back until to-day. Complexion naturally dark, but the skin has become very much darker since the illness commenced ; the skin generally is of a dirty brown colour and is especially dark over the abdomen ; the breasts are very small ; the areolæ of the nipples are not pigmented ; there are numerous pigmented patches on the buccal mucous membrane and on the lower lip at the junction of the skin with the mucous membrane.

No evidence of local disease in any of the viscera, except the suprarenal capsules.

Result.—Not known.

CASE VIII.—*Typical Addison's Disease: Profound Prostration ; Feebleness of the Heart's Action ; Occasional Vomiting ; Frequent Pains in the Back ; Pigmentation of the Skin ; Areolæ of the Nipples not dark ; One Pigmented Patch on the Buccal Mucous Membrane.*

Male, aged 46, factory worker, seen as an out-patient at the Edinburgh Royal Infirmary on 23rd June 1889.

Complaints.—Great weakness.

Duration.—Four months.

Previous history.—Enjoyed good health until the present illness commenced ; the weakness developed gradually and without any obvious cause.

Present condition.—Extreme prostration and weakness; considerable anæmia; no loss of flesh. Heart's impulse weak, first sound short and sharp ; pulse small and weak. Patient looks somewhat anæmic ; conjunctivæ pearly ; the red corpuscles (not counted) for the most part normal in size and shape, a few tailed (slight poikilocytosis), no excess of whites. Tongue clean, appetite poor, occasional vomiting, no diarrhœa. Frequent pain in the small of the back. Skin generally much darker ; the areolæ of the nipples not darker ; well marked pigmented patch on the buccal mucous membrane. Urine contains a trace of albumen and becomes very dark on the addition of nitric acid. No evidence of local disease in any of the viscera.

Result.—Not known.

CASE IX.—*Addison's Disease, Complicated with Enlargement of the Lymphatic Glands, Liver and Spleen (? Hodgkin's Disease or Tubercle) and Dermatitis Herpetiformis : No Post-mortem.*

Female, aged 19, admitted to the Edinburgh Royal Infirmary on 18th August 1893.

Complaints.—Great weakness, emaciation, pigmentation of the skin, itching, sweating and cough.

Duration.—One year.

Previous history.—Two years ago the patient began to suffer from itching of the skin ; it commenced on the heels and soles ; little vesicles developed from time to time ; the eruption and itching gradually extended, involving the legs, thighs, arms, and finally the trunk, head, face and neck. Small red papules which were very itchy appeared from time to time on the legs and arms, but never on the face or trunk. It was a year before the itching extended over the whole body.

Soon after the itching commenced, she began to sweat profusely, first on the face and then all over the body. She also noticed that her skin was becoming darker, and that her hair, which was previously very luxuriant, was coming out ; at the same time her hair got lighter in colour and drier in texture. The loss of hair was not confined to the head but affected the eyebrows, axillæ, and pubes.

In August 1892, she had an attack of influenza and since then has gradually got weaker and thinner ; for the past year she has been almost confined to bed.

In December 1892, some enlarged glands were noticed in the axillæ. About a year ago, the menstruation stopped. For the past three months, she has had a cough, but little or no expectoration.

Family history.—She inherits a strong rheumatic tendency ; one brother had scrofulous glands in the neck. No other relations, so far as she knows, have been tubercular.

Present condition.—Extreme prostration and weakness and appearance of profound lassitude ; marked emaciation—height = 5 ft. 1½ ins. ; weight = 5 st. 12 lbs. Temperature continuously above the normal (morning temperature about 99°, evening temperature about 101.5°). Pulse quick, small and weak (78 to 130). Appetite very good, no dyspepsia, no vomiting, no diarrhœa. Occasional pain in the back.

Heart's impulse not perceptible ; heart sounds very feeble. Red corpuscles number 3,980,000, normal in size and shape ; hæmoglobin = 62 per cent. ; slight excess of white corpuscles.

Skin thin, but dry and harsh ; very deeply pigmented, of a dirty brown colour like that of some of the darker races ; many minute black points (freckles) ; some larger white spots about the size of a very small pea, apparently the result of former vesicles or scratchings ; no papules or vesicles ; areolæ of nipples very deeply pigmented ; no pigmented patches on the buccal mucous membrane. Head almost bald, and hair of eyebrows, axillæ and pubes very scanty.

The patient complains of great itchiness of the skin.

Enlarged glands on both sides of the neck, and in both axillæ ; an enlarged gland in the second right intercostal space. The enlarged glands are hard and painless.

A solid mass, apparently enlarged glands, in the upper part of the right thoracic cavity (marked dulness and resistance on percussion from the right clavicle to the 3rd rib in front and in the supraspinous and right axillary regions) ; no moist sounds ; over the dull area the breathing was in places bronchial and the vocal resonance and fremitus increased. Some cough and shortness of breath when lying on the back ; very scanty frothy expectoration ; no tubercle bacilli. No evidence of phthisis.

Liver somewhat and *spleen* considerably enlarged.

Urine normal, except that it gave Ehrlich's reaction on several occasions.

Diagnosis.—The case seemed to be one of Addison's disease, with Hodgkin's disease or solid tubercular enlargement of the glands, and dermatitis herpetiformis.

Treatment.—A great number of remedies (cod-liver oil, quinine, iron, carbonate of guaiacol, strychnine, arsenic, thyroid extract, atropin, sulphate of atropia, morphia, bromide of potassium, together with menthol and other local remedies) were employed, but with no benefit.

Result.—The patient remained in hospital until 28th December 1893 (five months) ; there was no improvement ; during the whole of her stay in hospital, the temperature was above the normal (99° to 102°): she became thinner, weaker and more anæmic ; on 15th November the red corpuscles numbered 1,179,000 and the hæmoglobin = 38 per cent.; the skin became darker. She was, contrary to advice, taken home by her friends, and died, in Orkney, on 10th January 1894. The true nature of the case was consequently not verified by post-mortem examination.

CASE X.—*Suspected Addison's Disease : Extreme Debility without Obvious Cause ; Feebleness of the Heart's Action ; Pain in the Back ; Marked Pigmentation of the Skin ; Pearliness of the Conjunctivæ ; No Anæmia ; No Obvious Visceral Disease.*

Male, aged 49, seen on 14th August 1895.

Complaints.—Great weakness.

Duration.—Eighteen months.

Previous history.—The debility commenced eighteen months ago without obvious cause ; some anæmia developed, but disappeared under arsenic and iron.

Family history.—Unimportant.

Present condition.—Extreme debility ; very slight loss of weight ; no vomiting ; no diarrhœa ; some pain in the back over the region of the capsules ; conjunctivæ very pale and pearly, but lips not anæmic ; heart's impulse and sounds feeble ; pulse weak ; sleeps too much ; skin of face, hands, thighs and genitals very dark—much more so than they used to be ; areolæ of nipples somewhat dark ; no pigmented patches in the mouth ; no visceral disease detectable in any of the organs ; knee-jerks exaggerated ; gait rather unsteady.

Diagnosis.—Difficult, but condition suggestive of Addison's disease.

Result.—Not known.

CASE XI. — *Suspected Addison's Disease (Extreme Asthenia, Emaciation, Paroxysmal Attacks of Gastric Pain and Vomiting without Obvious Stomach Cause, Pain in the Back and Tenderness on Pressure over the Suprarenal Capsules, Pigmentation of the Skin and Palate): Recovery.*

Female, aged 25, was seen in October 1885.

Complaints.—Extreme debility, emaciation, pain in the back, paroxysmal attacks of gastric pain and vomiting.

Duration.—Three and a half years.

Previous history. — Six or seven years ago, patient had two attacks of bronchitis. Three and a half years ago, she suffered from severe gastric pain, going through to the back, with persistent vomiting for a day or two. There have been two similar attacks since ; the last occurred four months ago, and was followed, for several weeks, by pain after food and extreme irritability of the stomach ; this attack was attended with marked collapse. For the past year, she has suffered from pain in the lower dorsal region increased by exertion.

Family history.—Good ; her father died of pneumonia at the age of 56.

Present condition.—Extreme debility and lassitude ; considerable emaciation; heart's action feeble ; pulse small and weak ; temperature subnormal ; somewhat anæmic ; tongue clean, appetite poor, no pain or tenderness in the epigastric region ; the attacks of gastric pain and vomiting occur, sometimes at all events, without any obvious gastric cause ; one, which I had the opportunity of seeing, appeared to be due to over-exertion ; it resembled one of the gastric crises of locomotor ataxia ; no diarrhœa. There is distinct tenderness on pressure in each lumbar region (*i.e.*, over the suprarenal capsules). No spinal caries. Several pigmented patches on the skin of the arms, thighs and over the dorsal vertebræ ; one pigmented patch on the soft palate. Skin somewhat dry and rough. Menstruation profuse and attended with a good deal of pain. No evidence of disease in any of the viscera.

Diagnosis.—Difficult ; it lay between gastric ulcer and Addison's disease. The marked emaciation, the rough and dry condition of the skin, and the fact that the patient has recovered are against Addison's disease ; but the other symptoms, more especially the pigmented patch on the palate, were in favour of that condition. When the patient was under my observation I was of opinion that she was suffering from Addison's disease.

Result.—Under cod-liver oil, maltine, arsenic, the local application of iodine over the region of the suprarenal capsules and residence in a warm climate, the patient slowly but gradually improved. Though not robust, she is now (October 1898) in the enjoyment of fair health.

CASE XII.—*Pigmentation of the Skin, Exactly Resembling that of Addison's Disease, with Caseous Destruction of One Suprarenal Capsule, the other being healthy.*

In this very interesting but complicated case, the skin was deeply pigmented, exactly as it is in advanced Addison's disease, and after death the left suprarenal capsule was found to be twice the natural size and transformed into a putty-like mass, the right suprarenal capsule being normal.

The patient suffered from an intrathoracic tumour which closely simulated an aneurism. During the course of his illness right-sided hemiplegia and aphasia developed ; also pericarditis.

On post-mortem examination, the following conditions, in addition to the lesion of the left suprarenal capsule, were found :—Recent pericarditis ; a sacculated dilatation of the upper part of the pericardium ; a tumour involving the root of the left lung ; a large cyst in the left frontal lobe ; a recent embolism in left middle cerebral artery.

The notes are as follows :—

W. A., a pitman, aged 45, was admitted to the Newcastle Infirmary on 1st October 1874, suffering from right-sided hemiplegia, cough, emaciation, and debility.

Previous history.—At the age of 22, he had an attack of "inflammation of the chest." With this exception, he enjoyed excellent health until *November* 1873, when he caught cold. His eyes and nose began to run, and continued to do so for some time. *In April* 1874, he began to cough and lose flesh. *In August*, he commenced to spit; the sputa were white and frothy, never blood-tinged. He rapidly lost flesh; complained occasionally of pain in the chest and of palpitation. He never seemed very short of breath. *Six weeks before admission to hospital*, a marked change took place in his mental condition; he became very irritable and obstinate; slept badly; would sit silent for hours together; when spoken to, he answered in monosyllables. *A week before admission*, he partly lost the use of his right hand. A few days afterwards, the leg became affected. He was at work, off and on, as a pitman, until a fortnight before admission to hospital.

Family history.—Good; none of his near relatives have died of cancer or consumption.

Condition on admission.—The skin was of a dirty brown colour. His wife said it was much darker than it used to be. There were no pigmented patches on the buccal mucous membrane. He was very thin and emaciated. He was unable to give any account of himself or of his complaints. He said "Yes," "No," "Nicely," or some short word, in answer to all questions. He seemed to understand fairly well what was said to him. There was partial loss of power in the right arm and leg. Sensibility was apparently natural. The muscles of the right hand and arm were not more wasted than those of the body generally. Muscular irritability was very marked. His sight seemed good. The pupils were equal and contracted. (At this time, I was not in the habit of using the ophthalmoscope in all cases, for I had not then realised the truth of Dr Hughlings Jackson's observation that optic neuritis is often present with perfect vision. I regret, therefore, that I cannot state what was the condition of the optic discs.) The other special senses seemed natural. The tongue was protruded in the middle line. He was very irritable and obstinate, slept badly, and often ground his teeth. The anterior wall of the left chest was unduly prominent from the second to the sixth rib. It measured, at the level of the nipple, half an inch more than the right, being eighteen inches. Pulsation could be seen and felt over the prominent area. *The pulsation seemed to come to a focus* at a spot an inch and a half above and slightly outside the left nipple. It was apparently distinct from the cardiac pulsation and quite as forcible. On percussion, there was absolute dulness over the left chest—anteriorly, from the clavicle to the sixth rib; laterally, in the axillary region; posteriorly, in the suprascapular, upper half of the scapular, and upper half of the interscapular region on the left side. Pain was complained of on percussion about the left nipple. On the right side, there was dulness over an area an inch square below the sternoclavicular articulation. This dulness was directly continuous on its inner side with the dulness on the left side. The cardiac dulness could not be exactly defined by percussion, owing to the surrounding dulness. The apex-beat could be seen and felt between the fifth and sixth ribs an inch and a half below the nipple. On auscultation, the respiratory murmur was scarcely perceptible over any part of the left chest; it was entirely absent from the second to the sixth ribs anteriorly. Over the rest of the dull area, faint bronchial breathing was heard. Vocal resonance was greatly diminished all over the left chest; absent over the dull area. At the aortic cartilage, the first sound was replaced by a soft bellows-murmur. The second sound was well marked. Over the pulmonary area, the systolic murmur was heard, being fainter than over the aorta. The second sound was louder than the aortic. At the apex, the sounds had a dull thudding character. At the point of pulsation, an inch and a half above the left nipple, both cardiac sounds were very distinct, but free from murmur. The radial pulse numbered 92, was weak, regular, equal in the two wrists. The respirations numbered 20. The temperature was normal. There was no excess of the white blood-corpuscles. The red corpuscles did not form *rouleaux*, but adhered wherever they came into contact. The urine contained an excess of phosphates. The other organs were normal.

The subsequent progress of the case was as follows :—

17th October.—His mental condition was much worse. The paralysis of the arm and leg was now complete. There was also distinct loss of power in the muscles of the right side of the face. The heart was situated more to the left side. The apex was now an inch outside the left nipple. The dulness over the upper half of the left lung was more absolute and extensive.

19th October.—A well-marked pericardial friction-murmur was heard over the greater part of the left chest anteriorly ; it was very abruptly defined. The cardiac sounds were heard, free from murmur, in the axillary region.

21st October.—The left chest now measured an inch and a half more than the right.

28th October.—He was very much better, and was gaining power in the right arm and leg. The friction-sound was now almost gone.

4th November.—He could move the arm and leg freely.

5th November.—He had again lost all power in the right arm and leg. His face was very much congested ; breathing very difficult. He had been several times severely purged without medicine.

6th November.—He was again severely purged. He died at 9.30 P.M.

Temperature.—The temperature never exceeded 100 deg. Fahr. until 5th November ; on that day, it reached 101 deg. ; and on 6th November, 102 deg.

Post-mortem examination, made eighteen hours after death.—Body much emaciated ; rigor mortis well marked ; the left pupil dilated, the right contracted.

Both lungs were firmly adherent throughout. The left was scarcely visible on opening the chest, its anterior edge being much retracted. Between the sternum and adjacent parts, there was a quantity of recent lymph. The *pericardium* was adherent over the greater part of the heart. Along the right border and at the apex, it was free. The adhesions were recent and thick. Around the great vessels, the pericardium was dilated, and formed a sort of cyst, which projected to the left side. The sac was about the size of an orange, and was filled with pinkish semi-fluid matter. The *heart* weighed twelve ounces. Its valves were healthy. The outer coat of the aorta and pulmonary artery, where surrounded by the cyst, were roughened and coated with lymph.

Around the root of the left lung, and extending into the substance of the organ, was a growth of brain-like consistency, and composed of numerous nodules. The growth radiated into the lung-substance in all directions, and seemed to follow the course of the bronchi, the walls of which were much thickened. The terminal portions of the aortic arch and pulmonary artery were surrounded by the growth, which passed over to the right side. On section, the nodules were of a pink colour; one was caseous. The *left lung* was of a jet-black colour. The black fluid which escaped did not stain the fingers. After the black fluid had been washed out, the lung-substance was tough and non-crepitant, resembling the compressed lung from a case of copious pleuritic effusion. The *right lung* was congested, otherwise healthy. There were no tubercles.

The *mesenteric glands* were much enlarged, of a dark purple colour, and studded here and there with white nodules. A chain of enlarged glands surrounded the abdominal aorta. In the lower part of the ileum, there was an oval nodule of fully the size of a large walnut; it formed a well-defined tumour; its free surface was of a yellow colour, evidently stained by fæces. Several Peyer's patches were enlarged, but none were ulcerated.

The *left suprarenal capsule* was about twice the natural size and transformed into a cheesy putty-like mass. The *right suprarenal capsule* was normal.

The surface of the *brain* was considerably congested. An abscess of the size of an egg was situated in the middle of the left frontal lobe. The white matter was extensively destroyed. At one point corresponding to the middle of the superior frontal convolution, the grey matter was invaded and partly destroyed. The abscess contained a grumous yellow liquid of the consistency of thin cream; it was lined by a ragged membrane. Both lateral ventricles contained an excess of fluid. A clot was found in the left middle cerebral artery just at its commencement.

On *microscopic examination*, the intrathoracic growth was found to consist of :— 1. Cells, round and angular in form, about the size of white blood-corpuscles, and containing numerous highly refractive granules; 2. Free nuclei and granules; 3. Fibrous tissue; many of the fibres were nucleated. The pericardium, the cerebral abscess, and the lymphatic glands, contained the same corpuscular elements as the tumour.

Remarks.—It may, perhaps, be objected, that the discoloration of the skin was due to some other cause than the lesion of the left suprarenal capsule; in short, that it was not the bronzing of Addison's disease. But I see no reason to adopt this view; for the condition of the capsule was exactly similar to that which so frequently results from the "peculiar quasi-tubercular change which produces the symptoms of Addison's disease." It is an unfortunate fact that there is not in my case-book a more minute description of the discoloration, and I cannot at this distant period trust my memory to fill in details. I cannot, for instance, say whether the discoloration was more marked in the axillæ and genitals than elsewhere. There certainly were no pigmented patches on the buccal mucous membrane.

I do not make any mention of the constitutional symptoms, the anæmia, etc., which are characteristic of Addison's disease, the case being so very complicated. The emaciation is fully accounted for by the complications which were present. It is unnecessary for my present purpose to refer to the many other interesting features of the case; they are considered in the original record of the case.

Recorded in the "British Medical Journal," 3rd March 1877, p. 256.

MYXŒDEMA.

Definition.—The term myxœdema in reality represents a group of clinical symptoms and pathological changes which may result from any condition which causes arrested development of the thyroid gland or which produces abolition of the function of the thyroid gland. But since, in the vast majority of cases of idio-pathically developed myxœdema in man, the myxœdematous state is the result of one particular morbid process in the thyroid gland, viz., cirrhotic atrophy, the term myxœdema (like epilepsy) may be retained and applied in particular to this, the usual, form of the condition.

Historical Note.—The clinical features of this remarkable disease were first described by the late Sir William Gull, in the year 1873, in a paper read before the Clinical Society of London, entitled "*A cretinoid state supervening in adult life in women.*" In the year 1878, Dr Ord published an important paper on the subject and discussed the pathology of the disease. In consequence of the large quantity of mucin which was found in the subcutaneous tissues of one of his cases he proposed the name "myxœdema," which the disease now bears; and although subsequent analyses have for the most part failed to confirm Dr Ord's observations on this point, the name myxœdema has been retained. In the year 1888, the Clinical Society of London issued a very valuable report upon the subject. During the past seven years, in consequence of the great attention which has been directed to the subject since the introduction of the thyroid plan of treatment, our knowledge of the disease has been rendered very complete by the observations of many different physicians. The literature of the disease is now most extensive.

It is remarkable that the first account of myxœdema was only published some twenty-five years ago; for, in this country at all events, the disease is comparatively common, its clinical features are very striking, and, when the disease is fully developed, different cases present an extraordinary resemblance one to another.

It can hardly be doubted that the clinical features of myxœdema must have been regarded as peculiar by many observers before the first written description was published by Sir William Gull in the year 1874; and that other physicians must have come to the same conclusion that Gull did, viz., that the condition was a definite and distinct disease. I know that this was so in one instance at any rate, for in the year 1869, when I joined my father in practice, he showed me a splendid example of the disease and demonstrated to me in that patient many of the clinical features which are now known to be most important and characteristic, viz.:—The peculiar (solid) character of the œdema; the normal condition of the urine; the pink blush on the cheeks; the translucent, ivory-like appearance of the skin of the face and eyelids; the dulness of the intellect; the remarkable slowness of thought and speech; the debility and lassitude for which there was no obvious cause; the persistent low temperature, and the extreme susceptibility to cold, which most myxœdematous patients complain of. He told me that he believed the condition was a new disease—a disease which had never been described.

Since the disease was recognised as a distinct clinical entity many physicians have been able to recall typical cases which were previously under their observation, and which they had regarded as peculiar without knowing exactly what they were. Thus, Dr Ireland, of Prestonpans, tells me that in the year 1854, he attended a lady in Edinburgh, who was suffering from a peculiar form of dropsy which did not conform to any of the then recognised types; and that on looking back to that case (which proved fatal a year after he first saw it) he distinctly remembers that it presented all the characteristic peculiarities of myxœdema. Another medical friend wrote me as follows (and I have had several other communications to the same effect):—

"I have been reading the description of myxœdema in your 'Atlas of Clinical Medicine' with great interest and am much instructed thereby. My reason for troubling you with this letter is, that I have had good reason for knowing the symptoms well, as my dear old mother without doubt died from the disease as far back as 1871—two or three years before the disease was properly described. It used, I remember, to worry me greatly that Warburton Begbie and Sir R. Christison were unable to give any satisfactory explanation of her great feebleness, especially as she had, as they said, no organic disease. Begbie was always giving her iron as he said she was anæmic. The legs were œdematous, but the urine, which I frequently tested, was always free from albumen. I enclose a photo taken about six months before her death. You will notice the marked double ptosis and the elevation of the eyebrows. She had most of the characteristic symptoms you mention—unaccountable feebleness, constant subjective sensation of cold, slow speech, and gait. A hot sea-water bath used to brighten her up more than anything else. The immediate cause of death was obstruction of the bowels. She had been fifteen years in India, but had eight or nine years of good health after her return to this country; then, about eleven years before her death, the disease (myxœdema) developed."

ETIOLOGY.

Locality.—Myxœdema is, comparatively speaking, a common disease, in this country at all events, and it is perhaps nowhere more prevalent than in the neighbourhood of Edinburgh. During the past ten years I have seen in hospital and consulting practice thirty-three cases of adult myxœdema, one case of juvenile myxœdema, and six cases of sporadic cretinism—a very large number for any individual physician. Before the thyroid treatment was introduced I used frequently to see well-marked cases of myxœdema in the streets. At that time, there were almost always some cases of the disease to be met with in our large hospitals. The thyroid treatment has changed all this. Well-marked examples of the disease are now comparatively rarely met with in Edinburgh. The "full-blown cases," as I am in the habit of terming them, have all been recognised and treated. The cases which we now see are, with rare exceptions, imperfectly developed cases. It is probable that in the future the fully developed cases will seldom be met with except in remote districts, away from the centres of medical education and thought.

From statements made to me by several medical friends in Dundee, I gather that the disease is quite as prevalent in that city as in Edinburgh. The disease is also comparatively common in the north of England—Dr George Murray thinks more common in this than in other parts of England. The Clinical Society's Report seemed to show that the disease was very rare in Ireland; but I feel very doubtful as to this, for when I was collecting illustrations for my "Atlas of Clinical Medicine," I found that there were three cases in the town of Londonderry alone.

In Germany, America, and some other parts of the world, the disease seems to be much less common than it is here. A few years ago, Professor Hoffmann told me that the disease was rare in Heidelberg. Up to that time he had only met with one case of the disease. At the same time, he stated that within the past few years he had seen eight cases of acromegaly, all, with one or two exceptions, collected from a radius within twenty miles round Heidelberg. Now, acromegaly (which seems to have some relationship with myxœdema), although probably less rare than is usually supposed, is in this country much less common than

T

myxœdema.* In some parts of America myxœdema seems to be almost unknown. Dr Mackenzie, of Cincinnati, for example, tells me that he has never seen a case either in hospital or private practice, and he is visiting physician to a hospital which contains more than four hundred beds.

It is difficult to account for the remarkable prevalence of the disease in this country, unless it be due to some endemic, telluric, or climatic condition. Possibly the cold and damp of our climate predisposes to the production of the disease. And in confirmation of this it may be stated that the disease seems very rare in hot and tropical climates. I have, however, met with one case of myxœdema and one case of sporadic cretinism in which the disease developed in India.

Sex.—Myxœdema is at least six times as frequent (perhaps ten times as frequent) in women as in men. Of 109 cases tabulated in the Clinical Society's Report, 94 were women and 15 were men ; while of 150 cases tabulated by Drs Henry Hun and T. Mitchell Prudden, 113 were females and 32 were males, the sex not being stated in 5. Of 370 cases analysed by Dr George Murray, 322 were women and 48 were men. In my series of 33 cases of adult myxœdema, 29 were females and 4 males ; and all of my (7) cases of juvenile myxœdema and sporadic cretinism were females.

In its preference for the female sex, myxœdema resembles exophthalmic goitre. Professor Victor Horsley has suggested that the greater prevalence of myxœdema and exophthalmic goitre in women is due to the fact that the thyroid gland functionates more actively and is liable to more sudden variations (ups and downs) in functional activity in the female than in the male. He adds :—" It is well known that enlargement of the thyroid gland is not uncommon in women during menstruation and pregnancy ; and it may be laid down as a pathological law that the greater the physiological activity of an organ, and more especially the greater the variability of that activity, the greater the liability to certain diseased processes."

So far as my observation enables me to judge, sporadic cretinism is also much more common in girls than in boys.

Marriage and Child-bearing.—The disease seems to occur

---

* In reference to this point, Dr Sidney Kuh kindly wrote me on 8th March 1893 as follows :—" I have read your remarks on myxœdema (Meeting of Edinburgh Medico-Chirurgical Society, 15th February 1893), in which you refer to a statement of Professor Hoffmann that myxœdema is very rare in Heidelberg. Permit me to state that I have seen two or three cases of the disease in the Heidelberg Insane Asylum (Clinic of Prof. Kraepelin) within a few months, in 1892, which, I think, would prove that your conclusion is not quite correct."

more frequently in married women who have borne families than in the unmarried, though it is by no means uncommon in single women. Of the 115 female cases analysed by Drs Hun and Prudden, 84 of the women were married and 14 were single; while in 17 there was no mention made of this point. The 84 married women had had more than 300 children and 29 miscarriages. In my 29 cases of adult myxœdema in females, 23 were married and 6 were single. The 23 married women had had 119 children, or on an average 5.1 child each. Marriage, therefore, and especially the bearing of children, seems to have a distinct influence in favouring the development of the disease.

Age.—Myxœdema is most frequently developed during the middle periods of life—between the ages of 35 and 45; but the symptoms are usually so insidious in their mode of onset that there is probably a tendency to over-estimate the age at which the disease actually does commence; in other words, to think that it begins later than it really does. According to Hun and Prudden's statistics, the average age at which the disease commenced in seventy-six women was 38 and in twenty men 42 years. In my own 33 cases,* the average age at which the disease commenced was in women 41 years and in men 43 years. But the disease is by no means confined to middle-aged adults. It may develop at any age, and it is comparatively common in young children, for there can be no doubt that the condition which is termed sporadic cretinism is merely the infantile form of myxœdema. In stating that sporadic cretinism is the infantile form of myxœdema, I do not mean to imply that the pathological process (the lesion in the thyroid gland) which produces myxœdema and sporadic cretinism is necessarily one and the same in all cases. Myxœdema is a clinical condition due to abolition of the function of the thyroid gland; and any pathological process which produces arrest of the thyroid secretion will produce myxœdema. In some cases of infantile myxœdema (sporadic cretinism), the condition is doubtless due to congenital absence or arrested development of the thyroid gland during intra-uterine life; in others, to a process of cirrhotic atrophy similar to that which produces myxœdema in the adult. Myxœdema very rarely indeed develops between early childhood and the age of 20; in other words, the "*juvenile*" form of myxœdema, as I term it (to distinguish the condition from sporadic

---

* One case of juvenile myxœdema, in which the disease seemed to commence at the age of 10 years, and the cases of infantile myxœdema, are not included in this calculation.

cretinism or "*infantile*" myxœdema), is very rare. One case only has come under my own notice.

The disease is occasionally met with in old people. A few years ago I saw, with my friend Dr Mackie Whyte, of Dundee, a woman, aged 72, who was suffering from the disease. In her case the characteristic symptoms were first noticed at the age of 60. One of my series of cases treated by thyroid extract is now aged 70, and another at the time of her death was aged 73.

Hereditary influence.—In a few instances, hereditary predisposition can be directly traced, but this is extremely rare. Amongst the cases analysed by the committee of the Clinical Society two were sisters, two were relatives, and in one the father, and in another the mother, probably died of myxœdema. Some years ago a young unmarried lady, aged 26, was sent to me by Dr Halliday Croom, suffering from all the characteristic symptoms of the disease. Some ten or eleven years previously I had seen, with Dr Croom, the paternal uncle of this patient ; his case was quite typical ; he died from the disease, and I examined his body post-mortem. In another case, seen with Dr Aitchison Robertson, the mother of the patient had died some years previously from myxœdema, and a brother had a swollen heavy face suggestive of myxœdema. In more than one case of myxœdema which has come under my notice, a sister or other near female relative of the patient had suffered from exophthalmic goitre. In rare cases, of which Case XVII. is an example, the disease follows exophthalmic goitre.

Other predisposing conditions.—With regard to the other conditions which predispose to the production of the disease, little can be said. In a considerable proportion of the cases, the subjects of myxœdema seem to inherit a tendency to nerve disease. Tubercular disease also seems somewhat more common in the relatives of myxœdematous patients than in the general mass of the population. Depressing influences of all kinds, mental strain, anxiety, nerve shock, have preceded the development of the disease in a considerable number of the recorded cases. In quite a number of my own cases (6 out of 33) the patients have of their own accord laid great stress upon this point. In a considerable number of cases the onset of the disease is attended with, or preceded by, menorrhagia ; in others, by an excessive loss of blood after delivery. I have been much struck with the frequent history of menorrhagia in my own cases—whether that was a cause or a consequence of the disease is, however, doubtful. Some authorities state that a tendency to hæmorrhage is a highly characteristic feature of the disease. I have not observed this in any one of the thirty-three cases which have come under my notice, though in eight there was menorrhagia either at the onset or during the course of the disease. In some of my cases, the disease developed after influenza; in one, after a "severe illness," the exact nature of which I could not ascertain; in one case, after confinement without loss of blood ; in another case, after post-partum hæmorrhage and mental worry.

Injuries, and especially head injuries, have in some instances been blamed as a cause of the condition.

It can hardly be questioned that in the human subject exposure to cold favours the development of the disease in those cases in which the thyroid gland has been removed by operation, just as it undoubtedly does in the lower animals. It seems certain, too, that exposure to cold hastens the development of idiopathic (primary) myxœdema, and aggravates the symptoms once the disease has become established ; but whether exposure to cold favours the degeneration and atrophy of the thyroid gland, which is the pathological substratum of the disease, is another matter. It is not unlikely that this is so, but so far as I know there is no direct evidence in favour of such a proposition, unless the great prevalence of the disease in our cold and inclement climate is taken as a sufficient proof.

Morbid Anatomy and Pathology.

The essential pathological lesion in myxœdema is degeneration and atrophy of the thyroid gland. That the disease is due to diminution or abolition of the function of the thyroid gland is proved by the following facts :—

1. In the bodies of patients who have died of myxœdema, the thyroid gland is invariably found to be degenerated and usually atrophied and smaller than normal.

In some cases, though degenerated and atrophied as regards its secreting structure, the thyroid gland is enlarged. This was the case in Dr Mackie Whyte's patient to whom I have previously referred. The same condition has been observed in some other instances.

2. This degeneration and atrophy of the thyroid gland is the only constant and invariable lesion to be found in the bodies of patients who have died with myxœdema which can adequately account for the symptoms of the disease.

3. *Total* extirpation of the thyroid gland in many of the lower animals is followed (provided the animal survives a sufficient

length of time) by symptoms which closely resemble and appear to be identical with those of myxœdema in the human subject.

4. *Total* extirpation of the thyroid gland in man is also followed by the development of symptoms identical with those of idiopathic (spontaneously developed) myxœdema.

In those cases in which the symptoms of myxœdema have not been developed after extirpation of the thyroid gland, it is probable either (*a*) that the gland was not entirely removed, or (*b*) that supernumerary thyroid glands were present, and that they were not recognised at the time of the operation.

5. The symptoms of myxœdema rapidly disappear, and the disease can be completely cured and kept in abeyance by the introduction into the bodies of affected persons,* of a sufficient quantity of the thyroid secretion, either in the form of the raw gland, in the form of a liquid, or of a solid extract. And, what is still more remarkable, the beneficial effects are still obtained when the thyroid secretion is introduced through the stomach, either in the form of the raw or partially cooked gland, or as a liquid or solid extract.

The nature of the lesion of the thyroid gland.—The morbid change in the thyroid gland which produces the idiopathic myxœdema of adults seems to begin as a small-celled infiltration of the walls of the vesicles, which is accompanied or soon followed by epithelial proliferation in the vesicles themselves. In a more advanced stage, the gland becomes converted into a mass of delicate fibrous tissue, in the midst of which clumps of small round cells, clearly the remains of the vesicles, are scattered.†

Changes in other organs and parts.—In addition to these changes in the thyroid gland itself, pathological alterations are present in other organs. In most cases in which the condition of the pituitary gland has been noted, the gland has been enlarged; the thymus gland is in some cases also enlarged; well-marked pathological changes are developed in the skin and its appendages; and in certain cases of the disease, cirrhotic changes have been found in the kidney and blood vessels — endarteritis obliterans or atheroma. In one case which I examined some years ago, the spinal cord was markedly shrunken; and it is probable that more detailed and accurate investigation, with modern methods of staining and preparation, will show definite histological changes in the nervous tissues, particularly in the nerve cells; indeed, it is,

---

* Provided that the patient is not too old, that the heart and arteries are sound, and that there are no associated lesions or complications.

† Report by the Committee of the Clinical Society of London, p. 44.

I think, highly probable that minute changes are present in all of the tissues of the body.

Most of the pathological changes which I have just mentioned are obviously either secondary or mere associated lesions ; they are not the primary and essential causes of the disease.

As to the conditions which determine the atrophy and degeneration of the thyroid gland, which is the primary and essential lesion of the idiopathic or acquired form of myxœdema in the adult, we are at present ignorant. As I have already stated, exposure to cold seems to favour the production of the disease and to aggravate the symptoms when the disease is already developed. This fact was strikingly demonstrated by two experiments made by Professor Horsley, the one on a sheep, the other on a donkey. He completely removed the thyroid gland in two sheep. The result in No. 1 was survival, without the production of symptoms of myxœdema, $2\frac{1}{3}$ years after the removal of the thyroid. The result in No. 2 was death from acute myxœdema, brought on by accidental exposure to cold, $1\frac{3}{8}$ years after the extirpation. Professor Horsley makes the following statement regarding the latter case :—

"The fatal case in the second sheep is one of much interest, since it entirely negatives the view that the effects of total extirpation are due to injury of neighbouring structures in the course of the operation, and proves that the myxœdematous state is produced by the loss of the thyroid. It is worth while, therefore, to mention the leading features in this instance. The thyroid was removed (3rd October 1885) with the usual precautions, and primary union of the wound resulted. The sheep emaciated, and was weak a fortnight later, but its temperature was normal and appetite good. No marked change was observable in the animal, except that it gradually recovered its general nutrition, and apparently became more stupid, even than before the operation. In the meanwhile the wool grew, and not being cut covered the animal very thickly. In view of the approaching summer weather it was shorn in the first week of May 1887. The weather, which had been mild, became very cold ; the animal was then observed to become ill, it lost its appetite, then exhibited the usual symptoms of the acute cachexia, viz., spasms, paralysis, coma, anæsthesia, tetanoid contracture, and fall of temperature to 25° C. It died on 20th May 1887, i.e. 569 days after the operation. The post-mortem examination showed 'gelatinous' infiltration of all the subcutaneous tissue, which under the microscope was evidently mucinous degeneration of the ground substance, and by chemical analysis was shown to be actually mucin. The thyroid gland had been completely removed. In this instance we have the well-known influence of cold evoking the phenomena of the cachexia in its most acute form. It is interesting to note that the companion animal, sheep No. 1, which was similarly treated, but a much stronger and bigger animal, still survives, and will be preserved as long as it will live. Professor Horsley made one experiment upon a donkey, which supports the points established by the experiment just quoted of sheep No. 2. 'The thyroid was removed on 25th August 1885. After the operation the animal emaciated in spite of excessive appetite, became weaker, lay down, and the temperature was low. (Most of the wound healed by the first intention, the remainder—about one-sixth—by suppuration ; cicatrisation was complete by about the end of September 1885.) After the general appearance of illness had lasted two months the nutrition improved, and no obvious change was noted (the psychical analysis being difficult) until the beginning of March 1886, when, the weather becoming suddenly severely cold, the animal fell ill ; and anorexia, tremors, fall of temperature, &c., occurring in the order given, death with all the characteristic symptoms occurred within a week of their being first noted, *i.e.* 205 days after operation. Post-mortem.—The thyroid gland was found to have been completely removed. All tissues and organs appeared normal.'"

PATHOLOGICAL PHYSIOLOGY.

Two theories have been advanced to explain the exact manner in which abolition of the function of the thyroid gland produces myxœdema.

According to one, the thyroid gland secretes and pours into the blood some substance or substances essential for the healthy and satisfactory nutrition of the tissues, and more especially of the cerebral and nervous tissues. When the function of the gland is abolished or defective, a widespread change in the metabolism of the tissue, more particularly in the skin and its appendages and in the nervous tissues, is produced. The functional alterations which result from these derangements of metabolism and from the minute structural changes which are produced in the tissues and organs of the body and the structural and functional alterations which are due to the pressure of the myxœdematous infiltration, as it may be termed, on the tissue elements are the cause of the symptoms which characterise the disease.

According to the second view, the function of the thyroid gland is to separate from the blood some substance or substances which, if left to circulate in the blood, exert a poisonous influence upon the tissues, more especially upon the cerebral and nervous tissues. Atrophy and abolition of the function of the gland lead, according to this view, to a kind of intoxication which in some respects may be compared to chronic uræmia. As a result of this intoxication, the nervous and other tissues degenerate and the symptoms of the disease are produced.

There can, I think, be little doubt that the former view is the correct one ; this is shown, I think, by the beneficial effects which result in cases of myxœdema and sporadic cretinism from thyroid feeding—even from the introduction into the stomach of a few grains of the dried extract.

That the thyroid gland is in some manner or another (either

directly or indirectly) concerned in the regulation of the metabolism of mucin or of substances which form mucin, or that it is concerned in separating from the blood some substance or substances which either directly or indirectly (possibly through the nervous system) favour the production of mucin in the tissues, seems proved by the following facts :—

In Dr Ord's original case, an excessive quantity of mucin was found in the subcutaneous and other tissues ; and although most of the analyses which have been subsequently made have failed to confirm this, at all events in the same degree, it seems probable that during the "swollen stage" of the disease such excess is present. And here it may be noted that in some cases of myxœdema during active thyroid treatment, large quantities of mucus are excreted by the kidneys. In one of my cases, for example, I state in the clinical report :—" The amount of mucus was quite extraordinary ; it reached, in the form of a gelatinous-looking mass, like a coagulum, almost to the top of the tall urine glass in which the urine was placed." I have observed the same result, though in less degree, in more than one other case.

After extirpation of the thyroid gland in the lower animals the amount of mucin in the tissues is in some instances enormously increased.

Professor Victor Horsley found that after total extirpation of the thyroid gland the secretion from the parotid gland, which under normal circumstances contains no mucin, may contain large quantities of mucin.

It is important to note that, while in acute experimental myxœdema the tissues contain a large excess of mucin, in chronic experimental myxœdema no such excess is found. In chronic experimental myxœdema, fibroid or cirrhotic changes in the tissues seem to take the place of the mucinous degeneration which occurs in the acute form of the disease. These facts perhaps explain the result of different analyses in the primary and idiopathic myxœdema of man ; for while in Dr Ord's case (which died, be it observed, during the swollen stage of the disease) a large excess of mucin was found in the skin and subcutaneous tissues, in other cases which have since been analysed no such excess was found. But in these chronic cases, fibroid and cirrhotic changes in the skin and viscera have been invariably observed.

From these statements it will be gathered that recent observations have confirmed the view, which physiologists have long held, that the thyroid gland is a blood gland, and that the thyroid secretion is essential for the proper nutrition of the body. I would particularly emphasise the fact that this great advance in our physiological and pathological knowledge, which has thrown a flood of light upon the function of the so-called blood glands and ductless glands, and has opened up such a wide field for scientific research and therapeutic investigation, is very largely the result of clinical observation.

CLINICAL HISTORY.

Onset and Mode of Development.—The onset of myxœdema is usually very slow and insidious, though in exceptional cases the symptoms appear to develop rapidly. In a case recorded by Charcot, for example, the disease was ushered in by attacks of shivering, and in the first case reported by Ord, the onset of the disease was attended with shivering, and, according to the patient, with the passage of bloody urine. In one of my cases (Case IV.), the patient, an intelligent young lady, 26 years of age, stated that the swelling of the face, and the other symptoms of the disease developed in the course of a few days after an attack of influenza. In another case (Case XXVIII.), all the characteristic symptoms were developed in the course of four months.

But in most cases such as these, in which the myxœdematous symptoms appear to develop rapidly, it is highly probable that the disease has been in existence in an unrecognised form for some time previously. In my own case, for example, I found, on careful cross-examination of the patient, that for two or three years before the attack of influenza to which she attributed the onset of the disease, she had been unduly susceptible to cold. In this, as in many other cases, the date at which the symptoms are first perceived by the patient is often a very fallacious guide to the actual date of onset of the disease. The patient naturally dates the onset of the disease from the time at which he becomes conscious of the symptoms, or at which the results of the disease first become distinctly noticeable to others ; but the disease may have been slowly and gradually developing for years before the symptoms are sufficiently marked to attract attention.

Initial Symptoms.—A feeling of intense lassitude and debility, a repugnance to exertion both of body and mind, increased bulk of the body, an increased susceptibility to cold, and dryness of the skin, are, so far as my observation enables me to judge, usually the first symptoms. In some cases, headache, usually frontal, is an early symptom. In consequence of the debility and disinclination for exertion, most myxœdematous patients feel unable, even in the earlier stages of the disease, to attend to their household duties.

Debility and lassitude were prominent symptoms in every one of my 33 cases of adult myxœdema.

As the disease advances, a striking change takes place in the appearance of the patient, and when the myxœdematous condition is fully developed the physiognomy is highly characteristic.

The body as a whole is increased in bulk, the face, trunk, and limbs all being involved. The increase is due to a solid œdema. The parts affected by this œdema do not pit on pressure, and, it is said, do not exude a watery fluid on puncture; though, as has been previously stated, ordinary dropsical swelling (watery œdema) of the feet and ankles is sometimes also present. Ordinary dropsy (œdema of the feet and ankles) was present in 8 of my 33 cases of adult myxœdema.

Facial Appearance.—On looking at the face, one is at once struck with the heavy stolid expression of countenance. The face is full, coarse, broad-looking, and round; it has been termed "moon-shaped." As a whole it looks puffy and swollen. In many cases, the wrinkles are flattened out, but this is by no means always the case. The skin of the eyelids in particular has a translucent and wax-like appearance. Baggy swellings, highly suggestive of a dropsical œdema, are often present beneath the lower eyelids. These swellings are at first sight highly suggestive of Bright's disease. The upper lids in many cases droop over the eyeballs; and, in order to prevent the loss of sight which is occasioned by the falling of the upper lids over the pupils, there is often a compensatory elevation of the eyebrows and transverse wrinkling of the forehead. The same compensatory elevation of the eyebrows is seen in cases of paralytic ptosis. In one of my cases, the upper lids were so much swollen that they completely covered the eyeballs; the patient, in order to see, had to raise the swollen lid with the finger so as to expose the pupil. The upper eyelids are either swollen or wrinkled-looking. The cheeks are in some cases pendulous; in describing his condition before treatment, one of my patients wrote me, "I had great bags under my eyes and my cheeks were puffy and hanging, bobbing up and down as I walked along." The lips are, in the great majority of cases, swollen and usually of a bluish or purple colour; the lower lip in particular is unusually full; it usually feels firm, tense, and elastic; to the touch it resembles more or less closely a piece of indiarubber. The nose is broad and coarse-looking. The ears are in some cases large and swollen.

Dr Ord states that "the total effect (of these changes in the face) is that of a mask of sorrowful immobility." *

As I have just remarked, the appearance of the eyelids and the swollen condition of the face are highly suggestive of Bright's disease; and there is no doubt that before the clinical features of the disease were clearly differentiated, cases of myxœdema were often diagnosed as cases of kidney disease. But on close scrutiny, the facial appearance is very different from that of kidney disease. In typical cases of myxœdema, a pink blush is present on each cheek; in exceptional cases, the blush is not confined to the cheeks; in one of my cases it involved the nose; in two other cases a bright pink blush was diffused over the whole of the cheeks and nose. The colour of the face, too, is usually different from that of Bright's disease. The skin has in many cases a dingy yellow tinge (except about the eyelids, where it is usually translucent and wax-like), quite different from the white pallor which is such a striking feature in those cases of Bright's disease in which the face is much swollen; while the baldness of the scalp or the thin, dry, harsh condition of the hair, the dirty brown encrustation of the scalp, and the thinness or absence of the eyebrows, which are such important characteristics of the disease in its advanced stages, are absent in Bright's disease.

The tawny yellow discoloration of the skin is chiefly seen on the face, neck, and other parts of the body which are exposed to the atmosphere. This discoloration may persist after the œdematous condition has completely disappeared under treatment. Yellow discoloration of the skin of the face was present in 32 of my 33 cases of adult myxœdema.

In my 33 cases of adult myxœdema, a pink blush was present on the cheeks in 26 cases; in the 4 male cases included in the series, a pink blush was present in only one case.

I have now referred to the more important changes which myxœdema produces in the face. The alterations which occur in other parts of the body are no less striking and characteristic.

The *body as a whole*, is increased in bulk, and has a clumsy, heavy appearance. In many cases, the *tongue* is large and swollen, some patients say that it feels too large for the mouth. The *gums, buccal mucous membrane*, the *fauces, uvula, pharynx*, and *larynx* are in many cases also œdematous. The swelling of the soft parts at the back of the mouth may be so considerable that the patient may experience considerable difficulty in swallowing; some patients complain of a choking feeling when they swallow.

---

* "Lancet," 12th Nov. 1898, p. 1243.

The *neck* is usually broad and thick. Puffy elastic swellings, which are usually thought to be due to localised collections of fat, are in many cases present at the root of the neck above the clavicles. These elastic supra-clavicular swellings are usually more marked in children (cases of sporadic cretinism) than in adults. They were present in 22 of my 33 cases of adult myxœdema.

Although the neck is usually short, thick, and swollen, the rings of the trachea can generally be very distinctly felt ; in the great majority of cases of the disease no evidence of the *thyroid* can be detected during life. This is just what we would expect, for in the great majority of cases of myxœdema the thyroid gland is markedly atrophied ; while in the juvenile form of the disease it may be altogether absent. In those exceptional cases in which the thyroid is present or enlarged, its structure is altered and destroyed—in other words, the gland is functionally inert.

In none of my cases of myxœdema or sporadic cretinism could the thyroid gland be felt.

I may say in passing that it is very difficult to determine by palpation during life whether the thyroid is actually present or not. This difficulty was very clearly realised at a post-mortem examination on a case of myxœdema which I made in conjunction with Dr Thomson a few years ago. In that case, even after deflecting the skin of the neck, we were unable to feel the thyroid body ; but on further dissection, we found that the gland was present. At first sight, it looked of normal size ; its superficial extent was quite equal to that of a normal thyroid ; but it was so thin, soft, and flabby, and so closely applied to the trachea, that, even after the skin had been deflected, it could not be differentiated by palpation from the rings of the trachea with which it lay in close contact.

The *hands* are enlarged and broad—"spade-like" as it has been termed. The fingers are broad, flat, and thick ; many patients complain of their inability to perform fine movements (button their clothes, sew, etc.) ; some patients say that they cannot close the hand in consequence of the swelling. The *feet* present similar changes ; they are broad and thick. The *abdomen* is usually full and large, and the *trunk* as a whole looks markedly increased in size. The *vulva* and *external genitals* are in some cases swollen.

In my 33 cases of adult myxœdema, increased bulkiness of the body as a whole was present in 30 cases ; swelling of the face was present in 32 cases ; of the hands in 27 cases ; of the feet in 26 cases ; of the abdomen in 29 cases ; of the tongue in 27 cases ; and of the throat in 19 cases.

The increased bulk of the body and the swollen condition of the tissues, which are such striking features of the disease, are not the result of an ordinary œdema, such as the œdema of cardiac or renal dropsy, which pits on pressure and exudes fluid on puncture, but of a solid œdema, which in the early stages of some cases at least, is associated with a notable increase of mucin in the tissues. But as Drs Hun and Prudden have pointed out, the peculiar nature of the œdema does not always depend upon an infiltration of the skin with mucin.   They explain the solid character of the œdema and the absence of pitting on pressure in the following manner :—

"A possible explanation of the fact that in myxœdema the skin, although œdematous, does not pit on pressure is contained in Dr Prudden's observations, that the separation of the fibres, and the dilatation of the lymph spaces in the skin of the two myxœdematous cases which he examined, were in those superficial layers of the corium in which inter-fibrillary spaces are much smaller, and the interlacement of the fibres much finer, than in the deeper layers, which seem more frequently to be the seat of ordinary œdema.   From these smaller spaces, surrounded by a finer network of interlacing fibres, fluid is neither so easily driven by pressure, nor so easily affected by gravity, as it is from larger spaces surrounded by a coarse network of fibres.   Probably in this difference in the situation of the fluid lies the difference between the swelling of the skin in myxœdema and in ordinary œdema." *

I have already stated that in some cases of the disease, and chiefly in the later stages, a true watery œdema is present, especially about the ankles.

Such are the gross alterations and the more striking changes in the physiognomy which myxœdema produces in its advanced and fully developed stages.   When we come to study the condition more minutely, we find that the nutrition of the skin and its appendages is profoundly modified, and the functional activity of the nervous apparatus markedly impaired.

The Condition of the Skin and its Appendages.—The skin is coarse, harsh, dry, rough, and scaly looking.   It may be split up by superficial wrinkles and cracks into lozenge-shaped areas not unlike those which are seen in some cases of ichthyosis.   In one of my cases I have noted that when the finger was passed over the skin of the forearm it felt like a piece of sandpaper, and in another as rough as a file.   The skin of the heels in some cases becomes greatly thickened ; one of my patients stated that he " used to pare it with a big iron file."   In one case there was distinct ichthyosis of the heels.   In several cases eczematous eruptions, both dry and moist, have been present.

---

* " International Medical Journal," August 1888, p. 152.

In all of my 33 cases of adult myxœdema, the skin was harsh and dry ; and in 32 of the 33 cases there was absence of sweating.

The *electrical resistance of the skin* is, as one might expect, very greatly increased ; and this, be it observed, is the very reverse of the condition which obtains in exophthalmic goitre.

In well-marked cases of myxœdema the *secretion of sweat* is very much diminished or altogether in abeyance. The absence of sweating is a very characteristic feature of the disease, though in some cases the palms may occasionally feel moist. The *sebaceous secretion* is also in many cases said to be arrested or very much diminished. *Flat moles* and *warts* are sometimes developed on the face, neck, etc. In some cases, stalked moles are also present. In one of my cases, a projecting swelling of some size, like a stalked wart, projected from the gum ; and in another case, a flat button-like wart was present on the dorsum of the tongue close to the tip.

The *hair* becomes thin, dry, brittle, and harsh ; in many cases, the eyebrows are entirely wanting ; in the advanced stages of the disease, the scalp may be almost entirely bald, and, whether this is so or not, it is usually covered with dirty brown crusts. This *encrustation of the scalp* is of considerable diagnostic importance. On one occasion I recognised the presence of myxœdema in the person of a gentleman who was sitting immediately in front of me in church, by the coarseness of the skin of the back of his neck, the dry, scanty, ragged character of the hair on the back of his head, and the dirty-looking brown patches which were present on his scalp. The correctness of my opinion was amply confirmed when I obtained a full view of his face, for it was in every way typical and characteristic of the disease. It is often possible to recognise myxœdema merely by looking at the back of the neck and scalp. The thin, ragged, dry condition of the hair, the shrivelled, yellow, wrinkled appearance of the skin at the back of the neck, and the dirty brown crusts or scales on the scalp have in more than one case, in addition to that which has been mentioned above, enabled me to recognise the disease before I had the opportunity of looking at the patient's face.

In some cases, the colour of the hair changes as the disease advances ; in one of my cases the hair, which in health was brown, became black ; the change was so marked that the patient's brother thought she was dyeing it. In this case, the hair soon began to regain its natural brown colour under thyroid treatment. In another case, the hair, which was nut-brown before the disease commenced, became so black after a course of thyroid treatment that the patient's sister said to her children, "Why is your mother dyeing her hair?" In several other cases, the luxuriant crop of hair which developed after the myxœdematous symptoms had been removed by the administration of thyroid extract was dark and black ; in one case in which this took place the patient was an old woman 66 years of age.

In my 33 cases of adult myxœdema, loss of hair was present in 31, and encrustation of the scalp in 19 cases.

In some cases, the *nails* become dry and lustreless, brittle, ragged or cracked ; the *teeth* are apt to become carious and loose ; in some cases they drop out.

The altered nutrition of the skin and its appendages is associated with, and doubtless depends upon, definite histological changes, which are by the Committee of the Clinical Society described as follows :—

"Very marked changes are seen in the majority of cases and the changes were very similar, whatever the region of the body examined. In the coiled tubes of the sweat glands, the epithelium becomes swollen, then nuclear proliferation takes place, and the lumen of the tubes becomes obliterated. In the later stages, a nucleated fibrous growth is seen in the tissue outside the tubes. The change in the sebaceous glands resembles very closely that in the sudoriparous glands, and is probably identical with it. The sebaceous glands are represented by irregular masses of nuclei, and sometimes there are cellular accumulations in the tissues outside them. These cellular accumulations in some cases seem to undergo partial or complete absorption. Around the hair-follicles a nuclear growth is apt to develop, and external to this growth an abundant nucleated fibrous tissue is sometimes seen."*

In some cases, there is an *increased flow of saliva* from the mouth, especially at night ; whether this is due to an actual increase of the amount of saliva secreted or merely to the fact that the saliva which is secreted flows out of the mouth instead of being swallowed is, however, doubtful. In other cases, the *nose* or *eyes* "*run*" without any apparent cause. One of my patients stated, " My eyes were constantly weeping and my nose running."

This (?) increase of the salivary secretion and of the discharge from the nose and eyes is in remarkable contrast with the diminished or abolished secretion of sweat.

In my 33 cases of adult myxœdema, running at the eyes and nose was noted in 3 cases, and increased salivary secretion in 4 cases.

The condition of the motor nerve apparatus.—The stolid, heavy-looking, and puffy appearance which the face presents reflects

---

* " Medico-Chirurgical Transactions," Vol. lxi., p. 60.

the condition of the sensorium. One of the most striking features of the disease in its fully developed stages is the slowness with which all the cerebral processes, especially speech and muscular movements, are carried out.

The *gait* is heavy and clumsy ; I am in the habit of terming it "hippopotamus-like." The muscular power is markedly impaired. Some patients experience from time to time a sudden giving way in the legs. In consequence of the feebleness of the muscles of the neck, and perhaps also of the sleepy apathetic condition, the head may fall down on to the sternum. Dr Ord seems to lay considerable stress on this symptom. I noted its presence in 2 only of my 33 cases.

In most cases, the patients have difficulty in performing fine movements with the fingers ; this may no doubt be due to several different causes (*i.e.*, swelling of the fingers, defective sensibility, want of cerebral concentration and attention, deficient muscular power, inco-ordination), or a combination of some of these conditions.

The *articulation* is slow and measured ; the *tone of voice* is monotonous, thick, "leathery," as it has been termed, harsher and hoarser than it is in health ; the patient often speaks as if she had something in the mouth. Patients who have been in the habit of singing find that with the development of the disease they lose their voice.

Characteristic thickness of speech was present in 31 of my 33 cases of adult myxœdema.

These alterations in movement, and in speech, seem to depend partly upon the increased bulk of the body and limbs, and on the swelling of the lips, tongue, palate, and larynx, and partly upon the slowness with which the motor nerve apparatus functionates. The swelling of the tongue and fauces also, in part at least, accounts for the difficulty in swallowing which is complained of by some patients.

The condition of the cerebral and mental functions.—All the *cerebral actions* of myxœdematous patients appear to be carried out in an unusually slow and deliberate manner. After being asked a question, they often take an extraordinarily long time to answer it ; the "reaction time" is no doubt greatly prolonged. The acuteness of all the higher cerebral activities is blunted. In most of the cases which have come under my own notice, the memory and mental activity were more or less impaired. The patients often complain that it is an effort to think. My artist, Mr Williamson, who has painted several cases for me, volunteered the statement that myxœdematous patients are remarkably good sitters ;

U

they will remain for a long time, sometimes for hours together, in the same position without uttering a word and without exhibiting any change of expression. In consequence of the mental and bodily inertia, the subjects of myxœdema are apt to keep to themselves and to shun society. This is perhaps, as Murray has suggested, one reason why they are apt to become morose, depressed and melancholic.

In 31 of my 33 cases of adult myxœdema, the memory was more or less impaired.

This slowness of thought and action is also very striking in many cases of sporadic cretinism. Children affected with sporadic cretinism often sit for hours perfectly quiet, apparently taking no notice of, or interest in, their surroundings, and yet quite happy, comfortable, and contented, so long as they are sitting in the sun or before a hot fire.

It should further be noted that in many cases of myxœdema there is an excessive tendency to sleep. In one of my cases, the patient, a medical man, stated that he was always dreadfully sleepy, that he could hardly keep his eyes open when going his rounds, and whenever he got into his gig he used to drop off to sleep.

In my 33 cases of adult myxœdema the patients slept well in 23 and badly in 6 cases; in the remaining 4 cases the condition of sleep is not mentioned. In 2 cases, sleep was disturbed by very unpleasant dreams.

The placidity and stolidity of myxœdematous patients contrasts very remarkably with the perpetual unrest and hyperexcitability of patients affected with exophthalmic goitre. After I have described exophthalmic goitre, I will point out the difference between the two diseases in more detail. But I may here say that nervousness, tremor, and unrest are striking features of exophthalmic goitre; whereas, stolidity and placidity are characteristic features of myxœdema. It should, however, be stated that in some cases the patients state that they are more easily agitated and " put about " than formerly.

In some cases of myxœdema *more profound mental alterations* (delusions, hallucinations, insanity, which may take the form of acute or chronic mania, though more frequently of melancholia or dementia) are developed. The mental deterioration is sometimes so great that the patient has to be sent to an asylum. But I cannot help thinking that the frequency with which well-marked mental disturbances of this kind occur is probably somewhat less than the statistics of the Clinical Society seem to show.

In 5 of my 33 cases of adult myxœdema, the patients were mentally depressed; in one case, a condition of partial psychical blindness was present. One patient, who had, previously to her admission to hospital, been much depressed, but who presented no suspicious symptoms at the time of her admission, jumped out of the window of the ward two days after her admission and killed herself. This unfortunate accident occurred before the patient had been placed on thyroid treatment.

It must not, however, be supposed that slowness of thought and mental deterioration are essential features of the disease. In a well-marked case which I saw with Dr Menzies, and in which a complete cure has been established under the thyroid treatment, the mental faculties of the patient were quite keen and acute. It is, too, important to remember that in those cases in which the cerebral functions are profoundly altered, the mental alteration is usually the result of functional derangement and not of organic disease. The fact that as the result of thyroid treatment in cases of myxœdema the mental symptoms may entirely clear off in the course of a few days or weeks, and that in cases of sporadic cretinism an undoubted development may occur in the mental condition in the course of a few weeks, proves this.

I should also state that in some cases *temporary conditions of garrulousness, irritability or mental excitement* occur. But in my experience this is rare.

The condition of the sensory nerve apparatus.—Sensory symptoms are in most cases less striking and important. *Numbness* in the hands and feet is often complained of, but objective disturbances of sensation (either to touch, pain, heat, or cold) can rarely be demonstrated. The *tactile sensibility of the skin* is in some cases delayed or diminished; whether this is due to an alteration in the sensory nerve apparatus or merely to an altered condition of the skin is, I think, doubtful; both conditions probably account for the alteration. *Sight* and *hearing* are in many cases impaired. In one of my cases the eyesight was so bad that the patient could scarcely see at night during the winter months. In one case temporary paralysis of the external rectus muscle and diplopia were developed; but whether this was the result of the disease or merely an accidental complication I am unable to say. *Taste* and *smell* are in some cases impaired, though rarely in a marked degree.

In 13 of my 33 cases of adult myxœdema, numbness of the hands and feet was complained of; in 13 cases sight was impaired; and in 11 cases hearing was impaired.

Headache, which is usually frontal though sometimes occipital, is not uncommon; *neuralgic pains* and *cramps* are occasionally experienced; *faintness, giddiness, tinnitus aurium* are in some cases complained of.

Headache was complained of in 16 of my 33 cases of adult myxœdema.

The condition of the reflex nerve apparatus.—The *reflexes* do not present any changes of importance; they are usually diminished; in some cases the knee-jerks are abolished.

Temperature.—*Increased susceptibility* to cold is highly characteristic. Myxœdematous patients are almost invariably worse in cold and better in warm weather. One patient, for example, volunteered the statement that she felt quite a different person in warm weather, that in cold weather she seemed unable to think or exert herself. Several of my patients have told me that they could not get warmed up even if they roasted themselves before a hot fire, that the hands and feet were always cold; one patient said she frequently felt as if cold water were being poured down her back; another complained every now and again of shivering, followed by running at the eyes and nose and debility. Some myxœdematous patients dislike drinking anything cold. Increased susceptibility to cold was present in all of my 33 cases of adult myxœdema.

There are, however, exceptions to some of these statements. The husband of one patient, who, when I first saw her, complained greatly of the cold, for example, wrote (and this, be it observed, was before the thyroid treatment was commenced), "The advent of frost caused her to rally to such a degree that she went out, and enjoyed herself immensely when everybody felt the intense cold to be slightly inconvenient." He added, "In this connection I may mention that she rarely has cold limbs or feet now. There is a great change for the better in this respect." In another case, the patient, who first suffered from exophthalmic goitre and then from myxœdema, stated that "several times in the course of the day a feeling of flushing and heat passed over" her. In a third case, the patient complained of the frequent occurrence of flushing (burning) of the cheeks.

The increased susceptibility to cold is not merely a subjective symptom, for the *temperature*, as measured by the thermometer, is subnormal (in one of my cases, for example, it was usually about 96.5° F.), and the diurnal variations in temperature are much less marked than normal. The morning and evening temperatures are in many cases practically the same; the diurnal rises and falls which occur in health may be almost entirely absent. I have noticed, too, that in many cases of the disease the temperature does not rise above normal as the result of conditions which, under ordinary circumstances, would produce very considerable pyrexia. In connection with the diminished temperature, it is important to remember that in consequence of the remarkably dry condition of the skin the amount of heat which is given off from the surface of the body must be very much less than normal. When we take these two facts in association—the subnormal temperature and the diminished surface loss—it is obvious that the heat production in cases of myxœdema must be much below the normal.

In all of my 33 cases of adult myxœdema, the temperature was subnormal.

The condition of the circulatory system.—The *pulse* is usually slower than normal, and in many cases soft and weak ; the respirations are in some cases less frequent than normal.

The *heart's action* (impulse and sounds) is usually very feeble ; the aortic second sound is not unfrequently accentuated. In old patients, and in the advanced stages of long standing cases, the cardiac muscle may be degenerated and the arteries atheromatous.

This is a very important point so far as treatment is concerned ; for, as I shall presently point out, thyroid treatment is apt to produce very marked depression. In those cases in which there is any reason to suspect disease or degeneration of the heart or arteries, the thyroid treatment has to be conducted with very great care.

Fainting occasionally occurs. The patients usually complain of shortness of breath on exertion. *Palpitation* is sometimes troublesome ; one of my patients, a medical man, stated that he used to wake with "a tremendous sensation of oppression in the region of the heart." Palpitation on exertion was complained of in 9 of my 33 cases of adult myxœdema.

Some *anæmia* is usually present, but it is rarely marked. Both the red blood corpuscles and the hæmoglobin are usually moderately diminished in number. The red corpuscles are, so far as I have observed, normal in size and shape ; the white corpuscles are, in some cases, slightly in excess in number. In the case represented in Plate I. of my Atlas of Clinical Medicine, the red blood corpuscles numbered 3,320,000 per cubic millimetre, the white blood corpuscles were slightly, but only slightly, in excess, and the hæmoglobin equalled 70 per cent. In a second most typical case the red corpuscles numbered 3,820,000, and the hæmoglobin equalled 65 per cent.

More or less marked anæmia was present in 26 of my 33 cases of adult myxœdema.

The condition of the digestive apparatus.—The *appetite* is usually much impaired ; dyspepsia is not uncommon. In most cases there is *constipation ;* in exceptional cases the patients suffer every now and again from attacks of *diarrhœa ;* piles are occasionally complained of. In my 33 cases of adult myxœdema, the appetite was poor or bad in 29 cases, and good in 3 cases ; the bowels were regular in 8 cases, constipated in 22 cases, and loose in 3 cases.

The condition of menstruation : hæmorrhages.—As I have already stated, myxœdema is most usually developed in married women who have borne families ; in some cases there is *amenorrhœa ;* in others, *menorrhagia.* The onset of the disease is, as I have already remarked, often preceded by menorrhagia. In some cases, the amenorrhœa is without doubt the direct result of the disease ; this is proved by the fact that in some cases of myxœdema in which menstruation has been arrested, the menstrual flow is restored as the result of the thyroid treatment ; in other cases, the amenorrhœa may be explained by the circumstance that the myxœdematous symptoms only become fully developed after middle age, *i.e.,* at a time when menstruation would naturally cease. Myxœdematous women who happen to become pregnant (but this is comparatively speaking rare) are apt to suffer from profuse and exhausting hæmorrhage after delivery. In some cases, there is a *tendency to hæmorrhage* (epistaxis, bleeding from the gums, etc.), quite independently of pregnancy and parturition ; but in the cases which have come under my own notice this tendency has very rarely indeed occurred in the later and fully developed stages of the disease. Menorrhagia is, however, in my experience not uncommon. In the 29 female cases of adult myxœdema which I have observed, the menstruation was regular and natural in 2 cases ; arrested in 19 cases (in 12 of these the amenorrhœa appeared to be due to the occurrence of the menopause); irregular in 1 case ; irregular and scanty in 1 case ; scanty in 1 case ; and too profuse (menorrhagia) in 5 cases. In 3 of the 12 cases in which the menstruation was arrested in consequence of the menopause, there had previously been menorrhagia.

The condition of the urine.—The *urine* is in some cases normal, although the amount of urea is usually diminished. In other cases a certain amount of albumen is present. This is sometimes doubtless due to associated cirrhosis of the kidney, but in the majority of cases the albuminous condition of the urine appears to be the direct result of the myxœdematous condition. That this is so is proved by the fact that the albuminuria may completely disappear in the course of a few weeks as the result of thyroid treatment. In one of my cases the urine contained a distinct trace of globulin, but no serum albumen; in another case a considerable quantity of peptone was present; in one case there was a distinct trace of sugar.

In 6 out of my 33 cases of adult myxœdema, the presence of albumen was noted; in 4 of these cases the amount was small—a trace; in 2 cases considerable.

In the cases tabulated by Drs Hun and Prudden, albumen was absent in ninety-one and present in twenty-two cases; in three of the twenty-one cases in which albumen was present it did not appear in the urine until late in the course of the disease; and in five of the twenty-one cases the albumen was not constantly present, but only appeared from time to time.

The relative frequence with which some of the more important symptoms occurred in my cases is shown in Table 8, pages 312 and 313.

Course.—The course of myxœdema is usually slow and chronic. In one case, the disease had been in existence for thirty-four years before the patient came under my notice. The profound alterations which diminished or arrested thyroid secretion produces in the organs and tissues of the body seem to be functional in character. The disease does not kill as a rule until it has been in existence for many years, and even in old people the symptoms of the disease may entirely disappear, and the health and activity both of body and mind be restored in a very remarkable way under a course of thyroid treatment.

Death is usually due to the occurrence of some complication, such as bronchitis, pneumonia, influenza, diarrhœa, &c.; to cardiac degeneration, an atheromatous condition of the arteries or the structural changes associated therewith; or to the development of some associated disease, such as cirrhosis of the kidneys. In a few cases cerebral hæmorrhage is the immediate cause of death. In some cases, the patients appear to die purely from the exhaustion, debility, and defective nutrition which the myxœdematous condition entails; and particularly perhaps from the impaired nutrition and degenerative changes in the heart muscle which the myxœdematous condition and the anæmia, which is apt to be associated with it, occasion.

No.	Age.	Sex.	Married, Widow, or Single.	Number of Children.	Duration when First Seen.	Apparent Cause.	Debility.	Increased Sensitiveness to Cold.	Impairment of Memory.	More marked Mental Symptoms.	Impairment of Sight.	Impairment of Hearing.	Headache.	Numbness of Hands and Feet.	Thickness of Speech.	Sleep.	Running at Eyes and Nose.	Increased Salivary Secretion.	Bulkiness of Body as a Whole.	Myxœdematous Swelling of Face	Hands	Feet	Abdomen	Tongue	Throat	Supra-clavicular Swellings
1	52	F.	S.	..	12 years	Grief	1	1	1	0	1	1	0	0	1	B.²	0	0	1	1	1	1	1	1	1	1
2	59	M.	M.	..	5 ,,	o	1	1	1	0	?	?	?	?		G.²	0	0	1	1	1	1	1	1	?	?
3	63	F.	W.	6	20 ,,	o	1	1	1	0	1	1	1	1		G.	0	0	1	1	1	1	1	1	1	1
4	26	F.	S.	..	4 ,,	o	1	1	1	0	0	0	1	1		G.	0	0	1	1	1	1	1	1	1	1
5	41	F.	M.	1	4 ,,	o	1	1	1	0	0	0	1	1		G.	0	0	1	1	0	0	1	1	1	1
6	40	F.	M.	..	2 ,,	{ Mental anxiety }	1	1	1	1	0	0	1	?	1	G.d³	0	1	1	1	1	1	1	1	1	1
7	42	F.	M.	8	2 ,,	{ A severe illness }	1	1	1	0	1	0	1	1	1	B.	0	0	1	1	1	1	1	1	0	1
8	35	M.	M.	..	2 ,,	o	1	1	1	0	?	?	0	0	1	?.	0	0	1	1	1	1	1	1	1	0
9	48	F.	W.	1	5 ,,	{ Mental distress }	1	1	1	0	0	0	1	1		G.	1	1	1	1	1	1	1	1	1	1
10	33	F.	M.	7	3 ,,	{ Loss of bl'd and mental worry }	1	1	1	0	1	1	1	0	1	?	1	1	1	1	1	1	1	1	1	1
11	61	F.	M.	7	3 ,,	o	1	1	1	1	1	1	1	1		B.	0	0	S.⁴	0	0	0	0	0	0	1
12	61	F.	M.	2	8 ,,	o	1	1	0	0	0	0	0	0	1	G.	0	0	1	1	1	1	1	1	0	1
13	50	F.	M.	15	3 ,,	o	1	1	1	0	1	1	1	0	1	?	1	0	1	1	1	1	1	1	1	1
14	73	F.	M.	7	34 ,,	o	1	1	1	0	1	1	0	0	1	B.d³	0	1	1	1	1	1	1	1	1	1
15	51	F.	M.	7	20 ,,	o	1	1	1	0	0	0	0	0	1	G.	0	0	1	1	1	1	1	1	1	1
16	60	F.	M.	5	2 ,,	o	1	1	1	0	0	0	?	?	1	G.	0	0	1	1	1	1	1	1	1	1
17	55	F.	S.	..	2 ,,	{ Atrophy after exoph.goitre }	1	1	1	0	0	0	1	?	1	G.	0	0	1	1	1	1	1	1	0	1
18	67	F.	M.	6	4 ,,	o	1	1	0	0	1	0	1	0	0	G.	0	0	0	1	0	0	0	0	0	0
19	40	F.	W.	6	4 ,,	o	1	1	1	0	0	0	0	0	1	G.	0	0	1	1	1	1	1	1	1	1
20	60	F.	M.	2	2 ,,	o	1	1	1	0	1	0	0	0	1	G.	0	0	1	1	1	1	1	1	0	1
21	31	F.	M.	5	3 ,,	o	1	1	1	0	0	0	0	0	1	G.	0	0	1	1	1	1	1	1	1	1
22	60	F.	W.	9	3 ,,	o	1	1	1	0	1	1	?	1	1	G.	0	0	1	1	1	1	1	1	1	1
23	66	M.	M.	..	7 ,,	{ Mental shock }	1	1	0	0	1	?	?	1		G.	1	?	1	1	1	1	1	1	1	0
24	36	M.	M.	..	6 ,,	o	1	1	0	0	0	0	0	1	1	G.	0	0	1	1	1	1	1	1	1	1
25	33	F.	M.	..	3 ,,	o	1	1	0	0	1	0	1	1	1	G.	0	0	1	1	1	1	1	1	1	1
26	42	F.	W.	4	3 ,,	o	1	1	1	0	0	0	1	0	1	G.	0	0	1	1	1	1	1	1	0	1
27	50	F.	M.	3	12 ,,	o	1	1	1	0	1	0	1	1	1	B.	0	0	0	S.⁴	0	0	0	0	0	0
28	30	F.	M.	3	4 months	Grief	1	1	1	1	1	1	1	0	1	B.	0	0	1	1	0	0	1	1	0	0
29	64	F.	M.	10	3 years	? Influenza	1	1	0	0	0	0	0	0	1	G.	0	0	1	1	1	1	1	1	?	1
30	32	F.	S.	..	4 ,,	o	1	1	1	0	1	0	0	0	1	G.	0	0	1	1	1	0	1	1	0	0
31	41	F.	S.	..	14 ,,	? Inherited	1	1	1	0	0	0	0	0	1	G.	0	0	1	1	1	1	1	?	?	?
32	32	F.	M.	2	2 ,,	{ After confine't }	1	1	1	1	1	1	1	1	1	G.	0	0	1	1	1	1	0	0	0	0
33	48	F.	S.	..	4½ months	o	1	1	1	0	0	0	1	1	0	?	0	0	0	0	0	0	0	0	0	0
34	14	F.	..	..	4 years	o	1	1	1	0	0	0	0	0	0	G.	0	0	1	1	1	1	0	0	0	1
35	8½	F.	..	..	8 ,,	o	1	1	..	..	0	0	0	0	R.¹	G.	0	0	1	1	1	1	1	0	0	1
36	16½	F.	..	..	? From birth	o	1	1	..	..	0	0	0	0	R.	G.	0	1	1	1	1	1	1	1	1	1
37	3	F.	..	..	2½ years	o	1	?	..	..	..	..	..	..	..	G.	0	0	1	1	1	1	1	1	?	1
38	4	F.	..	..	3½ ,,	o	1	1	..	0	0	..	..	..	R.	G.	0	0	1	1	1	1	1	1	?	1
39	2 9⁄12	F.	..	..	Since birth	o	1	0	..	..	..	..	..	..	R.	G.	0	0	1	1	0	0	1	1	?	0
40	36	F.	..	..	? From birth	o	0	1	?	0	0	0	0	0	R.	G.	0	0	1	1	1	1	1	1	?	1

ADDITIONAL REMARKS.—*Case 1.* Formerly menorrhagia ; angina pectoris. *Case 2.* Right hemiplegia, ? from cerebral *Case 4.* Uncle died of myxœdema. *Case 5.* One cold winter felt better and brisker during the cold weather. *Case 17.* The myxœdema followed exophthalmic goitre ; has frequent flushings ; a sister also suffered from *Case 23.* Trace of sugar in the urine. *Case 24.* Frequently woke with feeling of terrible oppression in the region of Marked mental depression ; jumped out of the window and killed herself. *Case 30.* Acute eczema at the commence- suffered from ulceration of stomach. *Case 32.* Considerable mental depression. *Case 33.* Considerable anæmia menstruated regularly.

¹ R. = rough.   ² B. = bad or poor ; G. = good.   ³ G.d. = good, with dreams ; B.d. = bad, with dreams.   ⁴ S. = slight. Glob. = globulin.   * A.* = amenorrhœa, previously menorrhagia ; A. = amenorrhœa ; I. = irregular ; S. = scanty ;

Condition of thyroid	Yellowness of Face	Pink Blush on Cheeks	Loss of Hair	Encrustation of Scalp	Roughness of Skin	Absence of Sweating	Subnormal Temperature	Anæmia	Hæmorrhages	Ordinary Dropsy of Feet	Palpitation	Pulse	Appetite	Bowels	Albumen	Condition of Menstruation	Height	Mental Development	Speech	Anterior Fontanelle Unclosed	Milk Teeth	Umbilical Hernia
Cannot be felt	1	1	1	1	1	1	1	o	Men.⁵	o	1	70	B.²	C.⁶	o	A.*⁸	..	..	..	..	..	..
"	1	o	1	1	1	1	1	1	Cerebral	o	o	60	B.	C.	o	..	..	..	..	..	..	..
"	1	1	1	1	1	1	1	1	{ At last confinement }	1	1	60	B.	C.	T.⁷	A.⁸	..	..	..	..	..	..
"	1	1	1	o	1	1	1	1	o	o	o	68	B.	R.⁹	o	I.⁸	..	..	..	..	..	..
"	1	1	1	1	1	1	1	1	o	o	o	70	B.	Oc.D.⁶	o	A.	..	..	..	..	..	..
"	1	1	1	1	1	1	1	1	o	o	?	60	B.	C.	o	S.³	..	..	..	..	..	..
"	1	1	1	1	1	1	1	1	Men.	o	o	62	G.²	R.	o	M.⁵	..	..	..	..	..	..
"	1	o	1	1	1	1	1	1	o	o	o	?	B.	C.	o	..	..	..	..	..	..	..
"	1	1	1	1	1	1	1	1	o	o	1	46	G.	C.	Glob.⁷	A.⁶	..	..	..	..	..	..
"	1	1	1	?	1	1	1	1	Men.	o	1	60	B.	R.	T.	M.	..	..	..	..	..	..
"	1	o	1	1	1	1	1	1	o	o	o	60	B.	C.	o	A.men.⁸	..	..	..	..	..	..
"	1	1	1	?	1	1	1	?	o	o	o	72	B.	D.⁶	o	A.men.	..	..	..	..	..	..
"	1	1	1	?	1	1	1	1	{ Men. before menopause }	1	o	65	B.	C.	o	A.men.	..	..	..	..	..	..
"	1	1	1	o	1	1	1	?	o	o	o	64	B.	R.	T.	A.men.	..	..	..	..	..	..
"	1	1	1	o	1	1	1	1	o	1	1	58	B.	C.	o	A.men.	..	..	..	..	..	..
"	1	1	1	1	1	1	1	?	o	1	o	76	B.	R.	o	A.men.	..	..	..	..	..	..
"	1	1	1	o	1	1	1	1	o	1	1	70	B.	C.	o	A.men.	..	..	..	..	..	..
"	o	o	1	o	1	1	1	1	o	o	o	72	B.	C.	o	A.men.	..	..	..	..	..	..
"	1	1	1	o	1	1	1	1	Men.	o	o	70	B.	C.	o	M.	..	..	..	..	..	..
"	1	o	1	1	1	1	1	1	o	o	o	80	B.	C.	o	A.men.	..	..	..	..	..	..
"	1	1	1	1	1	1	1	1	o	o	o	70	B.	C.	o	R.	..	..	..	..	..	..
"	1	1	1	1	1	1	1	1	o	o	?	68	B.	C.	1	A.men.	..	..	..	..	..	..
"	1	o	1	o	1	o	1	1	o	o	1	60	B.	D.	o	..	..	..	..	..	..	..
"	1	1	1	o	1	1	1	o	o	1	1	72	B.	R.	1	..	..	..	..	..	..	..
"	1	1	o	o	1	1	1	1	Men.	o	o	63	F.	R.	o	M.	..	..	..	..	..	..
"	1	o	1	o	1	1	1	1	o	o	o	60	B.	C.	o	A.	..	..	..	..	..	..
"	1	1	1	1	1	1	1	1	Men.	o	o	72	B.	C.	o	A.*	..	..	..	..	..	..
"	1	1	1	o	1	1	1	?	o	o	o	72	B.	C.	o	A.	..	..	..	..	..	..
"	1	1	1	1	1	1	1	?	o	o	o	66	B.	C.	o	A.men.	..	..	..	..	..	..
"	1	1	1	o	1	1	1	1	o	o	o	44	B.	R.	o	I.S.⁶	..	..	..	..	..	..
"	1	1	1	o	1	1	1	1	Men.	o	o	..	B.	C.	o	M.	..	..	..	..	..	..
"	1	1	o	o	1	1	1	1	o	o	o	50	G.	C.	o	R.	..	..	..	..	..	..
"	1	1	1	1	1	1	1	1	o	1	1	100	B.	C.	o	A.men.	Ft. In.	..	..	..	..	..
"	o	1	1	1	1	1	1	1	o	o	o	56	G.	C.	o	N.M.⁸	4 2½	G.	G.	o	P.⁹	o
"	1	1	1	1	1	1	1	1	o	o	o	80	B.	C.	o		2 10½	S.	G.	o	P.	1
"	1	o	1	1	1	1	1	o	o	o	o	72	G.	C.	o		2 4¾	Nil	Nil	1	P.	1
"	o	o	1	o	o	1	1	o	o	o	96	B.	C.	..		2 2½	Nil	Nil	1	None	1	
"	1	1	1	1	1	1	1	1	o	o	o	80	G.	C.	o		2 3	Very little	Very little	1	Some	1
"	o	o	1	1	1	1	1	..	..	..	..	..	B.	C.	o	..	2 6	G.	Nil	1	Some	1
"	1	o	1	1	1	1	1	o	o	o	o	..	B.	R.	o	R.	3 o	Very slight	Little	o	Some	o

orrhage. *Case 3*. Menstruated only once since disease began twenty years ago; marked atheroma of superficial vessels.
9. Complicated with mitral regurgitation. *Case 10*. Frequent shivering attacks. *Case 11*. Marked mental depression.
bthalmic goitre. *Case 19*. Hair became darker during the disease. *Case 20*. Intercurrent paralysis of external rectus.
eart. *Case 25*. Has always had menorrhagia. *Case 27*. Amenorrhœa for three years; previously menorrhagia. *Case 28*.
of the disease; has daily flushings of cheeks. *Case 31*. Mother died of myxœdema; brother has a full heavy face; for years
mitral regurgitation. *Case 34*. Juvenile myxœdema. *Case 36*. A most extreme case. *Case 40*. Since the age of 25 has

n. and M.=menorrhagia. ⁶ C.=constipation; R.=regular; D.=diarrhœa; Oc.D.=occasional diarrhœa. ⁷ T.=trace;
en.=amenorrhœa due to menopause; I.S.=Irregular and scanty; N.M.=never menstruated. ⁹ P.=present.

DIAGNOSIS.

The diagnosis of typical cases of myxœdema presents no difficulty. In fully developed cases (*full-blown* cases, as I am in the habit of terming them), the facial appearance of the patient is so striking that the disease can be recognised at the first glance by any one who has seen cases before. The remarkable similarity in physiognomy which different cases of myxœdema present, and the facility with which the disease can in many cases be recognised, is well shown by the following facts :—In one of my cases, my son, a second year's medical student who had never seen a case of myxœdema, at once recognised the disease when I asked him what it was, without having told him that there was any case of myxœdema in the hospital, or given him any hint as to the nature of the disease with which the patient was affected. He was able to recognise the disease from the close resemblance to the plates in my Atlas of Clinical Medicine. In another case, the appearance of the patient was so typical and characteristic that while she was standing at the end of a long passage (away from me at a distance of 60 feet) I said to my assistant, Dr Douglas, " That old lady looks as if she had myxœdema." After I had examined and prescribed for her daughter, I questioned her, and found that my suspicion was perfectly correct.

The symptoms of which the patient complains, and the physical alterations which are produced in the body as a whole, and in the skin and its appendages in particular, are highly characteristic. Further, the diagnosis is confirmed by the absence of disease in any of the organs (other than the thyroid gland) capable of adequately and satisfactorily accounting for the condition—in particular, the absence of organic kidney disease. It must, however, be remembered that in some cases of myxœdema there is temporary albuminuria, and that in other cases—I refer more particularly to long-standing cases in old people—the disease is associated with cirrhosis of the kidney.

The most important symptoms and signs for the purposes of diagnosis are :—The general increase in bulk ; the broad (" moon-shaped "), swollen condition of the face, the swelling of the eyelids, lips, etc. ; the dingy yellow tint of the skin of the face ; the drooping of the upper eyelids, and the compensatory elevation of the eyebrows ; the pink blush on the cheek ; the large broad (" spade-shaped ") hands, and the short broad feet ; the solid character of the œdema ; the supraclavicular swellings ; the harsh, dry condition of the skin ; the absence of sweating ; the subnormal temperature ;

the increased sensibility to cold ; the dry, ragged, brittle con-dition of the hair ; the loss of hair on the scalp, eyebrows, eyelids, etc. ; the encrusted condition of the scalp ; the muscular feebleness; the slow monotonous speech ; the thick, " leathery" character of the tone of the voice ; and the remarkable slowness with which the act of thinking and, indeed, all the higher cerebral functions are carried out.

In the slighter cases in which the facial and other alterations are less characteristic and the symptoms less marked, the more important diagnostic features are :—The lassitude, debility and muscular feebleness for which there is no apparent cause ; the some-what " full " appearance of the face ; a tendency to increased bulk of the body as a whole ; the yellow colour of the skin of the face ; the dryness of the skin ; the diminution of the secretion of sweat ; the subnormal temperature ; the increased sensibility to cold ; the thin, harsh, dry condition of the hair (though this is not always present); and the slowness and thickness of articulation.

In doubtful cases the effect of a course of thyroid treatment is of the greatest diagnostic value. Case XXXIII. is an excellent illustration in point.

The differential diagnosis of myxœdema and Bright's disease.—Before the clinical features of myxœdema were clearly differentiated and recognised, the disease used frequently to be mistaken for Bright's disease. The same mistake in diagnosis is still occasionally made. The swollen condition of the face and especially the baggy dropsical swellings of the lower lids and the swollen (œdematous) condition of the limbs and trunk are at first sight—and especially in cases in which there is no cardiac lesion to account for the œdema—suggestive of kidney disease. Further, it must be remembered that in some cases of myxœdema the urine contains albumen. It is easy, therefore, to see how this mistake in diagnosis may arise.

The distinction between myxœdema and Bright's disease must be based upon the condition of the urine, the facial appearance, the peculiar character of the œdema, and the presence of other symptoms indicative of the disease, especially the dry condition of the skin, the increased sensibility to cold, the thickness of speech, etc.

The pink blush on the cheek is highly characteristic of myxœ-dema. The solid character of the œdema is another point of great diagnostic value ; but in this connection it is necessary to remember that in some cases of myxœdema ordinary dropsical swelling which pits on pressure is present in the feet.

In those cases of myxœdema in which the urine is free from albumen, an examination of the urine at once shows that the case is not Bright's disease; but, as I have already stated, in a considerable proportion of cases of myxœdema albuminuria is present. It is in these cases that the chief difficulty in diagnosis occurs, and it must be remembered that the two conditions (myxœdema and cirrhosis of the kidney) may be combined. This, however, is, so far as my experience enables me to judge, rare, except in the terminal stages of long continued cases in old people. In the great majority of cases of myxœdema in which the urine contains albumen, the albuminuria is merely functional and temporary; it may only be present after meals, and it disappears as the myxœdematous symptoms are removed under a course of thyroid treatment. In cases of this kind (cases of myxœdema complicated with functional albuminuria), the amount of albumen is rarely considerable and the urine does not as a rule contain casts. The presence or absence of tube casts, then, is one of the most important points in those cases in which there is difficulty and doubt. In some cases, a positive diagnosis can only be made by watching the effects of thyroid treatment. In those cases in which the albumen is merely temporary and functional—the result of the myxœdematous condition—it disappears under treatment ; whereas, in those cases in which it is due to Bright's disease it remains.

It is unnecessary to refer in detail to the many other points of distinction (condition of the skin, hair, voice, articulation, etc.).

The differential diagnosis of myxœdema and acromegaly is easy. Acromegaly usually develops during early adult life, most frequently between the ages of 18 and 27, and seems to be equally common in the two sexes ; while myxœdema is chiefly met with in middle-aged and old women. In acromegaly, the face is oval and elongated in its lower part ; whereas in myxœdema it is notably rounded (" moon-shaped "). The pink blush on the cheeks which is so characteristic of myxœdema (though not invariably present) is not seen in acromegaly. The facial expression in the two diseases is quite different. The thick monotonous speech of myxœdema is not met with in cases of acromegaly. In acromegaly, the skin is moist and the electrical resistance diminished; whereas, in myxœdema, the skin is harsh and dry and the electrical resistance markedly increased. In acromegaly, there is an increased growth of hair ; whereas, in myxœdema, atrophy of the hair and, in advanced cases, baldness of the scalp are highly characteristic features. In acromegaly, the enlargement chiefly affects the extremities ; whereas, in myxœdema, it involves the whole body.

In acromegaly, the bones, especially the short bones, are notably increased in size; whereas, in myxœdema, the increased bulk of the body is entirely due to a solid œdema of the soft parts. Bilateral temporal hemianopsia, which is such a frequent and characteristic symptom of acromegaly, does not occur in myxœdema.

PROGNOSIS.

Within the past six or seven years the prognosis of myxœdema has completely changed. When I wrote the article on myxœdema in my Atlas of Clinical Medicine, published in May 1891, I stated that, so far as our present knowledge enables us to judge, myxœdema is (with very rare exceptions) incurable. The exact reverse is now the case. Thanks to the thyroid treatment, the prognosis is now invariably favourable, provided always that the patient is not too old, and that there are no grave complications such as a diseased or degenerated condition of the heart, atheroma, kidney disease, etc.

By the administration of thyroid extract the myxœdematous symptoms can in the great majority of cases be removed in the course of a short time; and after the removal of the myxœdematous condition, the patient can be kept in good health by the systematic and regular administration of thyroid extract. Even in those cases in which the patient is old and in which the heart and arteries are degenerated or diseased, a carefully conducted course of thyroid treatment may produce the most remarkable improvement. In the case which is represented in Plate I., Atlas of Clinical Medicine (see Case III.), the patient was 66 years of age when the treatment was commenced, and she looked older than her years. The disease was of twenty-four years' duration; the patient was extremely debilitated, the scalp was almost entirely bald, the arteries were atheromatous, and the heart exceedingly feeble—in short, the case was a very aggravated example of the disease in an old woman with a weak heart and degenerated arteries. Now, at the end of six years, she looks at least ten years younger than her age; the myxœdematous symptoms have entirely disappeared, she has regained her mental activity, her articulation is sharp, she is able to attend to her household duties, her head is covered with a thick growth of long black hair, which is no doubt one of the reasons why she looks much younger than her actual age. Further, since her recovery, she has passed through a severe attack of influenza complicated with pneumonia, the attack being so severe that she was unconscious for days. No more remarkable illustration than this could be wished of the extraordinary benefit which may be obtained, even in very advanced and apparently unfavourable cases, by a carefully conducted course of thyroid treatment.

In connection with the prognosis in cases of myxœdema, I cannot too forcibly emphasise the fact that a course of thyroid treatment produces a very depressing effect upon the heart, and that in those cases in which the heart is degenerated or diseased, in which the patient is very old or debilitated, and in which the arteries are atheromatous, there is an undoubted risk of fatal syncope unless rigid precautions are taken to prevent cardiac failure during the early stages of the thyroid treatment.

SPORADIC CRETINISM.

Before leaving the clinical history of myxœdema it may perhaps be well to refer in more detail to the interesting condition which is termed sporadic cretinism. We now know that this disease is much more common than was supposed a few years ago. Since the introduction of the thyroid treatment a large number of cases have been reported, more especially in this country. Sporadic cretinism is merely the infantile form of myxœdema; the symptoms of myxœdema and sporadic cretinism are in many respects the same. Any differences which exist between the two affections, or which at first sight and on superficial observation appear to exist between them, are amply accounted for by the different ages at which the disease is developed. Myxœdema usually attacks the fully developed and adult organism, while sporadic cretinism attacks the non-developed and infantile organism. The profound disturbances in nutrition which result are attended with the arrest or non-development both of the body and mind.

Sporadic cretinism, like myxœdema in the adult, is due to diminution or abolition of the function of the thyroid gland. In some cases of sporadic cretinism the thyroid gland seems to be congenitally absent; in others, to be atrophied as the result of disease originating in early extra-uterine, or perhaps in some cases during intra-uterine life.

Sporadic cretinism, like the ordinary form of myxœdema, is much more common in females than in males. All of the six cases which have come under my own notice were females.

The symptoms characteristic of sporadic cretinism usually become apparent before the third or fourth year, sometimes during the first few months after birth, not unfrequently during the period of first dentition. In some cases, the symptoms of the disease are first noticed after recovery from an acute febrile disease, such as measles or scarlet fever; in rare instances, the disease appears to develop after an injury. In a few of the reported cases, the mother is stated to have received a fright during pregnancy; in a small proportion of cases, the birth of the child was attended with unusual difficulty, or the mother's health was seriously disturbed by sickness, traumatic injury, etc., during pregnancy. It has also been suggested that conception when one of the parents was in a state of intoxication may be a cause of the disease; but this appears to be quite exceptional. In a considerable number of recorded cases, the near relatives of the parents were tubercular or neurotic.

From this statement, it will be apparent that in some cases of sporadic cretinism the absence or atrophy of the thyroid gland is apparently due to arrested development or pathological conditions occurring during intra-uterine life; in others, to the result of pathological conditions during the first few months or years of extrauterine life. But in sporadic cretinism, as in the adult form of myxœdema, further information is required as to the conditions which cause, or predispose to the production of, the thyroid lesion.

Patients affected with sporadic cretinism, like patients affected with myxœdema, usually bear a remarkable resemblance to one another. It must, however, be remembered that the severity of the disease varies very greatly in different cases.

In typical and fully developed cases of sporadic cretinism, the appearance is very striking. The body is markedly stunted, dwarfed, heavy-looking, and podgy. At thirty-six years of age, the patient may only measure three feet in height (see Case XL.). The mental development is more or less, and in many cases almost entirely, arrested. The patient, though in years an adult, is, in respect to stature, mental condition, and sexual development, a mere child. The anterior fontanelle often remains unclosed. The milk teeth, which are usually very late in being cut and which are generally irregular, worn down, or carious, may persist even after adult age is reached. The face, abdomen, limbs and body generally are swollen, and the tissues are infiltrated with a solid œdema which does not pit on pressure. The facial appearance is highly characteristic and often extremely ugly. The expression is heavy and apathetic. The skin in some cases has a dingy hue; about the eyelids it is usually wax-like and translucent. The face is very broad ("moon-shaped") and coarse-looking; the eyes are set wide apart; the forehead is usually low and narrow; the cheeks are fat, pendulous and baggy ("jowl-like"); the nose flat and pug-shaped; the eyelids swollen; chronic inflammation of the lids (ciliary

blepharitis) is sometimes present; the mouth is unusually large, the
lips thick and swollen, the lower lip often everted and in many
cases blue ; the tongue is almost always very large and thick, and,
in some cases, is kept constantly protruded between the teeth.   The
pink blush on the cheeks which is such a striking feature in cases
of myxœdema is not usually present in cases of sporadic cretinism.
A fine growth of downy hair in some cases covers the forehead.
The head is usually large in proportion to the size of the body.   As
I have already stated, the anterior fontanelle often remains unclosed, even after the patient has attained the adult age.   The ears
are in many cases large, pale, and swollen-looking.   The hair, which
is in most cases fairly abundant, more especially on the back and
sides of the head, is usually straight, dry, and coarse; in some cases,
it looks like horse-hair.   During infancy, a scaly or eczematous
eruption is very generally present on the scalp; and this dry, rough,
scaly, and encrusted condition of the scalp persists, in many cases,
throughout life.   The neck is unusually short and thick; a depression
can often be felt in the position of the thyroid gland.   Elastic
swellings, which in some cases attain to such large size as to be
actual deformities, are in well-marked cases almost invariably present in the supraclavicular regions, sometimes in the axillæ or elsewhere.   A subcutaneous thickening, which is probably due to
deposits of fat, is in some cases present in the upper dorsal region
between the scapulæ.   A fine growth of hair is often seen in this
situation.   Enlarged veins are frequently present over the upper
part of the chest and limbs and venous mottling of the limbs is not
uncommon.   The abdomen is usually enlarged, often enormously
so ; an umbilical hernia is present in a large proportion of cases ;
it is generally of small size, but this is not always the case.   In
many cases, the belly is protruded and pendulous, while the back is
arched.   The limbs are short and broad, the lower limbs often curved
and apparently rickety.   The hands and feet are broad, thick, and
swollen-looking ("spade-like") ;   the forearms are in many cases
remarkably broad and thick ; the feet and hands are usually cold,
and often somewhat purple-coloured.   The skin of the face, neck,
and abdomen may be fine and wax-like, but over the limbs and back
it is usually rough, harsh, and dry.   The secretion of sweat is in
almost all cases greatly diminished or entirely abolished.   Moles,
warts, and nævi are in some cases present.   The voice is usually
rough, hoarse, and harsh, sometimes squeaky.   The temperature is
usually subnormal ; patients affected with sporadic cretinism are,
with rare exceptions, extremely susceptible to cold ; they like to bask
in the sun or roast themselves before a hot fire ; they are usually

much more active and lively in warm than in cold weather. The gait is clumsy and waddling ; in very extreme cases the patient may be unable to stand or walk. The back is often curved, and this deformity is apt to become more marked (apparent) after a course of thyroid treatment. The subjects of sporadic cretinism show a singular repugnance to exertion both of body and mind. In many instances they will sit perfectly still in one position for hours together, without speaking or apparently taking any notice of their surroundings, and yet perfectly happy and contented. They are usually of a placid and affectionate disposition and generally very unemotional ; they seldom cry and rarely shed tears. They are generally cheerful and easily amused, and are usually fond of playing with other children, animals and toys. Unless the case is a very aggravated one, they are generally cleanly in their habits, modest in their demeanour and, considering the low state of mental development, singularly careful of allowing themselves to be exposed. They usually sleep well, sometimes far too well.

The degree of mental development varies very greatly in different cases. Some are little better than idiots, unable to utter any intelligible speech sounds, unable to dress, feed themselves, etc. Others, though twenty-five or thirty years of age, resemble, as regards their mental development, a dull child of four or five. In very slight cases, the mental development may be comparatively little affected. Between the two extremes, all degrees of difference in the mental development are met with.

A notable and characteristic feature of the disease in the great majority of typical cases is the arrested development of the sexual organs ; even at twenty-five or thirty there are no hairs on the pubes or axillæ ; the testicles, ovaries, and uterus are in most cases entirely undeveloped. As a rule, the menstrual function is not established even when the patient is twenty-five or thirty years of age, but exceptions to this statement occasionally occur. In one well-marked case which came under my observation a few years ago, the patient, who was thirty-six years of age, and only thirty-six inches in height, menstruated regularly (Case XL.), but this is quite exceptional ; indeed I know of no other well-marked case of sporadic cretinism in which the menstrual function was established.

The appetite is in most cases moderate or capricious, the breath often foul ; flatulence is common ; constipation is usually a very prominent symptom, but in some cases diarrhœa is readily produced by slight dietetic errors.

A slight degree of enlargement of the lymphatic glands in the

X

neck and axillæ is not uncommon, but the internal organs (with the exception of the thyroid) are usually healthy. In some cases, the urine deposits a considerable quantity of mucus.

DIAGNOSIS.

In typical and well-developed cases of sporadic cretinism, the diagnosis presents no difficulty. The marked arrest in the physical and mental development, the peculiar and highly characteristic facial physiognomy, the earthy colour of the complexion, the thickness of the neck, the depression in the position of the thyroid gland, the supraclavicular fatty swellings, the large swollen abdomen, the umbilical hernia, the thickness and shortness of the limbs with the curvature of the lower limbs, the short broad swollen hands and small broad swollen feet, the rough harsh character of the voice, the dry harsh condition of the skin, the absence of sweating, the subnormal temperature, the marked susceptibility to cold and the love of warmth, the repugnance to exertion, the marked torpidity both of body and mind, the arrested sexual development, and the solid œdema which does not pit on pressure, form a clinical picture which it is impossible to mistake.

In slight cases, the retarded development of body, the retarded mental development (though in many cases this is by no means great), the dry condition of the skin and hair, the absence of sweating, the swollen condition of the eyelids, the large mouth, the large tongue, the large broad hands and feet, the subnormal temperature and the hyper-sensibility to cold, are the most important diagnostic points.

PROGNOSIS.

As yet it is hardly possible to make any definite statement with regard to the ultimate effects which thyroid treatment may produce in respect to the bodily and mental development in cases of sporadic cretinism. The length of time which has as yet elapsed since the introduction of the thyroid treatment is not sufficient to allow of any more definite statement. Much, no doubt, will depend upon the age of the patient when the treatment is commenced, and upon the severity of the case. In slight cases, and in cases in which the treatment is commenced at an early stage of the disease, there is every reason to expect marked improvement ; the effects which are produced by the thyroid treatment in two or three years are most remarkable. In cases of this kind, very considerable development, possibly the full development of body and mind, may ultimately be attained. But in severe cases, in which the disease is of long duration (as in Case XXXVI.), the degree of improvement which can be produced will probably be small.

These conclusions practically correspond to those arrived at by Dr John Thomson. In a thoughtful paper published in the "British Medical Journal," 12th September 1896, he says :—

"One of the next things wanted in our study of the thyroid treatment of cretinism is a clearer idea of the amount and exact nature of the improvement to be hoped for. Now, the improvement of cretins under thyroid is a much less simple thing than that of ordinary myxœdematous adults. In cretins, the treatment not only clears away the characteristic deformity and dulness, but also lets loose on the patient some at least of the natural impulses of growth which were in abeyance in his former thyroidless condition. This latent capability of reacting to thyroid treatment by a renewed growth and development seems to be present in all cretins, but its degree varies enormously, and is apparently in direct proportion to the youth of the patient when the treatment is first begun. It is very strong in children, less so in adolescents, and comparatively slight in those who have reached adult age."

In that paper Dr John Thomson directs attention to the fact, which was very marked in Case XXXVI., viz., that the spinal curvature and the tendency to bowlegs are apt to be increased during the thyroid treatment. He says :—

"This tendency to bowlegs may be due to too large doses of thyroid or to some other indiscretion in the treatment. It certainly seems likely to constitute a troublesome complication in the management of adolescent cretins. We should try to avert it by keeping the patient from walking too much at first and by giving him strengthening diet and medicine. Practically, however, these indications may be extremely difficult to fulfil. On the one hand, the great increase of energy renders it almost impossible to keep the patient off his feet, and, on the other hand, cretins are often extremely difficult to diet or to dose owing to their very fastidious tastes and the lax discipline to which they have always been accustomed."

These considerations show the great importance of early diagnosis and of early treatment.

The Treatment of Myxœdema and Sporadic Cretinism.

In the article on Myxœdema, in my Atlas of Clinical Medicine, published in May 1891, I made the following statements :—

"The statements which are to be found in the text-books, and indeed in the best and most extended monographs on the treatment of myxœdema, are of the most meagre and unsatisfactory character. . . . For the reasons given above, I cannot help hoping that, if attacked in a sufficiently early stage, the disease may, perhaps, in the future be found to be more amenable to treatment than we at present believe."

I then go on to say that from a consideration of the etiology, pathology, and clinical history of myxœdema, and the effects of removal of the thyroid gland both in man and the lower animals, it would appear that the main objects of treatment should be :— (1) To arrest the degenerative and atrophic process in the gland ; (2) to protect the patient against anything which is likely to aggravate the symptoms or facilitate the progress of the disease ; (3) to endeavour (as Victor Horsley has suggested) to supplement the function of the atrophied and degenerated gland by grafting a new and healthy thyroid gland tissue into the body of the patient.

When I wrote that article I had no doubt whatever that the myxœdematous condition was due to defective thyroid secretion.

In summing up the lengthened argument with regard to the pathology of the disease, I state :—" To my mind, then, it is satisfactorily and conclusively proved, both by clinical and post-mortem evidence in cases of primary myxœdema (by the results of extirpation of the goitrous thyroid gland in man and by the results of extirpation of the thyroid gland in animals), that the essential cause of myxœdema is abolition of the function of the thyroid gland."

Shortly after this article appeared (October 1891), Dr George Murray introduced the subcutaneous injection plan of treatment, and conclusively proved that the secretion of the thyroid gland, when introduced into the bodies of myxœdematous patients, in this way, produced rapid disappearance of all the myxœdematous symptoms and cured the disease, for if the treatment is regularly and steadily continued the patient is maintained in a condition of good health. This—the hypodermic method—was a great advance.

In October 1892, Drs Hector Mackenzie and Fox found that the same therapeutic effects (disappearance of the myxœdematous symptoms and cure of the disease) are produced when the secretion of the thyroid gland is introduced into the stomach. This was a still further advance, for the subcutaneous injection method is not only irksome and troublesome to the patient, but, unless extreme care is taken, is apt to be followed by injurious results (local inflammation, abscess, septic poisoning, etc.).

The effects produced in cases of myxœdema by the introduction into the organism of a relatively minute quantity of thyroid extract, the rapidity with which all the characteristic symptoms of the disease disappear under the influence of the thyroid treatment, and the extraordinary improvement, both in the physical and mental condition, of sporadic cretins, which results from the regular and prolonged administration of thyroid extract, are very remarkable.

Indeed, it is no exaggeration to say, that the cure of myxœdema by thyroid treatment is one of the greatest therapeutic achievements of this or any other age, and that the flood of light which has been thrown upon the functions of the thyroid gland by the experimental, pathological, and clinical researches of the past few years, and by the marvellous therapeutic results which have been obtained in cases of myxœdema and sporadic cretinism by the administration of thyroid extract, has opened up a wide field of investigation, alike for the physiologist, the pathologist, and the physician.

That the myxœdematous symptoms undergo immediate improvement after the introduction of a portion of living thyroid gland into the abdominal cavity or into the subcutaneous cellular tissue (the transplantation plan of treatment), and that myxœdema can be cured by the subcutaneous injection of a liquid extract of the thyroid gland, were remarkable discoveries ; but that the administration of the thyroid gland, given either in the raw or partly cooked state, in the form of a liquid extract, or even of a dry powder, is able, *when introduced into the body through the stomach*, to cause the rapid disappearance of all the myxœdematous symptoms and to lead to the cure of the disease, seems to me still more extraordinary.

At the end of this article I have appended the notes of thirty-four cases of myxœdema and of five cases of sporadic cretinism, which I have had the opportunity of treating during the past six years—*i.e.*, since the plan of thyroid feeding was introduced (see also Table 9). The remarkable results obtained in these cases speak more eloquently than words can do as to the specific value of the remedy. The husband of one of my patients wrote me :—" That thyroid extract appears to be the veritable *elixir vitæ* !"

The full details of most of these were published in the *Edinburgh Hospital Reports* for the year 1895, p. 116. At the end of that paper I summarised the results as follows :—

Therapeutic Conclusions.—The points which seem to me of most importance in connection with the thyroid treatment of myxœdema and sporadic cretinism are as follows :—

1. Myxœdema and sporadic cretinism being due to a deficiency of thyroid secretion (degeneration, atrophy, or absence of the thyroid gland), the thyroid extract is to be regarded as a true specific for the cure of the disease.

2. The specific effect may be produced either by (*a*) transplanting the living gland into the body of the patient ; (*b*) the subcutaneous injection of a liquid extract of the gland ; or (*c*) the introduction of the gland, either in the raw or partly cooked state,

TABLE 9.—SHOWING RESULTS OF TREATMENT IN THIRTY CASES OF MYXŒDEMA AND FIVE CASES OF SPORADIC CRETINISM.

No.	No. in Table 8.	Age.	Duration before Treatment.	Date of Commencement of Treatment.	Weight Lost during Treatment.	Immediate Result.	Subsequent Progress.	Ultimate Result.	Dose of Thyroid Extract which Patient continues to take.	Cause of Death.	Length of Time which has Elapsed since Treatment was Commenced.
1	1	52	10 years	Dec. 22, 1892	?	Rapid disap. of myx. symptoms.	Died 4 weeks after treatment com.	Death.	..	Syncope*	..
2	3	63	20 ,,	Jan. 25, 1893	?	Ditto.	Cont'd well.	Rem'ns well.	5 grains daily.		6 years.
3	4	26	4 ,,	Jan. 14, 1893	21 lbs.	Ditto.	Ditto.	Ditto.	2½ grains daily.		6 ,,
4	5	41	4 ,,	Feb. 9, 1893	?	Ditto.	Ditto.	Ditto.	5 grains every 3rd or 4th day.		6 ,,
5	6	40	2 ,,	?	?	Ditto.	Relapse: remains well.	Ditto.	10 grs. ext. daily.	..	6 ,,
6	9	48	5 ,,	Nov. 8, 1892	18 lbs.	Ditto.	Cont'd well.†	Death 5½ yrs. after treatment com.		Cerebral hæmorr.	
7	10	33	3 ,,	Jan. 5, 1893	7½ lbs.	Ditto.	Ditto.	Rem'ns well.	10 grains daily.	..	6 ,,
8	11	61	3 ,,	Jan. 18, 1893	?	Improvement.	Developed phthisis.	Death.	..	Phthisis.	
9	12	61	8 ,,	Jan. 23, 1893	?	Rapid disap. of myx. symptoms.	Cont'd well.	Rem'ns well.	5 grains every 3rd day.		6 ,,
10	13	50	3 ,,	Jan. 27, 1893	?	Ditto.	Ditto.	Ditto.	5 grs. every other day.	..	6 ,,
11	14	73	34 ,,	June 5, 1893	?	Some improvement.	*In statu quo.*	Died 6 mths. after treatment com.	..	Syncope‡	..
12	15	51	20 ,,	June 30, 1893	19 lbs.	Rapid disap. of myx. symptoms.	Cont'd well.	Rem'ns well.	10 grains twice or thrice a week.		5½ ,,
13	16	60	2 ,,	July 26, 1893	?	Ditto.	Ditto.	Ditto.	⅛ raw gland twice a week.		5½ ,,
14	17	55	2 ,,	Aug. 6, 1893	?	Ditto.	Ditto.	Ditto.	5 grs. every other day.		5⅓ ,,
15	18	67	4 ,,	Oct. 12, 1893	?	Ditto.	Ditto.	Ditto.	5 grains daily.		5¼ ,,
16	19	40	4 ,,	Jan. 10, 1894	?	Ditto.	Cont'd well, but d'v'lop'd melancholia	Ditto.	5 grs. every other day.		5 ,,
17	20	60	2 ,,	April 5, 1894	?	Ditto.	Cont'd well.	Ditto.	2½ grains daily.		4¾ ,,
18	21	31	3 ,,	May 9, 1894	?	Ditto.	Ditto.	Ditto.	5 grs. every other day.		4⅓ ,,
19	22	60	3 ,,	July 8, 1894	?	Ditto.	Ditto.	Ditto.	5 grains daily.		4½ ,,
20	23	66	7 ,,	Aug. 9, 1894	?	Ditto.	Ditto.	Ditto.	5 grs. every other day.		4⅓ ,,
21	24	36	6 ,,	Nov. 15, 1894	17 lbs.	Ditto.	Ditto.	Ditto.	5 grains daily.		4 ,,
22	25	33	3 ,,	Dec. 13, 1894	28 lbs.	Ditto.	Relapse.	Ditto.	10 grains daily.	..	4 ,,
23	26	42	3 ,,	Mar. 3, 1895	?	Ditto.	Cont'd well.	Ditto.	5 grains daily.		3¾ ,,
24	27	50	12 ,,	May 15, 1895	?	Gradual improvement.	Ditto.	Ditto.	10 grains daily.		3½ ,,
25	29	64	3 ,,	Mar. 29, 1896	20 lbs.	Rapid disap. of myx. symptoms.	Ditto.	Ditto.	5 grains daily.		2¾ ,,
26	30	32	4 ,,	Feb. 12, 1897	16 lbs.	Ditto.	Ditto.	Ditto.	5 grains once or twice a week.	..	1¾ ,,
27	31	41	14 ,,	Feb. 1893	?	Ditto.	Cont'd fairly well.	Death.	..	Ulcer'n of stom., etc.	
28	32	32	2 ,,	Apr. 15, 1897	15½ lbs.	Ditto.	Cont'd well.	Rem'ns well.	?	..	1½ ,,
29	33	48	4½ mnths	May 31, 1897	14½ lbs.	Slow but gradual improvement.	Cont'd fairly well.	R'm'ns fairly well: suffers from heart, etc.	0		1¾ ,,
30	34	14	4 years	Feb. 12, 1897	?	Rapid disap. of myx. symptoms.	Cont'd well.	Rem'ns well.	5 grains daily.		1¾ ,,
31	35	8½	8¼ ,,	Jan. 10, 1893	?	Ditto.	Ditto.	Still improv.	5 grains daily.		6 ,,
32	36	16½	16½? ,,	Apr. 1, 1893	3½ lbs.	Ditto.	Slight improvement.	*In statu quo.*	Nil.		5⅚ ,,
33	37	3	4¼ ,,	Mar. 30, 1893	?	Ditto.	Cont'd well.	Still improv.	3 grains daily.		5½ ,,
34	38	4	3¼ ,,	July 2, 1894	?	Ditto.	Ditto.	Ditto.	5 grs. every other day.		3½ ,,
35	39	2½	2½ ,,	Aug. 17, 1894	?	Slow disap. of myx. symptoms.	Ditto.	Ditto.	5 grs. every other day.	..	3½ ,,

* Total dose of thyroid administered = 2¼ sheeps' thyroids in the course of three weeks. Thyroid treatment stopped a fortnight before patient's death. On post-mortem examination, thyroid gland enlarged, pituitary gland enlarged; coronary arteries atheromatous; heart muscle extremely degenerated.

† Refused to take thyroid for two months before death. ‡ So long as continued to take the thyroid extract regularly.

in the form of a liquid extract or of a dry powder, into the body through the stomach.

3. The effects of transplantation—the first step in the development of the thyroid treatment—are merely temporary, owing to the fact that the transplanted portion of gland usually dies in the course of a short time and is absorbed. If the transplanted portion of gland could be engrafted so that it permanently lived and continued to secrete, the transplantation plan of treatment would, no doubt, be the best, since the result would be permanent and no further treatment would be required. But even if survival of the engrafted piece of thyroid gland could be ensured, there would still be the chance, as Murray has pointed out, of it becoming in its turn diseased, *i.e.*, affected with the same cirrhotic changes which produced the original degeneration and atrophy of the gland belonging to the patient. Fortunately transplantation is entirely unnecessary, for thyroid feeding is easy, cheap, and perfectly satisfactory in its results.

The subcutaneous injection method, which was the next step in the development of the treatment, has no advantages over thyroid feeding, and has several grave disadvantages, viz., the injection is attended with some pain ; it requires to be carefully performed, and should only be practised by a skilled observer ; it not unfrequently gives rise to local irritation and inflammation, and it may be, and has actually been, followed by general sepsis and death.

Thyroid feeding, which is quite as efficacious, is consequently the method of administration which should be preferred.

4. The dry extract in the form of tabloids, is an active and thoroughly reliable preparation ; its activity does not appear to be impaired by keeping ; the dose can be accurately regulated ; it is consequently a most convenient preparation, and is the one which I now almost invariably employ. Personally, I have had little experience with thyrocol which Dr Robert Hutchison claims is the active principle of the thyroid secretion ; but in the two cases (one case of myxœdema in an adult and one case of sporadic cretinism) in which I have tried it, while it produced marked headache, it certainly appeared to me to be less efficacious than the ordinary tabloids of dried extract.

5. Most patients affected with myxœdema and sporadic cretinism are very susceptible to the action of the thyroid extract ; and since it is rarely, if ever, advisable in the treatment of these diseases to produce the full physiological effects of the remedy (acute thyroidism), a small dose should be first administered. If the preliminary (small) dose is insufficient to produce any reaction or improvement, the dose should be gradually but carefully increased.

In cases of adult myxœdema, I usually commence by giving 5 grains of the dry powder once daily. In cases of sporadic cretinism, I usually commence by giving ¾ to 1½ grain once daily, in accordance with the age of the child.*

In some of my earlier cases the dose which was administered was too large, the result being acute thyroidism and serious disturbance (see Cases IX., X., and XXXVII.). The debility and cardiac depression which attend this acute thyroidism are often very great, and may, in old patients and in patients suffering from diseased hearts or arteries, be attended with danger.

Most patients suffering from myxœdema and sporadic cretinism seem to be much more susceptible to the action of thyroid extract than healthy people and patients suffering from skin diseases (psoriasis, ichthyosis, etc.).

In most cases of myxœdema, unpleasant symptoms and acute thyroidism are apt, in my experience, to be produced if the dose exceeds 4 tabloids daily (¼ of a sheep's thyroid gland); but in several cases of psoriasis and ichthyosis I have given 20, 30, 40, and in one case even 74 tabloids (a dose equal to one, two, or even five average sheep's thyroid glands) per diem.

6. **In cases of adult myxœdema the objects of treatment are :—**

(a) *To remove the myxœdematous condition without producing undue or serious depression of the action of the heart and strength, and without producing acute thyroidism.*

In most cases of myxœdema 1 (5-grain) tabloid, three times daily ($= \frac{1}{16}$ of an average sheep's thyroid gland) is the maximum dose which is required during this, the first, stage of the treatment.

I have only found it necessary to give large doses of the remedy in a few cases of myxœdema. In Case XXV., for example, 13 tabloids ($= \frac{3}{4}$ of a whole gland) were given for several days in succession without producing any distinct symptoms of thyroidism except vomiting.

(b) *After the myxœdematous symptoms are removed, to keep the patient in good health and prevent the redevelopment of the disease.*

In most cases of adult myxœdema, 1 (5-grain) tabloid every day or every second or third day is sufficient for this purpose ; but the dose which is required in each individual case can only be determined by experiment and observation.

---

* Burroughs, Wellcome & Co. supply two tabloids—one, suitable for adults, contains 5 grains of the dry extract $= \frac{1}{16}$th of an average sheep's thyroid ; the other, suitable for children, contains 1½ grains of the dry extract.

So far as our present knowledge enables us to judge, the systematic administration of the remedy must be continued throughout the whole future life of the patient; but this is no hardship; the remedy is cheap, and is as easily taken after or at a meal as a dinner pill or a pinch of salt.

So far as we know, a thyroid gland which is once atrophied and destroyed by the pathological process which is present in myxœdema, is never restored, but it is not unlikely that future observation may show that in some of the cases in which all the typical symptoms of myxœdema are present, the gland function is restored, at all events in some degree ; in other words, it is not improbable that the function of the thyroid gland may be temporarily arrested, suspended, or interfered with, and that myxœdematous symptoms may be the result of functional or structural changes of a temporary and removable kind. I do not see that it is necessary to suppose that in every case in which myxœdematous symptoms are developed, the secreting tissue of the gland is permanently and hopelessly destroyed.

7. **In cases of sporadic cretinism, the objects of treatment are :—**

(*a*) *To remove the myxœdematous condition without producing undue depression of the action of the heart and strength, and without producing acute thyroidism.*

In most cases of sporadic cretinism, 1 (5-grain) tabloid, once daily ($= \frac{1}{16}$ of an average sheep's thyroid gland), is a sufficient dose during this stage of the treatment.

(*b*) *To promote the development of the body and mind.*

(*c*) *To prevent the redevelopment of the myxœdematous symptoms ; and to keep the patient in good health until the full development of body and mind is attained, and during the remainder of life.*

One (5-grain) tabloid every second, third, or fourth day is probably a sufficient dose during this, the second, stage of the treatment. But it is impossible to speak with absolute certainty on this point. The length of time which has as yet elapsed since the introduction of the thyroid treatment is insufficient to allow of a definite statement.

And I may here say that as yet we do not know what effect the treatment may ultimately produce in respect to the bodily and mental development in cases of sporadic cretinism.

Much, no doubt, will depend upon the age of the patient when the treatment is commenced, and upon the severity of the case.

In slight cases, in which the treatment is commenced at an early stage of the disease, there is every reason to hope, judging from the remarkable effects which can be produced in two or three years, that a very considerable development—possibly the full development—both of the body and mind, will be ultimately attained.

But in very severe cases, in which the disease is of long duration, as in Case XXXVI., the degree of improvement which can be produced will probably be small. These considerations show the great importance of early diagnosis.

8. In most cases both of mxyœdema and sporadic cretinism, and in most cases of skin disease (psoriasis, ichthyosis, etc.), the susceptibility to the action of the drug seems, so far as my present experience enables me to judge, to diminish somewhat, rather than to increase, after the remedy has been given for a considerable length of time.

I have, however, met with several exceptions to this statement. The most remarkable is Case XI. From the commencement of the treatment this patient was very susceptible to the action of the remedy. After the drug had been administered for some months, the susceptibility became so great that $\frac{1}{8}$ of a tabloid ($= \frac{1}{128}$ of a gland) produced distinct effects (flushing of the face, a feeling of uneasiness and tension in the head, a rise of the temperature and pulse), even when the remedy was given without the patient's knowledge. The effect of these minute doses was so marked, that the medical attendant volunteered the statement that he believed one whole tabloid would have killed the patient at this stage of the case.

Between these two extremes—$\frac{1}{8}$ of a tabloid (in this exceptional case of myxœdema) and 74 tabloids (the largest dose which I have given in a case of psoriasis)—the therapeutic range is enormous. Hence the necessity of caution in prescribing the remedy, and of giving small doses at the commencement of the treatment.

9. In most cases of myxœdema and sporadic cretinism the beneficial effects of the remedy are rapidly manifested.

In some cases a distinct change for the better is apparent after the administration of a few grains of the dried extract. In one case of sporadic cretinism, for example (Case XXXVIII.), the myxœdematous swelling of the eyelids and lips was distinctly less, the expression was much brighter, and the colour of the lips and face distinctly improved, after the administration of two very small doses ($= 1\frac{1}{2}$ grains in all) of the dried extract.

Now, if a *visible* external change, a relatively coarse result, can be produced by $1\frac{1}{2}$ grains of the dried extract, it must, I think, be admitted that a distinct physiological effect can be produced by, relatively speaking, very minute doses.

Nor is the immediate effect altogether confined to cases of myxœdema and sporadic cretinism, for in one of my cases of psoriasis a distinct improvement was observed in the condition of the skin after the administration of two small doses of the extract (10 drops of Brady & Martin's liquid extract in all).

Further, in cases of myxœdema, a distinct improvement has been noted in the course of a few hours after the transplantation plan of treatment.

10. In cases of myxœdema, it is advisable to keep the patient in bed during the first three or four weeks of the treatment. Old and debilitated persons should remain in bed for a much longer period of time, and should be carefully warned against getting up suddenly, lest fainting or cardiac syncope should occur.

11. In all cases of myxœdema in which the action of the heart becomes much enfeebled during the thyroid treatment, it is advisable, I think, to give cardiac tonics and stimulants (strychnine, digitalis, strophanthus, alcohol, etc.).

12. During the first stage of the treatment of cases of myxœdema and sporadic cretinism, I usually keep the patient on a milk diet, or a milk-fish-white-meat diet.

13. **Immediate effects of the treatment.**—The more marked effects of the treatment in cases of myxœdema and sporadic cretinism are :—Rapid disappearance of the myxœdematous swelling ; loss of weight ; increased liveliness and activity ; a rise in temperature and pulse ; a feeling of increased wellbeing ; disappearance of the feeling of cold ; restoration of the secretion of sweat ; increased appetite ; disappearance of the constipation ; improvement in the general nutrition, and especially in the nutrition of the skin and its appendages ; and, in sporadic cretins, a rapid growth of the body, and a rapid development of the mental faculties.

The first effects of small doses are usually :—Decrease of the swelling of the eyelids, lips, and tongue ; increased brightness of expression and liveliness ; and improved colour in the lips and face. These alterations are usually quickly followed by a rise in temperature and pulse ; but the rise in temperature in some cases does not take place until later, or is only very slight. With the continuance of the treatment the myxœdematous swelling subsides, and finally disappears ; the skin becomes smooth ; the secretion of sweat is re-established ; and a feeling of pleasant warmth replaces the sensation of cold which the patient previously experienced. The disappearance of the increased sensibility to cold which is such a striking symptom of the disease is one of the most remarkable results of the treatment. One of my patients, a medical man, who before the treatment was commenced "felt the cold intensely," and whose "hands and feet were always icy cold," wrote me a month after the commencement of the treatment saying, "I have lost the cold feeling—in fact I always feel warm now." This patient resumed his professional duties three and a half months after the treatment was commenced; three weeks later he wrote me, on 22nd March, 1894, "I stood the intense cold which we have recently had as well as my neighbours I think, and where I was staying we had for some time a register 13° below zero (45 degrees of frost)."

The *loss of weight* which occurs during the course of the treatment is in many cases of myxœdema very great. Thus, in Case IV., the patient lost 21 lbs.; in Case IX., 18 lbs.; in Case XV., 19 lbs.; in Case XXIV., 17 lbs.; and in Case XXV., 20 lbs.

The administration of one or two large doses of thyroid extract is, in some cases of myxœdema and sporadic cretinism, attended with most marked diminution of the myxœdematous swelling and abdominal distension. Thus, in Case XXXVII. (sporadic cretinism), after three (10-drop) doses of Brady & Martin's liquid extract, the abdomen, which had previously measured 19 inches, only measured 14¾ inches.

This rapid loss of weight is usually attended with a feeling of great debility, languor, and depression; the heart's action and the pulse may become very feeble; and it is not uncommon for the patients to faint after getting out of bed suddenly, rising from the recumbent to the erect position, or after a free movement of the bowels.

Death may actually result from sudden failure of the heart's action in such conditions (see Case I.). In old and debilitated persons, and in patients whose hearts are diseased or weak, it is therefore of the utmost importance to guard against the occurrence of fainting during the course of the treatment, and to sustain the action of the heart by the administration of cardiac tonics and stimulants.

Further, it should be remembered that *anæmia* is apt to be produced by large doses of the remedy. In Case IX., for example, the red blood-corpuscles and the hæmoglobin underwent a marked diminution during the period of acute thyroidism, but rapidly increased under the subsequent administration of small doses of the remedy. The successive estimations were as follows :—

	Red Corpuscles.	Hæmoglobin.
October 28 (before treatment) - - - -	3,820,000	65 per cent.
November 28 (after acute thyroidism) - -	2,620,000	54 ,,
December 21 (during subsequent improvement)	3,850,000	68 ,,
January 13 (on discharge) - - - -	4,310,000	70 ,,

After the myxœdematous swelling has disappeared, and the patient begins to go about again, it frequently happens that the feet swell. This œdema, which is merely the result of the anæmia and cardiac enfeeblement, may be thought to indicate a return of the myxœdematous condition. Dr X., for example (Case XXIV.), became alarmed when he noticed the occurrence of this œdema of the feet. The œdema of the feet usually passes off in the course of a few weeks, when the patient regains strength; it should be treated by rest, and the administration of cardiac tonics and stimulants.

When the myxœdematous condition is completely cleared away, the alteration in the appearance of the patients is in many cases so great that their friends and relatives fail to recognise them. In several of my own cases I had absolutely no idea who the patients were, when they came to see me after having been for some weeks or months under treatment. In the first case which I treated, the patient's daughter, who had not seen her since the treatment was commenced, said to the nurse : "*I did not recognise her face ; I saw that her body was the same, but her face was so much changed that I did not know her.*"

As the result of the disappearance of the myxœdematous condition the difficulty in swallowing disappears.

The improvement in the condition of the general nutrition, and especially in the nutrition of the skin and its appendages, is one of the most striking effects of the treatment. It is no exaggeration to say that myxœdematous patients, in the course of a few weeks, get a new skin. The harsh, rough, dry skin becomes smooth, soft, and moist ; the secretion of sweat is re-established ; the fine, downy hairs, which in some cases of sporadic cretinism cover the forehead and back, disappear ; the warts which may have been developed on the surface of the skin in some cases, may also disappear. The dirty encrusted scalp becomes clean ; the hair begins to grow ; and the scalp, which was previously

quite bald, may, in the course of a few months, become covered
with a luxuriant crop of hair.   Case III. is a remarkable illustration
of the beneficial effects of the thyroid treatment.   The patient was
66 years of age when the treatment was commenced, and she looked
older than her years ; the disease was of twenty-four years' duration;
her arteries were atheromatous; she was extremely debilitated ;
the scalp was almost completely bald ; in short, the case was a very
aggravated example of the disease.   Two and a half years after the
treatment was commenced she looked at least ten years younger
than her actual age.   The myxœdematous symptoms had entirely
disappeared.   She had regained her mental activity ; her articulation was sharp; she was able to attend to all her household duties;
her head was covered with a growth of long black hair, which was
no doubt one of the reasons why she looked so much younger than
her actual age.   Further, after recovering from the myxœdema she
had a severe attack of influenza, complicated with pneumonia ;
during this illness she was unconscious for two or three days.

In two of my cases the hair, which had become dark and black
as the result of the myxœdematous condition, regained its normal
light brown colour as the result of the thyroid treatment.

Desquamation is, in my experience. always produced in those
cases of myxœdema and sporadic cretinism in which large doses of
the extract have been administered.   It is usually best marked on
those parts of the body on which the skin is thick—the soles of the
feet, for example.

The remarkable improvement in the condition of the nutrition
of the skin and the desquamation were the facts which led me to
suggest the administration of thyroid extract in psoriasis and other
skin diseases.

The improved state of general nutrition is remarkably seen in
some cases of sporadic cretinism.

The rapidity with which the body grows during the earlier
months of the treatment, is in many cases very extraordinary.
Thus, in Case XXXV. the patient grew 4 inches in one year, and 8
inches in two years and four months ; in Case XXXVII., 11 inches
in two years and one month ; in Case XXXVIII., 4½ inches in 11½
months (in this case the remedy was very irregularly given during
several months); and in Case XXXIX., 6½ inches in nine months.
In some of my cases of sporadic cretinism the increased growth
of the hands and feet was proportionately greater than the increased
growth of the limbs and trunk.

The improvement of nutrition is also manifested by the rapid
closure of the anterior fontanelle and by the cutting of the teeth.   In

Case XXXVII., for example, the patient, who before the treatment had no teeth, at the end of eight months had sixteen teeth. Further, in cases of sporadic cretinism, the teeth which are cut after the treatment is commenced are (usually) strong and healthy ; whereas the teeth which are cut before the commencement of the treatment, in most cases decay as soon as they come through the gum.

The increased appetite which occurs as the result of the treatment is, in some cases of sporadic cretinism, very noticeable. Thus, in Case XXXV., in the course of three weeks the patient was eating three times as much as she had eaten before the commencement of the treatment. During the course of the treatment some patients affected with sporadic cretinism get very fat.

I have already referred to the disappearance of constipation, which, in most cases of sporadic cretinism, is very marked. In Case XXXVII., for example, the bowels, which had never been opened without the aid of medicine or an enema, from the birth of the patient until the treatment was commenced, began to act regularly and naturally in the course of a few weeks after the regular administration of the thyroid extract.

In some cases of myxœdema, the menstruation, which had previously been in abeyance for many months, is restored, as the result of the treatment ; and in one case, as I have already pointed out, the breasts filled with rich milk during the course of the treatment.

With the disappearance of the myxœdematous symptoms the articulation becomes sharp and quick; the voice regains its normal tone, and patients who had been unable to sing for years may again get their voice. The mental condition is at the same time enormously improved. The sleepy feeling, which is in many cases a very conspicuous symptom, disappears ; the memory is regained, and the mental powers are quickened ; in some of the asylum cases, the mental deterioration, which was so marked as to necessitate their confinement, disappears. In many cases of sporadic cretinism, the rapid development of the mental faculties is one of the most remarkable results of the treatment.

The remarkable improvement in the memory and mental condition is well illustrated by Case XXVI. This patient stated that before the treatment was commenced her memory and mental powers were so much impaired that in the course of four weeks she was unable to get through the first volume of a three-volume novel ; she could not remember what she had read or where she had left off; several times, in going from her lodgings to the baths (at Buxton), which were close at hand, she lost her way. Two and a half months after the commencement of the treatment her memory and mental power had become as active and alert as they ever had been; in the course of a month or six weeks she read a number of books of different kinds and remembered what she read.

After the myxœdematous symptoms have been completely cleared away, the increased activity and capability for muscular exertion which some of the patients manifest is very remarkable. In one case the patient was able, six months after the thyroid treatment was commenced, to ascend a hill 1,700 feet high, and was less distressed than her husband and friends who accompanied her. Another patient, three months after the treatment was commenced, stated that she felt like a new person; this patient was able at the end of six months to dismiss her housekeeper and companion whom she had had for seven years, and to attend to all her household duties herself.

Alterations in the urine.—The albuminuria, which is by no means uncommon in cases of myxœdema, and which is usually, in my experience, functional, generally disappears during the course of the treatment (see Cases III. and XXIV., for example).

Several observers have noted an increased flow of urine as the result of the administration of the remedy, but in none of the cases which I have carefully observed in hospital has this been marked; and in some cases there has been absolutely no increased flow of urine. This was so in Case XXV., for example.

In one case the rapid disappearance of the myxœdematous swelling was attended with an enormous excretion of mucus and uric acid in the urine. In some of my other cases, the same result, though in a less degree, was noted.

Effects of too large a dose.—In cases of myxœdema and sporadic cretinism, large doses are very apt to produce acute thyroidism—profound gastro-intestinal disturbance (furred tongue, vomiting, diarrhœa, pain and tenderness in the epigastric region), great prostration, profuse sweating, great and rapid loss of weight, rapid destruction of the red blood corpuscles (in one patient there was a loss of 1,200,000 red corpuscles and $11\frac{1}{2}$ per cent. of hæmoglobin in three weeks), severe myalgic pains and headache, and a feeling of disagreeable flushing and discomfort. It is a curious fact that in one of my cases (Case IX.) the patient complained of great pain in the region of the thyroid gland. The same fact was also noted in another case.

In some cases I have observed an excited, hysterical condition produced by too large doses.

Effect of long-continued doses.—Whether the prolonged use of thyroid extract produces a deleterious effect upon any of the tissues and organs, it is perhaps, as yet, premature to say. Temporary glycosuria has been observed in more than one case, although no example has come under my own observation. In one of my cases of myxœdema (Case VI.), the patient, after taking the extract for more than a year, suffered from recurring attacks of acute congestion of the kidney, with albuminuria and hæmaturia, or rather, perhaps, hæmatinuria ; but whether this was a result of the prolonged administration of the thyroid extract, I am not prepared to say.

In one case of lupus, the patient has suffered from recurring attacks of syncope, pain in the stomach and retching, attended with alarming collapse and depression.

In Case XI., in which the patient became extremely sensitive to the action of the drug, acute tuberculosis developed. In this case, on several occasions a minute dose ($\frac{1}{8}$ of a tabloid $= \frac{1}{12\pi}$ part of a sheep's thyroid) was administered without the patient's knowledge. Half-an-hour after taking this small dose the face became red and flushed, the skin hot, the pulse-rate perceptibly increased, and the temperature elevated (from $\frac{1}{2}$ to 1 degree). This experiment was repeated on different occasions, and always with the same result. During the last two or three months of her illness the susceptibility to the thyroid was so great that Dr Menzies told me that he believed a whole tabloid ($\frac{1}{10}$ of a gland) would have killed her.

So far as my present experience enables me to judge, the beneficial effects of the treatment are most pronounced in those cases in which the myxœdematous swelling is most marked. In the atrophic cases, in which there is little or no myxœdematous swelling, the patients seem to be extremely susceptible to the action of the drug ; and in cases of this kind the treatment appears to produce very profound debility and depression. Cases XI. and XXVII. illustrate this fact, and it is interesting to note that the facial appearance and mental condition in both of these cases was very similar—the face was much wrinkled, the skin extremely dry and wrinkled, the memory greatly impaired, and mental depression very marked.

Y

ABSTRACT OF 34 CASES OF MYXŒDEMA AND OF 6 CASES OF SPORADIC CRETINISM, OBSERVED BY THE AUTHOR DURING LIFE.

A.—CASES OF ADULT MYXŒDEMA.

CASE I.—*Typical Myxœdema of Seventeen Years' Duration; Angina Pectoris; Rapid Disappearance of the Myxœdematous Swelling under Thyroid Treatment; Sudden Death from Cardiac Syncope; Extreme Degeneration of the Cardiac Muscle and Atheroma of the Coronary Arteries.*

Female, aged 52, single, first seen as an out-patient at the Royal Infirmary, on 2nd May 1888, suffering from typical myxœdema, and last on 27th January 1893, after the thyroid treatment had been carried on for four weeks by Dr John Thomson.

Duration.—17 years.

Apparent cause.—Mental strain and anxiety.

Present condition (2nd May 1888).—The case is a highly typical one. The swelling of the face, limbs, hands, feet, and abdomen is marked; the eyelids are swollen (bags of fluid beneath the lower lids); the skin of the face is of a sallow yellow hue, about the eyelids it is waxy and translucent; the lips are purple, *but not swollen;* the nose, too, is not flattened and broadened as it is in most cases of myxœdema; a well-marked blush is present on each cheek, and also over the nose; the hair of the head is scanty; the scalp is encrusted; the eyebrows are wanting; the tongue is large and flabby; the hands and feet are markedly enlarged; supraclavicular swellings are well marked. The patient states that she never sweats. She always feels cold; even on the hottest summer day she never can get warm; she much dislikes taking a drink of cold water. Her speech is typically slow, monotonous, and thick. The thyroid gland cannot be felt. Eyesight and hearing are impaired. The movements and gait are characteristically slow and deliberate. Muscular feebleness is a very marked feature of the case. The patient says that she sleeps badly. Her memory is impaired; all her intellectual processes seem to be carried on slowly. The urine, which has a specific gravity of 1015, does not contain albumen. The temperature is subnormal. The appetite is bad, the bowels constipated. The patient occasionally suffers from palpitation, and when she was able to go about more actively she used to feel short of breath on exertion. The first sound of the heart, as heard at the apex, is feeble, but there is no evidence of valvular disease. The heart is not enlarged, nor is the aortic second sound accentuated. The pulse tension is not increased; the pulse numbers 70 per minute. There is no ordinary œdema of the feet.

After this date, May 1888, I had, through Dr John Thomson's kindness, the opportunity of seeing the patient from time to time.

Noteworthy and exceptional symptoms.—In August 1892, she had a severe and typical attack of angina pectoris, and from August 1892 until 22nd December 1892 (when the thyroid treatment was commenced) several attacks, though less severe, of a similar kind.

Thyroid treatment commenced 22nd December 1892.

Preparation and Dose.—Raw gland (¼ twice a week), increased on 31st December to ½ gland twice a week.

Ultimate results of treatment.—*On 6th January* 1893, patient complained of severe angina-like pain, produced by over-exertion. Nitro-glycerine pre-scribed.

On 12th January, thyroid stopped, and ordered to remain in bed.

On 17th January, the myxœdematous symptoms had almost disappeared ; patient was very weak, complaining of epigastric pain.

On 27th January I saw her with Dr John Thomson and it was agreed to continue the digitalis, peptonised milk, and whisky which she had been taking.

At 9.30 the same evening, the patient, against express orders to the contrary, got up for the purpose of having her bed made, complained of feeling faint and died suddenly from cardiac syncope.

Post-mortem 29th January 1893. — Thyroid gland markedly atrophied ; pituitary enlarged ; kidneys healthy. The heart was very flabby ; the left ventricle dilated ; its walls in an extreme state of degeneration, especially towards the apex, where the muscular tissue appeared to be entirely replaced by a greenish-yellow looking material. The base of the aorta was studded with patches of atheroma, and the orifices of the coronary arteries were markedly narrowed. Both coronary arteries were atherosed, but no distinct clot was detected in the branch going to the degenerated portion of the left ventricle and to the septum.

Dr Gordon Sanders kindly undertook the microscopical examination, which showed that the heart muscle was in an advanced state of degeneration.

Remarks.—In this case, death resulted from sudden cardiac failure, and was undoubtedly due to the extremely degenerated condition of the heart muscle. The cardiac weakness was doubtless increased by the thyroid treatment, notwithstanding the fact that the thyroid extract had been stopped more than a fortnight before the patient's death, and the total dose of thyroid which was administered (2½ sheep's thyroids in the course of three weeks) was small. Nevertheless it had a very marked effect on the myxœdematous condition ; indeed, it may be stated that, so far as the myxœdematous symptoms were concerned, the treatment was eminently satisfactory.

The case shows the extreme importance of giving small doses of the remedy in all cases in which there is reason to suspect any degeneration of the cardiac muscle, and of rigidly avoiding all causes of cardiac syncope in cases in which marked cardiac feebleness and debility are produced as the result of the thyroid treatment. Though express directions to the contrary were given, the patient was, on the evening of the 27th January, injudiciously taken out of bed and allowed to sit up while her bed was being made. Immediately she got into the erect position she complained of feeling faint, and dropped down dead.

Recorded in full in the "Edinburgh Hospital Reports," Vol. iii., p. 192 ; and in "Atlas of Clinical Medicine," Vol. i., p. 15 (See Plate III.).

CASE II.—*Typical Myxœdema and Right-sided Hemiplegia. No Thyroid Treatment.*

Male, aged 59, turner, seen as an out-patient at the Edinburgh Royal Infirmary on 1st July 1889.

Duration.—5 years.

Apparent cause.—None.

Present condition.—The patient complains of weakness and a sensation of coldness ; the body is bulky ; the face moon-shaped, swollen under the eyes, and of a dingy yellow colour; there is no pink blush on the cheeks ; the tongue is very large ; the hands and feet broad ; the abdomen large ; the speech is charactistically thick; the hair very thin; the scalp encrusted; the skin dry and harsh; the patient does not sweat; the temperature subnormal; the memory impaired; the patient sleeps well; the appetite is impaired; the bowels constipated. The pulse is slow (60); the aortic second sound is accentuated; the mucous membranes are somewhat anæmic; there is no albumen in the urine. The thyroid gland cannot be felt.

Result.—Not known.

CASE III.—*Advanced and Typical Myxœdema of Twenty-four Years' Standing; Atheroma of the Superficial Vessels; Disappearance of the Myxœdematous Symptoms under Thyroid Treatment; Return of Mental and Bodily Activity; Severe Attack of Influenza Two Years Subsequently; Recovery.*

Female, aged 63, widow, six children, was first seen as an out-patient at the Edinburgh Royal Infirmary, 9th July 1890, and was admitted as an in-patient on 19th January 1893, suffering from typical and very advanced myxœdema.

Duration.—23 or 24 years.

Apparent cause.—None.

Condition on admission.—The patient complained of great debility, of loss of memory; failure of sight and hearing; and of great sensibility to cold. The features were broad and coarse; the face was markedly swollen, the skin of the face of a sallow yellow colour; the lips were swollen, the lower lip in particular being large, swollen, elastic-feeling, and to some extent pendulous and everted; the eyelids were markedly swollen, a bag of fluid being present beneath each lower lid; a well marked capillary blush was present on each cheek; the scalp was almost destitute of hair, and thickly covered with dirty brown scabs or crusts; the eyebrows were wanting, and the eyelashes had for the most part disappeared; the eyebrows were elevated; the forehead transversely wrinkled. At this date the baldness was much more marked than at the time when the painting which I have reproduced elsewhere ("Atlas of Clinical Medicine," Plate I.) was made. The body generally was large and swollen; the hands and feet broad and flat. Large elastic swellings were present above the clavicles; the thyroid gland could not be felt. The skin was dry and harsh, and the patient never sweated. The temperature was subnormal (97° to 97°.4 Fahr.). The speech was slow and thick. The patient was so weak and feeble that she could hardly walk. The memory and mental power were markedly impaired; sight and hearing were defective. The patient slept well. The appetite was poor, the tongue furred, the bowels always constipated. The urine was pale, sp. gr. 1.014; it deposited some mucus, but did not contain albumen. (In 1890, when the patient first came under my notice, a small quantity of albumen was present.) The superficial vessels were atheromatous, and the heart's action and impulse were weak; the pulse was rather slow (60); the patient was anæmic; red corpuscles numbered 3,320,000; hæmoglobin = 70 per cent.; the feet were swollen at night.

Noteworthy and exceptional symptoms.—Buzzing in head; superficial vessels atheromatous; sight and hearing much impaired.

Thyroid treatment commenced on 25th January 1893.

Preparation and Dose.—At first the raw gland (⅛th), subsequently B. & M. liquid extract (5-7 drops). Strychnine and strophanthus.

Immediate results of treatment.—Disappearance of the myxœdematous symptoms, sweating, desquamation of the skin, rise in temperature and pulse, growth of hair, etc., great improvement in strength, mental power, hearing, and seeing. Fainted twice on getting out of bed during the course of treatment.

Discharged 17th May, wonderfully well.

Subsequent progress of the case.—*During* 1893 (and subsequently) the patient did her housework (previously she had not been able to do anything for years).

In January 1895, had a severe attack of influenza and pneumonia, was unconscious for 2 or 3 days, but recovered (a remarkable fact in a woman of 68 with atheromatous arteries and a feeble heart, who had been myxœdematous for 25 or 26 years) ; was in bed for 6 weeks. Has since been well.

On 14*th May* 1895, shown to students at my clinique, looked at least 10 years younger than her age, whereas before thyroid treatment commenced (in January 1893) looked several years older than her age; hair of head black in colour, hardly a grey hair amongst it and nearly a foot in length (before treatment almost bald) ; memory very good; doing all her housework. Is taking 5 grains of dried extract daily.

Seen 8*th April* 1898.—Looking remarkably well and not her age (70 last August). Says on the whole she feels very well, though she has had several slight attacks of influenza during the past four years. She continues able to do light housework. There is still a little puffiness about the eyelids, but no evidence of myxœdematous swelling; the lips are thin, the tongue not enlarged ; the speech is quite sharp; memory and mental power very active; does not feel the cold at all, in fact face frequently flushes up especially on the least excitement or agitation; skin moist, sweats naturally, hair still growing thick, beginning to get grey. Her left eye is now quite blind (cataract). She continues to take the thyroid, gr. v., every day or every other day. She once left it off for 3 months, but had to begin it again as all the old symptoms began to return (weakness, swelling, feeling of cold, etc.).

Recorded in full in the "Edinburgh Hospital Reports," Vol. iii., p. 134 ; and in "Atlas of Clinical Medicine," Vol. i., page 13, where it is represented in Plate I.

CASE IV.—*Typical Myxœdema; Disappearance of all the Symptoms under Thyroid Treatment.*

Female, aged 26, single, seen 26th January 1891, suffering from typical myxœdema.

Duration.—4 years.

Apparent cause.—None.

Present condition.—The patient complained of debility, and she was somewhat anæmic. The eyelids, face, legs, abdomen, and body generally swollen. The face was of a dingy, yellow colour ; a pink blush was present on each cheek. The mouth was broad and large ; the lips were thick, elastic, and bluish in colour; the hair very scanty. The patient stated that she had not a third of the hair she had a few years previously. The colour of the hair has changed ; it was, she said, less golden than it used to be. Elastic swellings were present above the clavicles ; the thyroid gland could not be felt. The skin was dry and harsh, and the secretion of sweat, which used to be very profuse, almost entirely arrested. Several warts had developed on the skin during the past three years. The voice was rougher and harsher than it used to be ; the articulation was thick ; the buccal mucous membrane was swollen ; the whole appearance of the patient heavy and stolid. The hands were much larger, and the fingers much more swollen than they used to be. The patient stated that she felt quite a different person in warm weather; in cold weather she seems unable to think or exert herself. The tongue was large. The memory was impaired; the patient sleeps well. The thyroid gland could not be felt. The appetite was poor; the digestion bad; the bowels constipated. The temperature was subnormal (97°.6), the pulse small and weak, 68 per minute; the heart's action and sounds feeble. The urine was free from albumen. The menstruation was irregular.

Soon after this date the patient consulted me as to the advisability of going to Barbados. I advised her to do so, thinking that the warm climate would be beneficial.

Noteworthy and exceptional features.—Her uncle died from myxœdema. Colour of hair changed—it became less golden with the development of the disease.

Thyroid treatment commenced in Barbados, January 1892.

Preparation and Dose.—Raw gland.

Immediate results of treatment.—Rapid disappearance of all the myxœdematous symptoms.

Subsequent progress.—I saw the patient on 4*th September* 1893, and did not know her. She then told me that the sea air and damp had a most depressing effect upon her, and that too large a dose of the thyroid produced a severe aching pain like toothache in the left arm.

In *February* 1898, I met her in the street and did not know her; looks several years younger than she used to do and her facial appearance quite altered.

On 7th April 1898, she wrote me : "It will be three years next month since I left Barbados. During that time the greatest progress has been in *nerve*-strength. I am in every way less nervous, do not suffer such acute pain from any slight injury, am not so easily excited, and therefore less liable to nervous headache. In fact I fancy I am stronger nervously than I have been since I was a young girl. It is very seldom now that I have the old severe attacks of pain, but when they *do* come, I notice a marked difference in the way I revive after them, instead of being almost prostrated with exhaustion. I still have a great shrinking from cold, and am particularly sensitive to changes of *sunshine*. I am sometimes ashamed to feel and look really ill on a dull cold day, and next day—if the sun comes out—be quite well again! This sensitiveness to cold seems to have affected my *head* a good deal. Three times since returning to Scotland I have had long spells of a dull headache, the first one (December 1895) lasting nearly two months. In general health I am really well—probably as strong as, and I think more *steadily* strong than, I was at 17. I have lost the intense exuberant joy in living which astonished my Barbados friends so much, but it may have been partly due to my nervous condition, and might not return even if I went back to the heat and sunshine to-morrow. The only real traces of illness left are a constant tendency to indigestion, and a slight weakness of memory. The latter, however, is strengthening, and I begin to depend on my memory in teaching in a way which five years ago I should not have dreamt would have been possible. The oddest thing about my digestion is the way medicines disagree with me—frequently producing violent results, and occasionally acting in quite an opposite fashion from that intended. I have a horror of trying any remedy now, and the only thing reliable for indigestion, or as an aperient, is whisky and water !—

and that, as a strong total abstainer, I dislike taking. To keep myself well I depend on the thyroid and hot baths. For the last year and a half, half a tabloid (= 2½ grs.) of thyroid has been enough. I have sometimes tried doing without the thyroid for a day or two, but always by the second day weariness and headache have set in. Regular warm bathing helps me greatly. I take a hot bath on an average every second morning, and once in two or three weeks have a 'Russian (steam) bath.' I greatly enjoy exercise — particularly very *rapid* motion. I cannot afford to keep up my horseback-riding, but I cycle a great deal, and enjoy dancing like a girl of 15! In fact those years of illness seem to have been in a way missed out of my life, and in many ways I fancy I act and feel more like 25 than 33!

"I hope I have told you what you wish to know. If not, I shall be most happy to answer any special questions, as I owe you a great debt of gratitude for your help and kindness during a terribly dark time of my life."

Recorded in full in the "Edinburgh Hospital Reports," Vol. iii., p. 167.

CASE V.—*Typical Myxœdema; Rapid Disappearance of All the Symptoms under Thyroid Treatment.*

Female, aged 41, married, one child, seen in consultation 28th May 1891, suffering from typical myxœdema.

Duration.—4 years.

Apparent cause.—None.

Present condition.—The patient complained of great bodily weakness, and of loss of memory and mental power. The face and body were swollen, but the hands and feet were not characteristically misshapen. The eyelids were swollen, the lips thick and elastic-feeling, the hair of the head and eyebrows scanty, the scalp dry and rough. A pink blush was present on each cheek; several large brown pigmented patches were present on the forehead, and the skin of the neck was of a dingy yellow colour. The tongue and uvula were swollen; the speech was markedly thick, and the voice rough and hoarse. The skin was dry; the patient stated that she perspired much less than she used to do; the temperature was subnormal (96° Fahr.); she was very sensitive to cold. Elastic swellings were present above the clavicles. The thyroid gland could not be felt. The heart's action and pulse were very feeble, the aortic second sound accentuated; the pulse numbered 70 per minute; the patient was somewhat anæmic, and was subject to fainting attacks, and quite unable to undergo any exertion either of body or mind; the memory was impaired; the patient slept well; the menstruation, when the patient was first seen, regular, subsequently arrested. The urine was free from albumen, and there was no visceral disease. The appetite was poor; she was subject to attacks of diarrhœa, which came on without any obvious cause.

Various remedies were from time to time employed, but without any distinct benefit.

There is nothing of importance to note between May 1891 and February 1893, except that during the winter of 1892-93 "the advent of frost" (so her husband wrote me on 13th February 1893) "caused her to rally to such a degree that she went out, and enjoyed herself immensely when everybody felt the intense cold to be slightly inconvenient." He added: "In this connection I may mention that she rarely has cold limbs or feet now. There is a great change for the better in this respect."

Noteworthy and exceptional symptoms.— Hands and feet not swollen; occasional causeless diarrhœa; during 1892 (when the symptoms were all well marked and before the thyroid treatment had been commenced) she enjoyed the cold.

Thyroid treatment commenced 9th February 1893.

Preparation and Dose.—Liquid extract ʒi. daily (D. & F.'s)—equal to ⅛th of a gland—every other day.

Immediate result of treatment.—After four doses, a distinct improvement; in the course of a month her husband wrote : " Her bodily health and spirits have undergone such a change that she appears to be another creature. She is much thinner, and more healthy looking. The thyroid extract appears to be the veritable *Elixir vitæ !* " In the course of two months, the myxœdematous symptoms had completely disappeared; the hair was growing; the menstruation (absent for several months previously) had returned.

Subsequent progress.—*In August* 1893 (6 months after the commencement of the treatment) she ascended the highest of the Ochils (1700 feet); she was the least distressed and fatigued of the party, when they returned home in the evening. *In October* 1893, her hair, which before the commencement of the treatment was very scanty, was most luxuriant. She has continued in perfect health ever since.

On 2nd April 1898, when last seen, she looked the picture of health; continues to take the thyroid, as a rule, every third or fourth day, sometimes at longer intervals; always finds she must return to it again.

Recorded in full in the " Edinburgh Hospital Reports," Vol. iii., p. 164.

CASE VI.—*Typical and Advanced Myxœdema; Complete Disappearance of the Myxœdematous Symptoms under Thyroid Treatment.*

Female, aged 40, married, no children, seen on 23rd September 1891.

Duration.—2 years or more.

Apparent cause.—None, unless mental anxiety, of which she has had a great deal. Had typhoid fever at the age of 18, and says she has never been so strong since.

Present condition.—Patient complains of debility and muscular feebleness; body bulky; face markedly swollen, of a dingy yellow colour; baggy swellings of lower eyelids; pink blush on the cheeks; speech characteristic; tongue and throat swollen; some difficulty in swallowing; says the tongue gets very tired if she attempts to speak much, and if she is at all nervous can scarcely manage to swallow; fatty swellings above the clavicles; hands spade-like; feet broad and thick; used to have hot hands and feet, now always feels cold; temperature subnormal; skin dry, never sweats, but never did sweat much; hair thin and dry; scalp scaly; nails brittle; speech thick; appetite poor; bowels constipated; goes to bed feeling thoroughly exhausted; memory bad, has not noticed that it was worse in cold weather; thinks slowly; sleeps well, but has most distressing dreams; complains much of headache and " thudding " noises at the back of the head; distinctly anæmic; optic discs natural; menstruation scanty, has never had menorrhagia; the thyroid gland cannot be felt; pulse 60; urine normal.

Treatment.—The patient was treated, first, by the subcutaneous injection of thyroid extract, and subsequently, by the administration of the dried extract by the mouth.

Result.—Dr Robertson Crease of South Shields, who prescribed and conducted the treatment, wrote me on 8th April 1898 as follows :—" For two years after you saw her I injected twice weekly 15 m. thyroid extract; after that period she continued to take the thyroid tabloids twice daily. This treatment held her disease in check partly. She lost her husband 18 months ago, and had much family care and anxiety. The myxœdematous symptoms then returned, in spite of three doses (tabloids) per day. I was again asked to see her, and at her own request I began the thyroid extract injections, 15 m. twice a week. After five injections, the change in her appearance was marked—the skin is less dry and harsh; the temperature has risen; the flow of saliva has ceased; she says that she feels lighter; her spirits are better. I propose to give one injection per week and two tabloids per day. She has little faith in the tabloids; but she has great confidence in the injections."

CASE VII.—*Typical and Advanced Myxœdema; Death; No Thyroid Treatment.*

Female, aged 42, married, eight children, seen 19th October 1891, suffering from all the characteristic symptoms of typical and advanced myxœdema.

Duration.—2 years.

Apparent cause.—A severe illness, the exact nature of which I was unable to ascertain, seems to have preceded the development of the myxœdematous symptoms. Has suffered from menorrhagia since the birth of her last child.

Symptoms.—Complains of great weakness and giddiness; says she cannot get the limbs to work, cannot get them to move sharply. The body as a whole is bulky; the face is full; the eyelids are swollen and translucent-looking; the skin of the face is of a dingy yellow colour; a pink blush is present on the cheeks; the lips are swollen and blue; the nose, cheeks and hands are also somewhat blue; the ears are large; large elastic swellings are present above the clavicles; the hands and feet are broad and thick; the abdomen is large and pendulous; the under-surface of the tongue is swollen; the speech is characteristically thick; the throat is not swollen, but the buccal mucous membrane is anæmic; the eyebrows are scanty and ragged; the scalp is almost destitute of hair and thickly encrusted; the patient feels the cold very much; the temperature is subnormal; she does not feel sure that she is better in summer than in winter; the skin is very dry and rough; for some weeks she has experienced a severe pain behind the knee, nothing local can be detected to account for this; patient complains of numbness in hands and feet; the knee-jerks are exaggerated; there is frequent headache; the memory is impaired and the patient's mental condition is peculiar; at times she is very irritable, she mistakes people, sometimes thinks her husband is the nurse (psychical blindness); she sleeps badly; sight is quite good; the pupils are equal and active; there is no hemianopsia; hearing, taste and smell are unaffected; the heart is natural; radial pulse 62, small and weak; the appetite is good, digestion natural, bowels regular; the urine is normal; no thyroid gland can be felt.

Treatment.—Warmth and tonics were prescribed. As soon as the thyroid treatment was introduced, I wrote to the patient advising her to try it; and learned from her husband that she had *died* a short time previously.

CASE VIII.—*Typical Myxœdema. No Thyroid Treatment.*

Male, aged 35, married, bookbinder, seen as an out-patient at the Edinburgh Royal Infirmary on 22nd January 1892.

Duration.—2 years or more.

Apparent cause.—None.

Present condition.—The patient complains of great lassitude and repugnance to exertion; gait slow and ponderous; always feels cold; is somewhat anæmic; never sweats; body as a whole bulky; face swollen and of a yellowish tinge; no pink blush on the cheeks; tongue large; throat swollen; hands spade-like; feet broad and thick; abdomen large; no supraclavicular swellings; hair, which used to be thick before the disease commenced, very scanty, dry and brittle; scalp dirty; eyebrows almost absent; memory defective; speech thick; some difficulty in swallowing; skin dry and rough; temperature subnormal appetite poor; bowels constipated; knee-jerks present; thyroid gland cannot be felt, the rings of the trachea very distinct.   No albumen or sugar in the urine.

Subsequent progress.—Not known.

CASE IX.—*Typical Myxœdema; Rapid Disappearance of All the Symptoms under Thyroid Feeding; Profuse Desquamation of the Skin. Readmission to Hospital a Year after Discharge; Acute Bronchitis; Albuminuria; Hæmaturia and Hæmatinuria. Death Four Years Later.*

Female, aged 48, widow, one child, admitted to the Edinburgh Royal Infirmary on 28th October 1892, suffering from typical myxœdema.

Duration.—5 years.

Apparent cause.—Mental distress.

Family History.—A step-sister died of phthisis.

Condition on admission.—The case was most typical, all the characteristic symptoms of myxœdema being present. The patient complained of a feeling of debility, lassitude, and inability to exert herself. She always felt cold; even if she roasted herself before a hot fire, she could not get heated up. She stated that she was always worst in the winter and cold weather. The body as a whole was bulky; the movements heavy and clumsy; the abdomen large and pendulous. The face was moon-shaped, swollen and puffy, of a tawny-yellow colour, except about the eyelids, where it had the pale, transparent, waxy appearance which is so characteristic of the disease. A well-marked pink blush was present on each cheek. The lips were thick; the eyelids were swollen; the hair was scanty; the scalp dirty, and encrusted with brown scales and crusts; the hands were "spade-shaped"; the feet broad and thick. The speech was thick and drawling, as if the patient had something in the mouth or throat. The tongue was large and flabby; the throat was swollen. She stated that saliva used frequently to flow out of her mouth, especially during the night; and that her nose often ran, without any cold or other apparent cause. Elastic swellings were present above the clavicles. The skin was harsh and dry; she never sweated, though the palms of the hands were at times moist. The pulse was slow; it varied from 40 to 50 in the minute, the average being 46. The temperature was always subnormal (average, 97° Fahr.). The respirations averaged 14 per minute. The urine contained a distinct trace of globulin, but no serum albumen. The memory and mental activity were much impaired. The patient stated that she felt it an effort to think; at the same time she added that she was more easily agitated than she used to be; she slept well. The appetite was good; she had not had any indigestion for two months; the bowels were constipated. The red blood corpuscles numbered 3,820,000 per c.mm., and the hæmoglobin amounted to 65 per cent. The weight was 11 st. 4½ lbs.

Noteworthy symptoms.—The urine contained a distinct trace of globulin, but no serum albumen. Menstruation, which had been arrested for several months, returned immediately under thyroid treatment, and the urine contained an excessive quantity of mucus.

Thyroid treatment commenced on 8th November 1892.

Preparation and Dose.—Raw gland; at first half a gland daily, subsequently smaller doses.

Immediate result.—The production of acute thyroidism (severe headache, pain in the position of the thyroid, in the back and limbs, anorexia, pain in stomach, vomiting, diarrhœa, thickly furred tongue), rise in temperature and pulse, profuse sweating, menstrual flow which had been arrested for 8 months, diminution of red blood corpuscles and hæmoglobin (from 3,820,000 and 65 % to 2,620,000 and 54 °/₀), the rapid disappearance of the myxœdematous swelling, loss of 18½ lbs. in weight, the profuse discharge of a very large quantity of mucus in the urine, disappearance of globulin.

Subsequently.—Growth of hair, profuse desquamation of the skin which became quite soft and natural, increase of red blood corpuscles and hæmoglobin (from 2,620,000 and 54 °/₀ to 4,310,000 and 70 °/₀), restoration of strength, etc.

Weight on admission 11 st. 4½ lbs.; on discharge 10 st. 12 lbs.

The patient was discharged from hospital *on 18th February* 1893, saying that she felt quite well and "equal to anything." The change in her appearance was so great that her daughter said when she saw her, " I did not recognise her face; I saw that her body was the same, but her face was so much changed I did not know her."

Subsequent progress of the case.—Patient who had not been able to do any work for 5 years, worked during the summer of 1893.

In November and December 1893, had several attacks of bleeding from the kidney.

On 18th February 1894, was re-admitted to E.R.I., suffering from bronchitis, hæmaturia, albuminuria and loud systolic murmur, due to exposure to cold and wet. Discharged from the E.R.I., urine normal, 21st April 1894.

On 16th June 1896, when I last saw patient, she was keeping well, better than for years before the thyroid treatment, but still had a somewhat myxœdematous look. She was taking the thyroid (dried extract) fairly regularly. The urine still contained at times a small quantity of albumen.

On 27th May 1898 her medical attendant wrote me :—" You will be sorry to hear that Jessie G. *died last week*. Her heart became very flabby and ceased to respond to digitalis, etc. She was in very poor circumstances and refused to go into the poor-house, and consequently received inadequate nourishment. Four-and-twenty hours before her death she was affected with left hemiplegia (cerebral hæmorrhage) and she was also slightly jaundiced. The myxœdematous symptoms were always easily controlled by thyroid extract, but when she was unable to obtain the remedy for any length of time the peculiar symptoms of the disease asserted themselves."

Recorded in full in the "Edinburgh Hospital Reports," Vol. iii., p. 116.

CASE X.—*Typical Myxœdema ; Rapid Disappearance of All the Symptoms under Thyroid Treatment.*

Female, aged 33, married, seven children and one miscarriage, admitted to the Edinburgh Royal Infirmary on 26th December 1892, suffering from typical myxœdema.

Duration.—3 years.

Apparent cause.—Loss of blood last confinement and mental worry.

Family History.—A brother died of diabetes ; another had swollen glands.

Condition on admission.—All the characteristic symptoms of myxœdema are present. The patient complains of debility. The body as a whole is bulky, the hands and feet are broad and thick ; the face is broad, and the lower lip swollen and firm ; the eyelids are swollen. The skin of the face is of a dingy yellow hue ; a pink blush is present on the cheeks and nose. The hair of the head is very thin, the eyebrows scanty. A pigmented mole has developed on the right cheek since the illness commenced. A patch of dry eczema is present on the back of the right hand and wrist. The tongue and buccal mucous membrane are swollen ; the speech is slow and thick ; the patient has some difficulty in swallowing. The skin is harsh, rough, and dry, except on the face, where it is smooth. The patient says that she never sweats except on the head and forehead, which are occasionally cold and clammy. Her nose frequently "runs" without any apparent cause ; this, she says, relieves her headache, which is often very severe. Since her illness commenced, the secretion of saliva has, she says, been more profuse than it used to be ; it often runs from her mouth through the night. She complains of feeling cold, and of numbness in the hands and feet. She says that she always feels better in warm weather. Her memory is impaired, and sight and hearing are less acute than they were three years ago. Her gait is slow and clumsy. The thyroid gland cannot be felt. The temperature is subnormal (97° to 97°.6) ; the pulse rather slow (56 to 68 per minute) and soft. The heart's impulse is feeble. The urine contains a small quantity of albumen (both serum albumen and peptone). The appetite is poor, the abdomen large (the result of flatulent distension), the bowels regular. The red blood corpuscles numbered 4,210,000 per cubic millimetre, and the hæmoglobin (estimated by Gowers' instrument)= 56 per cent. The menstruation, which recommenced three months after the birth of the last child, has since been regular, but too profuse.

Noteworthy and exceptional symptoms.—Frequent attacks of shivering and running at eyes and nose, dry eczema on hand, severe headaches. During the treatment, the breasts filled with rich milk.

Thyroid treatment commenced on January 1893.

Preparation and Dose.—At first the raw gland ($\frac{1}{8}$th, subsequently increased to $\frac{1}{2}$ and finally reduced to $\frac{1}{4}$ of a gland).

Immediate results of treatment.—Complete disappearance of the myxœdematous symptoms, desquamation of the skin, growth of hair and complete cure.

During the course of the treatment, the patient suffered from headache, severe myalgic pains in the back, chest and limbs, anorexia, furred tongue, sickness, vomiting, epigastric pain, diarrhœa ; rapid filling of the breasts with rich milk.

Was discharged from E.R.I. *on 6th March* 1894, feeling quite well. Weight on admission 9 st. 6½ lbs., on discharge 9 st., greatest loss of weight during the treatment 7½ lbs.

Subsequent progress of the case.—Patient continued to take the thyroid and continued well. Was confined in 1894.

Seen on 2nd October 1897 ; was then quite free from myxœdematous symptoms, and feeling strong and well ; says she has been very well since she left the hospital ; able to do her housework ; was confined 3½ years ago ; now menstruates regularly : she feels vigorous and active ; her speech is not thick ; she does not feel the cold ; she sweats naturally ; her hair is as thick as it ever was. She continues to take one gr. v. tabloid night and morning.

Recorded in full in the "Edinburgh Hospital Reports," Vol. iii., p. 129.

CASE XI.—*Typical Myxœdema of Three Years' Duration; Intense Mental Depression; Peculiar Susceptibility to the Thyroid Extract; Disappearance of the Myxœdematous Symptoms under Thyroid Treatment; Continuation of the Bodily Prostration and Mental Depression; Acute Tuberculosis; Death a Year After the Commencement of the Thyroid Treatment.*

Female, aged 61, married, seven children and one miscarriage, seen in consultation 17th January 1893, suffering from advanced atrophic myxœdema; confined to bed for several months.

Duration.—3 years.

Apparent cause.—None.

Present condition.—The face was pale, and of a dingy yellow colour; the patient was somewhat anæmic; the eyelids and lower lips were somewhat swollen, but the swelling was less marked than in most typical cases of the disease; there was no pink blush on the cheeks; the hair was scanty, and the scalp covered with dirty crusts and scales; the skin was harsh and dry; the patient never sweated; she complained much of cold; the speech was thick; memory, sight and hearing were somewhat impaired; there was frequent headache; some numbness in hands and feet; she occasionally felt some difficulty in swallowing; fatty swellings were present above the clavicles; the thyroid gland could not be felt. The general state of nutrition was fairly good; the appetite poor; the bowels constipated. The temperature was subnormal (average 95° to 96°); the pulse 60, and very feeble. The patient was very debilitated; mental depression was a very marked symptom. The urine was free from albumen.

Noteworthy and exceptional symptoms.—No pink blush on cheeks, myxœdematous swelling slight, face wrinkled, mental depression very marked, extreme susceptibility to thyroid extract.

Thyroid treatment commenced 18th January 1893.

Preparation and Dose.—Raw gland ($\frac{1}{2}$ daily at first, dose gradually reduced); the patient became extremely susceptible to the remedy, until finally $\frac{1}{3}$th of a tabloid = $\frac{1}{15}$th part of a gland, once a week, was too much.

Immediate results of treatment.—Rapid disappearance of the myxœdema, growth of hair, but increase of bodily and mental depression.

Subsequent progress.—After some months, profuse sweating and diarrhœa, pain in the back, a feeling of heat and flushing all over the body, a sensation as if the head would burst, a marked rise of temperature and pulse; dyspepsia and diarrhœa resulted from the remedy even in small doses.

On several occasions, a minute dose ($\frac{1}{3}$th of a tabloid = $\frac{1}{45}$th part of a sheep's thyroid gland) was administered to the patient without her knowledge. Half an hour after taking this small dose the face became red and flushed, the skin hot, the pulse-rate perceptibly increased, and the temperature elevated (from $\frac{1}{2}$ to 1 degree). This experiment was repeated on different occasions, and always with the same result. During the last two or three months of her illness the susceptibility of the patient to the thyroid extract was so great that Dr Menzies told me that he believed a whole tabloid ($\frac{1}{15}$th of a gland) would have killed her. The remedy had consequently to be discontinued.

Acute phthisis then developed and patient *died on 4th January* 1894.

Post-mortem examination.—Not allowed.

Recorded in full in the "Edinburgh Hospital Reports," Vol. iii., p. 158.

CASE XII.—*Typical Myxœdema of Seven or Eight Years' Duration, but Mental Condition Not At All Impaired; Rapid Disappearance of All the Myxœdematous Symptoms, and Complete Cure under Thyroid Treatment.*

Female, aged 61, married, two children, seen in consultation January 1893, suffering from typical myxœdema.

Duration.—7 or 8 years.

Apparent cause.—None.

Present condition.—The body is bulky, the face broad, the hands spade-like; the feet broad and thick; elastic swellings are present above the clavicles; a well-marked pink blush is present on each cheek; the lips are thick, elastic, and bluish in colour; the skin of the face is of a characteristic dingy yellow colour; the hair is scanty; the skin is extremely rough and dry; the patient never sweats; she complains of always feeling cold; the temperature is always subnormal (97°); the pulse small and weak. The tongue is distinctly swollen; the speech is thick; she says she feels as if she could not get the words out; she occasionally has some difficulty in swallowing; but the throat does not appear to be swollen. Her mental condition is quite active and bright; throughout the whole course of her illness there has never been the least sign of mental impairment; sleep natural. She is very feeble, and slow in her movements. For the past seven years she has been quite unable to attend to her household duties, and has had to have a housekeeper and companion. The urine is free from albumen; the appetite is poor; she occasionally suffers from diarrhœa. The heart's action is very feeble, but the organs appear to be healthy. No thyroid gland can be felt.

Noteworthy and exceptional symptoms.—Mental condition quite active and bright; throughout the whole course of her illness there had never been the least sign of mental impairment; occasional diarrhœa.

Thyroid treatment commenced 23rd January 1893.

Preparation and Dose.—At first raw gland (⅓th daily); afterwards dried extract (gr. v. every second or third day).

Immediate results of treatment.—Rapid improvement and complete disappearance of all the myxœdematous symptoms.

Subsequent progress.—At the end of six months, she felt so well and active that she was able to dismiss the housekeeper and companion whom she had had for seven years, and to undertake all her household duties herself. She looked many years younger than she did before the treatment commenced.

Continues to take gr. v. thyroid extract every third day.

On 27th May 1898 her medical attendant wrote me:—"The patient is quite well both in body and mind, able to do all her household duties herself; takes her food well; her hair has grown in thick and of the natural shade, not grey. She takes one tabloid every second night."

Recorded in full in the "Edinburgh Hospital Reports," Vol. iii., p. 160.

CASE. XIII.—*Typical Myxœdema; Rapid Disappearance of All the Symptoms under Thyroid Treatment.*

Female, aged 50, widow, fifteen children, seen in consultation 26th January 1893, suffering from typical myxœdema.

Duration.—3 years.

Apparent cause.—None; ? cessation of menses.

Present condition.—All the characteristic symptoms of myxœdema are present. The patient complains of debility, and is somewhat anæmic. The body

is bulky; the face is broad and swollen, the lips thick, the eyelids puffy, the
skin of the face of a dingy yellow colour; a pink blush is present on each cheek.
The hair is scanty and dry. The hands are spade-like; the feet large and
swollen. The tongue and buccal mucous membrane are swollen; the speech
thick and slow; the tongue feels too big for the mouth; the patient often experiences a choking sensation when she swallows. Elastic swellings are present
above the clavicles. Her eyes and nose often run, but there is no increased
secretion of saliva. The skin is harsh and dry; she never sweats; the temperature is subnormal; she feels the cold intensely. Her memory, sight, and
hearing are distinctly impaired; she frequently suffers from headache. The
feet swell at night. The heart's action and sounds are feeble, pulse 65. The
appetite poor; bowels constipated. The urine does not contain any albumen.
The thyroid gland cannot be felt.

Thyroid treatment commenced 27th January 1893.

Preparation and Dose.—At first the raw gland (⅓th) twice a week; then 5
grs. of dried extract every other day.

Immediate results of treatment.—In the course of six weeks the myxœdematous symptoms had almost entirely disappeared and the hair was growing.
In the course of six months, the patient was quite well.

Subsequent progress.—The patient has continued quite well. On 3rd
December 1896 she looked many years younger than she previously did. Is
taking one gr. v. tabloid about once a week.

On 15th April 1896 her medical attendant wrote me saying that she was quite
well, and that she still continues to take 5 grs. of the dried extract every other day.

Recorded in full in the "Edinburgh Hospital Reports," Vol. iii., p. 161.

CASE XIV.—*Very Advanced Myxœdema of Thirty-Four Years' Duration in a
Patient aged 73; Decided Improvement under Thyroid Treatment;
Death Two Months after Discharge from Hospital.*

Female, aged 73, widow, seven children, was admitted to the Edinburgh
Royal Infirmary on 3rd June 1893, suffering from typical and advanced myxœdema; for fifteen years almost entirely confined to bed.

Duration.—34 years.

Apparent cause.—None.

Condition on admission.—The case is highly characteristic of myxœdema in
its advanced (atrophic) stage. The swelling, though still considerable, is much
less marked than it was fifteen years ago; the body is very bulky; the hands
and feet swollen; the upper eyelids are more swollen than in any other case of
myxœdema which I have seen. The patient is extremely weak; her movement, speech, and intellectual processes are very slow and deliberate; the memory
is bad. The face is markedly swollen; the upper eyelids completely cover the
balls; when the patient is asked to look at an object, she raises the swollen
lid with the finger, so as to expose the pupil. The lips are large, tense, and
elastic, the lower lip markedly pendulous. The skin of the face has a dingy
yellow tint; a pink blush is present on each cheek. Supraclavicular swellings
are present. The scalp is almost entirely bald, but is not covered with crusts
or scabs. The eyebrows and eyelashes are entirely wanting. The skin is very
harsh, rough, and dry. The patient feels the cold intensely, and never sweats.
She complains that her feet and hands are always cold, and that she frequently
feels as if cold water were being poured down her back. Many flat and stalked
warts are present on different parts of the body. They have for the most part

developed since the disease commenced. A large smooth wart-like projection, the size of a small cherry, protrudes from the gum of the lower jaw, between the incisor teeth. The tongue is large and swollen ; a flat button-like wart projects from the dorsum, close to the tip. The speech is very characteristic, thick, slow, and monotonous, the voice harsh and rough ; the patient says she feels as if the words stuck in her mouth. She has considerable difficulty in swallowing ; the throat is swollen ; saliva flows from the mouth at night. Memory, sight, and hearing are impaired. The temperature is subnormal (average 97°) ; the pulse slow (64) ; the respirations normal (22). There is some ordinary œdema of the feet. The urine contains a slight trace of serum albumen, no globulin, and no casts. The appetite is poor. She sleeps very badly, and is often disturbed by unpleasant dreams. The thyroid gland cannot be felt.

Noteworthy and exceptional symptoms.—In order to see, the patient has to raise the greatly swollen eyelid with the finger ; a large smooth wart-like projection the size of a small cherry protrudes from the gum of the lower jaw, between the incisor teeth ; a flat button-like wart is present on the dorsum of the tongue near the tip.

Thyroid treatment commenced on 5th June 1893.

Preparation and Dose.—B. & M.'s liquid extract, 5-7 minims daily. Strychnine and strophanthus. The thyroid was not well borne and had to be given intermittently.

Immediate results of the treatment.—Faintness, sickness, headache, epigastric pain, diarrhœa, rise in temperature and pulse, difficulty in breathing, marked diminution of the myxœdematous symptoms, growth of hair, some desquamation of skin. Fainting attack when up at stool during the course of treatment.

Date of discharge.—Patient insisted on leaving the hospital on 31st August 1893.

Subsequent progress of case. The myxœdematous symptoms lessened, the hair continued to grow, the diarrhœa continued, patient refused to continue the thyroid. She *died suddenly,* apparently from cardiac syncope, *on 26th November* 1893. Had not taken any thyroid for more than 2 months before death.

Recorded in full in the "Edinburgh Hospital Reports," Vol. iii., p. 143.

CASE XV.—*Typical Myxœdema ; Rapid Disappearance of All the Symptoms under Thyroid Treatment.*

Female, aged 51, married, seven children, seen 24th June 1893, suffering from typical myxœdema. She brought her daughter to consult me, and was surprised when I told her she herself was suffering from a definite disease (myxœdema) ; she thought her condition was due to "fat and debility."

Duration.—20 years.

Apparent cause. None.

Present condition.—The patient complained of debility, and was somewhat anæmic. Supraclavicular swellings large. The body was very bulky ; the face, hands, feet, and abdomen swollen. Her eyelids were swollen ; the skin of the face dingy yellow in colour ; a pink blush was present on each cheek ; the lips were thick, elastic, and of a bluish colour; the tongue large ; the throat swollen. The hair was scanty ; the scalp not encrusted ; the skin dry. The patient stated that she felt the cold intensely, and never sweated. The temperature was subnormal. The speech was thick and characteristic. The memory was bad. The feet and legs were œdematous. The appetite poor ; the bowels constipated. The urine was free from albumen. The pulse was small and weak; the heart sounds very feeble, and the cardiac impulse imperceptible, probably the result, in part at least, of the thickness of the chest walls; the pulse slow (58). The thyroid gland could not be felt.

Noteworthy and Exceptional Symptoms.—An extremely stout woman.

Thyroid treatment commenced 30th June 1893.

Preparation and Dose.—Liquid extract (D. & F.'s) ʒi ter die (= ⅓th gland).

Immediate results of treatment.—Rapid disappearance of myxœdematous symptoms; lost 1 st. 5 lbs. during the treatment. Says she looks and feels a different person, so active and energetic.

Subsequent progress.—*On 19th April* 1898, she wrote me saying that she was keeping well though short of breath; she had had one attack of dyspnœa (apparently cardiac) through the night; she had discontinued the tabloids for about 4 months, but had to begin them again as she felt she was getting stouter; she now takes two 5 grain tabloids twice or thrice a week; her present weight is 15½ st.

Recorded in full in the "Edinburgh Hospital Reports," Vol. iii., p. 172.

CASE XVI.—*Typical Myxœdema of Two Years' Duration; Rapid Disappearance of All the Myxœdematous Symptoms under Thyroid Treatment.*

Female, aged 60, married, five children, seen in consultation on 25th July 1893, suffering from typical myxœdema.

Duration.—About 2 years.

Apparent cause.—None.

Present condition.—The appearance is highly characteristic. The body is bulky, the face moon-shaped, the hands spade-like, the feet broad, the abdomen large and pendulous, the eyelids markedly swollen (bags of fluid), the lips thick and elastic, and of a bluish tint, the hair scanty, the scalp covered with dirty brown crusts. A pink blush is present on each cheek. The tongue is very large, and the buccal mucous membrane swollen; the speech is very thick, the memory impaired, the cerebration slow; she sleeps well. The skin is harsh and dry, and of a dingy yellow colour. The patient states that she feels the cold intensely, and that she never sweats. She feels very debilitated, and unequal to any exertion. Large elastic swellings are present above the clavicles. The temperature is subnormal (97° to 97°.8). The feet swell at night. The appetite is poor; the bowels regular. The urine is free from albumen. The radial pulse is 76, and of good strength. The aortic second sound is markedly accentuated. The thyroid gland cannot be felt.

Thyroid treatment commenced 26th July 1898.

Preparation and Dose.—Raw gland (⅓th) every other day.

Immediate results of treatment.—Rapid improvement; in the course of three months the myxœdematous symptoms had completely disappeared.

Subsequent progress.—The patient has continued in excellent health.

On 10th April 1898 she wrote me:—"I have much pleasure in stating that my health has been pretty good for some time back; but I find that the thyroid has to be taken regularly once a week, otherwise the old symptoms become noticeable. I have been in the habit of taking either the half of a small or the third of a large one (lobe). For several weeks, however, I have felt the necessity of taking that quantity twice in the week. I have not been so much troubled with sickness as formerly, and though not feeling very strong (patient is 65 years of age) my health has been pretty fair."

Recorded in full in the "Edinburgh Hospital Reports," Vol. iii., p. 163.

Z

CASE XVII.—*Typical Myxœdema, following Exophthalmic Goitre; Disappearance of the Myxœdematous Symptoms under Thyroid Treatment.*

Female, aged 55, single, seen in consultation 5th August 1893, suffering from typical myxœdema.

Duration.—2 years; had previously suffered for 6 years from typical exophthalmic goitre and heart.

Apparent cause.—Atrophy of the thyroid gland following exophthalmic goitre.

Present condition.—The patient complains of debility and loss of mental vigour; she is distinctly anæmic. The eyelids are markedly swollen, bags of fluid are present below the eyes; the lips are full and thick; the skin of the face is of a yellow tinge; a pink blush is present on each cheek; the eyebrows are scanty and elevated; the hair of the head is thinner than it used to be. Elastic swellings are present above the clavicles. The thyroid gland cannot be felt. The patient states that she usually feels chilly, and is more susceptible to cold than she used to be; but that several times in the course of the day a feeling of heat and flushing passes over her. She states that she is very easily tired, and unfit for any exertion. Her memory is bad; she sleeps well; frequent headache. The tongue is enlarged; the speech highly characteristic— thick and slow. The skin is harsh and dry. She does not sweat. The hands are swollen; she is obliged to wear larger gloves than she did a year ago. The feet are broad, and there is some ordinary œdema of the ankles. The abdomen and body generally are much swollen. The temperature is subnormal. The menstruation ceased ten years ago. The urine is free from albumen. The heart's action is natural, except that the first sound appears to be reduplicated; the pulse 70; still occasionally has palpitation. The appetite is poor; the bowels constipated.

Noteworthy and exceptional symptoms.—The thyroid gland cannot be felt; several times a day a feeling of heat and flushing passes over her, though she usually feels chilly and is more susceptible to cold than she used to be.

Thyroid treatment commenced 6th August 1893.

Preparation and Dose.—Dried extract, gr. v. daily.

Immediate results of treatment.—Rapid disappearance of the myxœdematous symptoms; desquamation of the skin and growth of hair.

Subsequent progress.—*7th May* 1895.—Continues perfectly well; the only thing she complains of is the unpleasant feeling of heat and flushing which passes over the body sometimes twenty times a day.

9th April 1898.—Though 60 years of age does not look more than 45. For the past year has been dyspeptic and troubled with her heart, but otherwise quite well. The flushings continue. She continues to take one tabloid (gr. v. of dried extract) every other day.

Recorded in full in the "Edinburgh Hospital Reports," Vol. iii., p. 170.

CASE XVIII.—*Imperfectly Developed Myxœdema; Rapid Improvement under Thyroid Treatment.*

Female, aged 67, married, six children, consulted me on 11th October 1893, suffering from slight myxœdema.

Duration.—Probably 3 or 4 years; worse for 6 months.

Apparent cause.—None.

Present condition.—The patient complained of giddiness, an uneasy feeling in the head, lassitude, debility, loss of appetite, uneasiness in the region of the stomach, and dimness of vision. The face was pale, the eyelids were distinctly puffy and swollen; the urine was, and always had been, free from albumen; the skin was harsh and dry; the patient had become very susceptible to cold, and did not perspire as she used to do. The hair of the head and eyebrows had got markedly thinner. Physical examination failed to reveal evidence of disease in any of the viscera.

Thyroid treatment commenced 12th October 1893.

Preparation and Dose.—Liquid extract (D. & F.'s) ʒss. ter die (= ¹⁄₁₂ of a gland); subsequently dried extract (gr. v.) daily.

Immediate results of treatment.—Marked and rapid improvement.

Subsequent progress.—*On 8th April* 1898 her doctor wrote me—"Patient continues in fairly good health; she goes out walking most days, and is bright and cheerful. I have just been attending her for a fairly smart attack of influenza from which she has made a good recovery. Continues to take one thyroid tabloid (5 grs.) every day; if she ceases taking them she misses them."

Recorded in full in the "Edinburgh Hospital Reports," Vol. iii., p. 174.

CASE XIX.—*Typical Myxœdema; Rapid Disappearance of All the Symptoms under Thyroid Feeding.*

Female, aged 40, widow, six children, seen in consultation on 9th January 1894, suffering from typical myxœdema.

Duration.—3 or 4 years.

Apparent cause.—None.

Present condition.—She complains of a feeling of great languor and depression, weakness and inability to exert herself. She says that she feels scarcely able to walk across the floor, she is getting so heavy and weak. There is some anæmia. The body, abdomen, face, hands, and feet are much larger than they used to be; supraclavicular swellings well marked; tongue large; throat swollen. The eyelids and lips are swollen. The skin of the face is yellow in colour; a slight pink blush is present on each cheek. The hair is thin and scanty, and much darker than it used to be; skin also darker. The skin is very rough; she no longer perspires as she used to do. She feels the cold very much; her temperature is subnormal. Appetite poor; bowels very much constipated. Her memory is much impaired; she sleeps well. The voice is much rougher and harsher than it used to be; the articulation is slow and thick. Menorrhagia; urine normal. Thyroid gland cannot be felt.

Noteworthy and exceptional symptoms.—Skin and hair became markedly darker as disease advanced.

Thyroid treatment commenced 10th January 1894.

Preparation and Dose.—Dried extract; at first gr. x. daily; after five days, reduced to gr. v. every other day. The larger dose produced severe aching pains in the head, back, and limbs and in the position of the thyroid.

Immediate results of treatment. — Rapid disappearance of all the myxœdematous symptoms and complete restoration of health.

Subsequent progress.—*On 22nd May* 1895, when I next saw the patient, I did not know her. She says she feels perfectly well. She states that her skin is much darker than it used to be (Dr Lundie confirms this), and that her hair is so much darker that her sister said to one of the children, "What! is your mother dyeing her hair?" Her hair is now quite black; it used to be dark brown in colour. She showed me a specimen of the hair cut off twelve years ago; it was then nut-brown in colour. The contrast between the present black and the former brown is very striking. Since she commenced to take the thyroid, her hair has got much thicker; it is also much softer than it used to be. The nipples are not any darker than they used to be.

She states that during the past eighteen months she has twice omitted to take the tabloids for some weeks at a time, but has always been obliged to return to them again. After omitting the remedy for a month, she on both occasions began to suffer from the old symptoms. She felt on each occasion as if there was something at the bottom of the throat (placing her hand over the region of the thyroid) which ought to come away. For the last four months she has taken one thyroid tabloid every other day.

12th April 1898.—Called to see me to-day. Looks quite well. Says she has been perfectly well ever since the last note ; able to do hard work both of body and mind ; her skin is quite smooth, but the skin and hair continue to get darker ; she still feels the cold a good deal ; menstruation regular, but much more profuse than it used to be. About a year ago left off the thyroid for a month, and felt the same pain and choking feeling in the throat that she used to have; it passed off as soon as she again resumed the medicine. Is taking 2 or 3 tabloids a week.

Recorded in full in the "Edinburgh Hospital Reports," Vol. iii., p. 185.

CASE XX.—*Typical Myxœdema ; Temporary Paralysis of the Right External Rectus Muscle ; Rapid Improvement, and Disappearance of the Myxœdematous Symptoms under Thyroid Treatment.*

Female, aged 60, married, two children, seen in consultation 4th April 1894, suffering from typical myxœdema.

Duration.—2 years at least.

Apparent cause.—None.

Present condition. — The right external rectus was partly paralysed ; the double vision developed suddenly, and without obvious cause.

The case presented all the characteristic symptoms of myxœdema. The patient complained of great debility. The body was bulky ; the abdomen, hands, and feet were enlarged. There was some anæmia. The face was swollen, the skin of a dingy yellow hue, the eyelids puffy, the lips were thick and firm, the tongue large, the speech deliberate and thick. There was no pink blush on the cheeks. The tongue was large. Elastic swellings were present above the clavicles. The eyebrows were very scanty, and the hair of the head thin, it had been coming out for the past two years; the scalp was covered with dirty brown crusts, the skin generally harsh and dry. The patient stated that she felt the cold much more than she used to do a few years ago, and that she never sweated. The temperature was subnormal (97.4° F.) ; the radial pulse 80, and of good strength ; the aortic second sound accentuated. Her memory was impaired, and her cerebration slow ; sight and hearing impaired ; sleep natural. The urine was free from albumen. The optic discs were natural. The appetite was poor ; bowels constipated. There was no evidence of any intracranial or other visceral disease. The thyroid gland could not be felt.

Noteworthy and exceptional symptoms.—Temporary paralysis of the right external rectus muscle.

Thyroid treatment commenced 5th April 1894.

Preparation and Dose.—Dried extract ; at first gr. v. afterwards gr. x., daily.

Immediate results of treatment.—In the course of a fortnight the dyspepsia and paralysis of the external rectus disappeared and all the myxœdematous symptoms rapidly disappeared.

Subsequent progress.—*2nd January* 1898.—Patient seen to-day and looks a very young woman for her age. She tells me that she has been perfectly well since the treatment was commenced. She says the result has been wonderful. She was blind and deaf and had lost her hair ; these symptoms have all disappeared. She has taken the thyroid from time to time, but not regularly. Advised to take half a tabloid (gr. 2½ of dried extract) every day.

Recorded in full in the "Edinburgh Hospital Reports," Vol. iii., p. 175.

CASE XXI.—*Typical Myxœdema ; Rapid Disappearance of All the Symptoms under Thyroid Treatment.*

Female, aged 31, married, five children, seen in consultation 9th May 1894, suffering from typical myxœdema.

Duration.—3 years.

Apparent cause.— None.

Present condition.—The patient complains of weakness, and says that she is unfit for any exertion. She feels the cold very much more than she used to do, and is always worse in winter. She is distinctly anæmic. The face, hands, feet, abdomen, and body generally are swollen. The lower lids are puffy; the lips large, swollen, and thick ; the skin of the face of a dingy yellow colour ; a pink blush is present on each cheek. Supraclavicular swellings present. The hair of the head is very dry and harsh ; the scalp dry and dirty ; the skin is remarkably harsh and dry ; on the face, hands, knees, and legs it is so rough, that when the finger is passed over it it feels like a file. The patient states that for some time past she has never sweated, and that she always feels cold. The speech is thick, the tongue large ; she often has a choking feeling, as if the tongue were too large for the mouth ; the throat swollen. At night the saliva often flows out of the mouth, "because," she says, "it does not go down." The memory is not impaired; she sleeps well. The appetite is poor ; the bowels constipated. The temperature is subnormal (98° F.) ; the pulse 70, and weak. The urine is free from albumen ; the menstruation regular. The thyroid gland cannot be felt.

Noteworthy and exceptional symptoms.—Increased flow of saliva from the mouth at night.

Thyroid treatment commenced 9th May 1894.

Preparation and Dose.—Dried extract gr. v. daily, increased to gr. x. for a time.

Immediate effects of treatment.—Rapid disappearance of all of the myxœdematous symptoms and restoration of health and strength.

Subsequent progress.—*On 2nd January* 1898, her doctor wrote me :—"The patient has continued quite well ; she had a child lately and lost much blood after delivery; this has pulled her down a good deal, but she has picked up again since. She continues to take one tabloid (gr. v. thyroid extract) every other day."

Recorded in full in the "Edinburgh Hospital Reports," Vol. iii., p. 176.

CASE XXII. — *Typical Myxœdema ; Rapid Disappearance of all the Myxœdematous Symptoms under Thyroid Treatment.*

Female, aged 60, widow, nine children, was seen as an out-patient at the Edinburgh Royal Infirmary on 7th July 1894, suffering from typical myxœdema. Her appearance was so characteristic that while she was standing at the end of a long passage (away from me at a distance of 60 feet) I said to my assistant Dr Douglas, "That old lady looks as if she had myxœdema."

Duration.—3 years.

Apparent cause.—None.

Condition on admission.—The patient complains of great debility. The body is very bulky; abdomen, hands, and feet enlarged. The face is broad, swollen, and of a dingy yellow colour; the lips are thick, elastic, and tense; the eyelids are so markedly swollen that all of the students who saw the patient came to the conclusion that she was suffering from Bright's disease; a pink flush is present on each cheek. The buccal mucous membrane is anæmic. Large elastic swellings are present above each clavicle. The hair is scanty; the scalp covered with dirty brown crusts; the skin is very dry and harsh; the patient states that she never sweats; she says that she always feels cold, and that when the room is so hot that other people complain of the heat, she only feels comfortable. The temperature is subnormal. The speech is thick, and highly characteristic. The tongue is large and the throat swollen; the patient complains of difficulty of swallowing. The memory, sight, and hearing are considerably impaired. The appetite is poor; the bowels constipated. The urine contains a considerable quantity of albumen, but no casts; its specific gravity is 1008. The thyroid gland cannot be felt.

Noteworthy and exceptional symptoms.—The urine contained a considerable quantity of albumen but no casts.

Thyroid treatment commenced 8th July 1894.

Preparation and Dose.—Five grains of dried extract daily.

Immediate results of treatment.—Complete disappearance of all the myxœdematous symptoms, free desquamation of skin, growth of hair, etc.

Subsequent progress.—*10th May* 1895.—Looks 10 years younger; all the myxœdematous symptoms have disappeared. Stated :—"Every one that sees me could not believe it was me, such a change." Can now do her housework; was not able to do this for 10 years previously. Advised to continue gr. v. of the dried extract every other day; also arsenic and iron as is anæmic.

9th April 1898.—Seen to-day. Says she has been keeping very well since last seen until 3 weeks ago; she then left off the tabloids and has not taken them since. Has felt a return of the old symptoms—languor, numbness in legs, swelling of abdomen and face. Has on several previous occasions left off the tabloids for a week, but always had to resume them again because she did not feel so well. One tabloid (gr. v.) every night keeps her in good health. Lower lip to-day rather swollen; head still scaly; otherwise seems all right. Advised to resume the thyroid at once and take it regularly.

Recorded in full in the "Edinburgh Hospital Reports," Vol. iii., p. 150.

CASE XXIII.—*Commencing Myxœdema, Complicated with Diarrhœa; Rapid Improvement under Thyroid Treatment.*

Male, aged 66, married, seen in consultation on 8th August 1894, suffering from myxœdema.

Duration.—Several (probably 7) years.

Apparent cause.—Mental shock.

Present condition.—The patient complains of debility, and inability to undergo either physical or mental exertion. His face is pale and sallow looking, the lower eyelids markedly swollen, the lips thick, swollen, and slightly blue; his hair has been getting thinner lately; his speech is distinctly slow and thick, but he has not himself noticed that it is different to what it used to be when he was well. His hands and feet are larger than they used to be. The skin is thick and coarse, but he says that he perspires easily on exertion. He complains that he feels the cold much more than he used to do; he says that he never feels warm even in summer. The temperature is normal. His eyes and nose frequently run. His memory and hearing are impaired; sleeps excessively. The tongue is large, the throat somewhat œdematous, the appetite poor, the bowels frequently loose. The urine is free from albumen; it contains a slight trace of sugar. No thyroid gland can be felt.

The case was not typical, but some of the symptoms, notably the swelling of the face, hands, and body generally, the increased thickness and roughness of the skin, the increased sensibility to cold, and loss of hair, were highly suggestive of commencing myxœdema.

Noteworthy and exceptional symptoms. — Occasional attacks of severe diarrhœa; perspires on exertion; urine contains a trace of sugar.

Thyroid treatment commenced on 9th August 1894. Also salicylate of bismuth for diarrhœa.

Preparation and Dose.—Dried extract, gr. v. daily.

Immediate results of treatment.—Rapid improvement. On 20th August was better than he had been for 6 months previously.

Subsequent progress.—*On 14th May* 1895, the patient wrote to me :—" I saw Dr Miller yesterday, and he suggested that I should write out a statement of my case, which I do so much the more willingly that I consider myself, and those whose breadwinner I am, under very great obligation to you. This is the state I was in just about a year ago :—

To begin at the top. My hair was getting fluffy, and coming out rapidly. My eyes were constantly weeping, and my nose running. I had great bags under my eyes, and my cheeks were puffy and hanging, bobbing up and down as I walked along. My whole body was enormously swollen, especially my hands, which I could scarcely shut, and my legs from the knee downwards. My legs were so heavy that I had literally to drag them along. Once at Birnam, thinking I was going to miss the train, I tried to run; the impetus sent my body forward, but the legs would not go—result, a very heavy fall. For at least two years, but especially during the last year of my illness, I suffered very much from cramp. If I did not lie straight in bed, if I put up my feet to get my boots laced (I had got terribly awkward in stooping), or going downstairs, my legs got terribly cramped; you could quite distinctly *see*, sticking out under my trousers, in the front part of my thighs, lumps as big as a large egg. These cramps have now entirely disappeared. I had a terrible catarrh; every time I coughed or sneezed I felt intense pain, as if my inside were being torn to shreds. The action of the heart was very unsatisfactory; it took me two hours one day to walk, panting and puffing, from Broughty Ferry to Monifieth—2½ miles—whereas I used quite easily to walk 4 miles an hour. Always, after about ten minutes' walk, my left arm got perfectly benumbed, quite dead. My hands and my lips were constantly blue, my feet always intensely cold, the heels very painfully so, as if they were plunged in ice-water. The skin on my heels grew to an abnormal thickness; I used to pare it with a big iron file. I was frequently obliged to make water— had always to get up twice during the night. A heavy torpid sleep two hours and a half after dinner; no sooner in bed than I was asleep. Sometimes stayed in bed on Sunday, sleeping the whole day, and all the time a tremendous snore which could be heard all over the house. (Never used to snore before.) Finally, a terrible diarrhœa, which began about the middle of August 1894, and culminated towards June in five or six stools a day, perfectly liquid, the smell of the evacution being most offensive. I got so weak that I frequently staggered across the pavement like one drunk. The Rev. Mr —— told me a few days ago that one day he said to his astonished family, 'If I did not know Mr D. to be a sober man, I should say he was drunk this afternoon.' He had seen me in one of my staggers. I was under the impression, until a few days ago, that my mind had not been affected, but it seems I was wrong. Dr Miller told me he noticed that I was getting slow in taking up an idea, and slow in expressing myself. I was also getting deaf. Dr M'Bride, whom I consulted on 18th October 1894, told me that my deafness arose from the myxœdema, and would be cured by the tabloids, and my hearing is decidedly better.

I commenced your treatment on the 10th of August. By the end of the month I was, I may say, well. The swelling of my body was fast disappearing, and then the terrible drain on my system (diarrhœa) began to show itself; there was nothing left of me but skin and bone. My strength returned rapidly. All the ugly symptoms mentioned above have disappeared, and Saturday three weeks ago I played two rounds on the Monifieth links with a young and strong player, a fast walker, and *improved considerably in the second round.* I still continue the tabloids, one every other night.

I fancy my illness must have been brewing for years. So far as I can recollect, the bags under my eyes, which have now quite disappeared, began to form about seven years ago; then I got eczema, and finally myxœdema."

On 10th April 1898, patient again wrote :—"I continue taking the tabloids, generally three times a week, one at a time. There seems to be no trace of myxœdema about me, I am looking remarkably well and vigorous; the only unfavourable symptom is that my hands are frequently blue. You may recollect that when I first consulted you I was terribly bloated; at the end of three weeks under your treatment, all that puffing had gone down and I weighed exactly ten stone, which, for a man of 5 ft. 9½ ins., broad-shouldered and deep-chested, is uncommonly little. Now I weigh 12 st. 4 lbs., all healthy substantial stuff. I am extremely obliged to you for the interest you are taking in my wellbeing, and infinitely grateful to you. There is not the slightest doubt in my mind that if I had not consulted you when I did, I should not have lived another two months."

Recorded in full in the "Edinburgh Hospital Reports," Vol. iii., p. 178.

CASE XXIV.—*Typical Myxœdema; Rapid Disappearance of All the Symptoms under Thyroid Feeding.*

Male, aged 36, married, consulted me on 14th November 1894, suffering from typical myxœdema. Though a medical man, the patient was surprised when I told him without asking any questions that he was suffering from myxœdema.

Duration.—6 years.

Apparent cause.—None.

Present condition.—The patient is a tall, big-made man. He weighs 16 st. 7 lbs.; he has increased rapidly in weight of late. Three months ago he only weighed 15 st. His appearance is most characteristic. His face is broad and round (moon-shaped): the lips are very thick; the lower lids are markedly swollen (bags of fluid beneath the eyes); a pink blush is present on each cheek; the eyebrows and hair of the head are scanty; the skin of the face has a dingy yellow colour. The hands are very broad and large; the feet and legs and body generally swollen. No fatty swellings are present above the clavicles. The tongue is very large; the throat œdematous; the speech thick and slow. The skin is very harsh and dry; the patient states that he never sweats, and that he feels the cold intensely; his hands are always icy cold. The temperature is subnormal. He feels so debilitated that he can hardly walk; his mental power and memory are markedly impaired; he feels unfit for exertion either of body or mind. He says that he is always dreadfully sleepy; he can hardly keep his eyes open when he is doing his rounds; whenever he gets into his gig he drops off to sleep. The appetite is poor; the bowels regular. The abdomen measures at the umbilicus 38 in.; the chest, at the level of the nipples, 37 in.; the neck, round the middle, 17 in. He is short of breath on exertion, and frequently suffers from palpitation. On waking "he always feels a tremendous sensation of oppression in the region of the heart." He wakes up several times through the night with this horrible feeling of oppression, and great difficulty of breathing. On physical examination, the heart appeared to be normal. A specimen of urine passed in my consulting-room was of specific gravity 1010; it contained a very decided quantity of albumen, but no sugar or casts. I may here say that the albumen was merely temporary, and only present after meals. Many specimens were subsequently examined. The thyroid gland cannot be felt.

Noteworthy and exceptional symptoms.—Very sleepy, especially when driving in his gig; frequent palpitation; on waking, he always feels "a tremendous sensation of oppression in the region of the heart"; he wakes up several times through the night with this horrible feeling of oppression, and great difficulty of breathing; heart normal.

Thyroid treatment commenced 15th November 1894.

Preparation and Dose.—Dried extract; 1 to 3 tabloids daily.

Immediate results of treatment.—Rapid disappearance of the myxœdematous symptoms; maximum loss of weight during the treatment 2 st.

Subsequent progress.—The patient has continued quite well.

On 22nd March 1895 (four months after the commencement of the treatment) he wrote me :—"The truth is, life seems and feels quite a different thing now. When I compare myself now with what I was when I left off work, I am indeed a different man. I am taking a tabloid every other night at bedtime, and am taking as much care of myself as possible. I have ceased to look for and expect swelling of my legs, and am not short of breath now. I stood the intense cold, which we have recently had, as well as my neighbours, I think; and where I was staying we had for some time a register of 13° below zero. My feet and hands skinned freely. My hair is now as thick as ever it was, and I do not feel the cold now. In fact, I feel quite well—better and different from what I have been for years. When I resumed work, many people did not know me. I feel very grateful to you for putting me in the way of wellbeing."

On 1st March 1898, the patient again wrote :—"I am well, and enjoy life and active work—night or day, and I have plenty of both. I drive without unduly feeling the cold as I used to, and I cycle a lot and enjoy it. Life is one long pleasure after previous years of illness. The struggle was something fearful when I look back upon it. Perhaps I am a trifle heavy—in weight I mean—but I am convinced it is not myxœdematous swelling, simply obesity.

I take one five-grain tabloid of Burroughs & Wellcome every night."

Recorded in full in the "Edinburgh Hospital Reports," Vol. iii., p. 181.

CASE XXV.—*Typical Myxœdema Treated by Thyroid Extract; Large Dose Required to Produce the Full Therapeutic Effect; Disappearance of the Myxœdematous Symptoms; No Increase in the Amount of Urine under the Treatment.*

Female, aged 33, married, no children, admitted to the Edinburgh Royal Infirmary, 19th November 1894, suffering from typical myxœdema.

Duration.—3 years.

Apparent cause.—None.

Condition on Admission.—Height, 5 ft 1¼ in.; weight, 12 st. Most of the characteristic symptoms of myxœdema are well developed. The body is bulky; the face is swollen; the lips are full, thick, elastic, and of a bluish colour; the eyelids are swollen, a faint pink blush is present on each cheek; the skin of the forehead is pigmented; the tongue is large and thick, and the buccal mucous membrane and uvula œdematous. The abdomen is much swollen; the hands are much larger than formerly (the patient states that she is now unable to get gloves sufficiently large to fit her); she says that she is unable to make fine movements with the fingers because of the feeling of stiffness and swelling. There is no difficulty in swallowing, but she states that she occasionally feels an obstruction at the back of the throat; the articulation is slow, monotonous, and thick; there is no loss of hair (it is abundant and dark on the scalp). The skin is exceedingly rough and dry; on the forearms it is so rough that on touching it one is reminded of a piece of sandpaper; the patient says that since her illness commenced she has only once perspired, and that was after a heavy day's washing, in a hot, moist wash-house. The palms of her hands are the only parts which are moist. She feels the cold much more intensely than she used to do; the temperature is subnormal (97°). Elastic swellings are present above the clavicles. The patient complains of a numb feeling in the fingers, but the objective sensibility to touch, pain, heat, and cold is unimpaired. She often complains of a frontal headache. She thinks slowly. Her memory has become impaired. The patient has not noticed that she is worse in winter than in summer. The mucous membranes are well coloured; the hæmoglobin = 66 per cent. The menstruation is regular; it is, and always has been, profuse. The amount of urine is scanty; she says that she only makes water twice during the twenty-four hours, and only passes a small quantity at a time. The specific gravity is 1018. It deposits a thick cloud of mucus, but contains no albumen and no sugar. The urea was estimated every day; the amount varied from 4 to 6 grs. to the oz. The heart sounds are weak; the pulse slow (63 per minute); tension good. The appetite is fair; digestion good; no constipation. The thyroid gland cannot be felt.

Noteworthy and exceptional symptoms.—Patient's knee excised for "white swelling" in childhood.

Family history.—Two sisters deaf-mutes.

Thyroid treatment commenced 13th December 1894.

Preparation and Dose.—B. & W.'s solid extract; one tabloid (gr.v.), gradually increased to 14 tabloids (70 grs.) per diem. Strychnine.

Immediate results of treatment.—Sickness, vomiting, loss of appetite, furred tongue, severe frontal headache, large deposit of mucus in urine, profuse perspiration, rise of temperature and pulse, slight jaundice, disappearance of myxœdematous symptoms, desquamation of skin, large deposit of urates in urine, no increase of the amount of urine.

Date of discharge.—24th January 1895; the myxœdematous symptoms have completely disappeared; her appearance has quite changed; she says she feels like a new person—"so much more active." Maximum loss of weight during the treatment, 2 st.

After her discharge from the Infirmary she continued to take the thyroid regularly for more than a year, and during the whole of this time kept well. She then discontinued the drug for several months and gradually fell back, all the old symptoms returning.

During May, June and July 1897 she was as bad as ever and confined to bed for the greater part of the day. At the end of July, she again commenced the thyroid, at first 3, then 4 tabloids daily; the symptoms rapidly disappeared, and since then she "has been in splendid health, better than ever since her illness commenced six years ago."

Seen *8th April* 1898.—She looks remarkably well; there is absolutely no appearance of myxœdema. She states that since the end of July she has been in splendid health. She is now taking two tabloids daily; one does not seem to be sufficient. She is able to do all her housework (she had not done this for three years before admission to the Infirmary); she does not feel the cold; she sweats naturally and feels vigorous and strong.

Recorded in full in the "Edinburgh Hospital Reports," Vol. iii., p. 152.

CASE XXVI.—*Typical Myxœdema: Complete Disappearance of All the Myxœdematous Symptoms under Thyroid Treatment.*

Female, aged 42, widow, four children, seen in consultation on 11th March 1895, suffering from typical myxœdema.

Duration.—3 years.

Apparent cause.—None.

Present condition.—The patient complains of great languor and debility, of loss of memory, and extreme sensitiveness to cold. She is somewhat anæmic. Her appearance, she says, is so much altered that many of her friends and acquaintances have failed to recognise her when she meets them. She used to have very fine features. The skin of the face has a yellow tinge; there is no pink blush on the cheeks. Her face is now decidedly puffy-looking, almost twice as full, she says, as it used to be; the lower lip is thick, the tongue much larger than it used to be. There are fatty swellings above the clavicles. The hands and feet are also considerably swollen. The abdomen is markedly enlarged. The speech is characteristically thick. She says that her memory is much impaired, that she always feels sleepy, and that she is always worse in cold weather; she feels the cold intensely; during the whole of last summer she had to wear her fur cloak in addition to her winter flannels, and yet she never could get warm; the temperature is subnormal. The skin is very harsh and dry, and the patient has, for the last three years, ceased to sweat. Hair much thinner and darker in colour. The pulse is slow, 56 per minute; the temperature subnormal. The appetite poor; bowels constipated. The urine does not contain albumen; amenorrhœa for two years. The thyroid gland cannot be felt.

Noteworthy and exceptional symptoms.—Since her illness commenced her hair has become black; it used to be brown; the change was so great that her brother thought she was dyeing it. Menstruation returned under the treatment. After the myxœdematous symptoms were removed became melancholic.

Thyroid treatment commenced 3rd March 1895.

Preparation and Dose.—Liquid extract (D. & F.'s) ʒi. (= ⅓ of a gland) daily, afterwards increased to ʒiii. daily.

Immediate results of treatment. — Marked and rapid improvement; free desquamation.

Subsequent progress.—*On 16th May* 1895, the patient called to see me and I did not recognise her. She said that she felt a different being; before the treatment was commenced she was unable to do anything; her memory and mental powers were so much impaired that in the course of four weeks she was unable to get through the first volume of a three-volume novel; she could not remember what she had read, or where she had left off. Now her memory and mental powers are quite as active and alert as they ever were. She has read, she says, a large number of books of all kinds during the past month or six weeks, and remembers what she reads. She was advised to protect herself from cold and to take 1 tabloid (5 grs. of the dried extract) daily.

15th December 1895.—For the past two or three months the patient has been in a very depressed condition of mind, taking a very morbid view of things, saying she is tired of life, etc.—she is in fact in a condition of marked melancholia. The myxœdematous symptoms have completely disappeared; she perspires very freely on the least exertion; she continues to take 5 grs. of thyroid extract daily. A change of scene, with proper nursing, and a course of tonics were prescribed. This treatment was quite successful.

On 6th April 1898, her medical adviser wrote me :—"Patient is very well indeed in every respect. I have not seen her professionally for a long time. The other day, however, she told me that she still continues to take one 5-grain tabloid daily; if she omits it she does not feel well."

Recorded in full in the "Edinburgh Hospital Reports," Vol. iii., p. 187.

CASE XXVII.—*Typical Myxœdema of the Atrophic Form; Great Prostration Produced by the Thyroid Treatment.*

Female, aged 50, married, three children, seen in consultation 14th May 1895, suffering from advanced atrophic myxœdema.

Duration.—12 years.

Apparent cause.—None. Ten years ago she lost a good deal of blood after the pulling of a tooth; this aggravated the condition, which seems to have increased rapidly afterwards. She ceased to menstruate three years ago. For some time previously she suffered from profuse menorrhagia.

Present condition.—The patient's appearance is so typical that I recognised the condition at the first glance, without having asked her any question. The skin of the face is of a dingy yellow colour; there is a pink blush on the cheeks; the hair on the scalp is very thin, and the scalp is covered with dirty scales and crusts. She is somewhat anæmic. There is slight puffiness under the eyes, and the lower lip is a little full, elastic-feeling, and blue in colour; but the myxœdematous swelling of the face is very slight, and there is no swelling of the hands or feet. There are no elastic swellings above the clavicles. The skin is remarkably harsh and dry; the face is very much wrinkled. The patient says that she never sweats, that she is very sensitive to cold, and that she is very much worse during the cold weather; she stood the intense cold of the past winter very badly, and has been much worse since. Her appetite is very poor; the bowels are constipated. The temperature is subnormal; pulse 72; heart's action weak. The speech is highly characteristic, slow and thick; the patient often feels a choking sensation in the throat. The skin of the fingers is remarkably dry, the nails very small and narrow. The memory is very much impaired; the patient is very slow in her mental processes as well as in her movements, and at times is very depressed. She sleeps badly; often has headache; complains of numbness in hands and feet. The urine is free from albumen. The thyroid gland could not be felt. The condition of this patient, both physical and mental, reminded me strongly of Case XI.; and it is very interesting to note that both of these patients were peculiarly susceptible to the action of the remedy.

Noteworthy and exceptional symptoms.—Little myxœdematous swelling, but all the other symptoms of the disease very marked; face and hands wrinkled; mental depression; marked susceptibility to thyroid extract.

Thyroid treatment commenced 15th May 1895.

Preparation and Dose.—Dry extract; five grains and then ten grains daily. The latter dose upset the stomach and produced great depression and debility; had to be stopped for a time. On 4th June, resumed the remedy, 1 tabloid (gr. v.) at first every third and subsequently every day.

Immediate results of treatment.—Gradual and marked improvement.

Subsequent progress.—*On 8th April* 1898, the patient called to see me, looking very much better, brighter and younger. She told me that since the treatment was commenced three years ago she has been on the whole very well, a great deal stronger, more active and mentally brighter than she had been for 10 or 12 years. The pink blush on the cheeks has disappeared, the face is much less wrinkled; the scalp is still scurfy, the skin still rather harsh and dry. She no longer feels the cold. She continues to take 2 tabloids (10 grains of the extract) daily; she is much less susceptible to the remedy than when the treatment was commenced. On several occasions during the past three years she has discontinued the remedy for a few weeks at a time; but always had to resume it in the course of a short time as she soon began to notice a return of the myxœdematous symptoms (weakness, coldness, increased bulk of the body, roughness of the skin), etc.

Recorded in full in the " Edinburgh Hospital Reports," Vol. iii., p. 190.

CASE XXVIII.—*Acute Myxœdema with Marked Symptoms of Mental Depression ; Suicide by Jumping out of Window.*

Female, aged 30, married, three children, admitted to the Edinburgh Royal Infirmary on 16th November 1895, suffering from myxœdema and mental depression.

Duration.—4 months.

Apparent cause.—Grief due to the sudden death of her sister. Patient is naturally nervous and has been at times depressed mentally. Since her marriage seven years ago, has suffered a good deal from headaches. Was confined five months ago; labour easy and no loss of blood; recovered well. She was in her usual state of health four months ago, when she suddenly lost her sister, became very depressed, and has since developed the symptoms from which she now suffers (myxœdema). Has become much weaker, body more bulky, face heavy and swollen, colour yellow; speech thick; appetite poor; mentally very depressed.

Present condition.—Body bulky; facial appearance highly characteristic; face and eyelids swollen; skin of face yellow coloured; pink blush on cheeks; eyebrows scanty and elevated; forehead wrinkled transversely; lower lip swollen; tongue and throat swollen; complains of a choking sensation in throat; hair coming out, very brittle and dry; neck thick; no supraclavicular swellings;

hands thinner; feet not enlarged or swollen; legs slightly swollen; abdomen swollen and large. Skin dry and harsh; absence of sweating; temperature subnormal; complains of feeling cold; very sensitive to cold. Speech characteristically thick; memory very much impaired; frequent headache; great mental depression; sleeps badly. Appetite very poor; bowels constipated; pulse 72; no visceral disease; urine normal; has not menstruated since last pregnancy. Thyroid cannot be felt.

Result.—The patient was observed and the diet and bowels carefully regulated for the first few days after her admission to hospital, prior to the commencement of the thyroid treatment. At times she was depressed, at other times more bright and natural. On 20th November, while the nurses were engaged at the other end of the ward, she got out of bed, opened the window and jumped out. Both legs were fractured, and she received severe internal injuries from which she died in the course of twenty-four hours.

Post-mortem examination not allowed.

CASE XXIX.—*Typical and Advanced Myxœdema; Complete Disappearance of the Myxœdematous Symptoms under Thyroid Treatment.*

Female, aged 64, married, ten children, seen in consultation on 1st April 1896.

Duration.—3 years.

Apparent cause.—The symptoms were first noticed after an attack of influenza.

Present condition.—The patient, who is naturally a big stout woman, complains of a feeling of excessive exhaustion and debility, of a sensation of coldness, and of loss of memory. The body as a whole is markedly large and swollen; her movements are ponderous and slow; the face is very full and moon-shaped; the lower eyelids are puffy and swollen; the skin of the face is of a dingy yellow colour; there is no pink blush on the cheeks; the lower lip is markedly swollen and slightly blue; the hands and feet are large and broad; the abdomen is large; the tongue is considerably enlarged; the scalp is almost destitute of hair and thickly encrusted; the eyebrows are very scanty; supraclavicular swellings are very marked. The skin is harsh and dry; the patient says that she never sweats; the temperature is subnormal (95°); pulse 66. The articulation is characteristically slow and thick; the memory is very markedly impaired and cerebration very slow; she sleeps well. The appetite is poor; the bowels constipated. The urine is normal. The thyroid gland cannot be felt.

Thyroid treatment commenced 29th March 1896.

Preparation and Dose.—Five grains of the dried extract once a day, increased for a few days to ten grains (but this dose was too large, it produced extreme debility); strychnine and digitalis.

Immediate result.—Marked and rapid improvement. In the course of a few weeks, the myxœdematous symptoms completely disappeared and the hair began to grow.

Subsequent progress.—The patient continues well.

On 28th May 1898, her doctor wrote me:—"She is very well, lively and intelligent, able to go about and do her household duties; skin moist, hair well grown. She continues to take one five-grain tabloid daily."

CASE XXX.—*Myxœdema; Disappearance of most of the Myxœdematous Symptoms under Thyroid Extract.*

Female, aged 32, assistant in a shop, single, admitted to the Edinburgh Royal Infirmary on 31st January 1897.

Duration.—4 years.

Apparent cause.—None. Three years ago was in hospital under Dr Bramwell's care suffering from acute eczema. At that time her cheeks were very pink in colour, but the presence of myxœdema was not suspected. It is interesting, however, to note that the eczema was treated and got well under the administration of large doses of thyroid extract (gradually increased from one to fourteen tabloids = 70 grains of the dried extract, daily); and it seems probable that the myxœdema had been gradually coming on for at least a year previously.

Condition on admission.—Patient complains of debility, swelling and heaviness of the eyelids, and flushings of the face. The body is bulky; the abdomen is moderately swollen. The face is full and swollen looking. The flushings occur very frequently; they are usually worse in the after-part of the day or after eating; she feels as if the blood were rushing to her cheeks, which feel hot; the feet become cold and the cheeks burning; the forehead, nose and chin are not, she says, affected. The flushings do not appear to have any relationship to menstruation. The skin of the face is thin and translucent looking, yellowish (creamy) in colour; the cheeks are uniformly tinted of a bright pink colour; the eyelids are swollen, the eyebrows raised, the forehead transversely wrinkled; the eyes partly closed as if the lids could not be raised; the tongue is large, the lips are not swollen; there are no supraclavicular swellings; the hands are square and spade-shaped; the ends of the fingers are very square; the nails furrowed transversely, very brittle and apt to crack; the feet appear to be normal. The eyebrows are scanty; hair of head scanty, coarse and dry; no scabs on the scalp; skin very rough, dry, and inclined to be scaly; the palms are particularly dry, fissured and cracked. The patient never sweats; she feels the cold very much; suffers much from cold hands and feet; the temperature is subnormal. The voice is rough, and the articulation very slow and thick. Memory is much impaired; her mental processes are all slow; she is very slow in replying to questions; she is more easily irritated than she used to be. Appetite poor; bowels regular; menstruation usually regular in time, but very scanty and pale. Some anæmia. Urine normal. Pulse slow, 44 per minute. Thyroid gland cannot be felt.

Thyroid treatment commenced 12th February.

Preparation and Dose.—Thyrocol; at first, one grain three times daily, subsequently increased to twelve grains three times daily, it produced little effect except intense headache and vomiting. On *20th February*, dry thyroid extract substituted; at first, five grains three times daily, gradually increased to thirty grains (on 28th February) three times daily. This dose was continued till 25th March, when the dose was reduced to fifteen grains three times daily; on 29th March, the thyroid was stopped for several days; five grains daily were subsequently given.

Immediate results of the treatment.—The thyrocol produced intense headache and vomiting. Under increasing doses of the dried extract the myxœdematous symptoms gradually disappeared; the temperature and pulse rose; the skin became moist and less rough; the swelling of the face disappeared; the flushing and injection of the face diminished; the patient lost 16 lbs. in weight.

On 30th March 1897 the patient was discharged.

Subsequent progress.—Continues well.

On 8th April 1898, she stated that she has been keeping well ever since her discharge and has been able to follow her employment (assistant in a shop). She feels much stronger ; but has not perspired since the hot weather of last summer ; her hair has not grown much ; the skin is still harsh and dry ; the bright pink discoloration of the cheeks is still present (but she was always very highly coloured) ; is sleeping well ; appetite and digestion good ; bowels regular ; menstruation still scanty. Until lately, she took one tabloid (five grains of the dried extract) every other day ; of late, she has only taken one tabloid every week, as she thought it made her "shaky."

Remarks.—In this case the myxœdematous swelling was not very marked ; the flushing of the face was very intense ; the roughness and dryness of the skin very great. Large doses of the extract were tolerated and required. Acute eczema occurred in the early stages of the disease.

CASE XXXI.—*Typical Myxœdema, Complicated with Ulceration of the Stomach and Peritonitis.*

Female, aged 41, single, was seen in consultation on 13th March 1897, suffering from incessant vomiting and peritonitis.

Duration.—14 years at least.

History and apparent cause.—Her former medical attendant kindly gave me the following account of the previous history of the case :—"The patient has never been very strong ; she was frequently absent from school because of illness ; at the age of 20 she suffered from anæmia, ulceration of the stomach and profuse hæmatemesis ; the myxœdematous symptoms developed some time after this (the exact date could not be fixed) ; before the thyroid treatment was commenced (February 1893), she was frequently confined to the house for months at a time, and had frequent attacks of severe pain in the stomach and vomiting. She was worse during cold weather.

Family history.—*Her mother died at the age of* 68 *of myxœdema,* of seven years' duration ; her father died at the age of 54 of apoplexy ; three brothers died at the ages of 28, 17½ and 12, respectively, of tubercular meningitis, phthisis, and tubercular disease of the glands ; one sister died at the age of 21 of diabetes ; one brother is alive and said to be healthy, *he has a full heavy face suggestive of myxœdema ;* three sisters are alive and fairly healthy. Before the myxœdematous patient was born, the mother, who was very nervous, passed through a severe mental strain.

Symptoms.—All the characteristic features of myxœdema were present, the mental symptoms being particularly pronounced.

Thyroid treatment commenced at the end of February 1893.

Preparation and Dose.—Ten drops of thyroid extract daily; subsequently increased to fifteen drops.

Immediate result.—Rapid improvement. On *17th May* 1893 (eleven weeks after the treatment was commenced), the following note was made regarding her condition :—"The result has been satisfactory, the most marked improvement being mental. She sweats freely and does not remember sweating before the treatment ; the face has become changed ; the hair is growing rapidly ; the gastric symptoms seldom trouble her, and she walks and goes up a stair better than she has done for years ; the temperature is normal in the morning and down to 97° in the evening ; the evening fall took place when she began to get up for the day; changing the time for giving the thyroid does not raise the temperature in the evening."

Subsequent progress of the case.—The gastric symptoms continued to recur, and although the myxœdema was to a considerable extent kept in abeyance by the thyroid extract the patient never got strong.

During the years 1895 *and* 1896, she continued to suffer from her stomach. The menstruation, which, prior to the thyroid treatment, had been too profuse (menorrhagia), became irregular ; she frequently missed three periods at a time, and the menstruation, when present, was always scanty.

During the spring of 1897, the patient on two or three occasions vomited small quantities of blood.

Condition on 13th March 1897.—The patient is in a very debilitated condition ; the feet are swollen ; well marked myxœdematous symptoms are still present ; the patient complains of feeling cold ; the skin is rough and dry ; the skin of the face has a dingy yellow tinge ; a pink blush is present on the cheeks ; the lips, hands and feet are swollen ; there are no supraclavicular swellings ; the hair is thin, but not markedly so ; before the treatment the patient was quite bald ; there is no encrustation of the scalp ; the memory, which, prior to the commencement of the thyroid treatment, was very bad, was still somewhat impaired ; the articulation was characteristically thick ; the bowels were constipated ; the urine was free from albumen ; the heart was weak, but there was no valvular disease ; no thyroid gland could be felt.

Incessant vomiting was present, almost everything being rejected ; the patient complained of intense pain and tenderness over the abdomen, which was swollen ; the temperature was 101.6° ; the pulse 108.

Treatment.—Peptonised milk and ice by the stomach ; nutrient enemata and suppositories ; morphia hypodermically ; strychnine and strophanthus.

Result.—The stomach symptoms, though somewhat relieved, continued, and the patient died, apparently from subacute peritonitis and exhaustion, on 22nd April 1897.

Post-mortem examination.—None.

CASE XXXII.—*Typical Myxœdema; Rapid and Complete Disappearance of the Myxœdematous Symptoms under Thyroid Treatment.*

Female, aged 32, married, four children, admitted to the Edinburgh Royal Infirmary on 30th March 1897.

Duration.—2 years.

Apparent cause.—The symptoms began to develop after the birth of her last child ; was quite well before this ; the labour was easy, and was not attended with any excessive loss of blood ; for five days after her confinement she suffered severe pain in the lower part of the abdomen ; was up on the fourteenth day, but feeling very weak.

Present condition.—Patient complains of debility, mental depression, severe headache, a feeling of cold, etc. Looks considerably older than her age, and is somewhat anæmic. The body as a whole is bulky ; the facial appearance typical ; face full and slightly swollen ; skin slightly yellow in tint ; a pink blush on the cheeks ; lower lip full, tense, and slightly purple in colour ; tongue not large ; throat not swollen ; ears natural ; no supraclavicular swellings ; hands and feet broad and large ; abdomen large and pendulous ; eyebrows elevated and scanty ; forehead transversely wrinkled ; hair of head very dry and coarse, but not thinner than it used to be ; scalp scaly, but not encrusted ; skin, except on face, very dry and rough; no sweating; feels the cold very much; worse in cold weather; temperature subnormal; complains of numbness of the hands and feet; sensation delayed; sight and hearing somewhat impaired; memory bad; marked mental depression and listlessness; voice rough; articulation thick and leathery; knee-jerks normal; sleeps well; pulse slow, 50; appetite good; bowels slightly constipated; urine normal; menstruation regular in time, but since the onset of the disease attended for the first two days with great pain in the back and right flank; no visceral disease. No thyroid to be felt.

Thyroid treatment commenced 15th April 1897.

Preparation and Dose.—At first the dried extract (maximum dose sixteen tabloids = eighty grains, daily); subsequently the raw gland ($\frac{1}{4}$ of a gland daily, subsequently reduced to $\frac{1}{8}$th of a gland).

Immediate result.—Little improvement under the dried extract; marked and rapid improvement (rise in temperature, pulse, and respirations, sweatings, disappearance of the mxyœdematous swelling; great improvement in memory and mental condition, etc.) under the raw gland.

On 24th May 1897, the patient was discharged looking fifteen years younger than before the treatment; skin smooth; headache much less frequent and severe; the mental depression quite gone; feeling bright and lively, laughing and talking continually; voice and articulation natural. Loss of weight during the treatment = $15\frac{1}{2}$ lbs.

Subsequent progress.—Remains quite well.

Remarks.—Large doses of the dried extract produced so little effect that I was disposed to think the tabloids were bad. The raw gland produced an immediate and marked effect.

CASE XXXIII.—*Imperfectly Developed Myxœdema; Marked Improvement under Thyroid Treatment.*

Female, aged 48, single, lady's maid, admitted to the Edinburgh Royal Infirmary on 19th May 1897. Weight = 7 stone $8\frac{1}{2}$ lbs.

Duration.—$4\frac{1}{2}$ months.

Apparent cause.—None.

Family history.—Two brothers died of phthisis.

Present condition.—Patient complains of debility, palpitation, shortness of breath, a sensation of cold, and swelling of the feet. The body as a whole is not swollen; the face is full and round; the skin of the face markedly yellow in colour; a well-marked pink blush (more bright and diffused than in most cases of myxœdema) covers the cheeks and chin; the upper eyelids are swollen; the skin of the face is thin and translucent looking; the lips, tongue, throat, ears, hands, and abdomen are not swollen; the feet and ankles are slightly swollen (ordinary œdema); there are no supraclavicular swellings; the thyroid gland cannot be felt; the patient is extremely sensitive to cold; the temperature is subnormal; the skin (except on the face) is very harsh and dry; she never sweats; the mouth and throat are drier than formerly; the head is almost bald, the hair having come out since the disease commenced; the hair is dry and brittle; the scalp is encrusted; the eyebrows and eyelashes are scanty; the nails are brittle and cracked; the voice and articulation are natural; the memory is much worse than it was 5 months ago; there is considerable anæmia and a soft systolic murmur in the mitral area; the pulse is quick, 100 to 110; the appetite is poor; digestion fair; bowels constipated; the patient has never menstruated regularly, and ceased entirely to menstruate several years ago ; the urine is normal.

Thyroid treatment commenced on 31st May 1897.

Preparation and Dose.—Dried extract, five grains, gradually increased to twenty-five grains, daily ; arsenic ; strychnine ; strophanthus.

Immediate result.—With some ups and downs, the patient gradually improved, and was discharged from hospital on 28th July 1897.

On her discharge, the patient felt much stronger, more active, and better in every way ; her face had entirely lost the myxœdematous appearance ; skin softer and more moist ; no growth of hair ; temperature normal ; pulse, which on admission was quick (100 to 110), had fallen to 60 ; memory better. Loss of weight during treatment = 14½ lbs.

Remarks.—A peculiar feature of this case was the fall in the pulse-frequency during the treatment ; it did not seem to be satisfactorily accounted for by the small doses of strophanthus which were administered.

B.—*CASE OF JUVENILE MYXŒDEMA.*

CASE XXXIV.—*Juvenile Myxœdema; Complete Disappearance of the Myxœdematous Symptoms under Thyroid Treatment.*

Female, aged 14, admitted to the Edinburgh Royal Infirmary on 26th January 1897, complaining of debility and arrested growth.

Duration.—At least 4 years.

History.—Patient's birth was easy and non-instrumental. Nothing was noticed wrong with her until four years ago. She then stopped growing, and has not grown at all since. At the age of 7, she had measles ; at the age of 12, herpes zoster (scars very marked). Up to the age of 10, she was a well-grown and well-developed child.

At the age of 11 she was, by the advice of her medical attendant, taken from school "because she was too advanced for her age and was not growing" ; she was very clever at her lessons, seldom requiring to prepare them, and was then in the 5th Standard. (The absence of any mental defect at this date is remarkable, for the myxœdematous condition must have been present in some degree before this time ; on inquiry it was ascertained that the patient did not shed any of her milk teeth till the age of 11.) Since the arrest in her growth occurred, she has lost all her old energy, has given up playing, is inclined to sit by the fire and has been very quiet and sedate. During the past two years, her face has become puffy and swollen, the skin dry ; she has felt the cold very much, has ceased to sweat ; her hair has come out. For the past three months, she has complained of (? rheumatic) pains in the small of the back, and in the elbow, knee, and ankle joints.

Family history.—Her father and paternal grandmother died of phthisis ; a sister died of scrofulous disease of the knee and spine ; a brother takes fits ; a maternal aunt died in an asylum from fits.

Present condition.—Height = 4 ft. 2½ ins. ; weight = 4 st. 6¾ lbs. ; temperature 97° ; pulse 56 ; somewhat anæmic ; red corpuscles = 2,800,000 per c.mm. ; hæmoglobin = 30 per cent.

Body short and broad ; expression dull and heavy ; face broad and puffy ; eyelids slightly swollen ; face pale ; very faint malar blush ; nose short and thick at the tip, nostrils wide, slightly pug-shaped ; lower lip slightly swollen ; tongue not specially large ; ears small and well shaped ; hands and feet somewhat broad ; slight tumefactions above the clavicles ; neck very thick ; the abdomen is not specially large ; there is no umbilical hernia. Head large (circumference $= 21\frac{1}{2}$ inches); fontanelle closed ; hair fairly thick, short and very dry ; some scurfiness of scalp ; the hair was cut nine months ago and has not grown at all since ; eyelashes long and thick ; eyebrows scanty. Teeth :—The lateral incisors on the right side, in both the upper and the lower jaw, are reduplicated ; there is only one molar tooth in each lower jaw ; the double teeth are rather decayed. The teeth which she has at present are, with the exception of the four upper and the three lower incisors, those of the first set. She had no teeth of the second set when ten years old ; the first tooth was shed when she was eleven years old ; the two new upper incisors appeared when she was twelve years old ; they took a very long time to grow in. The skin is rough and dry except on the face ; she never sweats ; she feels the cold very much ; the feet and hands are often blue and cold. The voice and articulation are normal ; the mental development good, but the memory is not nearly so good as it used to be ; she sleeps well. The thyroid gland cannot be felt. Gait, motor functions and sensory functions all normal. Knee-jerks active. Appetite very good ; breath foul ; tongue coated ; bowels apt to be constipated. Urine normal. No visceral disease.

Thyroid treatment commenced 12th February 1897.

Preparation and Dose.—Thyrocol was first given (one grain daily, increased to three grains daily); it caused headache and sickness and had comparatively little effect on the myxœdematous condition. *On 20th February*, the dried thyroid extract was substituted ; at first, five grains three times daily, gradually increased to four tabloids (20 grains) three times daily, *on 26th February ;* reduced to ten grains three times daily *on 4th March ;* five grains three times daily *on 24th March ;* and five grains twice daily *on 29th March.*

Immediate results.—Rapid disappearance of the myxœdematous symptoms, after the full effect of the thyroid was obtained (rise in temperature, sweating, growth of body and hair).

On 9th March, the patient had grown half an inch in height, and her hair had grown one inch and a half in length. Temperature 99°, pulse 108.

On 29th March was discharged. Height = 4 ft. $3\frac{1}{2}$ ins. (a gain of $\frac{1}{2}$ in.) ; weight = 4 st. (a loss of $6\frac{3}{4}$ lbs.).

Subsequent progress.—Continues well.

On 9th February 1898 she was quite well ; height = 4 ft. $6\frac{1}{2}$ ins. ; weight = 4 st. $6\frac{1}{2}$ lbs. (without clothes); is very bright ; never feels the cold ; sweats naturally ; skin smooth ; hair growing ; eats well ; bowels natural. Has lost one double tooth.

C.—CASES OF SPORADIC CRETINISM (Infantile Myxœdema).

CASE XXXV.—*Typical Sporadic Cretinism ; Rapid Disappearance of All the Myxœdematous Symptoms under Thyroid Treatment ; Continued and Progressive Improvement.*

Female, aged $8\frac{1}{2}$, admitted to the Edinburgh Royal Infirmary, 7th January 1893.

Duration.—$8\frac{1}{2}$ years ; symptoms first noticed at age of 4 months.

Apparent cause.—None. Labour difficult (instrumental) but head not injured; when 3½ months old, nearly choked in bath; frightened by nurse at 9 months old.

Family history.—Patient is the eldest of four children; one died of measles; the two survivors healthy. Father aged 41, mother aged 43; both healthy. Father lame from poliomyelitis anterior acuta; mother nervous; four children of a sister of father affected with Friedreich's ataxia.

Present condition.—Height = 34½ inches; weight = 1 st. 12¾ lbs.; somewhat anæmic. Body short and squat; face swollen, mouth large, nose pug-shaped, eyelids much swollen, skin translucent and ivory-looking; a slight pink blush present on the cheeks; tongue not enlarged; milk teeth present; neck short and thick; elastic swellings above the clavicles; abdomen very large; small umbilical hernia; hands and feet large, broad and short; back curved; a fine growth of hair between the shoulders. Anterior fontanelle closed; head covered with a considerable quantity of dark, lank, coarse hair; scalp dry and encrusted. Calves and forearms large, firm and elastic; skin of palms and soles wrinkled; skin dry and harsh; patient never sweats; very sensitive to cold; worse in cold weather; likes heat, and enjoys basking in the sun or roasting before a hot fire; temperature subnormal. Voice rough and hoarse; splendid sleeper. Appetite poor; bowels obstinately constipated. Urine free from albumen; a mucous deposit sometimes present. The thyroid gland cannot be felt. Venous mottling present on the chest, arms, abdomen and thighs. Very dull and apathetic; never smiles or takes any notice of what is going on around her. Placed in any position, will remain for hours quiet, without making any spontaneous movement. Understands what is said to her, recognises objects, and knows their names; her vocabulary is fairly good, but she seldom exerts herself to speak. Her mother says that her intelligence is not much more advanced than that of a child of three years of age. General state of nutrition good; though dwarfed, fat. Always passes urine in bed. When her parents came to see her she took no notice of them, and did not answer them when spoken to. Pulse regular, 80. Thyroid cannot be felt.

Thyroid treatment commenced 10th January 1894.

Preparation and Dose.—⅛th of raw gland, increased to ½ on 18th January.

Immediate result of treatment.—The first dose produced a rise in temperature; this was soon followed by the rapid disappearance of the myxœdematous symptoms; rise in pulse; sweating; increased appetite; disappearance of constipation; great improvement in mental condition.

10th March 1894.—Discharged; parents greatly pleased with the extraordinary change in patient's condition. To take ten drops of B. & M.'s liquid extract, every other day.

Subsequent progress.—*1st April.*—Very irritable, bad-tempered and excited; dose of extract reduced to five drops.

30th June 1894.—Height = 36¾ inches; weight = 2 st. 6½ lbs.

8th February 1895.—Quite well since last note. Very lively; skin smooth; height 38½ inches.

11th May 1895.—Perfectly well since last note, and taking one tabloid every other day. Began to go to school last September, and has made fair progress with her lessons; is now a lively child, active both in body and mind; instead of being sullen and quiet, is now irritable and often bad-tempered; appetite and digestion very good; bowels regular; skin perfectly natural; still some encrustation of scalp; hair long, silky, and quite healthy.

8th April 1898.—Quite well since last note; no appearance of myxœdema; umbilical hernia gone; skin moist and smooth; hair long and black; perspires naturally; does not feel the cold; has not been once absent from school during the past two years; doing well at her lessons; in the 2nd Standard; temper rather peculiar; appetite good; bowels regular; height=46 inches.

Both feet very high in the instep and short from before backwards (suggestive of commencing Friedreich's ataxia); left knee-jerk exaggerated, right normal.

The height at different dates was as follows :—29th June 1890=31⅞ in.; 19th March 1891=32¼ in.; 8th January 1893 (thyroid treatment commenced)= 34½ in.; 13th February 1893=35½ in.; 30th June 1893=36¾ in.; 8th February 1894=38½ in.; 11th May 1895=42½ in.; 8th April 1898=46 in.

Recorded in full, "Atlas of Clinical Medicine," Vol. i., p. 23; and "Edinburgh Hospital Reports," Vol. iii., p. 198.

CASE XXXVI.—*Extreme Sporadic Cretinism in a Patient aged* 16 $\frac{7}{12}$; *Disappearance of the Myxœdematous Symptoms under Thyroid Feeding; Increase in Height: Very Slight Improvement in the Mental Condition.*

Female, aged 16 $\frac{7}{12}$, admitted Edinburgh Royal Infirmary, 30th March 1893.

Duration.—? 16 years or from birth. Nothing definite, except enlargement of tongue and mottling of skin, noticed till child was 9 months old.

When 3½ years old, very ill with "stoppage of the bowels"; at 5, had chickenpox; at 7, measles; at 8, whooping-cough; at 10, scarlet fever; and at 12, a large glandular abscess in neck. Her hair, which was previously pretty thick, began to come out after the scarlet fever; it has not grown since.

Apparent cause.—None.

Family history.—Excellent in every way.

Present condition.—Though 16 years of age, does not look more than 2 or 2½ years old; height=29¾ inches; weight=2 st. 5½ lbs.; no anæmia; anterior fontanelle widely open (6 × 5½ cm.); stumps of first set of teeth still present; unable to stand; can support herself in a semi-erect position by leaning on her chest and arms; unable to creep in the ordinary way, but pulls herself along for a short distance on her belly by her arms. Mental development is completely arrested; grunts and barks like one of the lower animals, but does not seem to be able to produce any intelligible articulate sound; seems to have some sort of dull intelligence. Can see, hear and taste.

Looks more like one of the lower animals than a member of the human race, the facial appearance and expression resembling that of a bull-dog more than anything else. Head large in proportion to the body; mouth of enormous size, and always open; saliva frequently dribbles away from it; cavity of mouth very capacious; lips very thick and blue; lower lip everted; tongue of enormous size, both in length and breadth, and of a dark, purple colour, constantly projected between the teeth; nose very small, sunken, and snub-shaped; nostrils large, dilated, and set widely apart. Eyes small and bead-like, partly closed by œdematous swelling of the lids. No pink blush on the cheeks; face yellow and pale; skin of the body generally of a dingy yellow hue; scalp over the position of the anterior fontanelle destitute of hair; a considerable quantity of coarse, dry, shaggy hair covers the back and sides of the head; eyebrows hardly perceptible; eyelashes in the lower lids scanty; slight blepharitis. Belly large; an umbilical hernia of (relatively) great size. Hands and feet very broad, thick and wrinkled; legs, thighs, arms and forearms firm; the tissues infiltrated with solid œdema. Skin mottled, very harsh and dry; patient never sweats ; several moles and warts, some of them pigmented, scattered over the surface of the body; sensibility of the skin seems normal. Neck very thick ; very large elastic swelling above the clavicles. Spine curved towards the right ; left knee-joint distorted; tibiæ bent as if from rickets. Appetite good, but patient often vomits; disagreeable odour of breath; bowels very costive. Temperature subnormal; always worse during winter, somewhat better and brighter during summer. Pulse of normal frequency. Urine contains a small quantity of globulin. Pays no attention to the calls of nature. Sleeps well. Thyroid cannot be felt.

Thyroid treatment commenced 1st April 1893.

Preparation and Dose.—B. & M.'s liquid extract, five drops daily, subsequently increased to seven and ten drops (for a few days) ; afterwards B. & W.'s tabloids, gr. v., every other day.

Immediate result of the treatment.—Rapid disappearance of the myxœdematous swellings, rise in temperature and pulse, skin less harsh and dry, loss of $3\frac{1}{2}$ lbs. in weight, looks brighter and more intelligent.

17th May 1893.—Discharged, distinctly improved.

Subsequent progress of the case.—*15th November* 1893 (six months after the commencement of the treatment).—Looks much bigger and older than she did three months ago. Before the thyroid treatment was commenced did not look more than 2 or $2\frac{1}{2}$ years of age ; now looks at least 4 or 5. Has grown $6\frac{1}{2}$ inches since 1st April ; now measures 36 inches in length. The curvature of the spinal column is much more apparent. Her father and mother say that she is much brighter and more intelligent. The anterior fontanelle is much smaller than it used to be, very firm and evidently being filled in with bone. The hair has grown over the bald part of the scalp; the eyebrows are also much thicker, stronger, and longer. Has got four new teeth; the legs are firmer, but still very soft. Is able to support herself on her legs much better than she used to do, but is still unable to stand erect even with support. In some respects the patient does not seem so well as she was at the end of July. The skin is more dry and harsh, the tongue is larger, and the supraclavicular swellings are more marked. The dose of thyroid was consequently increased from 1 to $1\frac{1}{2}$ tabloids every other day.

April 1898.—Since the last note, there has been little or no improvement ; the thyroid has only been very intermittently given, the parents being afraid of the emaciation and depression which it produces.

The height at different dates was as follows :—3rd April 1893 (before thyroid treatment commenced)=$29\frac{1}{2}$ in. ; 8th April 1893=$29\frac{3}{4}$ in. ; 7th June 1893 = 32 in. ; 15th Nov. 1893 = 36 in. ; 12th May 1895 = $37\frac{1}{4}$ in.

Note.—In this case, in which the disease was most extreme and the patient comparatively advanced in age, one could hardly expect any considerable degree of improvement.

Recorded in full, "Edinburgh Hospital Reports," Vol. iii., p. 203.

CASE XXXVII.—*Typical Sporadic Cretinism ; Rapid and Continued Improvement under Thyroid Treatment.*

Female, aged 3 years, seen in consultation 13th March 1893.

Duration.—$2\frac{1}{4}$ years ; the disease was first noticed when the child was 8 or 9 months old.

Apparent cause.—None ; born in India ; birth easy ; two attacks of fever in early infancy.

Family history.—Excellent.

Present condition.—Does not look more than 8 or 9 months old; slightly anæmic; anterior fontanelle widely open; no teeth; mouth large, usually open; lips thick and slightly bluish in tint; tongue very large, usually protruding between the teeth; face and eyelids puffy and swollen; skin translucent and waxy looking; gums thick and hard; hands and feet short and stumpy; abdomen very large; small umbilical hernia; hair very scanty, but sufficiently long and soft, and of a golden-brown colour; a thick growth of fine downy hairs, ⅜ of an inch in length, extends over the forehead as far as the eyebrows, which have only grown in during the last few months; eyelashes long, but somewhat scanty. Temperature subnormal; *skin soft and smooth; sweats freely;* constipation very marked; large elastic swellings above the clavicles; appetite small; general state of nutrition good; temper placid; likes to be fondled, and strokes the nurse's face with its hands, but this seems to be the only evidence of intelligence; sleeps well; cannot say a single word, not even " Ba-ba "; makes no attempt to creep; radial pulse cannot be felt; heart numbers 96 per minute. Thyroid cannot be felt.

Thyroid treatment commenced 30th March 1893.

Preparation and Dose.—Ten drops of B. & M.'s liquid extract once daily; the second dose produced vomiting, collapse, a marked rise of temperature and pulse. Dose reduced to two drops.

Immediate result of the treatment.—Complete disappearance of the myxœdematous symptoms, followed by rapid and continuous improvement.

Subsequent progress.—*26th May.*—Hair growing; has cut one tooth.

3rd July.—Has six teeth; the umbilical hernia has entirely disappeared. Beginning to say a few small words.

3rd November.—Thriving splendidly; has fourteen teeth; looks perfectly bright and intelligent; talks a great deal in a language peculiar to herself.

11th May 1895.—Height = 37½ inches; has therefore grown 11 inches since the treatment was commenced two years ago, and 3 inches during the past year; weighs 36 lbs. In excellent health and spirits; legs getting stronger daily, and quite straight; walks fully a mile every day; very musical; always good-tempered; very slow at talking; can say plenty of words, but does not string them together. Cheeks rosy; eyes bright; mouth is now always kept shut; tongue never protrudes; teeth strong; hair long and thick; skin beautifully clear and soft; cannot yet feed herself, unless her hand is guided to her mouth; appetite excellent; bowels quite regular; sleeps splendidly.

April 1898.—Continues to improve; physically strong; has lost two of her first teeth; mentally improved, but still backward.

The height at different dates was as follows:—30th March 1893 (before thyroid treatment) = 26½ in.; 18th May 1893 = 29 in.; 23rd Nov. 1893 = 31¾ in.; 2nd April 1894 = 34½ in.; 11th May 1895 = 37½ in.

Recorded in full, " Edinburgh Hospital Reports," Vol. iii., p. 217.

CASE XXXVIII. — *Typical Sporadic Cretinism; Immediate Improvement under Small Doses of Thyroid Extract; Rapid Disappearance of All the Myxœdematous Symptoms.*

Female, aged 4, admitted Edinburgh Royal Infirmary, 6th June 1894.

Duration.—3½ years; symptoms first noticed when 7 months old.

Apparent cause.—None; birth easy.

Family history.—Six other children; three alive and well; three dead (one still-born, one died immediately after birth, one at age of 9 weeks from gastro-intestinal catarrh). No evidence of inherited syphilis. Since the birth of patient, mother has had occasional epileptic fits.

Condition on admission.—Height = 27 inches; weight = 1 st. 8 lbs.; slightly anæmic; face ugly; mouth very large; lips thick and of a bluish colour; lower lip everted; tongue very large and always protruding; eyelids markedly swollen; a slight pink blush on each cheek and over the tip of the nose; anterior fontanelle widely open; hair, which is fair, ragged and coarse, scanty over the greater part of the head; more plentiful at the sides over the parietal bones than over the occiput or vertex; scalp encrusted; neck short and thick; thyroid cannot be felt; elastic swellings above the clavicles; thick pad of fat at the root of the neck behind; masses of fat or myxœdematous swellings below the chin; abdomen very large; a small umbilical hernia; pelvis very narrow in proportion to the abdomen; chest walls seem to be infiltrated with solid œdema; arms short and broad; forearms colossal; hands large, broad and spade-shaped; thenar and hypothenar eminences tense, and evidently distended with myxœdematous swelling; hands cold, and occasionally cyanosed; skin of palms wrinkled and dry; legs short and stout; calves very large, hard and swollen; feet always cold and cyanosed; skin of soles wrinkled; ends of long bones thickened; no beading of ribs; spine markedly curved; some fatty or myxœdematous swelling between the shoulders; a growth of fine hair down the back; skin dry; no moles, warts, or nævi. Temperature subnormal; is always worse in cold weather and more lively in warm weather. Cry harsh and low-toned—a rough grunt; takes very little notice of anything that is going on around her; seems pleased with toys; can say "Ta-ta" and "Da-da"; is placid in disposition; sleeps a great deal. Is unable to creep, stand, or walk. Well nourished, but has great difficulty in swallowing; appetite good; has to be fed with a spoon; bowels constipated; urine free from albumen, but deposits mucus; pulse 80. Thyroid cannot be felt.

Thyroid treatment commenced 2nd July 1894.

Preparation and Dose.—¾ gr. solid extract daily, subsequently increased to 2¼ grs. daily.

Immediate result of treatment. — A distinct alteration produced by two doses (1½ grains of thyroid extract); rapid disappearance of the myxœdematous swelling, rise in temperature, pulse, etc.

On 4th July, the child looked distinctly better; eyes more widely open; tongue and lips slightly less swollen; colour better; lips less blue; the swelling of the thenar and hypothenar eminences distinctly less marked; taking its food better. No change in temperature and pulse.

Subsequent progress.—On *1st September* was discharged, very much improved in every way; myxœdematous swelling gone; much more intelligent and lively; anterior fontanelle closing; umbilical hernia gone; skin soft; the dirty brown crusts had almost disappeared from the scalp.

11th May 1895.—The mother says she has been very well since her discharge; is a fat, plump child; skin perfectly smooth and soft; sweats naturally; head covered with a quantity of long, soft, perfectly healthy light brown hair; anterior fontanelle closed; scalp quite clean; eight teeth which she cut while in the Infirmary under thyroid treatment are sound and good. All the teeth which were cut before the treatment was commenced rotted away as soon as they came through the gum—a striking proof of the improved state of nutrition. Appetite good; the bowels still somewhat constipated; can stand and walk a few steps with the help of a hand, but not by herself ; says a few baby words. Lips still thick, mouth still large, expression still suggestive of sporadic cretinism ; only grown 2 inches in the past nine months, whereas in the two months previously (the first two months of the treatment) she grew 2½ inches. On inquiry, I found that the thyroid had not been given regularly ; the importance of regular administration insisted upon.

The height at different dates was as follows :—28th June 1894 (before thyroid treatment commenced) = 27 in. ; 18th July 1894 = 27½ in. ; 30th July 1894 = 28 in. ; 31st August 1894 = 29½ in. ; 11th May 1895 = 31½ in.

Recorded in full, " Edinburgh Hospital Reports," Vol. iii., p. 224.

CASE XXXIX.—*Comparatively Mild Case of Sporadic Cretinism ; Marked Improvement under Thyroid Treatment.*

Female, aged 2 1⁄12, seen in consultation on 16th August 1894.

Duration.—Since birth. First child ; labour easy ; a small child ; at birth, the doctor noticed that there was something peculiar about it. As a young infant always cold, different from other babies. Has not grown and developed.

Apparent cause.--Congenital.

Family history.—Excellent ; a second child, also a girl, born a week ago, seems quite healthy, but has a small umbilical hernia.

Present condition.—A big, stout, fat child ; height = 30 inches ; limbs sturdy-looking ; abdomen relatively large ; hands small ; feet of good size ; a small umbilical hernia which has existed since birth. Has several teeth ; all have decayed as soon as they came through the gum. Nose squat ; eyelids swollen ; skin translucent and waxy-looking ; mouth not unduly large ; tongue rather large ; voice rough and harsh. Anterior fontanelle still open ; head covered with a good deal of brown hair ; slight encrustation of scalp ; skin dry and rough ; absence of sweating. Neither the nurse, the parents, nor the doctor have noticed that the child is worse in cold weather. No supraclavicular swellings. Temperature subnormal. The child is said to be quite intelligent, to understand what is said to it, and to play with its toys ; does not speak ; is fond of animals ; good-tempered ; sleeps well. Appetite very small ; bowels obstinately constipated ; urine normal. Thyroid gland cannot be felt.

Thyroid treatment commenced 17th August 1894.

Preparation and Dose.—Dried extract, 1½ grains daily, gradually increased to 5 grains daily.

I am indebted to the patient's medical attendant for the following notes of the progress of the case.

Immediate result of the treatment.—Slow improvement ; rise in temperature, etc.

Subsequent progress.—Marked and steady improvement.

7th May 1895.—Looks far more intelligent, very bright and happy, and the picture of robust health. Walks with almost a natural step, and holds herself beautifully erect ; seems to take an interest in everything, and to understand what is said to her, but cannot talk yet, though she makes various attempts— inarticulate sounds. Is still taking 1 tabloid (5 grs.) daily. Is quite a different child to what she was last August, and would apparently be perfect if she could only talk. None of the milk teeth which have been cut since the thyroid treatment was commenced have crumbled or decayed.

28th April 1898.—Since last note has made steady and continuous progress, and is now not very different from any ordinary child of her years. Head proportionately a little large ; features somewhat plain and a little coarse ; voice still husky and harsh, but can talk quite distinctly, intelligently, and nicely. Intelligence quite up to the average standard of a child of her age (6). Knows the alphabet ; can read and spell words of three or four letters. Her mother says her memory is not very good. Is fond of playing and amusements, but does not perhaps enter into them with the same eagerness and excitement as her younger and only sister does. Has grown ten inches during the last three years. Is strong and robust and enjoys very good health. Her figure is perfectly erect; limbs straight though in walking, the legs are kept slightly more apart than normal. Most of the milk teeth have now decayed; has several teeth of the permanent set—all the incisors and several molars; the latter are rather large teeth and not very evenly set. Constipation occasionally still troublesome.

About twelve months since, the parents thought they would like to try the experiment of leaving off the daily dose of thyroid extract (five grains). At the end of a few weeks, the mother thought the legs were not quite so straight; this observation I confirmed. I also noticed that the skin was markedly coarser and the flesh more bulky. I advised that the experiment should not be continued further, but that the daily dose of thyroid should be again commenced.

The height at successive dates was as follows :--16th August 1894 = 30 inches ; 4th October 1894 = 31¼ inches ; 7th November 1894 = 32 inches ; 17th December 1894 = 33½ inches ; 19th May 1895 = 36½ inches ; 21st May 1898 = 46¼ inches.

Recorded in full, "Edinburgh Hospital Reports," Vol. iii., p. 232.

CASE XL.—*Typical and Very Severe Sporadic Cretinism ; the Menstrual Function Regularly Performed ; No Thyroid Treatment.*

Female, aged 36, seen 26th January 1895.

Duration.--From birth or early infancy.

Apparent cause.—None.

Family history.—Mother died aged 31, of phthisis ; father aged 54, of gangrene of the foot following rheumatism. Six children in the family ; two sisters aged 40 and 38, alive and quite normal in every respect ; a brother (a fine, tall man, 6 ft. high) died, aged 28, of phthisis ; a brother and sister died a few months after birth—causes of death unknown. Six step-brothers and sisters, all well developed and strong.

Previous history.—Birth easy. Several attacks of bronchitis in infancy. Did not walk till three years old. Has hardly grown in height since that time, but has become much broader. At 7, abscess in leg ; at 16, abscess in neck. Has not had any children's diseases ; has been exposed to scarlet fever.

Present condition.—Height = 36 inches. Body very broad and bulky. Back markedly curved in the lumbar region ; abdomen large and prominent ; no umbilical hernia. Face full and swollen ; eyelids swollen and translucent ; no pink blush on the cheeks ; nose squat and broad (pug-shaped); ears rather large ; mouth large, lower lip pouting, but lips not much swollen ; tongue large but not protruded between the teeth ; palate very broad and flat ; teeth in the upper jaw all wanting. Head covered with a profusion of very coarse, dark brown hair. Scalp encrusted till the age of 25 ; since menstruation has become much cleaner. Anterior fontanelle closed ; it was very late in closing. Neck very broad ; enormous elastic swellings above the clavicles ; thyroid gland cannot be felt; some fatty or myxœdematous swellings in the anterior fold of the axilla. Forearms colossal; hands enormously broad and large; fingers very broad and flat; feet very broad and short; tibiæ somewhat bent. Complexion somewhat earthy coloured; skin generally dark, dingy, very brown in colour; very dry, coarse and harsh. Patient never sweats; however near the fire she gets, is always cold; worse in cold weather; temperature subnormal; hands and feet often blue and cold. Is of a cheerful disposition; fond of fun and company. Intellectual development is that of a child of five or six; understands a great deal that is said to her; vocabulary limited; does not speak much. Is vain and fond of dress. Sleeps well. Appetite small; does not like sweets; bowels quite regular. Urine natural.

The nipples and areolæ are somewhat developed; fulness in the position of the breasts; no pubic hairs. Since the age of 25 has menstruated every month; on one occasion, a year and a half ago, the discharge stopped for three months. The exact measurements were as follows :—

		Inches.
Height	- - - - - - -	36
Circumference round abdomen at level of umbilicus	-	24
,, ,, chest at level of nipples	- -	22
,, ,, neck over thickest part of glandular swellings	- - -	19
,, ,, neck, higher up	- -	14
,, ,, upper arm in middle	- - -	$6\frac{3}{4}$
,, ,, forearm, thickest part	- -	$7\frac{3}{4}$
,, ,, hand	- - - -	$9\frac{1}{8}$
Length of hand from wrist to tip of middle finger	- -	4
Circumference of foot, thickest part	- - - -	8
Length of foot	- - - - - -	6

Subsequent progress.—Patient remains *in statu quo*. The relatives refused to allow her to undergo thyroid treatment. They said they had known her so long in her present condition and were so much attached to her, that they would not like to have her changed, even for the better.

Recorded in the *Lancet* 10th December 1898, p. 1547.

Additional Note on the Treatment of Myxœdema.

—On page 324 I have inadvertently omitted to state that Dr Hovitz of Copenhagen was the first to introduce the method of thyroid feeding. In March 1892 he successfully treated a case of myxœdema by the administration of minced raw thyroid in the form of sandwiches.

EXOPHTHALMIC GOITRE.

Definition or Short Description.—Exophthalmic goitre, to which the synonyms *Graves' disease* and *Basedow's disease* are also applied, is a very interesting affection. In typical and fully developed cases, it is characterised by:—(1) increased frequency of the heart's action and palpitation ; (2) enlargement of the thyroid ; (3) prominence of the eyeballs ; (4) general nervousness ; (5) a fine muscular tremor ; together with, in many cases, (6) a number of other less important symptoms which will be afterwards described in detail.

The disease is much more common in women than in men, and is usually developed in young women (*i.e.*, during the period of active sexual life).

There is still much difference of opinion as to its exact pathology, though of recent years the theory, that *many* of the symptoms are due to over-activity or perverted activity of the thyroid gland, has gradually been gaining ground and may now be accepted as sufficiently well established. This statement does not, however, imply that the enlargement of the thyroid gland is the primary or initial lesion ; it is more probable, I think, that the primary cause of the disease is a lesion, or rather perhaps a functional disturbance, of some part of the nervous system, and that the enlargement of the thyroid gland is the result of this nervous derangement.

Historical Note.—Although cases of exophthalmic goitre had been previously described, the credit of recognising the connection between the accelerated and violent action of the heart and the enlargement of the thyroid—two of the great cardinal symptoms of exophthalmic goitre—undoubtedly belongs to the celebrated Dublin physician Graves ; hence the term *Graves' disease.* In a clinical lecture on the subject, published in the year 1835, Graves pointed out that the disturbance of the heart's action was not (necessarily) associated with organic disease of the heart. Five years later, a German physician, Basedow, published a more complete and elaborate account of the clinical features ; consequently in Germany the disease is usually termed *Basedow's disease.*

ETIOLOGY.

Sex.—Exophthalmic goitre is essentially a disease of the female sex, though males are occasionally affected. It is probably not far from the truth to say that the disease is nine or ten times more common in females than in males. In my series of 79 cases, 73 were females and 6 males. (I have also had under observation two other male cases, but since the notes have been mislaid they are not included in the series. Consequently in 81 cases 73 were females and 8 were males.)

Age.—Exophthalmic goitre may occur at any age, but in the great majority of cases the disease is developed during active sexual life. If I may judge from my own experience, the most common period for its commencement is, in women, between the ages of 15 and 35, and, in men, between the ages of 30 and 45. Though cases have been observed both in children and old people, all observers are agreed that the disease is extremely rare before the age of 12 and, comparatively speaking, very rarely developed after the age of 50. Divel has reported a case in a child aged 2½ years, and Charcot a case at the age of 68.

In my series of 79 (male and female) cases, the average age of the patients when they came under my notice was 34 years; the average age of the females was 33 and of the males 41 years.

The average *age of onset* in 76 (male and female) cases was 31 years; the average age of onset in 70 female cases was 30 years, and in 6 male cases 36 years.

The age at onset in the 76 cases (male and female) in which the date of commencement was ascertained, is shown in the following table.

TABLE 10, SHOWING THE AGE AT THE ONSET IN SEVENTY-SIX
CASES OF EXOPHTHALMIC GOITRE.

Below 12 years - - -	=	0 cases
Between 12 and 14 years inclusive	=	2 „
„ 14 and 19 „ „	=	10 „
„ 19 and 24 „ „	=	13 „
„ 24 and 29 „ „	=	11 „
„ 29 and 34 „ „	=	14 „
„ 34 and 39 „ „	=	9 „
„ 39 and 44 „ „	=	9 „
„ 44 and 49 „ „	=	3 „
„ 49 and 54 „ „	=	3 „
„ 54 and 59 „ „	=	2 „
		‾
Total	=	76

In the 76 cases in which the age at onset was ascertained, the disease developed in 69 cases (or 90.7 °/₀) between the ages of 15 and 49. In two cases (or 2.6 °/₀) the disease developed before the age of 15, viz., at 12 and 14 years of age respectively; and in 5 cases (or 6.6 °/₀) after the age of 49, viz., at the age of 50 in two cases, at 51 in one case, at 55 in one case, and at 56 in one case.

Influence of Marriage and Child-bearing.—In the 73 female cases included in my series of 79 cases, 47 were single women, and 26 were married women or widows. In the 26 cases in which the patients were married or widows, the disease commenced in 2 cases before the patients were married; consequently in the 73 female cases, the disease developed in single women in 49 cases (or 67.1 °/₀), and in married women in 24 cases (or 32.8 °/₀). In my series, therefore, the disease was twice as common in single as in married women.

In 25 out of the 26 cases in which the patients were married women and in which the number of pregnancies was noted, the average number of pregnancies was 3.2. In the two cases in which the disease was already in existence before the patients married, marriage seemed in one case (Case XVI.) to be followed by permanent, and in one case (Case XXII.) by temporary, benefit; in the latter case, a relapse occurred immediately after the birth of the first child; in another case (Case L.), the disease developed immediately after pregnancy.

Mode of Onset; Exciting and Predisposing Causes.—In some cases the symptoms develop insidiously and without any obvious cause; but in others the onset is more acute. In many cases, the exciting cause appears to be a fright, profound emotional disturbance or mental shock, over-fatigue, etc.; and in connection with the influence of fright and mental shock it is interesting to note, as Dr Hector Mackenzie has pointed out, that the physical effects of sudden fright and terror closely resemble the symptoms and appearances characteristic of exophthalmic goitre. Thus he states:—"The descriptions given by Darwin and Sir Charles Bell of the condition presented by persons under the influence of intense fear at once suggest the symptoms of exophthalmic goitre. The heart beats quickly and violently, so that it palpitates or knocks against the ribs. There is trembling of all the muscles of the body. The eyes start forward and the uncovered and protruding eyeballs are fixed on the object of terror; the skin breaks out into a cold and clammy sweat, and the face and neck are flushed or pallid. The intestines are affected." *

---

* Clifford Allbutt's "System of Medicine," Vol. iv., p. 490.

Occasionally the exhaustion produced by an acute illness, especially influenza, or a loss of blood seems to be the exciting cause. In exceptional cases, the disease has developed after a head injury. Anything which lowers the nerve tone and produces exhaustion and debility may probably act as an exciting cause in persons who are predisposed to the disease. Peripheral irritation originating in the nose or in the abdominal or pelvic viscera seems in some cases to be the exciting cause. Some of the patients affected with exophthalmic goitre are anæmic, and almost all observers are agreed that anæmia is apt to play a part in the production of the disease.

Gautier has suggested that cases of exophthalmic goitre should be divided into two great groups, viz., (1) Cases of *primary* exophthalmic goitre (these he regards as due to a functional disturbance of the nerve centres); and (2) Cases of *secondary* or *symptomatic* exophthalmic goitre (these he thinks are the result of some obvious peripheral lesion); but I doubt whether it is possible to draw a sharp line of distinction between these so-called primary and secondary forms of the disease, though the fact that in some cases the disease appears to have its exciting cause in some form of peripheral irritation should be kept in view for the purposes of treatment.

It may, I think, be doubted whether some of the conditions which have just been enumerated were the actual primary cause of the disease. It is probable that, in some cases at all events, in which a fright, emotional disturbance, or peripheral irritation appears to be the cause of exophthalmic goitre, the disease was already present in a slight and modified form, and that the emotional disturbance merely aggravated the symptoms and brought them into prominence, perhaps by deranging the tissue metabolism or upsetting the nervous balance.

In 78 of my series of 79 cases, the presence or absence of a cause for the disease was noted. In 45 of these 78 cases, there was no apparent cause; in 15 cases, the disease developed immediately after, and apparently as the result of, a nervous shock, profound mental anxiety, etc.; in 7 cases, after an attack of influenza; in 2 cases, after loss of blood; in 2 cases, immediately after childbirth; and in 1 case the following causes respectively were blamed, viz.:—sleeping in a damp bed, the occurrence of the menopause, an attack of rheumatic endocarditis, over-exertion shooting, an attack of bronchitis, privation and starvation. In 1 case, the patient, aged 27 when the symptoms of exophthalmic goitre developed, had had an enlarged thyroid (without any other symptoms) since she was 9 years old.

Hereditary and Family Influences.—Many of the subjects of exophthalmic goitre inherit a tendency to nerve disease. In rare cases, the disease appears to be directly handed down from parent to child ; but direct inheritance (mother and daughter both affected) is extremely rare. Cases are not very uncommon in which more than one member of the same family is affected. In the great majority of cases in which a patient who is affected with exophthalmic goitre inherits a tendency to nerve disease, the parents or near relatives have been affected with some other form of nervous malady, such as general nervousness, hysteria, epilepsy, or insanity.

In my series of 79 cases, a hereditary or family tendency to the disease was noted in 5 instances. In one case (Case XXI.), a sister had a large goitre ; in one case (Case XLVIII.), an aunt suffered from exophthalmic goitre ; in one case (Case LXXVIII.), a cousin had exophthalmic goitre ; in Cases LXXIII. and LXXIV., the patients were sisters ; in Case L., the patient's sister also suffered from exophthalmic goitre, and it is interesting to note that in both of these cases the disease developed after pregnancy and that in both cases the patients suffered during pregnancy from albuminuria.

In a considerable number of my cases, the patients came of markedly neurotic families, and in several instances were, prior to the commencement of the disease, themselves markedly neurotic. In a few instances, they were the subjects of other forms of nervous disease ; one patient, for example, suffered from epilepsy, another from asthma, a third from diabetes, etc. In several of my cases, there was a marked hereditary history of tubercle (phthisis, etc.), but I doubt whether this tendency was greater than it would have been in any other series of 79 cases of medical disease.

CLINICAL HISTORY.

Until comparatively recently, three symptoms—viz., (1) Increased frequency of the heart's action ; (2) Enlargement of the thyroid ; and (3) Prominence of the eyeballs—were considered to be the cardinal or fundamental symptoms of the disease ; but of recent years it has been generally recognised that in typical and fully developed cases other symptoms are also present. In a very large proportion of cases, a peculiar form of tremor, the special features of which I shall presently describe in detail, occurs ; this tremor is so constant that Charcot considered it to be one of the primary or fundamental symptoms. Another symptom, which is so constant and characteristic that it must undoubtedly be considered to be a primary or fundamental symptom, is nervous irritability and instability—a condition of general nervousness, as it may be termed.

In the following table, which is modified from Charcot, the symptoms of exophthalmic goitre are enumerated and classified. It is almost unnecessary to say that *all* of the symptoms enumerated in the table are rarely present in the same case.

TABLE 11, SHOWING THE SYMPTOMS WHICH MAY BE PRESENT IN CASES OF EXOPHTHALMIC GOITRE.

PRIMARY OR CARDINAL		Increased frequency of heart's action, palpitation, throbbing of the vessels, etc.
		Enlargement of the thyroid.
		Prominence of the eyeballs.
		General nervousness.
		Fine rhythmical vibratory tremor.
SECONDARY	*Digestive organs.*	Diarrhœa.
		Vomiting.
		Loss of appetite ; Bulimia ; Sudden fits of hunger.
		Thirst.
		Jaundice.
	Respiratory organs.	Cough.
		Increased frequency of respiration.
		Diminished inspiratory expansion (Bryson's symptom).
	Nervous system.	Von Graefe's symptom.
		Stellwag's symptom ; Absence of reflex blinking.
		Defective convergence (Möbius).
		Ophthalmoplegia externa.
		Paralysis ; Peculiar form of paraplegia.
		Epileptiform convulsions ; Chorea.
		Headache ; Neuralgia ; Angina pectoris.
		Psychical modifications (mental depression, maniacal excitement, etc.).
	Integumentary system.	Sweatings ; Flushings ; Sensations of heat ; Rises of temperature.
		Diminished electrical resistance.
		Increased pigmentation.
		Leucoderma ; Other skin eruptions.
		Loss of hair ; Atrophy of nails.
	Urinary system.	Polyuria.
		Albuminuria.
		Glycosuria.
	Generative system.	Menstrual derangements.
		Loss of sexual desire ; Impotence.
	General.	Debility ; Loss of weight ; Anæmia ; Cachexia ; Œdema of the lower extremities.

The Primary Symptoms of Exophthalmic Goitre.—The great primary, fundamental symptoms of exophthalmic goitre are, then, (1) Increased frequency of the heart's action; (2) Enlargement of the thyroid; (3) Prominence of the eyeballs; (4) A condition of general nervousness; and (5) Fine rhythmical tremor.

The appearance which a patient who is affected with exophthalmic goitre, in its typical, classical and fully developed form, presents, is highly characteristic. Graves' disease is, in fact, one of the few diseases which can, usually, be recognised at a glance. In typical and fully developed cases, the physiognomy of the patient is pathognomonic. The remarkable prominence of the eyeballs and the startled, staring, and in some cases almost savage appearance of the face, are very peculiar. These features and the obvious enlargement of the thyroid gland are admirably represented in my Atlas of Clinical Medicine, Plates XLIX. and L.

It must not, however, be supposed that one can recognise all cases of exophthalmic goitre at the first glance. In some cases, there is no prominence of the eyeballs; in others, there is no perceptible enlargement of the thyroid; while, in others again, there is neither prominence of the eyeballs nor enlargement of the thyroid. The symptoms which in my experience are constant are debility, general nervousness, and increased frequency and irritability of the heart's action. Without these symptoms a diagnosis of Graves' disease is, so far as we at present know, never justifiable. The fine muscular tremor and increased secretion of sweat are also very frequent and constant symptoms. Cases in which the disease is developed in a fragmentary or imperfect manner are, if I may judge from my own experience, somewhat more common in men than in women. It would appear that males are not only less frequently affected with exophthalmic goitre than females, but that, when the disease does develop in the male, its clinical features are apt to be less perfect and complete. It must not, however, be supposed that the disease is less severe or less serious in men than in women, for this is by no means the fact.

Several well marked but atypical or rudimentary cases of exophthalmic goitre in males have come under my observation. The first case of the kind which I clearly recognised—only, however, after its true nature had been pointed out by Sir William Jenner—was that of a gentleman whom I saw in consultation with my friend Dr Croom many years ago. He was a dark-skinned, very nervous man, some 45 or 50 years of age; his pulse was habitually very frequent, and the characteristic nervousness and tremor were well marked; but the eyeballs were not prominent, and the thyroid was not enlarged. Another case, in which the symptoms were almost identical with those of the case to which I have just referred, was that of a clergyman, under the care of Dr Millard ; he had been seen some time previously by Professor Charcot, who had given a written diagnosis of Graves' disease.*

In my series of 79 cases of exophthalmic goitre, enlargement of the thyroid was absent in 5 cases ; prominence of the eyeballs was absent in 14 cases ; and both enlargement of the thyroid and prominence of the eyeballs were absent in 5 cases.

Let us now consider the more important symptoms in detail.

Increased Frequency of the Heart's Action and Disturbance of the Circulation.—In many cases, these are the first symptoms which are complained of. In fully developed cases, the *pulse* usually numbers 120, 130, or 150 in the minute ; in some cases indeed, it is more frequent—180, 200, or even more in the minute. In the slighter forms of the disease and in those cases in which the symptoms are subsiding, the pulse may number only 100 or 90 in the minute. It is important to note that slowing of the pulse is perhaps the most certain sign of improvement which we possess ; *vice versâ*, a very quick pulse or increasing rapidity of the pulse, are unfavourable indications. The behaviour of the pulse under treatment is a most important guide for prognosis. The nervous equilibrium of patients affected with Graves' disease is so unstable that the slightest emotional disturbance or excitement, such, for example, as that occasioned by the presence of the doctor, is apt to produce an attack of palpitation and to cause a marked increase in the frequency of the pulse. In trying to form an estimate of the severity of any given case from the condition of the pulse, this must, of course, be allowed for. The extreme irritability of the heart is, indeed, one of the most striking features of the disease. In exophthalmic goitre, the heart seems to run loose ; it would appear that its action is no longer restrained or reined in by the inhibitory influence of the vagus ; the accelerating influence of the sympathetic seems to have the upper hand, and irritations and stimuli, emotional or other, which produce little or no effect upon a normal heart, may lash it, as it were, into an altogether unnatural and furious activity.

In rare cases, the increased frequency of the cardiac action appears to be paroxysmal and intermittent. In cases of this kind, more especially if the thyroid was not enlarged and the eyeballs were not prominent, the diagnosis would be most difficult. If the

---

* These two cases are not included in the series of 79 cases (see Table 12).

physician should happen to see such a case during an a-frequent interval (*i.e.*, at a time when the paroxysm of accelerated action was not present), a positive diagnosis could not (in the absence of exophthalmos and thyroid enlargement) be made. Such a difficulty in diagnosis is not, however, likely to occur. It is, I fancy, more theoretical than real. In the vast majority of cases of exophthalmic goitre, the agitation and nervous excitement, which the patient feels under the examination of the physician, would, even if the pulse were at times slow, set the heart off at a gallop and excite a paroxysm of increased frequency.

In my series of 79 cases, the pulse frequency was noted in 74 cases. The average frequency in these 74 cases was 129 per minute; but it should be stated that this probably represents a higher frequency of pulse than was actually present, for many of the cases were only seen once in consultation and the pulse was consequently in many of these cases temporarily increased by nervous excitement. I have, however, endeavoured to eliminate this error so far as possible, by counting the pulse at the end as well as at the beginning of the visit. The lowest pulse frequency which was noted in these 74 cases was 86 and the highest 240.

Many patients affected with exophthalmic goitre complain of a feeling of *throbbing or pulsation in the vessels* of the head and neck, and in some cases in the vessels of the whole body; but they do not, as a rule, appear to suffer in the same degree and to feel the same sensations of anxiety and dread as patients often do who are *suddenly* seized with a severe attack of ordinary functional palpitation. I have emphasised the word suddenly, for the sudden, intermittent, and unaccustomed character of an ordinary attack of palpitation seems to me to be a sufficient explanation of the very different character of the subjective sensations which the patient experiences in the two cases. There can be little doubt that, if the heart of a healthy individual were suddenly made to beat in the way in which the heart of a patient affected with severe Graves' disease beats, the healthy individual would experience all the alarming symptoms which are apt to be associated with an ordinary attack of functional palpitation. In exophthalmic goitre, the irritability of the heart continues for months or years; it becomes, as it were, part and parcel of the individual. It is natural, therefore, to suppose that, when a heart whose action is habitually increased and unduly irritable becomes temporarily still more accelerated— accelerated to a degree which, in a normal individual, is usually attended with the alarming sensations of a violent attack of palpitation—the discomfort would be, comparatively speaking, slight.

In my series of 79 cases, *palpitation* was present in 77 cases, absent in 1 case and not noted in 1 case. *Throbbing of the vessels of the neck* was present in 58 cases, absent in 10 cases, and not noted in 11 cases.

In exophthalmic goitre, the pulse is usually small in size and regular in rhythm. In some cases, it is more or less dicrotic. In the later stages of the disease, the pulse may become irregular or intermittent, as the result of cardiac failure, dilatation, or organic valvular disease; but it is important to remember that in the majority of cases of exophthalmic goitre there is no organic valvular lesion.

In some cases, the heart is found after death to be little, if at all, larger than normal; but in other cases, and I am disposed to think that they comprise the great majority of severe and long-continued cases, the heart becomes dilated or (but this is, I think, less frequent) to some extent hypertrophied. In a large proportion of the severe cases which have come under my own observation, the heart was more or less enlarged; and in some of them there was distinct evidence of mitral or (but this was less frequent) of tricuspid regurgitation.

Towards the termination of the case *œdema of the feet* is not unfrequently developed. In my series of 79 cases, œdema of the feet was present in 13 cases, absent in 56 cases, and not noted in 11 cases.

In most well marked cases of exophthalmic goitre, some *shortness of breath on exertion*, which is, in part at least, of cardiac origin, is complained of. In my series of 79 cases, shortness of breath was complained of in 39 cases, was said to be absent in 20 cases, and was not noted in 20 cases.

On *physical examination*, the area of visible impulse is usually increased, and in many cases an abnormal degree of epigastric pulsation is present. The action of the heart is usually sharp and flapping in character. The first sound is usually short in duration and accentuated in tone; in rare cases, the heart sounds are so loud as to be auto-audible. A systolic murmur can frequently be heard in the mitral or pulmonary areas, and in some cases in the tricuspid or aortic areas. In some cases, these murmurs are no doubt hæmic in character; in others, they seem to be independent of anæmia, and perhaps due to the altered character of the cardiac contractions. Systolic murmurs in the mitral and tricuspid areas are probably, in many cases, the result of dilatation of the ventricles. In exceptional cases, organic lesions, the result of endocarditis, are present; but, in my experience, the subjects of

Graves' disease comparatively rarely suffer from acute articular rheumatism or endocarditis.

In my series of 79 cases, the presence or absence of *enlargement of the heart* was noted in 71 cases; in 21 cases the heart was more or less enlarged, and in the remaining 50 cases it was not (so far as could be judged from clinical examination) enlarged.

In the 79 cases, *valvular murmurs* were present in 23 cases, absent in 49 cases, and not noted in 7 cases. In the 23 cases in which valvular murmurs were present, the murmur was a systolic mitral murmur in 11 cases, a pulmonary systolic murmur in 4 cases, a mitral and pulmonary systolic murmur in 3 cases, a mitral pre-systolic murmur in 2 cases, a mitral and tricuspid systolic murmur in 1 case, and a systolic murmur audible in all the valvular areas in 2 cases.

Exaggerated pulsation in the vessels of the neck is in many cases a striking symptom; the pulsation may be hammering in character. *Pulsations and thrills* can, in a certain proportion of cases, be felt *over the enlarged thyroid*. Inordinate pulsation (palpitation) of the abdominal aorta is frequent. In some cases the patients complain of excessive pulsations all through the body. *The veins of the neck* are, in some cases, unduly prominent, and, in the advanced stages of the disease, true venous pulsation in the neck is occasionally present. *Blowing systolic murmurs* can often be heard in the *carotids, over the enlarged thyroid*, and sometimes *over the enlarged eyeballs*. In many cases, a loud *venous hum* is audible at the root of the neck. Tinnitus, headache and, less frequently, vertigo, which are not uncommon, are probably in many cases due to these derangements of the circulatory system.

The exact cause of the increased frequency of the heart's action is a matter of dispute. According to one view, it is the result of overaction (irritation) of the sympathetic; according to another, of diminished action (paralysis) of the vagus; perhaps both views are correct.

Enlargement of the thyroid.—In typical and fully developed cases, this is a striking feature. The enlargement of the thyroid may be developed before, simultaneously with, or after the increased frequency of the heart's action and the exophthalmos, though it is sometimes the first symptom which attracts the attention of the patient; in other cases, the patient is not aware of the alteration until her attention is directed to it by the physician. In some cases, as I have already more than once stated, the thyroid does not appear to be enlarged; but in this connection it must be remembered that slight enlargement of the thyroid gland is difficult to detect and may easily escape notice. In some of the cases in which the thyroid is not obviously enlarged, exophthalmos is also wanting.

The enlargement of the thyroid is usually moderate in degree ; the gland rarely attains to such a large size as in ordinary goitre. The enlarged gland usually feels elastic and in some cases soft, but in others it is hard and even nodulated. Dilated veins may sometimes be seen coursing over the enlarged thyroid ; and pulsations and thrills can often be felt and blowing murmurs heard over the enlarged gland. It used to be supposed that the enlargement of the gland was chiefly due to the dilatation of the thyroidal vessels, but the correctness of this opinion is very questionable. In many cases at all events, the gland is not nearly so vascular as is commonly supposed. Nevertheless, I am quite satisfied that in some cases the thrills and murmurs are actually produced in the thyroid itself, and are not merely, as has been suggested, in the adjacent vessels.

In the later stages of exophthalmic goitre, the enlarged thyroid not unfrequently becomes firmer and harder than it was in the earlier stages of the case ; this is doubtless due to the development of hyperplastic and sclerotic changes ; and it is very interesting to note that in some rare cases, in which these sclerotic and interstitial changes are well advanced, and in which the glandular tissue has presumably become atrophied and destroyed, the symptoms of exophthalmic goitre may disappear and be replaced by the characteristic symptoms of myxœdema. One case of this kind has come under my own notice (see Case XVII., p. 354). As I have already pointed out, many of the symptoms of exophthalmic goitre are the direct opposite of those which characterise myxœdema.

All parts of the gland are usually enlarged, but the enlargement is not unfrequently more marked on one side than the other. The right lobe, which is normally, it is said, slightly larger than the left, is, as a rule, more enlarged than the left.

In rare cases, the enlargement of the thyroid and the exophthalmos are *unilateral ;* in cases of this description, the enlargement of the thyroid and the exophthalmos are usually on the same side of the body ; but this is not always the case. A remarkable case has been reported and figured by Dr Burney Yeo, in which the exophthalmos was limited to the left eye and the enlargement of the thyroid to the right lobe.

In my series of 79 cases, the thyroid was enlarged (when the patient came under my notice) in 71 cases ; there was no enlargement in 5 cases (in one of these cases, the gland had been, at a previous stage of the case, enlarged). In the 72 cases in which the thyroid was (or had been) enlarged, the enlargement was very slight in 8 cases, and more or less considerable (but very rarely great) in 64 cases.

In the 71 cases in which the thyroid was enlarged when the patients came under my notice, the enlargement was symmetrical in 36 cases, the right lobe was more enlarged than the left in 28 cases, and the left lobe more than the right in 7 cases.

In the 71 cases in which the thyroid was enlarged, the consistency of the gland was soft in 36 cases, firm or hard in 19 cases, and not noted in 16 cases.

Murmurs were present over the enlarged thyroid in 23 cases, absent in 35 cases, and not noted in 13 cases.

Thrills were present over the enlarged thyroid in 21 cases, absent in 36 cases, and not noted in 14 cases.

The degree of enlargement, like the prominence of the eyeballs, undoubtedly varies from time to time. I am satisfied that a decided increase can in some cases be observed during emotional excitement. In some cases, the enlargement of the thyroid increases and, in others, diminishes during menstruation or immediately after menstruation. In Case XX. of my series, in which the disease developed a few months after the first menstruation and in which the menstruation was irregular in time, the enlargement of the thyroid and the prominence of the eyeballs subsided and almost entirely disappeared during the menstrual period; if the patient went longer than four weeks without menstruating, the prominence of the eyeballs and the enlargement of the thyroid became much more marked. Temporary enlargements of this kind are no doubt due to temporary dilatation of the thyroidal vessels.

Prominence of the Eyeballs.—The exophthalmos is usually developed simultaneously with the enlargement of the thyroid and later than the increased frequency of the heart. The degree of prominence varies considerably in different cases. In typical cases, the prominence of the eyeballs is very striking and characteristic. In exceptional cases, there is no exophthalmos. When the exophthalmos is great, and especially when the upper lid is at the same time spasmodically retracted, the countenance acquires a wild, staring look. The protrusion of the eyeballs is occasionally so great that the insertions of the recti muscles are exposed; and cases have actually been reported in which it was said that the exophthalmos was so extreme that the eyeball was dislocated out of the orbit, and had to be pushed back into its place by the fingers. As I have already stated, the exophthalmos is, in rare cases, unilateral.

The degree of prominence appears to vary from time to time, as the result of emotional excitement, etc. It must, however, be remembered that in many cases the increased protrusion which appears to result from excitement is apparent only, and due to the fact that under excitement the upper lid becomes more retracted and a larger portion of the sclerotic exposed than under ordinary conditions.

It is said that in some cases the eyeballs are actually enlarged, but if such is the fact, the degree of enlargement is probably inconsiderable.

In my series of 79 cases, prominence of the eyeballs was present in 64 cases, absent in 14 cases, and not noted in 1 case. In the 64 cases in which the eyeballs were prominent, the exophthalmos was more or less considerable in 55 cases, and very slightly marked in 9 cases. In 2 cases, one eye only was prominent.

In those cases in which the exophthalmos is so great that the lids, when closed, are unable completely to cover the eyeball, conjunctivitis or ulceration of the cornea may be ultimately produced. Mr George Berry states that a certain degree of anæsthesia of the cornea is sometimes present; and he suggests that it is a symptom which deserves special attention, since it may favour the production of ulceration of the cornea.

In the great majority of cases of exophthalmic goitre—provided of course that the cornea is not ulcerated, but this condition is extremely rare—vision is unaffected. The retinal vessels are in some cases dilated, and pulsation in the retinal arteries can, it is said, in some cases be seen with the ophthalmoscope.

Increase of the orbital fat and dilatation and engorgement of the vessels at the back of the orbit are usually considered to be the chief causes of the exophthalmos. Spasm of the fibres of Müller's muscle is another condition to which the prominence of the eyeballs has been attributed.

The Condition of the Pupil.—The pupils are, as a rule, normal in size and in many cases extremely mobile. Marked and persistent dilatation, though it occasionally does occur, is rare. In some cases the pupils are unequal in size, but this, too, is in my experience very exceptional.

The absence of any marked and persistent dilatation of the pupils is strongly opposed to the view that the disease is due to irritation of the cervical sympathetic.

In my series of 79 cases, the condition of the pupils is noted in 72 cases ; in 37 cases the pupils were of medium size ; in 25 cases contracted ; and in 10 dilated.

Before leaving the condition of the eyeballs it may perhaps be well to refer to some of the other ocular symptoms which are frequently present.

Stellwag's sign.—In many cases, the upper eyelid is spasmodically retracted and the aperture between the eyelids is wider than normal. This spasmodic retraction of the upper lid (which is admirably seen in Plates XLIX. and L., Fig. 1, of my Atlas of Clinical Medicine) varies in degree from time to time, and is often markedly increased under emotional excitement. This retraction of the upper lid goes by the name of Stellwag's sign, and appears to be due to spasmodic contraction of Müller's muscle. Its diagnostic value is considerable, since it does not appear to occur in other forms of exophthalmos. But it must not be supposed that this (Stellwag's) symptom is a constant feature of the disease. Further, I have met with it in a few other cases in which there was no suspicion of exophthalmic goitre ; it cannot, therefore, be considered pathognomonic.

In my series of 79 cases, the presence or absence of Stellwag's symptom is noted in 70 cases ; it was present in 37 and absent in 33 cases.

In some cases, an *absence of reflex blinking* has been observed. This is perhaps due to the spasmodic retraction of the upper lid, or to anæsthesia of the cornea.

Von Graefe's sign.—In many cases of exophthalmic goitre, the upper lid fails to follow the eyeball downwards in a steady coordinate manner ; the movement of the lid hangs fire, as it were, or follows the downward movement of the eyeball in an uncertain, jerky manner. In health, the downward movement of the eyeball is accompanied by a simultaneous and exactly co-ordinated movement of the upper lid. If one stands in front of a healthy individual and makes him fix and follow one's finger with his eye, as it is moved slowly from above the horizontal line of vision downwards towards the ground, it is seen that as the eye is depressed the upper lid moves simultaneously with the ball.

In my series of 79 cases, the presence or absence of Von Graefe's symptom is noted in 69 cases ; it was present in 30 cases and absent in 39 cases.

Other ocular derangements.—Möbius has pointed out that in a considerable proportion of cases of exophthalmic goitre the patient is unable to converge for near objects. *Ophthalmoplegia externa*, or paralysis of one or more of the external muscles of the eyeball, has occasionally been observed.

In my series of 79 cases, the ability to converge for near objects was noted in 43 cases; in 17 of these cases, the power of convergence was impaired or lost; and in the remaining 26 cases was normal.

In 3 of my 79 cases, ophthalmoplegia externa was present; in 2 cases the degree of paralysis was slight; in 1 case very marked.

Muscular tremor.—This symptom, which was first particularly described by Marie and Charcot, is highly characteristic. The tremor consists of fine rhythmical muscular movements which appear to be nearly twice as rapid (eight or nine per second) as those which produce the tremor of paralysis agitans (in which the muscular contractions number four or five per second).

The tremor usually affects the muscles of the lower limbs and of the trunk as well as those of the upper extremities. In many cases the whole body can be felt to shake, when the hand is placed on the top of the head or on the shoulder. According to Charcot, the individual digits do not tremble, but I am not satisfied that this statement is always correct. This, he states, is a point of distinction between the tremor of exophthalmic goitre and that due to alcohol and general paralysis of the insane, in which conditions the tremor is also very rapid (eight or nine per second). In rare cases, the tremor is said to be unilateral; personally, I have never observed this. I am in the habit of demonstrating the tremor to my students by making the patient hold out the arm at right angles to the body, and then balancing a stethoscope, with the chest end uppermost, on the back of the hand.

In some cases, in addition to the fine rhythmical tremor which has just been described, *irregular jerking spasmodic movements of the fingers and also of the toes* may be noted if carefully looked for.

The muscular tremor is not usually developed, at all events in a sufficient degree to be readily perceived, until the other symptoms of the disease (palpitation, etc.) have become pronounced; but, in some cases, it appears to be the first symptom to be developed.

The tremor is of considerable diagnostic importance, especially in some of the imperfectly developed forms of the disease in which there is no enlargement of the thyroid and no exophthalmos.

In my series of 79 cases, fine tremors were present in 66 cases, absent in 5 cases, and not noted in 8 cases.

General nervousness.—Nervousness, excitability and irritability are, as I have already stated, constant and highly characteristic features of the disease. The contrast in this respect between exophthalmic goitre and myxœdema is very striking and highly suggestive.

In my series of 79 cases, general nervousness was present in 77 cases (in two of these cases the nervousness was very slight), and not noted in 2 cases.

Secondary Symptoms of Exophthalmic Goitre.—In addition to the five great primary symptoms to which I have just referred, quite a number of other symptoms may be present.

In describing the "secondary" symptoms of Graves' disease, I do not propose to follow in regular sequence the order of the symptoms as set forth in Table 11 (see p. 386). In that table, the symptoms are arranged in accordance with the particular system (integumentary, digestive, urinary, etc.) to which they belong. It is preferable, I think, to regard the manner in which the symptoms are produced, rather than the special organ, part of the body, or "system" which they implicate. Almost all the "secondary" symptoms of Graves' disease are the result of derangement of some part of the nerve apparatus. Even the diarrhœa, which is in some cases a very striking symptom, is clearly due to perverted innervation.

In connection with the exophthalmos, I have already referred to two of the most common and important of the secondary symptoms, namely, Stellwag's sign and Von Graefe's sign. I have also mentioned the not unfrequent occurrence of defective convergence, and the occasional occurrence of ophthalmoplegia externa. To these conditions I need not further refer.

Many of the secondary symptoms of Graves' disease appear to be due to the disturbance of the vasomotor nerve apparatus.

Excessive Sweating, Subjective Sensations of Heat, Elevations of Temperature.—*Excessive sweating* is a very characteristic and constant symptom. During the attacks of sweating, the skin is often warm as well as moist. In many cases, *sensations of warmth* and *flushings* of the face, feet, hands or body generally are complained of; and in some cases, though this is exceptional, distinct *rises of temperature*, which are apparently of nervous origin, for they may occur independently of any discoverable local inflammation or visceral complication, occur. They are said to be more common at the menstrual periods. In rare cases, these elevations of temperature appear to be associated with grave cerebral symptoms, though no case of the kind has come under my own notice.

In my series of 79 cases, *excessive sweating* was present in 64 cases, absent in 7 cases, and not noted in 8 cases. *Flushings* were present in 40 cases, absent in 10 cases and not noted in 29 cases. In 18 of the 79 cases (all hospital patients), the *course of the temperature* was carefully observed; in 4 of these 18 cases, the temperature was subnormal; in 5 normal; and in the remaining 9 cases (in which the temperature was usually normal or subnormal) elevations of temperature, for which there was no apparent cause (other than the nervous disturbances associated with the disease), and which were usually of temporary duration, occurred.

Diminished Electrical Resistance of the Skin.—In cases of exophthalmic goitre the resistance which the skin offers to the passage of electrical currents is markedly diminished ; this appears to be due to the fact that the epidermis, which in the dry state is such a bad conductor of electricity, is, in consequence of vasomotor alterations and the dilatation of the capillary vessels which results therefrom, bathed in fluid, its resisting power to electric currents being thereby greatly reduced.

Dr Wolfenden (quoted by Sajous) found that the average resistance of the normal skin to the passage of a galvanic current of moderate strength was from 4,000 to 5,000 ohms, while in eight cases of exophthalmic goitre the resistance which the body (skin) offered to the passage of the same strength of current was only 500 to 700 ohms ; in two of these cases, the resistance was as low as 200 and 300 ohms respectively. The measurements are, of course, made by means of an accurately graduated galvanometer or galvanoscope.

Diminished electrical resistance of the skin is not peculiar to Graves' disease; it occurs in many other conditions, such as chronic alcoholismus and acromegaly, in which the superficial capillaries are dilated and the skin bathed in moisture. But, so far as I know, such an extreme degree of diminution as that noted by Wolfenden in exophthalmic goitre has not been as yet observed, except as a mere temporary occurrence, in other diseased conditions.

Diarrhœa.—In some cases of exophthalmic goitre, diarrhœa is a prominent symptom. The characters of the diarrhœa are peculiar ; it is apt to occur in paroxysms, suddenly and without any apparent cause ; it usually persists for several days and then spontaneously disappears. The motions are frequent, copious and watery ; in one of my cases the motions were of a pinkish colour, probably due to the presence of blood. The diarrhœa is usually unattended by pain or colic ; but in some cases colicky pains are complained of immediately before the evacuations take place. In one of Charcot's cases, the attacks of diarrhœa recurred at regular periodic intervals. During the attacks of diarrhœa, the tongue may be quite clean and the appetite unimpaired; indeed the appetite may be increased, even voracious, during the attacks. In some cases, the diarrhœa is not easily restrained by ordinary astringent remedies, such as laudanum. When the diarrhœa is severe, a good deal of exhaustion may result. It seems probable that, in many cases of exophthalmic goitre, the diarrhœa is of nervous origin, and, like the sweating, due to some vasomotor derangement.

In rudimentary or imperfectly developed cases of exophthalmic goitre, the diarrhœa may be of diagnostic value, just as the gastric and intestinal crises are of diagnostic value in some obscure and undeveloped cases of locomotor ataxia.

In my series of 79 cases, the bowels were regular in 38 cases and constipated in 11 cases; in 21 cases occasional attacks of (nervous) diarrhœa occurred; in 9 cases the condition of the bowels is not mentioned in the notes.

Vomiting.—In other cases, vomiting, apparently of nervous origin, occurs. Dr Dreschfeld states that in some cases of this kind the breath has the sweet apple-like odour characteristic of acetonæmia, and that the urine contains diacetic acid.

In my 79 cases, vomiting was absent in 46 cases, present occasionally in 9 cases, and not noted in 24 cases.

Pigmentation of the Skin.—Dr David Drummond in particular has directed attention to this condition which is developed in a considerable proportion of cases of Graves' disease. In some cases, the pigmentary deposits are distributed in patches, a common situation being round the orbits; in others, the whole skin is uniformly discoloured, the pigmentation being most marked in those situations, such as the areolæ of the nipples and the genital organs, in which pigment is normally most abundant. In several cases which have come under my own notice, the dirty, dingy, yellowish-brown, or earthy tint of the face was very striking. In one of these cases, the disease existed in a rudimentary form, the enlargement of the thyroid and the prominence of the eyeballs being absent. I am disposed to think that the skin pigmentation is in some cases of considerable diagnostic value.

In my series of 79 cases, abnormal pigmentation of the skin was present in 29 cases, absent in 39 cases, and not noted in 11 cases.

Patches of leucoderma, urticaria, and other skin eruptions have been observed in some cases of exophthalmic goitre; and in this connection it is interesting to note that in some cases of Addison's disease leucoderma is also present.

In a considerable proportion of cases the *hair* becomes *thin;*

atrophic changes in the nails also occasionally occur, but in my experience appear usually to be due to anæmia associated with the exophthalmic goitre, rather than to the exophthalmic goitre itself.

In my series of 79 cases, a skin eruption was present in 8 cases, absent in 45 cases, and not noted in 26 cases. In the 8 cases in which a skin eruption was present, the eruption was leucoderma in 3 cases, eczema in 2 cases, erythema in 2 cases and psoriasis in 1 case.

Loss of hair was present in 14 cases, absent in 14 cases and not noted in 51 cases.

Urinary derangements.—Polyuria, albuminuria and glycosuria occasionally occur. In two of my cases in which the amount of albumen was considerable, there were no tube casts and none of the ordinary symptoms of Bright's disease; and it is perhaps worth noting that in both of these cases ophthalmoplegia externa was present. It is probable that these urinary derangements, which are usually merely temporary and intermittent, are, like so many of the other symptoms, due to vasomotor alterations. As has been already stated, Dreschfeld found diacetic acid in some cases during the attacks of (? nervous) vomiting.

If, as seems probable, the nerve centres in the medulla oblongata are deranged (either primarily or secondarily) in cases of exophthalmic goitre, the occasional occurrence of glycosuria (and I may perhaps also add of polyuria and albuminuria) is not difficult of explanation.

In my series of 79 cases, the urine was normal in 64 cases; albumen (only a trace in 4 cases) was present in 6 cases, and not noted in 9 cases.

Respiratory derangements.—*A short, dry (nervous) cough* is sometimes present. In one of my cases, a profuse, pink, watery secretion was poured out from the bronchial mucous membrane. The pulmonary œdema and profuse bronchial secretion in that case appeared to be the immediate cause of death. I have always regarded the pulmonary œdema and the profuse bronchial secretion which were present in this case, as the result of vasomotor paralysis. The condition was, I believe, exactly comparable to the profuse sweating and copious diarrhœa to which I have already referred.

In my series of 79 cases, cough was present in 12 cases, absent in 44 cases and not noted in 23 cases.

Increased frequency of the respirations is not uncommon. In some cases it seems to depend upon anæmia or cardiac complications; in others to be of nervous origin. *Diminished expansion of the chest during inspiration* has been observed in some cases (Bryson's symptom).

Nervous derangements not previously described.—*Psychical symptoms* are prominent in some cases of Graves' disease. I have already referred to the nervous irritability and unrest. The least thing " puts the patient into a tremble." The most casual observer cannot fail to be struck with the extreme "nervousness" of patients suffering from exophthalmic goitre. Their nervous equilibrium is eminently unstable. Little things, which would be unnoticed by any ordinary individual, are sufficient to agitate and disturb them. They are fidgety and irritable. And yet, they are not, as a rule, hysterical. Charcot, indeed, states that some patients, who, prior to the onset of the disease, were distinctly hysterical, cease to be so when the symptoms of Graves' disease become fully developed ; he further states that, with the decline of the disease and the disappearance of its characteristic symptoms, hysterical manifestations may again make their appearance ; but, in some cases, hysterical manifestations are undoubtedly developed during the course of the disease.

Mental alterations of a more decided kind are sometimes observed, such as mania, melancholia, and, more rarely, general paralysis of the insane.

Headache is a frequent symptom. The condition of *sleep* varies ; in some it is bad, in others good ; in some cases the patients complain of unpleasant dreams. *Neuralgia* is not uncommon. *Migraine, angina pectoris, epilepsy* and *chorea* are occasionally developed in the course of the disease. Charcot mentions the occurrence of *paraplegia*, which, he states, presents certain characters which seem to show that it is peculiar to the disease. The paralysis is usually incomplete ; but in one case it was complete and absolute at the time of the patient's admission to hospital ; in that case, the paralysed muscles were flaccid and moderately atrophied ; the reflexes, both deep and superficial, were abolished ; the electrical reactions were normal ; there were no fibrillary twitchings ; sensibility was unimpaired, and the bladder and rectum were unaffected. In those cases in which the paralysis was incomplete and the patient was able to move about (either with or without the aid of crutches), a sudden giving way of the legs, due to sudden and unexpected flexion of the knees, was apt to occur ; this sudden failure of the legs seems to be a characteristic and peculiar feature of the condition. The paraplegia is not permanent ; it seems to be functional ; the absence of hysterical symptoms and the characters of the paraplegia itself (especially the fact that there are no sensory disturbances) seem to show that it is not hysterical.

In my series of 79 cases, *headache* was complained of in 26 cases, was absent in 31 cases and was not noted in 22 cases. *Sleep* was good in 26 cases, bad in 35 cases (in 2 of these cases there were unpleasant dreams), excessive in 1 case and not noted in 17 cases. *Neuralgia* was complained of in 10 cases, absent in 39 cases and not noted in 30 cases.

The general health; condition of appetite, etc.—In some cases of exophthalmic goitre, the general health is comparatively little affected, though, as I have already said, general nervousness is always a prominent symptom. Languor, debility, and inability for sustained exertion are usually very marked features. In most cases, there is some loss of flesh, and in some cases, more especially acutely developed cases and severe cases, there is marked emaciation; in others, especially in the later stages of the disease, a cachectic condition is developed. If I may judge from my own experience, marked debility, great emaciation and cachexia, are more apt to be developed in the early stages of the disease in those cases in which the patient is a male. In many cases a certain degree of anæmia is present.

In my series of 79 cases, *debility* was present in 74 cases and not noted in 5 cases. *Anæmia* (usually slight in degree) was present in 27 cases, absent in 37 cases and not noted in 15 cases. *Loss of weight* was present in 51 cases, absent in 14 cases (in 1 case, Case XXV., the patient got fatter as the disease progressed) and not noted in 14 cases. In several cases, the loss of weight was considerable; in Case XV., the patient lost 16½ lbs.; in Case XXI., 14 lbs.; in Case XXIV., 14 lbs.; in Case XL. (this patient was a male), 3 st. 10 lbs.; in Case XLII., 14 lbs.; in Case XLIV., 2 st.; in Case LXI., 1½ st.; and in Case LXXVI., 2 st. 3 lbs.

In some cases, the *appetite* remains good; in others, it is impaired; in others, there is complete anorexia; occasionally an inordinate appetite for food, or sudden fits of hunger, occur; in other cases, the appetite is capricious or peculiar. Loss of appetite, distaste for food, and complete anorexia are in my experience usually associated with cachexia and emaciation. *Thirst* is in some cases a prominent symptom.

In my series of 79 cases, the appetite was good in 26 cases, fair in 4 cases, bad in 28 cases, excessive in 4 cases, and not noted in 17 cases.

Jaundice has been described as occurring in a few cases. In a male case of rudimentary or imperfectly developed exophthalmic goitre which came under my notice some twenty years ago (but which is not included in the series, for I have unfortunately mislaid the notes), the motions were habitually pale and devoid of bile. Sir William Jenner seemed to attach considerable importance to this condition as a sign of Graves' disease.

Menstrual derangements.—Amenorrhœa, menorrhagia, and irregularities of menstruation occur in a certain proportion of cases ; but in most cases of exophthalmic goitre the menstruation is quite natural. Leucorrhœa is not uncommon. In the male, loss of sexual power or even complete impotence may occur.

In my series of 79 cases, the condition of menstruation is noted in 65 cases. In these 65 cases, the menstruation was regular and natural in 29, regular and scanty in 5 cases, irregular in 2 cases, irregular and scanty in 5 cases, irregular with menorrhagia in 3 cases ; menorrhagia was present in 5 cases ; amenorrhœa in 5 cases ; amenorrhœa due to the occurrence of the menopause in 8 cases ; amenorrhœa due to pregnancy in 1 case ; in 1 case the patient (aged 14) had only menstruated once, and in 1 case the patient (aged 24) had never menstruated.

Other Visceral Derangements.—*Enlargement of the lymphatic glands* and of the *spleen* has been noticed in some cases.

Endocarditis and *organic valvular lesions* are occasionally, but rarely, developed. *Angina-like pains* occasionally occur.

Asthenia, asystole, relative and muscular incompetence at the mitral or tricuspid orifices, with *œdema of the feet* and *general dropsy,* and *pulmonary complications,* such as bronchitis and œdema of the lungs, are not uncommon in the later stages of the disease, and are often the immediate cause of death.

It is doubtful, I think, whether some of the conditions to which I have just referred should be regarded as complications. I am disposed to think that many of them are the direct result of the disease, due to the same nerve derangements, developed in a very intense form, which are the cause of the other symptoms which have been previously described.

The frequency of the more important symptoms in my series of 79 consecutive cases of exophthalmic goitre is shown in Table 12.

Course.—The course is usually chronic ; the disease generally persists for several years ; some cases have been recorded in which the symptoms developed very rapidly after a sudden fright or emotional disturbance, and, after being present for a short time, as rapidly disappeared.

TABLE 12.—SHOWING THE RELATIVE FREQUENCY OF THE

Sex.	Single, Married, or Widow.	Duration.	Apparent Cause.	Enlargement of Thyroid[1]	THYROID.		Murmurs.	Thrills.	Prominence of the Eyes[4]	Size of Pupils[a]	Von Graefe's Symptom.	Stellwag's Symptom.	D'fective C'vergence.	Ophthalmoplegia Externa[6]	Palpitation.	Throbbing of Vessels.
					Lobe chiefly affected[2]	Firm or Soft[3]										
F.	S.	8 months.	Mental anxiety.	1	S.	..	..	..	1	D.	..	..	..	o	1	1
F.	S.	2 years.	Sleeping in damp bed.	1	R.	S.	o	o	1	C.	..	..	..	o	1	1
F.	M.	2 years.	o	1	R.	S.	1	1	1	M.	..	..	..	o	1	1
M.	..	12 years.	o	1 V.S.	R.	..	o	o	1	C.	..	..	..	o	1	..
F.	S.	4½ years.	o	1	R.	S.	1	1	1	M.	1	1	..	o	1	1
F.	M.	(?)	o	1	S.	..	..	..	1 S.	..	..	..	..	o	1	..
F.	S.	3 weeks.	o	1	S.	..	..	..	1	M.	o	o	..	o	1	..
F.	S.	Some months.	o	1	R.	..	..	..	1 S.	D.	o	o	..	o	1	1
M.	..	1 year.	o	1	R.	S.	..	..	1	M.	1	1	..	o	1	..
F.	S.		o	1	S.	..	..	..	1	C.	1	o	..	o	1	1
F.	M.	....	....	1	S.	..	..	..	1	..	1	1	..	o	1	1
F.	S.	5 years.	o	1	S.	..	..	..	1	..	1	1	..	o	1	1
F.	S.	2½ years.	o	1	L.	F.	..	..	1	..	1	1	..	o	1	1
F.	M.	2 years.	o	1	R.	F.	1	1	o	..	o	˙o	..	o	1	
M.	..	2 years.	o	1 V.S.	R.	..	o	o	1	C.	o	o	1	1 and ptosis.	1	1
F.	M.	6 years.	o	1	S.	F.	o	o	1	..	..	..	..	o	1	1
F.	S.	1 year.	o	1	S.	..	..	..	1	M.	1	..	..	o	1	1
F.	M.	Few months.	Loss of blood : miscarriage 7 months previously.	1	S.	F.	1	1	1	M.	1	o	1	o	1	1
F.	M.[*]	4 years: married 10 months.	o	1	R.	S.	1	1	1	C.	1	o	..	o	1	1
F.	S.	9 months.	o	1	S.	..	..	..	1	M.	o	o	..	o	1	1
F.	S.	7 years.	o	1	R.	S.	1	1	1	C.	1	1	1	o	1	1
F.	M.	20 years.	After birth of 2nd child.	1 S.	S.	F.	o	o	1	M.	1	1	1	o	1	1
F.	S.	2 years.	o	1	S.	S.	1	1	1	D.	1	o	..	o	1	1
F.	S.	4½ years.	o	1	L.	S.	1	1	1	M.	1	1	..	o	1	1
F.	S.	6 months.	o	1	S.	S.	o	o	1	M.	1	1	..	o	1	1
F.	W.	1 year.	Mental shock.	1	S.	S.	o	o	1	C.	1	o	..	o	1	1
F.	S.	1 year.	o	o	..	..	..	..	1 R. only	M.	1	o	1	o	1	o
F.	S	6 months.	Influenza.	1	S.	F.	1	1	1	C.	1	1	..	o	1	1
F.	S.	4 months.	Endocarditis, ? rheumatic.	o	o	o	o	o	o	M.	o	o	o	o	1	1
F.	S.	2½ years.	Influenza.	1	R.	F.	o	o	1	M.	1	1	1	o	1	1
F.	M.	6 years.	Overwork and mental anxiety.	1	S.	S.	1	1	1	M.	1	1	1	o	1	1
F.	S.	10 years.	o	1	R.	F.	o	o	o F.	M.	o	o	o	o	1	1
F.	S.	9 months.	Menopause.	1	L.	S.	..	..	o	C.	o	o	o	o	1	1
M.	..	Several months.	o	1	R.	S.	1	1	1	C.	o	o	o	o	1	1
F.	M.[*]	4 years.	o	1	R.	S.	1	1	1	M.	o	o	..	o	1	1
F.	M.	16 years.	o	1	R.	F.	o	o	o	M.	o	o	o	o	1	1
F.	S.	6 years.	Mental worry.	1	S.	S.	o	o	1 S.	M.	o	o	..	o	1	1
F.	S.	10 months.	Influenza.	1	S.	S.	o	o	1	D.	1	1	1	o	1	1
F.	M.	16 months.	Mental shock.	1	S.	..	..	..	o	M.	o	o	o	o	1	o
M.	..	1 year.	Over-exertion,	1	R.	S.	o	o	1	M.	o	1	o	o	1	1

Shortness of Breath on Exertion.	Cough.	Nervousness.	Tremor.	Headache.	Condition of Sleep[9]	Neuralgia.	More Marked Mental Symptoms.	Flushings.	Excessive Sweating.	Pigmentation of Skin.	Skin Eruptions.	Loss of Hair[10]	Temperature[11]	Loss of Weight.	Debility.	Anaemia.	Appetite[12]	Bowels[13]	Vomiting.	Urine[14]	Menstruation[15]	Number of Pregnancies.
1	o	1	..	1	B.	..	o	..	1	o	Psoriasis.	..	..	1	1	1	G.	R.	o	N.	R.	1
1	..	1	..	o	B.	o	o	..	..	..		..	F.	1	1	1	B.	D.	o	N.	..	o
1	o	1	..	o	G.	o	o	..	..	1	o	..		o	1	o	G.	R.	o	N.	I.S.	3
1	1	1	1	o	D.	o	o	1	1	1	o	..		1	1	..	D.	D.	..	T.A.	..	..
1	o	1S	1	1	B.	o	o	1	1	o	o	..		1	1	..	P.	R.	o	N.	R.S.	o
..	..	1	..	..	..	..	..	..	..	..		..		..	..	..	..	..	..	..	..	..
..	..	1	..	..	..	..	..	..	..	..		..		..	..	..	..	..	..	N.	..	o
..	..	1	o	o	..	..	o	..	..	o		..		..	1	..	R.	..	..	N.	Once only 3 mos. ago	o
..	..	1	1	..	..	..	Impair. of memory.	..	1	1		1		1	..	..	D.	..	..	..	..	..
..	..	..	..	..	..	..	..	..	..	..		..		..	1	..	D.	..	..	..		o
..	..	..	..	..	..	..	..	..	..	..		..		..	..	..	..	..	..	..		o
1	..	1	1	..	..	..	o	1	o	1	Leucoderma.	..	..		1	..	..	D.	..	..	R.S.	o
..	..	1	1	..	..	..	o	1	1	1	..	..	..		1	..	..	R.	..	..	I.	o
..	..	1	1	1	..	..	..	1	1	..		..	..		..	..	..	D.	..	..	R.	o
1	o	1	1	..	B.	1	o	1	1	o	o	o	..	1 16½ lbs.	1	..	P.	D.	o	A.	..	..
1	1	1	1	1	B.	..	..	..	1	..	o	..		..	1	1	..	..	..	..	..	..
..	..	1	1	..	B.	..	o	..	1	o		..		..	1	1	..	..	..	N.	R.	o
1	o	1	..	..	B.	..		..	1	o	o	..		..	1	1	..	..	..	N.	R.	4
1	1	1	1	..	R.	..	..	..	1	o	o	..		..	1	1	..	D.	..	..	R.	o
..	..	1	1	..	B.D.	..	o	..	1	..		..		o	1	1	B.	R.	..	N.	I.	o
1	..	1	1	..	G.	..	o	1	1	o		..		1 14 lbs.	1	1	P.	D.	..	N.	R.	o
1	1	1	o	..	G.	..	o	..	1	1		..		1	1	o	..	R.	..	N.	R.	9
1	o	1	1	1	B.	..	o	1	1	o		..		o	1	1	P.	C.	..	N.	A.	o
1	o	1	1	1	B.	..	o	1	1	1	o	1 Grey.		1	1	..	P.	D.	..	N.	R.	o
1	o	1	1	..	B.	..	o	1	1	o	o			14 lbs. o fatter.	1	o	E.	R.	o	N.	R.	o
1	1	1	1	..	B.	..	o	..	1	1	o	1		1	1	o	B.	R.	1	N.	R.	?
1	o	1	1	1	G.	..	o	..	1	o		..		o	1	1	G.	C.	o	N.	R.	o
1	1	1	1	..	..	..	o	..	1	o		..	..		1	o	G.	R.	..	N.	R.S.	o
1	1	1	1	1	B.	1	o	1	1	1	o	1		1	1	1	G.	C.	o	N.	I.S.	o
1	o	1	1	o	..	..	o	1	1	..		..		1	1	o	F.	D.	o	N.	..	o
1	o	1	1	1	B.	1	o	1	1	1	o	..	..	1	1	1	P.	D.	..	N.	R.	o
1	1	1	1	o	B.	o	o	1	1	o	o	1	..	1	1	1	B.	D.	1	N.	R.S.	o
o	o	1	1	1	B.	1	o	..	1	1		..	..	1	1	o	B.	D.	o	T.A.	l. men.	o
..	o	1	1	o	..	..	o	1	1	1		1	..	1	1	o	B.	R.	1	N.	R.	1
1	o	1	1	1	B.	1	o	1	1	1		1		o	1	o	B.	R.	o	T.A.	I.M.	7
o	o	1	1	o	G.	o	o	o	1	o	..	..		1	1	o	B.	R.	o	N.	N.M.	o
o	o	1	1	1	B.	o	o	1	1	1	Leucoderma.	1		1	1	1	F.	D.	o	N.	A.	o
o	o	1	1	o	G.	o	o	1	1	o	o	o	..	1	1	o	G.	R.	o	N.	R.	o
1	o	1	1	1	G.	1	o	o	..	o	o	o	..	o	1	o	G.	R.	o	N.	R.	5
o	o	1	1	o	G.	o	o	1	1	1	o	o		1 52 lbs.	1	o	P.	R.	o	N.	..	

No.	Age.	Sex.	Single, Married, or Widow.	Duration.	Apparent Cause.	Enlargement of Thyroid.	THYROID. Lobe chiefly affected.	Firm or Soft.	Murmurs.	Thrills.	Prominence of the Eyes.	Size of Pupil.	Von Graefe's Symptom.	Stellwag's Symptom.	D'fective C'vergence.	Ophthalmoplegia Externa.	Palpitation.	Throbbing of Vessels.	Pulse Frequency.	HEART. Enlarged.	Murmurs.
41	32	F.	S.	9 years.	o	o F.	o	o	o	o	1 S.	M.	o	o	o	o	1	o	90	1	M. I
42	54	M.	..	3 years.	o	o	o	o	o	o	1	C.	1	1	..	o	1	o	96	1	M.S
43	35	F.	S.	Several months.	Bronchitis.	1	R.	S.	1	1	o	M.	o	o	o	o	1	o	130	o	o
44	22	F.	S.	2 years.	o	1	S.	S.	1	1	1	C.	1	1	1	o	1	1	140	o	M.S
45	57	F.	S.	11 months.	Nervous shock.	o	o	o	o	o	o	M	o	o	o	o	1	1	150	o	o
46	37	F.	S.	3 months.	o	1	R.	S.	o	o	o	M.	o	o	o	o	1	1	140	o	o
47	48	F.	S.	10 years.	o	1	R.	S.	1	1	1	C.	1	1	o	o	1	1	120	1	S.a
48	26	F.	S.	2 years.	Fright.	1	L.	S.	1	o	1	M.	1	1	1	..	1	1	130	o	o
49	37	F.	M.	1 year.	o	o	o	o	o	o	o	M.	o	o	o	o	1	1	140	o	o
50	31	F.	M.	4 years.	Birth of only child.	1	S.	S.	o	o	1 S.	C.	o	o	o	o	1	o	120	o	o
51	27	F.	S.	18 months.	o	1	S.	S.	1	1	1	D.	1	1	o	o	1	1	156	o	o
52	20	F.	S.	Some months.	o	1	S.	S.	..	..	1	M.	o	1	..	o	1	1	120	o	o
53	43	F.	M.	3 years.	o	1	S.	S.	..	..	1 S.	C.	o	o	..	o	1	o	120	o	o
54	45	F.	M.	9 months.	Influenza.	1	R.	F.	1	1	1 S.	C.	1	1	o	o	1	1	120	o	o
55	33	F.	M.	9 years.	Fright.	1 S.	S.	F.	o	o	1	C.	1	1	1	1 S.	1	1	104	o	o
56	51	F.	M.	18 months.	Influenza.	1 S.	S.	..	o	o	1	C.	..	..	1	1 S.	1	1	240	..	..
57	41	F.	M.	3 years.	Typhoid and fright.	1	S.	S.	1	1	1 S.	M.	o	o	o	o	1	o	96	1	S.N
58	29	F.	M.	2½ years.	Grief.	o	o	o	o	o	o	C.	o	o	o	o	1	o	140	o	S.N
59	12	F.	S.	3 years.	Privation and starvation.	1 V.S.	L.	S.	o	o	1	M.	1	1	..	o	1	1	114	o	o
60	42	F.	M.	2 years.	Enlarged thyroid since 9 years old.	1	S.	F.	o	o	1	C.	1	1	..	o	1	1	108	o	o
61	24	F.	S.	7 months.	o	1	S.	F.	1	1	1	C.	o	1	..	o	1	1	126	o	o
62	52	F.	S.	22 years.	o	1	S.	F.	o	o	1	C.	..	..	..	..	1	1	108	1	o
63	27	F.	S.	6 months.	o	1 S.	S.	S.	o	o	1	M.	1	1	o	o	1	1	110	o	S.?
64	39	F.	S.	2 years.	Mental shock.	1	L.	S.	..	..	1	D.	1	1	o	o	1	1	120	o	o
65	34	F.	M.	6 months.	Mental worry.	1	L.	S.	1	1	1	M.	o	o	..	o	1	1	110	1	o
66	27	F.	M.	2 months.	Influenza.	1	R.	F.	1	..	..	M.	..	..	..	..	..	..	120	1	S.? &S.
67	22	F.	S.	2 years.	Mental shock.	1	R.	S.	o	o	1	M.	1	1	1	o	1	o	90	1	S. D.
68	28	F.	M.	5 years.	o	1	R.	S.	o	o	1 S.	M.	1	1	o	o	1	1	120	o	o
69	20	F.	S.	1 year.	Mental agitation.	1	R.	F.	1	1	1	D.	1	o	o	o	1	1	120	1	S. &
70	36	F.	W.	2 years.	Loss of blood.	1	S.	F.	o	o	1	D	1	o	1	o	1	1	120	o	o
71	24	F.	S.	5 months.	o	1 S.	S.	S.	o	o	1	D.	1	1	o	o	1	1	110	o	o
72	57	F.	S.	2 years.	o	1	S.	S.	o	o	o	M.	o	o	1	o	1	1	150	o	o
73	25	F.	S.	2 months.	o	1	R.	F.	o	o	o	C.	o	o	o	o	1	o	150	o	o
74	44	F.	S.	8 years.	o	1	R.	F.	o	o	o F.	C.	o	o	o	o	1	o	140	o	o
75	20	F.	S.	5 years.	o	1	R.	..	..	..	1 R.	M	o	o	1	o	1	1	140	o	o
76	23	F.	S.	6 months.	o	1	S.	..	..	..	1	D.	1	o	1	o	1	1	120	1	S.
77	53	F.	S.	3 years.	Influenza.	1	S.	..	..	o	C.	o	o	o	o	1	1	112	o	o
78	38	F.	S.	6 months.	Excessive strain nursing.	1	R.	S.	..	..	1	M.	o	o	o	o	1	1	120	o	o
79	47	F.	S.	5 months.	o	o	o	o	o	o	o	..	o	o	o	1	..	120	1	o

Shortness of breath on Exertion.	Cough.	Nervousness.	Tremor.	Headache.	Condition of Sleep.	Neuralgia.	More Marked Mental Symptoms.	Flushings.	Excessive Sweating.	Pigmentation of Skin.	Skin Eruptions.	Loss of Hair.	Temperature.	Loss of Weight.	Debility.	Anæmia.	Appetite.	Bowels.	Vomiting.	Urine.	Menstruation.	Number of Pregnancies.
1	o	1	o	o	G.	o	o	o	o	o	o	..	..	o	1	o	B.	R.	o	N.	R.S.	o
o	o	1	1	o	G.	o	o	o	1	o	o	..		14 lbs. 1	1	o	G.	C.	o	N.	..	..
o	o	1	1	o	G.	o	o	o	o	1	o	..		1	1	o	G.	C.	o	N.	R.	o
1	o	1	1	o	B.	o	o	1	1	1	o	1		1	1	o	G.	D.	o	N.	A.	o
o	o	1	1	1	B.	o	o	o	1	o	o	o		1	1	o	D.	D.	o	N.	A. men.	o
1	o	1	1	o	G.	o	o	o	1	o	o	o		1	1	o	G.	R.	o	N.	R.	o
1	o	1	1	o	B.	o	o	1	o	1	o	..	..	1	1	o	B.	R.	o	N.	R.	o
1	o	1	1	1	B.	1	o	1	1	1	o	1	E.	1	1	1	B.	C.	1	N.	A.	o
o	o	1	1	1	D.	o	o	1	1	o	o	o		1	1	o	B.	R.	o	N.	R.	5
o	o	1	1	o	E.	o	o	1	1	o	o	1		28 lbs. o	1	1	1	G.	R.	o	N.	R.	1
..	..	1	1	o	G.	o	o	1	1	..	o	o		o	1	o	G.	R.	o	N.	I.S.	o
o	o	1	o	o	G.	o	o	1	1	o	o	o		o	1	o	G.	R.	o	N.	R.	o
o	o	1	1	..	..	o	..	o	o	1	..	..			1	..		D.	..	N.	..	..
o	o	1	1	1	G.	o	o	1	1	1	o	o	N.	1	1	o	B.	C.	1	N.	A.	8
o	o	1	1	o	..	o	o	..	1	o	o	..		1	1	o	G.	R.	o	N.	A. men.	3
..	..	1	1	..	..	..	..	..	1	1	o	..	..	1	1	..			..	A.	A. men.	7
o	o	1	1	1	B.	..	o	1	1	1	o	o	S.N.	1	1	o	F.	R.	o	N.	A. men.	3
o	o	1	1	o	B.	o	Depression.	o	o	o	o	o	..	o	1	o		..	..	N.	R.	1 (married 5 years).
1	1	1	..	1	G.	o	o	o	1	o	o	o	N.	1	1	1	G.	R.	o	N.	P.	1 (3rd m.).
1	1	1	1	o	B.	o	o	..	1	1	o	..	E.	1	1	o	B.	D.	o	N.	R.	5
1	o	1	1	o	B.D.	o	o	..	1	o	o	..	S.N.	21 lbs. 1	1	1	B.	R.	o	N.	R.	o
1	1	1	1	o	B.	o	o	..	1	1	o	..	S.N.	1	1	1	B.	D.	1	A.	A. men.	o
o	o	1	1	o	G.	o	o	..	1	o	o	..	N.	o	1	o	G.	C.	o	N.	R.	o
o	o	1	1	1	B.	o	o	1	1	o	o	..	E.	1	1	o	B.	C.	o	N.	M.	o
o	o	1	1	1	B.	o	o	1	1	o	Erythema.	..	S.N.	1	1	o	G.	R.	o	N.	A.	6
o	o	1	1	o	G.	o	o	1	1	o	o	..	E.	1	1	1	G.	R.	o	N.	R.	4
1	o	1	1	1	B.	1	o	1	1	1	Leucoderma.	1	S.N. & E.	1	1	1	E.	R.	o	N.	I.S.	o
1	o	1	1	o	G.	o	o	1	1	o	Eczema.	1	E.	1	1	1	G.	R.	1	N.	M.	5
1	1	1	1	1	B.	1	o	1	1	1	o	o	N. & E.	o	1	o	E.	R.	1	N.	R.	o
1	o	1	1	o	B.	1	Depression and impair. memory.	1	1	1	o	1	S.N.	1	1	1	P.	R.	o	N.	M.	3
..	..	1	1	o	G.	o	o	..	1	o	Erythema.	o	S.N.	1	1	1	G.	R.	o	N.	I.S.	o
o	o	1	1	1	G.	o	o	1	1	o	o	..		1	1	o	G.	C.	o	N.	A. men.	o
..	..	1	1	..	..	..	..	1	1	o	..	..		1	1	..	G.	R.	o	N.	R.	o
..	..	1	1	..	..	..	..	1	1	o	o	..		1	1	o	G.	R.	o	N.	R.	o
..	..	1	1	1	G.	o	o	1	1	o	o	1	..	1	1	o	B.	D.	o	N.	I.M.	o
..	..	1	1	1	G.	o	o	..	1	o	o	o	E.	1	1	o	E.	R.	1	N.	R.	o
..	..	15	o	o	G.	o	o	1	1	o	o	..		31 lbs. 1	1	o	G.	D.	o	N.	A. men.	o
1	..	1	1	o	G.	o	o	1	1	1	Eczema.	1	..	1	1	o	G.	R.	o	N.	M.	o
..	..	1	1	o	G.	o	o	..	o	o	o	..		1	1	o	F.	C.	o	N.	A. men.	o

F. = Firm or hard. ⁴ S. = Slight; 1 R. only = Right eye only; o F. = Absent when seen, formerly present. ⁵ D. = Dilated; T. = Tricuspid; D. = Diastolic; S. all = Systolic murmur in all the areas. ⁹ B. = Bad; B.D. = Bad with dreams; G. = Good. P. = Poor; E. = Excessive. ¹⁵ R. = Regular; C. = Constipated; D. = Occasional diarrhœa. ¹⁴ N. = Normal; A. = Consider-
I. = Irregular; A. = Amenorrhœa; I.M. = Irregular and menorrhagia; I. men. = Irregular due to menopause; A. men. =

MORBID ANATOMY AND PATHOLOGY.

From the foregoing description, it is obvious that the symptomatology of exophthalmic goitre has of recent years been so fully elaborated that we may now be said to possess a very complete and accurate knowledge of the clinical features of the disease. The pathology and pathological physiology of the affection are in a very different position, for as yet we have no certain knowledge as to the exact position and nature of the lesion.

The most striking pathological alteration found in the bodies of patients who have died from exophthalmic goitre is the *enlargement of the thyroid gland.* This enlargement is not merely the result of increased vascularity, for it is attended with an increase of the glandular tissue. The increase is not, however, a simple hypertrophy. The microscope shows that the normal structure of the gland is materially modified. The normal cubical epithelium is replaced by epithelium of a columnar form, resembling more in form that of a tubular secreting gland. Catarrhal changes in the epithelium which lines the glandular spaces, alterations in the colloid material, which becomes, it is said, more mucinous in character, or even disappears to a great extent, and proliferation and cellular infiltration of the connective tissue have been described by Professor Greenfield and Dr Robert Muir. Greenfield states that in some cases new-formed tubules are developed which give the structure a resemblance to that of the salivary gland. In two of my own cases very similar changes were present.

The *heart* is often less affected than one would expect from the very marked character of the cardiac disturbances which are present during life. In some cases, the organ is normal both in size and weight ; in others, it is dilated ; in others again, it is to some extent, but not usually in any marked degree, hypertrophied. Organic changes in the valves and appearances indicative of old or recent endocarditis are comparatively rarely met with.

According to some observers the arteries throughout the body are dilated. In some cases, the arterial coats have been thickened.

The *thymus gland* is usually (? always) persistent and enlarged. The significance of this fact is as yet unknown.

The *orbital fat* is usually increased in amount. As I have previously stated, the exophthalmos is generally thought to be due to this increase and to the dilated condition of the vessels at the back of the orbit. The *external muscles of the eyeballs* are, it is said, in some cases affected with fatty degeneration.

Pathological changes have also been described in the *cervical sympathetic, the floor of the 4th ventricle,* etc.; but so far as I am able to judge, such alterations are in no way characteristic; some of them are probably mere associated or accidental alterations; others, such as recent hæmorrhages, which have been met with in several cases, are probably the result of the profound vasomotor and vascular alterations which are such prominent features in the later stages of severe and fatal cases, and are not the cause of the disease. It is important, however, to note that in one case the resti-form body was atrophied and that in two cases (one described by Mendel and the other by Marie and Marinesco) the solitary bundle of fibres in the medulla oblongata was atrophied.

In a few cases the *lymphatic glands* have been enlarged, but this change is, so far as our present knowledge enables us to judge, inconstant and perhaps merely an accidental or an associated lesion.

Pathological Physiology.—The exact pathology of exoph-thalmic goitre is still unsettled. Many different theories have from time to time been advanced to account for the phenomena of the disease.

The old view, which for long held the field, is that exophthalmic goitre is due to an irritative lesion of the sympathetic in the neck. The widespread character of the symptoms seems opposed to the view that a localised lesion of the sympathetic in the neck is the primary cause of the disease. Careful microscopical examination has failed to show that the thoracic and abdominal portions of the sympathetic are the seat of any definite and constant lesion; although pathological alterations have by some observers been described in the cervical ganglia, other observers have found these structures entirely normal. Further, the absence of any marked and persistent dilatation of the pupils is, as has already been pointed out, opposed to this view. Again, some of the symptoms (such, for example, as the dilatation of the blood vessels, which is usually thought to be a conspicuous feature of the disease) seem to indicate a paralytic rather than an irritative lesion. It must, however, be remembered that Benedict has suggested that the vascular dilata-tion may be due to an irritative lesion of the vaso-dilator nerves, which run in the sympathetic.

It has also been theorised that the disease is due to the pressure of the enlarged thyroid upon the cervical sympathetic, and it has recently been claimed that section of the sympathetic in the neck is followed by disappearance of the symptoms.

Friedreich theorised that a paralytic condition of the vasomotor nerves, by causing an increased flow of blood through the coronary arteries and thereby increasing the excitability of the cardiac ganglia, is the cause of the increased action of the heart.

A lesion of the nuclei of the pneumo-gastric nerves and the other nervous structures in the medulla oblongata has also been suggested as a cause of the disease, and, as has already been stated, small superficial hæmorrhages have been described by more than one observer as occurring in the floor of the fourth ventricle. But I see no reason for supposing that these lesions (hæmorrhages) were other than accidental or secondary results ; such hæmorrhages are by no means uncommon in other diseased conditions, and their occasional occurrence just before death in a disease in which the vascular and vasomotor alterations are so profound is not to be wondered at.

Experimental evidence has also been advanced in favour of the view that the disease is due to disease or derangement of the medulla oblongata. Filene and Bienfait state that sections in the neighbourhood of the restiform body in some cases result in the production of exophthalmos, enlargement of the thyroid and tachycardia ; and in one case all the three great primary symptoms (increased frequency of the heart's action, enlargement of the thyroid and prominence of the eyeballs) were simultaneously developed. But the validity of these experimental observations has been vigorously questioned.

The widespread distribution of the vasomotor alterations, the character of many of the other symptoms (such as Von Graefe's symptom, Stellwag's symptom, defective convergence and ophthalmoplegia externa), and the fact that in rare instances the symptoms (such as the exophthalmos and the tremor) are unilateral, are highly suggestive of a lesion or functional disturbance of the central nervous system.

But even granting that organic or functional changes of this kind are actually present, it does not necessarily follow that they are the primary cause of the disease ; although they support, they do not necessarily prove, its nervous origin.

The exact cause of the increased frequency of the heart's action is a matter of dispute. According to one view, it is the result of overaction (irritation) of the sympathetic; according to another, of diminished action (paralysis) of the vagus ; perhaps both views are correct.

The theory which has been advanced by Möbius and strongly supported by Greenfield—that the primary cause of the disease is the lesion (hypertrophy) of the thyroid gland—is very plausible. In support of this view, George Murray argues that the condition of the thyroid gland in exophthalmic goitre may fairly be compared to that of the mammary gland during lactation, and that we may reasonably conclude that a far larger quantity of thyroid secretion is poured into the circulation than in health.

That many of the symptoms of exophthalmic goitre are due to an excessive or perverted secretion of the thyroid seems to me to be supported by the following facts :—

1. Many of the symptoms of exophthalmic goitre are the direct opposite of those which characterise myxœdema (see below) ; and, since the symptoms of myxœdema are due to defective thyroid secretion, it is reasonable to suppose that those symptoms of exophthalmic goitre which are the direct opposite of myxœdema are due to an excessive or perverted thyroid secretion.

2. In some cases of exophthalmic goitre the enlargement of the thyroid, after persisting for a time, subsides, the gland becomes atrophied and sclerosed ; and, with this atrophy, the symptoms of exophthalmic goitre disappear and those of myxœdema are developed.

Several cases of this kind have been recorded. Case XVII. (see page 354) is an example in point.

3. In some cases of exophthalmic goitre, excision of the enlarged thyroid is undoubtedly followed by marked improvement or cure.

The Points of Contrast between Myxœdema and Exophthalmic Goitre.—In a paper read before the Medico-Chirurgical Society of Edinburgh on 3rd March 1891, and published in the "Transactions" of that Society (Vol. x., p. 126), and in my Atlas of Clinical Medicine (Vol. i., p. 26), I was, so far as I know, the first to publicly direct attention to the points of contrast between myxœdema and exophthalmic goitre. The more important points of similarity and difference are as follows :—

In both affections, the thyroid gland is diseased, and both diseases occur much more frequently in women than in men.

But the character of the thyroid lesion, the mode of development and the nature of many of the symptoms are very different in the two diseases.

In myxœdema, the thyroid gland is atrophied and its secreting structure destroyed ; whereas in exophthalmic goitre the thyroid gland is enlarged and its secreting structure, though modified in character, is increased in quantity. In short, in myxœdema the secretion of the thyroid gland is greatly diminished or suppressed ; whereas in exophthalmic goitre the secretion of the thyroid gland is (apparently) increased and perhaps altered in character.

The symptoms of myxœdema are almost always developed in a slow, insidious, and gradual manner ; * whereas the symptoms of exophthalmic goitre not unfrequently develop with considerable rapidity, sometimes, indeed, suddenly, after a fright or other profound emotional disturbance.

Myxœdema is usually developed at a later age than exophthalmic goitre. The ordinary adult form of myxœdema is usually developed between the ages of 35 and 45, rarely during adolescence and early adult life (between the ages of 15 and 25). Exophthalmic goitre, on the contrary, is most frequently developed between the ages of 15 and 35—very rarely after the age of 50. In my series of 34 cases of adult myxœdema, the average age at which the disease developed in women was 41 years and in men 43 years; while in my series of 76 cases of exophthalmic goitre (in which the age of onset was noted) the average age at which the disease developed in the female cases was 30 years, and in the male cases 36 years.

Myxœdema is most frequent in married women who have borne children or have had large families ; while exophthalmic goitre is most common in unmarried (single) women, and (?) in married women who have not borne children or have had small families. Pregnancy seems, as a rule, to exert a prejudicial influence on patients who are affected with myxœdema ; while, in some cases of exophthalmic goitre, it seems to prove beneficial or even curative. This is not, however, always the case ; in two of my cases at least pregnancy seemed to aggravate or to excite the development of the disease.

In my series of 29 cases of adult myxœdema in females, 23 were married and 6 were single ; whereas in my 73 female cases of exophthalmic goitre, 49 were single (when the disease developed) and 24 married. The 23 married women affected with myxœdema had, on an average, 5.1 children each ; while the 25 married women affected with exophthalmic goitre had, on an average, 3.2 children each.†

In myxœdema, the temperature is subnormal, unusually stable, and the patients are extremely susceptible to cold ; whereas in exophthalmic goitre, temporary elevations of temperature, appa-

---

* A few cases have been reported, and I have myself met with two instances, in which the symptoms of myxœdema were developed more or less rapidly, but in some of these cases the disease had probably been in existence for some time unknown to the patient.

† This difference is probably in part at least (possibly altogether) accounted for by the difference in age ; the myxœdematous patients were older and had been married longer than the exophthalmic goitre patients.

rently of nervous origin, occasionally occur, the temperature equilibrium is easily disturbed, and the patients often complain of a feeling of heat and flushing.

In myxœdema, the skin is extremely dry and harsh and the secretion of sweat abolished or greatly diminished; whereas in exophthalmic goitre, the skin is soft and moist, and excessive sweating is, in the great majority of cases, a prominent symptom.

In myxœdema, the electrical resistance of the skin is greatly increased, whereas in exophthalmic goitre it is greatly diminished.

In myxœdema, the bowels are usually constipated; whereas in exophthalmic goitre, attacks of (nervous) diarrhœa are apt to occur.

In myxœdema, placidity, diminished emotional activity, and slowness of all nerve processes, are conspicuous features; whereas in exophthalmic goitre, emotional excitability, irritability, nervous instability and general nervousness are always very marked.

In myxœdema, the administration of thyroid extract produces immediate and marked improvement; whereas in exophthalmic goitre, if I may judge from my own experience, the administration of thyroid extract rarely produces any improvement and in fact in many cases aggravates the symptoms of the disease.

It must, however, be stated that cases have been reported in which the symptoms of exophthalmic goitre have improved under the administration of thyroid extract. This is directly contrary to my own experience; and it must be remembered that, even if it does occasionally occur, it does not necessarily prove that the symptoms of exophthalmic goitre (or rather, to speak more correctly, those symptoms of exophthalmic goitre which are the direct opposite of the symptoms of myxœdema) are not due to increased activity of the thyroid gland, i.e., to excessive thyroidal secretion. In this connection it is important to remember that in exophthalmic goitre the secretion of the enlarged thyroid is perhaps abnormal in character. If this view is correct, the introduction into the bodies of healthy persons of (normal) thyroid extract will not be likely to produce the symptoms of exophthalmic goitre. If the thyroidal secretion is not merely increased but is altered in character, there is no difficulty in understanding the fact that in some cases thyroid feeding exerts a beneficial influence upon the symptoms of the disease.

Further, in healthy persons the prolonged administration of thyroid extract may produce not only increased frequency of the heart's action and palpitation, but a condition of general nervousness and tremor which resembles very closely, and is perhaps identical with, the nervousness and tremor which are such characteristic symptoms of exophthalmic goitre.

So far as I know, prominence of the eyeballs (exophthalmos) has only once been noticed after thyroid feeding; M. Gagnevin, a healthy medical student, who submitted himself from the 15th to the 23rd of March to full doses of raw thyroid gland, suffered from palpitation, increased frequency of the heart's action, tremors, sweatings, flushings and exophthalmos, " sa famille s'aperçoit que les yeux lui sortent de la tête." *

I am fully prepared to grant, then, that many of the symptoms of exophthalmic goitre are probably the result of an increased or perverted action of the thyroid gland, but it does not necessarily follow that the enlargement of the thyroid is the primary and fundamental lesion. It is possible that the enlargement of the thyroid gland is itself the result of a primary nervous change.

Taking all the facts into consideration, I see no reason to alter the opinion expressed in my article on exophthalmic goitre (Atlas of Clinical Medicine, Vol. ii., p. 99) that the most probable view of the pathology of the disease which it is possible in the present state of our knowledge to advance is :—

First, that the primary cause of the disease is a lesion or rather perhaps a functional disturbance in some part of the nervous system, probably some part of the medulla oblongata.

Second, that as the result of this lesion or functional nervous derangement, the thyroid gland becomes enlarged or functionates in an abnormal manner, so that its secretion is increased and perhaps altered in character.

Third, that the increased or perverted secretion of the enlarged thyroid leads to the production of a widespread disturbance of function in the nervous and other tissues, and that it is to the secondary disturbances produced in this way that many of the characteristic symptoms of the disease are due.

Further information is required before any more dogmatic statement can be made.

Although, then, in the present position of our knowledge I am disposed to think that the *primary* cause of the disease is probably nervous, I am by no means prepared to deny that future observation may perhaps show that the view advanced by Möbius and supported by Greenfield, viz., that the enlargement of the thyroid gland is the primary and fundamental lesion, is correct.

---

* " Le Myxœdème," par le Dr A. Combe de Lausanne, p. 117.

DIAGNOSIS.

In typical cases the diagnosis of exophthalmic goitre presents no difficulty. In such cases, the appearance of the patient is pathognomonic. It is only in the rudimentary and atypical cases in which there is no enlargement of the thyroid and no prominence of the eyeballs that any real difficulty in diagnosis is likely to occur.

The Differential Diagnosis of Ordinary Goitre and of Exophthalmic Goitre.—In ordinary goitre, the enlargement of the thyroid is usually greater in degree and firmer in consistency than that of Graves' disease. In ordinary goitre, pulsations and thrills are not usually present over the enlarged gland. While the increased frequency of the heart's action (without which a diagnosis of exophthalmic goitre is not justified), the prominence of the eyeballs, the characteristic general nervousness and tremor and the numerous secondary symptoms, some of which are almost certain to be present in every case of Graves' disease, are not observed, or, perhaps, to speak more accurately, are only accidentally present. In ordinary goitre, shortness of breath and other symptoms due to the pressure of the enlarged thyroid upon the adjacent organs and parts (sympathetic, etc.) may be developed ; these pressure symptoms are rarely developed in exophthalmic goitre, at all events in any marked degree.

It must, however, be remembered that in ordinary goitre when the thyroid is very much enlarged, the nerves (sympathetic and vagus) in the neck may be pressed upon and irritated. It is said that increased frequency of the heart's action, and prominence of the eyeball on the side on which the sympathetic is irritated, may be produced in this manner. In cases of this description, a satisfactory conclusion as to the true nature of the case could probably be arrived at by attention to the following points :—The large size and firm consistency of the enlarged thyroid ; the age and sex of the patient ; the history of the case ; the duration of the disease ; the locality in which the patient lived (for ordinary goitre is apt to be endemic) ; the fact that the exophthalmos would probably be unilateral (for it is not likely that the nerves—sympathetic and vagus—on both sides of the neck would be pressed upon and involved) ; the presence of other distinctive signs of irritation of the sympathetic in the neck, and especially dilatation of the pupil and unilateral sweating ; together with the absence of the other secondary symptoms, some of which are almost certain to be present in every case of exophthalmic goitre.

The Differential Diagnosis of Exophthalmic Goitre and of Simple Functional Palpitation.—Difficulty in distinguishing these two conditions is chiefly apt to occur in atypical cases of exophthalmic goitre in which the exophthalmos and enlargement of the thyroid are wanting. In Graves' disease, the increased frequency of the heart, though subject to paroxysmal exacerbations, is, with rare exceptions, more or less continuous and persistent; while in functional palpitation and hysterical palpitation, it is essentially paroxysmal and intermittent. The subjective sensations which are associated with ordinary functional palpitation are, too, as a rule, much more pronounced than those associated with the palpitation of Graves' disease.

In doubtful cases, the presence of the following symptoms should be diligently looked for :—General nervousness ; the characteristic tremor ; flushings and sweating ; nervous diarrhœa ; pigmentation of the skin ; and the other less important and suggestive secondary symptoms of exophthalmic goitre.

The history of the case, the exciting cause of the palpitation and the effects of treatment, together with the age and sex of the patient, may in doubtful cases also afford corroborative evidence as to the true nature of the condition.

The Differential Diagnosis of Organic Disease of the Heart and of Exophthalmic Goitre.—Careful consideration of the history and whole facts of the case will in the great majority of cases enable a competent and judicially-minded observer to distinguish the two conditions without difficulty. In the somewhat exceptional cases in which Graves' disease is complicated with organic disease of the heart, a correct diagnosis can only of course be arrived at by detecting the presence or absence of the other primary and secondary symptoms which are characteristic of exophthalmic goitre.

PROGNOSIS.

This is usually a matter of much uncertainty. In most cases, the disease runs a chronic course, lasting for months or years, with perhaps temporary periods of improvement. In some cases (some authorities state a third or fourth of the whole, but according to my own experience this is too high an estimate), the symptoms after a time subside and a complete cure is ultimately established. In a large proportion of cases in which improvement occurs, and under this head I would include the great majority of cases, the cure is incomplete ; after advancing up to a certain point, the improvement seems to stop and the symptoms, or some of them, persist in a less severe form. In cases of this description, there is always the risk of a relapse. In some rare cases in which the disease begins acutely, the symptoms disappear almost as rapidly as they were established. In other cases, the disease steadily progresses from bad to worse until it terminates in death.

Probably, in the future, the prognosis will be more hopeful than it has been in the past, for some recent methods of treatment (such, for example, as the electrical treatment, excision of the gland and the administration of phosphate of soda and thymus extract) seem to be attended with more satisfactory results than the therapeutic measures which were formerly employed.

In trying to form an opinion as to the probable duration and course of the disease in any particular case, the following are the chief circumstances which have to be taken into account :—The age and sex of the patient ; the rapidity of development and the length of time which the disease has lasted ; the degree of general nervousness ; the rapidity of the pulse ; the severity of the general constitutional symptoms, more especially the presence or absence of emaciation, marasmus and cachexia ; the effects of treatment ; and the presence or absence of complications.

Other things being equal, the fact that the patient is middleaged or old is, I think, unfavourable, as regards the duration at all events. In my experience, the cases which occur in men are usually difficult to cure. The more rapidly the disease is developed, in a severe form, the worse perhaps the prognosis ; but I speak with great reserve on this point, for in some cases in which the symptoms of the disease are suddenly developed, they suddenly subside.

The degree of the exophthalmos and the extent of the enlargement of the thyroid do not seem to afford any true criteria as to the severity of the case and the length of time which the disease is likely to continue ; for in atypical ("fruste") cases, in which there is no goitre and no exophthalmos, the disease is often severe and of long duration. The degree of general nervousness and the frequency of the pulse are more certain guides to the prognosis. Other things being equal, the greater the general nervousness and the greater the frequency of the pulse, the greater the severity of the case ; vice versâ, diminution of the pulse frequency and of the general nervousness are usually favourable indications. Pregnancy seems in some cases to exert a favourable influence upon the course of the disease ; but in a small proportion of cases the disease is developed during or immediately after pregnancy. Profound debility, marked emaciation, marasmus and cachexia, severe and intractable diarrhœa or vomiting, are unfavourable indications. Asystole, considerable œdema of the feet, bronchitis and œdema of the lungs, which are usually only developed towards the termination of bad cases, are still more unfavourable indications.

The manner in which the disease behaves under treatment is in Graves' disease, as in so many other affections, a point of the greatest prognostic importance—and is so obvious that it need not be further insisted upon.

The presence or absence of complications must always, of course, be taken into account. It is unnecessary to go into details; the exact nature of the complication must guide the opinion in each particular case.

Mode of Death.—In most cases in which the patient dies from the disease itself and not from some intercurrent complication or associated lesion, the death is more or less gradual ; but in some cases the patients die suddenly. In one of my cases the patient while seated at dinner suddenly complained of severe pain in the head, became hemiplegic and died in a couple of hours ; in this case there was, so far as I could judge, no organic valvular lesion. In rare cases, the patient dies still more suddenly from cardiac syncope.

TREATMENT.

The indications for treatment are :—*Firstly*, to remove all causes of peripheral irritation, excitement, etc. ; *secondly*, to improve the condition of the general health ; and *thirdly*, to employ such drug remedies and other measures of treatment as experience has shown to be useful and salutary.

Persons suffering from exophthalmic goitre should be instructed to lead routine and quiet lives : everything (such as bodily exertion or mental excitement) which is found to accelerate the action of the heart, to produce palpitation, and to increase the general nervousness, should, so far as possible, be avoided. In aggravated cases, and probably in all cases during the early stages of the disease, the patients should be confined to bed, or at any rate be made to spend the greater part of their time in the recumbent position.

The diet should be easily digestible and nutritious. All articles of diet which are likely to produce flatulence or gastro-intestinal irritation should be prohibited. Tea, coffee, tobacco, and alcohol should be either prohibited altogether or very sparingly indulged in.

A climate which is neither too cold nor too warm is perhaps the most suitable. A long sea voyage, provided the patient is a good sailor, would probably, in some cases, be beneficial. Stiller, quoted by Sajous, reports a remarkable amelioration of the symptoms in two cases of exophthalmic goitre under the influence of high altitudes.

All causes of debility should if possible be removed. Any uterine or ovarian derangement which may be present should be attended to. Any cause of peripheral irritation which is present should, if possible, be removed.

In those cases in which there is much anæmia, arsenic, or arsenic and iron, should be administered. The effect which iron produces on the patient should be carefully watched, for some observers have stated that it is apt to disagree and aggravate the symptoms, but I am satisfied that in some cases iron is beneficial.

Arsenic, strychnine, quinine, the mineral acids, by improving the tone of the general health and of the nervous system in particular, are undoubtedly useful in some cases ; but so far as my experience enables me to judge, they do not seem to exert any distinctly curative effect upon the diseased condition.

Of drug remedies, belladonna is one of the most reliable. I believe that digitalis, or digitalis combined with iron, is in some cases beneficial. Some writers state that digitalis is contraindicated in Graves' disease, but in most of the cases in which I have prescribed it, I have failed to observe any prejudicial effect. In some cases, strophanthus appears to be useful. Aconite and the sulphate of sparteine have also been recommended ; in the few cases in which I have tried these remedies, I have failed to observe any beneficial effect from their use. Ergot of rye, sulphonal and antipyrin have also been said to be beneficial. Phosphate of soda or phosphate of potash (ten to twenty grains three times daily) seems in some cases to produce distinct benefit. I have usually employed phosphate of potash, for phosphate of soda is more apt to produce diarrhœa. In several of my cases, extract of thymus gland has appeared to produce decided improvement. I usually begin with one five-grain tabloid three times daily, increasing the dose gradually but continuously, and carefully observing the effects of the remedy upon the pulse, general nervousness, thyroid enlargement, etc. The experience of different observers, however, differs with regard to the effects of this remedy. Dr Hector Mackenzie, for example, states that in none of the cases in which he employed the remedy (thymus extract) was any improvement noted.

Some years ago Charcot recommended the application of icebags to the præcordia ; but latterly he seemed to have abandoned this method of treatment in favour of electricity, which has been specially recommended by M. Vigoroux, and which has also yielded satisfactory results in the hands of other physicians. On the whole it would appear that the electrical plan of treatment is one of the most satisfactory which has yet been introduced. Vigoroux and Charcot recommend that the constant current should be applied to the neck, and the interrupted current to the præcordial region. In using the constant current, the electrodes should be firmly pressed deep into the neck, beneath the angle of the jaw on each side. The current may be allowed to pass from five to seven minutes at each sitting. Care must be taken that the skin is not vesicated under the negative electrode. A current which, after it has been allowed to pass from five to seven minutes, gently reddens, but which does not vesicate, the skin and which is not painful, is, for practical purposes, sufficient. The strength of the faradic current should be regulated by the sensations of the patient. The strongest interrupted current which can be comfortably borne may be employed. In employing electricity in the treatment of exophthalmic goitre, it is well to remember that the patients are highly nervous and very easily agitated ; it is therefore advisable to commence with weak currents. As the patient becomes accustomed to the treatment, the strength of current may be gradually increased.

Excision of the enlarged gland or of part of the enlarged gland seems to have been followed by remarkable improvement in some cases ; but it remains to be shown whether this somewhat serious surgical procedure, which in more than one case has been followed by sudden death, is advisable in any considerable number of cases. It seems to me that, even granting that the results which Dr Lemke and some other surgeons have obtained are confirmed by subsequent experience, excision of the gland should only be practised in aggravated cases of the disease, in which medical and electrical treatment has been fairly and diligently employed for a considerable period of time and has failed to give relief; or in those cases in which the pressure of the enlarged thyroid on the trachea is attended with dangerous dyspnœa.

Other methods of surgical procedure have also recently been recommended, viz., ligature of the thyroidal vessels, division of the isthmus of the gland, stripping off the capsule and exposing the gland so as to cause it to atrophy, division of the cervical sympathetic, and complete excision of the whole sympathetic on both sides of the neck. My personal experience does not enable me to pronounce an opinion upon any of these methods of treatment. Jonnesco states (Centralbl. f. Chir., Leipsig, 1897, No. 2) that in ten cases in which he excised the whole sympathetic on both sides of the neck, complete recovery resulted in six cases and marked improvement in four cases.

ACROMEGALY.

Historical Note.—This rare disease, to which the synonyms *megalacria, pachyacria, pachyæmia*, and *Marie's disease*, have also been applied, was first systematically described in the year 1885 by a French physician, Dr Pierre Marie, who termed it acromegaly because of the enlargement of the extremities (ἄχρον = extremity, and μέγας = great), which is its most striking feature.

The disease is not a new one; for, as Marie has himself pointed out, cases which were without doubt typical examples of acromegaly had been met with before the year 1885. Several are recorded in medical literature. But to Marie belongs the merit of being the first to recognise that the disease is a distinct clinical entity and to give a systematic description of its peculiar clinical features.

ETIOLOGY.

Age.—In the great majority of cases which have been recorded, the disease seems to have commenced between the ages of 15 and 40; but occasionally the onset is earlier or later than the fifteenth and fortieth years respectively. In the cases analysed by Hinsdale, the age at onset was as follows:—"0-10 years, 4 cases; 11-20 years, 19 cases; 21-30 years, 33 cases; 31-40 years, 22 cases; 41-50 years, 10 cases; 51-60 years, 2 cases; 61-70 years, 1 case; 71 years, 1 case."

Sex.—Acromegaly seems to occur with equal frequency in the two sexes. In this respect it contrasts very remarkably with myxœdema, with which perhaps it has some relationship, and with which it is sometimes confounded; for myxœdema, as has been already pointed out, is very much more common in women than in men.

Race and Locality.—Acromegaly is said to occur amongst all races and in all parts of the world; but there are some grounds, I think, for supposing that it is more common in some countries and some localities than in others. In Scotland, if I may judge from my own observation, the disease is extremely rare; whereas, in the neighbourhood of Heidelberg it appears to be comparatively speaking common.

Heredity.—Acromegaly appears rarely to be inherited, though in exceptional instances more than one case has occurred in the same family. Virchow mentions a case in which two brothers were affected; in another case a father and daughter suffered from the disease.

Exciting or Aggravating Causes.—Exposure to cold, traumatic injuries, grief, anxiety and other causes of mental depression or excitement have preceded the onset (or rather the apparent onset) in some cases; but it is exceedingly doubtful whether these conditions, traumatic injuries to the head perhaps in some cases excepted, are real causes of the disease. They are probably rather contributory exciting causes which aggravate the condition and favour its more rapid development in the early stages.

Mode of Onset, Course and Duration.—The *onset* is usually very gradual and insidious. In many cases, the disease has already been in existence for some time before its presence is suspected either by the patient or the doctor. Occasionally, the onset is more rapid. In one of my cases (Case I.), the characteristic enlargement of the hands and feet and the marked alteration in the shape and appearance of the face seem to have developed, in a sufficient degree to attract attention, within the comparatively short period of three months. The *course* is usually very slow and chronic, but in most cases progressive. The *duration* is usually long; cases may go on for ten, twenty, thirty years, or even longer. In rare cases, in which the enlargement of the pituitary body is perhaps not merely simple but malignant (sarcomatous or cancerous) in character, the course may be much more rapid.

CLINICAL HISTORY.

The most striking characteristic feature of the disease is an enlargement of the extremities of the body; hence the term acromegaly. The hands, feet and the "cephalic extremity" (as French writers term the face) are the parts which are chiefly affected; but other parts are also involved. The tongue, for example, is in some cases of great size, and the sternum, ribs and clavicles are often also very much enlarged; while, in fully developed cases, the trunk presents characteristic alterations.

The enlargement is, in the great majority of cases, due to an increase of all the tissues composing the affected parts—the bones as well as the soft tissues; though in rare cases the bones of the hands and feet do not appear to be enlarged.* The enlargement is not due to œdema ; there is no pitting on pressure. The palms and soles, in which the enlargement of the soft tissues is most noticeable, feel firm and elastic as if cushioned with a thick layer of firm elastic tissue and fat.

Let me now describe the condition of the individual parts in more detail.

The upper extremities.—The hands and fingers are greatly enlarged, particularly in breadth. The *hands* are, in most cases, enormously broad ; they have been termed " spade-shaped," " battle-dore-shaped," " paw-shaped," etc. The increase of the soft tissues is usually well seen in the palms, which appear to be thickly padded with fat. The creases in the palms and soles and the interphalan-geal folds on the upper surface of the fingers are usually deeper than normal. The *fingers* are usually very broad and somewhat flat ; they have been termed sausage-shaped. Though nodosities are sometimes present on the phalanges, giving the hand and fingers a rugged appearance, the enlargement of the fingers is, as a rule, uniform ; there is very little if any tapering off at the extremities ; and it should be particularly noted that there is no clubbing of the finger tips. In this respect acromegaly differs from the condition to which P. Marie has given the term *hypertrophic pulmonary osteo-arthropathy*.

The *nails* usually appear small in proportion to the size of the fingers ; they are usually broad, flattened out transversely, and in many cases grooved in the longitudinal direction.

The *wrist joints* are not as a rule markedly affected, though in some cases they are moderately enlarged.

The lower extremities.—The lower extremities are affected in the same way as the upper. The *feet* are very much enlarged and the increase is chiefly in breadth. The *toes*, particularly the great toe, are often much enlarged, flattened and square at the end. The *nails* of the toes are square and in some cases grooved ; in others, buried, as it were, by the great increase of the soft parts.

The *ankles*, like the wrists, may be enlarged, but in most cases they are not affected, at all events in any marked degree.

The head and face.—The *face* usually undergoes a notable alteration in shape as the disease advances ; it becomes lengthened, especially below the forehead, and assumes an elongated oval shape. In most cases, the *expression* is somewhat sad, heavy

---

* Sir William Broadbent has recently reported a case of this kind, "Lancet," Vol. i., 1896, p. 846.

and apathetic. In typical and well-marked cases of the disease, the *forehead* looks low in proportion to the rest of the face ; the *nose* becomes thickened, flattened and increased in size, and this increase is due to an enlargement of all the tissues which enter into its composition—the bones, cartilages and soft parts all being involved ; the *cheek bones* are prominent ; the *lips*, especially the lower lip, are thick ; in many cases the lower lip hangs down and is everted ; the *superciliary ridges* are in some cases markedly enlarged ; the *eyes* are set wide apart ; in some cases they appear to be, relatively to the large face, unduly small and more prominent than normal ; the orbital and temporal ridges may become thick and prominent. In some cases the *eyebrows* are thick. The *upper lid* sometimes has a full swollen appearance ; the lower edge is in many cases increased in size. The *lower jaw* is usually markedly enlarged ; this is one of the most constant and characteristic changes. The chin usually projects forwards ; the angle of the jaw is less acute than normal. In some cases, the alveolar process in both jaws is considerably thickened ; in others, it is more or less atrophied in consequence of the falling out of the teeth. Owing to the increased size and width of the lower jaw, the front teeth are set widely apart ; in many cases they are separated from one another by considerable spaces which did not exist before the disease commenced. The *palate* is in many cases not only high but very broad, the space at the roof of the mouth being very capacious. As has been previously stated, the *tongue* is in some cases markedly enlarged.

The *neck* is usually short and thick and the *larynx* large and prominent.

The *voice* is generally low toned, rough, and harsh.

In some cases the *thyroid gland* is of normal size ; in others atrophied ; in others hypertrophied.

The *long bones* are not usually affected, except in the "giant form" of the disease.

The trunk—.In the advanced stages of the disease the trunk presents marked and characteristic changes. The *sternum, clavicles* and *ribs* are enlarged, the manubrium sterni being increased in length and breadth, and probably also in thickness. In many cases, as Professor Erb has shown, *a pyramidal area of dulness* can be demonstrated on percussion over the upper part of the bone ; in some cases, it appears to be due to the presence of a persistent and enlarged thymus gland ; in others, to the increased thickness of the bone.

As the disease progresses, the thorax becomes enlarged ; it is usually somewhat flattened from side to side ; the antero-posterior diameter is to some extent increased, and the chest seems to project forwards.

The *ribs* are not only increased in thickness, but in some cases they are notably enlarged in all directions and elongated.

The *vertebræ* may be markedly enlarged, and the thickening and enlargement of the spinous processes can in some cases be made out during life.

The *pelvis* is not always affected in any marked degree, though in some cases it is unusually broad, the pelvic bones being notably enlarged ; the iliac crests and spinous processes are in some cases thickened.

The attitude in the erect position.—When the patient stands in the erect position, the shoulders are seen to be rounded ; the head is usually bent forwards towards the chest ; in some cases it can only be held erect with difficulty. The dorso-cervical portion of the spine is in many cases much curved (cervico-dorsal kyphosis), and there is sometimes a compensatory lordosis in the lumbar region. In consequence of the development of these changes in the spinal column, the patient shrinks in height as the disease advances. As Dr Hinsdale states : " The peculiar deformity due to kyphosis, taken in connection with the enormous hands and feet, may give an ape-like appearance to the subject." *

Changes in the long bones, joints, and muscles.—It must be noted that the alterations in the bony skeleton which constitute such striking and characteristic features of acromegaly are for the most part confined to the short bones. In many cases the long bones seem to undergo comparatively little change.

In some cases the *joints*, more particularly the knees, are enlarged ; but the articular surfaces of the bones are usually quite normal. In some cases the joints creak on movement.

The *muscles* are usually soft and flabby. In typical and fully developed cases of the disease, muscular weakness and debility are highly characteristic symptoms ; but in the earlier stages of some cases, the muscles are hypertrophied and the muscular power very great.

Complaints.—Patients affected with acromegaly usually complain of " weakness," " debility," " loss of muscular power," " loss of strength," etc. In many cases, headache is a prominent symptom ; in others, pains, which are often described as rheumatic or neuralgic in character, are complained of in the bones and muscles. In

---

* " Acromegaly," by Guy Hinsdale, M.A., M.D., p. 11.

almost all of the cases which have been reported, an excessive tendency to sweat on exertion has been noted. In many cases, there is dimness of vision, or rather a peculiar defect of vision (bilateral temporal hemianopsia) to which I will presently refer in more detail.

The condition of the skin and its appendages.—I have already stated that an increased tendency to sweat is a characteristic feature of most cases of acromegaly; it seems to be due to a vasomotor alteration. In some cases, the hands feel cold, moist and clammy to the touch; they sometimes become dead and blanched. Owing to its moist condition, the electrical resistance of the skin may be somewhat diminished—a fact which was pointed out by Erb, who also states that the electrical excitability of the muscles is increased.

In many of the cases of acromegaly which have been recorded, numerous small stalked warts were developed on the surface of the body; they are probably the result of the vasomotor and nutritive alterations in the skin. The term "molluscum fibrosum" has been applied to them, but in those cases which have come under my own notice the little cutaneous outgrowths appeared to be true warts, and not molluscous tumours. The warty nature was demonstrated in one of my cases by Dr Gulland, who kindly removed one of the little outgrowths, and made microscopical sections of it. In reference to this point Souza-Leite says:—"A certain number of patients present on the upper part of the body, especially on the upper part of the trunk, little cutaneous tumours, sometimes pedunculated. They are the size of a millet or hemp seed, or even larger. They are of a red colour, sometimes violet, and very numerous. The condition presented is that of molluscum fibrosum or pendulum. A patient of Verstræten presented numerous flat warts round the neck and waist. At first Marie was inclined to regard molluscum as a simple coincidence of acromegaly, but having since found it in all his patients he questions if it is not one of the phenomena of acromegaly, due to changes in the nutrition of the skin." *

In some cases, the skin of the face, more especially about the eyelids, and of the nose, and it may be of other parts of the body, is more deeply pigmented than normal. In many cases it is of a dingy, dirty, sallow hue, often coarse in texture, and in some cases thickly studded with sebaceous points. The scalp is in some cases thickened and hypertrophied.

---

* "Acromegaly": Pierre Marie and Souza-Leite. Sydenham Society's Translation, p. 54.

The *hair* of the scalp is usually abundant and thick, coarse and wiry ; the hairs of the body and pubis are usually strong, probably thicker than normal but not more numerous ; in women the little hairs round the nipple and between the breasts are in some cases larger and longer than normal.

The condition of the nervous system.—The skin sensibility rarely presents any characteristic alterations.

The *reflexes*, both superficial and deep, are usually normal ; but in some cases the knee-jerks are markedly diminished or even abolished. The *functions of the bladder and rectum* are rarely, if ever, affected.

The condition of the special senses.—In a considerable number of the cases of acromegaly which have been recorded, *bilateral temporal hemianopsia* was present. From a diagnostic point of view, this is a very important symptom, and is due to the pressure of the enlarged pituitary body upon the optic chiasma. In some cases, the optic nerves are atrophied ; in others (but this is quite exceptional) there is double optic neuritis. In those cases in which optic atrophy is developed, the defect of vision may ultimately involve the nasal as well as the temporal half of the fields of vision in one or both eyes, complete blindness being finally produced.

In many cases of acromegaly *headache* is a prominent symptom, and in some cases *vomiting* and *giddiness* are also present.

The *hearing* is occasionally impaired, but this is exceptional. Tinnitus aurium and noises in the ears are in many cases complained of ; but it is doubtful if these conditions, which are so common in anæmia, are of any great importance.

Smell is rarely, and *taste* very rarely, if ever, affected.

Now, headache, vomiting, and giddiness, when associated with optic atrophy, are highly suggestive of the presence of an intracranial tumour.

Further, when temporal hemianopsia—a very definite localising symptom—is present in addition to these general and non-localising symptoms (headache, vomiting, and giddiness), the diagnosis of a coarse lesion (usually a tumour of the pituitary body or a tumour or aneurism at the base of the brain which is pressing on the central fibres of the optic chiasma) is warranted.

The headache, which is such a common symptom in acromegaly, has been described as one of the fundamental symptoms of the disease ; but I am disposed to think that it is more probably a secondary symptom, due to the presence of the enlarged pituitary body within the skull. What I mean to suggest is, that the headache, vomiting, giddiness, temporal hemianopsia and optic atrophy or optic neuritis are due to the pressure or irritation produced by the pituitary tumour, and that they should not be placed in the same category with (*i.e.*, that they have not the same pathological significance as) the enlargement of the extremities, the increase of the soft parts and some of the other symptoms, which are, so far as our present knowledge enables us to judge, probably due to derangement of the function of the pituitary gland, and which should therefore be regarded as primary and fundamental symptoms of the disease.

The mental condition.—In most cases of acromegaly, the mental faculties do not present any alterations of importance, at all events during the earlier stages of the disease. In some cases, an excessive tendency to sleep, drowsiness, and symptoms indicative of mental depression or melancholia have been noted; but these symptoms are probably in no way peculiar or characteristic; they are probably due to the disturbance of the cerebral functions produced by the presence of a cerebral tumour (the enlargement of the pituitary), or to the mental dejection and depression which the patients experience in consequence of the loss of sight and the progressive and incurable character of the disease.

The condition of the urine.—In many cases of acromegaly, the urine is notably altered. It is usually increased in amount, not infrequently contains sugar, occasionally peptone, or an excess of phosphates, rarely serum albumen. In rare cases, the amount of urine is less than the normal. It is probable I think that these conditions (polyuria, glycosuria, peptonuria, etc.) are, like the headache and vomiting, not primary and fundamental but merely secondary symptoms, due to the pressure of the enlarged pituitary body upon the surrounding nervous tissues. It is well known that temporary glycosuria and peptonuria are sometimes met with in cases of intracranial tumour, and especially in those cases in which the tumour is situated in the neighbourhood of the pituitary body or the floor of the fourth ventricle. Possibly, however, these urinary alterations are fundamental and primary—part and parcel of a widespread vasomotor disturbance which is the direct result of the disease, *i.e.*, of the derangement of the functions of the pituitary gland.

The condition of the organs of circulation.—In some cases, the heart is enlarged and the superficial arteries atheromatous; in some cases, the cardiac enlargement seems to be a simple hypertrophy, in others, the result of fibrosis and myocarditis. Piles and varicose enlargement of the veins of the leg are not unfrequently present. The pulse is often quicker than normal.

The condition of the digestive apparatus.—The digestive organs are as a rule normal. In some of the recorded cases, the stomach was dilated and the appetite inordinately large, but whether the latter symptom has any real significance I am unable to say. Excessive thirst is, too, in some cases a prominent symptom, and is perhaps the result of the polyuria and glycosuria above described.

The general state of nutrition.—Since the most characteristic feature of acromegaly is an increase not only of the bones but also of the soft parts, it is unnecessary to say that, in the early stages at all events, patients affected with the disease appear to be well nourished.

The condition of the blood.—This does not, so far as I know, present any characteristic changes, though a certain degree of anæmia is sometimes present.

The condition of the ductless glands.—In many of the typical cases of acromegaly which have been examined post mortem, the *pituitary gland* has been much enlarged. During life the existence of this enlargement is in many cases proved by the presence of bilateral temporal hemianopsia. In some cases, the *thyroid gland* is also enlarged; in others (and this is perhaps more common), atrophied. In some cases, the *thymus gland* not only persists but is notably enlarged. In some cases, the *pineal gland* has been found enlarged after death, but so far as I know this enlargement is not attended with any distinct symptoms during life. In one of the recorded cases the *lymphatic glands* beneath the jaws were very much enlarged.

The condition of the sexual organs.—In females affected with the disease, amenorrhœa is almost always present, and is in many cases the first symptom to attract attention. The ovaries and uterus are usually atrophied. The mammæ are in some cases atrophied, but the nipples are usually of large size and often surrounded by an increased growth of coarse hair. The external genitals (labia majora, nymphæ and especially the clitoris) are in some cases enlarged. In men, the penis is sometimes increased in size; the testicles are in some cases enlarged, but more frequently atrophied. There is usually complete loss of sexual desire and virile power.

Summary of the chief symptoms.—To sum up, the chief characteristics of this remarkable disease are :—

(1) An enlargement or overgrowth of the extremities (hands, feet and face), and (though this is less evident) of the ribs, sternum, vertebræ, iliac bones, and in fact of all the bony structures of the body; it must be remembered that the overgrowth is not confined to the

osseous structures, for the soft parts—notably the soft tissues of the palms and soles, the tongue, and in some cases the clitoris and penis—are also involved ; (2) gradually increasing weakness ; (3) a tendency to excessive sweating, especially on exertion ; (4) in women, arrested menstruation which often occurs at an early stage of the disease ; and in men, loss of sexual desire and impotence, conditions which are usually developed in the later stages ; (5) vasomotor disturbances (a "dead" condition of the fingers, &c.) ; (6) the development on the surface of the body of little warty tumours ; (7) an increased growth of hair ; (8) neuralgic and myalgic pains ; (9) atrophy of the mammary glands and ovaries, and in some cases of the testicles ; (10) headache, with which vomiting and vertigo are sometimes associated ; (11) bilateral temporal hemianopsia and it may be optic atrophy or (but this is rare) optic neuritis ; (12) glycosuria, polyuria and peptonuria ; (13) inordinate appetite and thirst ; (14) mental depression, stupor, and less frequently maniacal excitement, &c.

As I have previously stated, it is doubtful whether all of these symptoms should be placed in the same pathological category or not. It is possible that some of them, such as the enlargement of the extremities, the debility, the excessive sweating, are primary, i.e., the direct result of a derangement of the function of the pituitary gland ; and that others, such as headache, bilateral temporal hemianopsia, polyuria, etc., are secondary, i.e., the indirect result of, and due to, the increased size of the pituitary body and to the derangement of the cerebral functions which the tumour (the enlarged pituitary body) produces.

Varieties.—Two forms or varieties of acromegaly have been described, viz., (1) the *massive* type, and (2) the *giant* or *long* type of the disease ; for it has been shown that in some giants the pituitary body is enlarged and the symptoms, or some of the symptoms, of acromegaly are present. With regard to this point Hinsdale says :—"As to the two types of acromegaly, there is a disposition to assume the long or giant type of acromegaly, if the disease originated in the period of adolescence ; but if the onset is delayed until later life, the type will be large (Brissaud and Meige)." *

Dr Hinsdale throws out the suggestion that there is perhaps a relationship, in some cases at all events, between giantism and dwarfism. On this point he says :—"Cases have arisen which have suggested that there is, paradoxical as it may seem, a relation

---

* "Acromegaly," by Guy Hinsdale, A.M., M.D., p. 51.

between giantism and dwarfism. Such cases are those described by Mr Jonathan Hutchinson in 1866 and by Mr H. Gilford in 1896. In the latter case, while the patient was clearly a dwarf, there were parts that were more than fully developed; and Mr Gilford was led by this case to the study of dwarfism and giantism. He sees a close relationship between these deviations in nutrition, and suggests the term micromegaly as descriptive of his case and others allied to it. He thinks it not impossible that the cause of acromegaly operating before birth may bring about micromegaly; for many giants have evidently owed their proportions to the former. May the one be the congenital condition of the other, or are the two opposite states?" *

Morbid Anatomy and Pathology.

In addition to the enlargement of the bony structures which is such a striking feature of almost every case of acromegaly (but which is evidently a result of the primary lesion, whatever it may be, which is the cause of the disease), the most constant and noticeable pathological change found after death is enlargement of the pituitary body. The gland is usually so much increased in size that the sella turcica (the bony bed in which it is embedded) is greatly enlarged.

In some cases, morbid changes have also been found in the sympathetic, in the peripheral nerves and in the spinal cord. In some cases, the heart, arteries, and some of the abdominal and thoracic viscera have also been found affected (enlarged, sclerosed, etc.), after death. Further, as has been already stated in connection with the clinical history, the ductless glands, other than the pituitary gland, are in some cases affected; though the thyroid gland is in some cases normal, in other cases it is enlarged, in others again atrophied; the thymus gland in some cases persists and may be considerably enlarged; in one case at least, the pineal gland was increased in size.

The exact significance of many of these morbid changes is at present doubtful; but the weight of evidence seems strongly in favour of the view that the enlargement of the pituitary body is the primary and fundamental lesion of the disease. According to this view, the pituitary, like the thyroid, is a blood gland, which is, in some way or another, actively concerned in the regulation of the nutrition and metabolism of the body, and perhaps especially

---

* "Acromegaly," by Guy Hinsdale, A.M., M.D., p. 51.

concerned in the regulation of the nutrition and metabolism of the nervous tissues.

Another view, which seems, however, much less likely, is that acromegaly is the result of nervous changes—a trophic neurosis—and that the enlargement of the pituitary body is merely part and parcel of the trophic (or, perhaps, to speak more correctly, of the hypertrophic) change which affects many of the tissues and organs of the body. Further, it has been supposed that the enlargement of the pituitary body which is primarily the result of a nervous change, produces in its turn (by the disturbance—diminution, increase, or perversion—of its internal secretion) nutritional changes in the tissues and organs of the body.

The exact manner in which the lesion of the pituitary body produces the symptoms of the disease has not, however, as yet been definitely determined. It has been suggested that the disease (acromegaly) is due to :—(1) arrested, (2) increased, or (3) perverted pituitary secretion.

If the enlargement of the pituitary body is a true hypertrophy, the view which supposes that the symptoms of acromegaly are due to an increased or perverted action of the pituitary gland is very plausible. The pituitary body closely resembles in structure the thyroid gland, but our knowledge of the function of the pituitary body is as yet altogether indefinite. It is possible that the study of acromegaly may throw some light on this obscure physiological problem, just as the study of myxœdema has thrown so much light on the function of the thyroid gland. The remarkable influence which the thyroid gland undoubtedly exerts upon the nutrition of the body suggests that the pituitary and other ductless glands may, like the thyroid, exert a powerful influence on nutrition.

Further, there seems to be some sort of functional relationship between the thyroid and the pituitary—a fact which lends some corroboration to the view that the pituitary body is in some way or another concerned in the regulation of the nutrition and metabolism of the body. As has been already pointed out, in some cases of acromegaly the thyroid gland is hypertrophied, while in others it is atrophied; while in some (? all) cases of myxœdema the pituitary body is in some degree enlarged.

In the present state of our knowledge, it is impossible to form a definite conclusion as to the exact influence which the enlargement of the pituitary body exerts in the production of acromegaly. Every enlargement of the pituitary body is not attended with symptoms of acromegaly. Two cases of this kind have come under my own observation. Complete destruction of the pituitary body, the result, for example, of sarcomatous tumours, does not necessarily produce acromegaly, though in some cases of acromegaly, the enlargement of the pituitary gland has been sarcomatous in nature. Again, it is important to note that the results which have up to the present time been obtained from the administration of pituitary extract in cases of acromegaly are very contradictory. In a few cases marked benefit has resulted from the treatment, but in the majority of cases there has either been no improvement, or the improvement has been so slight as to be insufficient to warrant any definite conclusions.

In one of my cases, pituitary feeding seemed to do harm, and in another to be attended with benefit. In the former case thyroid extract appeared to do good, and in the latter harm.

The exact significance of the pathological alterations which have been found after death in the sympathetic, peripheral nerves and spinal cord is doubtful; it is possible that these changes are secondary results of either perverted, increased, or possibly (though this is perhaps less likely) diminished action of the pituitary gland. It is quite conceivable that the pituitary gland, like the thyroid, may exert a marked influence upon the nutrition of the nervous system, and that an arrested, increased, or perverted functional activity of the pituitary body may lead to the production of important nutritive and structural changes in the nervous system and perhaps in the other tissues of the body. Further, the enlargement of the thyroid and thymus glands which is frequently present in cases of acromegaly may perhaps be compensatory in character. Some of the structural changes which occur in acromegaly, namely, the enlargement of the bones and soft parts, appear to be of the nature of a hypertrophy or overgrowth; others, such as the changes in the mammary glands, ovaries and testes, are clearly atrophic in character.

Whether the pituitary body exerts any influence upon the structural or functional condition of the generative organs, we do not at present know; but such a connection is by no means improbable, and the possibility of such a relationship should certainly be kept in view. The facts that menstruation is so frequently arrested in the earlier stages of acromegaly, and that the mammary glands, ovaries, and sometimes the testes atrophy as the disease progresses, are suggestive of this view. Further, the fact that there appears to be some sort of relationship between the thyroid gland and the ovaries and uterus, and perhaps the mammary glands (for in one of my cases of myxœdema the breasts became full of milk on the administration of thyroid extract), and between the pituitary and thyroid glands on the other, perhaps point in the same direction.

DIAGNOSIS.

In typical and well marked cases of acromegaly, the diagnosis does not present any great difficulty. The symptoms are quite peculiar and characteristic. The physical alterations which are of most importance from a diagnostic point of view are:—(1) The marked enlargement of the extremities (hands, feet, and face), an enlargement which is not merely due to an increase of the bones, but which, in part at least, is the result of an increase of the soft parts: (2) the shape of the hands and fingers, feet and toes, and of the nails; the absence of clubbing of the ends of the fingers and toes is, according to Marie, a distinguishing characteristic between acromegaly and hypertrophic pulmonary osteo-arthropathy: (3) the shape and conformation of the face; the marked elongation of the lower part of the face, the enlargement of the lower jaw, the projection of the chin, the fulness and evertion of the lower lip, and the heavy, somewhat sad, expression of countenance; (4) the increased growth of hair: (5) the development of small pedunculated warts on the surface of the skin: and (6) the atrophy of the mammary glands. While the symptoms which are chiefly characteristic are:—(a) the lassitude and debility; (b) the increased tendency to sweat; (c) the arrested menstruation; (d) the myalgic and neuralgic pains; (e) the peculiar defects of vision (bilateral temporal hemianopsia); (f) the headache; (g) the thirst; and (h) the polyuria or glycosuria and peptonuria which are in many cases present.

The Differential Diagnosis of Acromegaly and Myxœdema has already been considered (see p. 316).

The Differential Diagnosis of Acromegaly and of Hypertrophic Pulmonary Osteo-arthropathy. — This is much more difficult—indeed, according to some observers the two conditions are one and the same disease. This view, however, seems a mistaken one.

The chief distinction between the two diseases seems to be as follows :—

In acromegaly the ends of the fingers are not clubbed; whereas in hypertrophic pulmonary osteo-arthropathy marked clubbing of the fingers is always present. In pulmonary osteo-arthropathy the enlargement of the fingers is especially noticeable at the last phalanx, the nails being considerably widened, lengthened and, more especially, curved. In pulmonary osteo-arthropathy the toes are affected in a similar manner, though usually in a less degree. In acromegaly the enlargement of the hands is chiefly in breadth (carpo-metacarpal region); whereas in hypertrophic pulmonary osteo-arthropathy the enlargement is chiefly of the last or terminal phalanges of the fingers and of the wrist joints.

In hypertrophic pulmonary osteo-arthropathy the face, and particularly the lower jaw, are not affected (enlarged). In hypertrophic pulmonary osteo-arthropathy the wrists and ankles are notably enlarged ; whereas in acromegaly the enlargement of these joints is rarely marked.

As the term hypertrophic pulmonary osteo-arthropathy denotes, the enlargement of the hands, feet, &c., is associated with, and apparently is the result of, some form of pulmonary disease—usually chronic bronchitis, empyema, &c. It has been supposed by Marie that the lung lesion leads to the development of the osseous changes by the production and absorption into the general circulation of micro-organisms, or some product of micro-organisms, and that the poison thus absorbed produces the structural changes which are characteristic of the disease. In acromegaly there is no pulmonary lesion.

PROGNOSIS AND TREATMENT.

The ultimate prognosis in cases of acromegaly is unfavourable. At the present time we do not know of any remedial measures which exert any distinctly beneficial effect upon the course of the disease. The course of the disease is in most cases very chronic, though, as has been previously stated, in rare cases the disease runs a more rapid course.

In some cases, nervine tonics, more especially arsenic and strychnine, appear to be beneficial. In those cases in which anæmia is prominent, iron or arsenic should be administered. In all cases of the disease, pituitary extract and thyroid extract deserve a thorough trial ; but, so far as our present information enables us to judge, the effect of these remedies is very uncertain. In some of the recorded cases in which these remedies were administered, improvement, usually slight in degree, resulted ; in others, there was no improvement, or the patients became worse. Thus, in eighteen cases tabulated by Hinsdale, in which either pituitary extract or thyroid extract or both extracts were administered, there was no improvement in 9 cases, slight improvement in 6 cases, and great improvement (as the result of the administration of pituitary extract) in 3 cases.

ILLUSTRATIVE CASES.

CASE I.—*Typical Acromegaly.*

Female, aged 27, single, admitted to the Edinburgh Royal Infirmary on 25th November 1892, complaining of general weakness and enlargement of the hands, feet and face.

Previous history.—The patient was perfectly well until July 1887. She attributes her illness to a fall. Just before the symptoms of the disease were first noticed, she fell from a swing and struck her right side; the injury was not severe. For three weeks before this accident, she had been subjected to a good deal of mental strain and overwork while nursing her grandmother and an uncle who were ill. A short time after the accident, her mother noticed that she was looking out of sorts, and that her facial appearance was changed. About the same time, the menstruation, which had always previously been quite regular, became arrested; it has never returned since. She then began to complain of increasing weakness. Before the disease commenced, she was fond of exercise and could easily walk six or eight miles without fatigue; during the past five years she has never been able to walk more than four miles; now, a walk of half a mile is as much as she can manage comfortably, more than that tires her.

Soon after the menstruation became arrested, her hands, feet and face began to enlarge. She does not know whether the enlargement first involved the hands, the feet, or the face. The enlargement soon became considerable. Her face used to be round; it is now long and oval; the alteration in her facial appearance is so marked that friends who have not seen her since the disease commenced now hardly recognise her.

Family history.—Unimportant. Her father suffers from rheumatism. She has three brothers and a sister, all healthy. So far as she knows, no case of acromegaly has occurred amongst any of her relatives.

Condition on admission.—The appearance of the patient is highly characteristic, the face, hands and feet all being markedly enlarged. The expression is sad and apathetic. When the patient stands in the erect position, the shoulders are rounded. The patient is well nourished; muscularity fair; temperature subnormal.

Complaints.—Debility, excessive perspiration on exertion, and dimness of vision are the chief complaints. The patient every now and again suffers from aching pains in the region of the left hip. There is no headache.

Detailed description of the appearance of different parts.—The *face* is oval in shape, being elongated from the nose to the chin. The nose is very prominent and aquiline; the nostrils and septum are broad, the soft parts as well as the bones being evidently enlarged. The lips, especially the lower lip, are thick. The lower jaw is considerably increased in size, and the chin prominent, the angle of the jaw being less acute than normal; the teeth in the lower jaw are separated from one another by considerable spaces. The eyes are set wide apart and are very prominent; the left eyeball looks a little lower than the right and diverges slightly outwards; the eyelashes are dark and abundant; the orbital fissures are comparatively narrow; the eyelids, especially those of the right eye, are somewhat swollen; the supra-orbital ridges are very thick, and the eyebrows are dark and bushy. The ears are not enlarged. The tongue is broad and flat; its upper surface is more ridged and grooved than normal. The uvula and soft palate appear to be slightly swollen. The bones of the skull are not enlarged.

The *neck* is short and thick; the head bent down on the thorax; the larynx is large and prominent; the thyroid gland can be distinctly felt. The clavicles and ribs are enlarged, and the antero-posterior diameter of the chest increased. The *sternum* is increased in size, the angle between the manubrium sterni and the lower part of the bone being very marked. There is little if any impairment of the percussion note over the manubrium sterni. The right side of the thorax measures considerably more than the left, possibly as the result of an attack of inflammation (? of the pleura) which occurred some two or three years ago.

The *pelvis* and pelvic bones appear to be enlarged.

The *hands* are markedly enlarged, increased in width and thickness rather than in length; the soft parts project like pads on the palmar aspect; the fingers are flattened. The hands present a "battledore" appearance; the hypothenar eminences are very prominent. The nails are wide but are not long, and do not seem to be hypertrophied. The wrist joints are slightly enlarged; they are increased in breadth.

The *feet* are markedly increased in size, especially in breadth; the soles very flat, the arch of the foot being almost entirely obliterated; the first phalanx of the great toe is much elongated, and the metacarpal bone is very large and lipped at its distal end. The nails of the great toes are square, and grooved transversely. The ankle joints are somewhat enlarged.

Integumentary system.—The *skin* of the eyelids and of the adjacent parts of the temples is of a yellowish brown colour, and there are dirty, brown-coloured patches on the front of the neck and over the anterior folds of the axillæ; the patient states that the discoloration of the neck and axillæ has existed since early life.

The hands are usually cold, moist and clammy to the touch. The feet are usually bathed in sweat. The hands frequently become cold, "dead" and blanched, even when the patient is sitting in a warm room; at other times, the feet and hands, and indeed the whole body, feel hot and flushed. Numerous small warts are scattered over the body. The patient sweats much more profusely than she used to do, especially after exertion.

The *hair* of the head, eyebrows and eyelashes is strong and wiry, but the axillary and pubic hairs are very scanty. There are no hairs round the nipple.

Nervous system.—Well marked *bilateral temporal hemianopsia* is present; hearing, smell, and taste are natural. There is no headache, no vomiting, and no giddiness. The reflexes are normal.

Alimentary system.—The *appetite* is good, but not excessive; the patient sometimes vomits before breakfast, and frequently suffers from dyspepsia.

Circulatory system.—Heart normal. Pulse somewhat slow; average morning frequency 60, evening 72; small, weak, of low tension, occasionally irregular in rhythm. The sphygmographic tracing shows a considerable degree of dicrotism. There is no atheroma of the superficial vessels. No œdema.

Urinary system.—The *urine* is normal; specific gravity 1,030; acid; free from sugar and albumen; it frequently deposits a large quantity of urates. The quantity of urine, instead of being increased, is greatly diminished. During twenty days in September (from the 4th to the 23rd inclusive) the average quantity passed in the twenty-four hours was 36 ounces, the lowest and highest amounts tested on any one day being respectively, 14 and 59 ounces.

Reproductive system.—Amenorrhœa.

The *mammary glands* are markedly atrophied, in fact they cannot be felt; the nipples, however, are large and prominent.

Blood.—On admission to hospital the red corpuscles numbered 3,830,000, and the hæmoglobin equalled 56 °/. After the administration of iron and arsenic the anæmia soon disappeared, and on 21st February 1893, the red blood corpuscles numbered 4,540,000 and the hæmoglobin equalled 84 %.

Progress of the case.—The patient remained in the hospital until 25th April. She was first treated with iron, arsenic, and thyroid extract, and subsequently with pituitary extract (at first $\frac{1}{2}$ a pituitary gland, subsequently $\frac{3}{4}$ of a gland daily). The pituitary gland did not produce any beneficial effect; under its use the sweating increased. The headache and other symptoms improved somewhat while she was taking the thyroid extract.

CASE II.—*Acromegaly in a Giantess.*

Female, aged 28, single, was admitted to the Edinburgh Royal Infirmary on 19th June 1893.

Previous history.—Up to the age of 16, the patient was no taller or broader than other girls of the same age. After the age of 16, she began to grow very rapidly, and at 20 was almost as tall as she is now; her shoulders became rounded and she began to stoop. About the same time (1885), her feet swelled and she began to suffer from debility, headache, and excessive sweating. During the summer of 1887, she became short of breath on exertion, and complained of pain in the left side of the abdomen, swelling of the front of the chest and of the breasts (which felt as if they were full of milk), and of pains in the back of the head. About the same time, she noticed that her hands, feet, and face were notably enlarged. Since the year 1887, the enlargement of the hands, feet, face, abdomen, and in fact of the whole body, has steadily increased. During the whole of this period, she has suffered more or less from headache, giddiness, profuse sweating, and gradually increasing debility. For the past two years she has been unable to do anything except knit.

Previous history prior to the present illness.—At the age of 10, she had scarlet fever, and at 20, measles; she made a good recovery from both of these diseases. She has had four attacks of inflammation of the bowels, each lasting about a week; two occurred before the age of 20, and two during the year 1888. Two years ago, she suffered from left-sided facial paralysis; it came on without any apparent cause.

Family history.—The patient comes of a healthy family. No case of acromegaly or giantism has occurred amongst her relations. Her brothers and sisters are all small (short) but robust country people.

Present condition.—The patient is a woman of enormous size. Height in her stockings 6 ft. 2 ins., and this does not represent her full height, for she is unable to stand erect owing to the curvature of the upper part of the spinal column. Her weight on admission was 24 st. 8½ lbs.

The whole body is increased in size, the hands, feet, and abdomen being especially large. The feet, ankles, and lower parts of the legs are surrounded by a solid œdema, which does not pit on pressure. The increased bulk of the body is obviously due to overgrowth of the bones as well as of the soft tissues.

While the patient stands in the erect position the shoulders are seen to be rounded, and the head is bent forwards towards the sternum.

Though well nourished, the patient is not excessively fat; the muscles are somewhat soft; the muscular power is very defective (dynamometer right hand = 43, left = 46). The gait is very slow, heavy and clumsy.

The temperature is subnormal, usually 97° Fahr.

Complaints.—Extreme lassitude, weakness, and disinclination for exertion (for the last two years, she has not been able to walk farther than the length of the Ward); headache; excessive sweating; thirst; vertigo; and neuralgic and myalgic pains in different parts of the body.

Detailed description of the appearance of different parts.—*Face.*—Expression sad and apathetic. The face, though massive, is not disproportionately large to the other parts of the body; the relative proportion between the upper and lower parts of the face is natural; the facial conformation is not typical of acromegaly; the lips are not specially thick, the chin is not enlarged, and the lower jaw is not prognathous.

The left side of the face is flatter than the right (old facial paralysis). The superciliary ridges are not thickened. The eyelids are large, heavy-looking, and drooping. The eyebrows, eyelashes, eyeballs, and ocular muscles are normal. The nose is large, even for the size of the face; its bridge is prominent, its tip large, and the septum massive. The cheeks are full and rounded, though not unduly prominent. The mouth is, relatively, small; the upper lip of natural size; the lower lip somewhat full but not everted; its colour is natural. The ears are not enlarged. The palate is very high and narrow, but not V-shaped. The lower jaw does not present any characteristic alterations. The teeth, many of which are decayed, are not "widely set." The gums are inclined to be spongy and to bleed. The tongue is rather large and flabby. The mouth is always dry, and there is consequently some difficulty in swallowing. The buccal mucous membrane, tonsils, uvula, and pharynx are normal.

The *head* is large (circumference 64 c.m.) but normally shaped; the scalp, which is dry and scaly, is thickly covered with dark brown hair.

The *neck* is thick, but not unduly short. The *larynx* is large, and the pomum Adami prominent. The *voice* is soft in tone, and has not changed since the disease commenced; the patient cannot sing so well as she used to do, being unable to get out high notes. The *thyroid gland* appears to be of normal size. There is no dulness over the manubrium sterni.

Upper extremity.—The hands are very large, but not unduly broad in proportion to their length; the fingers are tapered, the last phalanges being slightly dorsi-flexed. The nails are well shaped and slightly grooved in the longitudinal direction. The thenar and hypothenar eminences are large and soft, the palms thickly padded with fat. The wrists are large. The bones of the forearm and upper arm are of great length, but not, in proportion to their size, unduly thick.

The *clavicles* are well curved and very long.

The *chest* is well shaped. Its circumstance during free inspiration is 136, and during expiration 133, centimetres. The condition of the sternum, ensiform cartilage, and ribs does not call for any special remark.

The *mammæ* are large and pendulous; the nipples of normal size and colour; there are no hairs round the nipples.

The *abdomen* is very large and lax (circumference at the umbilicus 135 c.m.). The *pelvis* is very broad.

The *spinal column* is curved forwards in the upper dorsal and cervical regions; the spinous processes do not appear to be enlarged.

Lower extremity.—The feet, ankles, and lower part of the legs are surrounded with a solid œdema, which does not pit on pressure; the patient complains of pain when firm pressure is made over the swollen parts. The *feet* are very large, square and flat; like the hands, they have increased greatly in size during the past six years; the soles are very flat and thickly padded with fat; before the disease commenced the instep was high. The toes are clubbed, the first meta-carpal bone extended (dorsi-flexed) and the last phalanx flexed (plantar-flexed). The great toes are large. The nail of the pollux is, relatively to the size of the toe, small, but well formed; those of the other toes are small and almost com-pletely buried in the soft parts. The bones of the lower extremities are all enlarged, but not disproportionately so.

The *muscles* are poorly developed; the joints are normal.

Integumentary system.—The colour of the *skin* is pale and the texture much coarser than it was before the disease commenced. The skin is always moist; the patient perspires on the slightest exertion; the sweat has a heavy odour. On the face, abdomen, back and limbs, there is an excessive quantity of hair. On the abdomen two, and sometimes three, hairs, which measure on an average 3 centimetres in length, spring from a single hair follicle. The individual follicles are somewhat widely separated from one another. On the upper lip and chin, the growth of hair is very considerable. Numerous flat warts, moles, freckles and small stalked warts, some of them pigmented, are situated on the face, limbs, and back; many of them have developed since the disease commenced.

Nervous system.—*Headache*, which in the early stages of the case was con-stant and chiefly felt at the back of the head, has for the last three or four years been intermittent; it occurs daily and lasts for a few hours; it is usually worse during the afternoon. The pain is sharp and lancinating in character, and is chiefly felt at the back of the head and over the left temple. *Vertigo* is a pro-minent symptom, and is chiefly felt on going to bed. *Temporary dimness of vision* and *ringing in the ears* are also occasionally experienced.

The *superficial reflexes* are normal; the *knee-jerks* rather sluggish.

The skin *sensibility* to touch, pain, heat and cold is normal.

Sight.—The acuity of vision is normal. On admission, the area for white was markedly contracted in the temporal half of the right field; on 20th October, the constriction had disappeared. The conjunctivæ are healthy. The pupils and fundi oculi are normal.

Smell, taste and *hearing* are normal.

The *memory* for recent events is impaired. The patient sleeps badly and often wakes with a start.

Genito-urinary system.—The *urine* is scanty in amount (the average amount for the six days ending 25th July, was 21¼ ounces; and for the seven days ending 24th September, 27 ounces); the specific gravity of the urine is high (on 22nd July, amount = 12 ounces, specific gravity = 1,043); the amount of urea excreted in the 24 hours is very small, (on 20th September = 87.6 grains). The urine contains neither albumen, sugar, nor peptones. It frequently deposits a copious sediment of urates and mucus.

Menstruation first appeared at the age of 23; for the first year it was irregular; it is now regular; the flow continues for a week and is always profuse.

Circulatory system.—The patient is breathless on the least exertion, and is often troubled with palpitation. The *heart* is of normal size, the impulse feeble, the sounds somewhat indistinct. The *pulse* averages 67 per minute and is easily compressible. *Hæmorrhoids* are occasionally troublesome.

Blood.—The reds number 4,880,000 per c.mm.; hæmoglobin = 80 per cent.; whites not increased; reds normal in shape.

Respiratory system.—Normal. The nose often bleeds.

Digestive system.—Appetite small, patient has a distaste for butcher meat; very thirsty; digestion good; bowels constipated. The *stomach, liver,* and *spleen* are of normal size.

Treatment and progress of the case.—On 10th July, ten drops of thyroid extract (⅓th of a gland) once daily were prescribed; but it was discontinued on 16th July, the headache, sweating and feeling of lassitude having become markedly aggravated.

On 21st July, 10 drops of pituitary extract (₉⅟₄th part of a sheep's pituitary gland) were given once daily. The dose was gradually increased to 15 drops on 1st September; to 30 drops on 26th October; to two fluid drachms, three times daily (⅔ths of a gland) on 8th November. The remedy was steadily continued for several months. During the administration of this remedy, the symptoms (with the exception of the giddiness) were undoubtedly relieved; the headache disappeared; the sweating diminished; the feeling of debility and lassitude lessened; the constriction of the field of vision disappeared; and the weight decreased from 24 st. 8 lbs. to 24 st. But whether the improvement was entirely due to the pituitary extract it is, of course, impossible to say; I am disposed to think that the long continued rest and careful treatment in hospital were in part at least responsible for the improvement.

On 8th December 1893, the patient was discharged. She was again admitted to the Infirmary in September 1895 and July 1898.

During the seven years that she has been under my observation, the severity of the symptoms (headache, lassitude, vertigo, sweating, etc.) has varied from time to time, but there has been no substantial change in her condition. There has been no increase in size either in the body as a whole, or in its individual parts. In short, she is practically in the same condition that she was seven years ago.

CASE III.—*Typical Acromegaly.*

R. L., aged 34, shopman, married, seen at the Edinburgh Royal Infirmary on 6th May 1896, suffering from typical acromegaly.

Previous history.—The disease commenced gradually seven years ago; its development was preceded by an attack of influenza, which the patient thinks was the cause. During the past seven years the patient has complained of general weakness and of headache; at first the pain was felt in the right temple; it is now felt all over the head. During the past three years, the fingers have occasionally become "dead."

Previous history prior to present illness.—When quite young, he suffered from inflammation of the bowels; this is the only serious illness which he has ever had. He had syphilis twelve years ago, but has had no "reminders" since.

Family history.—Unimportant. All his near relatives are healthy; none very tall; none of them have suffered from rheumatism or gout. His father, aged 69, and his mother, aged 69, are both alive and healthy. He has four brothers and one sister, aged 32 to 45, all alive and in good health. He has two children of his own, both girls; both are healthy. His wife has had no miscarriages.

Complaints.—He complains of great weakness, headache, occasional giddiness, deafness, and noises in the ears. He is able to walk very little; before the illness commenced he could walk ten miles without difficulty; now he feels tired if he goes ten yards; is inclined to sit whenever he gets a chance.

Present condition.—Height 5 ft. 7 ins.; weight 12 st. 7 lbs. He states that he has grown one and a half inches since the disease commenced, and that when he married seven years ago (this was just before the disease commenced) he only weighed 9 st.; he is much stouter and broader than he used to be. His *hands*, which are very broad and short, are much larger than they used to be; he used to take size 7¼ in gloves, he now takes 9½. His *head* has also increased in size; he used to take a hat No. 6⅞ in size, he now takes a hat No. 7 in size. His *feet* have also increased greatly in size; he used to take No. 6 in boots, he now takes No. 9. The feet are short. The toes are very big and broad at the tips.

His *face* has changed very much in appearance. The lower jaw has, he says, shot out; the forehead projects more than it used to do, the supra-orbital ridges being enlarged. The lower lip is enlarged. The nose is much broader than it used to be. Ears not much altered. The tongue is very much enlarged. The teeth of the lower jaw are separated from one another by large spaces. Gums natural. Cannot breathe through his nose.

The *neck* is short and thick; the thyroid gland is not enlarged; there is no area of dulness over the manubrium sterni. His tone of voice has become changed; it is much harsher and rougher than it used to be; he used to have a clear tenor voice.

There is a marked antero-posterior curvature of the *spine* in the cervical and upper dorsal regions; also slight lateral curvature towards the left.

Skin.—Every now and again, he has a feeling of heat and flushing, at other times of cold. The hair and eyebrows are not changed. He sweats a good deal, especially about the head. Numerous small warts have developed on the skin; there are also numerous freckles on the extensor aspects of the arms, on the buttocks and thighs. Slight petechiæ occasionally develop on the skin.

No increase of saliva. For some time has had a "terrible watering" from the eyes and nose.

Appetite is poor, much smaller than it used to be; he is very thirsty, especially at night. The bowels have become very constipated since the illness commenced.

Urine clear amber coloured; specific gravity 1,032; no sugar; slight trace of albumen.

Genital organs are not enlarged. *Sexual power* decidedly less than it used to be.

Nervous system.—Headache is more or less continuous, and is felt over the whole head. There has been no vomiting and very little giddiness. Complains of rushing noises in the ears and deafness. Sleeps fairly well, if it were not for the pains in the head.

Six months ago his *sight* was normal; he now complains of slight dimness in the left eye. Acuity of vision in the right eye = $\frac{20}{20}$, left eye = $\frac{20}{30}$; the fields of vision are normal. Pupils equal and active both to light and accommodation. He has been deaf in both ears for nearly two years.

Treatment.—The patient stated that during the course of his illness he had been treated both with thyroid extract and pituitary extract; these remedies brought down his weight, but did not relieve the headache. Was advised to continue the pituitary extract, which he has been taking in larger doses. He was only seen once. The subsequent progress of the case is not known.

APPENDIX.

The condition of the nails in chlorosis.—In many cases of chlorosis the nutrition of the nails is markedly affected; they are apt to become thin and flat, in some cases ridged longitudinally, in others concave instead of convex.

Pernicious anæmia.—*Case XXVI.* (page 120): this patient died in January 1899. *Case XLIII.* (page 133): this patient died in November 1898.

Addison's disease.—Since the article was written I have had another case in which the most marked improvement resulted from the administration of suprarenal extract. The case was shown at a recent meeting of the Edinburgh and neighbouring Branches of the British Medical Association, and will shortly be published in the *British Medical Journal.*

Leucocythæmia.—The case reported on page 171 relapsed and died soon after the sheet containing the report was printed. The result of the post-mortem examination will shortly be published in full.

INDEX.

APRIL, 1899.

CATALOGUE
No. 1.

CATALOGUE

OF

MEDICAL, DENTAL,

Pharmaceutical, and Scientific Publications,

WITH A SUBJECT INDEX,

OF ALL BOOKS PUBLISHED BY

P. BLAKISTON'S SON & CO.

(ESTABLISHED 1843),

PUBLISHERS, IMPORTERS, AND BOOKSELLERS,

1012 WALNUT ST., PHILADELPHIA.

SPECIAL NOTE.

The prices as given in this catalogue are absolutely net, no discount will be allowed retail purchasers under any consideration. This rule has been established in order that everyone will be treated alike, a general reduction in former prices having been made to meet previous retail discounts. Upon receipt of the advertised price any book will be forwarded by mail or express, all charges prepaid.

We keep a large stock of Miscellaneous Books relating to Medicine and Allied Sciences, published in this country and abroad. Inquiries in regard to prices, date of edition, etc., will receive prompt attention.

The following Catalogues sent free upon application:—

CATALOGUE No. 1.—A complete list of the titles of all our publications on Medicine, Dentistry, Pharmacy, and Allied Sciences, with Classified Index.

CATALOGUE No. 3.—Pharmaceutical Books.

CATALOGUE No. 4.—Books on Chemistry and Technology.

CATALOGUE No. 5.—Books for Nurses and Lay Readers.

CATALOGUE No. 6.—Books on Dentistry and Books used by Dental Students.

CATALOGUE No. 7.—Books on Hygiene and Sanitary Science ; Including Water and Milk Analysis, Microscopy, Physical Education, Hospitals, etc.

CATALOGUE No. 8.—List of about 300 Standard Books classified by Subjects.

SPECIAL CIRCULARS.—Morris' Anatomy ; Gould's Medical Dictionaries ; Moullin's Surgery ; Books on the Eye ; The ? Quiz Compends ? Series. Visiting Lists, etc. We can also furnish sample pages of many of our publications.

P. Blakiston's Son & Co.'s publications may be had through the booksellers in all the principal cities of the United States and Canada, or any book will be sent, postpaid, upon receipt of the price, or forwarded by express, C. O. D. No discount can be allowed retail purchasers under any circumstances. Money should be remitted by express or post-office money order, registered letter, or bank draft.

CLASSIFIED LIST, WITH PRICES,

OF ALL BOOKS PUBLISHED BY

P. BLAKISTON'S SON & CO., PHILADELPHIA.

When the price is not given below, the book is out of print or about to be published.
Cloth binding, unless otherwise specified. For full descriptions see following Catalogue.

ANATOMY.

Ballou. Veterinary Anat. $0.80
Broomell. Anatomy and
Histol. of Mouth and Teeth. 4 50
Eckley. Practical Anatomy. ——
Gordinier. Anatomy of Nerv-
ous System. Illustrated. 6 00
Heath. Practical. 7th Ed. 4.25
Holden. Dissector. ——
—— Osteology. 8th Ed. 5.25
—— Landmarks. 4th Ed. 1.00
Macalister's Text-Book. - 5.00
Marshall's Phys. and Anat.
Diagrams. 40.00 and 60.00
Morris. Text-Book of, 790 Illus.
Clo , 6.00; Sh., 7.00; ½ Rus., 8.00
Potter. Compend of, 6th
Ed. 133 Illustrations. - .80
Wilson's Anatomy. 11th Ed. 5.00
Windle. Surface Anatomy. 1.00

ANESTHETICS.

Buxton. Anæsthetics. - ——
Turnbull. 4th Ed. - 2.50

BRAIN AND INSANITY.

Blackburn. Autopsies. - 1.25
Gowers. Diagnosis of Dis-
eases of the Brain. 2d Ed. 1.50
Horsley. Brain and S. Cord. 2.50
Lewis (Bevan). Mental
Diseases. 2d Ed. 7.00
Mann's Psychological Med. 3.00
Régis. Mental Medicine. - 2.00
Stearns. Mental Dis. Illus. 2.75
Tuke. Dictionary of Psycho-
logical Medicine. 2 Vols. 10.00
Wood. Brain and Overwork. .40

CHEMISTRY.

See Technological Books, Water.
Allen. Commercial Organic
Analysis. New Revised Edi-
tions. Volume I. 3d Ed. 4.50
—— Vol. II. Part I. 3d Ed. 3.50
—— Vol. II. Part II. 3d Ed. ——
—— Volume III. Part I. ——
—— Volume III. Part II. 4.50
—— Volume III. Part III. 4.50
—— Volume IV. - - 4.50
—— Appendix Vol. ——
Bartley. Medical and Phar-
maceutical. 5th Ed. - 3.00
—— Clinical Chemistry. 1.00
Bloxam's Text-Book. 8th Ed. 4.25
Caldwell. Qualitative and
Quantitative Analysis. - 1.50
Groves and Thorp. Chemi-
cal Technology Vol. I. Fuels 5.00
—— Vol. II. Lighting. - 4.00
Holland. Urine, Gastric Con-
tents, Poisons and Milk Anal-
ysis. 5th Ed. - - 1.00
Leffmann's Compend. - .80
—— Milk Analysis. - 1.25
—— Structural Formulæ. - 1.00
Leffmann and Beam. Food
Analysis. - - 1.25
Muter. Pract. and Anal. 1.25
Oettel. Electro-Chem. - .75
—— Electro-Chem. Exper. .75
Richter's Inorganic. 4th Ed. 1.75
—— Organic. 3d Ed. 2 Vols.
Vol. I. Aliphatic Series. 3.00
Vol. II. Aromatic Series. ——
Smith. Electro-Chem. Anal. 1.25
Smith and Keller. Experi-
ments. 3d Ed. Illus. .60
Stammer. Chem. Problems. .50
Sutton. Volumetric Anal. 4.50
Symonds. Manual of. 2.00
Traube. Physico-Chem. Meth. 1.50
Ulzer and Fraenkel. Tech-
nical Chemical Analysis. 1.25
Woody. Essentials of 4th Ed. ——

CHILDREN.

Cautley. Feeding of Infants. 2.00
Hale. Care of. - .50
Hatfield. Compend of. .80
Meigs. Milk Analysis. - .50

Power. Surgical Diseases of. $2.50
Starr. Digestive Organs of. 2.00
—— Hygiene of the Nursery. 1.00
Taylor and Wells. Manual. 4.00

CLINICAL CHARTS.

Griffiths. Temp't're Charts.
Pads of 50 - - .50
Keen. Outline Drawings of
Human Body. - 1.00
Schreiner. Diet Lists. Pads, .75

COMPENDS

And The Quiz-Compends.
Ballou. Veterinary Anat. .80
Brubaker's Physiol. 9th Ed. .80
Gould and Pyle. The Eye. .80
Hall. Pathology. Illus. .80
Hatfield. Children. .80
Horwitz. Surgery. 5th Ed. .80
Hughes. Practice. 2 Pts. Ea. .80
Landis. Obstetrics. 6th Ed. .80
Leffmann's Chemistry. 4th Ed. .80
Mason. Electricity. .75
Potter's Anatomy. 6th Ed. .80
—— Materia Medica. 6th Ed. .80
Schamberg. Skin Diseases. .80
Stewart. Pharmacy. 5th Ed. .80
Warren. Dentistry. 3d Ed. .80
Wells. Gynæcology. - .80

CONSUMPTION.

Harris and Beale. Pulmo-
nary Consumption. - 2.50
Powell. Diseases of Lungs,
including Consumption. - 4.00
Tussey. High Altitude Treatment of. - - - 1.50

DENTISTRY.

Barrett. Dental Surg. - 1.00
Blodgett. Dental Pathology. 1.25
Broomell. Anat. and Hist. of
Mouth and Teeth. - 4.50
Fillebrown. Op. Dent. Illus. 2.25
Gorgas. Dental Medicine. 4.00
Harris. Principles and Prac. 6.00
—— Dictionary of. 5th Ed. 4.50
Heath. Dis. of Jaws. 4.50
—— Lectures on Jaws. Bds. .50
Richardson. Mech. Dent. 5.00
Sewell. Dental Surg. - 2.00
Smith. Dental Metallurgy. 1.75
Taft. Index of Dental Lit. 2.00
Talbot. Irregularity of Teeth. 3.00
Tomes. Dental Surgery. 4.00
—— Dental Anatomy. 4.00
Warren's Compend of. - .80
—— Dental Prosthesis and
Metallurgy. Illus. - 1.25
White. Mouth and Teeth. .40

DIAGNOSIS.

Brown. Medical. 4th Ed. 2.25
Fenwick. Medical. 8th Ed. 2.50
Tyson's Manual. 3d Ed. Illus. 1.50

DICTIONARIES.

Gould's Illustrated Dictionary
of Medicine, Biology, and Al-
lied Sciences, etc. Leather,
Net, $10.00; Half Russia,
Thumb Index, 12 00
Gould's Student's Medical Dic-
tionary. ½ Lea., 10th Ed.,
3.25 ; ½ Mor., Thumb Index. 4.00
Gould's Pocket Dictionary
medical words. New Edition.
Enlarged. Leather, - 1.00
Harris' Dental. Clo. 4.50; Shp. 5.50
Longley's Pronouncing. .75
Maxwell. Terminologia Med-
ica Polyglotta, - 3.00
Treves. German-English. 3.25

EAR.

Burnett. Hearing, etc. 1.00
Dalby. Diseases of. 4th Ed. 2.50
Hovell. Treatise on. - ——
Pritchard. Diseases of. 3d Ed. 1.50
Woakes. Deafness, Giddi-
ness,and Noises in the Head. 2.00

ELECTRICITY.

Bigelow. Plain Talks on Medi-
cal Electricity. 43 Illus. $1.00
Mason's Electricity and its
Medical and Surgical Uses. .75
Jones. Medical Electricity.
3d Ed. Illus. ——

EYE.

Arlt. Diseases of. - 1.25
Donders. Refraction. - 1.25
Fick. Diseases of the Eye. 4.50
Gould and Pyle. Compend. .80
Gower's Ophthalmoscopy. 4.00
Harlan. Eyesight. - .40
Hartridge. Refraction. 9thEd. 1.50
—— Ophthalmoscope. 3d Ed. 1.50
Hansall and Reber. Mus-
cular Anamolies of the Eye. 1.50
Hansell and Bell. Clinical
Ophthalmology. 120 Illus. 1.50
Jessop's Manual of Diseases
of Eye. - 3.00
Morton. Refraction. 6th Ed. 1.00
Ohlemann. Ocular Therap. 1.75
Phillips. Spectacles and Eye-
glasses. 49 Illus. 2d Ed. 1.00
Swanzy's Handbook. 6th Ed. 3.00
Thorington. Retinoscopy. 1.00
Walker. Student's Aid. 1.50

FEVERS.

Collie. On Fevers. - 2.00
Goodall and Washbourn. 3.00

HEALTH AND DOMESTIC
MEDICINE.

Bulkley. The Skin. - .40
Burnett. Hearing. - .40
Cohen. Throat and Voice. .40
Dulles. Emergencies. 6th Ed. 1.00
Harlan. Eyesight. - .40
Hartshorne. Our Homes. .40
Osgood. Dangers of Winter. .40
Packard. Sea Air, etc. .40
Richardson's Long Life. .40
Westland. The Wife and
Mother. - - 1.50
White. Mouth and Teeth. .40
Wilson. Summer and its Dis. .40
Wood. Overwork. - .40

HISTOLOGY.

Stirling. Histology. 2d Ed. 2.00
Stöhr's Histology. Illus. - 3.00

HYGIENE.

Canfield. Hygiene of the Sick-
Room. - - 1.25
Coplin and Bevan. Practi-
cal Hygiene. Illus. ——
Fox. Water, Air, Food. 3.50
Kenwood. Public Health
Laboratory Work. - 2.00
Lincoln. School Hygiene. .40
McNeill. Epidemics and Iso-
lation Hospitals. - 3.50
Notter and Firth. - 7.00
Parkes' (E.). See "Notter."
—— (L. C.), Manual. 2.50
—— Elements of Health. 1.25
Starr. Hygiene of the Nursery. 1.00
Stevenson and Murphy. A
Treatise on Hygiene. In 3
Vols. *Circular* Vol. I. 6.00
upon application. Vol. II. 6.00
Vol. III. 5.00
Wilson's Handbook. 8th Ed. 3.00
Weyl. Coal-Tar Colors. 1.25

MASSAGE.

Kleen and Hartwell. - 2.25
Murrell. Massage. 6th Ed. ——
Ostrom. Massage. 105 Illus. 1.00
Ward. Notes on. Paper Cov. 1.00

MATERIA MEDICA.

Biddle. 13th Ed. Cloth, 4.00
Bracken. Materia Med. 2.75
Coblentz. Newer Remedies. 1.00
Davis. Essentials of. - 1.50
Gorgas. Dental. 5th Ed. 4.00
Groff. Mat. Med. for Nurses. 1.25

Heller. Essentials of. - $1.50
Potter's Compend of. 6th Ed. .80
Potter's Handbook of. 7th
  Ed. Cloth, 5.00; Sheep, 6.00
Sayre. Organic Materia Med.
  and Pharmacognosy. -
White & Wilcox, Mat. Med.,
  Pharmacy, Pharmacology,
  and Therapeutics. 4th Ed.
  Enlarged. Cloth, 3.00; Sh. 3.50

MEDICAL JURISPRUDENCE.
Mann. Forensic Med. - 6.50
Reese. Medical Jurisprudence
  &Toxicology,5th Ed.3.00; Sh.3.50

MICROSCOPE.
Beale. How to Work with. 6.50
  —— In Medicine. - 6.50
Carpenter. The Microscope.
  8th Ed. 800 Illus. ——
Lee. Vade Mecum of. - 4.00
MacDonald. Examination of
  Water and Air by. - 2.50
Reeves. Med. Microscopy. 2.50
Wethered. Medical Micros-
  copy. Illus. - - 2.00

MISCELLANEOUS.
Black. Micro-organisms. .75
Burnet. Food and Dietaries. 1.50
Duckworth. On Gout. - 6.00
Garrod. Rheumatism, etc. 5.00
Gould. Borderland Studies. 2.00
Gowers. Dynamics of Life. .75
Haig. Uric Acid. - - 3.00
  —— Diet and Food. - 1.00
Hare. Mediastinal Disease. 2.00
Hemmeter. Dis. of Stomach. 6.00
Henry. Anæmia. - - .50
Leffmann. Coal Tar Products. 1.25
Lizars. On Tobacco. - .40
Marshall. Women's Med. Col. 1.50
New Sydenham Society's
  Publications, each year. - 8.00
Parrish. Inebriety. - 1.00
St. Clair. Medical Latin. 1.00
Sansom. Dis. of Heart. - 6.00
Treves. Physical Education. .75

NERVOUS DISEASES, Etc.
Beevor. Nervous Diseases. 2.50
Gordinier. Anatomy of Cen-
  tral Nervous System. - 6.00
Gowers. Manual of. 2d Ed.
  530 Illus. Vol. 1,3.00; Vol. 2,4.00
  —— Syphilis and the Ner-
  vous System. - - 1.00
  —— Diseases of Brain. 1.50
  —— Clinical Lectures. 2.00
  —— Epilepsy. New Ed.
Horsley. Brain and Spinal
  Cord. Illus. - - 2.50
Ormerod. Manual of. - 1.00
Osler. Cerebral Palsies. 2.00
  —— Chorea - - 2.00
Preston. Hysteria. Illus. 2.00
Watson. Concussions. 1.00

NURSING.
Brown. Physiology for Nurses. .75
Canfield. Hygiene of the Sick-
  Room. - - - 1.25
Cuff. Lectures on. 2d Ed. 1.25
Cullingworth. Manual of. .75
  —— Monthly Nursing. .40
Domville's Manual. 8th Ed. .75
Fullerton. Obst. Nursing. 1.00
  —— Nursing in Abdominal
  Surg. and Dis. of Women, 1.25
Gould. Pocket Medical Dic-
  tionary. Limp Morocco. 1.00
Groff. Mat. Med. for Nurses. 1.25
Humphrey. Manual. 16th Ed. 1.00
Shawe. District Nursing. 1.00
Starr. Hygiene of the Nursery. 1.00
Temperature Charts. - .50
Voswinkel. Surg. Nursing. 1.00

OBSTETRICS.
Bar. Antiseptic Midwifery. 1.00
Cazeaux and Tarnier. Text-
  Book of. Colored Plates. 4.50
Davis. Obstetrics. 3d Ed. -
Landis. Compend. 6th Ed. .80

Schultze. Obstetric Diagrams.
  20 Plates, map size. *Net*, $26.00
Strahan. Extra-Uterine Preg. .75
Winckel's Text-book. 5.00

PATHOLOGY.
Barlow. General Pathology. 5.00
Blackburn. Autopsies. 1.25
Blodgett. Dental Pathology 1.25
Coplin. Manual of. 265 Illus. 3.00
Gilliam. Essentials of. .75
Hall. Compend. Illus. 2d Ed. .80
Hewlett. Bacteriology. 3.00
Virchow. Post-mortems. 1.00
Whitacre. Lab. Text-book. 1.50
Williams. Bacteriology. 1.50

PHARMACY.
Beasley's Receipt-Book. - 2.00
  —— Formulary. - 2.00
Coblentz. Manual of Pharm. 3.50
Proctor. Practical Pharm. 3.00
Robinson. Latin Grammar of. 1.75
Sayre. Organic Materia Med.
  and Pharmacognosy. -
Scoville. Compounding. 2.50
Stewart's Compend. 5th Ed. .80
U. S. Pharmacopœia. 7th
  Revision. Cl. 2.50; Sh., 3.00
Select Tables from U. S. P. .25

PHYSIOLOGY.
Brown. Physiol. for Nurses. .75
Brubaker's Compend. Illus-
  trated. 9th Ed. - .80
Kirke's New 13th Ed. (Halli-
  burton.) Cloth, 3.00; Sh., 3.75
Landois' Text-book. 845 Illus-
  trations.
Starling. Elements of. - 1.00
Stirling. Practical Phys. 2.00
Tyson's Cell Doctrine. - 1.50
Yeo's Manual. 254 Ill. 2.50

POISONS.
Murrell. Poisoning. - 1.00
Reese. Toxicology. 4th Ed. 3.00
Tanner. Memoranda of. .75

PRACTICE.
Beale. Slight Ailments. 1.25
Fowler's Dictionary of. - 3.00
Hughes. Compend. 2 Pts. ea. .80
  —— Physicians' Edition.
  1 Vol. Morocco, Gilt edge. 2.25
Roberts. Text-book. 9th Ed. 4.50
Taylor's Manual of. - 4.00
Tyson. The Practice of Medi-
  cine. Illus. Cl. 5.50; Sheep, 6.50

PRESCRIPTION BOOKS.
Beasley's 3000 Prescriptions. 2.00
  —— Receipt Book. - 2.00
Davis. Materia Medica and
  Prescription Writing. - 1.50

SKIN.
Bulkley. The Skin. - .40
Crocker. Dis. of Skin. Illus. -
Impey. Leprosy. - 3.50
Schamberg. Compend. .80
Van Harlingen. Diagnosis
  and Treatment of Skin Dis.
  3d Ed. 60 Illus. - 2.75

**SURGERY AND SURGICAL
DISEASES.**
Cripps. Ovariotomy and Ab-
  dominal Surgery. - 8.00
Deaver. Appendicitis. - 3.50
  —— Surgical Anatomy. - 21.00
Dulles. Emergencies. - 1.00
Hamilton. Tumors. 3d Ed. 1.25
Heath's Minor. 10th Ed. 1.25
  —— Diseases of Jaws. 4.50
  —— Lectures on Jaws. .50
Horwitz. Compend. 5th Ed. .80
Jacobson. Operations of. - 3.00
Lane. Surgery of Head. 5.00
Macready on Ruptures 6.00
Maylard. Surgery of the Ali-
  mentary Canal. - 7.50
Morris. Renal Surgery. 2.00
Moullin. Complete Text-
  book 3d Ed. by Hamilton,
  600 Illustrations and Colored
  Plates. Cl. 6.00; Sh. 7.00

Roberts' Fractures. - $1.00
Smith. Abdominal Surg. 10.00
Swain. Surgical Emer. - 1.75
Voswinkel. Surg. Nursing. 1.00
Walsham. Practical Surg. 3.00
Watson's Amputations. 5.50

TECHNOLOGICAL BOOKS.
Cameron. Oils & Varnishes. 2.25
  —— Soap and Candles. 2.00
Gardner. Brewing, etc. 1.50
Gardner. Bleaching and
  Dyeing. - - 1.50
Groves and Thorp. Chemi-
  cal Technology. Vol. I.
  Mills on Fuels. Cl. 5.00
  Vol. II. Lighting. 4.00
  Vol. III. Lighting Contin'd.

THERAPEUTICS.
Allen, Harlan, Harte, Van
  Harlingen. Local Thera. 3.00
Biddle. 13th Edition - 4.00
Field. Cathartics and Emetics. 1.75
Mays. Theine. - - .50
Napheys' Therapeutics. Vol.
  1. Medical and Disease of
  Children. - Cloth, 4.00
  ——Vol. 2. Surgery, Gynæc.
  & Obstet. - Cloth, 4.00
Potter's Compend. 6th Ed. .80
  ——, Handbook of. 5.00; Sh. 6.00
Waring's Practical. 4th Ed. 2.00
White and Wilcox. Mat.
  Med., Pharmacy, Pharmacol-
  ogy, and Thera. 4th Ed. 3.00

THROAT AND NOSE.
Cohen. Throat and Voice. .40
Hall. Nose and Throat. 2.50
Hollopeter. Hay Fever. 1.00
Hutchinson. Nose & Throat. ——
Mackenzie. Throat Hospital
  Pharmacopœia. 5th Ed. 1.00
McBride. Clinical Manual,
  Colored Plates. 2d Ed. - 6.00
Potter. Stammering, etc. 1.00

URINE & URINARY ORGANS.
Acton. Repro. Organs. 1.75
Allen. Diabetic Urine. 2.25
Beale. Urin. Deposits. Plates. 2.00
Holland. The Urine, Milk and
  Common Poisons. 5th Ed. 1.00
Memminger. Diagnosis by
  the Urine. 2d Ed. Illus. 1.00
Morris. Renal Surgery. 2.00
Moullin. The Prostate. -
  —— The Bladder. - 1.50
Thompson. Urinary Organs. 3.00
Tyson. Exam. of Urine. 1.25
Van Nüys. Urine Analysis. 1.00

VENEREAL DISEASES.
Cooper. Syphilis. 2d Ed. - 5.00
Gowers. Syphilis and the
  Nervous System. - 1.00
Jacobson. Diseases of Male
  Organs. Illustrated. - 6.00

VETERINARY.
Armatage. Vet. Rememb. 1.00
Ballou. Anat. and Phys. .80
Tuson. Pharmacopœia. 2.25

VISITING LISTS.
Lindsay & Blakiston's Reg-
  ular Edition. 1.00 to 2.25
  —— Perpetual Ed. 1.25 to 1.50
  —— Monthly Ed. .75 to 1.00
  Send for Circular.

WATER.
Leffmann. Examination of. 1.25
MacDonald. Examination of. 2.50

WOMEN, DISEASES OF.
Byford (H. T.). Manual. 2d
  Edition. 341 Illustrations. 3.00
Byford (W. H.). Text-book. 2.00
Dührssen. Gynecological
  Practice. 105 Illustrations. 1.50
Lewers. Dis. of Women. 2.50
Wells. Compend. Illus. .80

P. BLAKISTON'S SON & CO.'S
Medical and Scientific Publications,

No. 1012 Walnut St., Philadelphia.

ACTON. The Functions and Disorders of the Reproductive Organs in Childhood, Youth, Adult Age and Advanced Life, considered in their Physiological, Social and Moral Relations. By WM. ACTON, M.D., M.R.C.S. 8th Edition. Cloth, $1.75

ALLEN, HARLAN, HARTE, VAN HARLINGEN. Local Therapeutics.
Being a practical description of all those agents used in the local treatment of diseases of the Eye, Ear, Nose, Throat, Mouth, Skin, Vagina, Rectum, etc., such as Ointments, Plasters, Powders, Lotions, Inhalations, Suppositories, Bougies, Tampons, and the proper methods of preparing and applying them. By HARRISON ALLEN, M.D., late Laryngologist to the Rush Hospital for Consumption. GEORGE C. HARLAN, M.D., Surgeon to the Wills Eye Hospital, and Eye and Ear Department of the Pennsylvania Hospital. RICHARD H. HARTE, M.D., Surgeon to the Episcopal and St. Mary's Hospital; Ass't Surg. University Hospital; and ARTHUR VAN HARLINGEN, M.D., Professor of Diseases of the Skin in the Philadelphia Polyclinic and College for Graduates in Medicine; Dermatologist to the Howard Hospital.   Cloth, $3.00; Sheep, $4.00; Half Russia, $5.00

ALLEN. Commercial Organic Analysis. New Revised Editions. A Treatise on the Properties, Proximate Analytical Examination and Modes of Assaying the Various Organic Chemicals and Products employed in the Arts, Manufactures, Medicine, etc., with Concise Methods for the Detection and Determination of Impurities, Adulterations and Products of Decomposition, etc. Revised and Enlarged. By ALFRED H. ALLEN, F.C.S., Public Analyst for the West Riding of Yorkshire; Past President Society of Public Analysts of England, etc.

Vol. I.   Preliminary Examination of Organic Bodies. Alcohols, Neutral Alcoholic Derivatives, Ethers, Starch and its Isomers, Sugars, Acid Derivatives of Alcohols and Vegetable Acids, etc. Third Edition, with numerous additions by the author, and revisions and additions by DR. HENRY LEFFMANN, Professor of Chemistry and Metallurgy in the Pennsylvania College of Dental Surgery, and in the Wagner Free Institute of Science, Philadelphia, etc., with many useful tables: 8vo. *Just Ready.*   Cloth, $4.50

Vol. II—Part I.   Fixed Oils, Fats, Waxes, Glycerol, Soaps, Nitroglycerin, Dynamites and Smokeless Powders, Wool-Fats, Dégras, etc.   Third Edition, with many useful tables. Revised by DR. HENRY LEFFMANN, with numerous additions by the author.   8vo. *Just Ready.*   Cloth, $3.50

Vol. II—Part II.   Hydrocarbons, including Terpenes, Resins and Camphors, Benzene Derivatives, Phenols, etc.   Third Edition, by HENRY LEFFMANN, M.D., with many additions by the author.   *Nearly Ready.*

Vol. III—Part I.   Acid Derivatives of Phenols, Aromatic Acids, Dyes and Coloring Matters.   Third Edition, Revised by DR. HENRY LEFFMANN, with additions by the author.   *In Preparation.*

Vol. III—Part II.   The Amines and Ammonium Bases, Hydrazines and Derivatives. Bases from Tar. The Antipyretics, etc. Vegetable Alkaloids, Tea, Coffee, Cocoa, Kola, Cocaïne, Opium, etc.   Second Edition. 8vo 1892.   Cloth, $4.5

Vol. III—Part III.   Vegetable Alkaloids concluded, Non-Basic Vegetable Bitter Principles. Animal Bases, Animal Acids, Cyanogen and its Derivatives, etc.   Second Edition.   8vo. 1896.   Cloth, $4.50

Vol. IV.   The Proteids and Albuminous Principles. Proteoïds or Albuminoïds.   Second Edition, with elaborate appendices and a large number of useful tables. *Just Ready.*   Cloth, $4.50

SPECIAL NOTICE. These editions of Allen are issued by us in connection with him and his London Publishers; they include much new material and copyright matter, and are the only authorized and up-to-date editions. Circular upon application.

ARLT. Clinical Studies on Diseases of the Eye. By Dr. FERD. RITTER VON ARLT, Authorized Translation by LYMAN WARE, M.D., Surgeon to the Illinois Charitable Eye and Ear Infirmary, Chicago. Illustrated. 8vo.   Cloth, $1.25

ARMATAGE. The Veterinarian's Pocket Remembrancer. By GEORGE ARMATAGE, M.R.C.V.S. Second Edition. 32mo.   Boards, $1.00

BALLOU. Veterinary Anatomy and Physiology. By WM. R. BALLOU, M.D., Late Prof. of Equine Anatomy, New York Coll. of Veterinary Surgeons, Physician to Bellevue Dispensary, and Lecturer on Genito-Urinary Surgery, New York Polyclinic, etc. With 29 Graphic Illustrations. 12mo. *No. 12 ? Quiz-Compend? Series.*   Cloth, .80. Interleaved, for the addition of Notes, $1.25

BAR. Antiseptic Midwifery. The Principles of Antiseptic Methods Applied to Obstetric Practice. By Dr. PAUL BAR, Paris. Authorized Translation by HENRY D. FRY, M.D., with an Appendix by the author. Octavo.   Cloth, $1.00

BARRETT. Dental Surgery for General Practitioners and Students of Medicine and Dentistry. Extraction of Teeth, etc. By A. W. BARRETT, M.D. Third Edition. 86 Illustrations. 12mo.   Cloth, $1.00

BARTLEY. Medical and Pharmaceutical Chemistry. Fifth Edition. A Textbook for Medical and Pharmaceutical Students. By E. H. BARTLEY, M.D., Professor of Chemistry and Toxicology at the Long Island College Hospital; Dean and Professor of Chemistry, Brooklyn College of Pharmacy; President of the American Society of Public Analysts; Chief Chemist, Board of Health, of Brooklyn, N. Y. Revised and Improved. With Illustrations. Glossary and Complete Index. 12mo.   Cloth, $3.00; Leather, $3.50

　　Clinical Chemistry. The Chemical Examination of the Saliva, Gastric Juice, Feces, Milk, Urine, etc., with notes on Urinary Diagnosis, Volumetric Analysis and Weights and Measures. Illustrated. 12mo.   Cloth, $1.00

BEALE. On Slight Ailments; their Nature and Treatment. By LIONEL S. BEALE, M.D., F.R.S., Professor of Practice, King's Medical College, London. Second Edition. Enlarged and Illustrated. 8vo.   Cloth, $1.25

　　The Use of the Microscope in Practical Medicine. With full directions for examining secretions, etc. 4th Edition. 500 Illus. 8vo.   Cloth, $6.50

　　How to Work with the Microscope. A Complete Manual of Microscopical Manipulation. Fifth Edition. Over 400 Illustrations. 8vo.   Cloth, $6.50

　　One Hundred Urinary Deposits, on eight sheets, for the Hospital, Laboratory, or Surgery. New Edition. 4to.   Paper, $2.00

BEASLEY'S Book of Prescriptions. Containing over 3100 Prescriptions, collected from the Practice of the most Eminent Physicians and Surgeons—English, French, and American; a Compendious History of the Materia Medica, Lists of the Doses of all Officinal and Established Preparations, and an Index of Diseases and their Remedies. By HENRY BEASLEY. Seventh Edition.   Cloth, $2.00

　　Druggists' General Receipt Book. Comprising a copious Veterinary Formulary; Recipes in Patent and Proprietary Medicines, Druggists' Nostrums, etc.; Perfumery and Cosmetics; Beverages, Dietetic Articles and Condiments; Trade Chemicals, Scientific Processes, and an Appendix of Useful Tables. Tenth Edition. Revised.   Cloth, $2.00

　　Pharmaceutical Formulary and Synopsis of the British, French, German, and United States Pharmacopœias. Comprising Standard and Approved Formulæ for the Preparations and Compounds Employed in Medical Practice. Twelfth Edition.   Cloth, $2.00

BEEVOR. Diseases of the Nervous System and Their Treatment. By CHAS. EDWARD BEEVOR, M.D., F.R.C.P., Physician to the National Hospital for Paralyzed and Epileptic; Formerly Assistant Physician University College Hospital, London. Illustrated. 12mo.   Cloth, $2.50

BIDDLE'S Materia Medica and Therapeutics. Including Dose List, Dietary for the Sick, Table of Parasites, and Memoranda of New Remedies. By Prof. JOHN B. BIDDLE, M.D., Late Prof. of Materia Medica in Jefferson Medical College, Philadelphia. Thirteenth Edition, thoroughly revised in accordance with new U. S. P., by CLEMENT BIDDLE, M.D., Assistant Surgeon, U. S. Navy. With 64 Illustrations and a Clinical Index. Octavo. Cloth, $4.00 ; Sheep, $5.00

BIGELOW. Plain Talks on Medical Electricity and Batteries, with a Therapeutic Index and a Glossary. By HORATIO R. BIGELOW, M.D., Fellow of the British Gynæcological Society, etc. 43 Illus., and a Glossary. 2d Ed. Cloth, $1.00

BLACK. Micro-Organisms. The Formation of Poisons. A Biological study of the Germ Theory of Disease. By G. V. BLACK, M.D., D.D.S. Cloth, .75

BLACKBURN. Autopsies. A Manual of Autopsies, Designed for the use of Hospitals for the Insane and other Public Institutions. By I. W. BLACKBURN, M.D., Pathologist to the Government Hospital for the Insane. Illustrated. Cloth, $1.25

BLODGETT'S Dental Pathology. By ALBERT N. BLODGETT, M.D., Late Prof. of Pathology and Therapeutics, Boston Dental Coll. 33 Illus. 12mo. Cloth, $1.25

BLOXAM. Chemistry, Inorganic and Organic. With Experiments. By CHARLES L. BLOXAM. Edited by J. M. THOMPSON, Professor of Chemistry in King's College, London, and A. G. BLOXAM, Head of the Chemistry Department, Goldsmiths' Institute, London. Eighth Edition. Revised and Enlarged. 281 Engravings, 20 of which are new. 8vo. Cloth, $4.25 ; Leather, $5.25

BRACKEN. Outlines of Materia Medica and Pharmacology. By H. M. BRACKEN, Professor of Materia Medica and Therapeutics and of Clinical Medicine, University of Minnesota. 8vo. Cloth, $2.75

BROOMELL. Anatomy and Histology of the Human Mouth and Teeth. By DR. I. N. BROOMELL, Professor of Dental Anatomy, Dental Histology, and Prosthetic Technics in the Pennsylvania College of Dental Surgery. With 284 Handsome Illustrations, the majority of which are original. Large Octavo. Cloth, $4.50

BROWN. Medical Diagnosis. A Manual of Clinical Methods. By J. J. GRAHAM BROWN, M.D., F.R.C.P., Asst. Physician Royal Infirmary ; Lecturer on Principles and Practice of Medicine in the School of Medicine of the Royal Colleges, Edinburgh, etc. Fourth Edition. 112 Illustrations. 12mo. Cloth, $2.25

BROWN. Elementary Physiology for Nurses. By MISS FLORENCE HAIG BROWN. Late in Charge Nurse Department, St. Thomas' Hospital, London. With many Illustrations. Cloth, .75

BRUBAKER. Physiology. A Compend of Physiology, specially adapted for the use of Students and Physicians. By A. P. BRUBAKER, M.D., Adjunct Professor of Physiology at Jefferson Medical College, Prof. of Physiology, Penn'a College of Dental Surgery, Philadelphia. Ninth Edition. Revised, Enlarged, and Illustrated. *No. 4, ? Quiz-Compend ? Series.* 12mo. Cloth, .80 ; Interleaved, $1.25

BULKLEY. The Skin in Health and Disease. By L. DUNCAN BULKLEY, M.D., Attending Physician at the New York Hospital. Illustrated. Cloth, .40

BURNET. Foods and Dietaries. A Manual of Clinical Dietetics. By R. W. BURNET, M.D., M.R.C.P., Physician to the Great Northern Central Hospital. With Appendix on Predigested Foods and Invalid Cookery. Full directions as to hours of taking nourishment, quantity, etc. Second Edition. Cloth, $1.50

BURNETT. Hearing, and How to Keep It. By CHAS. H. BURNETT, M.D., Prof. of Diseases of the Ear at the Philadelphia Polyclinic. Illustrated. Cloth, .40

BUXTON. On Anesthetics. A Manual. By DUDLEY WILMOT BUXTON, M.R.C.S., M.R.C.P., Ass't to Prof. of Med., and Administrator of Anesthetics, University College Hospital, London. Third Edition, Illustrated. 12mo. *In Press.*

BYFORD. Manual of Gynecology. A Practical Student's Book. By HENRY T.
BYFORD, M.D., Professor of Gynecology and Clinical Gynecology in the College
of Physicians and Surgeons of Chicago; Professor of Clinical Gynecology,
Women's Medical School of Northwestern University, and in Post-Graduate
Medical School of Chicago, etc. Second Edition, Enlarged. With 341 Illustrations, many of which are from original drawings and several of which are colored. 12mo. 596 pages. Cloth, $3.00

BYFORD. Diseases of Women. By the late W. H. BYFORD, A.M., M.D. Fourth
Edition. 306 Illustrations. Octavo. Cloth, $2.00

CALDWELL. Chemical Analysis. Elements of Qualitative and Quantitative
Chemical Analysis. By G. C. CALDWELL, B.S., PH.D., Professor of Agricultural
and Analytical Chemistry in Cornell University, Ithaca, New York, etc. Third
Edition. Revised and Enlarged. Octavo. Cloth, $1.50

CAMERON. Oils and Varnishes. A Practical Handbook, by JAMES CAMERON,
F.I.C. With Illustrations, Formulæ, Tables, etc. 12mo. Cloth, $2.25
  Soap and Candles. A New Handbook for Manufacturers, Chemists, Ana-
lysts, etc. 12mo. 54 Illustrations. 12mo. Cloth, $2.00

CANFIELD. Hygiene of the Sick-Room. A book for Nurses and others. Being
a Brief Consideration of Asepsis, Antisepsis, Disinfection, Bacteriology, Immu-
nity, Heating and Ventilation, and kindred subjects, for the use of Nurses and
other Intelligent Women. By WILLIAM BUCKINGHAM CANFIELD, A.M., M.D.,
Lecturer on Clinical Medicine and Chief of Chest Clinic, University of Maryland, Physician to Bay View Hospital and Union Protestant Infirmary, Baltimore. 12mo. Cloth, $1.25

CARPENTER. The Microscope and Its Revelations. By W. B. CARPENTER,
M.D., F.R.S. Eighth Edition. By Rev. DR. DALLINGER, F. R. S. Revised and
Enlarged, with 800 Illustrations and many Lithographs. Octavo. *Preparing.*

CAUTLEY. Feeding of Infants and Young Children by Natural and Artificial Methods. By EDMUND CAUTLEY, M.D., Physician to the Belgrave Hospital
for Children, London. 12mo. Cloth, $2.00

CAZEAUX and TARNIER'S Midwifery. With Appendix, by Mundé. The
Theory and Practice of Obstetrics, including the Diseases of Pregnancy and
Parturition, Obstetrical Operations, etc. By P. CAZEAUX. Remodeled and re-
arranged, with revisions and additions, by S. TARNIER,M.D. Eighth American,
from the Eighth French and First Italian Edition. Edited by ROBERT J. HESS,
M.D., Physician to the Northern Dispensary, Phila., etc., with an Appendix by
PAUL F. MUNDÉ, M.D., Professor of Gynecology at the New York Polyclinic.
Illustrated by Chromo-Lithographs, Lithographs, and other Full-page Plates
and numerous Wood Engravings. 8vo. Cloth, $4.50; Full Leather, $5.50

COBLENTZ. Manual of Pharmacy. A Text-Book for Students. By VIRGIL
COBLENTZ, A.M., PH.D., F.C.S., Professor of Chemistry and Physics; Director of
Pharmaceutical Laboratory, College of Pharmacy of the City of New York.
Second Edition, Revised and Enlarged. 437 Illustrations. Octavo. 572 pages.
Cloth, $3.50; Sheep, $4.50; Half Russia, $5.50
  The Newer Remedies. Including their Synonyms, Sources, Methods of
Preparation, Tests, Solubilities, and Doses as far as known. Together with
Sections on Organo-Therapeutic Agents and Indifferent Compounds of Iron.
Third Edition, very much enlarged. Octavo. *Just Ready.* Cloth, $1.00

COHEN. The Throat and Voice. By J. SOLIS-COHEN, M.D. Illus. 12mo. Cloth, .40

COLLIE, On Fevers. A Practical Treatise on Fevers, Their History, Etiology,
Diagnosis, Prognosis, and Treatment. By ALEXANDER COLLIE, M.D., M.R.C.P.,
Lond., Medical Officer of the Homerton and of the London Fever Hospitals.
With Colored Plates. 12mo. Cloth, $2.00

COOPER. Syphilis. By ALFRED COOPER, F.R.C.S., Senior Surgeon to St. Mark's Hospital; late Surgeon to the London Lock Hospital, etc. Edited by EDWARD COTTERELL, F.R.C.S., Surgeon London Lock Hospital, etc. Second Edition. Enlarged and Illustrated with 20 Full-Page Plates containing many handsome Colored Figures. Octavo. Cloth, $5.00

COPLIN. Manual of Pathology. Including Bacteriology, the Technic of Post-Mortems, and Methods of Pathologic Research. By W. M. LATE COPLIN, M D., Professor of Pathology and Bacteriology, Jefferson Medical College; Pathologist to Jefferson Medical College Hospital and to the Philadelphia Hospital; Bacteriologist to the Pennsylvania State Board of Health. Being the Second Edition of the author's "Lectures on Pathology." Rewritten and Enlarged. 265 Illustrations, many of which are original. 12mo. 638 pages. Cloth, $3.00

COPLIN and BEVAN. Practical Hygiene. By W. M. L. COPLIN, M.D., and D. BEVAN, M.D., Ass't Department of Hygiene, Jefferson Medical College; Bacteriologist, St. Agnes' Hospital, Philadelphia, with an Introduction by Prof. H. A. HARE, and articles on Plumbing, Ventilation, etc., by Mr. W. P. Lockington. 138 Illustrations. 8vo. Second Edition. *In Preparation.*

CRIPPS. Ovariotomy and Abdominal Surgery. By HARRISON CRIPPS, F.R.C.S., Surgical Staff, St. Bartholomew's Hospital, London. With 17 Plates, several of which are Colored and 115 other Illustrations. Large Octavo. Cloth, $8.00

CROCKER. Diseases of the Skin. Their Description, Pathology, Diagnosis, and Treatment, with special reference to the Skin Eruptions of Children. By H. RADCLIFFE CROCKER, M.D., Physician to the Dept. of Skin Diseases, University College Hospital, London. 92 Illustrations. Third Edition. *Preparing.*

CUFF. Lectures on Medicine to Nurses. By HERBERT EDMUND CUFF, M.D., Late Ass't Medical Officer, Stockwell Fever Hospital, England. Second Edition, Revised. With 25 Illustrations. Cloth, $1.25

CULLINGWORTH. A Manual of Nursing, Medical and Surgical. By CHARLES J. CULLINGWORTH, M.D., Physician to St. Thomas' Hospital, London. Third Revised Edition. With Illustrations. 12mo. Cloth, .75

    A Manual for Monthly Nurses. Third Edition. 32mo. Cloth, .40

DALBY. Diseases and Injuries of the Ear. By SIR WILLIAM B. DALBY, M.D., Aural Surgeon to St. George's Hospital, London. Illustrated. Fourth Edition. With 38 Wood Engravings and 8 Colored Plates. Cloth, $2.50

DAVIS. A Manual of Obstetrics. Being a complete manual for Physicians and Students. By EDWARD P. DAVIS, A.M., M.D., Professor of Obstetrics in the Jefferson Medical College; Professor of Obstetrics in the Philadelphia Polyclinic; Clinical Professor of Pediatrics in the Woman's Medical College of Philadelphia; Attending Obstetrician to the Philadelphia Hospital and to the Jefferson Hospital; Member of the American Gynæcological Society, of the American Pediatric Society, of the International Congress of Gynæcology and Obstetrics, of the College of Physicians of Philadelphia, of the Philadelphia Obstetrical Society, etc. Third Edition, Revised. With many Colored and other Illustrations, a large number of which have been drawn for this edition by a special artist. 12mo. *Nearly Ready.*

DAVIS. Essentials of Materia Medica and Prescription Writing. By J. AUBREY DAVIS, M.D., Ass't Dem. of Obstetrics and Quiz Master in Materia Medica, University of Pennsylvania; Ass't Physician, Home for Crippled Children, Philadelphia. 12mo. $1.50

DOMVILLE. Manual for Nurses and others engaged in attending to the sick. By ED. J. DOMVILLE, M.D. Eighth Edition. Revised. With Recipes for Sick-room Cookery, etc. 12mo. Cloth, .75

DONDERS. Refraction. An Essay on the Nature and the Consequences of Anomalies of Refraction. By F. C. DONDERS, M.D., late Professor of Physiology and Ophthalmology in the University of Utrecht. Authorized Translation. Revised and Edited by CHARLES A. OLIVER, A.M., M.D. (Univ. Pa.), one of the Attending Surgeons to the Wills Eye Hospital; one of the Ophthalmic Surgeons to the Philadelphia Hospital, etc. With a very handsome Portrait of the Author and a series of Explanatory Diagrams. Octavo. *Just Ready.*
Half Morocco, Gilt, $1.25

DEAVER. Surgical Anatomy. A Treatise on Human Anatomy in its Application to the Practice of Medicine and Surgery. By JOHN B. DEAVER, M.D., Assistant Professor of Applied Anatomy, University of Pennsylvania; Surgeon-in-chief to the German Hospital; Surgeon to the Children's Hospital, and to the Philadelphia Hospital; Consulting Surgeon to St. Agnes', St. Timothy's, and Germantown Hospitals, etc. With about 400 very handsome full-page Illustrations engraved from original drawings made by special artists from dissections prepared for the purpose in the dissecting rooms of the University of Pennsylvania. Three large volumes. Royal square octavo. Sold by Subscription. Orders taken for complete sets only.

Cloth, $21.00; Half Morocco or Sheep, $24.00; Half Russia, $27.00

Appendicitis. Its History, Anatomy, Etiology, Pathology, Symptoms, Diagnosis, Prognosis, Treatment, Complications, and Sequelæ. A Systematic Treatise, with Colored Illustrations of Methods of Procedure in Operating and Plates of Typical Pathological Conditions drawn specially for this work. 32 Full-Page Plates. 8vo.   Cloth, $3.50

DUCKWORTH. On Gout. Illustrated. A treatise on Gout. By SIR DYCE DUCKWORTH, M.D. (Edin.), F.R.C.P., Physician to, and Lecturer on Clinical Medicine at, St. Bartholomew's Hospital, London. With Chromo-lithographs and Engravings. Octavo.   Cloth, $6.00

DÜHRSSEN. A Manual of Gynecological Practice. By DR. A. DÜHRSSEN, Privat-docent in Midwifery and Gynecology in the University of Berlin. Translated from the Fourth German Edition and Edited by JOHN W. TAYLOR, F.R.C.S., Surgeon to the Birmingham and Midlands Hospital for Women; Vice-President of the British Gynecological Society; and FREDERICK EDGE, M.D., M.R.C.P., F.R.C.S., Surgeon to the Wolverhampton and District Hospital for Women. With 105 Illustrations. 12mo.   Cloth, $1.50

DULLES. What to Do First In Accidents and Poisoning. By C. W. DULLES, M.D. Fifth Edition, Enlarged, with new Illustrations. 12mo.   Cloth, $1.00

ECKLEY. Practical Anatomy. A Manual for the Use of Students in the Dissecting Room. Based upon Morris' Text-Book of Anatomy. By W. T. ECKLEY, M.D., Professor and Demonstrator of Anatomy in the College of Physicians and Surgeons; Professor of Anatomy in the Dental Department, Northwestern University, Chicago. With over 200 Illustrations. Octavo.   *Nearly Ready.*

FENWICK. Guide to Medical Diagnosis. By SAMUEL FENWICK, M.D., F.R.C.P., Consulting Physician to the London Hospital; and W. S. FENWICK, M.D., M.R.C.P., Physician to the Out-Patients, Evelina Hospital for Children. Eighth Edition. In great part rewritten, with several new chapters. 135 Illustrations.
Cloth, $2.50

FICK. Diseases of the Eye and Ophthalmoscopy. A Handbook for Physicians and Students. By DR. EUGEN FICK, University of Zurich. Authorized Translation by A. B. HALE, M.D., Ophthalmic Surgeon, United Hebrew Charities; Consulting Ophthalmic Surgeon, Charity Hospital, Chicago; late Vol. Assistant, Imperial Eye Clinic, University of Kiel. With a Glossary and 158 Illustrations, many of which are in colors. 8vo. Cloth, $4.50; Sheep, $5.50; Half Russia, $6.50

FIELD. Evacuant Medication—Cathartics and Emetics. By HENRY M. FIELD, M.D., Professor of Therapeutics, Dartmouth Medical College, Corporate Member Gynæcological Society of Boston, etc. 12mo. 288 pp.   Cloth, $1.75

FILLEBROWN. A Text-Book of Operative Dentistry. Written by invitation of the National Association of Dental Faculties. By THOMAS FILLEBROWN, M.D., D.M.D., Professor of Operative Dentistry in the Dental School of Harvard University; Member of the American Dental Assoc., etc. Illus. 8vo. Clo. $2.25

FOWLER'S Dictionary of Practical Medicine. *By Various Writers.* An Encyclopedia of Medicine. Edited by JAMES KINGSTON FOWLER, M.A., M.D., F.R.C.P., Senior Asst. Physician to, and Lecturer on Pathological Anatomy at, the Middlesex Hospital, London. 8vo.   Cloth, $3.00; Half Morocco, $4.00

GARDNER. The Brewer, Distiller and Wine Manufacturer. A Handbook for all Interested in the Manufacture and Trade of Alcohol and Its Compounds. Edited by JOHN GARDNER, F.C.S. Illustrated.   Cloth, $1.50

Bleaching, Dyeing, and Calico Printing. With Formulæ. Illustrated. $1.50

FULLERTON. Obstetric Nursing. By ANNA M. FULLERTON, M.D., Demonstrator of Obstetrics in the Woman's Medical College; Physician in charge of, and Obstetrician and Gynecologist to, the Woman's Hospital, Philadelphia, etc. 41 Illustrations. Fifth Edition. Revised and Enlarged. 12mo. Cloth, $1.00

Nursing in Abdominal Surgery and Diseases of Women. Comprising the Regular Course of Instruction at the Training School of the Woman's Hospital, Philadelphia. Second Ed. 70 Illustrations. 12mo. Cloth, $1.50

GARROD. On Rheumatism. A Treatise on Rheumatism and Rheumatic Arthritis. By ARCHIBALD EDWARD GARROD, M.A. (Oxon.), M.D., M.R.C.S. (Eng.), Asst. Physician, West London Hospital. Illustrated. Octavo. Cloth, $5.00

GILLIAM'S Pathology. The Essentials of Pathology; a Handbook for Students. By D. TOD GILLIAM, M.D., Professor of Physiology, Starling Medical College, Columbus, O. With 47 Illustrations. 12mo. Cloth, .75

GOODALL and WASHBOURN. A Manual of Infectious Diseases. By EDWARD W. GOODALL, M.D. (London), Medical Superintendent Eastern (Fever) Hospital, Homerton, London, etc., and J. W. WASHBOURN, F.R.C.P., Assistant Physician to Guy's Hospital and Physician to the London Fever Hospital. Illustrated with Charts, Diagrams, and Full-Page Plates. Cloth, $3.00

GORGAS'S Dental Medicine. A Manual of Materia Medica and Therapeutics. By FERDINAND J. S. GORGAS, M.D., D.D.S., Professor of the Principles of Dental Science, Oral Surgery and Dental Mechanism in the Dental Dep. of the Univ. of Maryland. Sixth Edition. Revised and Enlarged, with many Formulæ. 8vo. Cloth, $4.00; Sheep, $5.00; Half Russia, $6.00

GOULD. The Illustrated Dictionary of Medicine, Biology, and Allied Sciences. Being an Exhaustive Lexicon of Medicine and those Sciences Collateral to it: Biology (Zoology and Botany), Chemistry, Dentistry, Pharmacology, Microscopy, etc. By GEORGE M. GOULD, M.D., Editor of *The Philadelphia Medical Journal;* President, 1893–94, American Academy of Medicine, etc. With many Useful Tables and numerous Fine Illustrations. Large, Square Octavo. 1633 pages. Fourth Edition now Ready. Full Sheep, or Half Dark-Green Leather, $10.00; With Thumb Index, $11.00; Half Russia, Thumb Index, $12.00

The Student's Medical Dictionary. Tenth Edition. Enlarged. Including all the Words and Phrases generally used in Medicine, with their proper Pronunciation and Definitions, based on Recent Medical Literature. With Tables of the Bacilli, Micrococci, Leucomains, Ptomains, etc., of the Arteries, Muscles, Nerves, Ganglia and Plexuses; Mineral Springs of U. S., etc. Rewritten, Enlarged, and set from new Type. Small octavo, 700 pages. Half Dark Leather, $3.25; Half Morocco, Thumb Index, $4.00

The Pocket Pronouncing Medical Lexicon. (21,000 Medical Words Pronounced and Defined.) A Student's Pronouncing Medical Lexicon. Containing all the Words, their Definition and Pronunciation, that the Student generally comes in contact with; also elaborate Tables of the Arteries, Muscles, Nerves, Bacilli, etc., etc.; a Dose List in both English and Metric Systems, **a new table of Clinical Eponymic Terms,** etc., arranged in a most convenient form for reference and memorizing. A new edition, completely revised and set from new type. 200 pages new material. Thin 64mo. (6 x 3¾ inches.) *The System of Pronunciation used in this book is very simple.* Full Limp Leather, Gilt Edges, $1.00; Thumb Index, $1.25
⁎ *Sample pages and descriptive circulars sent free upon application. See page 4*

Borderland Studies. Miscellaneous Addresses and Essays Pertaining to Medicine and the Medical Profession, and Their Relations to General Science and Thought. By GEORGE M. GOULD, M.D. 350 pages. 12mo. Cloth, $2.00

Compend of Diseases of the Eye and Refraction. Including Treatment and Operations, with a Section on Local Therapeutics. By GEORGE M. GOULD, M.D., and W. L. PYLE, M.D. With Formulæ, Glossary, and several Tables. 111 Illustrations, several of which are Colored. *Being No. 8 ? Quiz-Compend ? Series.* Cloth, .80. Interleaved for Notes, $1.25

GORDINIER. **The Gross and Minute Anatomy of the Central Nervous System.** By H. C. GORDINIER, A.M., M.D., Professor of Physiology and of the Anatomy of the Nervous System in the Albany Medical College. With many full-page Plates and other Illustrations, a number of which are printed in colors and the majority of which are original. Large Octavo.
> Handsome Cloth, $6.00; Sheep, $7.00; Half Russia, $8.00

GRIFFITH'S Graphic Clinical Chart. Designed by J. P. CROZER GRIFFITH, M.D., Instructor in Clinical Medicine in the University of Pennsylvania. *Printed in three colors.* Sample copies free.   Put up in loose packages of 50, .50 Price to Hospitals, 500 copies, $4.00; 1000 copies, $7.50. With name of Hospital printed on, 50 cents extra.

GROFF. Materia Medica for Nurses. With Questions for Self-Examination and a very complete Pronouncing Glossary. By JOHN E. GROFF, Pharmacist Rhode Island Hospital, Providence. 12mo. 235 pages.   Cloth, $1.25

GROVES and THORP. Chemical Technology. A new and Complete Work. The Application of Chemistry to the Arts and Manufactures. Edited by CHARLES E. GROVES, F.R.S., and WM. THORP, B.Sc., F.I.C., assisted by many experts. In about eight volumes, with numerous illustrations. *Each volume sold separately.*
> Vol. I. FUEL AND ITS APPLICATIONS. 607 Illustrations and 4 Plates. Octavo.
> > Cloth, $5.00; Half Morocco, $6.50
> Vol. II. LIGHTING. Illustrated. Octavo. Cloth, $4.00; Half Morocco, $5.50
> Vol. III. LIGHTING—Continued.   *In Press.*

GOWERS. Manual of Diseases of the Nervous System. A Complete Text-book. By WILLIAM R. GOWERS, M.D., F.R.S., Physician to National Hospital for the Paralyzed and Epileptic; Consulting Physician, University College Hospital; formerly Professor of Clinical Medicine, University College, etc. Second Edition. With many new Illustrations. Two Volumes. Octavo.
> VOL. I. **Diseases of the Nerves and Spinal Cord.** 616 pages.
> > Cloth, $3.00; Sheep, $4.00; Half Russia, $5.00
> VOL. II. **Brain and Cranial Nerves; General and Functional Diseases.** 1069 pages.   Cloth, $4.00; Sheep, $5.00; Half Russia, $6.00

***This book has been translated into German, Italian, and Spanish. It is published in London, Milan, Bonn, Barcelona, and Philadelphia.
> **Syphilis and the Nervous System.** Being a revised reprint of the Lettsomian Lectures for 1890, delivered before the Medical Society of London. 12mo.   Cloth, $1.00
> **Diagnosis of Diseases of the Brain.** 8vo. Second Ed. Illus. Cloth, $1.50
> **Medical Ophthalmoscopy.** A Manual and Atlas, with Colored Autotype and Lithographic Plates and Wood-cuts, comprising Original Illustrations of the changes of the Eye in Diseases of the Brain, Kidney, etc. Third Edition. Revised, with the assistance of R. MARCUS GUNN, F.R.C.S., Surgeon, Royal London Ophthalmic Hospital, Moorfields. Octavo.   Cloth, $4.00
> **The Dynamics of Life.** 12mo.   Cloth, .75
> **Clinical Lectures.** A new volume of Essays on the Diagnosis, Treatment, etc., of Diseases of the Nervous System.   Cloth, $2.00
> **Epilepsy and Other Chronic Convulsive Diseases.** Second Edition. *In Press*

HAIG. Causation of Disease by Uric Acid. A Contribution to the Pathology of High Arterial Tension, Headache, Epilepsy, Mental Depression, Gout, Rheumatism, Diabetes, Bright's Disease, Anæmia, etc. By ALEX. HAIG, M.A., M.D. (Oxon.), F.R.C P., Physician to Metropolitan Hospital, London. 65 Illustrations. Fourth Edition.   Cloth, $3.00
> **Diet and Food.** Considered in relation to Strength and Power of Endurance.
> > Cloth, $1.00

HALE. On the Management of Children in Health and Disease.   Cloth, .50

HALL. Compend of General Pathology and Morbid Anatomy. By H. NEWBERY HALL, PH.G., M.D., Professor of Pathology, Post-Graduate Medical School, Chicago. 91 Illus. 2d Edition. *No. 15 ? Quiz-Compend ? Series.   Preparing.*

HALL. Diseases of the Nose and Throat. By F. DE HAVILLAND HALL, M.D., F.R.C.P. (Lond.), Physician in charge Throat Department Westminster Hospital; Joint Lecturer on Principles and Practice of Medicine, Westminster Hospital Medical School, etc. Two Colored Plates and 59 Illus. 12mo.   Cloth, $2.50

HAMILTON. Lectures on Tumors from a Clinical Standpoint. By JOHN B. HAMILTON, M.D., LL.D., Professor of Surgery in Rush Medical College, Chicago; Professor of Surgery, Chicago Polyclinic; Surgeon Presbyterian Hospital, etc. Third Edition, Revised with new Illustrations. 12mo.   Cloth, $1.25

HANSELL and REBER. Muscular Anomalies of the Eye. By HOWARD F. HANSELL, A.M., M.D., Clinical Professor of Ophthalmology, Jefferson Medical College; Professor of Diseases of the Eye, Philadelphia Polyclinic, etc., and WENDELL REBER, M.D., Instructor in Ophthalmology, Philadelphia Polyclinic, etc. With 1 Plate and 28 other Illustrations. 12mo.   Cloth, $1.50

HANSELL and BELL. Clinical Ophthalmology. By HOWARD F. HANSELL, A.M., M.D., and JAMES H. BELL, M.D. With Colored Plate of Normal Fundus and 120 Illustrations. 12mo.   Cloth, $1.50

HARE. Mediastinal Disease. The Pathology, Clinical History and Diagnosis of Affections of the Mediastinum other than those of the Heart and Aorta. By H. A. HARE, M.D., Professor of Materia Medica and Therapeutics in Jefferson Medical College, Philadelphia. 8vo. Illustrated by Six Plates.   Cloth, $2.00

HARLAN. Eyesight, and How to Care for It. By GEORGE C. HARLAN, M.D., Prof. of Diseases of the Eye, Philadelphia Polyclinic. Illustrated.   Cloth, .40

HARRIS'S Principles and Practice of Dentistry. Including Anatomy, Physiology, Pathology, Therapeutics, Dental Surgery and Mechanism. By CHAPIN A. HARRIS, M.D., D.D.S., late President of the Baltimore Dental College, Author of "Dictionary of Medical Terminology and Dental Surgery." Thirteenth Edition. Revised and Edited by FERDINAND J. S. GORGAS, A.M., M.D., D.D.S., Author of "Dental Medicine;" Professor of the Principles of Dental Science, Oral Surgery, and Dental Mechanism in the University of Maryland. 1250 Illustrations. 1180 pages. 8vo.   Cloth, $6.00; Leather, $7.00; Half Russia, $8.00

  Dictionary of Dentistry. Including Definitions of such Words and Phrases of the Collateral Sciences as Pertain to the Art and Practice of Dentistry. Sixth Edition. Rewritten, Revised and Enlarged. By FERDINAND J. S. GORGAS, M.D., D.D.S., Author of "Dental Medicine;" Editor of Harris's "Principles and Practice of Dentistry;" Professor of Principles of Dental Science, Oral Surgery, and Prosthetic Dentistry in the University of Maryland. Octavo.   Cloth, $5.00; Leather, $6.00

HARRIS and BEALE. Treatment of Pulmonary Consumption. By VINCENT DORMER HARRIS, M.D. (Lond.), F.R.C.P., Physician to the city of London Hospital for Diseases of the Chest; Examining Physician to the Royal National Hospital for Diseases of the Chest, Ventnor, etc., and E. CLIFFORD BEALE, M.A., M.B. (Cantab.), F.R.C.P., Physician to the City of London Hospital for Diseases of the Chest, etc. 12mo.   Cloth, $2.50

HARTRIDGE. Refraction. The Refraction of the Eye. A Manual for Students. By GUSTAVUS HARTRIDGE, F.R.C.S., Consulting Ophthalmic Surgeon to St. Bartholomew's Hospital, etc. 104 Illustrations and Sheet of Test Types. Ninth Edition. Revised and Enlarged by the Author.   Cloth, $1.50

  On The Ophthalmoscope. A Manual for Physicians and Students. Third Edition. With Colored Plates and 68 Wood-cuts. 12mo.   Cloth, $1.50

HARTSHORNE. Our Homes. Their Situation, Construction, Drainage, etc. By HENRY HARTSHORNE, M.D. Illustrated.   Cloth, .40

HATFIELD. Diseases of Children. By MARCUS P. HATFIELD, Professor of Diseases of Children, Chicago Medical College. With a Colored Plate. Second Edition. *Being No. 14, ? Quiz-Compend ? Series.* 12mo.   Cloth, .80
     Interleaved for the addition of notes, $1.25

HELLER. **Essentials of Materia Medica, Pharmacy, and Prescription Writing.** By EDWIN A. HELLER, M.D., Quiz-Master in Materia Medica and Pharmacy at the Medical Institute, University of Pennsylvania. 12mo. Cloth, $1.50

HEATH. **Minor Surgery and Bandaging.** By CHRISTOPHER HEATH, F.R.C.S., Holme Professor of Clinical Surgery in University College, London. Tenth Edition. Revised and Enlarged. With 158 Illustrations, 62 Formulæ, Diet List, etc. 12mo. Cloth, $1.25

> **Practical Anatomy.** A Manual of Dissections. Eighth London Edition. 300 Illustrations. Cloth, $4.25

> **Injuries and Diseases of the Jaws.** Fourth Edition. Edited by HENRY PERCY DEAN, M.S., F.R.C.S., Assistant Surgeon London Hospital. With 187 Illustrations. 8vo. Cloth, $4.50

> **Lectures on Certain Diseases of the Jaws,** delivered at the Royal College of Surgeons of England, 1887. 64 Illustrations. 8vo. Boards, .50

HEMMETER. **Diseases of the Stomach.** Their Special Pathology, Diagnosis, and Treatment. With Sections on Anatomy, Analysis of Stomach Contents, Dietetics, Surgery of the Stomach, etc. By JOHN C. HEMMETER, M.D., PHILOS.D., Clinical Professor of Medicine in the University of Maryland ; Consultant to the University Hospital ; Director of the Clinical Laboratory, etc.; formerly Clinical Professor of Medicine at the Baltimore Medical College, etc. With Colored and other Illustrations. Cloth, $6.00 ; Leather, $7.00 ; Half Russia, $8.00

HENRY. **Anæmia.** A Practical Treatise. By FRED'K P. HENRY, M.D., Physician to Episcopal Hospital, Philadelphia. Half Cloth, .50

HEWLETT. **Manual of Bacteriology.** By R. T. HEWLETT, M.D., M.R.C.P., Asst. Bacteriologist British Institute of Preventive Medicine, etc. With 75 Illustrations. Octavo. Cloth, $3.00

HOLLOPETER. **Hay Fever and Its Successful Treatment.** By W. C. HOLLO-PETER, A.M., M.D., Clinical Professor of Pediatrics in the Medico-Chirurgical College of Philadelphia, Physician to the Methodist Episcopal, Medico-Chirurgical, and St. Joseph Hospitals, etc. 12mo. Cloth, $1.00

HOLDEN'S Anatomy. Seventh Edition. A Manual of the Dissections of the Human Body. By JOHN LANGTON, F.R.C.S., Surgeon to, and Lecturer on Anatomy at, St. Bartholomew's Hospital. Carefully Revised by A. HEWSON, M.D., Demonstrator of Anatomy, Jefferson Medical College, etc. 311 Illustrations. 12mo. 800 pages. *Preparing.*

> **Human Osteology.** Comprising a Description of the Bones, with Colored Delineations of the Attachments of the Muscles. The General and Microscopical Structure of Bone and its Development. 8th Ed., carefully Revised. With Lithographic Plates and Numerous Illustrations. Cloth, $5.25

> **Landmarks.** Medical and Surgical. 4th Edition. 8vo. Cloth, $1.00

HOLLAND. **The Urine, the Gastric Contents, the Common Poisons and the Milk.** Memoranda, Chemical and Microscopical, for Laboratory Use. By J. W. HOLLAND, M.D., Professor of Medical Chemistry and Toxicology in Jefferson Medical College, of Philadelphia. Fifth Edition, Enlarged. Illustrated and Interleaved. 12mo. Cloth, $1.00

HORWITZ'S Compend of Surgery, including Minor Surgery, Amputations, Fractures, Dislocations, Surgical Diseases, and the Latest Antiseptic Rules, etc., with Differential Diagnosis and Treatment. By ORVILLE HORWITZ, B.S., M.D., Professor of Genito-Urinary Diseases, late Demonstrator of Surgery, Jefferson Medical College. Fifth Edition. Very much Enlarged and Rearranged. Over 300 pages. 167 Illustrations and 98 Formulæ. 12mo. *No. 9 ? Quiz-Compend ? Series.* Cloth, .80. Interleaved for notes, $1.25

** *A Spanish translation of this book has recently been published in Barcelona.*

HORSLEY. The Brain and Spinal Cord. The Structure and Functions of. By VICTOR A. HORSLEY, M.B., F.R.S., etc., Asst. Surg., University College Hospital, London, etc. Illustrated. Cloth, $2.50

HOVELL. Diseases of the Ear and Naso-Pharynx. A Treatise including Anatomy and Physiology of the Organ, together with the treatment of the affections of the Nose and Pharynx which conduce to aural disease. By T. MARK HOVELL, F.R.C.S. (Edin.), M.R.C.S.(Eng.), Aural Surgeon to the London Hospital, for Diseases of the Throat, etc. 122 Illus. Second Edition. *Preparing.*

HUMPHREY. A Manual for Nurses. Including general Anatomy and Physiology, management of the sick-room, etc. By LAURENCE HUMPHREY, M.A., M.B., M.R.C.S., Assistant Physician to, and Lecturer at, Addenbrook's Hospital, Cambridge, England. Sixteenth Edition. 12mo. Illustrated. Cloth, $1.00

HUGHES. Compend of the Practice of Medicine. Sixth Edition. Revised and Enlarged. By DANIEL E. HUGHES, M.D., Chief Resident Physician Philadelphia Hospital; formerly Demonstrator of Clinical Medicine at Jefferson Medical College, Philadelphia. In two parts. *Being Nos. 2 and 3, ? Quiz-Compend? Series.*

PART I.—Continued, Eruptive and Periodical Fevers, Diseases of the Mouth, Stomach, Intestines, Peritoneum, Biliary Passages, Liver, Kidneys, Blood, etc., Parasites, etc., and General Diseases, etc.

PART II.—Physical Diagnosis, Diseases of the Respiratory System, Circulatory System, Diseases of the Brain and Nervous System, Mental Diseases, etc.

Price of each Part, in Cloth, .80 ; interleaved for the addition of Notes, $1.25

Physicians' Edition.—In one volume, including the above two parts, a section on Skin Diseases, and an index. *Sixth revised, enlarged Edition.* *568 pages.* Full Morocco, Gilt Edge, $2.25

" Carefully and systematically compiled."—*The London Lancet.*

HUTCHINSON. The Nose and Throat. A Manual of the Diseases of the Nose and Throat, including the Nose, Naso-Pharynx, Pharynx and Larynx. By PROCTER S. HUTCHINSON, M.R.C.S., Ass't Surgeon to the London Hospital for Diseases of the Throat. Illustrated by Lithograph Plates and 40 other Illus., many of which have been made from original drawings. 12mo. 2d Ed. *In Press.*

IMPEY. A Handbook on Leprosy. By S. P. IMPEY, M.D., M.C., Late Chief and Medical Superintendent, Robben Island Leper and Lunatic Asylums, Cape Colony, South Africa. Illustrated by 37 Plates and a Map. Octavo. Cloth, $3.50

JACOBSON. Operations of Surgery. By W. H. A. JACOBSON, B.A. (Oxon.), F.R.C.S., (Eng.); Ass't Surgeon, Guy's Hospital; Surgeon at Royal Hospital for Children and Women, etc. With over 200 Illust. Cloth, $3.00 ; Leather, $4.00

Diseases of the Male Organs of Generation. 88 Illustrations. Cloth, $6.00

JESSOP. Manual of Ophthalmic Surgery and Medicine. By WALTER H. H. JESSOP, M.B. (Cantab.), F.R.C.S., Ophthalmic Surgeon to and Lecturer on Ophthalmic Medicine and Surgery at St. Bartholomew's Hospital, London. With 5 Colored Plates, Test Types, and 110 other Illustrations. 12mo. Cloth, $3.00

JONES. Medical Electricity. A Practical Handbook for Students and Practitioners of Medicine. By H. LEWIS JONES, M.A., M.D., M.R.C.P., Medical Officer in Charge Electrical Department, St. Bartholomew's Hospital. Third Edition of Steavenson and Jones' Medical Electricity. Revised and Enlarged. 112 Illustrations. 12mo. *Preparing.*

KEEN. Clinical Charts. A series of seven Outline Drawings of the Human Body, on which may be marked the course of any Disease, Fractures, Operations, etc. By W. W. KEEN, M.D., Professor of the Principles of Surgery and Clinical Surgery, Jefferson Medical College, Philadelphia. Put up in pads of 50, with explanations. Each pad, $1.00. Each Drawing may also be had separately gummed on back for pasting in case book. 25 to the pad. Price, 25 cents.

*** *Special Charts will be printed to order. Samples free.*

KIRKE'S Physiology. (*15th Authorized Edition. 12mo. Dark Red Cloth.*)
A Handbook of Physiology. Fourteenth London Edition, Revised and Enlarged.
By W. D. HALLIBURTON, M.D., F.R.S., Professor of Physiology King's College,
London. Thoroughly Revised and in many parts Rewritten. 668 Illus., many
of which are printed in Colors. 872 pages. 12mo. Cloth, $3.00; Leather, $3.75

IMPORTANT NOTICE. This is the identical Edition of "Kirke's Physiology," as published
in London by John Murray, the sole owner of the book. It is the
only edition containing the revisions and additions of Dr. Halliburton, and the new and original
illustrations included at his suggestion. It is the edition of which the London *Lancet* says:
"The book as now presented to the student may be regarded as a thoroughly reliable exposition
of the present state of physiological science."

KENWOOD. Public Health Laboratory Work. By H. R. KENWOOD, M.B.,
D.P.H., F.C.S., Instructor in Hygienic Laboratory, University College, late Assistant
Examiner in Hygiene, Science and Art Department, South Kensington, London,
etc. With 116 Illustrations and 3 Plates.   Cloth, $2.00

KLEEN. Handbook of Massage. By EMIL KLEEN, M.D., PH.D., Stockholm and
Carlsbad. Authorized Translation from the Swedish, by EDWARD MUSSEY HART-
WELL, M.D., PH.D., Director of Physical Training in the Public Schools of Boston.
With an Introduction by Dr. S. WEIR MITCHELL, of Philadelphia. Illustrated
by Photographs made specially for the American Edition. 8vo.   Cloth, $2.25

LANDIS' Compend of Obstetrics; especially adapted to the Use of Students and
Physicians. By HENRY G. LANDIS, M.D. Sixth Edition. Revised by WM. H.
WELLS, M.D., Instructor of Obstetrics, Jefferson Medical College; Member
Obstetrical Society of Philadelphia, etc. With 47 Illustrations. *No. 5 ? Quiz-
Compend? Series.*   Cloth, .80; interleaved for the addition of Notes, $1.25

LANDOIS. A Text-Book of Human Physiology; including Histology and Microscopical Anatomy, with special reference to the requirements of Practical Medicine. By DR. L. LANDOIS, Professor of Physiology and Director of the Physiological Institute in the University of Greifswald. Fifth American, translated
from the last German Edition, with additions, by WM. STIRLING, M.D., D.Sc.,
Brackenbury Professor of Physiology and Histology in Owen's College, and Professor in Victoria University, Manchester; Examiner in Physiology in University
of Oxford, England. With 845 Illustrations, many of which are printed in
Colors. 8vo.   *In Press.*

LANE. Surgery of the Head and Neck. By L. C. LANE, A.M., M.D., M.R.C.S.
(Eng.), Professor of Surgery in Cooper Medical College, San Francisco. Second
Edition, with 110 Illustrations. Octavo.   Cloth, $5.00

LAZARUS-BARLOW. General Pathology. By W. S. LAZARUS-BARLOW, M.D.,
Demonstrator of Pathology at the University of Cambridge, England.
795 pages. Octavo.   Cloth, $5.00

LEE. The Microtomist's Vade Mecum. Fourth Edition. A Handbook of
Methods of Microscopic Anatomy. By ARTHUR BOLLES LEE, formerly Ass't in
the Russian Laboratory of Zoology, at Villefranche-sur-Mer (Nice). 887 Articles.
Enlarged and Revised, and in many portions greatly extended. 8vo. Cloth, $4.00

LEFFMANN'S Compend of Medical Chemistry, Inorganic and Organic. Including Urine Analysis. By HENRY LEFFMANN, M.D., Prof. of Chemistry in
the Woman's Medical College in the Penna. College of Dental Surgery and
in the Wagner Free Institute of Science, Philadelphia; Pathological Chemist
Jefferson Medical College. *No. 10 ? Quiz-Compend? Series.* Fourth Edition.
Rewritten.   Cloth, .80. Interleaved for the addition of Notes, $1.25

　　The Coal-Tar Colors, with Special Reference to their Injurious Qualities and
　　the Restrictions of their Use. A Translation of Theodore Weyl's Mono-
　　graph. 12mo.   Cloth, $1.25

　　Examination of Water for Sanitary and Technical Purposes. Third Edition.
　　Enlarged. Illustrated. 12mo.   Cloth, $1.25

　　Analysis of Milk and Milk Products. Arranged to suit the needs of Analyt-
　　ical Chemists, Dairymen, and Milk Inspectors. Second Edition, Revised
　　and Enlarged, with Illustrations. 12mo.   Cloth, $1.25

　　Handbook of Structural Formulæ for the Use of Students, containing 180
　　Structural and Stereo-chemic Formulæ. 12mo. Interleaved. Cloth, $1.00

LEFFMANN and BEAM. Select Methods in Food Analysis. *In Preparation.*

LEWERS. On the Diseases of Women. A Practical Treatise. By Dr. A. H. N. LEWERS, Assistant Obstetric Physician to the London Hospital; and Physician to Out-patients, Queen Charlotte's Lying-in Hospital; Examiner in Midwifery and Diseases of Women to the Society of Apothecaries of London. With 146 Engravings. Fifth Edition, Revised. Cloth, $2.50

LEWIS (BEVAN). Mental Diseases. A text-book having special reference to the Pathological aspects of Insanity. By BEVAN LEWIS, L.R.C.P., M.R.C.S., Medical Director, West Riding Asylum, Wakefield, England. 18 Lithographic Plates and other Illustrations. Second Edition. 8vo. Cloth, $7.00

LINCOLN. School and Industrial Hygiene. By D. F. LINCOLN, M.D. Cloth, .40

LIZARS (JOHN). On Tobacco. The Use and Abuse of Tobacco. Cloth, .40

LONGLEY'S Pocket Medical Dictionary for Students and Physicians. Giving the Definition and Pronunciation of Words and Terms in General Use in Medicine, with an Appendix, containing Poisons and their Antidotes, Abbreviations Used in Prescriptions, etc. By ELIAS LONGLEY.
Cloth, .75; Tucks and Pocket, $1.00

MACALISTER'S Human Anatomy. 800 Illustrations. Systematic and Topographical, including the Embryology, Histology and Morphology of Man. With special reference to the requirements of Practical Surgery and Medicine. By ALEX. MACALISTER, M.D., F.R.S., Professor of Anatomy in the University of Cambridge, England. 816 Illustrations. Octavo. Cloth, $5.00; Leather, $6.00

MACDONALD'S Microscopical Examinations of Water and Air. With an Appendix on the Microscopical Examination of Air. By J. D. MACDONALD, M.D. 25 Lithographic Plates, Reference Tables, etc. Second Ed. 8vo. Cloth, $2.50

MACKENZIE. The Pharmacopœia of the London Hospital for Diseases of the Throat. By SIR MORELL MACKENZIE, M.D. Fifth Edition. Revised and Improved by F. G. HARVEY, Surgeon to the Hospital. Cloth, $1.00

MACREADY. A Treatise on Ruptures. By JONATHAN F. C. H. MACREADY, F.R.C.S., Surgeon to the Great Northern Central Hospital; to the City of London Hospital for Diseases of the Chest; to the City of London Truss Society, etc. With 24 full-page Plates and numerous Wood-Engravings. Cloth, $6.00

MANN. Forensic Medicine and Toxicology. A Text-Book by J. DIXON MANN, M.D., F.R.C.P., Professor of Medical Jurisprudence and Toxicology in Owens College, Manchester; Examiner in Forensic Medicine in University of London, etc. Illustrated. Octavo. Cloth, $6.50

MANN'S Manual of Psychological Medicine and Allied Nervous Diseases. Their Diagnosis, Pathology, Prognosis and Treatment, including their Medico-Legal Aspects; with chapter on Expert Testimony, and an abstract of the laws relating to the Insane in all the States of the Union. By EDWARD C. MANN, M.D. With Illustrations. Octavo. Cloth, $3.00

MARSHALL'S Physiological Diagrams, Life Size, Colored. Eleven Life-size Diagrams (each 7 feet by 3 feet 7 inches). Designed for Demonstration before the Class. By JOHN MARSHALL, F.R.S., F.R.C.S., Professor of Anatomy to the Royal Academy; Professor of Surgery, University College, London, etc.
In Sheets, $40.00 Backed with Muslin and Mounted on Rollers, $60.00
Ditto, Spring Rollers, in Handsome Walnut Wall Map Case (Send for Special Circular), ... $100.00
Single Plates, Sheets, $5.00; Mounted, $7.50; Explanatory Key, 50 cents.
No. 1—The Skeleton and Ligaments. No. 2—The Muscles and Joints, with Animal Mechanics. No. 3—The Viscera in Position. The Structure of the Lungs. No. 4—The Heart and Principal Blood-vessels. No. 5—The Lymphatics or Absorbents. No. 6—The Digestive Organs. No. 7—The Brain and Nerves. Nos. 8 and 9—The Organs of the Senses. Nos. 10 and 11—The Microscopic Structure of the Textures and Organs. (*Send for Special Circular.*)

MARSHALL. The Woman's Medical College of Pennsylvania. An Historical Outline. By CLARA MARSHALL, M.D., Dean of the College. 8vo. Cloth, $1.50

MASON'S Compend of Electricity, and its Medical and Surgical Uses. By CHARLES F. MASON, M.D., Assistant Surgeon U. S. Army. With an Introduction by CHARLES H. MAY, M.D., Instructor in the New York Polyclinic. Numerous Illustrations. 12mo. Cloth, .75

MAXWELL. Terminologia Medica Polyglotta. By Dr. THEODORE MAXWELL, assisted by others in various countries. 8vo. Cloth, $3.00

The object of this work is to assist the medical men of any nationality in reading medical literature written in a language not their own. Each term is usually given in seven languages, viz.: English, French, German, Italian, Spanish, Russian and Latin.

MAYLARD. The Surgery of the Alimentary Canal. By ALFRED ERNEST MAYLARD, M.B., B.S., Senior Surgeon to the Victoria Infirmary, Glasgow. With 27 Full-Page Plates and 117 other Illustrations. Octavo. Cloth, $7.50

MAYS' Theine in the Treatment of Neuralgia. By THOMAS J. MAYS, M.D. 16mo. ½ bound, .50

McBRIDE. Diseases of the Throat, Nose and Ear. A Clinical Manual for Students and Practitioners. By P. McBRIDE, M.D., F.R.C.P. (Edin.), Surgeon to the Ear and Throat Department of the Royal Infirmary; Lecturer on Diseases of Throat and Ear, Edinburgh School of Medicine, etc. With Colored Illustrations from Original Drawings. 2d Edition. Octavo. Handsome Cloth, Gilt top, $6.00

McNEILL. The Prevention of Epidemics and the Construction and Management of Isolation Hospitals. By DR. ROGER McNEILL, Medical Officer of Health for the County of Argyll. With numerous Plans and other Illustrations. Octavo. Cloth, $3.50

MEIGS. Milk Analysis and Infant Feeding. A Treatise on the Examination of Human and Cows' Milk, Cream, Condensed Milk, etc., and Directions as to the Diet of Young Infants. By ARTHUR V. MEIGS, M.D. 12mo. Cloth, .50

MEMMINGER. Diagnosis by the Urine. The Practical Examination of Urine, with Special Reference to Diagnosis. By ALLARD MEMMINGER, M.D., Professor of Chemistry, Urinology, and Hygiene in the Medical College of the State of South Carolina; Visiting Physician in the City Hospital of Charleston, etc. Second Edition, Enlarged and Revised. 24 Illus. 12mo. Cloth, $1.00

MORRIS. Text-Book of Anatomy. Second Edition. 790 Illustrations, many in Colors. A complete Text-book. Edited by HENRY MORRIS, F.R.C.S., Surg. to, and Lect. on Anatomy at, Middlesex Hospital, assisted by J. BLAND SUTTON, F.R C.S., J. H. DAVIES-COLLEY, F.R.C.S., WM. J. WALSHAM, F.R.C.S., H. ST. JOHN BROOKS, M.D., R. MARCUS GUNN, F.R.C.S., ARTHUR HENSMAN, F.R.C.S., FREDERICK TREVES, F.R.C.S., WILLIAM ANDERSON, F.R.C.S., and Prof. W. H. A. JACOBSON. One Handsome Octavo Volume, with 790 Illustrations, of which many are printed in colors. Cloth, $6.00; Leather, $7.00; Half Russia, $8.00

"Taken as a whole, we have no hesitation in according very high praise to this work. It will rank, we believe, with the leading Anatomies. The illustrations are handsome and the printing is good."—*Boston Medical and Surgical Journal.*

"The work as a whole is filled with practical ideas, and the salient points of the subject are properly emphasized. The surgeon will be particularly edified by the section on the topographical anatomy, which is full to repletion of excellent and useful illustrations."—*The Medical Record, New York.*

Handsome circular, with sample pages and colored illustrations, will be sent free to any address.

Renal Surgery. With Special Reference to Stone in the Kidney and Ureter, and to the Surgical Treatment of Calculous Anuria, together with a Critical Examination of Subparietal Injuries of the Ureter. Illustrated. 8vo. Cloth, $2.00

MORTON on Refraction of the Eye. Its Diagnosis and the Correction of its Errors. With Chapter on Keratoscopy, and Test Types. By A. MORTON, M.B. Sixth Edition, Revised and Enlarged.   Cloth, $1.00

MOULLIN. Surgery. Third Edition, by Hamilton. A Complete Text-book. By C. W. MANSELL MOULLIN, M.A., M.D. (Oxon.), F.R.C.S., Surgeon and Lecturer on Physiology to the London Hospital; formerly Radcliffe Traveling Fellow and Fellow of Pembroke College, Oxford. Third American Edition. Revised and edited by JOHN B. HAMILTON, M.D., LL.D., Professor of the Principles of Surgery and Clinical Surgery, Rush Medical College, Chicago; Professor of Surgery, Chicago Polyclinic; Surgeon, formerly Supervising Surgeon-General, U. S. Marine Hospital Service; Surgeon to Presbyterian Hospital; Consulting Surgeon to St. Joseph's Hospital and Central Free Dispensary, Chicago, etc. 600 Illustrations, over 200 of which are original, and many of which are printed in Colors. Royal Octavo. 1250 pages.

Handsomely bound in Cloth, $6.00; Leather, $7.00; Half Russia, $8.00

" The aim to make this valuable treatise practical by giving special attention to questions of treatment has been admirably carried out. Many a reader will consult the work with a feeling of satisfaction that his wants have been understood, and that they have been intelligently met. He will not look in vain for details, without proper attention to which he well knows that the highest success is impossible."— *The American Journal of Medical Sciences.*

Handsome circular, with sample pages and colored illustrations, will be sent to any address upon application.

Enlargement of the Prostate. Its Treatment and Radical Cure. Illustrated. Second Edition. Octavo.   *Preparing.*

Inflammation of the Bladder and Urinary Fever. Octavo.   Cloth, $1.50

MURRELL. Massotherapeutics. Massage as a Mode of Treatment. By WM. MURRELL, M.D., F.R.C.P., Lecturer on Pharmacology and Therapeutics at Westminster Hospital. Sixth Edition. Revised. 12mo.   *Preparing.*

What To Do in Cases of Poisoning. Seventh Edition, Enlarged and Revised. 64mo.   Cloth, $1.00

MUTER. Practical and Analytical Chemistry. By JOHN MUTER, F.R.S., F.C.S., etc. Second American from the Eighth English Edition. Revised, to meet the requirements of American Medical and Pharmaceutical Colleges. 56 Illus.   Cloth, $1.25

NAPHEYS' Modern Therapeutics. Ninth Revised Edition, Enlarged and Improved. In Two Handsome Volumes. Edited by ALLEN J. SMITH, M.D., Professor of Pathology, University of Texas, Galveston, late Ass't Demonstrator of Morbid Anatomy and Pathological Histology, Lecturer on Urinology, University of Pennsylvania; and J. AUBREY DAVIS, M.D., Ass't Demonstrator of Obstetrics, University of Pennsylvania; Ass't Physician to Home for Crippled Children, etc.

VOL. I.—**General Medicine and Diseases of Children.**
Handsome Cloth binding, $4.00

VOL. II.—**General Surgery, Obstetrics, and Diseases of Women.**
Handsome Cloth binding, $4.00

NEW SYDENHAM SOCIETY Publications. Three to Six Volumes published each year. *List of Volumes upon application.*   Per annum, $8.00

NOTTER and FIRTH. The Theory and Practice of Hygiene. A Complete Treatise by J. LANE NOTTER, M.A., M.D., F.C.S., Fellow and Member of Council of the Sanitary Institute of Great Britain; Professor of Hygiene, Army Medical School; Examiner in Hygiene, University of Cambridge, etc., and R. H. FIRTH, F.R.C.S., Assistant Professor of Hygiene, Army Medical School, Netly. Illustrated by 10 Lithographic Plates and 135 other Illustrations, and including many Useful Tables. Octavo. 1034 pages.   Cloth, $7.00

*** This volume is based upon Parkes' Practical Hygiene, which will not be published hereafter.

OETTEL. Practical Exercises in Electro-Chemistry. By Dr. Felix Oettel.
Authorized Translation by Edgar F. Smith, M.A., Professor of Chemistry,
University of Pennsylvania. Illustrated.   Cloth, .75

    Introduction to Electro-Chemical Experiments. Illustrated. By same
    Author and Translator.   Cloth, .75

OHLEMANN. Ocular Therapeutics for Physicians and Students. By M. Ohle-
mann, M.D., late Physician in the Ophthalmological Clinical Institute, Royal
Prussian University of Berlin, etc. Translated and Edited by Charles A.
Oliver, A.M., M.D., Attending Surgeon to Wills Eye Hospital: Ophthalmic
Surgeon to the Philadelphia and to the Presbyterian Hospitals; Fellow of the
College of Physicians of Philadelphia, etc. 12mo.   Cloth, $1.75

*⁎*No attempt has been made for many years to treat exhaustively the remedial
agents used in ophthalmology. The aim of this book is to supply a treatise on this
subject that will serve as a guide to the practising physician; and in no branch of
therapeutics is the relative value of the remedies and formulæ to be employed so
worthy of careful consideration, and their results, when intelligently employed, of so
much importance to the physician and patient.

ORMEROD. Diseases of Nervous System, Student's Guide to. By J. A. Ormerod,
M.D. (Oxon.), F.R.C.P., Physician to National Hospital for Paralyzed and Epileptic
and to City of London Hospital for Diseases of the Chest, etc. With 66 Wood
Engravings. 12mo.   Cloth, $1.00

OSGOOD. The Winter and Its Dangers. By Hamilton Osgood, M.D. Cloth, .40

OSLER. Cerebral Palsies of Children. A Clinical Study. By William Osler,
M.D., F.R.C.P. (Lond.), Professor of Medicine, Johns Hopkins University, etc.
8vo.   Cloth, $2.00

    Chorea and Choreiform Affections. 8vo.   Cloth, $2.00

OSTROM. Massage and the Original Swedish Movements. Their Application
to Various Diseases of the Body. A Manual for Students, Nurses and Physicians.
By Kurre W. Ostrom, from the Royal University of Upsala, Sweden; Instructor
in Massage and Swedish Movements in the Hospital of the University of
Pennsylvania, and in the Philadelphia Polyclinic and College for Graduates in
Medicine, etc. Fourth Edition. Enlarged. Illustrated by 105 Wood Engravings, many of which were drawn especially for this purpose. 12mo. Cloth, $1.00

PACKARD'S Sea Air and Sea Bathing. By John H. Packard, M.D.   Cloth, .40

PARKES' Practical Hygiene. By Edward A. Parkes, M.D. Superseded by
"Notter and Firth" Treatise on Hygiene. See previous page.

PARKES. Hygiene and Public Health. A Practical Manual. By Louis C.
Parkes, M.D., D.P.H. Lond. Univ., Lect. on Public Health at St. George's Hos-
pital, Medical Officer of Health, Parish of Chelsea, London, etc. Fifth Edition,
Enlarged and Revised. 80 Illustrations. 12mo.   Cloth, $2.50

    The Elements of Health. An Introduction to the Study of Hygiene.
    Illustrated.   Cloth, $1.25

PARRISH'S Alcoholic Inebriety. From a Medical Standpoint, with Illustrative
Cases from the Clinical Records of the Author. By Joseph Parrish, M.D.,
President of the Amer. Assoc. for Cure of Inebriates.   Cloth, $1.00

PHILLIPS. Spectacles and Eyeglasses, Their Prescription and Adjustment. By
R. J. Phillips, M.D., Instructor on Diseases of the Eye, Philadelphia Polyclinic,
Ophthalmic Surgeon, Presbyterian Hospital. Second Edition, Revised and
Enlarged. 49 Illustrations. 12mo.   Cloth, $1.00

" This little work now appears in the form of a revised second edition of 101 pages. It
is of convenient size and is excellently printed. The book is issued as an aid to those who prescribe and who sell eyeglasses and spectacles, for the purpose of enabling them to reach the most
satisfactory and beneficial results in the adjustment of lenses to the eyes of patients. Since the
proper adjustment of spectacles and eyeglasses is of very great importance, it is desirable that
the rules and suggestions contained in this little volume should be familiar to every oculist and
optician."—*The Medical Record, New York.*

PHYSICIAN'S VISITING LIST. Published Annually. Forty-eighth Year (1899) of its Publication.

Hereafter all styles will contain the interleaf or special memoranda page, except the Monthly Edition, and the sizes for 75 and 100 Patients will come in two volumes only. The Sale of this Visiting List increased over ten per cent. in 1896.

REGULAR EDITION.

			Tucks, pocket and pencil, Gilt Edges,	$1.00
For 25 Patients weekly.				
50	"	"	" " " " "	1.25
50	"	" 2 vols. { Jan. to June } { July to Dec. }	" " " " "	2.00
75	"	" 2 vols. { Jan. to June } { July to Dec. }	" " " " "	2.00
100	"	" 2 vols. { Jan. to June } { July to Dec. }	" " " " "	2.25

Perpetual Edition, without Dates and with Special Memorandum Pages.
For 25 Patients, interleaved, tucks, pocket and pencil, ... $1.25
50 " " " " " " 1.50

Monthly Edition, without Dates. Can be commenced at any time and used until full. Requires only one writing of patient's name for the whole month. Plain binding, without Flap or Pencil, .75. Leather cover, Pocket and Pencil, $1.00

EXTRA Pencils will be sent, postpaid, for 25 cents per half dozen.

☞ This List combines the several essential qualities of strength, compactness, durability and convenience. It is made in all sizes and styles to meet the wants of all physicians. It is not an elaborate, complicated system of keeping accounts, but a plain, simple record, that may be kept with the least expenditure of time and trouble—hence its popularity. A special circular, descriptive of contents will be sent upon application.

POTTER. **A Handbook of Materia Medica, Pharmacy, and Therapeutics,** including the Action of Medicines, Special Therapeutics of Disease, Official and Practical Pharmacy, and Minute Directions for Prescription Writing, etc. Including over 600 Prescriptions and Formulæ. By SAMUEL O. L. POTTER, M.A., M.D., M.R.C.P. (Lond.), Professor of the Principles and Practice of Medicine and Clinical Medicine in the College of Physicians and Surgeons, San Francisco; Brigade Surgeon U. S. Vol. Seventh Edition, Revised and Enlarged. 8vo. *With Thumb Index in each copy.* Cloth, $5.00; Leather, $6.00; Half Russia, $7.00

Compend of Anatomy, including **Visceral Anatomy.** Sixth Edition. Revised, and greatly Enlarged. With 16 Lithographed Plates and 117 other Illustrations. *Being No. 1 ? Quiz-Compend ? Series.*
Cloth, .80; Interleaved for taking Notes, $1.25

Compend of Materia Medica, Therapeutics and Prescription Writing, with special reference to the Physiological Action of Drugs. Sixth Revised and Improved Edition, with Index, based upon U. S. P. 1890. *Being No. 6 ? Quiz-Compend ? Series.* Cloth, .80. Interleaved for taking Notes, $1.25

Speech and Its Defects. Considered Physiologically, Pathologically and Remedially; being the Lea Prize Thesis of Jefferson Medical College, 1882. Revised and Corrected. 12mo. Cloth, $1.00

POWELL. **Diseases of the Lungs and Pleuræ, Including Consumption.** By R. DOUGLAS POWELL, M.D., F.R.C.P., Physician to the Middlesex Hospital, and Consulting Physician to the Hospital for Consumption and Diseases of the Chest at Brompton. Fourth Edition. With Colored Plates and Wood Engravings. 8vo. Cloth, $4.00

POWER. **Surgical Diseases of Children** and their Treatment by Modern Methods. By D'Arcy Power, M.A., F.R.C.S. (Eng.), Demonstrator of Operative Surgery, St. Bartholomew's Hospital; Surgeon to the Victoria Hospital for Children. Illustrated. 12mo. Cloth, $2.50

PRESTON. Hysteria and Certain Allied Conditions. Their Nature and Treatment. With special reference to the application of the Rest Cure, Massage, Electro-therapy, Hypnotism, etc. By GEORGE J. PRESTON, M.D., Professor of Diseases of the Nervous System, College of Physicians and Surgeons, Baltimore; Visiting Physician to the City Hospital; Consulting Neurologist to Bay View Asylum and the Hebrew Hospital; Member American Neurological Association, etc. With Illustrations. 12mo.   Cloth, $2.00

PRITCHARD. Handbook of Diseases of the Ear. By URBAN PRITCHARD, M.D., F.R.C.S., Professor of Aural Surgery, King's College, London, Aural Surgeon to King's College Hospital, Senior Surgeon to the Royal Ear Hospital, etc. Third Edition, Enlarged. Many Illustrations and Formulæ. 12mo. Cloth, $1.50

PROCTOR'S Practical Pharmacy. Lectures on Practical Pharmacy. With Wood Engravings and 32 Lithographic Fac-simile Prescriptions. By BARNARD S. PROCTOR. Third Edition. Revised and with elaborate Tables of Chemical Solubilities, etc.   Cloth, $3.00

REESE'S Medical Jurisprudence and Toxicology. A Text-book for Medical and Legal Practitioners and Students. By JOHN J. REESE, M.D., Editor of Taylor's Jurisprudence, Professor of the Principles and Practice of Medical Jurisprudence, including Toxicology, in the University of Pennsylvania Medical Department. Fifth Edition. Revised and Edited by HENRY LEFFMANN, M.D., Pathological Chemist, Jefferson Medical College Hospital; Chemist, State Board of Health; Professor of Chemistry, Woman's Medical College of Penna., etc. 12mo. 645 pages.   Cloth, $3.00; Leather, $3.50
" To the student of medical jurisprudence and toxicology it is invaluable, as it is concise, clear, and thorough in every respect."—*The American Journal of the Medical Sciences.*

REEVES. Medical Microscopy. Illustrated. A Handbook for Physicians and Students, including Chapters on Bacteriology, Neoplasms, Urinary Examination, etc. By JAMES E. REEVES, M.D., Ex-President American Public Health Association, Member Association American Physicians, etc. Numerous Illustrations, some of which are printed in colors.   12mo. Handsome Cloth, $2.50

RÉGIS. Mental Medicine. A Practical Manual. By DR. E. RÉGIS, formerly Chief of Clinique of Mental Diseases, Faculty of Medicine of Paris; Physician of the Maison de Santé de Castel d'Andorte; Professor of Mental Diseases, Faculty of Medicine, Bordeaux, etc. With a Preface by M. BENJAMIN BALL, Clinical Professor of Mental Diseases, Faculty of Medicine, Paris. Authorized Translation from the Second Edition by H. M. BANNISTER, M.D., late Senior Assistant Physician, Illinois Eastern Hospital for the Insane, etc. With an Introduction by the Author. 12mo. 692 pages.   Cloth, $2.00

RICHARDSON. Long Life, and How to Reach It. By J. G. RICHARDSON, Prof. of Hygiene, University of Pennsylvania.   Cloth, .40

RICHARDSON'S Mechanical Dentistry. A Practical Treatise on Mechanical Dentistry. By JOSEPH RICHARDSON, D.D.S. Seventh Edition. Thoroughly Revised and in many parts Rewritten by DR. GEO. W. WARREN, Chief of the Clinical Staff, Pennsylvania College of Dental Surgery, Philadelphia. With 691 Illustrations, many of which are from original Wood Engravings. Octavo. 675 pages.   Cloth, $5.00; Leather, $6.00; Half Russia, $7.00

ROBERTS. Practice of Medicine. The Theory and Practice of Medicine. By FREDERICK ROBERTS, M.D., Professor of Therapeutics at University College, London. Ninth Edition, with Illustrations. 8vo.   Cloth, $4.50; Leather, $5.50

ROBERTS. Fractures of the Radius. A Clinical, Pathological, and Experimental Study. By JOHN B. ROBERTS, M.D., Professor of Anatomy and Surgery in the Philadelphia Polyclinic, etc. 33 Illustrations. 8vo.   Cloth, $1.00

RICHTER'S Inorganic Chemistry. A Text-book for Students. By Prof. VICTOR VON RICHTER, University of Breslau. Fourth American, from Sixth German Edition. Authorized Translation by EDGAR F. SMITH, M.A., PH.D., Prof. of Chemistry, University of Pennsylvania, Member of the Chemical Societies of Berlin and Paris. 89 Illustrations and a Colored Plate. 12mo. Cloth, $1.75

 Organic Chemistry. The Chemistry of the Carbon Compounds. Third American Edition, translated from the Eighth German by EDGAR F. SMITH, M.A., PH.D., Professor of Chemistry, University of Pennsylvania. Revised and Enlarged. Illus. 2 vols. 12mo. Vol. I. Aliphatic Series. 625 pages.
Cloth, $3.00
           Vol. II. Aromatic Series. *Preparing.*

ROBINSON. Latin Grammar of Pharmacy and Medicine. By D. H. ROBINSON, PH.D., Professor of Latin Language and Literature, University of Kansas. Introduction by L. E. SAYRE, PH.G., Professor of Pharmacy in, and Dean of the Dept. of Pharmacy, University of Kansas. Third Edition. Revised with the help of Prof. L. E. SAYRE, of University of Kansas, and Dr. CHARLES RICE, of the College of Pharmacy of the City of New York. 12mo. Cloth, $1.75

ST. CLAIR. Medical Latin. Designed expressly for the Elementary Training of Medical Students. By W. T. ST. CLAIR, Instructor in Latin in the Kentucky School of Medicine and in the Louisville Male High School. 12mo. Cloth, $1.00

SANSOM. Diseases of The Heart. The Diagnosis and Pathology of Diseases of the Heart and Thoracic Aorta. By A. ERNEST SANSOM, M.D., F.R.C.P., Physician to the London Hospital, etc. With Illustrations. 8vo. Cloth, $6.00

SAYRE. Organic Materia Medica and Pharmacognosy. An Introduction to the Study of the Vegetable Kingdom and the Vegetable and Animal Drugs. Comprising the Botanical and Physical Characteristics, Source, Constituents, and Pharmacopœial Preparations. With Chapters on Synthetic Organic Remedies, Insects Injurious to Drugs, and Pharmacal Botany. By L. E. SAYRE, PH.G., Professor of Pharmacy and Materia Medica in the University of Kansas, Member of the Committee of Revision of the U. S. Pharmacopœia, 1890. A Glossary and 543 Illustrations. Second Edition. *Preparing.*

SCHAMBERG. Compend of Diseases of the Skin. By JAY F. SCHAMBERG, Associate in Skin Diseases, Philadelphia Polyclinic; Quiz-Master at University of Pennsylvania. 99 Illustrations. Cloth, .80. Interleaved, $1.25

SCHREINER. Diet List. Arranged in the Form of a Chart on which Articles of Diet can be indicated for any Disease. By E. R. SCHREINER, M.D., Ass't Dem. of Physiology, University of Penna. Put up in Pads of 50 with Pamphlet of Specimen Dietaries. Per Pad, .75

SCHULTZE. Obstetrical Diagrams. Being a Series of 20 Colored Lithograph Charts, imperial map size, of Pregnancy and Midwifery, with accompanying explanatory (German) text, illustrated by wood-cuts. By DR. B. S. SCHULTZE, Professor of Obstetrics, University of Jena. Second Revised Edition.
   Price, in Sheets, $26.00; Mounted on Rollers, Muslin Backs, $36.00

SCOVILLE. The Art of Compounding. A Text-book for Students and a Reference Book for Pharmacists. By WILBUR L. SCOVILLE, PH.G., Professor of Applied Pharmacy and Director of the Pharmaceutical Laboratory in the Massachusetts College of Pharmacy. Second Edition, Enlarged and Improved.
Cloth, $2.50; Sheep, $3.50; Half Russia, $4.50

SEWELL. Dental Surgery, including Special Anatomy and Surgery. By HENRY SEWELL, M.R.C.S., L.D.S., President Odontological Society of Great Britain. 3d Edition, greatly enlarged, with about 200 Illustrations. Cloth, $2.00

SHAWE. Notes for Visiting Nurses, and all those interested in the working and organization of District, Visiting, or Parochial Nurse Societies. By ROSALIND GILLETTE SHAWE, District Nurse for the Brooklyn Red Cross Society. With an Appendix explaining the organization and working of various Visiting and District Nurse Societies, by HELEN C. JENKS, of Philadelphia. 12mo. Cloth, $1.00

SMITH. Abdominal Surgery. Being a Systematic Description of all the Principal Operations. By J. GREIG SMITH, M.A., F.R.S.E., Surg. to British Royal Infirmary. 224 Illustrations. Sixth Edition. Enlarged and Thoroughly Revised by JAMES SWAIN, M.D. (Lond.), F.R.C.S., Professor of Surgery, University College, Bristol, etc. 2 Volumes. Octavo.   Cloth, $10.00

SMITH. Electro-Chemical Analysis. By EDGAR F. SMITH, Professor of Chemistry, University of Pennsylvania. Second Edition, Revised and Enlarged. 27 Illustrations. 12mo.   Cloth, $1.25
** *See also Oettel and Richter.*

SMITH and KELLER. Experiments. Arranged for Students in General Chemistry. By EDGAR F. SMITH, Professor of Chemistry, University of Pennsylvania, and Dr. H. F. KELLER, Professor of Chemistry, Philadelphia High School. Third Edition. 8vo. Illustrated.   Cloth, .60

SMITH. Dental Metallurgy. A Manual. By ERNEST A. SMITH, F.C.S., Asst. Instructor in Metallurgy Royal College of Science, London. Illustrated. 12mo.
                    Cloth, $1.75

STAMMER. Chemical Problems, with Explanations and Answers. By KARL STAMMER. Translated from the Second German Edition, by Prof. W. S. HOSKINSON, A.M., Wittenberg College, Springfield, Ohio. 12mo.   Cloth, .50

STARLING. Elements of Human Physiology. By ERNEST H. STARLING, M.D. LOND., M.R.C.P., Joint Lecturer on Physiology at Guy's Hospital, London, etc. With 100 Illustrations. 12mo. 437 pages.   Cloth, $1.00

STARR. The Digestive Organs in Childhood. Second Edition. The Diseases of the Digestive Organs in Infancy and Childhood. With Chapters on the Investigation of Disease and the Management of Children. By LOUIS STARR, M.D., late Clinical Prof. of Diseases of Children in the Hospital of the University of Penn'a; Physician to the Children's Hospital, Phila. Second Edition. Revised and Enlarged. Illustrated by two Colored Lithograph Plates and numerous Wood Engravings. Crown Octavo.   Cloth, $2.00

   The Hygiene of the Nursery, including the General Regimen and Feeding of Infants and Children, and the Domestic Management of the Ordinary Emergencies of Early Life, Massage, etc. Sixth Edition. Enlarged. 25 Illustrations. 12mo. 280 pages.   Cloth, $1.00

STEARNS. Lectures on Mental Diseases. By HENRY PUTNAM STEARNS, M.D., Physician Superintendent at the Hartford Retreat, Lecturer on Mental Diseases in Yale University, Member of the American Medico-Psychological Ass'n, Honorary Member of the British Medico Pyschological Society. With a Digest of Laws of the Various States Relating to Care of Insane. Illustrated.
                    Cloth, $2.75 ; Sheep, $3.25

STEVENSON and MURPHY. A Treatise on Hygiene. By Various Authors. Edited by THOMAS STEVENSON, M.D., F R.C.P., Lecturer on Chemistry and Medical Jurisprudence at Guy's Hospital, London, etc., and SHIRLEY F. MURPHY, Medical Officer of Health to the County of London. In Three Octavo Volumes.
   Vol. I. With Plates and Wood Engravings. Octavo.   Cloth, $6.00
   Vol. II. With Plates and Wood Engravings. Octavo.   Cloth, $6.00
   Vol. III. Sanitary Law. Octavo.   Cloth, $5.00
** *Special Circular upon application.*

STEWART'S Compend of Pharmacy. Based upon "Remington's Text-Book of Pharmacy." By F. E. STEWART, M.D., PH.G., Quiz-Master in Chem. and Theoretical Pharmacy, Phila. College of Pharmacy; Lect. in Pharmacology, Jefferson Medical College. Fifth Ed. Revised in accordance with U. S. P., 1890. Complete tables of Metric and English Weights and Measures. *? Quiz-Compend ? Series.*   Cloth, .80; Interleaved for the addition of notes, $1.25

STIRLING. Outlines of Practical Physiology. Including Chemical and Experimental Physiology, with Special Reference to Practical Medicine. By W. STIRLING, M.D., SC.D., Professor of Physiology and Histology, Owens College, Victoria University, Manchester. Examiner in Physiology, Universities of Edinburgh and London. Third Edition. 289 Illustrations.   Cloth, $2.00

STIRLING. Outlines of Practical Histology. 368 Illustrations. Second Edition. Revised and Enlarged, with new Illustrations. 12mo. Cloth, $2.00

STÖHR. Text-Book of Histology, Including the Microscopical Technic. By DR. PHILIPP STÖHR, Professor of Anatomy at University of Würzburg. Authorized Translation by EMMA L. BILLSTEIN, M.D., Demonstrator of Histology and Embryology, Woman's Medical College of Pennsylvania. Edited, with Additions, by DR. ALFRED SCHAPER, Demonstrator of Histology and Embryology, Harvard Medical School, Boston. Second American from the Eighth German Edition, Enlarged and Revised. 292 Illustrations. Octavo. Cloth, $3.00

STRAHAN. Extra-Uterine Pregnancy. The Diagnosis and Treatment of Extra-Uterine Pregnancy. Being the Jenks Prize Essay of the College of Physicians of Philadelphia. By JOHN STRAHAN, M.D. (Univ. of Ireland), late Res. Surgeon Belfast Union Infirmary and Fever Hospital. Octavo. Cloth, .75

SUTTON'S Volumetric Analysis. A Systematic Handbook for the Quantitative Estimation of Chemical Substances by Measure, Applied to Liquids, Solids and Gases. Adapted to the Requirements of Pure Chemical Research, Pathological Chemistry, Pharmacy, Metallurgy, Photography, etc., and for the Valuation of Substances Used in Commerce, Agriculture, and the Arts. By FRANCIS SUTTON, F.C.S. Seventh Edition, Revised and Enlarged, with 112 Illustrations. 8vo. Cloth, $4.50

SWAIN. Surgical Emergencies, together with the Emergencies Attendant on Parturition and the Treatment of Poisoning. A Manual for the Use of Student, Practitioner, and Head Nurse. By WILLIAM PAUL SWAIN, F.R.C.S., Surgeon to the South Devon and East Cornwall Hospital, England. Fifth Edition. 12mo. 149 Illustrations. Cloth, $1.75

SWANZY. Diseases of the Eye and their Treatment. A Handbook for Physicians and Students. By HENRY R. SWANZY, A.M., M.B., F.R.C.S.I., Surgeon to the National Eye and Ear Infirmary ; Ophthalmic Surgeon to the Adelaide Hospital, Dublin. Sixth Edition, Thoroughly Revised and Enlarged. 158 Illustrations, one Plain Plate, and a Zephyr Test Card. 12mo. Cloth, $3.00
"Is without doubt the most satisfactory manual we have upon diseases of the eye. It occupies the middle ground between the students' manuals, which are too brief and concise, and the encyclopedic treatises, which are too extended and detailed to be of special use to the general practitioner."—*Chicago Medical Recorder.*

SYMONDS. Manual of Chemistry, for Medical Students. By BRANDRETH SYMONDS, A.M., M.D., Ass't Physician Roosevelt Hospital, Out-Patient Department ; Attending Physician Northwestern Dispensary, New York. Second Edition. 12mo. Cloth, $2.00

TAFT. Index of Dental Periodical Literature. By JONATHAN TAFT, D.D.S. 8vo. Cloth, $2.00

TALBOT. Irregularities of the Teeth, and Their Treatment. By EUGENE S. TALBOT, M.D., Professor of Dental Surgery Woman's Medical College, and Lecturer on Dental Pathology in Rush Medical College, Chicago. Second Edition, Revised. Octavo. 234 Illustrations. 261 pages. Cloth, $3.00

TANNER'S Memoranda of Poisons and their Antidotes and Tests. By THOS. HAWKES TANNER, M.D., F.R.C.P. 7th American, from the Last London Edition. Revised by JOHN J. REESE, M.D., Professor Medical Jurisprudence and Toxicology in the University of Pennsylvania. 12mo. Cloth, .75

TAYLOR. Practice of Medicine. A Manual. By FREDERICK TAYLOR, M.D., Physician to, and Lecturer on Medicine at, Guy's Hospital, London ; Physician to Evelina Hospital for Sick Children, and Examiner in Materia Medica and Pharmaceutical Chemistry, University of London. Fifth Edition. Cloth, $4.00

TAYLOR AND WELLS. **Diseases of Children.** A Manual for Students and Physicians. By JOHN MADISON TAYLOR, A.B., M.D., Professor of Diseases of Children, Philadelphia Polyclinic; Assistant Physician to the Children's Hospital and to the Orthopedic Hospital; Consulting Physician to the Elwyn and the Vineland Training Schools for Feeble-Minded Children; Neurologist to the Howard Hospital, etc.; and WILLIAM H. WELLS, M.D., Adjunct-Professor of Obstetrics and Diseases of Infancy in the Philadelphia Polyclinic; late Assistant Demonstrator of Clinical Obstetrics and Diseases of Infancy in Jefferson Medical College. With 8 Plates and numerous other Illustrations. 12mo. 743 pages. Cloth, $4.00

SYNOPSIS OF CONTENTS.—Physiology of the Infant and Child—Diseases Occurring At or Near Birth—General Hygiene of Infants and Children—Feeding and Food of Infants and Children—The Breeds of Cows Best Adapted for Infant Feeding—Diet of Children; Artificial Foods; Receipes, etc.—Diseases of the Digestive Organs—Diseases of the Peritoneum—Diseases of the Liver—Diseases of the Genito-Urinary System—Diseases of the Genital Organs—Diseases of the Blood—General Diseases—Diseases of the Heart—Diseases of the Respiratory Organs—Diseases of the Nervous System—The Acute Infectious Diseases—Diseases of the Skin—General Considerations on Physical Development—Diseases and Accidents Requiring Surgical Procedures.

TEMPERATURE Charts for Recording Temperature, Respiration, Pulse, Day of Disease, Date, Age, Sex, Occupation, Name, etc.　　Put up in pads; each .50

THOMPSON. Urinary Organs. Diseases of the Urinary Organs. Containing 32 Lectures. By Sir HENRY THOMPSON, F.R.C.S., Emeritus Professor of Clinical Surgery in University College. Eighth London Edition. 121 Illustrations. Octavo. 470 pages.　　　　　　　　　　　　　　　　　　　　　Cloth, $3.00

THORINGTON. Retinoscopy (The Shadow Test) in the Determination of Refraction at One Metre Distance with the Plane Mirror. By JAMES THORINGTON, M.D., Adjunct Professor of Diseases of the Eye in the Philadelphia Polyclinic; Ophthalmologist to the Vineland Training School and to the M. E. Orphanage; Lecturer on the Anatomy, Physiology, and Care of the Eyes in the Philadelphia Manual Training Schools, etc. With 38 Illustrations, several of which are Colored. Third Edition, Enlarged. 12mo.　　　　　　Cloth, $1.00

TOMES' Dental Anatomy. A Manual of Dental Anatomy, Human and Comparative. By C. S. TOMES, D.D.S. 263 Illustrations. 5th Ed. 12mo. Cloth, $4.00

　Dental Surgery. A System of Dental Surgery. By JOHN TOMES, F.R.S. Fourth Edition, Thoroughly Revised. By C. S. TOMES, D.D.S. With 289 Illustrations. 12mo. 717 pages.　　　　　　　　　　　　Cloth, $4.00

TRAUBE. Physico-Chemical Methods. By DR. J. TRAUBE, Privatdocent in the Technical High School of Berlin. Authorized Translation by W. D. HARDIN, Harrison Senior Fellow in Chemistry, University of Pennsylvania. With 97 Illustrations. 8vo.　　　　　　　　　　　　　　　　　Cloth, $1.50

TREVES. German-English Medical Dictionary. By FREDERICK TREVES, F.R.C.S., assisted by DR. HUGO LANG, B.A. (Munich). 12mo.　　　　½ Russia, $3.25

　Physical Education, Its Effects, Value, Methods, etc.　　　Cloth, .75

TUKE. Dictionary of Psychological Medicine. Giving the Definition, Etymology, and Synonyms of the Terms used in Medical Psychology, with the Symptoms, Pathology, and Treatment of the recognized forms of Mental Disorders, together with the Law of Lunacy in Great Britain and Ireland. Edited by D. HACK TUKE, M.D., LL.D., Examiner in Mental Physiology in the University of London. Two Volumes. Octavo. 1477 pages.　　　　　Cloth, $10.00

"This is an elaborate and valuable contribution to the literature of medical psychology, and will be found a valuable work of reference. . . . A comprehensive standard book."—*The British Medical Journal.*

TURNBULL'S Artificial Anæsthesia. A Manual of Anesthetic Agents in the Treatment of Diseases also their Employment in Dental Surgery; Modes of Administration; Considering their Relative Risks; Tests of Purity; Treatment of Asphyxia; Spasms of the Glottis; Syncope, etc. By LAURENCE TURNBULL, M.D., PH.G., Aural Surgeon to Jefferson College Hospital, etc. Fourth Edition, Revised and Enlarged. 54 Illustrations. 12mo. Cloth, $2.50

TUSON. Veterinary Pharmacopœia, including the outlines of Materia Medica and Therapeutics. By RICHARD V. TUSON, late Professor at the Royal Veterinary College. Fifth Edition. Revised and Edited by JAMES BAYNE, F.C.S., Professor of Chemistry and Toxicology at the Royal Veterinary College. 12mo. Cloth, $2.25

TUSSEY. High Altitude Treatment for Consumption. The Principles or Guides for a Better Selection or Classification of Consumptives Amenable to High Altitude Treatment, and to the Selection of Patients who may be More Successfully Treated in the Environment to which They were Accustomed Previous to Their Illness. By A. EDGAR TUSSEY, M.D., Adjunct Professor of Diseases of the Chest in the Philadelphia Polyclinic and School for Graduates in Medicine, etc. 12mo. Cloth, $1.50

TYSON. The Practice of Medicine. A Text-Book for Physicians and Students, with Special Reference to Diagnosis and Treatment. By JAMES TYSON, M.D., Professor of Clinical Medicine in the University of Pennsylvania, Physician to the University and to the Philadelphia Hospitals, etc. 8vo. Cloth, $5.50; Leather, $6.50; Half Russia, $7.50

" Few teachers in the country can claim a longer apprenticeship in the laboratory and at the bedside, none a more intimate acquaintance with students, since in one capacity or another he has been associated with the University of Pennsylvania and the Philadelphia Hospital for nearly thirty years. Moreover, he entered medicine through the portal of pathology, a decided advantage in the writer of a text-book. . . . The typography is decidedly above works of this class issued from our publishing houses. There is no American Practice of the same attractive appearance. The print is unusually sharp and clear, and the quality of the paper particularly good. . . . It is a piece of good, honest work, carefully conceived and conscientiously carried out."—*University Medical Magazine.*

*** Sample Pages and Illustrations Sent Free upon Application.

Guide to the Examination of Urine. Ninth Edition. For the Use of Physicians and Students. With Colored Plate and Numerous Illustrations Engraved on Wood. Ninth Edition. Revised. 12mo. 276 pages. Cloth, $1.25
*** *A French translation of this book has recently appeared in Paris.*

Handbook of Physical Diagnosis. 3d Edition. Revised and Enlarged. With Colored and other Illustrations. 12mo. 278 pages. Cloth, $1.50

Cell Doctrine. Its History and Present State. Second Edition. Cloth, $1.50

UNITED STATES PHARMACOPŒIA. 1890. Seventh Decennial Revision. Cloth, $2.50 (Postpaid, $2.77); Sheep, $3.00 (Postpaid, $3.27); Interleaved, $4.00 (Postpaid, $4.50); printed on one side of page only. Unbound, $3.50 (Postpaid, $3.90).

Select Tables from the U. S. P. (1890). Being Nine of the Most Important and Useful Tables, printed on Separate Sheets. Carefully put up in Patent Envelope. .25

ULZER and FRAENKEL. Introduction to Chemical-Technical Analysis. By Prof. F. ULZER and Dr. A. FRAENKEL, Directors of the Testing Laboratory of the Royal Technological Museum, Vienna. Authorized Translation by HERMANN FLECK, Nat. Sc.D., Instructor in Chemistry and Chemical Technical Analysis in the John Harrison Laboratory of Chemistry, University of Pennsylvania, with an Appendix by the Translator relating to Food Stuffs, Asphaltum and Paint. 12 Illustrations. 8vo. Cloth, $1.25

VAN HARLINGEN on Skin Diseases. A Practical Manual of Diagnosis and Treatment with special reference to Differential Diagnosis. By ARTHUR VAN HARLINGEN, M.D., Professor of Diseases of the Skin in the Philadelphia Polyclinic; Clinical Lecturer on Dermatology at Jefferson Medical College. Third Edition. Revised and Enlarged. With Formulæ and Illustrations, several being in Colors. 580 pages. Cloth, $2.75

"As would naturally be expected from the author, his views are sound, his information extensive, and in matters of practical detail the hand of the experienced physician is everywhere visible."— *The Medical News.*

VAN NÜYS on The Urine. Chemical Analysis of Healthy and Diseased Urine, Qualitative and Quantitative. By T. C. VAN NÜYS, Professor of Chemistry Indiana University. 39 Illustrations. Octavo. Cloth, $1.00

VIRCHOW'S Post-mortem Examinations. A Description and Explanation of the Method of Performing them in the Dead-House of the Berlin Charité Hospital, with especial reference to Medico-legal Practice. By Prof. VIRCHOW. Translated by Dr. T. P. SMITH. Illustrated. Third Edition, with Additions. Cloth, .75

VOSWINKEL. Surgical Nursing. A Manual for Nurses. By BERTHA M. VOSWINKEL, Graduate Episcopal Hospital, Philadelphia; Nurse in Charge Children's Hospital, Columbus, O. Second Edition, Revised and Enlarged. 111 Illustrations. 12mo. Cloth, $1.00

WALKER. Students' Aid in Ophthalmology. By GERTRUDE A. WALKER, A.B., M.D., Clinical Instructor in Diseases of the Eye at Woman's Medical College of Pennsylvania. 40 Illustrations and Colored Plate. 12mo. Cloth, $1.50

WALSHAM. Surgery; its Theory and Practice. For Students and Physicians. By WM. J. WALSHAM, M.D., F.R.C.S., Senior Ass't Surg. to, and Dem. of Practical Surg. in, St. Bartholomew's Hospital, Surg. to Metropolitan Free Hospital, London. Sixth Edition, Revised and Enlarged. With 410 Engravings. Clo., $3.00

WARD. Notes on Massage; Including Elementary Anatomy and Physiology. By JESSIE M. WARD, Instructor in Massage in the Pennsylvania, Philadelphia, Jefferson, and Woman's Hospitals; Clinical Lecturer at Philadelphia Polyclinic, etc. 12mo. Interleaved. Paper Cover, $1.00

WARING. Practical Therapeutics. A Manual for Physicians and Students. By EDWARD J. WARING, M.D. Fourth Edition. Revised, Rewritten, and Rearranged. Crown Octavo. Cloth, $2.00; Leather, $3.00

WARREN. Compend Dental Pathology and Dental Medicine. Containing all the most noteworthy points of interest to the Dental Student and a Chapter on Emergencies. By GEO. W. WARREN, D.D.S., Clinical Chief, Penn'a College of Dental Surgery, Phila. Third Edition, Enlarged. Illustrated. *Being No. 13 ? Quiz-Compend? Series.* 12mo. Cloth, .80
Interleaved for the addition of Notes, $1.25

Dental Prosthesis and Metallurgy. 129 Illustrations. Cloth, $1.25

WATSON on Amputations of the Extremities and Their Complications. By B. A. WATSON, M.D. 250 Illustrations. Cloth, $5.50

Concussions. An Experimental Study of Lesions arising from Severe Concussions. 8vo. Paper cover, $1.00

WELLS. Compend of Gynecology. By WM. H. WELLS, M.D., Instructor of Obstetrics, Jefferson Medical College, Philadelphia; Fellow of the College of Physicians of Philadelphia. 150 Illustrations. *?Quiz-Compend? Series No. 7.* 12mo. Cloth, .80; Interleaved for Notes, $1.25

WESTLAND. The Wife and Mother. A Handbook for Mothers. By A. WESTLAND, M.D., late Resident Physician, Aberdeen Royal Infirmary. Clo. $1.50

WETHERED. Medical Microscopy. A Guide to the Use of the Microscope in Practical Medicine. By FRANK J. WETHERED, M.D., M.R.C.P., Demonstrator of Practical Medicine, Middlesex Hospital Medical School; Assistant Physician, late Pathologist, City of London Hospital for Diseases of Chest, etc. With a Colored Plate and 101 Illustrations. 406 Pages. 12mo. Cloth, $2.00

WEYL. Sanitary Relations of the Coal-Tar Colors. By THEODORE WEYL. Authorized Translation by HENRY LEFFMANN, M.D., PH.D. 12mo. 154 pages.
Cloth, $1.25

WHITACRE. Laboratory Text-Book of Pathology. By HORACE J. WHITACRE, M.D., Demonstrator of Pathology, Medical College of Ohio, Cincinnati. Illustrated with 121 original Illustrations. 8vo. Cloth, $1.50

WHITE. The Mouth and Teeth. By J. W. WHITE, M.D., D.D.S. Cloth, .40

WHITE AND WILCOX. Materia Medica, Pharmacy, Pharmacology, and Therapeutics. A Handbook for Students. By W. HALE WHITE, M.D., F.R.C.P., etc., Physician to and Lecturer on Materia Medica and Therapeutics, Guy's Hospital; Examiner in Materia Medica to the Conjoint Board, etc. Fourth American Edition. Revised by REYNOLD W. WILCOX, M.A., M.D., LL.D., Professor of Clinical Medicine and Therapeutics at the New York Post-Graduate Medical School and Hospital; Visiting Physician St. Mark's Hospital; Assistant Visiting Physician Bellevue Hospital. Fourth Edition, thoroughly Revised. 12mo. 704 pages.
Cloth, $3.00; Leather, $3.50

WILLIAMS. Manual of Bacteriology. By HERBERT U. WILLIAMS, M.D., Professor of Pathology and Bacteriology, Medical Department University of Buffalo. With 78 Illustrations. 12mo. Cloth, $1.50

WILSON. Handbook of Hygiene and Sanitary Science. By GEORGE WILSON, M.A., M.D., F.R.S.E., Medical Officer of Health for Mid-Warwickshire, England. With Illustrations. Eighth Edition. 12mo. Cloth, $3.00

WILSON. The Summer and its Diseases. By JAMES C. WILSON, M.D., Prof. of the Practice of Med. and Clinical Medicine, Jefferson Med. Coll., Phila. Cloth, .40

WILSON. System of Human Anatomy. 11th Revised Edition. Edited by HENRY EDWARD CLARK, M.D., M.R.C.S. 492 Illustrations, 26 Colored Plates, and a Glossary of Terms. Thick 12mo. Cloth, $5.00

WINCKEL. Text-Book of Obstetrics; Including the Pathology and Therapeutics of the Puerperal State. By Dr. F. WINCKEL, Professor of Gynecology and Director of the Royal University Clinic for Women in Munich. Authorized Translation by J. CLIFTON EDGAR, A.M., M.D., Adjunct Professor to the Chair of Obstetrics, Medical Department, University City of New York. With nearly 200 Handsome Illustrations, the majority of which are original with this work. Octavo.
Cloth, $5.00; Leather, $6.00

WINDLE. Surface Anatomy and Landmarks. By B. C. A. WINDLE, D.Sc., M.D., Professor of Anatomy in Mason College, Birmingham, etc. Second Edition, Revised by T. MANNERS SMITH, M.R.C.S., with Colored and other Illustrations. 12mo. Cloth, $1.00

WOAKES. Deafness, Giddiness, and Noises in the Head. By EDWARD WOAKES, M.D., Senior Aural Surgeon, London Hospital; assisted by CLAUD WOAKES, M.R.C.S., Assistant Surgeon to the London Throat Hospital. Fourth Edition. Illustrated. 12mo. Cloth, $2.00

WOOD. Brain Work and Overwork. By Prof. H. C. WOOD, Clinical Professor of Nervous Diseases, University of Pennsylvania. 12mo. Cloth, .40

WOODY. Essentials of Chemistry and Urinalysis. By SAM E. WOODY, A.M., M.D., Professor of Chemistry and Public Hygiene, and Clinical Lecturer on Diseases of Children, in the Kentucky School of Medicine. Fourth Edition. Illustrated. 12mo. *In Press.*

YEO. Manual of Physiology. Third Edition. A Text-book for Students of Medicine. By GERALD F. YEO, M.D., F.R.C.S., Professor of Physiology in King's College, London. Third Edition; revised and enlarged by the author. With 254 Wood Engravings and a Glossary. Crown Octavo. Cloth, $2.50

BLAKISTON'S ? QUIZ=COMPENDS ?

The Best Series of Manuals for the Use of Students.

Price of each, Cloth, .80.   Interleaved for taking Notes, $1.25.

☞ These Compends are based on the most popular text-books and the lectures of prominent professors, and are kept constantly revised, so that they may thoroughly represent the present state of the subjects upon which they treat. The authors have had large experience as Quiz-Masters and attachés of colleges, and are well acquainted with the wants of students. They are arranged in the most approved form, thorough and concise, containing over 600 fine illustrations, inserted wherever they could be used to advantage. Can be used by students of *any* college, and contain information nowhere else collected in such a condensed, practical shape.

ILLUSTRATED CIRCULAR FREE.

No. 1. **HUMAN ANATOMY.**   Sixth Revised and Enlarged Edition. Including Visceral Anatomy. Can be used with either Morris's or Gray's Anatomy. 117 Illustrations and 16 Lithographic Plates of Nerves and Arteries, with Explanatory Tables, etc. By SAMUEL O. L. POTTER, M.D., Professor of the Practice of Medicine, College of Physicians and Surgeons, San Francisco; late A. A. Surgeon, U. S. Army.

No. 2. **PRACTICE OF MEDICINE.** Part I. Sixth Edition, Revised, Enlarged, and Improved. By DAN'L E. HUGHES, M.D., Physician-in-Chief, Philadelphia Hospital, late Demonstrator of Clinical Medicine, Jefferson Medical College, Philadelphia.

No. 3. **PRACTICE OF MEDICINE.** Part II. Sixth Edition, Revised, Enlarged, and Improved. Same author as No. 2.

No. 4. **PHYSIOLOGY.** Ninth Edition, with new Illustrations and a table of Physiological Constants. Enlarged and Revised. By A. P. BRUBAKER, M.D., Professor of Physiology and General Pathology in the Pennsylvania College of Dental Surgery; Demonstrator of Physiology, Jefferson Medical College, Philadelphia.

No. 5. **OBSTETRICS.** Sixth Edition. By HENRY G. LANDIS, M.D. Revised and Edited by WM. H. WELLS, M.D., Instructor of Obstetrics, Jefferson Medical College, Philadelphia. Enlarged. 3 Plates and 47 other Illustrations.

No. 6. **MATERIA MEDICA, THERAPEUTICS, AND PRESCRIPTION WRITING.** Sixth Revised Edition (U. S. P. 1890). By SAMUEL O. L. POTTER, M.D., Professor of the Practice of Medicine, College of Physicians and Surgeons, San Francisco.

No. 7. **GYNECOLOGY.** By WM. H. WELLS, M.D., Instructor of Obstetrics, Jefferson Medical College, Philadelphia. 150 Illustrations.

No. 8. **DISEASES OF THE EYE AND REFRACTION.** A New Book. Including Treatment and Surgery and a Section on Local Therapeutics. By GEORGE M. GOULD, M.D., and W. L. PYLE, M.D. With Formulæ, Glossary, several useful Tables, and 111 Illustrations, several of which are colored.

No. 9. **SURGERY, Minor Surgery, and Bandaging.** Fifth Edition, Enlarged and Improved. By ORVILLE HORWITZ, B.S., M.D., Clinical Professor of Genito-Urinary Surgery and Venereal Diseases in Jefferson Medical College; Surgeon to Philadelphia Hospital, etc. With 98 Formulæ and 167 Illustrations.

No. 10. **MEDICAL CHEMISTRY.** Fourth Edition. Including Urinalysis, Animal Chemistry, Chemistry of Milk, Blood, Tissues, the Secretions, etc. By HENRY LEFFMANN, M.D., Professor of Chemistry in Pennsylvania College of Dental Surgery and in the Woman's Medical College, Philadelphia.

No. 11. **PHARMACY.** Fifth Edition. Based upon Prof. Remington's Text-Book of Pharmacy. By F. E. STEWART, M.D., PH.G., late Quiz-Master in Pharmacy and Chemistry, Philadelphia College of Pharmacy; Lecturer at Jefferson Medical College.

No. 12. **VETERINARY ANATOMY AND PHYSIOLOGY.** Illustrated. By WM. R. BALLOU, M.D., Professor of Equine Anatomy at New York College of Veterinary Surgeons; Physician to Bellevue Dispensary, etc. With 29 graphic Illustrations.

No. 13. **DENTAL PATHOLOGY AND DENTAL MEDICINE.** Third Edition, Illustrated. Containing all the most noteworthy points of interest to the Dental Student and a Section on Emergencies. By GEO. W. WARREN, D.D.S., Chief of Clinical Staff, Pennsylvania College of Dental Surgery, Philadelphia.

No. 14. **DISEASES OF CHILDREN.** Colored Plate. By MARCUS P. HATFIELD, Professor of Diseases of Children, Chicago Medical College. Second Edition, Enlarged.

No. 15. **GENERAL PATHOLOGY AND MORBID ANATOMY.** 91 Illustrations. By H. NEWBERRY HALL, PH.G., M.D., Professor of Pathology and Medical Chemistry, Chicago Post-Graduate Medical School. Second Edition.

No. 16. **DISEASES OF THE SKIN.** By JAY F. SCHAMBERG, M.D., Instructor at Philadelphia Polyclinic. 99 Illustrations.

Price, each, strongly bound in cloth, .80.   Interleaved for taking Notes, $1.25.

THE PHYSICIAN'S VISITING LIST.

(LINDSAY & BLAKISTON'S.)

Special Improved Edition for 1899.

In order to improve and simplify this Visiting List we have done away with the two styles hitherto known as the "25 and 50 Patients plain." We have allowed more space for writing the names, and added to the special memoranda page a column for the "Amount" of the weekly visits and a column for the "Ledger Page." To do this without increasing the bulk or the price, we have condensed the reading matter in the front of the book and rearranged and simplified the memoranda pages, etc., at the back.

The Lists for 75 Patients and 100 Patients will also have special memoranda page as above, and hereafter will come in two volumes only, dated January to June, and July to December. While this makes a book better suited to the pocket, the chief advantage is that it does away with the risk of losing the accounts of a whole year should the book be mislaid.

The changes and improvements made in 1896 met with such general favor that the sale increased more than ten per cent. over the previous year.

CONTENTS.

PRELIMINARY MATTER.—Calendar, 1899–1900—Table of Signs, to be used in keeping records—The Metric or French Decimal System of Weights and Measures—Table for Converting Apothecaries' Weights and Measures into Grams—Dose Table, giving the doses of official and unofficial drugs in both the English and Metric Systems—Asphyxia and Apnea—Complete Table for Calculating the Period of Utero-Gestation—Comparison of Thermometers.

VISITING LIST.—Ruled and dated pages for 25, 50, 75, and 100 patients per day or week, with blank page opposite each on which is an amount column, column for ledger page, and space for special memoranda.

SPECIAL RECORDS for Obstetric Engagements, Deaths, Births, etc., with special pages for Addresses of Patients, Nurses, etc., Accounts Due, Cash Account, and General Memoranda.

SIZES AND PRICES.

REGULAR EDITION, as Described Above.

BOUND IN STRONG LEATHER COVERS, WITH POCKET AND PENCIL.

For 25 Patients weekly, with Special Memoranda Page,						. . . .		$1 00
50 " " " " " "						. .		1 25
50 " " " " " "						2 vols. {January to June / July to December}	. . . . .	2 00
75			"	"	"	2 vols. {January to June / July to December}	. . . . . .	2 00
100 " "			"	"	2 vols. {January to June / July to December}	. . . . . .	2 25

PERPETUAL EDITION, without Dates.

No. 1. Containing space for over 1300 names, with blank page opposite each Visiting List page. Bound in Red Leather cover, with Pocket and Pencil, ... $1 25

No. 2. Same as No. 1. Containing space for 2600 names, with blank page opposite, ... 1 50

MONTHLY EDITION, without Dates.

No. 1. Bound, Seal leather, without Flap or Pencil, gilt edges, ... 75

No. 2. Bound, Seal leather, with Tucks, Pencil, etc., gilt edges, ... 1 00

☞ All these prices are net. No discount can be allowed retail purchasers.

Circular and sample pages upon application.

P. BLAKISTON'S SON & CO., PUBLISHERS, PHILADELPHIA.

HEMMETER.

Diseases of the Stomach

COLORED ILLUSTRATIONS.

THEIR SPECIAL PATHOLOGY, DIAGNOSIS, AND TREATMENT. With Sections on Anatomy, Dietetics, Surgery of Stomach, etc. By JOHN C. HEMMETER, M.D., PHILOS.D., Clinical Professor of Medicine at the Baltimore Medical College, Consultant to the Maryland General Hospital, etc. With Colored and other Illustrations, many of which are original and have been specially prepared for this volume. Octavo, 778 pages.

Cloth, $6.00; Leather, $7.00; Half Russia, $8.00

*** This work has been prepared with great care and forms the only complete practical text-book in the English language. The author brings to his own large experience a vast knowledge of the literature of the subject. His chief effort has been to furnish the general practitioner with a work from which he can readily acquaint himself with all that has been done in this important branch of medicine, to fit himself to make examinations, to take advantage of new methods of diagnosis, and to treat this very difficult class of diseases rationally and successfully.

The illustrations have been selected and engraved with great care. A number of them are original; these have been drawn by the author or prepared by an artist under his immediate directions, and will, we believe, prove most satisfactory.

" The appearance of a work by an American author arouses an interest rather more than patriotic, an interest having its origin in the fact that the point of view of such a one is in many respects similar to our own, that he sees the same variety of disease acting under the same conditions of life, and that, therefore, his experience will be more helpful to us than the experience of a foreigner would be, and this interest is the keener when the field of such work is one in which but little has been published by our countrymen. All these conditions prevail in the present instance to make the book now at hand peculiarly attractive.

" The book is very conveniently divided into three parts. The first deals with anatomy and physiology and with methods of diagnosis; the second, with treatment and materia medica; and the third, with the diseases of the stomach as they present themselves clinically. Part I is very complete, and we wish to express an unqualified approval of the tendency that is shown to emphasize the simple and more practical diagnostic methods. . . .

" Part II, therapy and materia medica, devotes much space to dietetics, and contains a great fund of valuable information upon a subject far too little understood. The principles of dietetic treatment in gastric disease are discussed, and methods of cooking and diet lists in abundance are given. . . . The dietetics of alcohol and alcoholic beverages is the subject of a short but valuable chapter, and considerable attention is also given to mineral waters, and their use and abuse in diseases of the stomach. The remainder of the section is devoted to the discussion of medicinal and surgical treatment and of the effect of gastric diseases upon the rest of the organism.

" Part III treats of the diseases of the stomach from a clinical standpoint, and is by no means the least valuable part of the book. Much space is justly devoted to diagnosis, and the treatment is divided very conveniently into prophylactic, dietetic, and medicinal. Those derangements of the gastric function that, while not serious, are so very annoying, are here fully discussed, and what the author says will be read with interest by many who have found the usual text-books so unsatisfactory on this subject."—*From the New York Medical Journal.*